CUMBRIA COUNTY LIBRARY

This book is due for return on or before the
last date above. It may be renewed by personal
application, post or telephone, if not in demand.

C.L. 18

The Running Years

By the same author

Sisters
Reprise

The
Running Years

Claire Rayner

HUTCHINSON
London Melbourne Sydney Auckland Johannesburg

Hutchinson & Co. (Publishers) Ltd
An imprint of the Hutchinson Publishing Group
17–21 Conway Street, London W1P 5HL

Hutchinson Group (Australia) Pty Ltd
30–32 Cremorne Street, Richmond South, Victoria 3121
PO Box 151, Broadway, New South Wales 2007

Hutchinson Group (NZ) Ltd
32–34 View Road, PO Box 40-086, Glenfield, Auckland 10

Hutchinson Group (SA) Pty Ltd
PO Box 337, Bergvlei 2012, South Africa

First published 1981
© Claire Rayner 1981

Set in Linotron Bembo by
Computape (Pickering) Ltd, Pickering, North Yorkshire

Printed in Great Britain by The Anchor Press Ltd
and bound by Wm Brendon & Son Ltd,
both of Tiptree, Essex

British Library Cataloguing in Publication Data

Rayner, Claire
The running years.
I. Title
823′.914[F]   PR6068.A949
ISBN 0 09 146510 9

For Max and Muriel
With love and with gratitude
for just being there

ACKNOWLEDGEMENTS

The author wishes to thank the following for their help with the research: The Hebrew University of Jerusalem; The Israel Museum, Jerusalem; Eli Ben-Gal, Curator, Beth Hatefutsoth (Museum of the Diaspora), Tel Aviv; Tirtsah Levie, Curator, Joods Historisch Museum (Jewish Historical Museum), Amsterdam; The Curator, Anne Frank House, Prinsengracht 263, Amsterdam; The Imperial War Museum, London; The National Maritime Museum, London; Jewish Board of Guardians, London; Jewish Welfare Board, London; Education Department of the Jewish National Fund, London; Information Committee, Board of Deputies of British Jews; William J. Fishman, Historian, Morley College, London; Rabbi Michael Stanfield, Middlesex New Synagogue, Harrow, Middlesex; Dora Elliott, Debè Elliott, Alex Elliott, Rose Lee, Mary Moss, Minnie Guttenberg, the late Ronnie Elliott; Ben and Gertie Rosen, Brian Buckman, Max and Muriel Berk and many others too numerous to mention for their invaluable help with folk history.

And the Lord will scatter you among all peoples, from one end of the earth to the other; and there you shall serve other gods, of wood and stone, which neither you nor your fathers have known. And among these nations you shall find no ease, and there shall be no rest for the sole of your foot; but the Lord will give you there a trembling heart, and failing eyes, and a languishing soul; your life shall hang in doubt before you; night and day you shall be in dread, and have no assurance of your life. In the morning you shall say, 'Would it were evening!' and at evening you shall say, 'Would it were morning!' because of the dread which your heart shall fear, and the sights which your eyes shall see.

Deuteronomy xxviii, 64–7

The Dispersion

(from 72 AD)

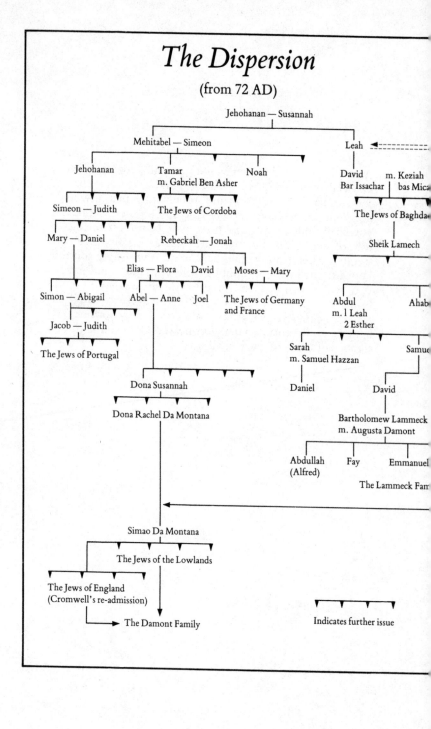

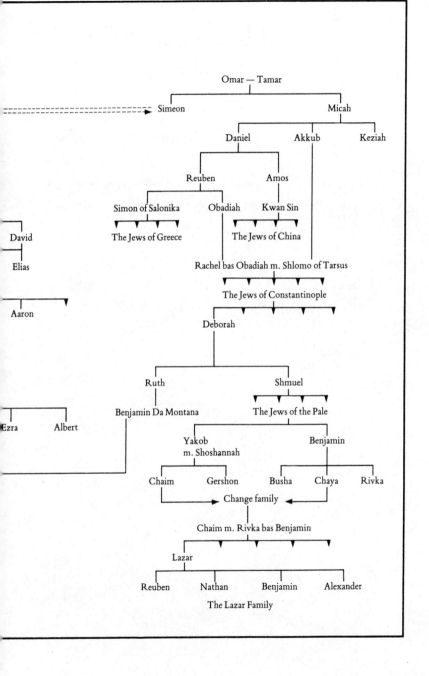

Omar — Tamar

Simeon

Micah

Daniel   Akkub   Keziah

Reuben   Amos

Simon of Salonika   Obadiah   Kwan Sin

The Jews of Greece   The Jews of China

David

Elias

Rachel bas Obadiah m. Shlomo of Tarsus

The Jews of Constantinople

Aaron

Deborah

Ruth   Shmuel

Benjamin Da Montana   The Jews of the Pale

Ezra   Albert

Yakob
m. Shoshannah   Benjamin

Chaim   Gershon   Busha   Chaya   Rivka

Change family

Chaim m. Rivka bas Benjamin

Lazar

Reuben   Nathan   Benjamin   Alexander

The Lazar Family

The Lammecks

(London from 1859)

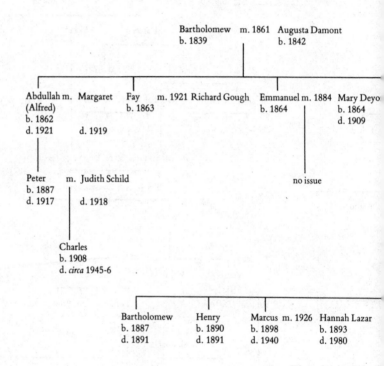

Bartholomew   m. 1861   Augusta Damont
b. 1839   b. 1842

Abdullah m. Margaret   Fay   m. 1921 Richard Gough   Emmanuel m. 1884 Mary Deyo
(Alfred)   b. 1863   b. 1864   b. 1864
b. 1862   d. 1909
d. 1921   d. 1919

Peter   m.   Judith Schild
b. 1887
d. 1917   d. 1918   no issue

Charles
b. 1908
d. *circa* 1945-6

Bartholomew   Henry   Marcus m. 1926   Hannah Lazar
b. 1887   b. 1890   b. 1898   b. 1893
d. 1891   d. 1891   d. 1940   d. 1980

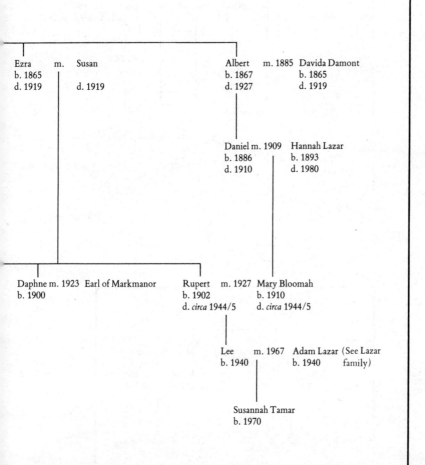

Ezra   m.   Susan
b. 1865
d. 1919   d. 1919

Albert   m. 1885   Davida Damont
b. 1867   b. 1865
d. 1927   d. 1919

Daniel m. 1909   Hannah Lazar
b. 1886   b. 1893
d. 1910   d. 1980

Daphne m. 1923 Earl of Markmanor
b. 1900

Rupert   m. 1927 Mary Bloomah
b. 1902   b. 1910
d. *circa* 1944/5   d. *circa* 1944/5

Lee   m. 1967   Adam Lazar (See Lazar
b. 1940   b. 1940   family)

Susannah Tamar
b. 1970

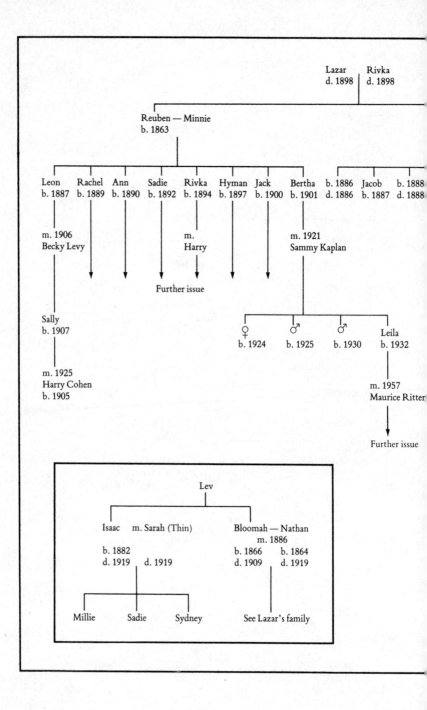

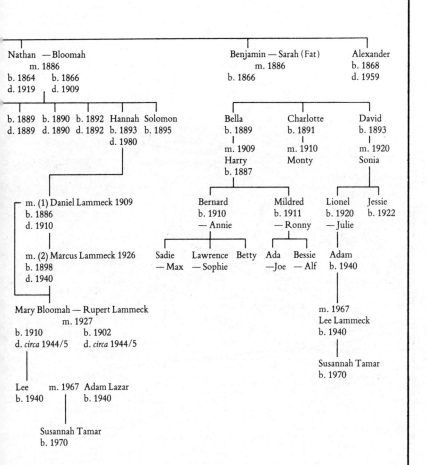

Lazar's Family

(London from 1900)

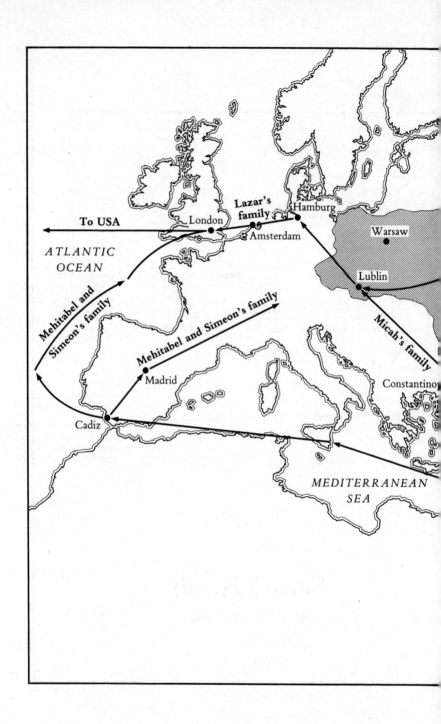

The Running Years

Travels of the children of Susannah and Jomar
70 AD—1881 AD

THE PALE
SETTLEMENT

Micah's family

CASPIAN SEA

BLACK SEA

Micah

Leah
Bagdad

David to Bombay and Shanghai

usannah   Jerusalem   Tamar   Pompeditha

Gaza

Cairo

Back to London

RED SEA

BOOK ONE

Scattering

1

They knew long before noon that they were widows. The fighting had been too violent, the noise too battering, the stench of dust and destruction as buildings crashed all around them too overwhelming for it to be otherwise. But not until late in the afternoon did they allow themselves to throw their robes over their heads and sit wailing in the sun-drenched rubble, luxuriating in their grief.

Not that the wailing helped Tamar much. She had always been the soft one, the tender one, the one who wept easily, so for her crying offered little comfort now she was faced with so grievous a loss. Omar dead. She could not really imagine it. But she knew it had to be true. So she sat and wept obediently beside Susannah as the children huddled close, and listened to Susannah's huge racking sobs and marvelled. Susannah, to weep like that? Big strong Susannah with her sharp sardonic tongue and her narrow black eyes that saw everything and sneered at most of it, to weep like that? She must have loved Jehohanan as much as Tamar loved – had loved, she corrected herself bleakly – her Omar.

The sun shifted slowly, lengthening the shadows of what was left of the city of Jerusalem, and still they sat, their knees hunched and the fabric of their clothes whitening along the folds as the dust of the dying city settled on them. Still, Susannah did not speak. She was not sobbing now, but sat hidden in her robes, a faceless heap of silent anguish.

Tamar moved, experimentally, and the baby Micah woke from the shallow sleep into which he had drifted and whimpered softly. She picked him up, holding him on her lap with his soft cheek against hers. Just holding him was enough to make her feel better; but he whimpered again and struggled in her arms, and she thought, 'He's hungry.' And as if he'd heard her say the words, Simeon at her other side said, 'Imma, I'm hungry. Where is Abba? Can we go

19

home now? I'm hungry.'

Tamar looked at him helplessly, and then at Susannah, and at the little girls beside her who sat silent and wide eyed, staring back.

'Susannah?' she said, softly, then more loudly. 'Susannah? The children are hungry. What shall we do?'

Susannah didn't seem to hear. Then, with a sharp movement, she straightened and pushed back her robe from her head. She looked ordinary again. The grimace of distress which had twisted her cheeks before was gone. There was a line of sweat beads along her upper lip, and some smears of dirt on her forehead, but otherwise she just looked like Susannah; sensible, capable, strong Susannah.

'They'll have to stay hungry for a while,' she said harshly. 'We must go. Come on.' She got to her feet and the little girls, moving almost absurdly in unison, stood up too and followed her as she went scrambling away over the pile of rubble.

Bad as the early part of the day had been, the next two hours were worse. They picked their way from one heap of desolation to another, hearing the cries of people buried beneath the debris and trying not to listen, hiding from the bands of Roman soldiers who were still roaming about singing and shouting their victory. They moved from the Temple shadows, past the first wall, and on southward into the Lower City, through what had once been recognizable streets where their friends and neighbours had lived, dodging among the wandering crowds of bewildered refugees like themselves, as the children became more and more weary, more fractious. And though Tamar comforted them as best she could, talking as softly and lovingly to her nieces as to her own two boys, Susannah said nothing. She just went relentlessly on, leading them away, away from home and Jehohanan and Omar and all that had made life real.

Tamar was not weeping now. She could not, for the terror was too real, the pain too much. She just went on doggedly, following Susannah, crooning to the children and trying not to think.

It was almost dark by the time they reached the southernmost wall, overlooking the Valley of Hinnom. Behind them the noise, the shouting and the moaning of the injured and dying, went on. Ahead of them the land lay low and unwelcoming in the deepening darkness. And still Susannah had said nothing.

They stopped then, as the wall lifted ahead of them. The attacks of Titus's soldiers had been concentrated to the north and east of the city, and here the great piles of hewn stone. fortifications remained unbreached. Or almost. Susannah lifted her chin and looked, and then nodding sharply at Tamar, turned west and began to hurry along in the wall's shadow, making for the deep embrasure they both knew lay a few thousand cubits ahead.

It was as they reached the curve of the embrasure that Leah spoke for the first time. Her smaller sister, Mehitabel, had cried and nagged and whined as they made their painful way, cubit by cubit, through the hubbub, but Leah had been as grimly silent as her mother. Now she lifted her small pointed chin and said almost conversationally, 'They're burning the Temple.'

'What?' Susannah too lifted her chin, looking very like Leah for a moment, and stared back over her shoulder. 'The Temple? You're mad. They couldn't. It couldn't happen.'

But behind them the dark eastern sky was lit with the glow of a sunrise such as none of them had ever seen; a rich red and yellow and orange and flaming crimson glory that even as they stared rose and roared and then sank, as though whatever it was the fire had consumed had succumbed as quickly as it could to the greed of the flames. The glow dropped almost as fast as it had risen, sinking to a dull sulking amber. But they could smell it now, the almost cheerful scent of timber burning, a new smell over and above the reek of destruction that had been in their nostrils all day.

'It's the ninth of Ab,' Susannah said. 'We were married on the ninth of Ab, Jehohanan and I. And now they've burned the Temple.'

'I'm hungry,' Simeon said plaintively, uninterested in fires, unless they were cooking fires. 'I want my supper. Where is Abba?'

'Dead,' Susannah said, brutally.

Tamar tried to reach out for her arm, tried to stop her, not wanting the child to know, just yet. 'He's had enough to suffer, don't tell him yet that he has no father. He's only five years old.'

But Susannah was not to be stopped. 'Crushed like a lizard

21

under a rock. Cut up and bleeding, and burned and dead. Like my Jehohanan. They're dead, like the Temple, like everyone but us.'

'Oh,' Simeon said. And then, plaintive again, 'I want my supper.'

They clambered through the wall, kicking aside the loose masonry, for Susannah had been right in her guess: other refugees had come this way ahead of them and had opened a breach. Beyond, in the dark valley, a few fires began to dot the blackness with points of light, and the distant scent of cooking came drifting back to them. Now, not only Simeon but Micah and Mehitabel began to cry in earnest and Susannah had to stop and lift her small daughter into her arms before she went hurrying on. Tamar settled Simeon on her back, his arms around her neck, as she clutched Micah as close and warm as she could, putting her hand on his round belly and pressing gently, hoping to stay the pangs of his hunger.

Susannah stopped barely three hundred cubits from the wall. There was a patch of scrub and beneath it a hollowed out sandy patch. She swung Mehitabel to her feet and then, moving with economy, untied the bundle of her skirts. Tamar, as ever following her powerful sister-in-law's lead, did the same.

They counted out their meagre store, the few things they had managed to snatch when they fled from the house they had shared in the shadow of the Temple, after Jehohanan and Omar had gone, kissing the children briefly, warning the women to go as fast as they could to the comparative safety of the Lower City, as far as they could get from Titus's marauders.

There was a bag of meal. There were a few dried fish, a handful of dried dates and figs, and some olives. There was a small leather bottle of thin olive oil and a couple more with water in them, and some almonds. Pitifully little to sustain two women and four children, but God alone knew where they would get more. Behind them the city with its shops and warehouses, its merchants' stores and the kitchens of ordinary people was being looted of what little food there was by the soldiers. Ahead of them lay the valley and then the open plain, and where were they to find the food there? Had not Jerusalem itself been starving for well over a month, as the siege had bitten harder and harder into the defences?

'We'll eat what there is, and then worry,' Susannah said and sent Simeon to collect sticks and build a fire, while Mehitabel searched for a flat stone on which they could bake some bread.

As the night wore on, the glow of the burning Temple sank ever lower into the horizon and the bitter desert cold crept into their bones. But their spirits lifted a little, for Simeon had found a good store of wood, and their fire burned bright and hopeful and the bread they mixed from meal and oil and water baked fast on the slab of stone that Mehitabel had found. So the children ate, and at last slept, exhausted with terror and running and the sheer extra-ordinariness of it all.

But their mothers did not. They sat and stared back at their dead city, and thought of their dead husbands.

Grim serious Jehohanan, the Zealot who was more passionate than any of his fellows, the fighter who had devoted his life to his belief in the rightness of the Great Jewish Cause, who had hated the Roman invader with a violence that made his body seem as though it was made of rock, so rigid did he become when he spoke of them.

And Omar, who had fought with him, and been as brave as any, if less committed; for Omar it had been his brother who had mattered. He had been at heart as gentle as his Tamar, an easy going, easy laughing man with hair as black and curly as Tamar's was straight and red, eyes as narrow and dark and laughing as Tamar's were blue and round and solemn. A lovely man, Tamar thought, and stared at the city where his corpse lay somewhere in the ruins. A lovely man. I wish his brother had not been so ...

But she pushed that thought aside and made herself think lovingly of Jehohanan, the fighter, the plotter, the spy and then the warrior. Ever since Omar had first come to her parents' house in far off Babylonia, all that time ago, six long years ago when she had been fourteen and her own dear Imma and Abba had been looking about for a good husband for her, Jehohanan had hung over their lives like a shadow. Omar had come to their house, a handsome and well spoken-of young merchant, sent by distant Jerusalem relations to make trading contact with the rich Jews of the Exile. A happy lot, were the Jews of Babylon. Once they had wept bitter tears of loneliness, longing for Jerusalem and home, but that had been long ago, well before Tamar's time. She had grown up comfortable and very satisfied with life in the town of Pumpeditha, where her father traded so happily and successfully. If her great-great-grandfather had wept by the waters of Babylon, she certainly had not.

And certainly not when Omar had come, and Tamar had looked at him and her fourteen-year-old heart had shattered at once, for he was the best of men, the handsomest of men, and so very kind and generous. He had brought her presents from the beginning, well primed by her father's friends, but he had talked of his brother Jehohanan. He had sat beside her in her father's house, holding her hand secretly so that her father might not see his boldness, but he had spoken of his brother Jehohanan.

And when they had come to Jerusalem, she an excited, frightened bride, the first person she had met had been Jehohanan. Serious, straight faced, handsome too, but not as Omar was. He had looked at her and nodded and said sharply to Omar, 'You have been gone too long. There is work to be done. In the warehouse and at the meetings.' And he had taken Omar away, and left the frightened girl to her sister-in-law, only one year her senior in years, but so much older in her knowledge of the world.

Not that Susannah had ever been unkind to Tamar. But hard, that she had been. She had not allowed her to weep when she missed her mother. She had chided her for being so sick as her pregnancy took hold of her. She had made her work in the big house the brothers shared when she yearned to go out into the busy streets to wander in the crowds and stare at the booths in the bazaars the way she had always done at home.

But Susannah had also been good. When Tamar's time had come and her labour pains had frightened her so, it had been Susannah who made them bearable by her presence. When the baby Simeon had been so ill, so frail that it seemed he might die, it had been Susannah who had taught his silly childish mother how to care for him, and rear him to sturdy toddlerhood. And when Omar had become more and more involved with Jehohanan's politics, it had been Susannah who had helped Tamar, sulky and pouting at being neg-lected, to see how foolish it was to chide a man for doing what he had to do.

And if she herself had ever yearned for her own people, far away in Gaza by the sea, if she had suffered the same homesickness in the bustle and danger of Jerusalem that Tamar suffered, no one, least of all Tamar, knew of it.

Dawn came with its usual suddenness, bearing with it the smell of old smoke and the sweet sickly scent of dead bodies, already rotting in the wreckage, and the children turned into the last sleep of the night as Susannah stood up and stretched.

'We must count what we have, share it and then part,' she said, as calmly as if they were still at home and she was instructing Tamar on how to arrange to deal with the day's laundry. 'We cannot go together, for there is no reason why my people should care for you, or yours for me.'

'Go where?' Tamar stared up at her, suddenly more frightened than she had been all night. To have lost Omar was agony. Lovely happy Omar. She would not think of him. But to part from *Susannah*? That was unthinkable.

'I'm not going anywhere without you!' she said shrilly. 'Susannah, you cannot ...'

'You must go home to your own people. Home to Babylon,' Susannah said. 'They are yours and they will care for you. If you go north, you should pick up a caravan. They will see you safe on your way. You are a handsome woman, and the children are tender. They will help you. If you're clever and sensible.'

'I don't want to go to Pumpeditha,' Tamar began, and then stopped. 'I mean, I do, but not without you. I want you to come too. My Abba will love you and look after you – '

'Don't be a fool,' Susannah said sharply. 'I have my own people, and they have a right. A right to the children I have borne.'

She stopped, sharply, staring at Tamar and then looking down at the four children, curled up together in the sandy hollow, sleeping like a litter of puppies in a basket; and then turned her head away.

'It must be so, my dear,' she said more gently. 'You must go to your people, and I to mine. It has always been so for widows. Who else can we ask to care for us? Come, let me see what shekels you have brought.'

Tamar felt the tears running down her cheeks and made no effort to hide them. Usually Susannah was infuriated by her

25

easy weeping, but today, Tamar felt, she would not scold her for it. Not when they were to part so soon. For Tamar knew she could not argue with Susannah. Dreadful, fearful, miserable as it would be to part from strong Susannah, to her own people each of them must go. It had always been so.

Together they untied their fortunes from about their waists and necks and fingers. Omar and Jehohanan had been successful merchants, for all they gave so much energy to their politics, and their wives had gone as decently bedecked as the wives of such men should; tinkling with gold pieces threaded on gold thread, their clothes glittering in secret places with carefully sewn on golden coins. They should have a goodly store.

And they did. When they counted it and shared it, they had more than enough to get back to their homes, even if they had to pay travellers they met on the way to accompany them. They even had enough to feed themselves on their arrival, for a little while at least.

And so it was that as the sun at last lifted the complete roundness of its disc above the wreck of Jerusalem on the tenth day of Ab that Tamar and Susannah stood in the Valley of Hinnom and looked at each other, saying goodbye. Tamar stood with Micah in her arms and Simeon clutching at her skirts, and Susannah with Leah and Mehitabel flanking her.

And then Susannah began to speak, her voice low and almost dreamy, and Tamar felt the chill of what she said rising from the pit of her belly into her throat. And could do nothing about it.

For what Susannah said was irrefutable. Had there been any argument that could have been marshalled against her, strong as she was, would not Tamar, weak as *she* was, have done so? Would she have let such a thing happen had it not been the ineluctable will of God? In years to come she was to tell the bitter angry Leah the same thing, over and over again. Not that it made any difference.

Jehohanan, said Susannah, staring back at what was left of Jerusalem, had died with his city. 'Never again shall he walk or breathe or eat or sleep beside me. Never again shall he make me a child.'

She had turned then and looked at Tamar. 'Is it not a cruel thing that there is no child to follow such a man, Tamar? Is it not? God could not have meant it so.'

'No child? But there are your lovely daughters,' Tamar said, looking anxiously at her small nieces, feeling the cut in Susannah's words, not wanting the children to feel hurt. 'You have your sweet daughters.'

· 'Ah yes, but no son. No boy to be called Bar Jehohanan. No son to bear the name of such a great man on into the world he fought for. It is a cruel thing, that. God could not have meant it so. Could he?'

'I do not know the ways of God,' Tamar said, frightened and not knowing quite why. 'How can I know the ways of God? I never understand men's doings ...' For indeed, in Tamar's eyes God was really just another man. Large, powerful, totally incomprehensible. Just another man. 'I don't understand you.'

'If your Omar had lived, the good Lord in his wisdom would have decreed that he give me a son for his dead brother. Is it not so, Tamar? Isn't that the law?'

'I told you, I know nothing of such things,' Tamar said, almost pettishly. 'I'm just a woman.'

'Ah, but I know, Tamar. I tell you it would be so. But Omar is dead, like Jehohanan.'

There was a silence then, and Tamar did not look at her. She was still frightened, still did not know why.

'But *you* have two sons to call Bar Omar. Haven't you, Tamar? Haven't you?'

And now Tamar understood. She pulled the boys closer to her, her soft-skinned brown eyed boys, and shook her head, furiously, violently, as though by doing so she could shake off Susannah and her soft implacable voice for ever.

'But it must be so, my dear,' Susannah said, with a voice full of infinite reasonableness, infinite patience. 'You know it, and so do I. It has to be so – you cannot take away two boys called Bar Omar, and leave me with no Bar Jehohanan. It would not be right. It would be an abomination in the face of the Lord.'

And so it was that on the tenth day of Ab, in the year 70 of the Common Era, Susannah, widow of Jehohanan, turned her back on Jerusalem and walked southward, her daughter Mehitabel scurrying along on her left, and her right hand firmly holding the dirty fist of a small weeping child who tried to pull away, and kept looking back piteously at Tamar. In Tamar's arms as she stared with stricken eyes at the

27

receding figures of her sister-in-law and the two children lay the baby Micah, burbling a little and reaching for the loose hair on her forehead to play with it. And at her side stood her niece, Leah, a stolid dark eyed girl with a still face and eyes as opaque as the pebbles that lay about them in the rough valley scrub.

Tamar never saw her son Simeon again, and Susannah never saw her daughter Leah. But the Will of God had been done, according to Susannah, and a son bearing Jehohanan's name was carried away from Jerusalem to the new world beyond. And Tamar, doing as she always did, which was the best she could, turned and walked blindly northward, bearing her baby Micah in her aching arms, barely noticing how cruelly the stones of the valley floor bit at her feet. She had lost her home and her husband and her son. There wasn't much else that could happen to her and her children. Was there?

2

And so it was that the wandering began. In truth, of course, it had begun long before, hundreds of years ago in the time of Nebuchadnezzar and Jehohaichin, when many thousands of the people of Judea had been deported to Babylon. Some of them had come back to Jerusalem in the time of Joshua, but later others had sickened of the hard labour of reconstructing the ruins of the first temple, and had returned to the lush life of the great eastern nation, sending money back to help the struggling builders in Jerusalem, just as some had gone to settle in the old land of bondage, Egypt, where life was good and easy.

But it was not good and easy for Tamar, walking doggedly northward from the Valley of Hinnom below burning Jerusalem, with the silent ice-cold Leah at her side, and Micah soft and heavy in her arms. Battered with loss, she could feel nothing but the pain in her feet and legs. The misery of Omar's death, the agony of parting from Simeon, and also from Susannah, strong and comforting Susannah, was so overwhelming that the only way she could comprehend any of it was by thinking of the sharp stones beneath her soles, the dragging in her ankles and the spasms that seized her shrieking calf muscles.

It was not good and easy, but for all that it was not impossible. As the evening shadows lengthened over the rising ground on that first day after the burning of the Temple of Jerusalem, Tamar fell in with a small group of travellers making their way eastward, from Damascus. Judeans, by great fortune, they were kind to her and did not kill her for the sake of her small store of gold, and the possession of the children who would have made useful slaves in time, but welcomed her, and gave her a bundle of goat skins in which the children could be put to sleep, and above all, fed them. They gave her goats' milk and coarse meal bread and dried figs, and asked in return only that she tell them in all the detail she could, of what had happened in Jerusalem.

They sat there in the thick black velvet night around a sulky cooking fire and listened attentively, their heads covered with the woollen cloths that showed the heavy wear of their travelling life. These five men were merchants in a small way of business who could only live by moving their goods from one town to another about the rich green half-moon through which the Euphrates and Tigris made their mighty ways to the Persian Gulf. What happened in Jerusalem mattered profoundly to them, for where Romans were, trade was not.

So they questioned and listened and sighed and looked upon Tamar with sad respect for her suffering and let her sleep secure that night, rolled in one of their own carpets for warmth, and did not molest her even though not one of them had lain with a woman these many weeks.

The next day they laughed at her, indulgently, for travelling north when she had wanted to go east, and took her up on their pack ass with Micah wrapped in her robe on her lap and Leah walking alongside and set off towards the rising sun, while she pondered on Susannah's wisdom; for had Tamar turned east she would have found no travellers to aid her, but would have had to walk the many miles alone, finding what food she could along the way.

Dear Susannah, she thought, and let tears prick her eyelids. Dear Susannah, I miss you so. And somehow she managed

29

not to think of how much she missed Simeon, too, he of the noisy shouting and sweet insolence that used to make her laugh with such delight. She thought only of her sister-in-law as the travellers made their way to Ava and then to Sippora and finally, bypassing Babylon and Sura, to Pumpeditha. It was the only way she could keep her head clear, thinking of Susannah.

And what did Susannah think of, so many miles west and south of her, in Gaza? As Tamar and Leah and Micah were being carried safe into the main market square of the dusty city of Ava, she was lying on her back on the hard stones of an alley off the Anthedon wharf of Gaza, her knees spread apart and her eyes wide open, staring up at the sky over the rise and fall of the heavy shoulders of the man who was pushing his body into hers. She was grimly not thinking of anything, just watching the sky appear and disappear as he grunted his way to his satisfaction, and cutting her mind off completely at the waist. She knew that somewhere behind her Simeon and Mehitabel were watching, alert and a little puzzled, but she did not think about them either. And certainly she did not think about dead Jehohanan.

The man rolled off at last, fumbling at her even though he had reached his peak and clearly found it good. This time she slapped at his hand, feeling safe now to do so, and he laughed and stood up and rearranged his robes, leaving her to scrub herself as dry and clean as she could, her back turned to him and the children in an attempt to maintain some dignity.

'No more till we are safe at sea,' she said then, turning around and staring at him, her head up and her dark eyes narrow in her white face. 'That was the bargain.'

'A bargain it is – though it won't be much of a one for me if you don't show a bit more enthusiasm.' He grinned, his broken teeth yellow against his dark lips. 'Got a lot to learn, you have.'

'I'm not a whore,' she said contemptuously, bending to pick up her bundle and jerking her head at the children to bring them to her side. 'Just a widow and orphan, trying to keep my soul in my body, and my children's too. When do you sail?'

'Sunrise.' His eyes slid away from her direct gaze. He

should be despising her, damn it, a woman he had just taken in such a way, but there was something in her face that made him uneasy. Not ashamed, precisely, for when did a man ever need to feel shame about his manhood? But something. 'Sunrise,' he repeated, then said abruptly, 'Did you hear what happened in Jaffa last night?'

'Last night? Last night I was sitting in my dead father's house, hearing that all my kin that live have fled. Gone to Egypt. I can't follow them there, for where will they be? They didn't know I was in need of them so they left no messages for me. And with my father dead, why should any of my brothers care for me? They have anguish enough with their own women and children – ' She was talking almost to herself now, staring out at the wharfside at the end of the alley, at the tangle of masts and rigging swaying against the greyness of the dawn sky. 'Anguish enough...'

'They took to their heels there,' he went on, 'heard the Romans were coming, piled into the ships, went out even though the wind was rising. Storm took 'em. Turned every last damned vessel on its side, and those that got themselves ashore were stuck on Roman swords along the beaches. Never put to sea at night – there's not a mariner anywhere as doesn't know that. Drowned for their pains – '

'Better than being spitted on a sword,' she said sharply, and pulled Mehitabel towards her, for the child had broken into a sudden wail. 'But there'll be no storms or drowning for us. God wouldn't bring me so far, not take such sacrifices from me just to tip me into the sea.'

And she led the way to the ship, with its owner trailing behind her, a little bewildered by the subservience she was able to create in him.

It was to be so for the next many weeks as they traversed the great sea, hugging the shores whenever they could, on their way to Cyprus where he had a cargo of dried fruit to exchange for one of olive oil which was to be taken on to Sicily, there to be exchanged for a load of cracked marble to be taken at last to Valencia in Spain. All through the journey it was she who in some subtle way seemed to control him, deciding when they should sail and what they should eat, when they should copulate (for she was scrupulous in paying her fare for herself and the children) what rates they should get for cargoes and what they should carry.

31

She left him in Valencia, taking her share of the cargo money – for, she told him firmly, it was her shrewd bargaining that had got him his prices and she was entitled. Turning her back on him, contemptuous still, she took the children, taller now and even fair skinned Simeon baked nut brown by the sun and sea winds, and made her way to the city of Cordoba.

She could have stayed in Valencia, for there were Jews there, but deep within her she was still afraid of the Romans. If she herself had come by sea from Gaza, could not they? Inland, it would be safe. So, inland she went, and with her cargo money bought a small house at the top of a long winding street and set herself up modestly as a merchant. The Jewish citizens of Cordoba, comfortable and settled people who traced their ancestors back to the days two hundred years before when a handful of Jewish slaves had been expelled from Rome and fled to the safety of the western peninsula, accepted her, and allowed her a widow's privileges. Even at this great distance news of the happenings in far away Jerusalem had penetrated. They felt she had a right to their tolerance.

And there, at last, she stayed. Sometimes she remembered her Jehohanan, in the dark wastes of the summer nights when her body stirred and reminded her she was a woman, had once had hungers and had been sweetened by the satisfaction of them, but that was not often. More of her thoughts she gave to Simeon.

Simeon Bar Jehohanan, for she always addressed him by his full name, was the most precious possession she had, in spite of her growing store of gold from her dealings in the Cordoban markets. But he – he hated her. He spent the rest of his life filled with a huge fury at the way he had been robbed in his infancy of that warm soft red headed mother, and given instead this implacable black eyed creature who brooded over him and watched him and stirred his deepest feelings into anger. His hate spilled over into hatred of her daughter Mehitabel too, but it was a different sort of hate, a mixture of contempt and disgust. Only when he realized, as he did eventually, how it would hurt Susannah to show any care for Mehitabel, did he do so.

Despite Susannah's rage, he married Mehitabel, timid cowed Mehitabel, and bred many children upon her, of whom nine survived. And one of them, just one, was a girl with red hair and round blue eyes, and he called her Tamar for the mother for whom he still yearned, and at last learned to love again, as well as to hate.

But Susannah stopped loving, and became harder and more shrivelled and more angry as the years dropped away, and died at last in the year 120 of the Common Era, with her full complement of seventy years, long after her daughter Mehitabel had succumbed to the exhaustion of her repeated childbirths and had closed her eyes in peace. And no one, not one of her grandchildren, and certainly not the nephew she had tried to make into her son, mourned her.

But Tamar mourned far away in Babylonia though she was never to know what had happened to her beloved Susannah; such messages as she sent to Gaza from time to time went unanswered, and she never did hear again of her son, or her niece. But all her life she remembered Susannah and spoke of her often with love and longing however much Leah stared at her with opaque black eyes and disgust in her face.

That was something that Tamar found it difficult to come to terms with, Leah's loathing. Micah grew up to be a gentle easy going boy, much like his dead father. Had there been any kinsman of her dead husband to whom Tamar could have been wed, her family would have arranged it, but there were none. The Romans had killed them all. So Tamar lived comfortably enough as a widow watching Micah grow up, and marry, loving his quiet little wife Sarah as if she had been her own, and exclaiming joyously over the fat babies who arrived with almost monotonous regularity, and trying hard to love Leah too.

But with each year Leah became colder and more bitter and more adamantine. She would sit in the kitchen of Tamar's house, consumed with hate, only her eyes gleaming in her white face to betray the heat of the fires within. Tamar would sit and watch her uneasily, and try to talk brightly to her about finding her a husband, but the look that always turned on her from those black eyes would make the words falter in her throat.

And then the time came when the festering hurt in Leah at last spilled over for all to see. Micah, now a prosperous weaver of fine silk, happy with his silent Sarah and vociferous brood of children, was accused by his neighbours of having robbed a fellow weaver. He protested, of course, for in truth Micah was too easy going a soul, too simple a man, to have the wit to plan a robbery. He demanded as was his right under the law to know his accuser. And his sister – as he had always considered her to be – stepped forward from the press of people standing about his doorway, and stared at him bleakly over the shawl that covered her head and which she kept close to her mouth and said, 'It is I.'

Tamar, pushing through the crowd to which she had been summoned, wept aloud at that, and ran to Leah's side, and begged her not to be so evil, not to turn against her own brother with such wicked lies, but Leah only said softly, 'Brother? He is no brother of mine nor ever was. He stole the silk. I saw him.'

The whole town of Pumpeditha rang with the scandal of it. Day after day, Micah, standing his trial before the priests and the elders, brought his friends to explain that he had been with them all evening, but failed to convince them, for if the man's own sister had informed on him did they not have to believe her? Blood of his blood, the sin she would be committing if she lied was so awesome they could not believe she could contemplate it. So they believed her, and stripped him of his loom and his tools, everything but the clothes on his and Sarah's and the children's backs, and left him, despised by his neighbours, grieved over by his kin, and totally bewildered by all that had happened to him.

And Leah? She returned to Tamar's house and sat in her kitchen and stared at her aunt with those bleak black eyes, but this time Tamar did not see hate in them, but a sick triumph, and for the first and only time in her life let anger fill her. From her earliest days, Tamar had been the easy gentle one. She had cried easily, yearned easily, smiled and laughed easily, but she had never raged easily. Until now, when she turned with her hands raised to strike the silent girl.

It was as though, at last, Leah had been given permission to let loose the bitterness that filled her. She stood up, suddenly tall in Tamar's eyes, and jerked her neck back so that her shawl slipped from her smooth black head. And moving so easily it was as though she had rehearsed every movement, took from the stone beside the fire a bone handled knife with a wicked long narrow blade and held it before her in such a way that Tamar, rushing headlong towards her in her pain and distress, ran straight upon it.

They stood there for a long moment, the two women, in the dimly lit kitchen on the south side of the courtyard of Tamar's mother's house, Tamar with her round blue eyes even more rounded in a sort of silly surprise, holding her belly with both hands and feeling the blood slide from beneath her fingers in bulging spurts, and Leah, the knife in her hand, still watching her with, for the first time that Tamar could ever remember, a smile curving her mouth. That was the last thing Tamar saw in this world, the smile on Leah's face. But the last word she ever said, breathily and in a childlike little voice was, 'Susannah ...'

Of course Leah had to go. Bearing false witness was one thing; easy to get away with that. But to kill – that was a Law of Moses much harder to flout. Go she must, and go she did.

To Babylon, a two and a half day's journey to the north, if she walked fast, and did not rest too long at night. There in the great bustling city where men from every corner of the modern world came to trade and cheat and womanize and sometimes to learn and worship, there where a woman with energy and limited scruples could build a personal fortune, there she would lose herself. Using the silver dishes she had taken from Tamar's house and gold ornaments she had taken from Tamar's cooling body she set herself up in the spice trade.

Not that it was easy for a woman to be a dealer in her own right. Women were for bed and children, nothing more; faced with any encroaching female trying to live a man's life the merchants of Babylon would have jeered and asked who she thought she was – Deborah come again? Leah knew that, and wasted no energy or time flouting established practice. It was simpler to circumvent it. A man named Issachar, a handsome indolent Moabite, was content to marry her, at her behest, and do as he was bid.

By the time she was forty, she was rich. Issachar had given her five children as well as cover for her spice dealing, and they were, by and large, satisfactory. The older two boys were twins, dour black eyed fifteen-year-olds with a sharp eye for dealing and a harsh reputation in the Babylonian markets. Then there were the girls, largely unregarded by their mother though useful about the house, both at thirteen and fourteen safely betrothed to men of substance in the community. And last of all ten-year-old David, the child of her age, a tall boy with her own dark eyes and hair and a watchfulness that was so like her own that in his company she could relax as she could with no one else. They were close, those two, so close that the older boys had long since learned to hate their brother.

Which should in a sense have helped them too to be close to their mother, for despite the prosperous years in the Babylonian spice markets, Leah had never lost her consuming hate for the two people who had so destroyed her life when she had been five years old. Micah and his mother. So faded was her memory and so warped had her imaginings become that Micah had become the focus of all her resentment, and even though she had destroyed his repute in Pumpeditha and killed his mother, she was not yet content. She wanted to do more, to drive him and all his kin away from his home as she had been driven out of hers.

One day, she would tell herself, sitting in her counting house with David by her side, one day I will destroy him. One day before I die.

3

When David was eighteen years old, Leah told him once again as she had told him many times before the story of her childhood sufferings, painting in vivid colours the agonies of unhappiness she had known, making graphic comparisons with his own easy love-lapped childhood. And David (who had indeed grown up in comfort, for by the time of his birth his mother had made the family tolerably well off, and by the time he was called to be a Son of the Commandment at thirteen, very rich) caught fire as she meant him to. Filled with the eagerness of his youth and the passion of his love for his mother and not a little by a desire for adventure to enrich his too secure life, David was ripe for instruction. Which

36

Leah duly gave to him.

Which was why in the year 118 of the Common Era he travelled from Babylon to Pumpeditha, retracing his mother's steps of a quarter of a century earlier, though he rode in a handsome leather saddle on the back of a large, well fed ass where she had gone barefoot on calloused soles. He was accompanied by two slaves and pack asses piled with bales of rich spices, notably the very precious pepper from India that had reached Babylon overland in one of Leah's caravans, from that far and mystic country. David knew exactly what he was to do.

He set up his auction of spices in the Pumpeditha market place, as Leah had said he should, announcing himself by his full name, David Bar Issachar. None, she said, would think he could be her son, so it would be safe. People came, as she knew they would. Though Pumpeditha was a city of importance, with many scholars from the neighbouring academies at Nehardia and Sura thronging its streets on market days, and comfortable merchants and vintners and farmers jostling there too, something new was a matter of excitement; and David Bar Issachar was new.

He auctioned part of his store for gold, then announced to the listening throng that he wanted no more gold; he wished to sell his spices for goods – especially silk and woollen cloth. Were there, he asked innocently, weavers of such cloth in the town?

And so David came face to face with his Uncle Micah – and Micah's daughter, Keziah. The youngest of his great brood, she was the joy of his life. After her grandmother's dreadful death, her mother, poor Sarah, had gone quite mad, and spent all her days huddled in a back room, listening to strange voices that none but she could hear. It was Keziah who ran the house and stretched its poor resources to feed them all, and who comforted her father as he struggled to make ends meet.

And struggle it was, for since the scandal of his sister's accusation and his mother's murder, Micah had been regarded with deep suspicion by his fellow citizens; far too few of them sold him good yarn to weave his cloth, and even fewer bought the cloth. But they managed well enough – but not so well that the news that a rich merchant was in town and willing to trade cloth for valuable pepper could be ignored.

Looking upon Keziah had a strange effect on David Bar Issachar. Because she was an unmarried girl, she went with her head uncovered, and as she stood in the sunlit market place her red hair shone in an aureole of wildly curling tendrils and her round blue eyes seemed to shine. Such colouring was not unheard of among the Jews of Babylonia, but it was not common, and to David's bedazzled eyes Keziah seemed the most exotic creature he had ever seen. Gazing at her, he did not think of his mother at all.

Afterwards, he was to smile wryly at how matters had transpired. His instructions had been clear – he was to discover which of the weavers was Micah, and exchange spices for cloth and then switch the cloth his uncle gave him for some trumpery stuff Leah had provided and accuse him loudly of cheating. 'After all that has gone before,' Leah had declared, 'He will be as an outcast. It will destroy him totally.'

But David did nothing of the sort. He traded Micah's cloth for the best of his pepper, making the older man's eyes open with delight, and asked himself to their house to deliver the sacks, and perhaps engage in further trading. By the time he had eaten Keziah's good cooking, served by Keziah herself, and had watched her moving about the small and mean living room of the family house, the discovery that he had managed to find the Wicked Uncle of whom his mother had spoken to him came too late.

Too late for Leah that is, for when David told Micah, with the disarming honesty of a young man fallen helplessly in love and desperately needing to please the man he sought to make into his father-in-law, who he was, Micah told him the truth about the past. Of Leah's false witness, and later, murder. Of the way Tamar had suffered in Jerusalem so long ago, and saved the children's lives.

'Why,' said Micah, 'if the exchange of my brother for your mother had not been effected, my boy, you would not exist. For it is clear that your mother's mother, Susannah, perished under the Roman sword in Gaza. You have a sorry heritage, my poor nephew, a sorry heritage, for Leah is a bitter twisted woman. Though I wish her no evil,' he added hastily. 'I just pray she will never come near nor by me or mine.' He made an ancient gesture, learned from the street boys of his youth, a sign that would keep evil from him.

What could David do but believe him, besotted as he was?

He smiled at Keziah, and then totted up the value of his mother's spices and the gold he had already gained, and his riding ass and his pack asses and his slaves, and decided he was ready to live his own life. He would renounce his father and his mother and cleave unto a wife.

They went to live many days' journey away eastward, far beyond the great Euphrates, on a tributary of which Pumpeditha lay, and the mighty Tigris, in a small village which was of so little importance it had no name though it was near the very ancient place where the patriarch Abraham had once lived, the city of Ur. David Bar Issachar laboured well and mightly there, planting olives and vines and rearing fat sheep, as did his children and his children's children, and their children after them. For David, the wandering ceased. Twenty-four generations later, in the year 762 of the Common Era when the Abbasid caliph Al-Mansur came and founded his great city of Baghdad there, the rich Jewish family that David had begun became great Princes of the Great City. They were to wander again, eventually, but for a while, a long while, it was all peace and comfort and increasing riches for the grandchildren of Leah, the great grandchildren of Susannah.

But not for Micah, son of Tamar and Omar. When David Bar Issachar bore away his beloved Keziah he let her go, for he knew it was inevitable. But he suffered dreadfully from loneliness and fear after she had gone – fear that Leah might try again to harm him, especially now she had lost her son to Micah's child.

So, Micah left poor demented Sarah to the care of her brother who agreed to take on the burden in exchange for Micah's precious loom and tools, and with his two surviving sons left Pumpeditha on foot, bearing his meagre store of gold tied to his waist on a leather thong.

They went west and north, making their painful way through scattered groves of olives and patches of grain fields, going – anywhere, as far as they could get from Leah's baleful influence. Micah by now was almost as mad as his poor Sarah, seeing Leah or her agents behind every tree, smelling her on every change of wind, hearing her whisper to him from every dawn breeze. But he was not completely mad –

he could still work, and did, together with his sons, Daniel and Akkub, hiring themselves out wherever they could. In Damascus they halted for a time, and there Micah died, weary, old before his time, and longing for his lost red haired Keziah.

Daniel, an energetic young man with great personal ambitions, decided he would be most likely to realise his ambitions if he went on. Almost a year after his father's death he reached the mighty city of Byzantium, and there he stayed. He married the daughter of a rich merchant, and seemed well set upon his plan for riches of his own to start with. But much was to happen to the children of Daniel before they were to be as comfortable as the children of his sister Keziah. Very much.

As for Akkub, he didn't get quite as far as Byzantium. He reached Tarsus, beyond Antioch, and there married a poor man's daughter (having no wealth of his own, he was lucky to get a bride at all) and laboured away his life in other men's vineyards. His children, the family of Akkub Bar Micah, became part of the grey background of Tarsus, poor, unremarkable, happy enough to fill their bellies, make children on their wives, and in their time, die quietly enough. Their time, too, would come, one day, but for many generations they simply existed. Nothing more.

And Leah? What of Leah? When David failed to return, and she could hear nothing of what had happened to him, her fury, her resentment, all the pain of her childhood, the protracted grief she still felt for the dead child she had once been, at last overwhelmed her. With no one else nearby upon whom she could vent her pain, she turned it all against herself so violently that even her indolent husband Issachar was alarmed, and had her put in chains to restrain her from self injury. For the rest of her life – and she lived to be seventy – she was lost in the world of her own madness.

She was put in her chains in the same year that her mother Susannah died far away in Cordoba. The Romans who had destroyed the Temple in Jerusalem almost fifty years before had destroyed them both.

It was strange how the patterns repeated themselves, as the generations of the children of Susannah and Tamar pleated down the years. As son followed father, as daughters kissed their weeping mothers goodbye and went away to enrich another family's nursery with the husbands chosen for them, the characteristics that had marked the two of them over-whelmed, time and again, those of the fresh blood that each marriage of each child brought to the tribes.

In the place that would become Baghdad, first; there, long after Keziah had died in her eighty-second year and been laid to rest in a tomb that was a good deal more sumptuous than was proper for a Jewess but upon which her grieving sons insisted, red haired and blue eyed babies were born in almost every generation. Cousin married cousin with almost mono-tonous regularity as the years moved on, and so strengthened and refreshed the red hair and the blue eyes.

But not all the marriages were so close. One or two of David Bar Issachar's and Keziah's great-great-great-grandsons brought Persian wives into the family, somewhat to the disapproval of some of their sisters, but they were biddable girls and did not disturb the even tenor of the family's ways. Still the old Jewish customs were observed – the Sabbaths and the festivals, the fasts and the celebrations – by children who had the liquid dark eyes and aquiline noses of their Persian ancestors as well as by the snub-nosed rust-topped cousins who were Tamar's memorial.

As Islam spread and flourished in the cities of Mesopotamia, so did the Jewishness of the family of Bagh-dad. The Caliphs of the city built themselves the most beautiful palaces, set in many acres of wooded parkland with singing fountains and brooks and lakes teeming with rare fish. They built peacock blue mosques and slender minarets and around them as Baghdad stretched itself along the right bank of great Tigris, streets of vaulted bazaars sprang up. Raw wool and cotton goods, spices and sugar, copper and precious stones came by camel and pack ass across the eternal deserts from China and the Indies, or arrived on the ancient goatskin rafts which twisted their way through the Tigris's tangled channels to bring pearls and silver from the Persian Gulf.

But among the minarets and great houses of the viziers were the synagogues of the Jews, rich yet elegant buildings which bore the most costly tiles, the handsomest cedarwood carvings in their dim cool interiors, and all that could ever be dreamed of in wrought gold and silver vessels and ornaments. The Jewish houses were mansions, built around paved courtyards where water tumbled from tiled fountains into marble basins, everywhere carpeted with the best products of Persia, the most exquisite porcelain from far China, the softest cushioned beds behind the cool lattice of the windows, and were inhabited by the most splendidly dressed men and women.

And none were more richly dressed nor more lavishly bestowed than the mighty family of David Ben Lamech. His great-great-grandfather had been nicknamed The Strong by a grateful vizier, whom he had helped to quell an uprising of local peasants by means of bribery paid to their allies, a nomadic tribe which had come sweeping into the city hell bent on robbery. The nickname had stuck, but had been translated into the ancient tongue of Judah, so that the sons of the vizier's friend became the 'Sons of the Strong' – Ben Lamech.

There were by the year 1150 over forty thousand Jews living in the city of Baghdad. Some had come to trade from Babylon, Sura, Pumpeditha and Ava, drawn by stories of the great wealth of this jewel on the Tigris, and stayed to prosper. Others had come from Persia, retracing their steps westward from their earlier migrations there, after the first Captivity that had taken their ancestors from Judah to Babylon. And many, of course, were the descendants of David Ben Issachar and Keziah.

The Elder, David Ben Lamech, could trace his ancestry back through the oldest son of an oldest son directly to their Patriarch, David Ben Issachar. It was said by those who wished to curry favour that they could trace their line further still, to King David himself, who had ruled so long ago in lost Jerusalem, but the family themselves never made any such claims. They just smiled into their beards, and let their neighbours talk and fawn and said nothing.

They did not need to. Whatever had been their ancient heritage, what they had now was enough for any family. Their senior member David (for the family liked to bestow this important name on someone in every generation) was the Nasi, the Prince of the Captivity who led all the forty thousand. When the Caliph wanted money for one of his schemes, and had to turn to his Jewish citizens to get it, it was to David Ben Lamech he spoke first, labelling that great man *Sarraf Bashi* – Chief Banker. The other Jews did not like the Caliph's taxes; who would? But paying them to David Ben Lamech was somehow less painful than paying them directly to the viziers of the haughty Caliph; and anyway, it was more than taxes; it was insurance. While the Nasi rode decked in gold tissue to the Palace and was greeted as 'Brother' by their temporal ruler, they had a friend at court who could speak for them in any civil argument, and who could protest – successfully – when some junior official allowed his rapacity to get the better of him. Life was good in Baghdad. Good and easy. The family of Ben Lamech had no reason to think it would ever be otherwise.

Patterns were being repeated elsewhere, also. In Cordoba, it was very similar to Baghdad, even down to the regular appearance of red haired blue eyed children. Simeon Ben Jehohanan enriched the inheritance Susannah had left him, garnered from her prudence and hard work, and then distressed his sons by giving the bulk of his possessions to his beloved daughter Tamar before he died, so that their own inheritance was meagre. They learned to hate their sister, Tamar Bas Simeon, because she took all her wealth into marriage with a Jew from Granada, Gabriel Ben Asher, leaving them to make their own fortunes, while she and her children went to live on a hill above Cordoba.

They too had children, many of them, who grew up and learned to copy the customs of their neighbours in marrying exceedingly young. The great great great granddaughters of that Susannah who had lain on her back and stared at the sky beside the wharf in Gaza learned before they were twelve years old to lie on theirs and stare up at ornately decorated ceilings while experiencing the same invasion of their bodies. But they seemed to come to little harm from it, and dutifully bore their many children before going to their graves on the Spanish hillside near their homes in the growing city of Cordoba. The Jews of the city called the country where they had come to rest *Sepharad*, identifying it with the place named in the Book of Obadiah. They still remembered home though, and spoke yearningly of Jerusalem. One day, they promised each other, they would return. One day. Meanwhile they buried their dead on the hillside and kept to the old rules of the old religion, and went on making their livings.

The Arabs came in 711 and spread themselves around the peninsula like olive oil spilled on a marble slab, rolling into every corner of every life. It was said by some of the Spanish Christians that the Jews had plotted with the invading strangers. The Jews denied that. In response, their Christian neighbours pointed to the way the Muslims left the Jews of Cordoba and Cadiz and Toledo and everywhere else well enough alone, in spite of the fact that Mohammed, their great founder, had been on less than ideal terms with some other Jews. He had tried unsuccessfully to convert the Jewish tribe of Nadir in the city of Yathrib, the town he had renamed Al Medina, the City. Mohammed had been angry, very angry. Yet, somehow his anger seemed to have been dissipated in his followers, and the invaders of Christian Spain, a country they called Andalus, dismissed the Jews there as mere slaves, and let them be.

So, the Islamic invasion pleased the Jews of Cordoba well enough; only thirty years before they had been sadly harrassed by the King Erwig, who had taken it upon himself to insist that all the Jews of Spain be baptised, or exiled. The King who followed him onto the throne reversed that rule, but insisted the Jews sell their property to Christians at fixed and very low prices. Thus, the arrival of the Muslims came as some sort of relief. They had indeed been reduced almost to slavery by their previous masters – a change could be nothing but a benefit.

Reduced to slavery – almost but not quite. The descendants of Tamar Bas Simeon had managed to hold on to much of her property in the form of gold and jewels, following a family tradition. It was said among them that because their first ancestors had always dealt in gold, they would too. Their memories were long, of the bad times all those years ago. No land-owning for them – they felt safer with their small delicate tools and their skill at spinning the precious metal into beautiful objects, for then if Romans or other marauders set about them again they could escape with most of their substance in their own hands.

Inevitably, under Islamic rule, they prospered. The Muslims came into the Jewish workshops and looked at the delicate tracery of the neck pieces and bracelets and platters and cups that the people of the Mountain made, and bought them at handsome prices. The family of the Mountain – everyone knew them as the Da Montana tribe – thrived. And went on thriving for many generations, rearing their dark haired children (many of whom bore a remarkable resemblance to the sharp eyed men from over the sea, but what could you do? These things happen in every family) and their red haired blue eyed ones, and marrying each other in succeeding generations, just as did their remote cousins, far away in Baghdad. They too were to go on prospering for many years, but not always. There, far ahead in the future, lay a cloud which would one day blot out the whole sky. But now, they had survived the Romans, the early Christian harrassment and finally the Islamic invasion.

That was God's goodness enough for the present.

4

Strange things happened to Micah's children in Byzantium, and not only to them; their distant kin in Tarsus, with whom they had long since lost any contact (indeed, none of the great-great-grandchildren of David Ben Micah even knew they *had* kin there) suffered upheavals too.

The world was changing. Teutonic tribes bore down on Rome, and destroyed that eternal empire; Islam, passionate, united by Mohammed, destroyed first the Byzantine army and so overran Syria and Palestine, and then defeated a vast Persian army. Great empires toppled.

In the north, far on the other side of the Black Sea, a tribe of Mongolians had swept into Southern Russian in the year 700 CE and conquered it to found the Kingdom of the Khazars, which stretched from the Black Sea to the Caspian. The Khazars built a capital city, Ityl (later to be called Astrakhan), at the mouth of the Volga river, and flourished and grew rich; rich enough to have time for such matters as culture and religion. Travellers from distant Muslim and Christian countries came, and so did Jews, and the king of the Khazars, Bulan, who saw himself as a man of high thoughtfulness, listened to all they had to say of their religions, and chose Judaism for himself, for was it not the mother of the other two? He and his nobles had themselves circumcised and read the Torah with eagerness and adopted the rituals of the Sabbath and the festivals with enthusiasm. So the kingdom that stretched deep into Great Bulgaria, among the pagans of the North with their brutish ways and ugly guttural speech, became known as the Jewish Kingdom of the Khazars – a matter of some amazement to the Jews of distant Sepharad when news of its existence filtered through to them, struggling as they were to maintain themselves amid the complications of life surrounded by both Christians and Muslims.

Once more, for a time, the scattered Jews dared to dream of a country of their own again. Yet the descendants of Micah dreamed no such dreams. They were living as they had for many generations; Daniel's children comfortable enough traders in rich Byzantium, and Akkub's children poverty-stricken work horses in Tarsus. Until the world around them tilted, stirring the waters of their lives, and sent them off again on the ripples, wandering yet again.

It was two of Daniel Ben Micah's more energetic progeny who set off first, in the year 880 AD, from the teeming wharves and jetties of Byzantium, bearing such gold as they could extract from their father Jethro, an old man who deeply distrusted this absurd project. They had visions, these two, Reuben and Amos Ben Jethro, of making their personal fortunes.

It was not as easy as they had dreamed without means and connections in the rich city of Ityl. Amos, disgruntled, was prepared to return at once across the Black Sea to Byzantium even though the journey he had already made had been hellish. He was even prepared to face his father's scorn. But to his own good fortune, he chose to take his evening meal on what he meant to be his last day in Ityl at a wharfside inn overlooking the broad Volga. Here he fell in with the servant of a Radhanite, one of the Jewish merchants who travelled, carrying others' goods and letters and money and a certain amount of political intrigue when it suited them.

The tales this man told impatient, twenty-three-year-old Amos fired him with new hope – stories of Radhanite life that seemed to him to match his private fantasies and promised their swift fulfilment. He persuaded his new friend to speak well of him to his master.

Thus Amos became the member of his family who would wander furthest of all from Jerusalem. His Radhanite master, Menahem Ibn Labrat, had come from the Islamic city of Granada. The ebbing and flowing of the barbarian tribes throughout Western Europe, the wars and the invasions culminating in the defeat of the Syrian Empire by Islam, had closed the trade routes once used by the Christian Syrians. For a time it looked as though the people of the West, even the richest of the landed gentry and the highest of the Church dignitaries, would have to do without luxuries – the silk and spice, sugar and slave girls they hungered for. It was this need that provided opportunity for many ambitious Jews.

Going overland in well protected caravans they set out from such cities as Burjan, in Great Bulgaria deep in the Khazar kingdom, and Cadiz, in Sepharad, and Damascus and Antioch and Baghdad, bearing furs and beaver skins from the remote Russians, swords and knives from Toledo in Spain, and honey, millet and dried grapes from the plains of Europe to China and India. And in time, they came back with cinnamon and musk and camphor, silk and above all, precious sugar.

They were not easy journeys. The roads were alive with robbers, and there were wild animals, and freaks of climate from dust storms to hailstones and thick clotting snowfalls to contend with as well as disease and death. Yet Amos was happier than he would ever have thought possible. He never took a wife, but he left his imprint in every town through which he passed. Brown eyed black haired children with the face of long dead Micah tumbled and shouted and wept and laughed and grew up in back streets of Cologne and Troyes, Champagne and Aachen, never knowing their father was a Jew, or that their remote ancestors had once fled from burning Jerusalem.

After many years of trading, Amos settled in the far city of Shanghai. There, when he was almost sixty years old, he had a son by a Chinese woman. Uncharacteristically, Amos took the child into his house and reared him lovingly. Later the boy, Kwan Sin – Sin meaning new, since he was a new sort of citizen – was taken to Kai Feng Fu, deep inside the Chinese

47

mainland, and there he joined the small cluster of other Jews who had arrived there from Persia and Turkestan, long before.

Kwan Sin was not the only Jew to have an oriental look; within a few dozen generations, even after they had built their synagogue in 1163 and become closer as a community, Jews of Kai Feng Fu married with the people of the town, absorbing them into their rituals and practices. They were to stay there for many years, worshipping in their synagogue. When the Chinese conducted memorials for their ancestors, the Jews of Kai Feng Fu did so too, filling bowls with incense in memory of Abraham, Isaac and Jacob, and Aaron and Joshua and Ezra. They used a ritual bath, as did their distant brethren of the West, and killed their animals for the table according to the laws of kashrus. But they ate their meals with chopsticks.

When Amos died at the age of eighty-three he left the world convinced that he had wrought well with his life; and indeed he had. Eventually his seed would peter out many centuries hence when the greatest war of all time engulfed the remnants of the people of Kai Feng Fu. But Amos could not know that, and so died contented.

After he had bade his brother Amos farewell, so many years before, Reuben had set off northward, taking ship as a deckhand on one of the many boats that plied the Volga, leaving the Caspian Sea behind, and making his way to the very edges of the Khazar kingdom, and beyond across two more great rivers, the Don and the Dneiper, before coming to rest eventually in a tiny village deep in the sheep rearing country north of Olbia.

Here at last he settled. He married a woman of the Khazars, and when she had given him eleven children and died of the effort, married another who was almost as fruitful and gave him six more. He was not always as grateful to God as he might have been for the richness of his family life, for it left him very poor in every other way; but they all loved him, and wept when they were old enough to be sent out to make their own ways in the world.

Some of his sons went to Olbia to make their livings, and did well enough; long after, when the town had been renamed Odessa, their children's children became pillars of the Jewish community there, for they had brought from their life with their father Reuben a great affection for the practices of their religion, and kept every festival and fast most faithfully.

Yet for Reuben, in his old age, the favourite of all his children was Obadiah. He was a thin young man with very large dark eyes set deep in a pale face, and a passion for the study of the Torah that sometimes awed his father. Reuben could of course read and write – every Jew could do that, for how could he be called to be Bar Mitzvah unless he was literate? – but the years of dealing with fleeces and recalcitrant rams and the killing of lambs for the tables of his neighbours had rusted his ability to find his way among the ancient scrolls. So when Obadiah sat hunched over them in the synagogue the old man would watch him and smile proudly into his prayer shawl.

Obadiah might never have married at all, had not Reuben become concerned for his future when he no longer had a father to feed and care for him. The old man entered into very complex and protracted negotiations with a family in Byzantium, using the services of one of the Radhanites who passed through Olbia, and after the exchange of many fat sheep sent the bemused scholar there, amid many fatherly tears, to settle down as the husband of a rich man's daughter.

Obadiah managed to sire six sons of his own, and spent the rest of his life happily in his books. One of his sons followed him, and so started a tradition of scholarship among the descendants of Micah that was to last for many generations. Long after Byzantium had lost its early glory and had become Constantinople, the family of Simon Ben Chazen, the 'son of the singer of Israel' as Obadiah's son was called, was respected for its scholarship, if despised for its poverty. It is a sad truth that learning and wealth make bad bedfellows.

It was there in Constantinople that eventually the descendants of Daniel Ben Micah met again the children of Akkub Ben Micah. They did not know that they were remote cousins. After so many years had passed, how could they? But so it was. Two of Akkub's children, starving in Tarsus, had decided at last that life anywhere must be better than the grinding soul-destroying poverty of that sour city and left their father behind, and like their kin, went travelling.

These great grandsons of Akkub found themselves in Constantinople and because one of them was as eager a scholar as Obadiah Ben Reuben and his son Simon Ben Chazan had been, it was inevitable they should meet. And that a daughter of Simon should wed a son of Akkub's seed.

So the web was woven and went on growing wider, tightening the bonds in every generation. As the years went by they all scattered far and wide about the lands between the three great rivers, Volga, Don and Dneiper, and settled in villages and small towns to raise even more children in the laws of lost Judah, teaching their sons the ancient language and the ancient rituals and their daughters the old rules of feminine submissiveness. And above all the ancient and yet ever new promises of future peace and happiness.

In the thousand years that had passed since Susannah and Tamar had fled the horrors of Roman conquest, forty generations of their children had spread about the world. And forty generations of the ninety thousand other fleeing Jews had also come and gone in the world, their numbers ebbing and flowing with the diseases and famines, heavy crops and good summers that so governed the lives of these struggling people. There were fortunate ones like the families of David Ben Lamech in Baghdad, and the Da Montana tribe of Cordoba in Spain who prospered, each generation adding something to the family's wealth. They grew in thought and learning as well, for riches give the human heart and mind room in which to grow.

But there were others, like the myriad children of Micah, Jews of central and western Europe who were too poor, too insignificant, too scorned by their gentile neighbours ever to have the dignity of a family name. The Jews who lived their lives out as their father's sons – Reuben Ben Jethro, succeeded by Absalom Ben Reuben, succeeded by Jacob Ben Absalom, and who cared any more who his great grandfather had been? It was enough to be alive, to have food to eat and a wife to warm your belly on a bitter night. Of course these poor Jews read their holy books and observed their holy laws, and when they could, found a few copper coins to give to the Rabbis, but there was no energy to spare to study literature or contemplate the art of the painter and the sculptor, the singer and the player of sweet music, as did their rich cousins in happier lands.

50

Yet a few of them – in these far lands of France and Bohemia, Hungary and Bulgaria and the myriad duchies from the Rhine in the west to the Elbe in the east, which were one day to be collected together as Germany – a few of them learned to live with their neighbours in such a way that they grew fat. Banned from the membership of the Guilds that would have admitted them to the mysteries of successful craft, because they could not, would not, swear the necessary Christian oaths, they turned to money dealing. It was a natural way to be, with the Radhanites travelling the world and able and willing to carry money and messages from one place to another. A Jew could trust another Jew, and that helped. So, some of them became money lenders, the earliest of bankers, financing nobles in their petty skirmishes, lending money to would-be builders of cathedrals, bustling about the markets of the cities; needed, used, and in time inevitably hated and feared. For it is a part of the darker side of the spirit of man to loathe most that upon which he most depends.

All of which added up to the horrors that were to be visited upon some of the children of Susannah and Tamar, and their fellow Jews. The fortunate ones in Spain and Baghdad were left in peace for a while, but their turn would come. First it was the children of Micah, the poor ones, who were to know the pain.

Because of Pope Urban, the second of his name.

5

Samuel Ben Israel, a descendant of Micah, who lived a quiet humble life in a tiny Jewish village not far from Blois, deep in the land of the Franks, had never heard of Pope Urban. How should he? He was an old man, who spent all his waking hours deep in study of the Torah and the Talmud. His five sons and his three daughters and their husbands made sure he had enough to eat, difficult though it was on the meagre livings they made as pedlars and small shopkeepers; so, for old Samuel, life was good. God had smiled on him. Yet when Urban the second stood up amid the listening clergy and aristocracy that made up the Council of Clermont on a

51

November afternoon in 1095, what he said was to mean much to Samuel and his children.

It was, said Urban, unthinkable that the Holy Places of Jerusalem, where Jesus Christ had suffered his Passion and had died for the sins of the sons of man, should be in the hands of the Infidel. There must be, said Urban, a Crusade. Men must take up their crosses, and go to Jerusalem, to free that great and holy city from its yoke. It would bring suffering and pain, warned Urban, to those who answered his call, but also glory and a life of eternal bliss. Those who did follow would have all their sins forgiven.

It was not a spark of a speech, but a conflagration. Within a matter of weeks great swathes of Europe were seething with excitement as everyone – even the children – took up the cry to the Crusade.

Who it was or when it was that the Christian peasants – and quite a few of the aristocrats too – pointed out that there were infidels nearer at hand to be killed for the Cross, no one ever really knew. Suffice it that someone did, saying that it was absurd to go to kill Christ's enemies in foreign lands when there were some so handy, and so rich, with wealth that could be used to further the ca se. The cry 'Kill a Jew and save your soul!' began to reverberate through the countryside and hills of Europe.

The Jews did their best. They called a Day of Fasting three months after the speech at Clermont, a place which the Jews came to label *Har Ophel*, 'The Hill of Darkness', making a mournful pun on its French name 'The Hill of Light'. Samuel Ben Israel did not fully understand why he had to fast and pray, but he did so with great enthusiasm, as he always did.

Not that it did him or his fellows much good; in Metz in February of 1096 twenty-two Jews were killed by a looting mob, precursors of the real Crusades, running amok among the peaceful Jewish community there. In May the synagogue at Spires was surrounded and attacked on the Sabbath. Two weeks later, in Worms, another attack was made, and this time some of the terrified Jews agreed to immediate baptism; but most didn't. So the community was almost totally destroyed, even those who had taken refuge in the palace of the Bishop, a true and caring Christian who had tried to protect his Jews. Eight hundred died there.

And in Mayence, just a week later, the same. In Cologne,

three days afterwards, more deaths. On the first of June, it was the turn of Treves. Before July was out, the mobs had reached as far as Salonika.

Poor old Samuel Ben Israel died lying in a pool of blood in the wreckage of his synagogue, his grey head almost severed from its scrawny neck, and so did three of his sons and twelve of his grandchildren. But there were survivors who limped away to hide in the more remote villages of the land in which they and their fathers and grandfathers before them had been born, to lick their wounds and ask their God, again, what they had done to deserve such suffering. And slowly, pick up the pieces of life and begin again.

Samuel's youngest surviving grandchild, Issachar, moved to Treves, and there married and raised a family By the time he was an old man, and the First Crusade was a sour memory, he had produced six children of his own, and they had given him twenty-two grandchildren. The line that had come from far off Micah seemed to have caught its breath, and put out new shoots. There were three little red headed blue eyed children in this generation, a girl called Deborah, and her cousins David and Isaac. They had heard the tales of the awful things that had happened fifty years before and been threatened with Crusaders when they were naughty, but it had never occurred to their young minds that they would ever suffer such experiences themselves. Until it all started again.

The Second Crusade was as bloody as the first had been for the Jews in Europe. In Cologne and Magdeburg, Halle and Würtburg, itinerant mobs fell on the traders and street pedlars, anyone who wore the gaberdine and grew the beards and long ear locks of the devout and pious Jew, and even on the not so pious, the fashionably dressed who looked and spoke and behaved exactly as their Christian neighbours did. And also upon their women and their children. The mob, led by a particularly virulent monk called Radulph hooted and screamed and killed them all, scattering thick blood to run in gutters and stain the cobble-stones of the old cities a sickening brown.

They came to Treves as well, of course, and Deborah's mother, frantic with terror after her sons' deaths, pushed her too-distinctive red headed surviving child into the arms of a visiting pedlar, one David of Odessa, a poor man who was

53

hoping to mend his fortunes by travelling as far as possible from his home. He had not meant, God knew, to travel into the arms of marauding Jew-baiters, and having inadvertently done so, he had turned tail to flee as fast as he could.

So, when the woman of Treves gave him her child to care for, as he took to his heels, he wanted to abandon her. A child of seven! How could he, a pedlar travelling the rough roads with his poor pack, cope with that? But the child looked so much like his niece, small Rachel far away at home in Odessa, with her round blue eyes and rough curly hair the colour of freshly cooked carrots, that he had not the heart to abandon her. So he carried her, weeping, away from the killers roaming the streets of her birthplace.

He fled before the hordes into northern France. Always just ahead of the massacres. Deborah took his hand and held it tightly, not understanding, but feeling his need for such contact, as well as her own. Neither of them knew of their relationship; that both had once, long long ago, shared a mother. Red headed Tamar somehow survived in them both. Just.

It was at Blois that at last they stopped. Deborah had come back to the home of her great great grandfather, had she but known it. They had covered many weary miles, over many weary frightened months, but the sounds of killing seemed to have died down behind them and David of Odessa was tired. It was a tiredness born of disease, though he did not know that. His lungs were shredded by consumption, and in a few months he would cough his life's blood up at the side of a road, and die alone leaving his pack to be seized by the next passer by. But first he left Deborah, now a taller and leggier creature than she had been when her mother had pushed her into the pedlar's arms, in the care of a harassed but kindly enough widow who barely kept her large family on what she could earn as washerwoman to her fellow Jews. One more made little difference, and another pair of working hands could be useful.

There Deborah stayed, sometimes remembering her parents in far away Treves and trying to remember David the pedlar who had been kind to her, but losing them in the haze of steam and soap that were her daily lot. And so she lived, in a daze of hard work and hunger until she had the good fortune to catch the eye of Mordecai Ben Yussef, a comfortably off silversmith, when she took his laundry to him. He had had a grandmother with red hair, and this child was like enough to her in looks to be interesting – and to wed a dowerless orphan, while it was not economic sense, made good personal sense to Mordecai, whose first wife had been one of a large and clannish family, whose demands had made his life less than peaceful.

So, fourteen-year-old Deborah married forty-five-year-old Mordecai and thought herself well off to do so. He made four children on her, much to his satisfaction, for his first wife had been not only a shrew but barren as well, and to Deborah with no parents or brothers or sisters to call her own it was a comfort to have children, however painful it was to bear them.

But there was still no peace for her. When her oldest son Micah was twelve (his father had chosen the name, telling Deborah it was one that had been in his family for many generations; as indeed it had been in hers and from the same source, though neither of them knew that) and the baby, Reuben, just five, a whisper began to hiss about the streets of Blois. It came from no one knew where, but it was the women who thronged the market place who knew most of it, and they told each other, and told their men and their children, and soon it came to the ears of the Jews themselves, who laughed at first, incredulous that anyone could imagine such a tale, let alone believe it.

The Jews, whispered the women, kill Christian babies. They kill them for the sake of their sweet blood, which they take into their houses, and using some strange and dreadful recipe, bake into their special Passover bread. Why, said the women of Blois, haven't you seen that hateful bread? It is thin and flat and bears brown blisters on it, blisters of Christian blood, burned brown in their evil ovens.

The people of Blois were determined to believe the blood libel, airily dismissing the absence of any mysteriously dead body that might have been adduced as evidence, and set on the small community.

It was a sunny day in May, in 1171, when Deborah was just a few days from her thirty-first birthday, when they did it. They built a pyre in the centre of the town, and dragged the Jews to it, all the men they could find, and seventeen women, and tied them to the stakes and set light to the brushwood round them. Deborah's last sight of Mordecai was his face upturned and his beard alight, his eyes closed as he cried aloud the '*Shema Yisrael, adonai alehenu, adonai echael*' – 'Here O Israel, the Lord is God, the Lord is one'. Had it not been for the children around her skirts, their eyes tight closed against the horrors and their small faces screwed up in terror, she would have hurled herself bodily upon the pyre with him, for old though he was, and despite the fact that she had never actually fallen in love with him, he was her husband and was deeply precious to her.

But the children were even more precious, and in the screaming hysteria that surrounded the smoking pyre and the flames that burned pallidly in the afternoon sunlight she slipped away, her four children wrapped in such clothes as she could salvage for them, and took to the road.

Refugees like them were not uncommon in those bad years. The roads of France and Germany were strewn with them; they were too commonplace to be interesting. It was that commonplaceness that was to keep Deborah alive. She made her way to Limoges first, feeding the children on roots and handfuls of grain garnered from the farms they passed, and later on fruit and nuts as the year turned golden. She managed to stay in Limoges for the winter, taking to her old trade of laundering, blessing the long dead foster mother who had taught her how, and hoped for a while to stay there, even sending Micah to the cheder, the school where he could learn his Hebrew, for he was close to thirteen and ready to be called to the Torah.

But times were hard there, too, as the contagion of Jew hating spread and the Jews of Limoges who once had employed the red headed washerwoman soon had to wash their own clothes, or go dirty, for they could not afford even her few coins. She managed to last till spring, and then, thinner, and with her eyes seeming even larger in her face, she set off again.

She reached the river Garonne, far inland from Bordeaux, making her way through the vineyards of that lush country-side, and grew a little stronger, for the rich farmers and vintners of these parts were more generous than their northerly neighbours. Indeed the children became quite plump, well filled with grain and eggs and milk. Micah and Reuben, when their hair was freshly washed in a brook and shone glossily black in the sun, would run about and laugh and play, while their mother and two sisters, Esther and Ruth, sat beside the road and rested, seeming much as other children were, whether Christian or Jew. It was Deborah and Ruth who caught the eye, for that little one, a vivid high spirited seven-year-old, had just her mother's colouring. It alarmed Deborah sometimes because of its strangeness among the dark haired people of these parts, and she would make the child keep her head covered, as she covered her own, as they travelled on.

Over the Pyrenees, and down at last into Navarre, where the heat of the sun beat cruelly on their heads and made their senses swim.

The children begged to stay there. 'Find us a house. Mamma, please find us a house,' Micah said. 'I want to go to school.' For all his sufferings and travels, Micah was still a child, and Deborah had to explain to him, painfully, that they must find a place where Jews were before he could do that. He sulked and shouted at her, but followed her when she set off again, though she feared he would rebel and run. And eventually they came to Toledo.

Toledo. Beautiful, sunlit Toledo, with its thriving metal workers' shops and tanners' yards, its streets of tailors and bookbinders, candlemakers and silk dealers, and so many of them Jews; it was a paradise to the exhausted Deborah and her children, who had become unruly and insolent to their mother through the long months of rough living. A city paradise.

She found a home for her family in a back room in the tailors' quarter, in the establishment of Laban Ibn Menahem, a widower with three children. He needed someone to keep house for him and she needed a roof, and though he was a taciturn embittered man, for he had loved his wife dearly and was ruined by her death, they managed well enough. He disciplined her errant sons, and saw to it that Micah was Bar Mitzvah, so deeply to Deborah's relief that she agreed to marry Laban.

It was a peaceful life, and she had a bed and a roof and so did the children. And there was Esther, quiet, sweet and biddable, to help her about the house, and to go looking for her naughty sister when she ran off to play boylike in the streets, so Deborah was happy enough.

57

Until Ruth, a glinting eyed creature with spirits which were one moment tearing away in the skies and the next sunk in the deepest of despair, reached maturity and found that she could sing. Oh, that was a shock and a shame to Deborah, who wanted only that her girls would be good daughters of Israel, and wed good men and rear their children. To have such a child as Ruth, who would slip away, however carefully she was watched, to wander the squares of the Christian quarter of Toledo and sing her wild and lilting songs, songs she made up for herself, for the coins men threw at her – how could Deborah have reared such a one? What sin had she committed in the eyes of the Lord, Blessed be He, that she should suffer so?

So she thought until it happened that Ruth was heard one hot August night by a rich merchant of Toledo who bade her come to his palace in the cool hills above the town and sing for his guests. He dressed her in silks and a rich soft woollen cloak and set leather shoes on her feet, and she sang, and his guests were entranced. Especially a visitor from Cordoba, a very rich goldsmith named Benjamin Da Montana. He was stirred deeply by the sideways glances of those round blue eyes and the way the candle light gleamed on that red hair, and decided he must have her. He was rich enough and powerful enough to outface the disapproval of his fellows in the synagogue at home in Cordoba, when he brought such a wife to them – and the girl was Jewish, after all! He would have had her even if she had not been, though perhaps not as a wife – but as it was, a wife she became. Deborah felt she had at last some recompense for all her suffering; to be mother-in-law to so rich a man was bounty indeed.

Which was how it happened that a child again changed from one side of Tamar and Susannah's scattered family to the other. The red hair wove its way deeper and deeper into the spreading tapestry. It always would.

Peace at last. There in noble, cultured Spain, where Moors lived tolerant lives and shared their minds with their Jews, peace at last.

For a little while.

6

Black as had been the lives of many of the families which had spread throughout the world since Tamar and Susannah had left Jerusalem, it had not been all bad. For Susannah's descendants, the Da Montana family, there were many tranquil years, during which they grew in beauty and wisdom and culture. And enjoyed themselves hugely.

The main trunk of the family lived always on their mountain; or so they called the hill which they had made their own. Looking down on the cluster of Cordoban roofs, a broad white walled villa built in the cool, airy Moorish style spread itself in every generation as extra rooms and patios were added, and the gardens grew – miniature groves of oranges set where the fragrance of their blossom could drift across to the screened patios; water gardens, with their cunningly contrived rills and waterfalls and pools full of lilies.

Doña Susannah Da Montana, a formidable lady who wore a black lace veil over her greying head at all times, and who commanded her many servants in a soft whispering voice which yet struck terror into each and every one of them, was a hard task master and always expected perfection of service.

She also expected – and received – respect as well as affection from her children, grown adults though they were. Her husband had died thirty-five years earlier when she was just forty, leaving her with four sons and two daughters to rear, the healthy remainder of the nine children she had borne. In this she had been like many of her ancestresses of the long contented generations which had lived in this house; fecund and fortunate, rearing more children than they lost, unlike their poorer neighbours.

Sometimes those neighbours whispered that the Jews had a special pact with the devil that allowed them to have so many healthy children. They saw no link between the ritual bathing and rules of eating and their avoidance of disease. When their children died of the flux after eating gamba brought up from the fishing boats that came into Malaga, far to the south, they did not blame the bad shellfish, but suspected the Jews of putting a spell on them – for why else should they refuse to eat them? But such whispers did not touch the Da Montanas too much. Let the ignorant peasantry mutter. They were aristocrats and cared nothing for such things.

In this year of 1390, Doña Susannah stood at the head of a large and powerful clan. Not all of them were rich by any means; the original family of the hill were still goldsmiths, and had amassed much property not only in gold and silver and precious stones, but in books and furniture, though they still preferred not to own land and buildings apart from their home on the hill. But they were not the richest either; one of the branches, a family that had sprung off the main trunk more than a hundred years earlier, were bankers in Madrid, running a sophisticated network of trade, financing Radhanite merchants and other travellers all over the world. Nor were they the poorest, for there were many who bore the good name of Da Montana who were small traders and had just modest workshops in the unimportant streets of Cordoba. And some were the poorest of all in material needs, however rich they were in culture – the students and the rabbis and the poets and artists who lived on what their more practically-minded relations gave them. All happy and all linked by an awareness of their common ancestors. They had long proud memories, these Jews of Cordoba. Unlike their further flung cousins, they carried an oral tradition of their origins. It was imperfect, and often garbled, but in essence they remembered, and each parent told each child, who told his children in their turn of the ancestress who had come so long ago to Spain from the Promised Land.

'We were here before the Moors,' they told their children with huge pride. 'Before most of the Christians too. They were heathens when we came here, already knowing God.'

Doña Susannah, who had been a second cousin of her husband's and so had been a Da Montana before as well as after her marriage, was as punctilious as any of her predecessors when she told the flesh of her flesh of their past. It meant a lot of telling for she had fifteen grandchildren, and they in their turn had already given her twenty-three great-grandchildren.

At present she was very anxious indeed about telling them all of their history, for times were uneasy in her golden land.

All those long years of peace which had brought her to this stage of her life were crumbling in fear and too many of her neighbours had become Conversos; Jews who, alarmed at the way the contagion of Jew-baiting had spread southward from France and Germany, chose the safer way of kissing the Cross and renouncing their past. What else could they do when news of massacres came to them? Like the one in Toledo, forty years ago, when, it was said, fully twelve thousand Jews had been put to fire and sword.

Not all of them were as whole hearted about their new religion as they might be, however; for all their attendance at Mass on Sundays they were still reluctant to eat pork and shellfish, still lit candles on Friday evenings, still left their chimneys smokeless on Sabbath days. Some even managed to fast on Yom Kippur and read the Seder on Passover while conforming outwardly to Christian manners, a way of life Doña Susannah was swift to condemn.

'For,' she would say in her haughty whisper, 'such creatures are an abomination in the sight of the Lord, Blessed Be He. To be both is to be neither.'

And she would try to strengthen her grandchildren's and great-grandchildren's love of their faith as much as she could, fearing for their future if they were to go the same way as those Converso neighbours.

And oh, but she was right! Fortunately for herself, she died just before Ferrand Martinez, father confessor in the court of the King of Castile, caught fire and started on his campaign in 1391 to bring the infidel Jews into the Christian fold. Repeating the words that had so fired the Crusaders long years before, he took up his cross and followed by a mob went from one city to another, marching through the Jewish quarters, right into the synagogues sometimes, offering every Jew he met the choice between the Cross and a disagreeable and immediate death.

That many chose the cross was not surprising; that some of them chose to be whole hearted about their acceptance into the Catholic Church was not surprising either. What did perturb the Christian clergy was that some were so stiff necked as to pay lip service to the new faith, while sticking as stubbornly as ever to the old. The secret Jews, they called them, the Marranos. Pigs.

Those who chose to become Conversos thought they were

61

choosing life. Perhaps they were, for themselves. Of those who put aside their phylacteries and prayer shawls and had their heads anointed in baptism many lived to die in their beds, in God's good time, unmolested if sneered at by both their new Christian brethren and their old Jewish ones. They might have died thinking all was well for their children's future, for those born to Conversos were brought up as Christian children. They went uncircumcised, were taught none of the old rules about what they might and might not eat, and were given no Talmudic teaching. They should have lived for ever after, happy and secure Spaniards, and of course some did; the old Jewish families gave birth to some surprising sprigs. Two hundred years after her ancestor had converted from Star of David to Cross, Teresa of Avila was born to become a great Christian saint, a founder of convents.

But not all did so well. Not by any means. For in 1476 a seed came into Spain from France and took root. It had first come to flower almost 250 years before in far away Lincoln in the windy cold island of England, far to the north. The archdeacons there had made an enquiry into the behaviour of the Jews in England. It was to spread, that inquiry. They called it the Inquisition.

Led by Queen Isabella's personal confessor, Tomas Torquemada, a train of priests and scribes and lesser and greater clergy, and not a few hangers-on ready to seize whatever fell from the skirts of the Inquisition's robe, moved through the land. There was nothing dramatic about it, really. Just a slow, methodic, even pernickety, process of law. Some cases lasted fourteen years or more. They would arrive in a town and set up their office in some convenient place – perhaps a shop loaned by a local merchant eager to curry favour, sometimes in the market place itself, sometimes even building a special Palace of the Inquisition, if they intended to remain a long time – and start their enquiries.

Who was there, they asked the local populace, among the New Christians, who wore clean linen on Fridays and Saturdays? Did any abstain from lighting fires on those days? Did they buy special wine or meat from known Jews? If there were such they must be brought before Torquemada and his minions and be questioned.

And what a great opportunity it all was for the people of

these commercial towns. Did you owe a debt to a man whose father or grandfather had been a Jew? Splendid! Never mind that he sat next to you in church at every Sunday's mass, or stood beside you to take his communion. Nod at Torquemada, and you could forget your debt forever.

Isabella and Ferdinand benefited too: from the confiscated wealth of convicted Marranos, secret Jews. To be pious was very good business, and not bad politics either. Poor people with secret Jews to root out were much less likely to show any interest in what went on at court. It was a good time and a bad time, depending on which side you were.

A confused time for the Da Montanas. About a third of the clan had converted. They came from a long line of survivors, drawing their determination to live from Susannah herself, that long ago fugitive from Roman cruelty who had brought them to this threat of Christian cruelty in Sepharad. What else should they do but convert?

The more far sighted, like Doña Rachel Da Montana, did not. Doña Rachel was a formidable old lady of more than ninety summers – no one ever asked her age any more; it seemed insulting to do so, for she was so lined and so bent that she seemed as desiccated and eternal as an olive tree. Doña Rachel could just remember her own great grandmother, Doña Susannah. Her views were clear and drawn directly from that long ago time when she had sat at the old lady's feet playing with a doll and listening to the words of wisdom, not really understanding them but storing them up all the same.

'Remember always that God cares for you,' Doña Susannah had told the infant Rachel and her brothers and cousins. 'If you remain true to him, he will be true to you. Do not abandon his protection for the false protection of a different faith. Not just because it would be wicked. Because it would be stupid.'

Ancient Doña Rachel told her sons and daughters and grandchildren and great-grandchildren the same.

'As long as we are Jews,' she said in her cracked old voice, which scratched on the listener's ear like a stone on slate, 'the Christians can have no jurisdiction over us. They can rob us and harry us, but they do not own us. But become Christian and you give up the only protection you have – of not being one of them.'

She was right, of course. Those of her kin who dismissed her words as the wanderings of an old fool, and what was worse an old fool of a woman, and converted soon found that their Christianity was their scourge. Never mind that in the early days after conversion they did well, Conversos had, in the past hundred years or so, spread themselves widely about Spain's upper echelons. They were financiers and physicians, professors and courtiers, friends of princes and much sought after marriage partners by less rich families. There were few noble dynasties anywhere in the whole of Spain which had no Marrano blood. Yet when Torquemada, his eyes on Isabella's soul and coffers, started on his work their high connections were useless to them. They did not tell Doña Rachel of what happened to her brother's great-great-grandchild Catalina. She had been fond of the girl, in spite of her high handedness and her attempts to deny their relationship. Doña Rachel's brother had been a Converso, and so his great-great-granddaughter Catalina regarded herself as very much a Christian.

They took her to the Offices of the Inquisition to face the Promoter Fiscal, after he had made his *clamosa*, the formal demand for the opening of the proceedings against her. She was just thirty years old, the mother of three fine sons and a plump daughter, the wife of a merchant of the city, a tall and handsome woman with her sleek dark hair and haughty black eyes. Because of the rule of secrecy which always surrounded Inquisition trials, none of her family knew what the charge was, who had laid it, what the *calificadores*, the lawyers who examined the charges, had presented in their *calidad de officio*, the justification for further proceedings.

All they knew was that one morning, while her husband Simão Da Montana was at his counting house, and she was sitting playing with her children in her richly appointed house in Cordoba, the arresting officers had come. Her sevants had shrieked and run away. Not until her husband came home to find his house abandoned and his children screaming and alone in their nursery did he know anything was amiss. Even then, he could not find out what had happened. He went of course to his priest to ask his help, but that did him no good. As the priest told him and he knew perfectly well, everyone involved in a trial before the Inquisition was sworn to total secrecy. Even, poor devils, the accused –

So, Doña Catalina, wife of Simão Da Montana, faced her trial. She did not of course know who her accuser was or what the accusations were. It was part of the complex rules of evidence that such facts should be withheld from the person before the court. She stood there, ice cold with fright, yet feeling the sweat trickling between her shoulder blades and breasts and heard the intoning voices, and tried to think what she had done. If she could do that and then confess to it, then the torture would be less, and the pain diminished. She had heard enough of the tortures that were done to fear the coming days, for although secrecy was supposed to be the hallmark of the Inquisition, of course the stories came out of those dark cellars where the officers went about their business.

Three times they asked her, each of the three Inquisitors in turn, to confess her crime. Three times she said, 'I have committed no crime, señores. I am innocent of any sin.' It was almost perfunctory, Catalina thought, staring up at the three men in red robes on their dais, seeing the clerks around the room with their heads together, chattering in whispers, laughing sometimes, ignoring her. 'I have committed no crime, señores. I am innocent of any sin ... ' And no one listened or cared.

'Strappado?' one of the clerks in the court said, almost conversationally. 'Strappado, senor? Cordeles?'

They read the sentence of torture to Doña Catalina, starting with the promise of the strappado, the rope, but she could not understand it. 'I have done nothing, señores. Nothing at all. What is it you wish me to say? Tell me and I will say it – I do not wish to be in such trouble, señores. Just tell me what you want of me and I will freely confess and make my penance to save myself.'

They carried her away to the cellar and stripped her and with her modesty in tatters at her feet she thought that was hell. They hung her from a beam by a rope tied about her wrists and she cared nothing any more for her nakedness, not even when one of the jailers flicked his forefinger at her nipples and laughed to see her breasts wobble as she slowly turned from side to side, for all the world like a beef carcass hung up to be drained of blood after killing. They let the rope go loose and then pulled it tight just before her feet touched

65

the ground so that her arms were pulled cruelly out of their sockets and she shrieked with the pain, forgetting her previous agony, and cried again, 'I have done nothing – tell me what I have done and I will confess it. I did, I did – I refused pork. I lit candles. Oh God, oh Christ, take my misery from me.'

No one took her misery from her. They poured water into her throat through a great funnel until she thought she would drown, or burst, or both, and then pressed it out of her, in time to save her life, and again she shrieked, but this time in a hoarse croak for they had nearly ripped her throat out of her with the great funnel, that she had done nothing, but tell her what she had done, and she would do all the penances they wanted.

They stopped at last, and threw her into a corner, naked, bleeding, in an agony of pain from her shoulders and her scarred throat and feet – for at one point in that long afternoon they had anointed her feet with tar and then held them to the fire so that the tar caught light. She lay there in her own blood and vomit, naked and shuddering, and yet lived long enough to go through it all again three days later.

Doña Catalina was lucky. She died that time, her heart leaping finally in her chest and giving up to release her from her agony. Not for her the auto da fe, the public scourgings and burnings of the final Act of Faith that day after day filled the market place of the city with curling tendrils of smoke, scented with charred human flesh.

And her death saved her children, for her husband, the bereft and frantic Simão Da Montana turned back to his Jewish family in his despair and renounced the church so that when the time came that Isabella and Ferdinand, seeking to rid themselves of Jews for good and all, issued their edict, he found he would live in consequence.

In Granada, on 31 March 1492, Isabella and Ferdinand signed their decree.

From Don Ferdinand and Doña Isabella to the Jews of all cities, towns, villages and places in our kingdom and under our rule. We hereby order all Jews, male and female of whatever age who live in our kingdom, those who were born here and those who were not, to leave our kingdom by the end of the month of July next. They must leave with their sons and their daughters, their Jewish servants and their families and abjure Spain. They shall not ever again be permitted to live in their former residence. . . .

The little boats began to leave, slipping away from Barcelona and Tarragon, Valencia, Alicante and Cartagena, Malaga and Cadiz and every port in between. They left their land and workshops behind them, but took some gold and jewels, tied around their middles, and all their families. Two hundred thousand of them went, some said.

Not so the Conversos. For the next four hundred years that hated Inquisition went on. Long after Torquemada closed his fanatically gleaming eyes in death his successors carried on his work with enthusiasm, though it dwindled in its later years. A later King of Spain, Ferdinand VII, abolished the Holy Office of the Inquisition in 1820, although it was not until 1834 it was finally to splutter and die. Not that it mattered to the people in the tightly packed ships bobbing about on the seas around Spain in 1492. They had more important matters to think about. Like living.

But Doña Rachel died at sea, crossing the Bay of Biscay, to be wept over by those of her family who had escaped with her. Yet she died content enough, for she had been right, as Doña Susannah had been. The true Jews, those who had resisted conversion, had lived. Stripped of almost all their riches, hungry and frightened, their few remaining possessions on their backs, they were again traversing a hostile world. But they were *alive*. They had a future, however grim.

7

Day succeeded day as water and food ran low, and babies were born and circumcised and old people died and were consigned to the sea as Kaddish, the prayer for the dead, was intoned over them. They slipped ashore where they could to refill the water barrels and barter what few bits and pieces of value they had left for sacks of grain and then took off again, hoping, praying, expecting daily to make a safe and final landfall.

Those who took to the Mediterranean were fortunate, by and large. Many died of course, if not of scurvy or fevers, then by being swept overboard from the crowded decks on blustery nights, and many of the wooden ships bucketed themselves to death and sank with all hands. But many of them managed to cross the threatening expanse of heaving water and find refuge.

There were those who reached Italy, to come ashore bedraggled and half dead at Genoa and Livorno, or even as far south as Naples. One group reached Sardinia and hoped to settle there, only to discover that there too the Jews had been expelled by decree and were on their way somewhere else. So they took to sea again, and went to the North African shore, to Tunis and Algiers, and so on inland to Fez.

One most brave captain, who had been prudent enough to take the biggest ship he could find, stock it high with food and water and limit the number of his passengers, however much they pleaded to be allowed to overcrowd themselves, struck far to the south east, delivering the remnants of his human cargo – for many died of sheer misery on the long way – to Smyrna and then to Salonika. Others, less ambitious but still far flung, plunged deep into the Adriatic and came ashore at Venice. Those who settled there did quite well. Not so their friends who had come to land on the other shore, on the Hungarian side; they were set on by bandits and killed for the rags of clothes they stood up in, and their few remaining trinkets.

Those who left Spain from the port of Cadiz, which included the majority of the Da Montanas who survived, fared better. Their captains opted to travel north, hugging the Portuguese coast for the first weeks – they travelled very slowly – as the frightened passengers discussed the possibility of coming ashore at Lisbon or Oporto. But good sense prevailed, for as Simão Da Montana pointed out, 'A kingdom so close to Spain – how can it escape the same infection as that which has fallen on us?' In which he was wise, for the Portuguese Jews were to be expelled barely five years later.

On they went, round past Corunna to Capo Ortegal, on into the Bay of Biscay. That was hell indeed, and there were those who found it in their hearts to envy old Doña Rachel her release by death there. What were they suffering this misery of sea sickness for, after all? A delayed death when they arrived God alone knew where?

Wicked thoughts, said Simão Da Montana, and he harangued them into strength again. His own suffering and status as a man bereaved by the Inquisition had given him another status, that of the leader of their shipload, and they listened to him, and huddled into the corners of the decks, slippery as they were with sea water and vomit, and prayed and wept and prayed again.

They reached the other side of the Bay as summer died in October gales, rounding Finisterre, beating across the Gulf of St Malo, going they did not know where any more. So long had they been on this floating slum that it had become home. There had been two weddings and half a dozen births and more deaths than Doña Rachel's, and a sort of government had been set up by Don Simão, and they were content enough. Here at sea where the world was safe and sure and the sun rose each morning and set each evening with its utterly predictable pattern, where there was no Inquisition to turn the world on its ears and perhaps force the sun one day to rise in the west, there was less fear, less need to cower against the sins of other men. Here there were just themselves and their God. It was not a bad way to be.

So, they took on more supplies at Cherbourg and went on, through the English Channel, staring with vague interest at the towering white cliffs of the cold dreary island that had given the narrow waters their name, and then curved southwards towards the coast of the Low Countries, as those white cliffs, beetling over the turbulent waters, sank into the mist. 'Shall we go there?' asked a child, who was beginning to feel restless, and was one of the ignorant young ones who wanted the journey to end. 'Shall we go there?'

'Not there,' said Simão. 'Not there. Too cold. Too northerly.'

In fact some of the ships that were behind them, which had also come bobbing cork-like and indomitable across the Bay of Biscay, did turn north and land in England, coming ashore at Hastings where, had they known it, some of their more remote ancestors had landed with William the Conqueror, four hundred years ago. They vanished into the raw mists and biting cold of that dank island, and found comfort and peace there. Their place at last had come.

Simão Da Montana's place came when their vessel, now

beginning to ship more water at a time than they could pump out, rounded the coast of Flanders. There were mists here too, spreading themselves wraithlike across the great sand spits and mud flats of that low-lying coast, but somehow he felt a beckoning there. Perhaps it was that he had had time to contain his grief for his dead Catalina. Perhaps it was because of a stirring of his old instincts to prosper rather than merely survive; whatever it was, he called a council of the men of the ship, and told them, rather than asked them, to settle there.

'I believe that God is telling us that this is where we shall find peace and hospitality,' he told them in great seriousness. 'I feel the goodness of God stirring in me. He is calling us to this place and we must heed Him.'

The other men, less mystical than Simão, whom they regarded as somewhat touched in his head by all his suffering, and lacking his sense of a personal relationship with Jehovah, yet agreed. So far, safety at sea had been enough. Now they too were ready for more. Anyway, they were hungry, and food was running out as fast as water was running in. They had barely enough left in personal gold and silver to start themselves up again in business wherever they happened to land. The place and time had come.

Which was how they arrived in Amsterdam, after twenty weeks at sea, slipping up through the Zuider Zee into its snug harbour, to come ashore and stand swaying weakly on its well found jetty as they looked about their new home. They found some Jews there to welcome them, secret ones of course, for practising Jews were welcome nowhere. They were wise people who had also come from Spain some years ago. They had seen the way the wind was blowing long before, and slipped out of their homeland before there was any compulsion to do so, while they had been able to bring much of their fortune with them.

They had brought their good hearts too, and took care of the new arrivals. 'Do not,' they warned them, 'make display of yourselves. You may not confess in public to being Jews, remember that. There remains here Spanish domination.'

'Then we must go on,' Da Montana said, alarmed. 'We can't stay. They've expelled us once, and will do it again. The Inquisition – '

'No,' said their mentors and laughed. 'No. The people of these low lands are not the peasants of Sepharad, and never you think it. They will not have the Inquisition here. They have refused it. Good Catholics though they are, they have no love for Spanish ideas or Torquemadas of their own. Keep quiet and be discreet and you will prosper here.'

Some of the travellers believed what they were told, but many didn't, and they restocked their poor old ship, and set off again, planning to go further north to Hamburg. Among those who stayed were Simão Da Montana and his three children (the baby girl had died three weeks out at sea). He stayed because he discovered that one of the party of Marranos who met them was a kinsman. Jacob Damont.

'It is better not to sound too Spanish, you know,' Jacob told Simão. 'I shall tell my friends and colleagues that you are Simon Damont, my cousin. They'll be glad to know you because they are glad enough to know me. I think we can find work for you. One way or another. And I have a daughter who in a year or so will be ripe for that lively looking lad of yours, the bigger one. How old do you say he is? Twelve? Hmm. Nearly ready for you to be thinking of a bride for him. Hey young Fernando? Another three years or so, and you can settle down nicely. Nicely ... '

Simão Da Montana felt surprisingly comfortable as he walked alongside his kinsman across the bridges towards his home in the east of the city of Amsterdam. He was no longer Simão Da Montana. Those bad days were gone, as dead as his Catalina. Now he was Simon Damont, a new citizen of a new land.

Times were good again for the children of Susannah. Life in the northern land was safe and easy as long as they were discreet about being Jews and did not publish their practices. Simon learned to live with the climate and its rains and mists and accepted with a philosophical shrug the rheumatism that came to plague his old age. 'Better to be racked by the screws of my own bones than to be pulled on a Spanish rack,' he would tell his grandchildren, and they would look at each other and make little grimaces, for they were bored, very bored, by Grandpapa's tales of the bad old days.

They weren't even sure they believed half of them; how could they believe, living as they did in their big comfortable houses alongside the canals of their beautiful Amsterdam, growing fat and sleek on their great meals of butter and cream cheese and good roast goose? They had busy happy lives, the young Damonts, in their hidden, private classrooms, learing the Talmud and the great stories and the complexities of industries and law, and scorned their ignorant old grandfather, who shared none of their scholarship. *He* told them that he was ignorant of the Books of the Law and the stories of Moses and Isaac and Jacob and all the Mishnah and the Midrash because of his past sufferings, because he had been forced to embrace the Cross. They did not believe that, for did he not sit with the other men when they prayed in their houses, secretly, his shawl over his head?

Simon did not object to their scorn. He knew of it, and smiled into his beard at it. To have children like these large and noisy downy-cheeked boys, tall and straight and free to walk with their heads up, looking everyone in the face, unafraid and even haughty, was what the hell of their grandmother's death and the journey that followed their expulsion had been about. He and his Catalina had suffered that the children might laugh at their stupid old grandfather.

That he had done quite well since his arrival in Amsterdam added to his self esteem, and so made him even more tolerant of his grandchildren's intolerance. By the time Jacob Damont had led him and his sons from the jetty towards their new home in the city, all his money had gone. What little he had been able to take away from Cordoba had gone in victualling the ship, buying tar and canvas for repairs, seeing his fellow passengers on their way to Hamburg.

But that had not mattered; Jacob had talked to him long into that first night in his snug house, while the children slept curled up together in their cousins' beds, and mapped out a plan. He would make a loan to Simon, a sizeable loan, for the purchase of gold and tools. Then Simon would employ three of his fellow travellers who had decided, like him, to remain in Amsterdam, and who were, God be praised, goldsmiths. They would make their necklaces and trinket boxes, their rings and bracelets, and Simon would sell them. There should be enough in the enterprise to make a profit and pay off the loan within a reasonable time.

Jacob was wise indeed. Within a couple of years Simon had a thriving business. His employees worked hard and made enough for themselves to buy small but comfortable houses in the less elegant parts of the city, and he had made enough to pay off his debt to his kinsman and buy an even more fashionable home for himself and his growing sons.

Another ten years, and he was even more established. Linked now to Jacob by the marriage they arranged between their children, and making enough profit to be able to enlarge his business, he employed seven goldsmiths, as well as dealing more and more in precious stones in addition to precious metal.

He never married again. He had been thirty years old when he lost his Catalina, but theirs had been a love match, and he could not contemplate ever sharing with another woman what he had known with her. It would have been a desecration of her memory. But he was content enough, looked after by a plump Dutch housekeeper, his sons and daughters-in-law treating him with the respect due to one of his importance, and with his growing brood of grandchildren.

They were as fecund here as they had been in Spain, the Da Montanas. By the time old Simon Damont was called to his fathers and to his Catalina again in 1517 there were fourteen grandchildren, born of his three sons, and the oldest of them, Simon (for in accordance with Sephardic custom the oldest grandchild was named for his paternal grandfather) was already betrothed.

This Simon, who mourned his grandfather the requisite number of days, although only his uncles actually sat on low chairs with their heads smeared with ashes and their garments torn, praying morning, noon and evening, felt a genuine sense of loss. In his young years he had with his brothers and his cousins laughed at the old man, but now he knew better. Though only twenty years old, he was, he felt, in touch with the realities of life in a way he never had been in his boyhood. 'They were stern realities,' he told himself, as he took spade in his hand and threw earth on his grandfather's body in its grave, then made way for his brothers to do the same. 'The new world the old man brought us to is full of promise for energetic people like me. I'll make it better for him.'

Confused thoughts, for who could make life better for a dead man? But young Simon Asher Damont knew what he meant, and he meant it wholeheartedly. He vowed that he would always remember the old man and his stories of

73

Spain, the ancient Sepharad of his people.

The future looked rosy for Simon, as he mourned his grandfather. The people of the mountain had come to a safe haven, and he was going to make sure it would be a rich and comfortable one as well as safe.

But despite his pretensions, Simon Asher was drawn away from the Sephardic practices of his grandfather's family. The magnet was a red-headed girl named Sarah Van Praag.

They were outlanders, the Van Praags, his wife's family, essentially coarse and uncultured. Not his precious Sarah, of course, but her father and brothers, newly come to Amsterdam from Hamburg, were a rough lot. Nevertheless, they had sent Sarah into marriage with a good dowry, and they were good businessmen, however uncouth they might seem to Simon Asher Damont's fastidious family. With their many cousins in not only Hamburg but also Leipzig and Lublin and Vienna, they offered a useful network for a young man with his eye on the newly developing trade routes that were opening up, and which needed financing. Simon's brothers Solomon and Elias were deeply entrenched in the family gold and precious stone business, and he could use them as part of his new business schemes.

They would, like his cousins by marriage, support and invest in him, though Simon Asher never truly understood what it was about these alien people that made them so *successful*. Indeed, the Van Praags themselves could not. They knew that they tended to prosper where others did not. That a few crowns in their hands could be doubled, trebled, quadrupled, in a fraction of the time it took some of their Christian neighbours. Not all of them; *some* of them. There were Christian merchants as hard working, as busy, as efficient as they were themselves and they too prospered. But by and large, it was the Jews and especially the Van Praags who did best. Why?

'It's because we never feel settled,' old Isaac Van Praag told his son-in-law. 'When you feel comfortable in a place, when you know tomorrow or the day after it doesn't matter, you'll still be there and able to collect your debts, it takes the edge off you. But us – how do we know what will happen next? Sure, sure I know, thirty-five years I lived in Hamburg. It's a long time. But I remember another time, when we had to leave Nancy, in France where my mother was born, because

74

they started baiting the Jews again. So we had to go. And debts we hadn't collected, we had to leave behind. My father told me then, it's a bad thing to leave your debts uncollected. They don't love you any the better for it, your neighbours, believe me. All the time they owe you, they hate you. So collect soon, and they hate you a shorter time – and you've got your money safe in your hand to lend again. Remember that, Simon Asher, and you'll be as good a banker as your brothers-in-law.'

That was not all the old man taught him. He showed him how to control complex transactions, and make them more and more complex, and therefore more profitable. And collecting his debts fast, as the old man had advised, meant that Simon always had money in his hand for new ventures. Inevitably, he prospered, with the aid of distant Van Praag cousins; in an illiterate world being able to write down your messages in your own script and consign it to the hand of one you could trust (for your own brethren, by and large, treated you fairly) meant you could take risks further afield. And risks brought money. Money begat money.

For Simon Asher Damont and the Van Praags and for others like them, but for by no means all Jews. There were many, poor pedlars, living hand to mouth, trying to earn enough each day to stock their meagre packs with a few trinkets and ribbons for the next day's trading. If they failed, the next day was one when their wives and children went unfed. Life was like that, they told each other, and shrugged. How could it be otherwise for poor Jews? For them the riches and sleekness of the merchants were as remote and envy provoking as for the peasants of the countryside.

Not that poor Jews remained poor always. Individuals would come pushing their way through the mass of struggling humanity that filled the Jewish quarters of the cities of Europe and emerge blinking to the notice of the richer folk.

That was how Isaac Van Praag's grandmother had become his grandmother. A thin creature, with red hair and blue eyes, she had come to Hamburg from Lublin with her family, her father being a poor Jewish pedlar who could not make enough to feed his large brood in that busy Polish town.

There in Hamburg old Van Praag had seen the girl with red hair and fallen in love with her and married her, in the

75

teeth of much family opposition, but much to the delight of the girl's mother. Clearly, leaving Lublin had been the right thing to do.

Thus it was that yet again, one small and slender strand of the family that had been started by Micah, son of Tamar, made contact again with the children of Micah's brother, Simeon. It was a tenuous link (just one red-headed girl producing a great-grandchild, Sarah, to wed a child of the family of the mountain, the children of Susannah) but a link none the less.

Sarah Damont vanished into the maw of that haughty tribe of grandees, learning to speak soft Ladino, the part Castilian Spanish, part Arabic, part Hebrew tongue the Marranos had brought to the low countries with them, instead of the harsh Judisch-Deutsch of her own family, the Van Praags. That Low German dialect, with its odd mixture of Slavic and Hebrew words as well as German was written in Hebrew characters and had found its birth in the middle Rhine, where Jews had once clustered together in large numbers. They had taken their language with them when they fled to the greater safety of Poland two or three hundred years earlier.

Not that Sarah cared. All she knew was that her marriage into aristocratic circles had ennobled her, and made her a better and more valuable person, and she preened and strutted her way through Amsterdam, more Spanish than any of the Damonts had ever been, wearing the most costly clothes Simon could provide for her, and the richest jewels, and quite ignoring her Van Praag relations when she could.

It was not easy. Her Ashkenazi ways remained with her always, however hard she tried to be Sephardi, and affected her husband Simon too. He lost some of the high gloss of the Marrano culture to her earthier ways. But she never admitted what she regarded as a taint in herself, and indeed once her old father died, tried to cut herself off altogether. She would speak slightingly of 'those Ashkenazis – so uncouth.' 'With such people about,' she would say, 'is it any wonder we Jews are sometimes looked upon askance by our neighbours? We really ought to try to keep them out of Amsterdam.'

Simon said nothing, of course. It was less trouble to be as she was, and anyway it amused him to see the airs she gave herself. But sometimes he looked across at those abandoned relations and thought wistfully of the energy and the connections that would have been so useful to him, if he had been able to use them as much as he would have liked, and sighed. Never mind. He was doing well enough to the memory of his old grandfather. He was making his mark in Amsterdam. He had time enough. He was still the right side of fifty, and the Damonts had always been a long-lived family as long as no Inquisitors were around to truncate their lives. He had time.

He became a revered figure in Amsterdam society. Simon Asher Damont indeed paid his grandfather's debt of pain before he died. He, together with his cousins, brothers and brother-in-law had built a bank with tendrils that stretched across the whole trading world. His sons developed the bank even further, and his grandsons were exceedingly rich, for they had become part of the great Dutch mercantile explosion. That small and tidy lowland country had become one of the great Colonial powers, and that meant trade, trade and more trade.

Out of Holland went muskets and gunpowder and hard working serious men with strong Protestant beliefs – for at last Luther had happened to the people of Europe – and excellent habits of prudence and thrift and acquisitiveness. They needed to be financed and it was the Damonts and their friends who financed them. Into those booming Dutch ports came sugar and spices, of course, the ever desirable trade goods of the ancient world, from the Dutch settlements in South America far across the heaving Atlantic, but also newer imports; rice and teak and above all diamonds from Borneo and Sumatra, Java and the Moluccas far away in the South China seas where the Dutch East Indies lay.

And that was not all. Dutch India – Cochin and Negpattan and Colombo in Ceylon – sent pearls to Amsterdam, as well as familiar cinnamon, pepper and ginger. Every ship load brought profits for the careful Damonts and their cousins. And not only for them; in every one of the cities where the Dutchmen traded, there were representatives of the great Jewish banking houses. Passover was celebrated in sweating steamy Borneo in the same special garments and with the same gold and silver dishes brought long ago from Spain, and in the same soft Ladino words, lisping their story of the long ago Exodus to children who thought their parents were talking about Amsterdam when they spoke yearningly of Jerusalem and Zion.

The progress and success of Dutch colonial effort had not gone unnoticed elsewhere. Across the cold English Channel the Commonwealth, which was busily trading too, was very aware of their success. Particularly Oliver Cromwell, its exceedingly shrewd and thoughtful leader. That the Dutch were successful was obvious. Why? What had they that England had not too?

There were no Jews in cold Britain, at least not officially. Some had crept in quietly of course, fleeing from Spain and later Portugal, and the local citizens had been content enough to close their eyes to their presence, for they were hard working people and brought their own prosperity with them. But they were all secret Jews and did not count. For Cromwell, a good Puritan who had taken himself back to first principles, which included the Old Testament, there was an appeal in the People of the Book, the source of his own true beliefs. Others, however, the theologians and the merchants, did not agree. They did not want Jews.

So Cromwell set about letting the Jews come in by the back door.

Quietly they started to come; from Amsterdam and Antwerp to join the already resident Marranos who, cautiously, started to be a little less secretive about their Jewishness. In March 1656 they petitioned Cromwell for permission to 'meet at our said private devotions in our Particular houses without feere of Molestation,' and to set up a cemetery 'in such place out of the cittye as wee shall think convenient.'

And Cromwell agreed – though only informally. No risks were to be taken by that wily man. He was wily again when he was asked for asylum by a Marrano merchant who would have been thrown out of the country on the grounds he was a Spaniard, when the wars between Spain and England began, by granting it on the grounds that the man was not a Spaniard, but a Jew. Tacit acceptance that, and who would dare to throw out such a man who had suffered so at the hands of England's enemy? He had to be given a home – and with him, his fellow Jews.

And so they came, in a trickle at first and then a small stream. One year later, they rented a house to use as a synagogue. A few months after that, they bought their patch of land for a cemetery. They imported a rabbi, from Hamburg.

Jacob Damont, a great-great-great-grandson of Simon Asher Damont, watched London's new little Jewish community thrive, and waited. 'I've always liked to have my bed warmed for me,' he used to say to his children, long after when telling them the story – and then went to buy himself a house in Houndsditch, in the City of London. He was one of the founder members of the new synagogue that was built in Bevis Marks nearby, and a noted benefactor of the community.

Before the end of the seventeenth century the name Damont was as respected in London as it had long been in Amsterdam, and for the same reasons. They were hard working and honest men, though shrewd and with an excellent eye for trade. They still dealt in goldsmith's work of the finest quality, and in diamonds, as had old Simão Da Montana, the founder of that clan. They lent money at reasonable rates to men concerned with world trade, and were not afraid to take a chance on merchants who showed as much energy and foresight as they did themselves. They looked after each other as well as their own. And they never lost contact with the other half of the family. In each generation, young Dutchmen left Amsterdam to come to London to work for a while with their uncles and cousins, and young Englishmen with Oxford accents went to Amsterdam to discover the mysteries of the diamond Bourse and reforge the links with the old people. But they regarded themselves as solely and wholly English through and through, and not in the least as expatriate Dutchmen.

The first of the English families had arrived.

8

In the many hundreds of years that had passed since David Bar Issachar had brought his red headed Keziah to the nameless village by the Tigris to found the great family that was to become the Princes of the Captivity, the Nasis of the mighty city of Baghdad, life had been comparatively peaceful for the Ben Lamech clan. Its tentacles had spread wide through the carefully planned marriages of its children, so that they were now related by both law and blood to virtually every Jewish family in the whole of that great city, and indeed over half of the Eastern world, for comfortable though life was in the land between the two rivers adventure and profit always beckoned from somewhere else. There seemed to be in many of the Jews of Baghdad a well of restlessness from which they were always drawing. By the time Jacob Damont's great-great-grandsons were settled in England as if they had been there for ever, David Ben Lamech, the Sarrif Bashi as well as Nasi of the City, had cousins in Madras and Calcutta and even far Shanghai, and every place of note in between.

Peaceful years over all, if not always good ones. The family had gone on about its business contentedly enough, running their lives as they always had.

The women stayed safely at home, in their tiled fountain-tinkling courtyards in the cooler winter months, and at other times in special sections of their underground thick-walled serdabs, the great warehouses full of the family's trade goods, where they hid from the cruel simooms, the hot dry suffo-cating sand winds that swept across the African and Asian deserts to broil the city to a purgatory of heat.

They bore their children and reared them, parting with the boys to send them to school as soon as they were six, and losing their company altogether when they were thirteen and joined the men's world, and teaching their girls how to be good daughters of Judah.

They had in their homes their private *mikvahs*, the ritual baths which they used to punctuate their menstrual lives and therefore their copulations, and servants to perform every function necessary for their comfort. So, they never needed to go out, and never did, except to go to synagogue, living in a purdah that no one man or woman ever questioned.

Some of them became petulant and bored, and comforted themselves with the sticky Persian and Turkish sweetmeats flavoured with rose water and orange flowers and almond oil and grew monstrously fat as a result, but others kept their dark-eyed sharp-nosed beauty well into their dried up useless years when they were grandmothers. Not a very exciting life perhaps, but one they had always known, and who were they to expect otherwise?

But the lives of their men were full of interest and drama, the drama of the souks and the trade routes, the caravanserais and the failures and successes of their enterprises.

Each small Lamech boy learned at school the language of his fathers, Hebrew. In recent years their Hebrew had taken on a hint of Spanish pronunciation as well as the purer tones brought from the Ancient Land of Canaan that they had always used. Marranos fleeing from the Spaniards had reached Baghdad just as they had reached every other part of the known world, and had brought with them their ways. The Jews of Baghdad were Sephardic in their practices now, and the children of the Lamech tribe learned its observances faithfully.

But that was not all they learned. By the time they were ready, at thirteen, to stand up in the cool arched synagogue to read a portion of the Law while their fathers nodded at them over their prayer shawled shoulders and their mothers and sisters, hidden away in the latticed gallery above, wept tears of pride, they had learned other languages besides.

Turkish of course, for Baghdad was part of the Ottoman Empire, but also Arabic and Spanish, and most important, the language of business – Persian. They could compute too, understanding the bewildering range of currencies that were common tender in the markets of Baghdad, and could swiftly convert from one to the other the different methods of weighing and measuring that were used there.

Each day, after morning prayers, carried out in the proper manner with phylacteries, the leather boxes containing the words of God, strapped to forehead and arms, they would leave their comfortable homes, their robes wrapped close around them, to find out what was afoot in the tangle of narrow streets lined with souks and booths which was the trading heart of Baghdad.

Who had arrived in the city, what was he selling and what was he buying? What, above all, was the state of the wool trade? For this was the most vital business in which the Lamechs dealt. They were interested in many things, and were happy to handle a few bales of vividly coloured silks when they came in from the mercers of Bushire, down the Gulf, or a pile of cotton goods from Calcutta or Madras and of course the spices that came by camel caravan from Java and Singapore; but it was wool that held the best place in their mercantile hearts. As soon as the sheep shearing time came among the Bedouins in Spring when lambing was over, Lamech agents were bustling about up-country, deep in the Mesopotamian uplands, bargaining and arguing and dealing, and always getting the best wool for the best prices.

But now times were not as they had been. The once beautiful city, with its needlelike minarets and great tiled palaces had dwindled sadly over the years of Ottoman domination. Before the Ottoman had come, there had been Persians to loot and destroy, and before them the Mongols. The once proud beauty that the Abassid Caliph Al-Mansur had caused to be raised on the banks of the Tigris had collapsed upon itself to become little more than a stinking huddle of brick houses where poor artisans lived, and derelict waterworks and broken sewers gave dumb evidence of the sophisticated splendour that had been old Baghdad.

Its physical decay was matched by its political state. The capital of the Empire of which Baghdad was but a part was far away in Constantinople. The Sublime Porte there, the central office of the Turkish Government, was the source of all power – and all misery too. Its officials used the ruined city of Baghdad as a gutter, depositing there the political malcontents they did not want to keep in Constantinople, the failed civil servants who had to be shuffled away into uselessness. Where better to send them than this sour desert pashalik? It might offer good trading opportunities for its resident Jews, but it offered nothing to its Turkish officials and civil servants.

Inevitably, there was discontent among them, struggles for power, and above all, greed for advancement. The more they could collect in taxes from the population of this hateful place, they argued, the sooner they would be forgiven and could return to civilized life on the Bosphorus. So, the officials of the Government became ever more rapacious, and the people who suffered most from their rapacity were inevitably the Jews, the richest of the city residents. Above all, their own tax collector, the Sarrif Bashi, David Ben Lamech.

They called him Sheik Lamech, and for more than forty years he struggled to keep the peace between the Jewish community for which he felt himself responsible and the greedy stupid sly officials who sat on his back and dug their cruel claws into his heart – or so he would tell his fellow Jews.

'They punish me, always they punish me,' he would cry. 'The pain I suffer for all of you!' Sheik Lamech expected a great deal of respect and gratitude from his flock, and indeed he got it from many. But not from all. Inevitably, there were others, less rich, less careful than he in the wool trade, with fewer than the nine clever sons with whom Sheik Lamech had been blessed, to back them up and learn the business. These less fortunate men watched him from under their skull caps as he inspected the ritual baths, the rabbis at his side, or reprimanded a citizen for allowing the mezuzzah – the scroll of the Holy Law in its silver or gold casing which adorned the doorstep of every Jewish house – to fall into bad repair, or licensed the ritual slaughterers to do their holy work. They came to hate the successful Lamech family, and plotted and talked and plotted again and eventually told the Government such tales of David Ben Lamech's wickedness that it was inevitable that action would be taken.

Sheik Lamech heard of what was happening, of course. After forty years as head of the Jews of Baghdad, he too had his spies and not so much as a goat died without his knowing of it. He plotted, too, sending special messages – and extra money – to Constantinople to appease the treasurer of the Sublime Porte, and held trouble off for a long time. But he was tired and old, and it could not be much longer before they succeeded, the men of the synagogue who wanted to see the haughty Lamechs toppled.

It was his grandson Abdul who was to carry the brunt of the trouble when it came. The second son of the younger son of the Sheik, he had long been the old man's favourite, for he was a bright boy with an awesome gift for figures and narrow black eyes that laughed a lot, and yet missed nothing of importance.

The Sheik made him head of the financial side of the house, when he was only seventeen; his uncles had their own interests, and his older brother like his father had died in the plague, so there was no problem of primogeniture to stop him, and the younger brothers would do as they were told. And Sheik Lamech felt safe having the boy there. He was a sensible responsible person, having been married since the age of fifteen to a girl of his own age, Leah, the daughter of a merchant of the city, and could be trusted to keep his mind on his business rather than on young men's nonsense.

By the time Abdul was twenty-eight, the old man was happy to sit at home with the women, or in the synagogue praying, while Abdul held all the reins of the family fortunes in his capable hands. His practical and very sensible wife had borne him four children, the oldest of whom, Sarah, now aged twelve, had inherited his great gift for numbers, and his life seemed to him to be good and comfortable.

But it was not. His younger brothers squabbled and plotted among themselves as much as some of the other Jews of the city plotted, and eventually, driven more by fraternal jealousy than good sense, they combined with the outsiders to pull Abdul Lamech down from his place.

He was lucky; he heard in time. Like his grandfather, he had always kept his spies active, and he was told almost on the day it happened how his younger brothers Ahab and Elias had laid a complaint before the Sultan in Constantinople about 'the Nasi who does not remember as he should the benefits which accrue to us from your magnificence, and who therefore witholds from your honour that which is yours.'

He thought carefully. He thought of the state of the city and the state of trade. He thought of his old grandfather, now almost senile and sitting among the women in his faded mansion where the tiles were falling from the walls and the fountains were blocked with verdigris. There had been so much decay in the past ten years; was there enough to salvage?

He decided there was not. The time had come to admit that

there was real danger to face and to leave it behind. For all the hundreds of years during which the Jews of Baghdad had lived in their city on the Tigris, there stirred in Abdul a deep racial memory; a sense of survival that told him when to move on. And of course, he was an educated and informed man. The traders who came to his souks brought more than silks and spices; they brought news as well. He had heard of the sufferings of other Jews in Europe, of the bloody massacres that had accompanied the Crusades, of the places in the west where his fellows had to live in huddled ghettoes, wearing a yellow star to mark them off as different, unwanted. And of course he knew well about the Inquisition. Abdul was well aware of the world he lived in, and was also aware that he was no more protected from danger than any other Jew, however long his lineage, however firm his grip on the city of his birth.

Leah had to do as she was told – which was to remain behind. 'I would take us all if I could,' Abdul said. 'I love you and the children too dearly to leave you willingly. But they will come to arrest me any day now, and if they take me, they will strip the house of all there is. If I am not here, they will go to seek me, and leave you in peace. I will take what I can carry, no more, and leave you all else. Take care of the old grandfather, and I will send for you. You understand?'

'Yes,' said Leah, and breathed a little more deeply, but it was not a sigh that he could see or interpret as a complaint. That was not Leah's way. 'What will you take?'

'As much gold as I can carry. The last consignment of pearls. And Sarah.'

'Sarah?' Now Leah did allow her feelings to show. Woman or not, she had her rights as a mother and Sarah was only thirteen – old enough to be betrothed, even wed, but still very young. 'You cannot be serious! Take Sarah?'

'She will get me away safe. And I will be in need of a companion. Better Sarah, surely, than – some other?'

And Leah, knowing of her husband's eager appetite for the pleasures of the body and the interest with which he looked at the other women in the family could say no more. The presence of his daughter would indeed keep him from misadventure, for he was a careful and concerned father.

'Furthermore,' Abdul went on, packing gold coins into tight wads, so that they could be tied about his body under his robes. 'She will be my disguise. I will travel as a deaf mute. She will be my tongue. I will send for you, Leah. Take care.'

They took a boat at the furthermost jetty along the Tigris, almost as far as the southern edge of the city, paying the captain a huge sum for their passage. It was the only way he could be persuaded to take them at all, especially as Abdul insisted, through Sarah, on having special food provided for him. Even in times as bad as this he could not contemplate eating any but the proper foods, prepared according to the laws of kashrus, and the captain needed much gold to soothe his hurt feelings at this; there is nothing that insults a man more than to despise his victuals.

They went aboard in the dark of night, when the moon had not yet risen, and sat huddled side by side in the belly of the ship, their feet awash in the bilge water and their heads half covered by stinking sodden fishing nets. The boat slipped away down river towards the Gulf just half an hour before the Sultan's men arrived at the house on the Kazimayah road to harangue Leah about her husband's disappearance. Even as she sat in her elegant courtyard, in the light of a yellow lantern, telling them with tranquil self assurance that no, she did not know where her husband was, though she thought he might have gone up country to Kirkuk to deal in wool, and yes, he often went away without telling her where, Abdul and Sarah were watching the black waters disappear beneath the keel and carry them away from the only home they had ever known.

It took them eleven days to make the journey down the widening Tigris to the waters of the Gulf and the port of Basrah where they halted for a while, and on at last to Bushire, a dirty reeking fishing port on the eastern side of the Gulf, with a landing stage in such shallow water that ships had to anchor three miles out and ferry their goods and passengers ashore in rowboats.

Sarah looked across the water to the huddle of buildings with peeling red roofs and took a violent dislike to it. She told the captain that she and her husband – for so they had decided she should pretend to be – would rather go further on. Abdul was furious. He could say nothing nor show any reaction to her words for he was supposed to be deaf and dumb, but his eyes when he looked at her spat venom and she paled and said hastily to the captain that perhaps it was not so bad after all...

They went ashore, and Abdul had to admit she had been right. The wharves were filthy, rat-infested and stinking. But they could not risk making any fuss or show themselves, for fear the Sultan would be looking for him even as far afield as this.

For the gently reared and protected Sarah it was hell on earth. They slept that first night and the three subsequent ones in a warehouse that was used to store drying fish, with rats running over their feet as they slept, and she wept herself to sleep each night, praying for the morning to come. When it came, and they had to go out stealthily into the streets to seek some sort of remedy for their situation, she ached for it to be night so that she need no longer tolerate the treatment meted out to her by passersby who regarded her and her father as the beggars they were pretending to be, spitting on her as she walked, jeering and plucking at her robe. Her misery was so intense that after a day or two she stopped feeling it, just plodding on from place to place as her father led her, tweaking her robe and pinching her hands to give her his instructions.

At last they found what he was seeking and for which they had not dared to ask in so many words; the synagogue. That there was a Jewish community here in Bushire was a fact known to Abdul. It was what made Bushire on the Persian Gulf, miserable though it was, a safe haven. The troubles in Baghdad had made all his business links with the more salubrious places suspect. Here in Bushire he could start again, and he hoped to find the people there willing to help him establish himself again, to make a home to which to bring his wife and three other children. That it had taken so long to find it dismayed him, for he had expected to see, as he walked about the streets, avoiding the glances of the Sultan's swaggering soldiers, a building of the same sort of quality as the synagogue in Baghdad. What they eventually found was little more than a hovel, a ramshackle wooden place with painted walls that peeled leprously in the sun and which looked about as inviting as a slaughterhouse.

But he prodded Sarah and she led him into the small

doorway, past the mezuzzah that his sharp eyes had noticed there and which had helped him identify the place, and into the shadowed interior. They could just see the light burning erratically before the ark, and Abdul took a deep breath and said aloud, 'God be praised,' the first spoken words that had crossed his lips since they had left Baghdad two weeks before. 'God be praised.'

An old man came shuffling towards them out of the shadows, his eyes glinting with suspicion. It took Abdul a long time to convince him that here before him stood one of the great family of Lamech of Baghdad, that he was in trouble and throwing himself onto the mercy of his fellow Jews, but when at last Sarah, unable to bear it any more, burst into a great wail of hysterical tears, the old man, alarmed, took action. He brought the rabbi who listened and nodded and believed that he was being told the truth, especially when Abdul, throwing prudence to the wind, untied his money belt from beneath his shabby robe and showed him.

They allowed him to stay, and assured him that there had been no whisper of any trouble from the Sultan. They agreed to send messengers back to Basrah, to see if there was news there, and another two weeks later they were told that Jews of that city, resourceful and concerned for the grandson of the great Sheik Lamech, had told the Sultan's men that indeed yes, Abdul had been amongst them, but had died only a few days after arrival. 'The plague,' they had said vaguely and the Sultan's men had taken fright and gone swiftly away, and sent the message back to Constantinople: the Nasi Lamech, the Sarrif Bashi of the Jews of Baghdad, was dead.

Abdul was safe.

'Never go back to Baghdad?' Sarah said miserably, when her father told her the news. 'Never go home to mother and the children? Must we stay in this hateful place always, father? Can we not go home?'

'We have no home, my child. No place that will always be home. We are Jews, and like other Jews, we live under the sufferance of those above us. You have heard the stories as much as I have – of what happened to those of your ancestors who came to Baghdad from Sepharad, long ago, and why they came. Well, it has always been so. We must stay here. I will find a house for us, and a souk, and in time I will send for your mother.'

'But we belong to Baghdad,' she said again, clutching at his robe. He pulled her hand away pettishly, and shook his head.

'We belong nowhere. We carry our homes on our backs – we as much as any other of the Lord's people. It is wicked of you to complain. Clean this place up, and prepare food. I will return tonight, when I've found a souk.'

So, she cleaned the two dirty rooms he had found for their lodging, and prepared goats' milk cheese and bread and olives for his return, and wept for her mother while she did it. She was a lonely homesick child, not the strong daughter of Judah she had been reared to be and she felt very young and very helpless and very very frightened.

9

By the time Abdul was ready to send for Leah, it was too late for her. The fretting that she had suffered in the eighteen months that had passed between his departure and the message to follow had ruined her constitution, already enfeebled by her many childbirths, for although she had only four living children, she had borne seven. She was, in truth, very frail for a woman of twenty-nine years.

It had been a bad eighteen months, with no word at all from Abdul or Sarah, and the children constantly asking for both of them. She'd had to hold off her brothers-in-law as they probed and prodded at her – and dismantled her husband's business before her helpless eyes.

One by one they came, each picking away for himself some aspect of Abdul's carefully structured business until all that was left for her and her children was a shambles.

The brothers kept her fed, of course; even Elias and Ahab would not have dared to let starve the wife and children of the brother they had already destroyed. Instead they put on a show of concern for her and made Leah's burden even heavier.

She ate less and less, slept less and less, worried more and more, burying her feelings as she had always been trained to do. So, when the message came and she had to bundle up her sons and whatever was left of her possessions that she could carry and take to a ship, she was in no condition to face a long journey.

The weather was appalling – so hot, even for a Baghdad summer, that the very stones in the street seemed to melt, and even the mighty Tigris seemed to have become diminished and oily. She sat in the stern of the ship with her robes over her head and refused steadfastly to eat at all, for unlike her far-sighted husband she had not thought to ask the captain to lay in special food for her, and could not, would not, eat what he was willing to provide.

The children did (their young hunger could not be gainsaid), and she prayed steadily for them that they might be forgiven their weakness, and reminded God as often as she could that they were not yet responsible for their own sins. The sin was hers, it was all her fault.

She survived her arrival in Bushire by just five days. They had to carry her from the rowing boat that brought her from the ship to the jetty where her husband was waiting for her, for she could not walk. The boys were silent and frightened, for they had never seen their mother in such a way, and it was so long since they had seen their father that he seemed like a stranger. As for Sarah, she seemed to have changed unbelievably. She stood beside her father on the jetty, her head and most of her face covered as modesty demanded, but her eyes were the eyes of a woman and not a child, and the boys were strangely shy of her.

Abdul took them all to the neat house he had bought for them on the far side of the stinking city, where the air was a little cleaner and where a few flowers could grow and watched Leah die and wept into his beard, and buried her as a virtuous Jewish wife should be buried, and mourned her as a devout Jew should mourn his dead, and then set about finding a new wife as fast as he could. Sarah was already betrothed to a local merchant and could not be expected to take on the burden of her younger brothers' care. They needed a mother, and he needed a wife – badly. It had been a long time, being virtuous under his daughter's eye –

He married Esther, the daughter of the most respected physician in Bushire. She was just two years older than her step-daughter, Sarah, and the two became close friends, which was a great comfort to Abdul, for he wanted peace now that the miseries were over and warring women in the household was no way to live in comfort. When Sarah married and his son-in-law, Samuel Hazzan (whose great-grandfather had come to live in Bushire from far away Constantinople), bought a house alongside his own, he felt all was well in his world again.

When he heard the news from Baghdad in the following autumn that Tigris had risen and flooded the city and that a plague had flared up in which four thousand people of the Jewish community had died, including his renegade brothers, he lifted his head piously and thanked his God – not for bringing disaster on others, of course, which would be wicked, but for saving him and his beloveds. To be honest, he had to make quite an effort to control his satisfaction, but he managed it. To be happy at another's downfall was not the way of a good Jew, and he wanted above all else to be a good Jew.

He had his family at his side, the hope of more children with Esther, a small but thriving business dealing with silks, and every hope of extending it further. God had smiled on him.

The years passed tranquilly. Esther bore him more children, although only three, two sons and a daughter, survived, and Sarah had three sons of her own. The business thrived, as Baghdad caught its breath and began to recover from its disasters, and trade with Bushire picked up once more. Now Abdul was dealing in wool again, sent to him from his old agents in Baghdad who were happy to work with him as in the old days, and was sending back to Baghdad shiploads of cotton which he was importing from India.

Quite when it was that his restlessness overtook him he was never to be sure. It all seemed enough, and yet, and yet . . .

He was bored, that was the truth of it. There was not enough for him here in this stagnant town. It seemed to him that however hard he tried in Bushire he could never achieve all of which he was capable, and at thirty-five he was far from old yet. His oldest son was now almost eighteen, and his next one seventeen, both well trained in business matters. He looked at David – named in the sephardic tradition for his grandfather – and Solomon and chafed at the way their

91

talents could not be put to good use.

His son-in-law Samuel Hazzan was doing very well, with Sarah to help him, for he was an unusual man; he had recognized his wife's remarkable gift for computation and made use of it. Other men might despise women and women's ways, but not Samuel. As long as she did all a woman should do in the house and with the children, he would permit her to do his number work as well. And she did it, superbly.

It was almost on an impulse that Abdul made the journey the first time in 1813. He had accepted a cargo of cotton goods from Madras, and by great good fortune had managed to pick up a return cargo of horses to Bombay. There was a great demand there for the best Arab animals, and when a rival trader's ship was lost at sea, Abdul was swift to seize upon the business. Above all he wanted to see Bombay. There was an instinct stirring deep inside him that told him his fortune was waiting for him there.

Bombay was all he could have ever hoped to find. A vast sprawl of buildings stretched over the seven islands which had given birth to the settlement, and on into the mud flats beyond. There was a fort which the British had built and still manned, and around it the city seethed, one vast bazaar. And the people – the sight of the people made Abdul's lips curve above his greying beard.

There were Muslims and Hindus; there were Parsees, still wearing the pointed shoes and bright silk pantaloons of their ancestors in Persia; there were Afghan horse dealers with their hair oiled to a glistening cap; there were Musselmen in bright turbans, Bokharan traders in long gaberdine robes with tall sheepskin caps on their heads, and Armenians who wore their beards dyed with henna. Abdul kept well away from them. Armenians were not people he had ever found congenial business partners. But the others, the others promised great possibilities. Everyone seemed to get on well with everyone else and there seemed little evidence of the rigid caste structure that he had been told made trade so complex in Madras, far away on the other side of the continent. Here indeed was hope for a lavish future.

He sold his cargo of horses for an excellent price, and negotiated another of cotton to take back to Bushire. But he did not hurry to go; there were other things to consider, first.

He found the synagogue easily enough, in the middle of a tightly packed Jewish quarter, and went to the service on Friday night to be at once invited, as a stranger should be, to share the Sabbath meal with one of the residents.

They talked long into the night, of Talmudic matters of course, but also of more mundane things. Like the amount of British trade there was available.

'Take a look at the wharfside, down beyond Bazaar Street,' his host advised him. 'The British traders have their warehouses there. There's business to be done – they buy more than any others. They tell me the island they come from is very small, but I tell you, the people there have such appetites – they buy so much, so much ... '

It was unusual for Abdul to wish the Sabbath over, but he did that week. He sat in his host's house and in the synagogue itching to be about the new business that he could see beckoning, and when at last Monday came (for the British Sabbath was carefully kept and that meant a wasted Sunday for him) he was on the wharfside again, watching, listening, thinking.

The port was so congested with shipping that men could go far out over the water by jumping from deck to deck. The most agile and busy jumpers were the Parsees, their tall shining *Khokas* on their nodding heads, accompanying the British.

Abdul stared at them, florid complexioned men in crumpled white suits, with hats pushed to the backs of their heads, cigars in their mouths – a very strange way to use tobacco, he thought, for to him tobacco was the solace of one's peace and leisure, not the accompaniment of work – and sweaty shiny faces. Some of them looked ill and yellow in the heat, and brushed away the omnipresent flies with a much greater irritation than their attentions seemed to warrant. The British, decided Abdul, were not comfortable in these climes. But they were busy, oh, but they were busy.

He found a boy in rags, a thin creature with a pointed chin and eyes so huge in his small face that he looked like a sprite; half starved, illiterate – and fluent in a dozen languages. Including English, and that was what Abdul did not speak, and needed.

With the boy at his side to tell him what was said he listened to conversations in which enormous amounts of money were discussed, huge cargoes were traded as casually as a sweetmeat would be sold from a wharfside barrow, and the promise he had smelled in this fetid port grew solid before his eyes.

Before he returned to Bushire with his cargo he had taken a house in Oleander Alley, just outside the Jewish quarter, as close to the wharves as he could get. It was small, but there was room for an office and living quarters above, and below there was a sizable godown, the warehousing space that the local people labelled with this old Malay word. He would need more space eventually if his plans were to come to fruition, but this would do to start with.

He left the small boy, who said his name was Sanjib and that he had no parents and that he lived on his wits and what he could steal, in the house in Oleander Alley and promised him a reward if he took care of the property. Sanjib, who knew a good thing when he saw it, swore passionately he would do so, defending it with his life for the sahib if necessary, and Abdul went back to Bushire.

Esther was not too pleased with the plans when she heard them, fearing that her Abdul was about to repeat his own history, but there was little she could do to affect them. She was only his wife, and though she had her own ways of showing her displeasure, could certainly not expect to deflect a man from his business. How could she? But she pouted all the same.

Abdul did not worry about that. She'd get over it, he told himself, and called his sons and his son-in-law and told them his plans.

They were eager, especially Solomon, who was to have the most exciting part of them. Briefly, Abdul's plan was to make a permanent link between Bushire and Bombay and ultimately with England.

'They tell me it's the biggest market anywhere,' Abdul said, pulling at his ear in the way he always did when he was excited. 'They buy and buy and buy, and the amount of goods that go through Bombay to get there is monumental.'

The sons' eyes opened wider.

'I will leave you, David, to head the Bushire office. You understand me? You will be responsible for all the goods incoming from Baghdad, and for preparing cargoes for Bombay. Also you will deal with the return cargoes. What they will be depends on what Solomon finds.'

He turned to his younger son. 'You will be in Bombay. You will see the incoming goods from Bushire into the godown in Oleander Alley, and then onto the ships for England. Then you will see the fresh cargoes for Bushire back onto the ships going back to David.'

'And I?' asked Samuel. 'What will I do?'

Abdul smiled. 'You will make the occasional journeys to Baghdad, to be sure we're getting the best goods from there. You and Sarah will keep the books, as well. And I – ' He smiled more widely. 'I will travel between Bombay and Bushire, regularly, and make sure we keep those ships going to England full of *our* goods instead of the Parsees'. It's time they gave up a share for us. And we will use our name in the English way. Sanjib told me the English buyers will say our name as Lammeck. We must make it easy for them. That's good business, isn't it?'

The Oleander Alley house was the first. They had seven more by the time Abdul was fifty and Lammeck and Sons owned a great swathe of the Bombay waterfront by the time he was seventy and ready to take life a little more easily. He had done well, the old man, shrewdly foreseeing the value of wharfside property long before any of his competitors. He had ploughed every rupee he could into those ramshackle buildings, slowly replacing them with better structures. Other merchants had watched him and laughed – until they realized that he was now better placed than any of them to get the best cargoes and the best prices.

Ships from England took five months to make the hazardous journey to India when Abdul first arrived in Bombay, but he had heard of the new steamship services that were being planned and knew what a difference they would make. They did. Ships poured into the docks, and needed space to tie up and unload. Abdul had it, and that meant he had the pick of their goods, long before the city dealers did. Also, because many of the ships were forced to hold port waiting for the monsoon to pass, their captains needed money to tide them over, Abdul provided it, and was repaid by being given first pick of cargo space going back to England.

No wonder he thrived.

Abdul and his sons dealt in everything and anything. If there was trade to do, they did it. Cotton and wool, hides and turquoises, silk and nankeen and muslin, opium and tea.

The opium trade was highly regarded despite the half-hearted attempts by China to control it, for it had the seal of approval of mighty Britain. No merchant of any sense, or any pretensions to standing in the Bombay mercantile community, could afford not to be part of it. Abdul and his sons were therefore part of it, sharing their responsibility with many other major firms, including the great British traders Jardine Mathieson. Why should Lammeck and Sons be any different? They had never seen the effect of opium on a regular user. They felt no more concern about opium than they did about silk; both were highly lucrative.

It was the opium trade that took the business to Shanghai. Sarah and Samuel's eldest son, Simon Hazzan, was sent there to open the first Lammeck office in China, with his cousin Moses and also the firm's oldest employee, the much trusted and highly experienced Sanjib, now a dapper well dressed family man enjoying great respect from his neighbours and fellow merchants, to accompany him. Soon branch offices sprang up in Hong Kong and Macao and Tientsin, and even, eventually, across the Sea of Japan in Yokohama. Indeed, there was not a corner of the world where the ledgers and lading notes of Abdul Lammeck and Sons did not penetrate.

Abdul had long since realized that the best thing that had ever happened to him and his family was the plotting and greed of his brothers and fellow Jews in old Baghdad.

'Had it not been for them,' he would tell his great-grandchildren, 'we would all be living in a half dead city, knowing nothing of the world outside, instead of here in our beautiful bungalow in Poonah where the wind is cool and the trees are shady in the summer.'

And he would look down from his terrace in the general direction of Bombay and think of his industrious sons working there to improve the family fortunes even more and smile.

When he died all mercantile Bombay, his rivals as well as his colleagues, turned out to watch his simple interment and to listen to the Kaddish being intoned over him by his sons and grandsons, and to see his daughter Sarah, a large and powerful lady now, standing there with her head covered in a silken sari, braving men's disapproval of her presence to mourn her father. Women did not usually go to gravesides, remaining in the house to wail and weep and greet the returning men with salt fish to remind them of the painful saltiness of tears and cooked eggs to remind them of the way the human spirit is toughened by tribulation, as an egg is made rocklike by boiling. But Sarah was no ordinary woman. She was the widow Sarah Lammeck Hazzan and a power in her dead father's great business.

As soon as the mourning month was over, she sent her own son, the youngest, Daniel, to take the place of his half nephew Bartholomew in Shanghai, and summoned Bartholomew home again.

He came home to Bombay, and kissed his aunt and listened with his mouth half open when he heard what she had to say. He went to his uncles and to his cousins and they talked and planned far into the night. The next day, they all went to call on Sarah, and talked and argued and talked more.

In the end she had her way. Bartholomew Lammeck, aged twenty, took ship on 17 February 1859 for Southampton, England, to open the first London office of Abdul Lammeck and Sons.

He arrived to a muggy rainy day when the town looked wary and unwelcoming, to stand on deck in his neat turban and silk robe shivering a little in the unaccustomed chill, for all it was now mid-spring. But this was not Bombay or Shanghai. This was the north and after a littlewhile he went below to change into the clothes that hitherto he had regarded as mere fancy dress, but now saw as inevitable.

When he came up again he looked awkward and miserable in his cutaway coat and stiff white shirt with its overlarge black cravat; his whiskers looked far too luxuriant against his yellowish skin and his eyes were bloodshot. He looked very alien to the other English passengers, very much a foreigner, but Bartholomew was not aware of their sideways looks and half smiles directed at each other. He just saw the bustling docks and felt the chill in his bones and thought gloomily of the years to come, a long way from all he had ever known. How could he ever enjoy life here?

The second of the families had arrived in England.

10

For most of the children of Micah, through his sons Daniel and Akkub, life had become circumscribed by the ghetto. In city after city throughout Europe, Jews had been forced to live in their own special quarters behind high walls with locked gates, observing curfews which were viciously enforced by the Christian community that surrounded them and wearing the yellow circle above the heart whenever they ventured outside to trade.

In some of the cities the ghetto was little more than a street or two; in others it was a widespread tangle of alleys where the houses were built ever higher in the most rickety of structures, for the Jews were never allowed to extend the ghetto boundaries as their communities grew. When a man's family enlarged all he could do to increase the living space to match was build another story on top of the house he lived in, which never bothered his Christian landlord (only Christians being allowed to actually own property, even inside the ghetto) for it improved his rents handsomely.

As a result some of the families suffered dreadful tragedies when they filled their houses to celebrate a wedding or a bris, the circumcision of a son, or observe the days of mourning after a death; the ramshackle buildings would creak under the strain of the influx of visitors, and all too often collapsed, or worse still caught fire. A fire in the ghetto was hell indeed, for none outside – apart from the landlords of course – cared enough to offer help to extinguish it, and it could spread like a crimson dye in a bowl of water, affecting every other house in no time at all.

But still the families survived, going on much as they always had. The ill fortune which had always dogged the footsteps of the children of Micah seemed as entrenched as ever; over and over again men appeared in the family tree who could make no money but could make lots of babies. For every one who could manage to scrape a respectable living as a pedlar of odds and ends, there was at least one other who subsisted largely on the goodwill of his brothers

98

and neighbours, whose children went bare-bottomed as well as barefoot and whose wives became grey and bent long before their time in the struggle to maintain a decent Jewish home. Not for the wives of Micah's great grandsons the handsome black stuff gowns and snowy white Sabbath aprons that other more fortunate women wore; not for them the gold earrings and bracelets and finger rings that glittered and flashed discreetly in the women's gallery of the synagogue on Sabbath mornings. They were lucky if they had the wherewithal to buy a chollah and a salt herring for the Friday evening meal, let alone the chicken for the pot more comfortably off families enjoyed.

Yet it was not all gloom. There were the scholars. Over and over again, in generation after generation, were boys who showed such a thirst for the Talmud and the Torah that it was inevitable that they became denizens of the yeshivas, the study places of the truly devout and learned.

The families were very proud of them. Women who were gaunt with hunger would preen themselves over their sons' scholarship. Men who could hardly hold their heads up in public for shame at their poverty gleamed with satisfaction in the synagogue on Sabbaths where every man was equal, rich and poor, and none more equal than the father of a true scholar.

And there were, too, the midwives. What it was about the women of Micah's descendants that made them so adept at matters to do with childbirth they never knew themselves; yet so it was, over and over again. The wise woman, the one the neighbours ran for when a young mother's time came and she began to grunt and push her baby out of her body, was a daughter of Micah. It was a most valuable gift, and one they tried to encourage in their own daughters to make sure they always had the skill, for as well as bringing the respect of the neighbours it also brought more concrete forms of gratitude. Many were the families that were maintained more by the nursing and midwifery skills of the mothers than by the acumen of the fathers.

Of course some did well enough, marrying into richer families – like the girl who became a Van Praag of Amsterdam. But never did any of the children of Micah become entrepreneurs in their own right; there seemed to be some deep defect in them that made that impossible.

They went on, limping through the generations as at last the ghettos of western Europe disappeared. Emancipation came, slowly, as statesmen and philosophers began to look at the way Jews had been ill treated for so long and felt compunction. In Holland first, and then parts of Germany, and Norway and Sweden and Denmark and Italy and Great Britain – all over the West the yellow circle disappeared and Jews came blinking out of the ghettos to become lawyers and doctors and musicians and philosophers and robbers and beggars and thieves just like everyone else. It was a heady time for some – but not for all. Not in eastern Europe.

Micah's family had mostly got it wrong again. Several of the branches of the children of Akkub had turned towards Poland in the good days when that country had offered the most civilized living conditions for Jews. Others went to Russia and settled there. So when, after yet another of the long struggles between Poland and Russia ended with the annexation by Russia of much Polish territory, the decision was made to push all the Jews together tidily into one place to solve for good and all the problems posed by their stubborn determination always to be different, these already poor families were the ones who suffered most.

Some of course were already living in what was to become known as the Pale of Settlement, the family who lived in Olbia, now called Odessa, for example. They'd been there for as long as any of them could remember, and when they were told that from now on they could not live anywhere else they shrugged their shoulders and went on as they always had, for what difference did it make? They had nothing to go anywhere else for.

Like the family of millers, distant cousins of the Van Praags, who lived in Lublin, they had been there for a dozen or more generations, so they felt that new laws made to compel them to stay there lacked force; though they were, like many of their neighbours, a little aggrieved at the way the Russian and Polish authorities sent hordes of newcomers pouring into their towns, until they were all crowded together into shtetls, the special townships and villages that were set aside for the Jews and the Jews alone. A million square miles running from the Black Sea to the Baltic, twenty-five provinces where one person in nine was a Jew. Which did not precisely endear them to the other eight.

The Russian government set about trying to Russianize their Jews. They looked at these people in their antiquely styled clothes based on a century old fashion, at their inability to speak any language but their own Judisch Deutsch, which they called Yiddish, and their stubborn refusal to regard any form of study except Talmudic as true scholarship, and frowned. Many of the Jews of the western countries outside agreed. Their brothers in the shtetls were so – well, so *rough*. To emancipated and cultured French and German and Dutch and English Jews it was very understandable that the Russian authorities would want to contain this alien presence in their midst. Even the way they did it made sense.

They made rules about their clothes and hair to try and iron out that difference first. Jews were no longer to be allowed to wear the full length coats, *capottes*, which were their traditional garb. It had to be short coats – and also short beards. So pious old Jews found themselves being chased in the streets by policemen with scissors, who, when they caught them, chopped first their beards and then their overcoats. The old men were puzzled, mortified, and no more Russian than they ever had been for all their shearing. They just let their beards and earlocks grow again, and patched their *capottes*, and stayed as stubbornly Jewish as ever.

The Russians tried other ways. They began to encourage handicrafts and agriculture, to get Jews away from their traditional pedlar's packs into more productive employment. They allowed the brighter young ones who were able to learn Russian to take up some municipal jobs. They leaned on the Jewish schools to teach the children Polish and Russian and mathematics – as well as traditional Hebrew and Talmudic lore; they tried to stop the ancient Jewish practices of self government which had grown up so inevitably during the ghetto years – in fact, they tried in a few short years to undo the grinding effects of centuries of misery and oppression.

And were angry when it didn't work.

The blank faced stares which greeted the Russian officials trying to enforce the new ways infuriated those gorgeously uniformed gentlemen. Even more maddening was the nodding smiling acceptance which some Jews offered, before going away to carry on precisely as they always had.

They got impatient, the Russians. They pushed harder and

harder. And in 1827 there was an Imperial Ukase. The privilege of conscription into the Tsar's army was to be extended to the Jews. The period of service which the Jews had to give was to be twenty-five years just like all the other soldiers. Not all that bad, really, when you considered that the recruits were to be taken from the age of twelve – even eight, sometimes – so that they could have special indoctrination before becoming true soldiers. There would still be a bit of life left over to live outside the army, wouldn't there? And a much better life, as an ordinary Russian, for it would be an exceedingly strange boy of twelve who could maintain his Jewishness under the care of a drill sergeant rather than his pious parents. And who would bother to keep up contact with them over the many many miles that separated army camps from the Pale.

Little wonder then, that parents whose sons were torn from them by the recruiters of the Canton regiments, as those to which Jewish boys went were called, mourned, and sat *shivah* for their lost sons.

For years after that Jewish parents became adept at hiding their sons from the Tsar's recruiters. Each shtetl had to produce its quotas of Jewish boys for the army, and sometimes kidnappers were employed to make sure the quota was up to strength. So the parents had to do *something*.

They tried all they could to keep their children by them. Those who were physically small were the easiest to protect; birth records were kept poorly and falsifying them was easy, especially with the rabbi to help you do it. So they fed them as little as they could, to keep them full while preventing their growth, and the streets of the shtetls filled up with deep-voiced hairy-chinned short statured youths who would stare strangers in the eye and swear they were only eleven years old, even though they had been telling the same story for the past five or six years.

Some even went as far as maiming their sons. A boy with his feet bound up so that they became deformed and made him limp made a poor recruit; one who had lost his right forefinger, the trigger finger, was even less useful. To destroy a baby's finger for such a reason was a painful thing to do, but not as painful as parting with a son forever, so there were those who did it. They would tie a ligature around the small finger, gradually tightening it so that the circulation was cut off and the finger was irreparably damaged. The parents would look at their boys and pray for forgiveness for having had to do what they had to do.

There were other ploys the frantic parents could use, like disowning their own much loved boys. That was what happened to Chaim Ben Yacob, of Lublin.

He was a handsome boy, right from his birth. Red hair with a saucy curl to it, and blue eyes that laughed a lot, and his mother Shoshannah would sit and twist locks of the coppery hair around her fingers and sing at him and pray that by the time he was of an age the miracle would have happened and the Tsar would have decided he wanted no more Jewish boys in his army.

Chaim reached two and his brother Gershon was born, and Shoshannah wept bitterly that the tragedy of another bris should be upon her, even as the men celebrated the birth of a man to the community.

Chaim reached three and then four and he and his brother grew like reeds, and looked every moment of their age and Shoshannah wept more than ever.

Chaim became old enough to start at cheder and learn his Hebrew, and still his mother prayed, and still her prayers showed no sign of being granted as boy after boy was spirited away from Lublin to disappear into the sea of platoons and regiments and battalions which was the hated army.

When Chaim was seven, she could wait no longer; whoever's prayers God was listening to they weren't hers, she told her Yacob. Chaim had to be looked after. *Now*.

They went to Benjamin, Yacob's brother. A lovely man, rich in many ways, with his successful butcher's business, his three roomed house behind the shop and slaughter yard, his real silver candlesticks and no less than three white Sabbath tablecloths. And his three daughters, poor man, lucky man.

When Yacob and Shoshannah had finished speaking, Benjamin shrugged and looked at his Rachel, who stared out at the children in the yard with her face blank, and then nodded as well.

Benjamin said, 'What else can we do?'

It was a common answer in these bad times to the dilemmas of parents of sons. The Tsar had humanity enough not to take only sons. The family that could produce one boy and thereafter girls only considered itself blessed indeed; they and their children could live together as families should. Others had to do as the brothers Yacob and Benjamin had done – exchange children, changing their names, altering the records with the rabbis' cooperation, so that when the officials came to take them they found that Chaim Ben Benjamin and Gershon Ben Yacob were cousins, not brothers.

Shoshannah had been wise; she did it in time. Gershon was only four and enough years would elapse for even the most perspicacious of the Tsar's men to be hoodwinked. Those who tried to keep their boys in their own homes until the last possible moment were more likely to see their trick uncovered and be punished as well as losing their beloved young.

So, Chaim grew up with his Uncle Benjamin and his Aunt Rachel, and visited his mother and father often, until even he could not quite remember to whom he belonged. Was Rachel Mamma, or was Shoshannah? Both were, really. With two adoring women to feed him titbits and spoil him above the girls, how could he fail to be content? Unlike his long ago ancestor, Micah, he had not lost a harsh mother to gain a tender aunt. He had gained *two* tender mothers. He was one of the rare fortunate ones.

The years drifted on, and life within the Pale remained as it always had been, while in the liberal world beyond, where emancipated Jews lived and worked and were respected, where one had even become Prime Minister of Great Britain (though he didn't really count as a Jew, for his father had left Bevis Marks synagogue in a huff and converted to Christianity even before the boy was born), the mood was changing. The Age of Reason which had seemed to sweep away the old hatreds and superstitions had been a thin bristled broom. It had seemed to have banished intolerance and stupidity in a great wave of philosophical wisdom and humanitarian politics, but it had left much behind, in the corners and under the carpets of Europe, and slowly another wave began to build up. Another wave of hatred for the Jews.

Perhaps it was the energy that had been realeased when the ghetto walls were razed. Out had come a people who had been unable to use their natural gifts for years, and in the sunlight of that much vaunted Age of Reason they had grown and blossomed, soaking up new ideas, new know-

ledge, new skills. They had married their old pent-up energies with their shining new abilities and gone into the society
that lay about them like hot knives through butter. There
wasn't a corner of endeavour that did not have Jews in it; new
Jews, looking and behaving like everyone else, on the surface,
but still stubbornly practising the old religion. Still maintain-
ing close ties with each other. Still forming a tight, threatening brotherhood.

It was this that seemed to be a menace to the middle classes
and the poor of western Europe. These urbane, rich Jews with
their quick tongues and their sleek good looks, what could
they not be capable of, given their heads? Had they not had
enough of their heads already? some started to whisper. Isn't
it time we looked to our defences? They will overwhelm us.

The cry of the xenophobe was heard everywhere, and the
wave rose and became a tide of antisemitism, a new and
pseudo-scientific name for an old game, the baiting of the
outsider.

The hatred was at its most intense in the Pale. How could it
be otherwise, in a place where Jews were in such numbers?

The Russians found a label for what happened. Pogroms.
The first was in Odessa, where individual men, probably
good in their own way, coalesced into a howling hysterical
mob; they ran through the Jewish quarter of the city, a place
which had hummed with excitement and creativity as young
men sang songs and wrote books and talked politics at each
other, and destroyed it. The shops which bore Jewish names
over their doorways were looted and then burned. The
houses where the mezuzzah was set proudly on the doorposts
were burned down. The women who ran shrieking into the
streets were chased and raped by jeering men, one after the
other, and then had their throats cut.

It went on, and became worse.

'One third should convert,' Konstantin Pobedonostsev,
Procurator of the Holy Synod said. 'One third should
emigrate. And one third should die.'

They died. In city after city the fashion of pogrom, started
in 1871 in Odessa, spread. The spring of 1881 turned into a
blood washed summer. In Kiev, in Odessa again, in any
number of insignificant townlets and villages the officials
stood by and watched, their eyes blank, as the peasants
burned synagogues, and looted and killed and raped and

105

enjoyed themselves greatly. The Jews, who had thought their suffering stopped at the rape of their religion and the induction into the army of their sons, discovered there were greater sorrows than even they had thought possible.

In Lublin, some did not wait to see what would happen. A tall red headed boy, one Nathan Ben Lazar, the seventeen-year-old grandson of that Chaim who had changed families to escape conscription heard what was happening, and kissed his mother and small brothers tenderly and hugged his father warmly and set off to walk over the border of the Pale in Galicia. His older brother had already made the journey, and he would follow him.

The town was full of others like him, refugees running from pogroms and the fear of pogroms. Bewildered women alone with children were herded along by the Galician authorities. There were old men and young men like himself, and every one of them was struggling to get a ticket to somewhere – anywhere away from the troubles.

Nathan bought a ticket for New York. It cost him every penny he had brought with him, but he thought it well worth while. When he arrived there, in the great land of promise about which they had all heard so much, then he would earn enough to reline his thin pockets. When he got there.

But a message came, an expensive message sent on the telegraph, by his father Lazar Ben Chaim in Lublin. It was a miracle the message reached him at all, in that hubbub of milling people, all with their luggage clutched in their hands, their bundles on their backs. But he was a noticeable sort of person, was Nathan, with his red hair and his blue eyes, and his father had directed the message very carefully.

When Nathan read it, standing there with the ticket to New York in one hand and the message from his father in the other, he would have cried, had he not been a man. He had to go home. The message was uncompromising in its urgency. They had need of him. He had to return.

11

Nathan had always been a sunny tempered individual. There had been no reason for him to be otherwise. His father, Lazar Ben Chaim, an easy going man with a friendly way, was a miller, so the family had always been well fed and shod, if not precisely rich, for everyone needs the miller.

Nathan's older brother, Reuben, had been kind as older brothers go; although he was stout and Nathan was slighter in build he hadn't beaten him more than most big brothers beat smaller ones, and had defended him in arguments with other boys at the cheder. His younger brothers were no threat to him either, for in many ways, he was his mother's favourite. She, a quiet shy little woman, had found her second son's charm and sense of fun much to her taste, when compared with solemn Reuben's rather dull heaviness.

Even the threats of danger, of pogroms happening in distant places, had not ruffled Nathan unduly. So far Lublin had not suffered, so although he listened with fascination to the stories that came from less fortunate places, they did not really touch him. He could not imagine such things ever happening in his home. For him the tales had been a useful lever to get his parents to allow him to travel. His brother had left because he was genuinely frightened; but that, Nathan had told himself scornfully, was just like Reuben. He, Nathan, was made of sterner stuff. He'd soon make his fortune but because he was hopeful, not because he was frightened.

Then the telegram had come and, like the obedient, cheerful boy he was, he had swallowed his anger and disappointment and returned to Lublin.

'Listen, Nathan,' his father said, his face pinched and grey in the dull morning light. 'The mill – it's burned down.'

Nathan cocked his head to one side and looked at his father intently. 'So? I thought that was the idea. I mean, before I left, you said all being well there'd be money coming one day, and you'd be able to follow Reuben and me when you had the money to buy the tickets for you and Mamma and the boys.'

His father shuffled his feet under the kitchen table and looked helplessly across the room at his wife who was sitting on a low chair by the fire with her shawl thrown over her head, rocking slightly as though she were praying.

'Rivka? Tell him, Rivka – don't just sit there. Tell him!'

'Tell him? Oh, I'll tell him all right!' Rivka lifted her head and Nathan stared at her, open-mouthed. Her usually quiet expressionless little face was suffused with fury, the cheeks blotched and the eyes red rimmed. 'What won't I tell him! That he's got an idiot for a father?' She turned to her son. 'I've told him, believe me, Nathan, time and again I've told him, *think* first, make sure, don't do things in a hurry. So what does he do? He makes up his mind the only way he can get enough money for the tickets is to burn down the mill, so he burns it. Does he find out first if it'll be all right, if there'll be problems? That shlemiel – does he? I ask you!'

'What more could I do? I make sure the premiums are paid, I make sure no one sees me when I go to the mill at night, I make sure there's no signs I been there. What more could I have done? It wasn't my fault!'

Nathan shook his head, confused. 'So, what's the problem? You say you'd paid up the insurance? That no one saw what you did? So what's the problem?'

'The army, that's the problem,' Rivka said in a tragic voice. 'The army!'

'What has the army got to do with it?'

'The insurance company say they can't pay us what's due on the mill because we've got no son in the army. They looked at the records, they say that Reuben is eighteen, he should live to a hundred and twenty, please God, and he's not in the army. So they say, no son in the army, no insurance money. It's a regulation. That's what it is. A regulation.'

'And I can't see Reuben coming back to go in the army, can you?' Lazar said and stared at Nathan with his chin tucked in so that he looked like a lugubrious dog waiting to be beaten. 'All the way from London ... '

'London?' said Nathan mechanically, trying to organize his thoughts. 'What's he doing in London? I thought he was going to New York.'

'So did he,' Rivka said, and sniffed as tears began to course again down her face. 'The letter he sent – the rabbi read it to us, you weren't here so the rabbi read it, and it said he thought he was going to New York, he bought a ticket for New York, but the captain of the ship, he cheated him. He arrived, he thought he was in New York already, until he went to a letter writer and the letter writer told him it was London. But he's all right, thank God. The letter the man wrote for him, it said he was all right. He's got work in a stick factory, he's all right.'

'But will he come back to make it all right for us? And where's the money to come from to pay his ticket back, if he does, which he won't? You, thank God, hadn't gone too far – Brody, I can get hold of you, London I can get hold of nobody – and it's not so bad, the army. Only three years it is now a soldier has to be. Only three years. And you're young, yet.'

Nathan shook his head, slowly. 'No, Papa. You can't mean it. Mamma! You can't mean it!'

But they did, and he knew and they knew there was no other way. Their livelihood had gone with the mill, and without the insurance money . . . It was every Jew's responsibility to dispense charity, but to receive it? That was something quite different. And looking at his mother, at the narrow face with the look of a frightened anger on it, Nathan knew he couldn't let it happen.

And maybe, he told himself as cheerfully as he could, maybe it wouldn't be so bad. The army – everyone talked about how awful it was, but it would be travel, wouldn't it? And a uniform, and the chance to swagger a bit. It couldn't be all bad.

Once he'd accepted the inevitable they treated him as a hero. His family, the people of the shtetl, all admired him, and all said so. He was the one who was to save his whole family from ruin. Without him where would they be, all of them? He and he alone was to see them on their way to comfort and peace of mind again. Nathan began to strut even before he got his uniform.

The day before he was to leave to join the training camp, he went to see Bloomah. Her father, Lev, was the innkeeper on the other side of the shtetl, a large and bonhomous man who liked Nathan almost as much as Nathan enjoyed the evenings he spent in his tavern, drinking schnapps. He welcomed the hero of the hour with loud cries of approval and heavy sweat-scented hugs when he arrived that evening, holding his hat in his hand and shuffling the mud off his boots on the old iron scraper by the kitchen door.

'Nathan!' Lev cried. 'So, my boy, you're going to the army, hey? Such a son for a man to have, such a son! Believe me, Lazar doesn't know what a lucky man he is – eh, Bloomah?'

Bloomah looked up from her sewing and blinked short-sightedly at Nathan and then went red and bobbed her head and returned to her sewing. Nathan preened even more; when Bloomah looked at him that way he knew she liked him. And when Lev looked at him the way he was looking now, it meant he could get away with behaviour that usually would cause great shaking of adult heads.

'Ah, good evening, Reb Lev. You keep well, I hope?'

'Thank God, thank God, I'm well enough, apart from a bit of rheumatism, you know how it is, a man gets a few twinges on a cold night – '

The pleasantries went on, as Nathan stood there and watched Bloomah's fingers flicker in and out of her sewing and when at last Lev had come to the end of his chatter, Nathan said daringly. 'I wanted to say goodbye, Reb Lev. That's why I came. Tomorrow, very early, I go to camp, to the army. So I came to say goodbye – could I – er, perhaps I could talk to Bloomah alone before – I mean, I'll say goodbye to you as well, of course, but ... '

Lev grinned, then shook his head and looked roguish. 'So, you want to say goodbye to my Bloomah, hmm? So who am I to stop a soldier from saying goodbye? I've got barrels to schlap from the cellar – so I'll schlap, and you can say goodbye ... '

It was a very satisfactory goodbye. Lev was gone for almost an hour, and Bloomah wasted only ten minutes on pretending to be a good girl who wouldn't dream of letting a boy touch her hand, let alone go any further, and then they were curled up together in the candlelight, kissing and hugging with an abandon which would have appalled the respectable. But, as Nathan said, looking deep into her brown eyes, 'These are bad times, Bloomah. How can we worry ourselves about the old ways when the old world is changing so fast? Tomorrow I'm in the army. The next day maybe you'll be gone too. Everyone else is going away –

maybe you, soon.'

'Papa says maybe. There's only us and my brother Isaac and his wife since Mamma died last year and he says soon the troubles will come here, and as soon as he can sell the inn, he's going to buy tickets for New York too.'

'Tell him to go to London,' Nathan nuzzled her ear. 'Because when I come out of the army, we'll be following Reuben, me and my family, and he's in London. Tell him to go to London, Bloomah.'

'Why should I?' she whispered, pretending she hadn't noticed the way his hands were wandering. 'America is better, they say.'

'Because when I come out of the army I'm going to marry you,' Nathan said recklessly and his hands became even more reckless than his words. 'I'll come to London, with my family, we'll soon be settled, we'll get married.'

'You'll tell Poppa that? Tonight before you go?' Bloomah said sharply. Nathan lifted his head from her neck and peered at her in the candlelight.

'You will then?'

'You talk to Poppa,' said Bloomah, and smiled up at him and stopped pretending that she didn't know where his hands were, and clasped her own about his neck and kissed him as eagerly as he was kissing her.

So, Nathan joined the army as a betrothed man, and he swaggered even more at the thought of it. Half the shtetl turned out to see him on to the train, and he felt good, even though Rivka was standing there clinging to Lazar's arm with her face white with misery, and even though his father had tears running down his cheeks and both his young brothers looked solemn. He was a hero, an affianced man who was to save his family and come back to marry his girl in just three years, just thirty-six short months, and then live happily ever after. To be Nathan Ben Lazar in that cold morning in March 1882 was a good thing to be.

It was not so good for the next few months, as Nathan, facing the rigours of army training and above all the loathing of his fellow recruits, quickly learned.

To most of the Russian peasants joining the army was a privilege, a step up in the social order, and to discover as they rapidly did that the Jews who were pressed into the army regarded it as an unmitigated disaster was an unpleasant shock. How dare these creatures, these Christ killers, how dare they despise their elite Russian army? They turned on every Jew with venom, and only those with considerable stamina withstood it.

Nathan was fortunate. He looked different from the other Jews. He was a respectable five feet ten, and reasonably well built with it. Furthermore there was that red hair and the blue eyes. Jews were supposed to have black oily locks and big dark eyes and noses that shrieked their origins, not this frank open-countenanced look that would have been as much at home on one of the Northerners who sometimes penetrated Russia from her Scandinavian borders.

And·he had charm and wit, when he wanted to use either of them. There was something about Nathan that disarmed the most suspicious of the soldiery, a drollery that they liked, though they never forgot he was a despised Jew. When they came in from hard training sessions on the frozen parade ground to collapse into their bunks, Nathan always had the worst place. Indeed he often had no bed at all.

And yet he was happy enough. He missed the good home food he had been accustomed to, the boiled chicken in its soup, the dumplings made of matzo meal and chicken fat and hot water, the special carrot tzimmes Rivka had made for Friday evening suppers, above all, the cholent, that heavy concoction of beans and onions and potatoes and sometimes meat that would cook all day beside the damped down fire on the Sabbath to be eaten after the men came home from shul; life without a cholent was hardly life at all, he sometimes thought.

But it could have been worse. There was black bread and salt herrings and cabbage borscht and the men were generous enough to let him have extra vegetables out of their shared ration to make up for the unclean meat he refused. It was no virtue in him and he knew it. It was just that his gorge rose at the sight of the chunks of meat floating in the stewpots. He would eat black bread and cabbage and settle for that.

The first year drifted into the second, and life became easier. There were no more long periods of enforced training on the parade ground, but real work to do. He and his fellows in the platoon would be shunted out from place to place, here to supervise the clearing out of a gang of bandits from a hideout in the Ural mountains, there to break up an illegal workers' meeting on the city street corner. They were as much civil police as military men but the Russian soldiers cared nothing for the niceties of such matters. They were well fed enough not to feel the pain suffered by those men they were ordered to shoot down in the name of the Tsar. Themselves mostly children of serfs, they cared little enough for the fate of other serfs.

It was midsummer in 1883 when Nathan set out on the longest journey of his life. He would have liked to tell someone about it, someone of his own. He wrote occasional letters to his parents at home in Lublin, for he was an educated man and could write not only Yiddish but also Russian and Polish. But they never replied to his letters, and he had to assume they couldn't raise the money to employ a scribe to do so. If letters could only have been directed in Yiddish, his father might have managed that. But that was not allowed; it had to be Russian. So communication between Nathan and his family had long since foundered, and now he missed them keenly. To be going to Siberia! No one in the shtetl had ever travelled so far. That would be something to tell them all about, indeed it would.

They collected the prisoners they were to escort the thousand and a half miles to Turachansk from the jail at Sverdlosk in the Ural mountains, and looked them over. Their sergeant, a beefy man from Moskva who despised each and every member of his platoon, snorted with disgust.

'Not even decent thieves and murderers,' he said and spat on the floor at the chained feet of the seventeen men. 'Just look at them! A bunch of useless political plotters – I could take the bastards to Siberia on my own!'

They indeed looked a sorry sight. Thin, bedraggled, many of them with scars on their faces, testament to vicious beatings during their interrogation and trials, they seemed too weak to hold up their manacled wrists. They sat in a huddle on the floor of the straw-strewn cattle truck on the train and stared silently at their feet, not even wincing when the sergeant's indiscriminate spitting hit them full in the face.

'You! Lazar,' the sergeant said. Since Nathan like most of

the Jews of the Pale had no family name, he had given his father's name as a surname. 'Stay here and keep your gun cocked. We'll relieve you at the next station. Maybe.' And he laughed and jerked his head at the rest of the platoon who laughed sycophantically back, and then followed him, jumping out of the cattle truck to the railway line to make their way further down the train to more comfortable quarters.

The train clanked and rocked its way through the mountains, and on through the swampy lowlands of Nizmennost towards Tomsk and the railhead, and he sat with his back against the corner, watching the men sleepily over his cocked rifle, a cigarette dangling between his lips, thinking of Bloomah. It was the only way he could keep himself awake, and it was important that he should because one thing Nathan knew about himself was his ability to sleep and sleep deeply. His brother Reuben had been used to joke about it, long ago at home in Lublin.

'Our Nathan sleep? He doesn't sleep! He *dies*. The sky could fall in and the Lord our God on top of it, and believe me, he'd not stir. Nathan sleeps like Lev the innkeeper drinks – like he *means* it – '

So he did not dare risk falling asleep. He thought instead of Bloomah.

That part of the journey took three days. The other men in the platoon relieved him for just three short bursts, so that he could eat and sleep, and spent the journey themselves mostly gambling over cards, sleeping, and eating everything they could get their hands on in the small stations they passed through. And the prisoners sat in their truck with Nathan.

At Tomsk they hosed the prisoners down with icy water that left them gasping and shivering and then loaded them into the truck on the roadside to start the longest part of the haul. They were to go as far north as the road would take them, moving slowly through the almost featureless tundra, until the road would peter out some two hundred miles south of Tirachansk. From then on they would have to walk, the prisoners in their chains, the soldiers marching glumly at their side. No one was looking forward to that stage of the journey.

For Nathan it was to mark the turning point.

12

The horse-drawn van was mud-encrusted and filthy inside as well as out, overcrowded and ill-sprung with solid wheels and so rickety and battered that the only way they could make themselves heard while it was moving was to shout. The soldiers were settled at the front of the truck, behind the driver's cab, in which the driver and sergeant were comfortably ensconced, and the prisoners were jammed in as small a space as possible in the middle while Nathan was forced to take up guard in the coldest place of all, at the rear.

They had been given a meal of potato soup and black bread at the railhead by order of the officer in charge of the couple of platoons which were stationed there. There would be no more food for soldiers or prisoners until they arrived at Belyi Jar the next day.

The driver of the van pushed the horses along the rough road so fast that they sweated great froths, and left a trail of dust far behind them, and they reached a small tributary of the river five miles from Belyi Jar at five in the morning. There were another five hours to go before they were expected at the guard post, and the sergeant was no fool. To report too early would be as heinous a sin as reporting late. And the horses were trembling with their exertion, and needed time to recover.

He ordered the driver to lead the animals over to the side of the road and the man did, grinning with the self-satisfaction of a cat. 'Now we all get some sleep,' he muttered.

Nathan looked over the silent wide flatlands, grey in the moonlight around them, and then shivered as much with loneliness as the bitter cold. June though it was, they were close now to the Arctic circle, only six hundred miles north across a bare tundra. Ice laden winds bit through their clothes, heavy though they were. The prisoners' faces looked as grey as the landscape, for they were wearing little more than rags, and were even worse fed than their guards. Yet they sat there huddled together in their chains looking as impassive as they had from the beginning of the journey;

no better, no worse.

'Lazar! Get these bastards out!' the sergeant bawled. 'They can lie under the truck till we go on in the morning. You watch 'em.'

Nathan, trying not to let his yawns be seen by the sergeant, shepherded his clinking prisoners out of the truck to the lee side, away from the wind. 'Lie together,' he told them roughly. 'It won't be so bad then. Against the wheels, you fools, that's it.'

He set himself against the other wheel, pushing his back against the spokes, and wrapped his greatcoat about his legs as best he could. The cold was still bitter but down here, out of the wind, it wasn't as bad as he'd feared, and at least the rocking and noise from the drive had stopped. Still, it wasn't going to be easy. Already his eyes were glazing and he stared hard at the road between his feet, trying to count the stones there, anything to keep himself awake.

Behind him in the van the platoon slid into noisy sleep. He could hear the snores as clearly as if they had been lying next to his ears, and the rhythm of the sound made his own sleepiness that much more imperative. But he had to stay awake, he had to.

His eyes were almost closed when the man at the end of the line of chained prisoners moved against the wheel and said hoarsely, 'Sir? Good sir, Lazar? Sir?'

Nathan's eyes snapped open.

'Sir, I've got to shit – please, sir?'

Nathan peered at him in the dimness. 'What?'

'I've got to, sir! Can't hang on much longer. Got to.'

'So? What do you want me to do? Wipe your arse?'

'No, sir, of course not, sir – but here – I mean, right here? Next to you?'

Nathan looked at him uneasily. So far on the journey the prisoners had been made to sit in their own ordure, but that had been little enough for they had hardly been fed enough to fill a sparrow's belly, let alone a man's. But it happened once or twice that a man's bowels had turned to water, and the railway truck had been nasty in consequence. The hosing down of the prisoners on Tomsk station had been hell for them, but not much worse than smelling as they had before it was done. And now – he thought of the van next morning, of the way they were all crowded in, and looked again at the man, who was sitting clutching his belly in both hands, looking agonized.

Nathan shook his head impatiently, but he leaned over and reached for the man's manacles. They were not locked with a key, but by a loop of metal so placed that it could only be opened from the outside by a man using two hands at once. The ankle manacles were fastened so that no prisoner with his hands chained together could operate the mechanism.

The chains fell clinking to the ground and the man scuttled across behind the truck, bent double, still clutching his belly. Nathan leaned against his wheel and tucked his hands into his pockets, leaving his rifle in the crook of his elbow. The metal had been cold against his fingers, and they needed warming up again so he could chain the man again when he'd finished doing what he had to do.

The silence was thick, and he shook his head to push it away, for it felt warm and velvety. Again he shook his head. Oh, God, the need to sleep. The need to sleep.

It was ineluctable. There was no way he could have fought it. He sat there, his back against the wheel, his rifle tucked into the crook of his elbow, and fell into a sleep so profound that the crack of doom could not have disturbed it.

What woke him was light on his eyes. Redness seeped into his vision behind his closed lids and he became aware of the dryness of his mouth and throat. He swallowed, hard, and then, slowly, opened his eyes.

The sky was a very vivid blue, and the ground now looked olive green rather than grey. He blinked at the horizon for a moment, trying to work out where he was.

He turned his head after a second to look at his prisoners and then as he saw the pile of empty chains on the road the memory came sliding back. He could see the bent shape of the man who had gone scuttling away behind the truck, bent double, clutching his belly.

'Oh God. Oh, my God.' He struggled to his feet, stiff and awkward with the cold, and pulled himself, hand over hand, around to the back of the truck.

It was unbelievable. Absolutely unbelievable. The men he had known so well, all still looking like the men he had known and yet totally different, like distorted images in broken stained mirrors. The sergeant with his throat cut so widely that his neck seemed to smile as well as his mouth, which was pulled wide in a grimace. The corporal curled up in death against the side of the truck and looking like a helpless baby, happily asleep, except for the stoved-in skull. There was blood everywhere, and he climbed into the truck, still muttering, 'ohmygod, ohmygod,' and pulled at the men's shoulders, clambering over their legs, getting their blood on his hands, on his greatcoat, smearing even his face as he pulled them against himself, praying still to find even one still alive. The stink of blood sat thickly in his throat and he could taste its sweetness, and all he could do was tug at heads and arms and shoulders and moan, 'ohmygod, ohmygod, ohmygod.'

He climbed heavily out of the truck at last, and let his legs sag under him so that he was sitting on the ground, his rifle still held in his bloody hands, his legs stuck out in front of him and his head drooping on his chest. The litany was still running through his head but he wasn't saying it any more. He had no energy left to move his lips.

That was how the patrol from Belyi Jar found him, when it came thundering along the road from the guardhouse to look for the missing van an hour after they should have arrived. The officer bent over him and pulled him to his feet, and Nathan managed to stand there swaying as the captain shouted at him, 'What happened? What happened? For the love of Christ, man, tell me what happened!'

He stared back at the officer, sick with terror. Would they shoot him now, or put him through the whole business of court martial and firing squad? Nathan's eyes turned upwards and he fainted.

When he came to, he found himself a hero. The officer had worked it all out to his own satisfaction; the prisoners had managed to overcome their brave guards and escape. That the guards had fought courageously was clear – look at the dreadful injuries they had suffered! That Private Nathan Lazar had fought bravely was even more evidenced by the state he was in, the dreadful shock he had clearly suffered, the exhaustion that so filled him.

Nathan said not a word. He nodded and looked noble and tried not to think about those thin half starved weaklings who had been prisoners. If this officer ever heard how pathetic they were, compared with the men of the platoon, surely he would realize that the only way the prisoners could possibly have overcome their superior strength was while they were asleep?

But the officer didn't hear, and no one was likely to tell him that a platoon of the Tsar's army had not acquitted itself nobly. Instead they told Nathan what a splendid fellow he was, and how brave and heroic, until even Nathan almost believed it. And when at a special ceremony they pinned a medal on him, making him the only Jew in the Russian army ever to be so honoured, he felt he'd earned it.

He never once asked himself why it was the prisoners had not dispatched him, as well. He just took it for granted that they'd liked him. Nathan was beginning to discover that people usually did.

Then at last, it was 1885. Nathan Lazar was twenty years old, thicker in the shoulders now and with thicker whiskers too than he had had when he had kissed his Bloomah goodbye in Lublin. The time had come at last to think of Bloomah again, for he had thought as little as possible about her this past year or so. Thinking about Bloomah, he had discovered, had aroused feelings and needs in him that could not be satisfied. Better not to think of her at all. . . .

Now he handed in his uniform and put on instead the cheap serge suit and coarse cotton shirt which was all he could afford to buy, along with a pair of stout black boots and a thick green woollen muffler. That left him just enough for a railway ticket to get him back to Lublin. He needed no more than that, he told himself confidently as he parted with the money and took his ticket from the clerk. Papa and Mama must have their insurance money by now, and be ready to buy tickets to London for all of them, himself included.

For there was no doubt in him that that was where he was going. The plan had been simmering at the back of his mind all through these past three years. Even if Papa and Mama had changed their minds, he would go. The Pale was no place for him to spend his life. London for him – especially if Bloomah had already gone there. If not, he'd take her.

Lublin looked exactly the same. He climbed stiffly out of the train and stood there at the railside staring out at the squat stone buildings, remembering the number of people who had been there to see him off that day three years ago, Mama and Papa and Benjamin and Alexander, and Bloomah and Lev, but now there was just the usual collection of passersby, porters and railwaymen who cared nothing at all for him, a Jew in a cheap suit.

Well, never mind, he told himself as he walked out of the station and turned towards the shtetl. Never mind. Today, a hero in disguise, tomorrow an obvious hero –

He did not believe it at first. So many changes, so many faces he did not recognize. The shtetl seemed to have shrunk, somehow. House after house had been boarded up. Family after family seemed to have disappeared completely.

The inn was closed, and no one seemed to know anything at all about Reb Lev and his daughter Bloomah. His father's house was boarded up, and he stood outside the door staring up at it, feeling very young again, not at all a twenty-year-old hero, but a lonely six- or seven-year-old who wanted his Mama and his Papa.

There was nothing here for him any more.

Before setting out on the long hike to Brody, where, with luck, he'd be able to sneak aboard one of the cattle trucks on the trains going north (and he was experienced in cattle trucks the good God knew), he walked once more around the shtetl, past the wooden houses with their narrow verandahs, past the inn with its boarded door, past the bakery where his mother used to send her cholent to be cooked on Sabbaths when there could be no fire at home, past the ramshackle building which had been his school. Lublin belonged to yesterday now.

The journey was easier than he had hoped. In the hubbub of refugees still streaming out through Brody, one young man was hardly noticed. He could slip on and off trains and keep moving once aboard them in a way that evaded even the most careful of ticket inspectors. He even managed to get aboard the cross channel steamer without paying, preferring to keep his money for food. The ship was so packed and so many were seasick that evading payment was easy.

He leaned over the rail as the boat steamed up the river Thames to Tilbury. It was November, and the air smelled heavy and sulphurous, and there was rain pattering on his forehead, for he had put his astrakhan hat – his single memento of his army years – in his pocket to keep it safe and free from damage. But he did not mind the way his hair curled damply on his forehead or the way his belly lurched queasily against the heavy swell of the river tide. He had arrived in the land of fortune. From now on, it was going to be a hero's life all the way.

The third family had arrived in London.

BOOK TWO

Gathering

13

On the same November day in 1885 that brought Nathan Lazar steaming up the sulphur-smelling Thames to Tilbury, Bartholomew Lammeck sat in his own special seat on the eastern side of the New West End Synagogue in St Petersburgh Place, just off the Bayswater Road. Outside there were shreds of fog swirling in the traffic-roaring streets, and the dripping trees in Hyde Park could hardly be seen beyond the railings, so shrouded was the park in thick greyness. But in here all was warmth and light and magnolia scented air and high excitement, for it was not every day that such a marriage as this was celebrated – the last time had been a quarter of a century ago. A Lammeck marrying a Damont! Such drama had not been known since the days long ago when Rothschilds were marrying Montefiores, and Gompertzes were marrying Mocattas.

He looked round the synagogue and almost unconsciously tipped his glossy top hat to a more rakish angle to match that of his oldest son, Alfred, who was sitting in deep conversation with his brother Emmanuel. Such well-set-up young men, both of them, Bartholomew thought fondly, though Emmanuel hadn't quite as much style as Alfred. Alfred, right from the beginning, had shown that he was special. He had flatly refused to be called by his given name, the one taken from his esteemed ancestor Abdul.

'I'm English,' he had told his father stubbornly, 'and English boys don't have such outlandish names.' He had hit on the almost Royal sounding Alfred, at the age of ten, and had insisted on being called it ever since.

Such a boy, thought Bartholomew again, even more fondly, so good looking, so gifted. It's been well worth it, well worth it all.

He looked across the synagogue to where high crowned hats alive with feathers and flowers and fruit bobbed over the smooth well fed faces and high collared coats and fur capes of the Damont and Lammeck women and their friends. There was his Augusta, half a head taller than every other woman sitting there, with the highest of hats – no wonder, Bartholomew thought wryly, they call 'em 'three storeys and a basement' – and the smoothest most gleaming of faces. The furs that lay across her shoulders were sables which quite outshone the marten and opossum of the women sitting on each side of her; her daughter Fay, looking quiet and cowed as she always did, and her daughter-in-law Susan, looking bored and impatient as she always did. Odd, thought Bartholomew, how it works out.

Inevitably his mind drifted back to his own wedding, twenty-four years before. That had not been in this handsome synagogue, for St Petersburgh Place had not been built until ten years ago. His wedding had been at the older establishment at Bevis Marks, in the City, just an hour's walk away, but an eternity away in experience and living. He had been so very young, so very doubtful, so very overawed.

At twenty-two, still speaking English with a heavy Bombay accent, he had regarded himself as very much an alien among these comfortable English Jews. They had been kind enough to him when he had first arrived. One of the Montefiore family had scooped him up at the very first service he had attended and introduced him round to the others. They had, he now realized, found him quaint and amusing. His clothes, his exotic speech sounds, his very un-English whiskers – and the weight of his very successful family business.

Bartholomew had never been in any doubt that the name of Lammeck mattered in the world. All his life it had been the most essential thing about him. In merchant circles in Bombay and Calcutta, Shanghai and Tientsin and Yokohama, to be a Lammeck was to be a prince among men, just as it had been in Baghdad for centuries.

But he was no fool, and had not expected quite such a warm welcome from these remote English people. After all, the new office of Lammeck and Sons, in Haunch of Oxen Yard just behind St Paul's Cathedral not far from Ludgate Hill, was far from elegant, and at first only a small amount of business passed through it. Bartholomew had been advised by his formidable Aunt Sarah Hazzan Lammeck and his cousins and brothers to be cautious, not to involve Lammeck's in enterprises that could not be properly handled from the London end.

'Wait till we know we can keep the business flowing as it should, and then we'll expand,' they had said.

And in those early days in London, in 1859 and 1860, that was just what he had done. He had lived modestly in simple chambers near Baker Street, and been unassuming in the company of the established community.

Yet, they had taken him up, and he was invited to every Jewish house of note, going to balls at the Rothschild mansions in Piccadilly and Grosvenor Gate, to crushes at the Montefiores' rented house in Hill Street in Mayfair, to picnics with the Goldsmiths. When the youngest Rothschild invited a glittering company to Mentmore for the weekend to sample the delights of that magnificent house with its running hot water and artificial ventilation, Bartholomew Lammeck was one of the company. When Jacob Damont, the patriarch of that numerous clan, celebrated his ninetieth birthday at his splendid house in Berkeley Square, Bartholomew's name was high on the guest list.

That had been where it had all happened. It was at her great-grandfather's birthday celebration that Augusta Damont made up her mind that this interesting little man was the one she wanted.

She was two inches taller than he, and proportionally larger in girth, and had a strong manner and a jutting chin to match. Her colour was as high as his was sallow, her energy as noisy as his strength was quiet. But she wanted him, as he was. Her name had been linked with several well set up young men, for she was a considerable heiress in her own right. But, she looked at Bartholomew – 'my Birdie,' she called him – and told her father coolly that she had made up her mind.

'He's going to be even richer than you are, Papa,' she told that tired widower. Isaac Damont had never really recovered from the loss of his wife, who had died giving birth to his masterful Augusta. 'And with me to help him, there's no knowing what we mightn't achieve.'

Isaac could never resist his daughter's pleas, and Bartholomew, a little bemused and not a little flattered, found himself swept up in Damont doings till his head rang with the social whirl. But not so much that he could not see the excellent business benefits that were accruing to him. He was able to tell them in Bombay within three months of that birthday party in Berkeley Square that 'We are now able to be quite confident about next year's business. I have made arrangements for the shipment of large quantities of pig iron as well as of some excellent Southdown wool – the sheep here are of a very superior strain – and would most earnestly advise a larger investment in this office for future development ... '

Sarah, ailing now but still as businesslike as ever, sat in her godown in Bombay and nodded in satisfaction, and sent back to London cargoes of spices that Bartholomew was able to turn to very handsome profit. The small office in Haunch of Oxen Yard spread to the buildings adjoining it on each side, and Augusta, visiting it, nodded in satisfaction and told her Papa that the time had come to arrange the wedding.

Bartholomew, waiting for his own son to appear and stand beneath the chuppa, the wedding canopy, on a foggy November day in 1885, looked back down the twenty-four years to Bevis Marks in 1861 and watched himself marrying Augusta Damont in full view of a richly dressed and somewhat amused congregation who had thought he had done well for himself, a Lammeck marrying the Damont heiress. Now that same congregation, looking only a little older themselves but with their small children grown into handsome young adults and wearing bustles and pelisses rather than crinolines and Balmoral mantles, waited to see a Damont marry a Lammeck, and thought the Damonts lucky to have so rich and promising a young man for their daughter.

For Augusta had been right in her view of her little Birdie. How the man had flourished! Dealings in commodities like pig iron and Southdown wool and imported spices occupied too little of his energy. He invested Lammeck money in the cotton mills of Lancashire and competed keenly with his own relations in the Indian trade. He loaned money to his fellow traders and so almost without intending it added merchant banking to his enterprises. He became interested in diamonds, through his wife's father, who was a diamond merchant of note with close family links on the Amsterdam diamond bourse, and started dealing in them too.

Haunch of Oxen Yard gave up building after building to feed the insatiable maw of the Lammeck office until, just five years ago, the metropolitan authorities had given up struggling and changed the name plate on the entrance to the Yard. Everyone had taken to calling it Lammeck Alley long before, and Lammeck Alley it was to be, officially.

That had been a moment of great pride for Bartholomew. He had not really intended to be quite so busy a businessman. In his young days in Shanghai he had been interested in many things that were not designed to make money, like horse racing and cards, and had always planned a life with minimal attention to work, maximum to enjoyment. But Augusta had different views, and the only way he could escape her loud and very definite reiteration of them was to go to the office.

Now his industry had given his family name to part of the greatest metropolis in the world. Baghdad had had many such labels, for Lammecks had been there for centuries, but this was London, a much older, much richer and altogether more important city. The years spent here working over ledgers and haggling with other merchants had seemed wearisome at times, but now he had Lammeck Alley to comfort him. It almost helped him feel less irritated with his dear Augusta.

There was a flurry at the entrance to the synagogue, Bartholomew pulled himself back into the present with a little start. Beside him his third son Ezra stood up, nervously pulling at his grey kid gloves. His brother had chosen him to be his best man (not entirely unprodded by Ezra's wife Susan, who had strong views on the way Ezra's older brothers tended to overshadow her beloved husband) and looked nervously along the line at Alfred and Emmanuel, both of whom were also standing now and staring up the synagogue to the entrance.

Bartholomew set his hat back at its more sober angle, and stepped forward at the same time that his wife did, her bustle curving with such richness of line that it seemed quite possible that she would be toppled flat onto her imperious nose at any moment, and they both turned to watch their youngest son, the bridegroom, come towards them.

Albert looked quite delightful. His hat shone with a satin rich gleam above a face as round and soft as a child's. His chin seemed to be as smooth as an infant's, with no sign on it of any hair, yet his upper lip was adorned with a silken black moustache. His linen was a startling white and the collar of his shirt was so high that his ears seemed to rest upon it. His black tail coat and impeccably cut trousers fitted his slender form as though he had been poured into them (and indeed his tailor was so uniquely gifted that even the excessively rich Bartholomew had been taken aback by the bill) and his boots did all they could to outshine his hat. Altogether he looked like every little servant maid's dream of male perfection, as Susan, ever waspish, enjoyed pointing out to her cowed sister-in-law behind Augusta's majestic back.

The wedding party took its place beneath the chuppah, and the rabbis – surely more than could fit under the velvet canopy? – came surging to join them. From somewhere behind a screen shrill tenors and rich basses lifted their voices in wedding melodies; the New West End Synagogue prided itself on its modern approach to the great traditions of religion, and its choral offerings were as splendid as any that could be heard in any church along the Bayswater Road, and indeed in all London. The mother of the groom took her place, smiling mistily, and the congregation stiffened and fell silent, waiting for the bride.

She stopped for a moment at the door where everyone could see her, ignoring the urging of her father's hand on her arm, and the sound of the music lifting in ecstasy. Davida Damont, twenty years old, a distant cousin of the man she was about to marry, had enough self confidence to be able to do things her way rather than anyone else's and her way was to give everyone plenty of opportunity to admire her gown of stamped white velvet, her headdress of the most price-less old Chantilly lace, and her cascade of magnolias entwined in silver ribbons. The decisions about the gown and the prolonged fittings and discussions had been such that the whole bridal ensemble deserved every scrap of attention and admiration it could get. And Miss Damont was determined it should get it.

And also that *she* should. That she looked enchanting she knew beyond any shadow of a doubt. Her eyes, wide and dark under the frosting of dark curls on her creamy forehead, her little pointed chin under the rosy parted lips (were they not rather particularly rosy? Susan whispered to Fay. Did dearest Davida use *rouge*? *Quelle horreur*!) her slender neck encased in

130

its lacy collar, the great rope of huge pearls that hung almost to her waist (dear Papa, so generous) and the great sweep of her ten-foot-long Brussels lace veil, added up to total magnificence. Everyone who saw her must be overawed by her.

The wedding went beautifully. The handsomest of young men married the most beautiful of young girls in the presence of the best dressed and most affluent people in the whole of London on that November afternoon, and everyone congratulated everyone else afterwards, and wept a few happy tears and told each other what a delightful affair it all was.

And at the reception, as the guests, now wearing even more splendid clothes than they had at the synagogue, moved slowly past the great tables laden with the wedding gifts, admiring their own contributions (and feeling somewhat slighted if they were not positioned to advantage) and curling their lips a little at everyone else's, the congratulating went on. This was a fine match, a joy for the respective families, a credit to the thriving and well-thought-of community that belonged to the New West End Synagogue, an event to be greeted with satisfaction.

Fay escaped from the hubbub as soon as she could, managing to hide in a window embrasure of the great drawing room of the Lammeck house in Park Lane where the reception was held by slipping into the shadow of a curtain. She was tired and unhappy and it was vital that her formidable mother should remain totally unaware of both facts.

Mary found her there not because she was looking for her sister-in-law, but because she too was seeking somewhere to hide. Mary was just a year younger than Fay. She had been married to Fay's brother Emmanuel for almost a year now, and the two women had much in common.

'Oh, my dear, how glad I am it is you!' Fay breathed as Mary put her hand on her arm. 'For one dreadful moment I was afraid it was Mama – I mean, I thought it might be Mama. And I do so wish to rest a little – the flowers in the synagogue were so strong, were they not? They gave me the headache.'

'Have you told them yet?' Mary was not usually so direct, but she was so concerned for Fay with her pale face and the blue shadows under her eyes growing larger every day that

131

she could not be as circumspect as she usually was.

There was a little silence as Fay looked bleakly out at the milling crowd of elegant people with their glasses of champagne in their hands and their bright eyes and their splendid gowns and monocled eyes and then she breathed in sharply through her nose.

'No. Nor shall I ever, I don't suppose.'

'Then you will never be anything but miserable, my dear one, and surely you cannot believe your parents wish such a thing!'

'Papa would not – he is most tender, truly he is. Dearest Papa.' Fay's sad face lifted for a moment. 'But he would be bitterly distressed. As for Mama ... '

Both girls fell silent, and Mary slipped one hand into her sister-in-law's and squeezed hard. Quiet, with soft mouse coloured hair and green eyes, she had been more than amazed when the elegant Emmanuel Lammeck had come courting her, even though she knew that as a member of the Deyong family, she was considered a respectable match. But Emmanuel, he of the bright and rather insolent black eyes and full red mouth and quick wits? He and his father worked closely together in Lammeck Alley, and he had no need of Mary's far from large dowry. Why had he chosen *her*?

Yet he had, and married her, and she had hoped to be happy with him, for she had found him exciting, if rather overwhelming. Now, just a year after her own wedding, with Emmanuel already showing his impatience with her and his interest in livelier company, she found all her comfort as a married woman in the company of her sister-in-law, Fay. She too had her problems, for Augusta Lammeck made no secret of the fact that she cared immeasurably for her sons and only incidentally for her daughter, regarding her somewhat as she would a tiresome puppy.

Fay, who had inherited her father's small build and quiet ways and none of her mother's more fiery nature, knew she enjoyed little but maternal contempt. For her the best thing that had ever happened was her brother Emmanuel's marriage, and not only because it took him out of the house where he had always teased and bullied her during her growing up years. It was all because of her dear sister Mary.

'We've got another one now,' she said then, staring across

132

the room to where Davida Damont, now Mrs Albert Lammeck, stood surrounded by admirers, her eyes glittering with
excitement and her cheeks aflame with pride and joy.

Mary nodded. 'Yes,' she said softly. 'But not like you and
me, I think.'

'No. Not like you and me,' Fay said, and squeezed Mary's
hand affectionately.

'So you will not tell them?' Mary said after a while. 'You
will just go on as you are?'

'What else can I do?' Fay said almost helplessly. 'They
would never understand. That I should wish to marry at all
would amaze Mama – but that I should wish to marry a
Christian . . . ' She shook her head. 'I cannot see how I can do
it.'

'Shall I help you, Fay? Would you come to stay with me in
my house for a few weeks? I could tell them I needed you,
because of my condition – they would let you come to me, I
think. And then you and your Richard could make a plan to
be wed. Once it was a fait accompli, surely they would accept
it?'

Fay looked at her, her forehead creased a little. 'Do you
really think so? Do you think you could stand what would
happen afterwards? They would torment you dreadfully, my
dear, would they not? They would blame you. Mama would
be . . . ' She shook her head. 'I love you for the good
heartedness of your plan, my dear one, but I cannot let you.'

'After the baby is born, perhaps.' Mary said uncertainly.
She wished nothing but happiness for her sister-in-law, but
of course Fay was right. Her redoubtable Mama-in-law
would be . . . oh, it couldn't be thought of. Even imagining
Augusta's rage that would ensue increased the sense of
queasiness she had been feeling all day, and tightened the pain
in her middle.

She longed suddenly for home and bed, even that stiff and
over-furnished house in Green Street that Emmanuel had
insisted they live in, and which was so unlike her own old
comfortable home in St John's Wood. But that home had
gone, now that Papa was dead, and all she had was
Emmanuel and Green Street and all these overpowering
Lammecks and Damonts. Really, she did not feel at all well.

'I cannot persuade you, my dear,' she said now. 'But
remember, do, that I am your friend. Whatever you wish me

to do for you, I will to the best of my ability.'

Fay kissed her gratefully, and then went away to behave as a daughter should and dance attendance on her Mama, and to try not to think of her beloved Richard, the son of the surgeon who had looked after her when she had had the whooping cough two years before, and whom she had adored ever since.

On the other side of the room Emmanuel was leaning against the overmantel of the wide fireplace, warming his buttocks at the flames and talking to his cousin James Damont.

'Something will have to be done, there's no doubt about that. I was told only last week, by the captain of one of the cargo boats m'father called in from Holland, that they're coming out in thousands, if not tens of thousands. He had some on his own ship – a more superior class, he said, paid a decent rate for their passage, don't you know, decently dressed small businessmen, as I understand it. But most aren't that sort.'

'I've seen them,' James said, and took another glass of champagne from the tray of a passing footman. 'Disgusting, really, quite disgusting. Women look like ragbags, children so underfed they're all eyes and mouths. Terrible business, terrible. They have a bad time of it.'

'My dear chap,' Emmanuel said strongly. 'Never think I lag behind any others in my sympathy for hardship. These poor devils have had a dreadful time, I well know that. Those damned Russians and their pogroms – ought to be put a stop to! But meanwhile, what good does it do them to come pouring in here this way? Jews have a good name in business here. Respected, don't you know. And now all these riff raff, because let us not be sentimental about it, James, riff raff they are, Jews or not. In they come and make everyone else in the country *very* dubious. I mean, look how it was when the Irish came.'

'I don't remember that,' James said, and gave a wolfish little grin. 'Forty years ago, m'boy. Before my time.'

'Dammit, James, before my time too! But I've heard the way people talk, ordinary men, don't you know, chaps one meets in one's club, fellows who work for the firm. Irish navvies and trouble makers they call them. Blame them for everything, and then respectable Irish citizens find themselves tarred with the same brush. The same will happen to us, you mark my words, if we don't do something about all these damned peasants coming pouring into London from Russia and Poland. They'll blame all of us, and then where will we be? People don't always know the difference between ... well, differences!'

'You may be right. But I can't see what we can do about it. Poor devils come here – they're here. Not much we can do then, is there?'

'There's a society being formed to do something very sensible – raising funds to help the poor devils. Most of them would gladly go back again, given enough to set themselves up in business. They haven't all come to escape pogroms, you know! I know for a fact there's plenty of them just with their eyes to the main chance.'

'Good Jewish businessmen?' James murmured.

'Don't be ridiculous, man! You know perfectly well what I mean! Don't he, Alfred?' Emmanuel's brother had joined them, a cigar clamped comfortably between his teeth, and one thumb hooked into the armhole of his otherwise elegant waistcoat.

'Are you talking about the Society for the Relief of Indigent Jews?' Alfred jerked his chin at a footman to bring his champagne. 'Good idea, that. They've sent letters already, seventeen of them, to the rabbis in those places.'

'Letters?' James asked.

'Indeed. Warning them about the conditions here. These poor devils are living in the most appalling housing, *appalling*. I've given several hundred pounds myself to the Society. You ought to do the same. It's going to be a bad lookout if the rush isn't stopped. I warn you – very bad. Funds to send 'em back, that's what they need.'

'You see?' Emmanuel said triumphantly. 'You see? I told you, James. What's going on with those people in the East End is going to make trouble for every one of us in this community. We really do have to do something about it.'

135

14

Nathan was puzzled. He had not thought a great deal about what would happen when they arrived in London, but he had assumed that it would be much as it had been when he left Brody. There would be men in richly braided official uniforms shouting and demanding to see papers, and herding them along from place to place; loud voices insisting on a constant perusal of lists and passports and an eternity of beady eyed questioning about place of origin, destination, means of support.

Yet here there was nothing. Just a wooden landing stage rising from the oily lapping waters of the river on rotting weed-encrusted posts. The ship sat there at her moorings further out, while small boat after small boat left her side, cluttered with people and bundles and screaming children, and made their way across the heaving water to the stage. The people clambered out, and that was it. They had arrived. No one in uniform, braided or otherwise, stepped forward; no one seemed interested in the bundles of papers the immigrants clutched in their hands; no one official seemed to care at all.

There were people about, of course; against one wall overlooking the landing stage were a collection of men who laughed and shouted raucously together, throwing occasional stones at the bewildered new arrivals standing in huddles at the water's edge, hangers-about with nothing better to do than stand and gawp at what was going on. There were children, barefoot and filthy, darting about in the crowds, pushing people out of the way and shrieking with excitement when they were sworn at, and there were other Jews, residents of London who had come to meet some of the arrivals.

Nathan looked at them eagerly. They were people who looked just like the old people, at home in the shtetl, with their round faces and dark eyes and heavy dark clothes. They spoke in the same tones, in the same loud Yiddish, and for a moment he felt a surprising pang of homesickness. After all,

he had been away from the shtetl for three years, a soldier, a
hero. He was used to being a traveller. How could he now
feel like a frightened child longing for home and Momma
this way?

Momma. Momma and Poppa. That was the trouble, of
course. He had given little thought to what he would do to
find his family once he arrived in London; he had used all his
energies to get here. In his imagination, the moment of
arrival had been a sun-glittering excitement bathed in a
golden haze of delight. He had not realized how big London
would be. He had supposed there was a place in it like the
part of Lublin in which he had lived, clearly defined, well
circumscribed by walls and gates and the types of houses
where Jews like his family would live. Now he knew better.

He had stood at the rail of the ship as she came slowly up
the river, watching the buildings on each side pass interminably. The place seemed to go on for ever. Row after row of
wharves and warehouses, row after row of houses and big
buildings that looked like factories, and traffic, traffic, traffic.

On the river, first, big ships, great freighters that looked to
Nathan like ocean going liners, so huge did they seem in his
eyes, and small fussy boats with oars that rose and dipped in
the filthy water so fast that Nathan felt his arms ache as he
watched them.

On shore there was the same bustle. Horses and carts and
carriages moved along the roads almost as far as the water's
edge. Nathan stared and marvelled and worried. How on
earth was he to find any familiar face in such chaos?

He lifted his chin now and looked around him. High on his
left rose a squat grey building with towers on each corner. It
looked imposing and rather alarming, though its threat might
have been due to the fact that someone on the boat had told
him it was the Tower of London, a place for malefactors. He
looked away quickly, and searched with his eyes for somewhere he could stand for a while where he wouldn't be
pushed and jostled by the boatload after boatloads of arrivals,
somewhere he could think, and decide what to do.

The short winter day was dwindling into darkness.
Somewhere on the far side of the landing stage a gas light
flared up and then another, nearer to him. He blinked and
coughed as a swirl of fog moved up from the river and
thickened in his throat. It made him want to cough and spit,

but he knew better than to do that; a filthy habit, his mother had told him, and he had always shared her opinion. So he breathed through his mouth carefully, trying not to notice the way the chill sulphurous air grated on his throat, and trying above all to ignore the smell.

It was not as bad here on the waterside as it had been on the ship. They had been huddled together below decks in bunks so close that he could feel the warmth of his neighbour's body, and as the first night had passed the stench had become worse and worse. Unwashed people, clothes dank with the ever present moisture in the air which sent rivulets of condensed water trickling down every plank and strut in the hold, babies with an ammoniacal smell from their soiled napkins, which made his eyes water, and, as the weather got worse, the sour acid smell of sea sickness. There were no lavatories for all the scores of people in steerage, and in their desperation they eventually used the floors; what else could they do? By the second day at sea he could bear it no longer and had crept up on deck to find a corner there, icy though it was, to sit curled up and live the journey away as best he could. Anything was better than that dreadful hold.

So here on the riverside the smell of sulphur laden fog and the taste of soot in his mouth, were tolerable, almost familiar. Winter nights in Lublin had created similar weather conditions, and similar smells.

Someone shoved against him in the dimness, and he moved obligingly, but the push came, again. He turned on the huddled shape beside him and snapped in Russian, 'Don't push!' You don't have to push.' A woman looked back at him with eyes red with fatigue and watering just like his own, and then shrugged and spat on the ground at his feet, and muttered something in a language he didn't understand. He frowned and spoke again, this time in Yiddish. 'There's no need to push. You'll get where you're going soon enough.'

This time she smiled, a little down-turning of her lips that made her look happier for a moment and then she said in Yiddish, 'It wasn't me. The bitch behind – she shoved me.'

He looked over her shoulder at the woman beyond her and nodded. She was a big stout creature with one small child clutching her neck, and another on her crooked arm, and she was carrying a big bundle in front of her. She could hardly help pushing for she was swaying with fatigue. 'Well, she didn't mean to, I dare say. Where are you from?'

'Tisza Eszlar.'

'Tis – where's that? I never heard of it.'

'Hungary,' she said, and spat again on the wooden landing stage and then reddened a little as she caught the expression of distaste on Nathan's face. 'I shouldn't do that, I know, but the stink – it's made my mouth so bad I can't swallow. It's horrible, the taste in my mouth. My mother, God rest her soul in peace, would be shocked to see me spit like some street drunk, but what can you do? When you're in bad places you do bad things.'

It was as though a tap had been turned on. She chattered on in a great tide of oddly accented Yiddish and he blinked and listened to her, trying to understand. She was not as old as he had thought at first. The shawl that had been over her head had slipped back and he could see that her hair was black and glossy, young hair above a face that was now animated and had recaptured some of its youth. She was hardly much older than he was himself.

'... so when Mama died, three years ago in the bad times, I said to my uncle, I'll go. You won't have to worry. I'll work, I'll learn to keep myself, I'll go and God rot you for your wickedness, thank God my mother didn't live to see how you treated her poor child.'

The crowd on the wharf thickened and Nathan stepped back automatically, still listening to her jabber. Gradually, he pieced the story together. Tiszla Eszlar was a town in the middle of Hungary, and there had been bad times there, sporadic outbreaks of house and shop burning in the Jewish quarter. Her father had been killed in one such episode and her mother had died soon afterwards and left the girl to the unwilling care of an uncle.

It was a pathetic little story, and he shook his head over it and tried to stop the flow of talk, for it was beginning to bore him and also to worry him. He had troubles of his own enough, surely. She had nowhere to go now that she had arrived here in London? No relations, no contacts? Was he any better off, not knowing where his family was, where he might meet any single person he knew? He contemplated his own situation mournfully as the girl beside him chattered on and on, and thought bleakly, 'A hero – some life for a hero – '

On his other side an old man in a ragged coat and a hat so

139

rusty with age that it seemed incredible it held together at all leaned against the wall and sighed deeply, and Nathan tried not to look at him, not wanting to get involved. I've got troubles enough of my own, he thought, troubles enough.

A shape came out of the darkness and materialized into a man with a worried expression on his face and a notebook in his hand. He peered at the knot of people of which Nathan was now the centre and said something in English. They all stared back at him, uncomprehending. The man spoke again, this time in awkward Yiddish.

'You are alone? No one to meet you?'

The old man beside Nathan rocked a little as though he were praying. 'Ay, ay, ay,' he keened. 'Alone! My son, my boy Itzik took ill in Hamburg – couldn't come further, he said go on alone, he'd come after me, someone will meet you, he said to me, *landsleit*. Someone will be sure to find you, take care of you till I come – '

'Alone.' The man nodded and took a notebook from his pocket, and Nathan felt his spirits rise. A man asking questions and writing things down. This was more like the way things should be!

'Name?' the man said to the old man, and then repeated it in his halting Yiddish.

'Yossel,' the old man said, eagerly. 'Yossel són of Chaim.'

'Family name?'

'Eh?'

'Family name? Do you have a family name? Mine is John Walker. My first name is John, my family name is Walker. What is your family name?'

The man shrugged. 'Family name? From where should I get a family name? Me, I'm Yossel son of Chaim! Everyone knows me.'

'No family name,' the man repeated. 'Then you'll accept the name I give you for identification purposes?' Again he spoke English and Yossel's eyes once more glazed with confusion.

'*Ich bin ein altemann*', he said helplessly. 'What do I know of such things? I'm an old man.'

'Altman,' said the man with the notebook, glad to have something to write in it. 'Altman, Yossell. Age? Don't bother, somewhere between sixty and seventy by the look of you. Call it sixty-five.'

140

He scribbled busily and then tore the page from the notebook and gave it to Yossel. 'Listen, Mr Altman,' he said earnestly. 'Over there, by the alleyway, you see?' He pointed. 'There are six other people waiting there – go there, wait, and soon I come to take you to a shelter, a good place where we'll look after you.'

'What sort of place?' Nathan pushed forward, very interested in all that was happening. The girl beside him pushed closer too, staring over his shoulder at the man with the notebook, as Yossel went obediently away.

'It's a mission,' Walker said after a moment and poised his pencil over his notebook again. 'Your name?'

'What sort of mission? What's a mission, anyway?'

'A Christian mission,' he said and smiled up at Nathan, half a head taller than he was, and bobbed his head. 'We come from the evangelical mission to the Jews, and we can give you a bed for the night, and a meal, and tomorrow we help you find a job and … '

Nathan backed away, staring at him. 'Christians? But we're Jews! What do you want with us? What do you want with the old man there? He's a Jew like me. What does he know of evangelists? You can't take him away with you, not an old man who doesn't understand.'

Walker peered up at him for a second and then the earnest smile faded. He turned and went weaving his way through the mob on the landing stage towards the alleyway, and Nathan tried to follow him, to catch his arm and to prevent him from taking the old man away, but he was hampered by his bundle, which he could not possibly let go, and by the fact that he did not know his way about in the dimness as well as Walker did.

By the time he reached the alleyway on the far side the man had gone, and so was Yossel Ben Chaim, now labelled Yossel Altman.

Nathan stood there for a moment, and then shrugged. It was none of his affair, after all. He couldn't imagine anyone would get far trying to convert the old man, anyway. He had troubles enough, he reminded himself.

He turned back into the crowds, still unsure how to resolve these troubles and looked about him again. It was thinning out a little now as those who had come to meet the boats bore off the lucky ones they had come to find, and the last boat made its way back to the parent ship out in the river, but there were still people standing about, seeming as aimless and confused as he was himself.

The men who had been throwing stones were still there, still throwing their stones and shouting their jeers, but he ignored them, for they were a familiar type; they might have been the sort of Russian peasants who had tormented the boys of the shtetl in Lublin except that they were wearing rough cloth trousers tied at the knee with string and broken boots and flat caps, instead of the long tunics and fur hats and high boots of the men he remembered.

But there were the others who were bustling about who interested him. There was a little man wearing some sort of official badge who seemed to be trying to talk to some of the immigrants and a couple of men in heavy overcoats who were moving purposefully from group to group, collecting luggage, harrying people into little knots, sending them on their way with boys to guide them. Nathan watched as the little groups went shuffling away down the dark alleyway, following the boy at their head.

After a while one of the men in overcoats came across to him and said in cheerful Yiddish, in an accent that was so familiar it could have been a Lublin one, 'So? Good to have arrived, hey? Out of the troubles at home, hmm? But it won't be easy here unless you've got people to meet you. You got people to meet you? Family? *Landsleit?*'

The little man with the badge appeared suddenly behind the man in the overcoat. 'Young man,' he said shrilly. 'You come with me! I'm an official of the Hebrew Protection Society, and I'll see to it you come to no harm. This man is no more than a crim – he'll get you into trouble – be advised, come with me – '

His voice was thick and grated on Nathan's ears, for though he spoke good Yiddish his accent was a heavy German one and Nathan disliked it. It had none of the friendly overtones of the overcoated man, and Nathan looked at the badge uncertainly. He needed help, obviously, but who was it safe to take it from? Apart from the risks of being converted, there were other risks; he'd heard stories enough in Brody of newcomers who'd been rooked and robbed by strangers and left penniless and in deep trouble.

The man in the overcoat laughed, then shrugged. 'Listen,'

he said easily. 'It's no skin off my nose. You want to go with this *farbissener*? This miserable twisted grizzler? So go.' He laughed again as the little man turned on him and started shouting at him in confused German.

Nathan grinned at the man in the overcoat. There could be no doubt who would be the best guide, of that he was now sure, and he said easily, 'So, tell me. If I say I've no one to meet me, and I don't know where my family are, what'll you do?'

'Get you a bed for the night', said the man in the overcoat promptly. 'Not a palace, you understand, but a bed, and a meal. Believe me, in this city it ain't easy. You need a *maven*, someone who knows the ins and outs. Me, I'm a *maven*.'

'What's in it for you?' Nathan said. He'd not been a soldier for nothing, he told himself, preening in his awareness of his own good sense. No one was going to put anything over on Nathan the hero. 'Why should you bother for me?'

'For a few pence, is all,' the man said, and shrugged. 'Listen, I find you a place to sleep, maybe point you at a job, all right? So you give me a couple of kopeks for my trouble. Say seventeen men do that in one day, I'm not doing so badly, am I? And I'm showing a bit of *rachmones*, a little compassion to my brothers in trouble. Is that so terrible?'

'It's not so terrible,' Nathan said judiciously, and thought for a moment. The old man with the badge on his shabby coat said urgently, 'He's a *gonif*, a thief, I tell you! He'll rob you blind! Me, I'm employed by the proper authorities to help greeners! I'll take you to a safe place where they'll look after you. You'll say Mincha, evening prayers, you'll eat.'

'Say Mincha?' Nathan said. He might not want to go with a convert-hunting Christian but he was equally unwilling to get deeply involved with a rabbi. It had been a long time since his religious practices had mattered much to Nathan. 'Listen, Zadah, I'm more interested in finding my family than getting any praying done, God should forgive me. If you think I've nothing better to do than say prayers, you've got another think coming. I'm a soldier! Got a medal – see it? You can't make a fool of me, you know!'

The old man threw his hands up in the air and turned away. 'I should worry! You want to be a fool, you be a fool – ' and he hurried across to another little knot of people to show them his badge and offer his services.

'What's your name?' Nathan asked his new friend, as he followed him across the cobbled yard back towards the dark alleyway.

'Ah, call me Sam. Everyone knows me. Just Sam.'

'Glad to know you, Sam,' said Nathan. 'Me, I'm Nathan Lazar. My father's name is Lazar, you understand, but in the army – you know how it is. Now, listen, I need to find my father. He's a miller by trade.' He looked over his shoulder for a moment as they reached the alleyway, wanting, oddly, to take one last look at the waterside, almost as though it were a last look at the old life in the old country. The water lapped as thick and oily as ever against the landing stage, and he stared at it for a long moment. Then, resolute once more, he began to speak to Sam again.

'My father, I was saying. He's a miller.' He stopped yet again. He had caught sight of the girl who had talked to him so eagerly. She was still standing there uncertainly against the wall, her small straw suitcase in one hand and her shawl held under her chin with the other. She looked even younger now than she had before and very lonely, and Nathan said impulsively, 'Listen, Sam, that girl there, she was talking to me – a kid on her own. Could you help her?'

Sam looked back, then made a little face. 'Not me,' he said. 'Don't deal with girls. Someone'll soon pick her up. Believe me. A girl on her own, she'll be all right. See? There's someone talking to her already. You don't need to worry.'

Indeed, there was a woman standing beside the girl now, a neatly dressed woman in a shabby hat and a tightly fitting rusty black coat over a full bustled skirt. She was talking earnestly to her, and after a moment the girl nodded and fell into step beside the woman.

Sam was pulling on his arm but Nathan held back, waiting for her.

'Hello,' he said as she caught up. 'Someone to meet you after all?'

The girl looked at him in alarm for a moment, and then, recognizing him, smiled in relief.

'Oh, it's you. No, no one to meet me. But this lady says she can help me, says there's a special hostel for girls alone in London and she can get me a job.'

Nathan nodded and looked at the woman and then, on an impulse, looked over his shoulder at Sam just in time to see one eyelid flicker at the woman in the rusty black coat. He shook his head, puzzled for a moment and looked back at the woman. She too had an expression on her face that aroused his doubts and then, sharply, his anger.

'Listen,' he said suddenly. 'You're coming with me.' The girl stepped back a little, her face tight with anxiety. 'No, don't look like that. There's something here I don't like. I've been around you know, I was in the army – got a medal – no one puts one over on me that easily, and there's something wrong here.'

It was all over in a matter of moments. He felt Sam's grip hard on his arms as his shoulders were pulled back and his bundle fell from his suddenly paralysed hands. Then there was a knee in his back and a pair of hands squeezing his throat and he really couldn't see anything any more. His eyes were bedazzled with black spots and the noise in his ears was deafening. He was really quite glad when he felt himself land on the cobbles with a jarring impact; it hurt less than those fingers round his throat.

When he opened his eyes he was alone. Sam had gone, the girl with the shawl over her head had gone, the woman had gone, and his bundle had gone. And when he put his hands in his pockets he found his money had gone, too.

15

He was found by the little man with the official badge sitting against the wall of the alleyway in a state of total bewilderment. The little man crouched beside him mopping his sweating face with a handkerchief and pouring out a stream of condolences and I-told-you-sos, not that Nathan listened. He needed all his strength to collect his scattered wits and come to terms with the fact that now he really was penniless. His bundle had contained little enough, a change of underwear, a pair of clean socks, a fresh shirt, some soap, a razor, but now he had only what he stood up in. Thank God he'd put his precious astrakhan hat in his sleeve, otherwise they'd have stolen that, too.

Worst of all he had no money. He had been scornful of the elaborately concealed money belts some of his fellow travellers had provided for themselves, and had felt safe enough with his money tucked tightly into the breast pocket of his shirt, inside his coat. No one could have picked that pocket without his immediate awareness, of that he had been sure, not Nathan the wily soldier. But they had, and taken not only his leather wallet, a Barmitzvah present, but even the small change that he had had in his trouser pockets.

The little man helped him to his feet as other immigrants stood about exclaiming and shaking their heads over him in sympathy and led him to the end of the alley and into a small, noisy eating house that stood tucked against the wall as though it were trying to hide from neighbouring shops. He settled Nathan at one of the oilcloth covered tables and bustled away, returning with a mug full of steaming tea, very strong and sweet and laced with milk. Nathan took it gratefully, and sipped it slowly.

By the time he was finished he felt less shattered. The old man looked at him and shook his head and said, 'Better? Good. Next time maybe you'll listen when you're warned – these people, they're evil villains, *gunovim*, every one of them. I warned you. I stood there and ... '

'Yes,' said Nathan. 'Please, mister. You were right, I was wrong, you don't have to go on and on about it, like a *yachner* in the market place – believe me, I know I was wrong. I've got a sore throat to remind me.' He touched the bruises on his neck gingerly and shook his head at his own stupidity.

'So now, will you come to the Shelter with me, hey? I've already seen the others on their way now, but there's room for one more. They'll take you, and you can pay towards your keep when you've got it – '

'Pay? How do I get with to pay? Nathan said. 'Isn't it bad enough I've been robbed? Do I have to run up a debt as well?'

'No debt. If you can't pay, you can't. But we say to people, as charity has done for you, so you do for charity when you can. When you get a job, get yourself together, you'll remember the Protection Society, give us a little something maybe. Come on.'

The walk helped revive Nathan. It was dark now, and they

had to move through ill lit alleys and narrow high walled streets which smelled fetid and were slippery underfoot. The old man seemed very sure of his way, and they moved swiftly, passing from street to street, plunging ever deeper into the warren. Nathan couldn't see the city beyond those high walls but somehow he could feel the weight of it. There was a distant roar that puzzled him and he asked the little man what it was and was taken aback when he said succinctly, 'Traffic.' Traffic to be so voluminous that it could sound like that? Cart wheels and horses' hooves to be rattling together in such numbers that the total effect was a constant din? It seemed incredible.

Some boys ran after them down one street jeering, and the little man turned on them and shouted. One of them threw a stone, but they made off, and when Nathan asked why they behaved so, the little man said shortly, 'Because we're Jews.' Nathan needed to be told no more. London was just like everywhere else, he told himself. Jews were for hating here as much as anywhere else. He felt more depressed than ever.

The main street into which they finally came made him blink, so wide and important did it look to his Lublin trained eyes.

'Where are we?' he asked, panting a little, for the little man was a fast walker and made no concessions to Nathan's recent adventure. 'Is this the main street of London?'

'Leman Street, the main street of London?' The man laughed then, turning to stare at Nathan over his shoulder. 'Oy, oy, but you really are a greener! A know-nothing! This is just Leman Street! If you make good, get some money together, dress right, maybe one day you'll really see the main street, one of them. Piccadilly, Regent Street, Bond Street, now those you call a street! This is just a hovel, a sty compared with them!' Laughing with delight at his own greater sophistication he led Nathan to a tall flat faced building with a short flight of steps leading up to its front door.

'The Jews' Temporary Shelter,' he said with some pride. 'How's this for a splendid place, hey? You never saw anything like this in the *haim*, did you?'

Nathan lifted his chin. 'I saw big places. Bigger than this,' he said with studied casualness. He was still smarting from the little man's scorn at his reaction to Leman Street. 'I was in the army, you know. Got a medal. I saw a *lot*.'

But the little man wasn't listening, hurrying up the steps to open the door and usher Nathan inside.

It was sparse and bleak. A big room where the residents prayed three times a day, and also ate their meals, an office for the superintendent, a tall rabbinical looking man with a soft blond beard and a richly embroidered satin yarmulka on his head, and uncarpeted stairs which led to a series of dormitories where beds, each equipped with a striped ticking pillow and a pair of rough blankets, stretched in silent rows.

The little man showed him into the office and nodding cheerfully at Nathan went bustling away. Not till after he had gone did Nathan realize he hadn't thanked him properly for his help, and he felt bad about that for a moment. 'I'll tell him next time I see him,' he promised himself (though in fact he never did see him again) and sat down on the only chair in the small, cluttered room, resting his head in one hand. He was beginning to feel the pain in his shoulders and neck more now.

The superintendent, who had followed the little man out, came back and Nathan, like the trained soldier he was, stood up and the superintendent looked approving and nodded at him.

'So, my boy, who are you?' he said. His voice was pleasant to listen to, a cultured yeshiva trained voice that Nathan found reassuring.

Without thinking, he drew himself up to his full height and snapped his arm into a salute, swinging his elbow wide so that his medal, still pinned firmly to his right breast, could be clearly seen. 'Lazar, Nathan, Private. The Fifteenth Regiment, *sir*,' he said, and then winced as the pain in his shoulders reminded him where Sam's thumbs had dug in so cruelly.

'No need for that,' the superintendent said sharply. 'None at all. Here we have no problems about the Tsar's army. So, let's get you registered.'

The questions were comprehensive. Place of birth, date of birth, father's name, grandfather's name, trade, previous occupation, everything that could be thought of. Nathan answered happily, feeling his sense of security growing. Proper documentation at last.

'So, you're looking for your family?' the man said finally, as he blotted his ledger. 'I can tell you, there's a small group of families from Lublin over in Chicksand Street, the other

148

side of Whitechapel Road. Came a while ago, I'm told. They may know some of your landsleit, hmm? People from your part of your shtetl? Tomorrow, after morning prayers, you go and see them. After the bath, of course.'

The bath turned out to be a Russian vapour bath a ten minute walk away to which Nathan and all the other new arrivals had to go in a line, like schoolchildren. Not that Nathan minded. He felt dirty, and was ashamed of his unshaven cheeks and grimy hands, and his dirty clothes. About them he could do nothing. No one could provide a change of linen, as they could loan a razor. But at least he emerged fresh faced, his scarf knotted round his neck to hide both his dirty collar and his bruises, to set about his first full day in London.

It was a better day than the previous one. The sky was a heavy leaden grey but the fog had gone leaving only a hint of sulphur behind it and he could see both ends of the street clearly. It was a bustling street, lined with shops and almost choked with traffic. He stared, fascinated. His native energy and hopefulness was rising in him again, and he felt capable of coping with anything. Anyway, any minute now he would find his family, of course he would. Hadn't that blond bearded rabbi said so last night?

Back at the Shelter they were given breakfast, black bread and margarine and that same stewed heavily sweetened tea he had had last night, with milk in it. He grimaced a little, preferring the familiar Russian style of tea, clear and weak with a lemon slice and drunk through a sugar lump held between the teeth. But it was plentiful fare and he was hungry. His next meal, he promised himself, would be of his momma's cooking.

In fact it took him three days to find them. It seemed to him an eternity of tramping down street after street, looking for people from his own shtetl, asking stranger after stranger. He went in and out of the little shops, places where they sold salt herrings and pickled cucumbers and soft sweet kierchel biscuits like those he had loved so at home in Rivka's kitchen; in and out of workshops and yards, where they thought he was looking for a job and sometimes offered one to him. But he wasn't interested in work. He had a family to find, a rich

149

family who would soon make all well, with the insurance money safely collected because he had gone into the army to make it possible.

Antcliff Street, someone told him. There are some Lubliners in Antcliff Street. A miller? No miller. Just an old man who sells a few things, from a tray, in Watney Street market. Go up the Commercial Road, they said to him, ten minutes, twenty minutes. You walk slow it's twenty minutes, you walk fast it's ten minutes, past Cannon Street Road and Cavell Street till you come to Sidney Street. That isn't it. It's not the next street either, you go into Bromehead Road the next one along, and the next on the right, this hand, not that one, the right hand, *that's* Antcliff Street ...

He escaped the garrulous women who were so eagerly giving him this information in an interval of buying a pair of salt herrings and a pound of black bread, and started walking, feeling hope skulking low in his belly. When he had started three days ago – was it so short a time? It felt an eternity – he had been sure he would find them at any moment. Now his hope was dwindling, and he was beginning to fear that something had gone dreadfully, horribly wrong. Maybe they hadn't come to London at all. Maybe they'd gone on to New York, for they had a lot of money, after all. The insurance money would have made them rich. Maybe they've gone to New York and I've got to get there too and where do I get money of that sort? And what happens if I don't? Do I never see Momma and Poppa again? Never see Bloomah again?

That was the first time he had allowed himself to think of Bloomah for a long time. Firmly he pushed the vision of her face away. Find Momma and Poppa first. First things first. And if he didn't find them today, he'd see what he could do about New York. Maybe he could manage it the way he'd managed the journey from Brody. It could be done, surely?

He walked on, brooding on ways and means of making the Atlantic crossing, and almost missed his directions. It was Bromehead Road he turned into at last, a narrow street with matching rows of small houses, each with a front door and one window at ground level and two windows on the level above. There were children playing in the street, running noisily from door to door and shrieking at each other as children always do. Feeling old, he picked his way among them till he was on the corner of Antcliff Street. Number nine, they had said. That's the house.

It was a tiny house exactly like all the others. The front door stood open and he banged on it with his fist a couple of times, peering into the narrow hallway. He could just see the bare boards of the floor and a door beyond, and on the left a staircase rising steeply into the darkness. The place smelled of cats and carbolic soap and the lingering smell of cooking, and suddenly he was at home again. His mother was rendering down chicken fat, cutting the yellow slabs into little lumps, throwing them in a pan with a chopped onion to fry until the fat ran liquid gold and could be poured safely into a basin, leaving the crisp fat pieces and the crunchy onion to be piled on a piece of fresh rye bread. His mouth watered at the memory, and so did his eyes.

The door at the end of the hallway creaked open and an old woman came shuffling towards him, staring suspiciously. He said carefully, 'I'm looking for my parents – Rivka and Lazar. From Lublin. You might know if they are here? I was told maybe ... '

The old woman turned and shuffled back the way she had come, wordlessly, but she jerked her head at the staircase and after a moment he stepped over the threshold and began to climb.

The smell of frying chicken fat and onions became stronger and for the first time in three days his hope began to burgeon. It really did smell so much like Rivka's kitchen.

The door at the top of the stairs was ajar and he pushed it open, and stood there looking in.

She was standing beside the fire, a pan in her hand. She turned at the sound of the door and stared at him, holding the pan awkwardly in front of her. After a moment she held it out towards him and said, '*Greben*, Nathan. You want some of Momma's *greben*?'

The tears were over. The hugging and the exclaiming and explaining were dying down. His shirt and underwear were drying in front of the fire, and he was sitting wrapped in a blanket, a glass of schnapps in one hand and a piece of freshly baked sugar-strewn kugel in the other. His mother was sitting on the other side of the fire staring at him as though it were the only way to keep him safe, as though turning her gaze away from him would make him disappear. He laughed with the sheer joy of looking at her, and drank his schnapps and held out his glass for more.

'So, tell me Momma, everything that's happened. I must know *everything*. Where's Reuben? Where are Benjamin and Alexander? And why do you live in this little place? I mean, with the money from the mill you should be better than this.'

He looked around, trying to see the home they had had back in Lublin. They hadn't been rich, but they had been comfortable enough. Solid furniture hewn from whole trees; rich red curtains in the windows, plenty of handsome gold decorated dishes on their shelves and a fine brass samovar on a lace clothed table in the corner. He could see it all clearly, superimposed on this tiny shabby place with its rickety table made of cheap pine and its four straight backed chairs, one with a rope tying in place the broken strut at the back. The wooden floor was bare, with a couple of old sacks spread over it, and the grimy window was uncurtained. Beside the open fireplace was an up-ended wooden box in which some pans, a kettle and a few coarse white plates stood. The fire was warm and the pot on it smelled good, but it wasn't what it had been at home.

'Why are you living here, Momma?' he repeated. 'With all that money?'

'You'll have to ask your Poppa,' she said and got to her feet. 'Listen, bobbalah, the clothes are dry. You put them on, hey? Better you should be dressed. I can't iron them, on account I got no iron, but I pulled them straight as I could. Soon maybe we get an iron and then you'll look better, hey? When we get an iron ... '

His father came in just as he was putting on his boots again, still nagging at his mother to explain. He straightened up as the old man came in and stared at him across the tiny room. And Nathan could have cried.

He had never been a big man, Lazar Ben Chaim. Spare and wiry, really. But now, he looked like a thread. His hair, a vigorous pepper and salt when Nathan had last seen him, had become a thin and straggly grey. His face was lined and bitten with fatigue and at the sight of him the words that had been pouring out of Nathan as he questioned Rivka dried up completely.

'Nathan?' Lazar said after a long moment. 'Nathan?' He

152

bent and set down the tray he was carrying on straps across his shoulders. It had toys on it, cheap little tin things with clockwork interiors that sat there, pathetic in their gaudy colours.

The exclaiming and weeping started all over again, but with less enthusiasm on Nathan's side this time. Something had obviously gone dreadfully wrong. His vision of a peaceful and comfortable life with parents made affluent by the insurance money his army service had brought them began to recede rapidly down the corridors of his imagination.

They ate then, the three of them round the rickety table, a bowl of soup and black bread to bulk it out.

'Not a proper soup, bobbalah,' his mother apologized. 'A whole chicken I can't manage this week. Giblets and a bit of *schmaltz* from the butcher, so I can make soup, a few *knaidlech* – you got to have chicken fat to make good dumplings, this you remember! – but a whole chicken? Next week maybe.' She shot a sideways glance at Lazar, silent on the other side of the table, and then clamped her lips tightly closed.

They ate silently, listening to Nathan telling them of his exploits. He told them of the medal, of course, and how he got it, though they were left rather confused about the details.

But even he couldn't keep it up for long, and by the time they were drinking tea, proper Russian tea with lemon and sugar lumps, all three were silent again, watching the candle in the battered pewter candlestick and the firelight as the last of the day's coal burned down.

When he'd finished his tea, Nathan took a deep breath and leaned forward in his chair, resting his elbows on the table.

'So, Momma, Poppa?' he said. 'What's happened? Where is Reuben? Where are Benjamin and Alex? And where's the insurance money I worked so hard for? I'm here now and it's time I had my share, isn't it? What happened to it?'

16

Mary Lammeck did not think she would ever be able to cry again. She had wept for three days, waking with tears in her eyes, feeling them trickle down her cheeks as her maid opened her curtains and the nurse came padding across the heavy carpet to start the day's fussing, continuing all through the morning and on into the long afternoon and evening.

When Emmanuel came, as he did punctiliously each morning before he left for the office, she did her best to hide her misery for she knew it angered him, but failed every time, for she was too weak and too drained to exert any control at all. He would stand beside the bed looking down at her as she lay there her face turned to the pillow and breathe in sharply through his nose and then pat her shoulder, at first awkwardly and then, as the days passed and the same pattern persisted, with some asperity and bid her to cheer up and escape with relief to Lammeck Alley.

It was worse when her mother-in-law came each day after the nurse had taken away her untouched luncheon tray, and sat there silent and majestic beside her. Mary knew perfectly well how much effort Augusta was putting into remaining silent. Had she given vent to her feelings Mary had no doubt at all that the result would have been a tidal wave of reproach. Hadn't Augusta herself given birth five times with no mishaps at all? Had not each and every one of her infants been born exactly when it should have been, bawling and lusty? How could she not fail to despise such a one as Mary, who could not even carry her first pregnancy beyond seven months, and then produced so puny a child that it had gasped but once and then died?

Yet Augusta sat silent, preventing any word of reproach from passing her lips, and that made Mary feel worse. Even complaint would have been better than silent contempt. And she would weep even more helplessly, lying there with her eyes closed and the tears pushing through her lids to slide down her pallid cheeks and soak her pillow.

In fact, she did Augusta an injustice. Augusta did in truth

feel sympathy for her daughter-in-law, little though she had ever found in her to admire. To have spent thirty-seven hours in painful labour only to have a dead baby at the end and then to be told by the doctors that she had been so appallingly damaged by her experience that she could never hope to have another pregnancy, was to Augusta, healthy vigorous Augusta, quite dreadful. Poor pathetic creature that Mary was. It really was too sad.

But her sadness for Mary was as nothing as compared to her distress on her son's behalf. That so splendid a boy as her Emmanuel should be deprived of children of his own blood was a dreadful thing; so dreadful that she had hoped for a couple of days after Mary was first delivered that the poor wretched child would succumb to loss of blood and general weakness. A wicked thought, she knew, but understandable, surely, for such an eventuality would have relieved the situation so ... well, so neatly.

But Mary somehow survived to weep the days away, and Augusta would come and sit beside her every afternoon as a mother-in-law should and watch her weep and failing to find anything useful to say would say nothing. Mary would lie there praying for her to go, and then when she had, weep for her to return for even a silent reproachful mother-in-law was better than having no mother at all.

Now, four days after they had taken away that scrap of red haired infant, so dead and helpless in her little white shawl, she at last stopped crying. It was as though the pool of tears that had filled her belly had at last dried up leaving her desiccated and incapable of further distress. She just lay and stared at the elaborate loops of Nottingham lace that swathed the three windows of her huge bedroom and listened to the way the traffic outside became muffled as it passed over the straw that had been laid in the street beneath. 'It would have been better for everyone if I had died,' she thought bleakly. 'Much better.' She didn't care at all that it was a wicked thought and ungrateful to a good God who had seen fit to spare her life.

That afternoon for the first time Fay came to see her. Mary had expressly asked in the beginning that she should not come; the only thought she had had for anyone apart from herself in those first dreadful days had been that she wanted Fay protected from her distress. The nurse and doctors had been glad enough to enforce her wish. They would have banished everyone but Emmanuel from visiting if they could, but even the most celebrated accoucheur in London and the most expensive physician could not prevail against Augusta Lammeck, and wisely had not tried to do so.

Now they felt a little agreeable company would be good for their patient, and Fay was ushered into the big front bedroom of the house in Green Street. She stood uncertainly at the foot of the bed, a great sheaf of white lilies on one arm.

Mary was touched at the sight of her small pale face above the dark blue of her mantle and framed in a sober gable bonnet trimmed with pleated dark blue silk. Clearly Fay had tried to choose clothes that would show how distressed she was without actually going into mourning. One did not wear black for a baby who had been born dead, for it did not count as a person. Augusta had told Mary that when she had arrived in a handsome crimson gown over which she had worn an emerald green covert coat. Mary, who cared little about such matters, had yet wept to know that her baby did not even warrant the wearing of black. Now, seeing Fay in her sober blue, she was grateful to her, and held out her arms in welcome.

Fay dropped her flowers and ran to Mary's side to kneel beside the bed and throw her arms across her and weep furiously. Mary stroked her hair and felt, for one brief moment, some comfort. Her own dear Fay, to care so much, so genuinely – she needed the warmth of Fay's tears, and basked in them.

They talked, desultorily, easily, about silly things; about a shopping trip Fay had undertaken, and the difficulty of buying comfortable boots, about Fay's visit to the Montefiores' for the weekend, of the family's plans to spend the week between Christmas and the New Year with the Rothschilds at Mentmore, for although of course none of them observed Christmas as a festival, it was an inevitable hiatus in the business world, and anyway, the Jewish festival of Chanucah, which coincided this year with Christmas, could be celebrated.

'They make a great deal of fuss of Chanucah at Mentmore,' Fay said, holding Mary's hand tightly now between both of her own. 'They have all those grandchildren and cousins to visit, and as they say, it is the children's festival – oh, my darling! I am so sorry! I should have bitten my tongue out before saying such – '

'Hush,' Mary said. 'You can't pretend there are no children in the world, my love, just because I – just because of me. That would be foolish. Of course Chanucah is for children – all those candles and the presents.'

'I can't bear it, Mary, really I can't. That you should suffer so. You've done nothing to deserve it.'

'Fay, listen to me.' Mary struggled to sit up, pulling herself up against her pillows with so much energy that for a moment her pale face reddened a little. She leaned forward and put her hands on Fay's shoulders. 'Listen to me. Do you still want to wed your Richard? Have you said anything to Mama about him?'

'Have I – ' Fay drew back. 'Of course I have said nothing! Why do you think of that now? You have more important things to think of, my love, like getting better and … '

'Fay, do please listen to me, before the nurse comes back and makes you go away – it really is important.' She leaned back on her pillows again, suddenly fatigued.

'Well, no, I haven't said anything to Mama,' Fay said. 'And I never can. I must just – ' Fay shrugged and let her eyes slide away from Mary's. 'I must just bear it, must I not? I was a fool ever to let myself … I am a fool. I know that. I must just forget him.' She managed a small smile. 'I shall devote myself to good works and be a maiden aunt and – oh, Mary! There I go again! How could I be so cruel!' Her eyes filled with tears once more.

Mary pushed that aside. 'Listen, my dear one. Please. I – I love you too well to let you be unhappy. I know it will be difficult for you, but please, do as I say. Tell your Richard you will come and stay with me as soon as they will let you, to keep me company. And he must make arrangements to take you away and marry you. Yes, I know it will be difficult and wicked but he must contrive something. You shall have your husband and your children and be happy. You hear me?'

'You're ill, Mary darling. Please don't excite yourself. It really isn't important enough and … '

'It is, it is,' Mary said fretfully, and turned her head on the pillow. Her eyes were very bright now, and the colour had returned to her cheeks in high red patches. 'It is. My little girl is dead and I shall never have another, but they shan't take your life away from you. I shan't let them. To live with a man you thought you loved and who ... well, never mind that. I mean, to love a man and not to be able to share your life with him. It must be like dying, a little. There's been enough of dying here, you understand me, Fay? My little girl is dead, but you mustn't be. You must have your Richard and the devil take them all. Please, Fay, will you? Will you be happy for me? I can't be happy, but if you are ... ' She shook her head, too weary to say more and Fay stared at her, and shook her head too and tried to argue, but there were no words she could think of. Mary seemed to be staring through her and beyond her to a world of misery she could not comprehend. She felt the urgency in her and for the first time allowed herself to think seriously of what Mary was suggesting.

It became a game between them, one they could play whenever they were together. After two weeks, when Mary was allowed to sit out of bed for an hour a day, and they permitted Fay to spend each afternoon with her (thus relieving Augusta of the need to come so often, an opportunity she was glad to seize), they began to make more detailed plans. At first Fay played along with Mary to mollify her. It all seemed an impossible fantasy that Mary in her weakened state seemed to need. But as the weeks turned into a month and the Christmas and New Year visit to Mentmore punctuated Fay's attendance at Green Street, it took stronger shape in her mind.

She could see what had happened; Mary, in losing her infant daughter, had seized on this scheme to further Fay's happiness as a way of atoning for her own guilt over her child's death. That she blamed herself was clear to Fay, and in a way she shared Mary's view of what had happened. Women were for having children; a woman who could not have children was pitiable, but also somehow culpable; to be so was to be like being a man who was incapable of earning a living. How could anyone fail to regard the barren woman otherwise than as a failure? Loving her sister-in-law as she did, Fay wanted to help her assuage her guilt, and if the way she wanted to do it was by opening the door of Fay's own private prison, who was Fay to argue with her?

So they plotted and planned, and Richard was brought in one Friday afternoon – when there was no risk of any of the family visiting, for the Sabbath came in early on these short winter days and they would be bustling about their synagogue affairs – to take his share of the organizing.

Fortunately for Mary's peace of mind, he was enthusiastic. Genuinely in love with the rather quiet and mouselike Miss Lammeck, he had been sadly hampered in his courting of her not so much by her religion – as the student son of a freethinking physician, religion had never played much part in his young life – as by her fortune. He had a comfortable competence of his own, enough on which to marry and run a simple home, as well as his future as a physician, but the Lammeck wealth had alarmed him. He had not believed he could possibly hope to marry her. Now, with Mary's help, he could see a way that made it very possible, for clearly a runaway heiress ceased to be an heiress. She would come to him penniless, and to Richard Gough that was a very attractive prospect.

'We can marry in a register office,' he said. 'None of your family nor your friends will notice the banns posted there and so will not stop us, and this way there can be no insult to anyone's religion.'

'Oh, they will consider me a bawd,' Fay said as equably as she could. 'Such a marriage will not be regarded by them as a marriage at all. But I don't care. Except perhaps for Papa . . . '

She made a little face, but there was excitement and a certain hardness in her eyes. What had started as a game to comfort an ailing sister-in-law had become the core of her life. She would marry her Richard, no matter what.

'But he will have the boys, and of course his precious Davida. I sometimes think he believes the sun shines out of her mouth, he's so besotted with her.'

The way the new Mrs Albert Lammeck had ingratiated herself with her father-in-law had rankled with Fay. She had returned from their short honeymoon in the Swiss lakes – for Emmanuel had said strongly that the firm could not spare its junior partner for longer than a fortnight – to pass her days in a whirlwind of spending as she decorated and equipped her handsome new house in Mount Street, and her evenings in the bosom of her husband's family, talking breathlessly and listening flatteringly to every word Bartholomew uttered. The only member of her immediate family with whom Fay had ever felt any rapport seemed to have turned away from her to a more exciting and attractive rival. Why should she concern herself, therefore, with the effect her departure to live her own life might have on him? She would not – and since in addition there was real pleasure to be found in contemplating what her mother's rage would be, Fay's resolve hardened. She would elope.

And elope she did, one February evening, walking calmly out of her sister-in-law's house with her valise in her hand to clamber into a four wheeled cab and rattle away with her Richard to a life of her own. She wept a little at parting with Mary, but not a great deal. She had seen enough of her sister-in-law's life at the hands of her husband during the weeks when she was staying at the house, ostensibly to help the ailing mistress of it to recover, to know what hell a loveless marriage could be. She wanted none of that chilly loneliness, that ever-present anxiety about the quality of her husband's mood that so obviously filled Mary's life. She felt some guilt at leaving her much loved sister-in-law to her dismal existence, when her own promised so much happiness, but since doing so meant that Mary felt better about the loss of her baby, that made it all right.

So Fay told herself, clutching Richard's arm, and staring out at the rainwashed streets clattering by and thinking of the little house in Croydon, where they were to live, and where she would experience the full joy of being Mrs Gough, rather than Miss Lammeck.

Mary watched them go, standing at her drawing room window and peering out at the cab wheeling away, and wept as she had not since her baby had died, and then sat down calmly to wait for the storm to break over her head. She sat up till three in the morning when Emmanuel at last came home, and went clattering up the stairs past the drawing room door. She had left it half open, and now called his name as he went by.

He came and peered in at her, staring in amazement at the sight of his wife fully dressed at this hour of the morning and snapped his brows down in a hard frown. He was very tired and in an evil mood. He had spent the evening at a card party at David Da Costa's house, a man he had never liked too well but who included among his friends many of the Marlborough House set.

Emmanuel was ambitious and wanted to move in the highest social circles, which meant those adorned by his Royal Highness the Prince of Wales. And that meant assiduous attendance at the sort of costly entertainments the Prince so much enjoyed. Which also meant that sometimes losses were incurred, losses which Emmanuel much resented. To gamble in business was one thing; he did it all the time, weighing one risk against another and putting down hard money to back his decisions, but to gamble on the turn of a card or the energy of a horse running pointlessly along a grassy track was quite another. He disliked it intensely. He had not yet learned how not to lose, let alone how to win, and he hated waste.

Tonight had been one of the bad nights. He had lost seventeen guineas at the card table, and the Prince had not even attended, even though he had been expected. Now the sight of his wife, white faced and clearly still far from well, looking owlishly at him sharpened his temper.

'What the devil are you doing there at this hour? Go to bed, Mary, for heaven's sake!'

'Fay has gone,' she said, standing there with her hands clasped lightly in front of her and her face expressionless. Indeed, she looked better than she had for some time, for her gown of soft brown silk did not underline her pallor too cruelly and there was an expression on her face that made her look much more interesting, somehow. Usually she had a slightly worried crease between her brows when she looked at Emmanuel and a hangdog expression in her eyes that irritated him profoundly. Tonight, looking at her, she seemed to him, just for a moment, the sweet and charming girl she had been when he first met her, at a party at her father's house. But then her father had died and her prolonged grief had irritated him, and somehow she had become more of a burden to him than a source of marital pleasure.

He shook his head at his own confused thoughts and said sharply, 'What did you say?'

'Fay has gone. Run away. Eloped.'

There was a silence. Then he came into the room and stood there with his top hat in one hand and his overcoat hanging open and said blankly, 'Fay has what?'

161

'Eloped. With Richard Gough. He is a Christian. Well, not precisely that – let's say he is not a Jew. She is very happy.'

The first storm broke. His rage was monumental as he shouted and roared at her, demanding more information about where his sister had gone, what had been planned, her own part in the affair. Servants were wakened and came running and messages were sent to Park Lane to alert his father and mother, and to his brothers' houses to rouse them to action. By six a.m. they had all congregated at Emmanuel's house and were sitting in the morning room in postures ranging from deeply dejected (Bartholomew) via puzzlement (Albert and his brother Alfred) and beady eyed relish (Davida and Susan) to total shock and outrage (Augusta and Emmanuel).

Mary sat quietly at the head of her own breakfast table pouring cups of coffee and letting them rant on and on, seeming quite unmoved. She answered their questions as calmly as she poured coffee: no, she did not know where they had gone, only that Fay had left a letter saying she was to wed Richard Gough in a registry office and it was a waste of time for anyone to seek her, and no, she had had no inkling that any such scheme was afoot and yes, she did feel very sad indeed that her beloved Fay had thrown away her life. At which she lowered her lids and sipped her coffee, not wanting anyone to see how triumphant she felt when she contemplated the way Fay had 'thrown away her life'.

It went on for days, with the brothers meeting and talking interminably. They could not decide how to handle it; should they send out detectives to search for their sister and bring her back? What would be the good of that? She was legally of age to marry, having passed her twenty-second birthday, and if a ceremony had been conducted at a registry office and the marriage had been consummated they had no jurisdiction over her. To institute a search, they decided, would be to institute a scandal to no benefit, and yet ... and yet, she was their sister.

It was Bartholomew who settled it. In the middle of Augusta's tightlipped fury and the soothing words Davida poured over him in his suffering and his sons' rage he sat silent, until four days after Fay's marriage. Then he left the house, quietly, to go to Bevis Marks synagogue in the City.

He sat there in its cool, stark interior, staring at the wooden

162

pews and the small light burning in front of the Ark, at the brass candle holders that hung across the centre of the quiet space, at the low railings that flanked the women's balcony, and thought of his family, at home in Bombay.

He thought of his aunt, the strong, resourceful Sarah Hazzan Lammeck, who had died twelve years ago, and of his brothers and cousins and the whole network of Lammecks that stretched from here, in the City of London, to the Middle and Far East, as far as Shanghai and beyond.

He thought of the sufferings of his grandfather Abdul, when he had escaped from Baghdad, of his own hard work and loneliness in this damp, alien land, and last of all, of his daughter Fay who had turned her back on all of them.

And went home and told them that she was dead. They would say the prayers for the dead over her, and tear their clothes and then never speak of her again. Even masterful Augusta, looking at the way his face had hardened under the narrow dark eyes said nothing, but did as she was bid. She had not lived so happily with her Birdie for so long without knowing when to give way to him.

And Mary – Mary breathed deeply and attended the mourning prayers for her sister-in-law and for the first time since her own hope of happy life had died in a breath taken by a scrap of a red headed infant, felt she could face existence again. She had paid the debt she owed her baby. She did not look at Emmanuel, however, as she thought this thought. Indeed she hardly ever looked at Emmanuel's face at all, now.

17

Nathan sat facing his brother Alex in Curly's café in Whitechapel Road, a buttered bagel on the plate in front of him and a cup of coffee beside it. It wasn't easy to leave them lying there untasted, yet it was even harder to eat food for which his young brother had paid.

He looked at Alex under his lashes; the brother he had last seen as a gawky fourteen year old was now very different. He had filled out physically, for a start. The bony cheeks were veiled in fat, and there was already a faint hint of double chin under the blueness of his morning shave. His shoulders were broad under a checked jacket – and that in itself was startling to Nathan, who had never worn anything but decent gaberdine or khaki uniform in his life – and his neck bulged a little over the edge of a very white shirt. His dark hair gleamed with oil, each ridged line of curls picking up the gaslight that hissed and popped overhead, and his hands looked well scrubbed and very large and capable as he pushed the last of his own bagel into his mouth and waved at Curly behind the counter at the back of the cafe to bring him another.

'So, Nathan, you aren't eating?' Alex said cheerfully, and took a long draught of his coffee. 'Believe me, you won't get a better bagel anywhere.'

'Speak Yiddish, for God's sake,' Nathan growled. 'You know I can't understand English.'

'And you never will if you don't try. So I'll talk some English to you, and you'll learn, and you'll do well,' Alex said, half in Yiddish, half in English.

'Don't you tell me what to do and what not to do!' Nathan snapped, his face darkening with the sudden urge of anger that rose in him. 'I'm your older brother, remember? Don't you go telling me.'

'All right, all right, I'm sorry.' Prudently Alex lapsed completely into Yiddish. 'You've had a bad time, Nathan, and I sympathize, I really do. It's a sin and a crime, that's what it is and Reuben, Reuben ought to be horsewhipped, I tell you. I'd do it myself, only it'd be a waste of time. He's so bone hard selfish it'd make no difference to him and so bone hard stupid he wouldn't even be hurt.'

Nathan grunted, a little mollified, but still ill at ease. To see this seventeen year old looking so changed, so *old*, so alien, depressed him.

'So how come you live with him?'

'On account I'm not stupid,' Alex said promptly and grinned at Curly who had brought him another bagel. 'Hey, Curly? Me, I'm not stupid, am I?'

Curly sniffed unappetizingly. 'You're stupid like I'm Lord Rosebery. You owe me fourpence ha'penny.'

'So I'll pay, I'll pay! Did I ever not pay? We're not finished yet. Eat Nathan, eat already. Then you eat more. Bring him another bagel, Curly.'

164

Nathan began to eat, unable any longer to resist the golden crispness staring up at him from the plate, but he chewed with a certain ferocity, anger still filling him.

'Listen, Nathan, I can understand how it is with you.' Alex leaned fowards over the wooden table, his elbows spread wide. 'You go off to the army – and I'll never forget the way you looked that morning you went away, so sad and sorry. You go off and do that for the old ones, and Reuben, he does nothing. *Nothing. Gornisht mit gornisht.* They lose everything, the *shlemeil* that Poppa is. I mean no disrespect, Nathan, so don't look at me that way! It's true, it's got to be said, ain't it? The old man was a *shlemeil*. I told him when I saw him with that man at the docks, I told him nothing but trouble will come. I could see the man was a *gonif*, a real thief, but Poppa, will he listen? Never does he listen to anyone, you know that. So the *gonif* took us of every penny we got, and we arrive in London broke. Finished. Ruined. Momma and Poppa and two kids and not a rouble, not a kopek, not a pfennig, not a farthing. And Reuben, he's the one in charge all of a sudden, the *gunsa macher*, the big one, who does it all. How can we argue?'

'I hate him. I'll give him a hiding. I'll ...' Nathan's voice was low, because however justified anger might be, to threaten to harm your own brother was a wicked thing to do. But the anger in him seethed and he swallowed his mouthful of bagel, pushing the rage back down.

'Much good that'll do you!' Alex leaned back in his seat, grinning. 'Be like me, Nate – clever! Use him, don't hate him! Momma and Poppa'll be all right, believe me.'

'In that place?' Nathan flared at him. 'Living in that disgusting place with Poppa walking the streets with a tray on his belly with that rubbish he tries to sell? That by you is all right?'

'No,' Alex said calmly. 'Not all right. Not now. But I said they *will* be. I'll take care of them.'

'You?' Nathan managed a sneering laugh. 'You, seventeen years old, and already he's going to run the world ...' But he couldn't look at his young brother, all the same. That jacket must have cost a lot of money, and the boy looked so well fed compared with everyone else he saw in these teeming Whitechapel streets. Maybe he could at that.

'Now, just you listen to me, Nate, and you won't go

wrong, believe me.' Alex leaned forwards in the confidential way that Nathan was beginning to realize had become characteristic of him. 'Move in with Reuben. He's got a whole house, for God's sake! A whole house, and there's only him and Minnie and four little kids. He's got space for Benjamin and me, he'll find space for you too. He can't refuse. And he can afford it, believe me. He's got, that man, I tell you. He's been here four years already. He's established! Anyway,' Alex leaned back again, folding his arms almost triumphantly. 'Where else are you going to go? Have you got money to pay rent to strangers?'

Nathan had to admit he had not. Alex had been tactful enough to say nothing about the way he had been robbed, but he knew his young brother was aware of how stupid he had been, and that rankled too. Altogether he found little to be glad of in finding this particular member of his family again.

'How come you're so ...' Nathan gestured awkwardly, a movement that took in the gleaming hair, the round cheeks, the air of satisfaction with which Alex was clothed.

'You like it?' Alex straightened the lapels of his jacket and squared his heavy shoulders slightly. 'Nice bit o' shmutter, hey? Worked it off.'

'Worked it off?'

'Sure! There's a mate of mine, got a stall down the Lane – I spiel a bit for him Sunday mornings, see? So I said to him when I saw this jacket come in, hardly worn. I said to Moishe, I'll work this morning for the jacket and a pair of shoes. Maybe I'll sell more, maybe less, you take a gamble. And Moishe, the *shlemeil*, he said yes!'

'Why *shlemeil*?' Nathan was confused, staring at his brother who seemed to inhabit a world different from his. 'People get paid for their work here, don't they?'

'Listen, Nate. The way it is, I sell on commission, see? What I sell for him, I get a few pennies on the deal. Right, that means I have a good morning I get more money than if I have not such a good morning. A bad one, I never have. See?'

Nathan shook his head. 'No.'

Alex sighed, like a mother trying to teach a recalcitrant child. 'Listen,' he said patiently. 'I sell good that morning – but I say to the customers, come back next Sunday, then you get the garment a few pence cheaper, my life you do. I'll hold

166

it for you. So, they put their markers on the garments, they go away, and I still get my jacket and my shoes even though I haven't sold quite so much this Sunday. Then the Sunday after the customers come back, I have a marvellous morning, and get the cash commission. You see?'

Nathan shook his head. 'I thought you said Moishe was your friend?'

Alex laughed, indulgently. 'Sure he's my friend. And he'd screw the *tochus* off me for a farthing. I should worry about him! Believe me, he does well with me, and he knows it. No one sells like me, no one.'

He looked thoughtfully at Nathan and then sighed again. 'Nathan, you were always a bit of a fool, you know that? A fool to yourself. There's a whole big world out there waiting to do you – unless you do 'em first. When we was kids I used to watch you, always the good one, always the one who fetched and carried for Momma, helped the neighbours and got nothing for your trouble. You still do it. Reuben never did, but you ...'

'Reuben!' Nathan's face darkened again. 'He was always too busy to do anything for anybody.'

'And so was I! Benjamin you can't count – he was like now, always with his nose in a book – but you never noticed that I could have been like you, but wasn't! Where d'you suppose I was all the time you were so busy with Momma and all?'

Nathan frowned. 'I never thought,' he said uncertainly. 'I always supposed – cheder – school...'

Alex laughed. 'Sometimes, sure, often enough so the rabbi wouldn't complain to the the family I was a truant. But whenever I could, I was doing other things. A bit here, a bit there. By the time we left Lublin, I had seven roubles tied in my shirt tail.'

'How much?' Nathan said, his eyes widening. 'You had ... but you said Momma and Poppa were robbed, had no money. How come you didn't give it to them?'

Alex shook his head. 'Believe me, I thought about it. Then I thought, I give them my seven roubles, we lose the lot, the way we lost the rest of the insurance money. Better I say nothing, see what Reuben does. So Reuben had to do, and I kept my roubles. Not that it helped all that much. I didn't get as much in pounds as I should have for 'em, I'll tell you that now. The bastards cheated me – but I learned. Now I got a few bob put away, invested.'

'How do you mean, invested?'

Alex looked cautious for the first time. So far he had had a boastful air about him but now he seemed to be in a little doubt. He looked at Nathan for a long moment and then, seeming to approve of what he saw, once more leaned forwards.

'I got an interest in a coffee stall. Outside the Yiddish theatre in Whitechapel Road, every night it's there, except Friday and Monday. After I finished the show, I come out, take a cup of coffee, the people see me, they want to be close to the performers, they buy coffee too! The man I got running it doesn't rob me more'n I can stand – a man's entitled to make his way, after all. If it goes on going as good as it is, I reckon I'll get another stall, put it down in the Commercial Road, near the hall where the boxing matches are. Then maybe another for the working men's club down by Leman Street. The card-players there, they like a little nosh. I tell you there's a lot I can do once I get enough money to buy more stalls. I'm telling you this, Nathan, in confidence, you understand. If Reuben finds out, he tells me to go find my own place. But it doesn't suit me to find my own place, not yet. It's noisy at Reuben's, with those bloody kids bawling and Reuben shouting and throwing himself around the way he does, but it suits me. I want to put every penny I got into my own affairs, you see? Now, listen, Nathan. Come in with me. I'd rather employ my own brother than some stranger. Come with me, work the stall and together we'll make a fortune, you'll see. Just you follow your little Alex, and we'll make a fortune.'

Nathan shook his head, bewildered. There was too much going on for him to get hold of properly; his father and mother living in dire poverty and yet one brother renting a whole house in this busy city, and another talking this way of his own business? It was more than he could grasp.

'Momma told me you were working in the theatre. She said that was why you were never able to come to see her evenings. How come you're talking about coffee stalls?'

Alex shook his head. 'You don't listen, Nate. Sure I work in the theatre. You come tonight, you'll see. Bit of singing, bit of dancing, a few jokes, they love it! But that doesn't take

168

a man all day, for God's sake! From seven o'clock till ten o'clock, I'm on a stage, or near enough on it. What should I do the rest of the time? Gamble the few bob they give me? I should be so stupid! No, Nate, the rest of the time I got affairs to deal with. The coffee stall, the Lane with Moishe on a Sunday morning, believe me, it's the best market for miles around, the best ... I got a fighter I'm training – Danny – on Sunday afternoons, the occasional fight Monday night – when I don't go to the theatre.'

'Fight?'

'I'm a partner with a man, a promoter. Fight promoter – people like to see a bit of skill, you know? There's some big fast boys here, these days. Got ourselves a couple of Dutch Jewish boys, their families been here twenty years maybe, more even, and they got some real muscle on 'em. So my partner sets up fights with a purse for the pair of 'em, and a percentage to the house – that's us – and we make a few bob. Nothing big, you understand, but why not if there's a profit to be made? That's the point, you see, Nathan! You got to look at all the opportunities, do what you can. A *bissel* here, a *bissel* there – the little bits they all add up. Another few months, I get a house of my own. I move Momma and Poppa in, and they're all right. Poppa can stop his peddling, take life easy a bit, and Reuben can go crawl up his own *tochus.*'

Nathan finished his coffee, now almost cold, and tried to organize it all in his head. He had paid so little attention to Alex at home in Lublin. He had been the baby, the young one, who would pay any attention to him? Certainly not his older brother, so busy about his own life. The boy had slipped in and out of the house, quiet, unobtrusive, what did Nathan know of him? And now this; he sounded like a whirlwind of activity. Could it all be true? Was he just making it all up as he went along? A boy's fantasy?

Nathan looked at the jacket and the gleaming hair and round face and knew it was true.

'So come work for me, hey, Nathan? I'll see you're all right. I'll look after you.'

It was an unfortunate choice of words. Alex meant well, very well. In his eyes his older brother was really rather a fool, though a very charming one, a lummox who went bumbling through life never seeing the opportunities that

169

fortune dangled in front of his nose. Clever enough, of course; no one else in the family spoke Russian and Polish so fluently, and certainly none could write in those languages as well as Nathan did. His gift for languages had remained with him, for even in the half dozen or so days since he had arrived in Whitechapel he had picked up some of the English words he heard around him. Yet for all Nathan's cleverness Alex believed he was a fool. He needed looking after.

But Nathan was proud. To contemplate being looked after by his youngest brother – it could not be. He pushed the empty plate away from him and said gruffly, 'No thanks, I'm no coffee maker. That's a woman's job.'

Alex shrugged. He wasn't going to waste energy on pushing a favour; he knew perfectly well that Nathan would be more of a hindrance than a help in any business activity. He just didn't have the spark that in Alex was a blazing inferno, a fire that made him determined to be rich, rich, rich. Rich enough not to care about money any more, rich enough to be the sort of gentleman he sometimes saw at the ringside at the fights, the men of the world from the fashionable West End who found pleasure in going slumming in the East End of London.

'It's up to you. I can give you a job if you want one. What'll you do, if you don't take this?'

'I don't know,' Nathan said. 'I'm still thinking. I'll decide soon. I'm not moving in with Reuben – better to stay with Momma and ·Poppa and sleep on the floor than go to that lousy ... I'll stay where I am in Antcliff Street. And I'll get a job.'

'You a tailor? Know how to use a machine? Can you hump one of those big goose-irons? So go work in the sweat shops, for tuppence an hour. You'll work eight in the morning till nine at night, later sometimes, in a stinking pigsty, crammed in worse than on the boat coming here, and you'll make enough to eat twice a day if you're lucky. Don't be a bloody fool, Nathan! You aren't the sort for that kind of work.'

'I'm no fool, Alex! Stop talking like I'm some sort of fool! I served three years, got a medal. You can't tell me what...'

'Nathan, listen to me,' Alex said as gently as he could. 'No one here will care about your medal. Here all they care about is can you work, can you pay your way. No one owes you a living, Nathan! Not even your family. Yeah, yeah, I know,

Reuben is a bastard. He got here and set himself up nicely in business making his lousy sticks, and he's sitting pretty on account you went in the army for him. But for God's sake, Nathan, that's all ancient history now. I got no time for Reuben neither, believe me. The man's as dull as – well, I got no time. But he's got his problems like you have. He's got four kids and a wife who looks like she's pregnant again, and a business to run. He's willing to give you a roof, food to eat, so as far as he's concerned he's done all that's necessary. I think he's a bastard, you think he's a bastard, but who are we to say he's wrong? If you were married, had kids, you'd be the same.'

Married, thought Nathan. Married. Bloomah. Oh, God, Bloomah.

'I'll find work,' he said stubbornly. 'My sort of work. I don't have to go to no sweat shops, I don't have to make coffee in the street. I'll do something suitable. You think you know it all, but you don't know everything. You've been here three years? So, you've been here three years. By the time I've been here so long, you'll see – you'll see.'

Alex sighed. 'Well, I hope so. Believe me, I wish you all you wish yourself. And if it doesn't work – well, let me know. I'm your brother, I'll always be your brother. I know what we owe you for what you did, even if Reuben doesn't.'

He stood up, and revealed his excessively pointed patent leather shoes under straight very narrow trousers in a spongebag check which looked a little uneasy in company with the much larger shepherd's check of his jacket. He tweaked his cravat, a neatly tied black satin creation, and looked as exotic as a parrot in a sparrow's cage as he stood there staring down at Nathan in his shabby suit, bought in Astrakhan with his army pay.

'Remember,' he repeated. 'I'm always here.'

'I'll remember,' Nathan said, and didn't look up. Alex sighed and went off about his multifarious affairs leaving Nathan to stare at his empty coffee cup and try to sort out his situation.

No matter what happened he wasn't taking anything from his young brother. There was no need now, and there never would be. No matter what.

So he promised himself, but uneasily, feeling somewhere

171

deep inside the truth of what Alex had said. He did have to find work, some sort of work, somehow. He couldn't go on living in his parents' two rooms, eating food they could barely afford to buy, much as he knew they wanted him there. Since his arrival years seemed to have fallen off Rivka. Even he could see that, and it made him feel worse somehow. He should have been able to make things better for them, after all they'd been through. To do for them what Reuben had so signally failed to do.

He tried not to think of Reuben with his heavy blustering manner and the look of constant anxiety on his face. He looked nearer forty than the age he was, just a year older than Nathan himself, but a man who marries when he is seventeen and then fathers a baby a year is likely to look anxious by the time he is into his twenties. That was no reason to feel sorry for him. Nathan had no right to feel sorry for him – only furious. How dare he marry and buy a house and have children, while Nathan had to join the army?

He shook his head at himself, and stood up. There was no point in thinking about Reuben or his parents or Alex, or even Benjamin, the only one of them who seemed to be happy with his lot. He was still the studious boy he had always been, still looked young and pale and bent, sitting there in the back room of Reuben's house with his head down over the dog-eared book that was his only really personal possession, or hurrying away to the yeshiva in Weston Street to study his days away in blissful unawareness of the world outside. No point in thinking of any of them, Nathan told himself, and moved towards the door, turning up his coat collar as he went. It was cold out there and the fog was coming back, curling up from the river in yellow tendrils.

'So, listen,' Curly's voice came from behind him, haranguing a customer who was standing in front of his high counter. 'What do you want already? I'm a seller of bagels and coffee and a bit of strudel! What do I know of letters? Go ask a rabbi, go ask a scholar, don't ask me!'

Nathan looked back over his shoulder as he reached the door and then stopped. A woman was standing at the counter, the steam from the big kettles on the stove at the back wreathing her head under the popping gaslight. She wore an old grey shawl which she had let slip to her shoulders to reveal the startling artificiality of her wig and in her hands was a sheet of paper at which she was peering with an anxious face.

'I can't go to the rabbi, Curly! How can I? I don't know what he's written here! It might be something the rabbi shouldn't know of. That's why I came to you. You I can expect to understand if he writes what he shouldn't. My brother, he always was one for doing what he shouldn't, saying bad words and all. Curly, please, I'll pay you – '

As Curly shrugged and turned away to fiddle with his kettles, Nathan realized that he was not unwilling to help, just unable. He had seen that look of baffled embarrassment too often before not to recognize it. He came back towards the counter.

'Can I help, boobah? Me, I read Russian and Polish, and write it, too. I was in the army, you see. Got a medal.' He smoothed his jacket lapel where the medal was pinned, casually, easily. 'Can I help?'

'Oy, can you help! If you can read Russian, you can help! Three days I've had this letter and no one to read it to me. I'm crippled with my joints, can't go more than a few yards down the road, and who else do I come to but my landlord Curly here? And will he read it for me?' She shot a look of pure venom at Curly. 'Like he'll get cholera for me he'll read it! Some friend, some landlord!'

'Too busy,' muttered Curly and began to slice and butter bagels with great energy. 'So let the scholar read for you. He's the clever one – go let him read.'

Nathan read, declaiming the sentences in fine rolling phrases, and with a great deal of expression. It was poor material on which to use his talents, a humdrum account of the troubles of a middle aged man living in Bialystock and struggling against considerable odds to save enough money to bring himself, his wife and his five daughters to London, but it fascinated the old woman, who sat at the table beside the counter, her mouth half open as she listened with great concentration to every word.

When he had finished, she demanded that he read it again, louder, which he did, enjoying the audience of half a dozen other customers. When he'd done that, she asked him if he'd write an answer for her, and sent a small boy to the shop next door to buy her a sheet of paper, an envelope, a bottle of ink and a pen.

Nathan wrote her letter, covering the page with his flowing script, and then read it back to her and the enthralled bagel chewing audience and finally sealed it with a drip of candle wax a now willing Curly provided, and addressed it.

'There,' he said. 'Your letter. I hope he gets it soon, and all should be well.'

'Sixpence,' the old woman said and held out her hand with the small silver coin in it. 'Sixpence, hey? Thruppence for reading, twice, thruppence for writing, once. That's what I used to pay Solly next door when he did it for me, before he moved away. Sixpence is all I pay.'

Nathan took it, turning it slowly in his hand as he stared down at it, and then blinked as one of the other customers said offhandedly, 'Tonight, you come to my place, hey? I got a letter from my sister in Vilna I should like to hear. And maybe you write me a fancy answer like that one, hey? Sixpence, she said?'

Nathan had found himself a job.

18

The room buzzed with voices and the susurration of silk, the sound rising and falling on the warm pot-pourri scented air in such a hypnotic way that Mary felt her lids slide heavily over her eyes and had to sit up to keep herself alert.

Across the room Davida was ensconced on a broad yellow satin upholstered sofa. She was wearing a spreading gown of blonde georgette trimmed with lace which she had arranged carefully so that the bulge of her belly could clearly be seen, and so that her high, now very plump, breasts were equally apparent. Mary stared at her, and remembered how she had been about her own pregnancy, how carefully she had chosen clothes that would disguise rather than accentuate her condition, how prudently she had sat so that no one would notice she was increasing. She had done so out of an innate shyness, and though she knew that Davida was anything but shy, she would have expected her to be equally as circumspect out of simple vanity. Surely, she had thought, Davida cares too

174

much for her appearance to want to look bloated and ugly?

But of course she didn't look bloated and ugly the way some other pregnant women did. She looked, as ever, enchanting, like a peach at the peak of its ripeness, all roundness and bloom; and also, Mary realized, looking away for a moment, very sexual. She sat there displaying the fact that she was loved, that she had been the object of a man's passion, in a way that seemed to Mary positively blatant. Since every woman in the room with her was married, and many of them had children, they too were as sexually experienced as young Mrs Albert Lammeck, but somehow Davida was the one who exuded an air of sensuality while they looked merely married.

Mary stared at them, the score or so women who had been called here to 'talk seriously about the problem' and tried to feel at one with them. They were her people, after all; some of them actually her family. Not only Davida Lammeck but Susan Lammeck, Ezra's wife, and Margaret, who was married to Alfred, had come, though Margaret hardly ever went anywhere apart from visits to her own mother and sisters, a particularly clannish section of the Goldsmith family. Probably Margaret had come because she had brought two of her sisters with her. There were a couple of Montefiores and several Damonts and a sprinkling of Cohens and Rothschilds. The cream of London Jewish society was in the drawing room of the Mount Street house of the Albert Lammecks, and Mary, for all she was as well connected as any of them, felt like an outsider. But then, since last December when her baby had died, she had felt an outsider to every aspect of living. It was nothing new.

The footmen removed the tea things, wheeling away Davida's trolley with its massive silver tea pots and creamers and sugar basins, and as the door closed behind the last of the servants Davida clapped her hands for silence.

'My dears,' she said. 'We really must start business, mustn't we? We haven't too much time and if we don't get this organized properly the men will be most scathing – and we don't want that!' She laughed a silvery little laugh and one or two of them joined in – those with husbands who needed to be on good terms with Albert Lammeck – and settled themselves into a listening posture.

There was no doubt who was in control. Davida's voice

went on and on, telling this one that she would make a superb secretary, and that one that she would be *so* grateful if she would take on the onerous task of treasurer, though of course it need not be too difficult for dear Albert had promised the loan of one of the clerks from Lammeck Alley for the tiresome bits, and perhaps darling Ann would be responsible for the selection of suitable stationery, while Davida herself would take on the heavy burden of the chairmanship, for she wanted above all to do her duty.

Mary let her mind wander, thinking about Fay. She usually did think about Fay wherever she had the chance, imagining her in her house in Croydon, seeing her sitting over her dinner table with Richard, visualizing her busy about her daily chores, and that comforted her.

Fay had written her three letters in the early weeks of her marriage, each one more lyrical than the last. Reading them had given Mary enormous pleasure and satisfaction. To know that she had, by her own action, created that happiness for someone she loved was balm to a painful wound. They could be as overwhelming as they liked, as impatient and successful and capable as they wanted, these Lammeck relations of hers; she, Mary, ordinary quiet Mary who couldn't give her husband a child, was able to give happiness to someone.

But sadly, there could be no more letters to receive. She had seen Emmanuel's face one morning when one of Fay's letters had arrived, and she had read suspicion on it. If they discovered she was in correspondence with Fay, now officially dead in her family's eyes, the uproar would be immense. Too much for Mary to tolerate, she knew; so, unhappily she had sent a letter to Fay begging her to write no more.

'For,' she had written in her neat rather childlike script, 'I am not as strong as I would wish to be, my dear one, and if they discover that I know your whereabouts and choose to torment me and forbid me to care for you I fear I will not be able to prevent myself from giving into them. I was strong enough to manage when you first went away, but that was because it was for a short time. But if they were to persist at me, I truly don't know what would happen, for you know that I am a useless creature. So, it will be better if you do not write again, though I will miss your letters sadly.'

But never mind, she thought now, staring dreamily at the yellow satin curtains that swathed the drawing room windows and kept out the humid July air; never mind, Fay is happy, and I know that I am part of it. That is what matters. Secretly, Mary carried those letters with her. They gave her security and comfort.

' . . . and Mary I am sure will also make it her business to check these applications most carefully, won't you, Mary?'

'I beg your pardon?' Davida was looking at her, her face pinched with irritation as Mary stared at her in puzzlement.

'My dear, have you not been listening?' Davida said. Her silvery laugh had a sharper note in it now. 'We have decided that the Daughters of Sarah shall have a settlement house, and that you shall go and find the best place for it – in the East End you know.'

'I? Go to the East End?' Mary said, alarmed. 'And what do you mean, the Daughters of Sarah?'

'Really, Mary, you are being tiresome!' Davida snapped and then went a little pink as she caught Margaret's rather fishlike stare. 'I know it's a warm day, but dear one, you really must concentrate, I'm finding it difficult too, I do assure you.' She fanned herself gently, and drooped her shoulders, thus displaying her own condition, her own patience, and her own immense efforts for others in one comprehensive gesture.

'The ladies' branch of the Society for the Relief of Indigent Jews is to be called The Daughters of Sarah, Mary, and it has been decided that you shall have the task of searching for the right house for us to use as a Settlement,' Susan said and smiled at Davida a little maliciously. 'Like Davida, I'm not able to perform the task – it's early days for me, of course, but still, one cannot be too careful, can one?'

'Oh, my dear, when?' one of the Goldsmith girls cooed at her. Susan, with a sharp little look at Davida who was clearly put out at having the limelight taken from her, said smoothly, 'December, please God. In time for Chanucah – '

'So, Mary, will you go? If you start at Aldgate, Albert said, you'll find plenty of possible places. He says he'll send someone from the office to help you. Indeed, he said the clerk could do it all, but I was most insistent that one of the committee should be in charge. It wouldn't do to leave it all to servants. One wishes to perform one's task properly, don't you agree?'

'What sort of building?' Mary said wretchedly. 'I mean –
what will it be used for?'

'Oh, offices, you know, and so forth,' Davida said airily.
'Somewhere we can see the applicants and make sure they're
entitled to benefit, you know, and perhaps some rooms
where those who are about to leave can stay the night. Albert
was very definite about that. He said that the main purpose of
any organization we girls ran was to encourage them to go
back, and that those we agreed to give money to for that
purpose should be properly supervised. So I said, I thought if
we have lodgings they could stay in the night before they left,
they'd have to come to them to get their tickets, you see, and
then we could be sure they went on the ships, and didn't just
sell the tickets. Albert said that's the sort of thing these people
do.'

Mary was all attention now, sitting up straight. 'I thought
this meeting was about a relief committee? I mean, you said,
when you told me of it, that the men's Society wanted us to
run the relief side.'

'Well, so we shall, my dear! That is precisely what all this is
about!'

'But tickets to go back. That isn't relief, is it?'

Davida shook her head impatiently. 'You really don't
understand, do you? Albert explained it all to me, and I am
sure Emmanuel would tell you the same, if you were to just
listen to him. These are aliens who are coming in.'

'Jews,' Mary said. 'Jews. Like us.'

'Of course, dear. Why else are we concerned? Alien Jews.
They can't find proper work here, and they live in dreadful
hovels and work in the most awful sweatshops. Albert went
with the men's Society, they said they must see for themselves. And he told me it really is dreadful. They work for
such terrible masters who pay them too little and make them
work for all the day and half the night and in such disgusting
places they can't be thought of, and it is all quite dreadful. So,
you see, they must be helped.'

'But how is it helping them to give them lodgings in a
Settlement and tickets?' Mary said stubbornly. 'Wouldn't it
be better to help them get better houses to live in and to make
the masters change the way they work?'

'Really, Mary, you've being very foolish! I've told you –

178

the men have talked about it all and they've decided that what they need is a relief organization. They're doing all the other things – about houses and workshops and so on.' She waved her hand in a vaguely comprehensive gesture. 'And they want us to apply direct relief. Now, we've been through all this, haven't we, ladies?'

There was a soft murmur of assent from the other women.

'And we've decided that we must have a Settlement House and that someone has to go and seek it out. I can't go – and of course Susan can't.' She managed a thin smile at her other sister-in-law. 'Everyone else has been give a task, and that leaves just you. Of course, if you don't *want* to, we must make other arrangements.'

'Oh, of course it isn't that I don't want to.' Mary was losing her grasp of it all, and was becoming anxious to escape as anyone else. 'It's just that I'm not quite sure I understand. But still ... '

'Then you'll do it. Good.' Davida leaned back on her sofa and fanned herself again. 'I'm sure Emmanuel will explain any more you need to know. So, girls! That's the end, then? We've settled everything? The men *will* be so pleased with us! I'm sure I am. I think the Daughters of Sarah will be a great success.' She yawned delicately and contrived to look weary and they surged to their feet in a greater than ever rustle of silk and kissed her and chattered at her and each other as they made their way down the stairs and on to home, or dressmakers' appointments or visits to the milliner. The Daughters of Sarah had been convened and had made decisions, and they felt the satisfaction of a job attempted and a job performed.

Mary felt no satisfaction at all. She had spent three days rattling around the streets of Whitechapel in the carriage her husband and brothers-in-law had sent from Lammeck Alley for her use. ('Don't use ours, for heaven's sake!' Emmanuel had said when she had told him what she planned to do. 'Those people'll wreck it! I'll send a hired one, with young Levy. He'll look after you. You need somewhere that is well into the quarter, but not too cut off. We don't want you girls having to deal with any problems – look around near the police stations. I'll tell Levy, anyway. He'll know what to do.') Now she was exhausted.

At first she had been horrified. That there should be streets and alleys like these in the same city as the one in which she had lived all her life was amazing. Her childhood had been spent in far from the rich surroundings she now enjoyed, for her family, though respectable (like the Damonts, the Deyongs had come to England from Holland, a very long time ago) had been of limited means, but she had never seen such poverty as this.

The streets were narrow and dirty, the gutters laden with garbage and the pavements slippery and greasy underfoot. The houses that were huddled so close together seemed to be filled to overflowing, for in street after street she saw hordes of children – ill dressed though tolerably well fed from their appearance – who obviously all managed to cram into these tiny dwellings. Outside the doors groups of women in black stuff dresses, their heads often covered in shawls despite the warmth of the weather, gossipped and squabbled and stared at her carriage as it went by, making her want to shrink back out of sight. There was in their boot-black eyes and in their pinched faces a despair that filled her with shame for her own comfort, for her neatly shod feet in their kid shoes, of her fine gown in cool silk, of her beringed fingers. In her own circle Mary was thought to dress quietly, even dowdily. But here she felt insultingly overdressed.

They found their building at last. She had given up searching for a place near a police station, for there was none suitable, and young Levy, a taciturn youth who clearly regarded this expedition with distaste and impatience, suggested she choose somewhere busy.

'There won't be any trouble with these people, anyway,' he said, looking out of the carriage window. 'They're too cowed to do anything but be a burden to everyone – no spirit in 'em at all.'

Mary said nothing, uneasy though she was about his scorn. Wasn't he a Jew too, like herself, like these very people he found so unpleasant? Did he not feel the shocked pity that filled her? Probably not; Mary had long since discovered that no one else seemed to behave or feel as she would expect them to. Her opinion of herself continued to sink.

In the end she settled on a tall brown fronted house in Hanbury Street, in Spitalfields, near the junction with Brick

Lane. It wasn't ideal, but it was available for rent on a long lease, and she was wearying rapidly. There was just so much misery that could be observed, just so much pity to be felt, and she had reached the end of her store of both when she told Levy with more authority than she usually displayed that this was to be the Settlement.

For the next weeks, it was Mary who seemed to be busiest of all the Daughters of Sarah. Davida was too exhausted by her pregnancy to do more than sit on her sofa and send long messages to Mary about how she should do what had to be done, and Susan complained that she was too smitten by nausea even to send messages. The other members of the committee helped a little but most of them pleaded the pressures of child care, or of husbandly demands for entertaining of business friends, and since everyone made it clear that Mary, in her childless state, was hardly likely to be as overworked as they were (an opinion she inevitably felt was fully justified) so the burden fell on her.

But she was still uneasy about the goals of the Daughters of Sarah, feeling that to send these poor creatures she saw in the streets back to where they came from must surely be an act of cruelty. If they actually preferred to live in these conditions, what must life have been like for them in the places they had come from?

It was Albert who soothed her fears best. He listened to her talking to Davida one evening, and shook his head and laughed in the way he so often did, a loud bluff laugh that made him seem even more boyish and handsome than he was.

'Dear Mary, you have got it all wrong, haven't you? Some of 'em actually do want to go back to Poland or Russian or wherever – but lots of 'em don't. They want to go anywhere they can do well for themselves – and it's obvious to them that they won't do well here. You've seen what it's like down there. It's like ... it's an inferno.'

'It's disgusting,' Mary said, and her face reddened a little with the intensity of her feeling. 'Quite disgusting. It ought to be ... '

'What?' Albert said reasonably. 'Burnt down, all those streets and alleys? What do you do about the people there then? Chuck them out forcibly? That wouldn't be justice, would it? That wouldn't be humane. No, Mary, it's coercion

181

that's the key. Compassionate coercion. We've got to try to persuade them they can do better somewhere else. Germany – I'm told that in Germany there's a lot of room for immigrants. Jews can do well there. And America. Now, there's the place to send 'em! You know what they call it, those people? The Goldeneh Medina – the Golden City – and why not? This is an old country, my dear, and we're established in it. In America, there's all that land to be opened up, and all that space. They're all immigrants there anyway, so we can send them more. It's a great place for them. Don't you think that we're not going to take care of the East End people there in your Settlement. Of course we are! Why, you should see the sort of contributions that are coming in – hundreds of pounds, hundreds. You stop worrying, Mary. Just get it all ready, the way Davida says, and you'll see. Everything will be fine.'

So, she did. The Settlement opened its doors on the third Monday in August 1886 after handbills, written in Yiddish, had been distributed around the neighbourhood, in Flower and Dean Street and Thrawl Street, Fashion Street and Heneage Street, all along the Commercial Road and Whitechapel Road.

She didn't know what the handbills said, for she neither read nor spoke Yiddish, only a little Ladino, and precious little of that, but clearly whoever had written them had worded them well. There was a line of more than seventy men, women and children standing there at nine o'clock when she arrived, alone, to take the first session with applicants for relief, and her heart sank.

They looked at her with eyes so blank, so unexpressive, that they frightened her; would they not turn on her, and try to drag the money that she had been given to distribute out of her hands? Would they not steal all the bread and flour and potatoes that the committee had bought for distribution? Would any of them accept the offer of their fare to some-where else – anywhere else – as long as they agreed to be escorted to their ships?

She need not have feared. They were a docile lot, these hungry aliens. They shuffled along the line and explained in their halting English, or through the Yiddish interpreters the Daughters had employed what their dilemma was and took gratefully and humbly whatever she chose to give them.

182

That day six men accepted the offer of a free ride out of England and when she reported back to Davida, she in her turn sent a fulsome account of the work of the Daughters to the executive of the men's committee, the Society for the Relief of Indigent Jews. Davida was well satisfied with the glowing letter and testimonial she got back.

Indeed, everyone was satisfied, even Mary, in her own way. She had at last found something to fill the gaping hole left by her baby's death and the loss of Fay. She was to spend the next fifteen years and more devoting almost all the energy she had to that brown faced house in Hanbury Street, and to the people who lived near. And, in a way she could never imagine, it would change her life.

19

Nathan's and Bloomah's marriage should have been a happy one. Heaven knew it started in a blaze of passion that should have kept it warm for many years. But somehow, it just didn't work out that way.

Finding her had been easy. Once he had found his parents, the whole jigsaw fell into place. The people they had known at home in the shtetl in Lublin lived scattered nearby; in Bromehead Road, Sidney Street and Jubilee Street the landsleit had found rooms in which to pack themselves and their children and the few possessions they had managed to bring with them from the Pale. They all spoke the same Yiddish with the same Lublin accent. They all took their wigs to the same wig dresser, who had found herself an attic in Musbury Street, all took their Sabbath cholents to the same baker, who had set himself up in an establishment on the other side of Commercial Road on the corner of Watney Street, all went to the same little synagogue tucked between two shops at the end of Bromehead Street. They carried on the same arguments and feuds they had started at home, the women muttering at their enemies, whispering to their cronies as they had always done, spreading the same calumnies.

Of course not all of them were able to pick up the threads they had been forced to drop when they took to the road, running away from the pogroms. There were many like Lazar the miller whose livelihood was lost for ever. Here in London there was no call for millers, or weavers or wine makers; only for tailoring workers who would sweat their guts out for masters who were little better off than the men they themselves employed.

Lev the innkeeper, like his old friend Lazar, had lost his way of life. He had assumed that he would be able to use the money from the sale of his tavern in Lublin to buy a new one in London, but bewildered by the system of public-house ownership run by the breweries, unable to understand the rules and regulations surrounding the lucrative business of making and selling beer, he had decided to 'look about' and see what better way he could invest his money.

He rented two rooms on the third floor of a house in Jubilee Street and split the bedroom with a curtain, so that his daughter could have privacy, and furnished the other room as best he could with second hand bargains.

His son Isaac tried to persuade him to invest what cash was left in his business; he had managed in the time he had been in Whitechapel to get a house of his own, for himself and his wife and four children. The family slept in one room, and had another for their kitchen and living room, while the other six rooms in the three storied building were crammed with machines and pressing tables and basters' benches, and workers, workers, workers. He put as many as he could in each box of a room, and kept them at work from eight in the morning until ten at night.

That was the trouble with the trade, Isaac explained; sometimes there's more work than you can handle, but that you've got to handle at the lowest possible prices, if you're to get enough to make a profit on, and other times you're scratching for work to do to feed yourself, let alone pay workers.

'I lay 'em off, in the slack times,' he told his father. 'I can always get new workers when I want 'em, at the *chazar* market.'

'The pig market?' Lev said, and frowned his disapproval, and Isaac laughed.

'They all call it that, Poppa. The men wanting jobs go down to Black Lion Yard, on a Shabbat morning, and the masters go and see what they can get, for how much. But you, Poppa, you I'd never lay off. Put a little money in the business and I can build a shed at the back, take on more work, get more profit – believe me Poppa, this is the only way we'll ever get anywhere. Build a business, that's the only answer – '

But Lev, looking at the crowded rooms reeking of tailor's soap and the grease from the heavy cloth that was used to make the army uniforms that were Isaac's speciality, and also of rats and cats and human sweat, declined. He had other better ideas, he told Isaac, and took himself off to sit with old cronies from the innkeeping days in Lublin, at the café on the corner where the card players were.

By the time Nathan arrived in London, Lev had gambled away most of the money he had brought with him. Isaac had long since given up trying to involve him in his business. He took on his sister, Bloomah, teaching her to be a felling hand, making the hems and oversewing the seams, her hands flickering in and out of the heavy cloth until her finger tips bled from being rubbed raw. He paid her what he could, which was very little, but enough to feed her and her father.

And so they managed, Lev spending all his time at the café, betting on horses and playing his eternal solo or klobiash or kaluki amid loud recriminations and shouts of excitement and Bloomah working her days and evenings away at Isaac's workshop, and her early mornings and late nights at the flat, for food had to be cooked and laundry had to be washed, for that was woman's work. She couldn't expect Lev to do it.

When Nathan arrived, one Shabbat afternoon, primed with her address by his unwilling mother (who was worried indeed by his interest in the girl; Rivka had only just got her boy back, after all! Was she to lose him again so soon?), she was sitting in her window, staring down at the children in the street below.

The two years she had spent as a felling hand had left their mark on her. No longer was she the round faced pretty girl she had been when Nathan bade her goodbye in Lublin. Now she was thin, her face hollowed under the cheekbones and her jawline as clean cut as a flint edge. Her eyes, always big and dark, now looked huge in her attenuated face, and her hair, fluffed out in a fashionable fringe on her forehead – like most of the East End girls she had studied pictures of Princess Alexandra in the illustrated papers – made her look particularly vulnerable and appealing. She was wearing a new georgette blouse which she was buying for a penny a week from the tallyman, the door to door pedlar who clothed almost all the girls of the quarter, and because it had not yet been washed to a limp rag it retained a pristine freshness that added greatly to her look of fragility. Nathan stood in the street looking up at her in the thin wintry sunlight of the December afternoon, his astrakhan hat on the back of his head, and felt sick with excitement.

Had he come later in the evening, Lev would have been at home, sitting snoring in his chair before the fire; had he come on any other day of the week, she would have been at Isaac's wearing her usual rep skirt and old grey shirtwaister, her hair tied up in a tattered scarf. But as it was, she was alone, and the excitement of their meeting and the intimacy of the small cluttered kitchen with its old horsehair sofa on one side of the coal fire and the light dwindling to a cosy dimness was more than either of them could resist.

It was not that Bloomah was in any way a bad girl. She had been carefully reared by her mother to be aware of her own sexual value. No respectable shtetl girl let boys take liberties. No respectable shtetl girl recognized any base urges in herself – or if she did, never dreamed of admitting that she had such. Certainly no respectable shtetl girl allowed any man to anticipate the pleasures of her marriage bed.

Yet on that winter afternoon in Jubilee Street, Bloomah did all those things. Maybe it was the combination of circumstances that overcame her; the fact that she was dressed in her finery, and was freshly clean, for it was only on a Sabbath afternoon that she had the privacy and the time and the energy to give herself the all over wash that was the nearest she could ever get to a bath; the fact that her body was poised at a peak of fertility that made her more than usually receptive; the fact that she was deeply tired, and so less able to control those deeper urges which are powerful enough always to overcome conscious will; above all the fact that Nathan looked so woebegone. Had he returned to her the strutting self-confident young buck she had said goodbye to so tearfully at Lublin railhead all that time ago, she would have been well able to deal with him. There would have been the age old ritual of flirting and repartee and pushing and giggling to protect her. There would have been some kissing and cuddling, just as there had been that night he had come to her father's inn to say goodbye, but no more than that.

But now, in Jubilee Street on a winter afternoon in a small front room fretted with flickering firelight he stood and looked at her, his astrakhan hat held in both hands, his chin tucked into his neck so that he had to look up at her from beneath worried brows, and he was thin and shabby and infinitely sad, and she opened her arms to him, and drew him into a maelstrom of feeling that burst the banks that he had put up inside himself to control his own need.

It was as though they had never been apart, so easy and natural was it. They pulled at their own clothes and at each other's, stripping them so quickly that they had no time to feel any shame at their nakedness. The sight of his white body, so very thin that the ribs made a trellis pattern against his skin, made tears come into her eyes, and she took his head in her arms and held it to her so that his face disappeared between her breasts and he could hardly breathe – but that was what he wanted. The smell of her, the faint animal scent that overcame the breath of the carbolic soap with which she had scrubbed herself, the heat of her skin against his cheeks were like all the dreams he had ever had in the long dark watches of his army days; and he let the dream carry him along, not really believing it was happening.

He knew there was some pain when he pushed himself into her body, felt the slippery blood that his urgency drew from her, but he also knew that she relished it, pushing herself against him ever more urgently, arching her back so that he was almost crouching over her, and grunting her need, and then, finally, with staring eyes and a mouth drawn back in a grimace to show her teeth, her satisfaction. And feeling her muscles grasping him so tightly and rhythmically, his own rising excitement at last broke over the top and he was thrusting himself into her with such vigour that it seemed to him he would pass right through her body to emerge on the other side.

And then they were lying there, he sprawling over her on the horsehair sofa breathless and sweating, their legs entangled and their eyes blank and staring. They lay so for a long time, dozing for a while until a coal shifted in the grate and collapsed into dull embers and the fire sank a little and the room seemed colder, and she woke and pushed him away.

187

She snatched her clothes from the floor and fled to the other room, leaving him to dress again as best he might, and then came back to stand in the doorway and stare at him with wide and now frightened eyes.

They managed to talk, at last, haltingly, carefully. He told her how much he had thought of her, how much he had always needed her, wanting desperately to let her know what had happened this afternoon had not been in any way a casual matter, but the natural climax of three long years of wanting her and needing her, and she told him that she too had thought of him every day, and most nights, too, ever since he had gone away. By the time Lev came home, in high good humour because this afternoon he had won (not actually taking the money, of course; one did not handle money on the Sabbath, even when you were a reprehensible hellbent gambler like Lev; but you could play the games, and settle the debts the day after) they had news for him. They would be married as soon as they could get a place to live in, as soon as Nathan could earn enough money from his new occupation to make a proper marriage home possible.

No one was pleased with their news. Lev, realizing that without Bloomah's earnings he would have to work to earn his own bread, objected strenuously. Where were they to find the money to pay for a home of their own? Where would they find the massive fee the rabbis demanded to marry people, three pounds ten shillings, an impossible amount! Where were they to find the strength to cope with the inevitable children that would result? 'You're young,' he shouted. 'Too young!'

Rivka said the same, though more quietly, and without any real hope of being regarded. For her, life had become blow after blow; her home disintegrated, her children flown, what more could she expect but the loss of the child so newly returned to her? As for Nathan's brothers – Reuben grunted and looked at his own Minnie, pale with nausea in her fifth pregnancy, and said nothing, and Alex threw up his hands and shook his head and told Nathan he was mad; didn't he have problems enough? Benjamin said nothing; he too was looking with more than a little interest at one Sarah, the daughter of the rabbi at his synagogue, for the first time in his life finding something more interesting than books and talmudic study, and thought it prudent to make no judgement at all on people who married young. After all, he was two years younger than Nathan.

The only one who offered any practical support was Isaac, who told Nathan he too could have a job with him.

But Nathan refused. Some of his old assurance had come back to him now, for he felt himself to be at last a man. He had his own occupation, which, he assured everyone, was developing nicely. Didn't he already have seven regular clients who paid him every week to write letters to their relations in the Pale? Weren't there more where they came from?

Of course, there was something else to sustain him, something he did not talk about. The memory of what had happened that dark afternoon. That single experience had lit a flame that clamoured ever more loudly for more fuel, but Bloomah steadfastly refused to allow any further such encounters until she was safely and respectably married. But never mind, he could remember it all, which he did in every vivid detail, whenever he could. And he planned and saved and scraped to raise the money for a wedding and to pay rent on a place of his own.

They could not manage it until March was moving into April and the Whitechapel streets were beginning to smell a little stronger as the warmer suns of Spring arrived. By that time it had become a matter of some urgency. Bloomah could not wait much longer. A six month baby she could perhaps persuade the *yentas*, the gossiping women of the shops, was just a very impatient premature one. Anything less than six months would announce to the whole of the shtetl that was Whitechapel that Bloomah, daughter of Lev the gambler, was an even bigger sinner than he was.

They were married on a hot afternoon in the first week in April after Nathan had painfully managed to collect the seventy shillings for the rabbi's fee, and enough to buy himself a black gaberdine coat that was only third hand. He had allowed Alex to select it for him though he insisted on paying the proper price for it, which Alex thought was mad, but he made up for his brother's lunacy by giving his new sister-in-law a handsome petticoat, two blouses and a set of copper saucepans, bought especially for her in the Lane on a Sunday when trade was bad and bargains were to be had for the bullying.

189

It was not to be the last time that Alex was Bloomah's friend and banker. Knowing he was there and could be trusted not to tell silly Nathan when she approached him, helped Bloomah a great deal in those early years of married life in Antcliff Street.

For that was where the newly weds went to live. Alex, good to his word, got himself a house of his own in Sidney Street and ensconced his parents there, and fitted out a room for himself with such elegance that people came to admire it from several streets around. He put up curtains with cord ties and silk tassels, a specially made wooden overmantel with two foot high blue lustre vases on it, and covered the floor not only with oil cloth but also with red carpet. He had polished wooden tables and chairs and a sofa upholstered in velvet and burned two scuttles full of coal a day. There was luxury for you, the neighbours told each other, and marvelled over the success of the young Lazar boy, and the good fortune of his parents to have such a son to look after them in their old age.

No one envied Nathan and Bloomah. They did their best with the furniture they had in his parents' old home in Antcliff Street, adding a pine desk for Nathan's work, and ornaments picked up from the Brick Lane stalls on rainy evenings when trade was slack and bargaining successful. Bloomah did the best she could with it, cleaning it lovingly each evening after coming home from Isaac's workshop and each morning before leaving to start her stint of shoulder hunched stitching, and cooking busily late into the night even when she was so pregnant that she could hardly fit herself in front of the stove which stood on the landing outside their kitchen door in a tiny recess. Nathan blossomed under her care, putting back some of his lost flesh and looking sleek and content with his new happiness.

For Bloomah, once married, displayed the same sexual fire he had warmed himself with that delicious afternoon in December.

But it was different after the first baby was born. A boy, puny and ailing from birth, he died when he was a month old, and some of Bloomah died with him. She became pregnant again fast enough, and seemed to have recovered from her first loss, but it was to haunt her always. No other pregnancy was ever to mean as much as that first one,

190

that failed one.

The years slipped through their fingers, winter succeeding summer but noticed by the residents of Whitechapel only as an alternation of busy times when there was plenty of money because people were earning, and slack times when everyone went short, not only the workers but also the bagel sellers, the cafe keepers, the stall-holders in the Lane, and inevitably, Nathan the scribe. His income, little as it was, was as much subject to the vagaries of the tailoring trade as anyone else's. Like everyone else, he did not notice whether the sky was blue or leaden, whether the air was fog laden or hot with the stink of melting asphalt from over-heated streets. He knew only busy times and slack times.

There were many times when he slipped away quietly from his home to Hanbury Street, to the 'Schnorrers' Shop' as the settlement run by the Daughters of Sarah was called. He hated it there; hated the richly dressed women with their turned up noses and niminy-piminy voices and refusal to understand a single word of Yiddish. The mean sharpness with which they questioned petitioners for money made his throat tighten with fury. But what can a man do, he would ask himself, trudging the long way back, when times were so impossibly hard? How could any man do well in such circumstances?

But Alex prospered. His one coffee stall became two and then three. His occasional successful boxing matches in narrow halls in side streets became regular bouts attended by half the neighbourhood and plenty of West End swells as well, held in the biggest main road venues. His dealing and selling in the Petticoat Lane market developed into a full scale supplies business for the stall holders. Whatever he did, he did successfully.

By the time he was twenty he was able to abandon his act as a song and dance and joke man in the Yiddish theatre. He had enjoyed it, and been a tolerably good performer, but now he had better ways to spend his time, better ways to make money. By the time he was twenty-seven he had left the house in Sidney Street to his parents, who now lived very comfortably on an income drawn from taking in lodgers, and lived in a much smarter establishment in Victoria Park Road in the elegant purlieus of Hackney. It was a newly built house well decorated with cupolas and iron railings and red tiles, in which every room was furnished with the best of everything, from plush upholstered furniture to mahogany sideboards and gas lights.

No one in the family had done as well as Alex; not even Reuben, though he had managed to enlarge his workshop almost as much as his family (he had seven children, did Reuben, which gave him and his exhausted Minnie a great deal to be proud of, of course) and now lived in a house set apart from the factory. Benjamin, who had married his Sarah on the understanding that the rabbi her father would take full responsibility for their keep, was content enough.

Not so Nathan, however. Still doggedly trying to make ends meet with his efforts as a letter writer, still begging sometimes from the Schnorrers' Shop, still dreaming his dreams of future recognition as the hero he was, he never forgave Reuben or, to be honest, his parents for what he regarded as the wicked way they had treated him. He never really forgave Alex either, for being so successful. Indeed, by the end of 1893, when he was twenty-eight years old, Nathan had lost much of the easy charm and good temper that had been so much a part of his young years. He was tired, resentful and bitterly angry at his own poverty. Only one of the many pregnancies his Bloomah had plodded through had resulted in a living child, and that too filled him with fury. There was Reuben with seven healthy brats, and he had only this one, Jacob. Why was it? What had he done to God that God should treat him so?

That was how it was on the foggy November evening in 1893 when Bloomah's sixth pregnancy ended in a successful delivery. The old woman from Christian Street, who acted as neighbourhood midwife, held up the baby by her heels and laughed at her, peering shortsightedly at the child who was bawling loudly, her mouth splitting her face in half, and shook her head with elderly roguishness at Bloomah.

'How come you made such a *boobalah* as this one, Bloomah? Maybe you gone a bit rusty, hey? Better have more babies after this, make 'em *schwartzkopfs* like you and your Nathan!' And she laid the red headed creature in Bloomah's arms, and laughed again.

So did Hannah Lazar make her first entrance into her world.

BOOK THREE

Growing

20

Hannah was dancing, light as a feather, drifting across the great sparkling ballroom in her froth of a dress, made all of lace that looked like beaten eggwhite and everyone, absolutely everyone, was watching her. Her eyes glittered with the brilliance that they had all come to expect of her, and her hair, her skin, her mouth, everthing about her was perfect, as the handsome young man with the rather shadowy face in whose arms she was floating, thistledown soft, whispered over and over again into her ear.

'Hannah?'

She tried to dance harder, squeezing her eyes a little to hold onto the vision of herself in the great chandeliered ballroom, but the voice was too insistent, calling her name again, and the image shattered into glittering shards which curled and drifted away to die in the dust of the yard.

'Hannah, how often have I told you? How often has your Momma told you? How often has everyone told you? It's dangerous to sit up there, a little girl like you! You could slip, you could tear yourself on a slate, you could do terrible damage. Terrible!'

Hannah peered down over the edge of the roof at Mrs Arbeiter, who was standing arms akimbo and staring up at her, her wig sliding slightly sideways as she craned her neck.

'I'm all right here, Mrs Arbeiter. It's easy, really it is. I won't slip.'

'Then you'll break the roof, and a nice thing that'll be, people down in the you should excuse me the you-know-what and all of a sudden there's a hole in the roof, people can look in, a nice state of affairs!'

'But no one could look in from up here,' Hannah said reasonably, 'and anyway – '

'Enough already! Down! You want I should tell your

Momma, your poor sick Momma no harm should come to her? Is that what you want?'

'No, Mrs Arbeiter,' Hannah said, resigned to the inevitable, and scrambled over the tiles to climb in through the half open window to the landing, sliding down between the sink that was just under the window and the narrow cupboard alongside it which held the family's dishes. Horrible Mrs Arbeiter! she thought. Horrible ugly stupid smelly Mrs Arbeiter, I hate her, I'll cut her up in little pieces with a very sharp knife and cover the bits in salt and then wash them and feed them to the cats in Jubilee Street market and then she'll be sorry!

Thinking her wicked thoughts with great relish she gave one last regretful glance over her shoulder at the rooftop that overlooked the yard. It was the only private place she had in all the world, and as soon as it had stopped raining this morning she had crept out there to sit with her eyes slitted against the dull March sky and her thin arms wrapped around her knees to keep what little warmth there was in her safe inside, and dream. It was almost the only pleasure she had, and now Mrs Arbeiter had spoiled it again. Cut her into *very* small pieces with an *extra* sharp knife...

She slipped into the room and looked across at Momma. She was propped up in bed against the white pillows, her head to one side and her mouth slightly open as she dozed. Seeing Momma look like that made Hannah feel bad. Scratchy and sharp inside and a little bit sick. Momma was always being ill, so Hannah often felt bad. And not knowing what it was made it worse.

When Auntie Minnie had been ill with the pneumonia everyone had known what it was and talked and talked about it, about her breathing and her heart and her crisis, please-God-soon-she-should-get-better. When Uncle Benjamin had broken his ankle and had to sit in a special wheelchair for weeks the whole family had sat around and talked for ever about his bones, and how God forbid a bit of the broken part might get back into his bloodstream (Hannah imagined a bloodstream looked rather like a gutter after the rain) and get to his heart and then *pfft*.

But no one ever talked out loud about Bloomah's illnesses. They just dropped their voices and whispered together and shook their heads and pursed their lips and said you shouldn't know of such things.

That it had to do with having babies Hannah knew. There had been so many babies over the years. Three brothers more than the ones she already had. Poppa had told her that and she could almost remember them being born. She tried to imagine what it would be like now to have three more Jakes and Sollies and was glad she hadn't. Not glad the other brothers had died, exactly, just glad they weren't here. Jake and Solly were enough for anyone, though it would be quite nice if they were here now, to play with. Playing with them usually meant being bullied by Jake and grizzled at by Solly but it would be better than being alone. She slipped across the room, moving quietly so as not to wake her mother and looked out of the window at the way the sodden London sky had lifted from slate to pearl as the rain at last stopped.

The gutters were running noisily with muddy water and swirling with scraps of garbage and the cobbles shone greasily beneath the hooves of dray horses and van wheels. But there was life down there as well, interesting busy life. She could see the bouncing black curls on Rachel Levin's plump neck as she lurched across the hopscotch squares scratched on the pavement in front of the corner shop, while the Stern boys, David and Sammy, watched eagle-eyed in case her toe went over a line. If Hannah went down there with them they'd jeer at her and tease in their usual silly fashion, making fun of her thinness and her carrotty hair and her narrow blue eyes while Rachel preened and flashed her big round brown eyes that the Stern boys so obviously admired. All the same, it would be better than sitting here.

Bloomah woke suddenly, her eyes snapping open. She stared at the window, her gaze seeming almost panic stricken and Hannah said quickly, 'Do you want something, Momma?'

Bloomah blinked and then, slowly, her staring eyes dulled a little and she looked like herself again.

'No dolly. No. Nothing. Listen, why don't you go down and play? It's stopped raining. Go down, play with the children.'

At once Hannah felt bad again. She'd been thinking how nice it would be to go down and play and wondering how she could get out, and now that Momma said to go, she couldn't. Not go and leave Momma all alone.

'No thank you, Momma,' she said and slid off the window sill. 'The Stern boys are down there, though they ought to be at school, and it wouldn't be proper to play with people who ought to be at school.'

Bloomah smiled and for a moment her face looked quite young and Hannah smiled back. 'Such a good little girl.'

The fire was beginning to die down and Hannah crouched in the grate, delicately picking at the ashes with the poker, the way Bloomah had showed her would make the fire last, and then, carefully, added a few pieces of coal. She didn't have to be told there wasn't any more after this bucketful was gone. She'd brought it up herself from the cellar, scraping the last bits of dust from the corners of the cellar so as not to waste any. But it was cold and Momma was ill, and the fire had to be kept going somehow –

She heard the door slam below and lifted her chin, and Bloomah did too, both of them looking oddly alike, although they were really so different, Bloomah with her round face and crinkly black hair and dark eyes and Hannah with her sharp bird-like looks.

Nathan's feet were heavy on the stairs, and Hannah knew at once it was bad. Really bad. It was the way his shoes slapped on the lino, the heavy thump of his hand on the rickety banisters. It was bad.

'Nothing doing, Nathan?' Bloomah said, and pulled herself up against her pillows awkwardly. 'Nothing doing.' That time it wasn't a question; just a statement. Nothing doing.

'So why should there be?' Nathan said. He threw his hat on the chair beside the fire. 'Why should there be? Who needs a professional man when every tuppenny ha'penny *shlemiel* goes to school, makes with the pen, thinks himself a scholar already? Who needs the work of a real professional when they all think they can do as good? And who needs me when the *mumsers* forget they got family anywhere except on their own doorsteps? Who cares any more about sending decent letters the people in the old shtetl can be proud they should get? Who needs...'

Hannah, still crouching by the grate, felt worse than ever. When Poppa started like this, shouting question after question at them, at the ceiling, at the whole world, things were extra bad. He'd gone out so happy too, so sure this time he'd find a lot of people ready to have letters to Warsaw and

198

Lublin and Plotsk written in his beautiful copper plate handwriting, because hadn't it been a good time in Whitechapel this past few weeks? Hadn't big orders come into Uncle Reuben's stick factory and Uncle Isaac's tailor's workshop down Commercial Road? 'Sure there'll be work,' he'd promised Bloomah, cheerfully kissing her, setting his hat on his head at a rakish angle. 'There'll be plenty. I'll come home with bagels and cream cheese and coffee and we'll have such a nosh.' So he had said this morning, and now he was shouting questions at them. Hannah wanted to cry.

Instead, she stayed in front of the fire, a small crouching shape, and let her mind slide away, far away from the small crowded room and sick white-faced Bloomah and shouting angry Nathan. She wasn't always going to be the good little girl they all thought she was. One day she'd be rich. Rich like Uncle Alexander in his bright tweed suits and his sparkling tie pins. *Richer* than Uncle Alex. She'd never eat black bread and herrings and onions ever again. Only the best Dutch cheese and chollahs. She'd never wear Jake's boots again, hard and rubbing her bare feet. They could go straight to Solly, because she'd have shoes and stockings of her very own, soft smooth stockings, like Rachel Levin's mother and like Auntie Minnie. Not long now. Just another three years, that was all. Three more years until she was thirteen and could go and work in the theatre, like Uncle Alex used to, and wear marvellous clothes, like the ones she drew on the blue paper bags the herrings from the corner shop came wrapped in. Oh, she'd show them! She'd have dresses in deep green taffeta and trim them with creamy lace and ...

The vision of a dress shaped itself in her mind's eye and she stayed there, unmoving, near the grate. Nathan had to say her name twice before she heard him and scrambled to her feet.

'Poppa?'

'Go get your coat on. We got to go out.'

'Out?' She flicked her eyes at Bloomah, puzzled. 'Who's going out?'

'Us! You and me! Go and put your coat on already. Don't give me aggravation! Haven't I got enough?'

Obediently, she shrugged into her coat, a heavy black rep garment that had once belonged to Auntie Minnie's youngest Ann, and which she hated for its lumpishness, for Ann was a solid square child, with legs like sturdy little tree trunks, and what had looked tolerable on her looked dreadful on skinny Hannah.

'The hat,' Bloomah said. 'It's raining again.'

'Oh, Momma, please, not the – '

'Do as you're told!' Nathan roared and almost in despair Hannah did, pulling onto her curling hair the pancake of black straw which creaked with every movement she made. To wear the coat was bad enough; the hat was hell on earth.

'Be a good girl, *bobbalah*,' Bloomah said, and smiled at her, her face looking even more tired and white than it had. 'You hear me? Be good, do what Poppa says. It'll be all right. It will, really.'

They went out into the street without a word to each other. Nathan stopped on the pavement and stared up at the sky. 'You see?' he said, almost triumphantly. 'You see? Bad enough we got to go to the schnorrers' shop. Has it got to start to rain again as well, already? What more do they want of me? I ask you, what more? Come on, Hannah, and keep your hat over your eyes. It'll keep the rain out.'

They began to walk, Hannah feeling her belly tighten into the sick familiar sensation it always got when they had to do what they were doing this morning.

Davida Lammeck had woken in a bad temper, as the entire staff knew before the clock struck ten. Her maid had been sent scurrying from her bedroom in tears; the butler had been mortally offended by the peremptory message she had sent him about last night's dinner for Edward Albert, once the Prince of Wales who had long been a friend of Albert's and who was now King; and the housekeeper had threatened to give her notice. Thirty-seven Park Lane was not a comfortable place to be on this wet March morning.

The trouble was, of course, Master Daniel. Most of the servants still thought of him that way, even though he was now very much a man of the world, a young man about town at nineteen with his own carriage and membership of his own clubs (one or two of which were decidedly fast, although, of course, irreproachable in a social sense).

Freddy, the third footman, who'd seen it all told them the story in the servants' hall with enormous relish, embroidering a little as he talked, but not all that much.

'There they was, Mr Albert and Mr Emmanuel, standing there all full o' themselves, talking to the King in the 'all, an 'im as bouncy as ever, the rip, for all 'e's been crowned an' all, and in comes Madam from the ballroom, all done up in 'er diamonds, lookin' as smart as paint, and draggin' that Miss Damont be'ind 'er – you know the one I mean. Lofty piece, she is, tall as a copper, an' twice as 'aughty!'

'Leontine,' said Ellen the fifth housemaid. 'She's Madam's cousin on 'er father's side, daughter of 'er Dad's youngest brother. He was in diamonds, 'ad interests in South Africa an' all that. Madam's took 'er up ever since 'er own mother died. 'Er mother was a Rothschild, you see.'

'Well, spare us the family trees,' the cook said. 'Or we'll never get to the really fruity bits. Go on, Freddy, tell us what 'appened.'

'Right,' said Freddy, with great gusto. 'I'll tell yer. Up comes Madam, right? With this Leontine Damont trailing be'ind 'er lookin' as bored as a pig in a bathroom.'

Ellen giggled. 'You shouldn't talk about pigs, not 'ere. Madam'd 'ave a fit. She'd say you wasn't kosher – '

'Yer bleedin' right I'm not,' Freddy said, and grinned. 'Got all my bits an' pieces the way they was born, ain't I? No one chopped no bits off o' me.'

'If you're goin' to talk dirty, you can get out o' my kitchens,' Cook said frostily. 'Tell us what 'appened, or shut up.'

'So, there she was, all bored lookin' – until Master Daniel comes down from the drawin' room, an' I tell you, 'e looked a right treat. I wish I 'ad an 'alf of 'is looks, I'll tell you. An' a tenth o' what 'e spends on 'is tailor – anyway, there 'e was, and you'd a' thought someone 'ad switched on the electricity inside that Leontine madam, that you would. Bright and eager as – well, I don't know. Stood there lookin' as though she'd got more front than Brighton. So, Madam smiles sweet as you like, sings out to young Daniel, 'Daniel, my dee-ar, come an' talk to dear Leontine – she's been dyin' to speak to you all evenin'.'

'I'd be ashamed to come on that strong with a fella, no matter 'ow much I liked the look of 'im,' Ellen said, self righteously.

'Different for the likes o' them,' Cook said, jerking her

chin up to indicate above stairs. 'They're arrangin' things all the time. Keeps the money in the family, don't it?'

'Are you interested or ain't you?' Freddy demanded. 'Right, then listen. Miss Leontine surges forwards like, and you know what Master Daniel did? 'E stands there on the steps lookin' at 'er, and then just nods, all cool like, and turns round and goes back up the stairs. Well! You should'a seen Madam's face! A study, it was, she was that put out, and Miss Leontine she goes as red as beetroot and then as white as a sheet and says as she's got an 'eadache and she'll go to the boudoir for a bit, and off she goes. The King, 'e sees all this, and 'e laughs and says all jovial like, "Well, Mrs Lammeck, it seems our young man isn't as h'interested in doin' 'is dooties by marriage as 'e should be, hey? You'll 'ave to start a lot h'earlier an' be a lot craftier to drag *that* young man into matrimony, I'm thinkin'!" And o'course Mr Emmanuel Lammeck 'e laughs too, and so does Mr *Albert*. Which makes Madam right livid, although she can't say nothin', can she, seein' as it's the King – but I wouldn't like to be in Mr Albert's shoes this morning, nor Master Daniel's come to that.'

'Our Master Daniel'll look after 'isself well enough, never you fear,' Cook said. "E's no Mama's boy, though *she'd* like to think it! No one makes 'im get married till 'e's good and ready.'

'They're funny, these Jews,' Ellen said knowledgeably. 'They reckon it's wrong for a man not to be married by the time 'e's twenty. That's why Madam's so keen. An' of course she'll want 'im to marry one of 'is own, won't she?' She launched herself into an account of the Lammeck family's connections, talking about Damonts and Rothschilds and D'Avigdors with great fluency. They all listened respectfully; Ellen was Park Lane's acknowledged expert on the aristocracy. She probably knew more about Mrs Lammeck's relations than Madam herself.

She, upstairs in her great blue and gold bedroom, was dressing, choosing clothes she could easily dispose of because today, to add to her general sense of being hard-done-by, was her day for the 'Girls'.

She thought, briefly, of the possibility of sending a message round to Eaton Square to tell Mary she just couldn't cope today, that she had a headache, but had to dismiss it.

Mary was often ill, genuinely so, and she never missed, while Davida had missed her last two days of duty. If she did that again, people would notice and start to talk, and no one was ever going to be given the chance to say that Davida Lammeck was less assiduous in her charitable duties than her sister-in-law. No matter how upset she was by Daniel's outrageous behaviour at last night's ball, and the King's silly comments, she would go to that dreadful Settlement and Do Her Duty.

But how nice it would have been if only they had succeeded in what they had tried to do when the Daughters of Sarah was first founded almost twenty years ago. They should have been able to keep those hundreds of thousands of Jews from the Pale out. It was absurd that they should have continued to pour in in such numbers, and so poverty stricken too. She had herself written many letters to the rabbis, far away in the hinterland of Eastern Europe, pointing out how bad it would be for all Jewry if England were overwhelmed with immigrants, but it had made no difference. Still they had come, and had become poorer and poorer. At least some of the earlier influx had had some property with which to support themselves. The later waves had been the dregs of the villages and tiny towns of Russia and Poland and still they came. Thank God the government had seen sense at last, and had brought in the Aliens' Bill. From next year it would be better, with checks at the ports and immigration officers with rules and regulations with which to turn the worst of them away. Meanwhile, the Daughters of Sarah had to work as hard as they ever had, and this morning Davida was in no mood for it. It was too bad, she told herself pettishly, that people should have to put up with such matters. As if she hadn't enough of her own problems to concern herself with.

'Esme! Fetch me the purple sarsanet. It's a shade out of date now I come to think of it, and will do perfectly well for the East End. You can send it to the Settlement immediately I get back.'

That was another thing; every time she went to that hateful East End she had to throw away every stitch of clothes she had been wearing, for how could any lady with any pretensions at all to self respect bear to wear such garments again? And it was irritating to have to do it, for often the gowns she had to part with she quite liked.

By the time she reached the Settlement house she did have a headache, for she had sat in the corner of her carriage and chewed over in her mind last night's episode again and again. What was the matter with the boy? What did he think was wrong with Leontine? A sweet child, and so well reared, and a considerable heiress, after all. Not that it mattered to Daniel, for he would eventually inherit all her own as well as Albert's money, but it would be silly to let Leontine's considerable wealth go to waste outside the family. Foolish, headstrong boy! She must talk to him. Today, when he collected her from the Settlement, as he knew he had to, after she had done her wretched tasks.

Mary was already there, wearing her deep blue serge with the French braid, and Davida sniffed slightly. She'd worn that gown for a whole season already, *and* had worn it here several times. Mary had no fastidiousness, none at all.

They had little time to talk, for the line of supplicants was already long, and Davida had felt her irritation increase as she sailed past the line of bent, shuffling figures, her handkerchief held delicately to her nose. Wretched creatures! Why couldn't they do a decent day's work and earn their keep? Coming begging like this. It was shocking. Really shocking.

'Mary, my dear. How are you? Better, I hope? I heard you'd not been well, and I was so wowwied, weally I was.' Davida could in fact pronounce her r's quite easily, but it was fashionable at present to make them redundant, so redundant hers were.

'I'm very well, thank you, Davida.' They clashed cheeks in the time honoured way of women who are related but do not particularly care for each other. 'And you? Last night was very splendid. I hardly spoke to you, of course, but ... '

'Yes, well, the King seemed to enjoy it,' Davida said, brushing it aside. She had no wish to give her wretched ball another thought. 'I suppose we'd better start. They're out there like flies.'

'Yes, and it's raining so hard too, poor things, I thought I'd let them all in and we'd just talk quietly, you know? I wouldn't want to distress them unduly, and it's never easy for them, with others listening, but the rain is really so dreadful.'

One of the more officious of the paid employees heard her,

and went at once to the doors and flung them open. The line at once broke up, became a pushing eager crowd thrusting its way in through the double doors. Immediately the heated room began to steam with the smell of wet serge and tired humanity. It was not an agreeable smell.

Davida sat behind her table, her cash box in front of her and her register of applicants beside it, her face as icy and controlled as a glacier and her eyes blank with disdain as she stared at the people who came before her. And she was harsh, very harsh indeed with all of them.

Mary, on the other side of the room with her own table and cash box and register was uneasily aware of Davida's voice, high and frosty as she questioned the people who slid into the bentwood chair in front of her. She sounded so cold, so angry, so very uncaring that Mary wanted to tell her to go away, that she would see all the people herself, that Davida didn't look well, should go home. But it had been a long time since Mary had tried to influence her masterful sister-in-law. As the years had gone by Mary had done more and more of the real work performed by 'the Girls', but never had Davida lost her grip on the organization. She came to Hanbury Street just often enough to keep her status as chairwoman of the Committee and her place in the men's eyes as the Most Important Member. Each year the Committee of the Society for the Relief of Indigent Jews sent Davida an illuminated address as their thanks for her sterling efforts. Each year Davida accepted it with a long suffering smile. And each year Mary looked at her, and liked her less and less, and said less and less. This morning was no exception. So she bent her head to her own cash box, and spoke as gently as she could to her own line of applicants.

By the time Nathan and Hannah reached the bentwood chair in front of Davida's table Hannah was feeling very miserable indeed. Her wet coat hung on her like a piece of dead ice, her feet were solid with the cold, bare inside Jake's old boots, and her ears ached with the chill. She was hungry too, for it was now almost noon and a long time since her breakfast of black bread and jam at seven.

She stared at the lady on the other side of the table. She had the smoothest thickest black hair, the whitest skin and most lustrous dark eyes she had ever seen. She also had a **very** disagreeable expression, her narrow nose seeming lifted at the tip with disapproval.

Hannah let her eyes flick sideways to her father, sitting on the edge of the chair with his hat held in both his hands on his lap, and his head bent a little nervously. Tell her not to stare at you like that! She wanted to say. Tell her to smile!

'Well?' Davida said. I don't like your dress, Hannah thought scornfully. That purple is *ugly*. But it wasn't really and she knew it. It was a beautiful gown, cut with perfect lines, with lace of the purest cream Chantilly on the high boned collar and on the bodice. A beautiful dress.

'What do you want? Have you been here before?'

Have we been here before? Oh, we have, we have. So many times, facing the jeers of the children who taunted people like them who went begging at the schnorrers' shop for handouts when they couldn't eat. We've walked the long painful miles all the way from Whitechapel to Spitalfields, our feet biting the grey pavements in an eternity of trudging. We've faced interrogation and nagging and the sheer shame of it, over and over again. We've been hungry more often than we've been fed. None of it came into ten year old Hannah's mind in so many words, but the feelings did. The humiliation did. The sheer sick misery did.

'Because we're not here to be made use of by the shiftless, and you may well know it,' Davida went on. 'Genuine hardship and twouble we tweat with compassion, of course, but it is hardly genuine hardship if the same person keeps coming over and over again. Have you no work you can do? You *look* able bodied enough.' She stared at Nathan and lifted one eyebrow.

He began, awkwardly at first and then gaining confidence, explaining about Bloomah and the need to be there to look after her, about the boys at their charity school, for boys must learn to read and write and be Barmitzvah, about the rent, about the way people in the streets and alleys no longer needed the services of a scribe like himself to write their letters for them. About his well off brothers and sisters-in-law who had cheated him of his rightful share, so long ago, and who did so little about his army service and his medal and ...

Don't. Oh, Poppa, don't. Don't crawl to this woman. Again it

206

wasn't words that filled Hannah's mind; just feelings. Raw angry desperately ashamed feelings.

It went on and on, the cold questioning, Nathan's almost whining answers and then it seemed to Hannah that the room was brightening as she stared at the table and the implacable face behind it and everything began to glitter with light and the glitter was inside her chest and belly, pushing upwards, needle sharp against her throat, trying to get out. And then it did, in one great shout of fury.

To the onlookers it was a commonplace enough sight. A small child screaming and kicking in rage.

To Nathan, though, it was the most amazing thing he had ever seen. His Hannah to behave so? His quiet sweet little Hannah? He put out one hand, almost tentatively, to try to stop her.

It made no difference. Hannah threw herself at Davida across the table and hit out at her horrified face. Her small fist made no contact at all, she was so tense, but her rage expressed itself in every taut line of her body. Then she scrambled off the table and turned and ran, not knowing where, just anywhere to be out of this dreadful place, and away from that hateful woman.

As she reached the door she cannoned into a hard firm shape. Strong hands gripped her beneath her arms and she was lifted high, dizzily high into the air, her head swinging and her vision still blurred by the glitter of her fury.

'Well, well, and what have we here?' Daniel Lammeck said, his voice a little high and drawled. 'A termagant? A little spitfire? How very quaint!'

He held her out at arms' length, while she kicked and struggled in his grip, one of her oversized boots falling from her foot in her struggles. She was silent now, her teeth clenched and her eyes like narrow blue slits in her chalk-white face, but she was still strong and her kicks were sharp and he had to hold her well away to avoid injury.

There was hubbub everywhere now as the waiting suppli-cants muttered and exclaimed and disapproved loudly, and then there was another voice, a quiet but somehow insistent one that cut through the noise. Hannah looked over her shoulder, aware of the calm in it, suddenly needing calm very much indeed.

'Give her to me, Danny. The poor child is upset. Give her

to me,' Mary said, and Daniel, with just a moment's hesitation, did. Hannah felt the strong arms go around her and after a second of rigidity, let her exhaustion take over. She relaxed back into those warm and welcoming arms, and drooped her head on Mary's shoulder, and closed her eyes.

21

'I don't understand,' Bloomah said again, and shook her head. 'It's *meshuggah* – a child her age! How can you even think of it? Bad enough children have to go to work when they do, but a ten year old? It's mad. I don't understand.'

'Listen, Bloomah, it isn't like it sounds!' Nathan said, and shook his head in some asperity. 'Eat some more, shut up and eat, and I'll tell you again.'

'You've told me already,' Bloomah said fretfully, but she reached for the plate and took one of the onion rolls from it and spread it thick with cream cheese. Watching her, Hannah could feel her delight. How often was it they had a full half pound at one time? How often was it they didn't have to spread it thin as an oil slick in the gutter?

'I'll tell you again. This woman – she says our Hannah could be a companion to her. Not all the time, but during the week. She'll collect her every Sunday morning, take her to her house in the West End, bring her back in time for shabbas, Friday night. That's all. A *companion*. For all her money, she's got no children, not one! What sort of woman is it got no children? Naturally she feels it, feels it bad. And this morning, she talked to our Hannah and that was how it happened. She wants a child she can look after a little bit, teach a little bit, have as a companion. She'll pay good money, Bloomah, and take such care of our Hannah. Believe me, it's a great opportunity for her. I saw the house, I know what I'm talking about.'

Hannah knew too. She sat there on the old piece of rug by the fire, now piled high with coal Poppa had bought with the money the lady had given him and thought about the morning. Already it didn't seem real. She stared inside her head at all that had happened and all that she had seen and she

208

couldn't tell whether it had been one of her private stories or an actual here-and-now event. It must have been real for Poppa kept talking about it as though it had all happened. And yet it felt like one of her dreams, just like one of the stories she lived on the roof outside the landing window.

The lady had carried her away somewhere and she had hung on, her eyes tight shut, feeling the crisp fabric of the lady's gown against her cheek and smelling the rich soft smell of her, and shaking inside as her tide of rage slowly subsided. She had taken her away from the big room where the people were lining up, away from the smell of steaming clothes and unwashed bodies to a smaller warmer room upstairs where there was a fire burning, and she had sat down on a wide chair, making a lap that was comfortable and safe.

There they had sat for what seemed a long time, Hannah huddled against the lady's serge bosom, her face buried in her neck as her shaking feelings slackened and at last died away. Finally she had sat up and looked at the lady's face, so near her own, and uncertain what to say had managed, in a very small voice, only 'Hello.'

'Hello,' the lady said gravely, and then smiled. She had a friendly smile, Hannah decided, though she wasn't pretty. Her hair was a faded colour, like the curtains in Mrs Arbeiter's room downstairs that had once been brown but which had hung at the window so long that most of the colour had been bleached out of them by the summer sun. Her eyes were faded too, though they might once have been a brighter green, and her face had a sort of melted look, as though the soft bits of it around her jaw were sliding off the bones underneath. But it was a friendly face, though it had a worried look on it, and suddenly Hannah felt the need to be nice to her, the way she was extra nice to Momma when Bloomah had her worried look. So she smiled, a wide and cheerful smile and nodded her head.

Mary looked at the child on her lap, and felt her chest tighten. She had red hair, a frizz of curls that stuck damply to her forehead, and a hideous black straw hat which had fallen off the back of her head and was held against her neck by a frayed elastic. She had a pointed chin and a wide gap-toothed smile, with her two front teeth very white and large in her small face. Her eyes were blue, a clear translucent blueness that made Mary feel she was looking right inside the child's head when she looked into them. It was exactly the sort of face that Mary envisaged on those long sleepless nights that still overcame her, when she thought of her dead red-haired daughter.

For as the years had gone on, she had allowed her dead baby to grow in her memory. With each passing year she had added to her vision of the child and would think of her and grieve for her not as a helpless scrap of newborn humanity but as a growing one-year-old, and then two-year-old and five-year-old, and six-year-old. . . .

Somehow, she had not been able to let her grow much beyond the age of ten. To imagine her dead baby as a gawky girl, with budding breasts and curving hips, a woman like herself, was too much even for her creative mourning. So she had, for the past decade, remembered her dead child as a ten year old, merry and intelligent, with red hair and blue eyes, and the roundness of childhood still about her.

Like the child now sitting on her lap and smiling at her. *Almost* like. The dead child in her mind was round and soft and dressed in pretty clothes. This child was sticklike, with wrists as thin as a bird's claws and a face that was shadowed by hunger. Her clothes, the ugliest Mary had ever seen, were much too large for her, and she had one bare foot and one adorned with a large very worn boy's boot. Yet behind her sat a shadow of the child she could be, if she were properly fed, and properly dressed and properly cared for.

Hannah was eventually to know of what happened to Mary that morning, with the March rain pelting down the window and the coal fire spitting cheerfully in the grate, but it was to be a long time before the knowledge came to her. All she knew that day was that the lady who smelled good talked to her, and asked her questions and fed her soft sweet biscuits and gave her a glass of milk to drink.

It was possibly the questions as much as the food that filled her with pleasure in Mary's company, for Hannah was at heart a chatterer. Her need to talk had long since been flattened, since Bloomah was often too exhausted with ill health to respond to her child's eagerness, and Nathan almost always was buried too deep in his own anxieties. As for her brothers, being boys they took their own superiority for granted and their own right to be heard first as obvious, and gave her little chance to express her needs to them. So, she had learned to be silent when it was necessary, talking to herself inside her own head instead. Still she could talk easily when someone allowed her to do so.

And this morning Mary allowed her to do so. The questions she asked were about herself, about what she liked and what she did and how she felt and how she lived. And she listened to the answers. So often, Hannah had found, people questioned you but weren't really interested in what you had to say; Mrs Arbeiter was like that. 'What're you doing? Where're you going?' but she never waited to hear what Hannah might want to tell her. 'Don't get into trouble. Don't talk to strangers. Come straight home.' Boring busy-body Mrs Arbeiter was one of the people the child hated most, because she was one of the people who listened to her least. This lady, she thought as she chattered on, telling her more than she knew of the bleakness of her life in Antcliff Street, this lady was not a bit like Mrs Arbeiter. She really wants to know about me.

'So you like dresses?' Mary said. 'Would you like to learn how to sew, so that you can make them?'

'I'll have to one day,' Hannah said. 'Poppa says I'll have to, because I'll have to work in a factory like the others. I don't want to do that. I want to be like Uncle Alex. He's rich.' Prudently she said nothing about her plans to act in a theatre. Even this warm and listening lady might not understand something as outrageous as that.

'I don't mean that sort of sewing,' Mary said, knowing exactly the sort of sweatshop that awaited Hannah. 'I mean real sewing – by hand, to make pretty things that you've chosen for yourself. Would you like that?'

'Sew dresses for myself?' Hannah's brow furrowed. 'Where do I get stuff from?'

'Well, I have an idea,' Mary said, and suddenly put her arms around the child and hugged her. After a startled moment Hannah hugged her back.

Still holding her by the hand, the lady took her back downstairs, and told her to sit with Poppa, and gave Poppa a cup of coffee and some biscuits too, which surprised and pleased Nathan so much that he was almost speechless. Then she crossed the room to talk to the hard faced lady with the black hair, still sitting at her table.

Hannah wouldn't look at her. She couldn't. The sight of

211

that smooth pale face with its sweeps of elegant black hair made the anger tremble in her again and she didn't want that. It was much nicer to feel warm and full of biscuits than cold with anger.

So, she turned away and felt her face go pink as she caught the eye of the tall young man leaning against the wall. He winked at her, a slow knowing wink, and she looked down, deeply embarrassed, and then, unable to resist, peeped back at him. He winked again, and this time smiled too, and almost against her will she found herself smiling back. It had really been very awful to shout and kick at him as she had done, and it was very nice of him not to be angry about it. She could tell he wasn't angry, and that comforted her, and she decided he must be there because of *her* lady; he looked nice enough and rich enough to belong to her.

Though she was by no means as expert on men's clothes as she was on ladies', Hannah knew nice things when she saw them. Hannah knew all about balls and gowns made of lace and people who rode in carriages. The illustrated papers were full of accounts of their doings, and she had taught herself, with Uncle Alex's occasional aid, to read them avidly, and believed implicitly every word in them, including the fiction. They had to be true, because why else would they be in the papers if they weren't? Now she had evidence they were true, for the young man who had caught her at the door and at whom she had aimed her kicks was clearly the hero of every story she had ever read. Even though he winked, which the men in the stories never did.

Mary came back to them, and Hannah looked up into her face, trying to see what she was thinking. The worried look had gone, and there was a blankness there that puzzled her. When they had been talking before the lady's face had told Hannah a great deal; that she was friendly, that she liked to listen, that she often worried. Now it told her nothing.

Mary's face was composed, but she was tense with excitement. Over the years, ever since she had connived in Fay's escape to her happy marriage, she had learned to dissimulate. What she most wanted must always be treated casually, for as sure as God had made Lammeck Alley the most important business thoroughfare in the whole of the City of London, she would lose it if anyone knew she really wanted something. Of that she was certain. And now she wanted something so desperately that she almost frightened herself with the strength of her desire.

She took Nathan away, bidding Hannah quietly to sit and wait. Obediently, Hannah waited, finishing the last biscuit that had been left on Nathan's plate, enjoying its soft crumbly sweetness against her tongue and relishing the warmth that now filled her. The room had largely emptied now, and the bustle would not start again till the afternoon when new applicants for charity came. Hannah swung her legs contentedly, glad there was no one there to stare at her and mutter about her bad behaviour. That she had behaved very badly she was well aware, but somehow it didn't matter. She was a little sleepy now, as the aftermath of her attack of rage moved into her, and she leaned back against the wall behind the bench and stared at the ceiling, not thinking very much at all.

When Nathan and her Lady came back she was wearing a mantle over her serge gown, and had a hat on, and Nathan was looking, well, Hannah wasn't quite sure how he was looking. Rather, she thought after a moment, like the stuffed bird in a cage that Uncle Alex kept in his window at the house facing Victoria Park; glassy eyed and not quite there.

What followed made her feel glassy eyed too. They went out of the Settlement into Hanbury Street, and with a nonchalance that left Hannah breathless Nathan held open the door of a carriage that was waiting outside so that Hannah's Lady could climb in, and then picked up Hannah, and put her inside too. She sat there with her eyes round with amazement as Nathan climbed in after them and the door closed behind him and the carriage went rattling away, so that she swayed and had to lean back against the leather padding. She, Hannah, in a carriage? Her *Poppa* in a carriage?

The streets through which they passed were a blur of traffic with carriages just as fine as the one in which she was riding thronging on every side, and here and there, amid the horse drawn traffic, motor cars with men in goggles moving majestically through the press. The shops they passed were breathtaking in their size and beauty, and she could not altogether believe they were real. The morning was getting more and more like the pages of the illustrated papers at every moment.

And then the house, a huge and unbelievable house in

Eaton Square, with tall windows and the most imposing front door Hannah had ever seen, and people, people, people. Men in sober suits holding doors open. Girls in dark stuff dresses and lacy aprons and caps with frills taking her coat from her, leading her to the largest, prettiest room she had ever thought to see, and sitting her down before the fire and giving her a bowl of bread and milk. She looked at it with the yellow spread of melting butter on the top and the memory of the biscuits disappeared at once. She seized the spoon and wolfed the plateful of hot sweet stuff faster than she knew she ought. Somehow it didn't matter, for the girls in lacy aprons just smiled and shook their heads at her in mock reproof and brought her more when she had finished.

She slept after that, curled up in the chair in front of the fire, and it was not until Nathan came and touched her shoulder to wake her that she gave any thought to what was happening. Only then did she ask for the first time, 'Poppa, when are we going home?'

'Soon,' he said and looked over his shoulder. 'Do you like it here, bobbalah?'

'It's nice,' she said. 'When are we going home to Momma?'

'Yes,' he said vaguely, and looked over his shoulder again, and this time her Lady answered, coming from the far side of the room where she had been standing against the door.

'Hannah, my dear,' she said softly. 'Your father and I have been talking. About you.'

'I didn't mean to be so rude,' Hannah said, wary now. Sooner or later everything had to be paid for, she knew that. 'I didn't mean to be ... I mean, it was all – '

The lady shook her head. 'That doesn't matter,' she said. 'That's not what we've been talking about, Hannah. My name is Mary Lammeck. Mrs Lammeck.'

'Yes,' Hannah said, not sure what was expected of her.

'I have no children of my own. I did have a girl, like you, but not now. And I've asked your father if I can ... well, I would like to share you with him and your mother. Just for a while. Would you like that?'

Hannah was sitting up very straight now, her hands rolled into tight fists. 'I don't know what you mean, share.'

'I thought maybe you would like to come to my house and learn to sew, and perhaps some music and things like that, and keep me company, and go home to your parents at the

214

end of each week. I would provide you with clothes, new clothes and stuff to make some, too, and we'd walk in the park and listen to the musicians there, you know, and go to the shops and out to tea at Gunter's.'

'Gunter's?' said Hannah, blankly.

'Well, never mind that, I'll explain that afterwards. Just now, I want to know, will you stay with me this way, for a while? It would be ... ' She looked uneasily at Nathan. 'It would be a help to your mother and father.'

'It's not right, a girl of your age sharing a bedroom with your brother. Jake's nearly sixteen already,' Nathan said. He sounded wretched.

'Shall I, Poppa?' Hannah said, and looked round the room. 'This is a very nice place and it's a big room, big enough for a lot of people.... '

'This room?' Mary said. 'Oh, my dear, you won't sleep here. This is the housekeeper's room. You'll have a bedroom all of your own. Come and see.' She leaned over and picked Hannah up, perching her on her arm, and carried her away, into the rest of the house.

That was almost more than Hannah could bear. Room after room went by her uncomprehending eyes as Mary carried her through the lower floor, and then, after she had insisted on being set on her feet, and Mary had taken one hand to hold it warmly in hers, she went through the upper rooms, staring at the great double drawing room in blank amazement at its vast fireplace and brocaded chairs and silken curtains in the richest yellow Hannah had ever seen outside the sun itself, and so many settees and chairs with little gilt backs and tables laden with ornaments. It was all much too much.

So much that when Mary said again, 'Would you like to visit me, then, Hannah? Just for a while? From Sunday morning to Friday afternoon. Then home to your parents, until Sunday again. Just to see how we get on? It would be ... I would like it very much.' And Hannah could say nothing, only moving nearer to Nathan to stand close beside him and stare up at the face of the lady who was turning her entire world upside down.

All the way home to Momma, all the time while she sat inside the carriage as Poppa made the driver stop on the way so that he could buy things to take home – including a sack of

215

coal, which made the carriage driver's face look very peculiar indeed – she sat silent. It was like the things that happened in her long lonely hours on the roof, but she could not get hold of it properly. When it was all inside her own head she knew exactly what to do, exactly how it all ought to turn out. But this was a dream inside someone else's head. Mrs Lammeck's head.

'Mrs Lammeck,' she said aloud, practising it, rolling it round her tongue. 'Mrs Lammeck.'

'Do you like her, Hannah?' Nathan asked. 'Is she a nice lady?'

'She's a very nice lady,' Hannah said. 'She smells nice.'

'Is that the best you can say? The woman offers you a future like no one can ever imagine, and all you can talk about is she *smells* nice?' Nathan suddenly seemed to have lost his temper. 'What sort of a child is it, tell me, that talks of smells in such a situation? So answer me? How do you deal with a child you give a sensible question, she gives you a stupid answer? How do you ...'

All the rest of the way Poppa asked the interior of the carriage questions, and she sat against the corner of the window, staring out and feeling oddly better. Poppa asking questions no one could answer, this was as it should be. This she could understand.

Then there was Momma, her face so white with worry for they had been gone so long that Hannah felt sick with shame. It was all her fault, she told herself, flinging her arms around Bloomah's neck. All her fault.

And then the explanations, the interminable talking, the displaying of the lavish purchases Nathan had made with the money he had been given, the talk about the chance that had been thrown at Hannah, to learn to be a lady.

'A Jewish home, Bloomah,' Nathan kept saying. 'Never forget that, a good Jewish home. Stinking rich they may be, but it's a Jewish home. That house – oy, oy, that house! You should see that house, Bloomah! It's amazing – a-*mazing*! With a *mezuzzah* on the door, just like us. Bigger and fancier I grant you, but a *mezuzzah*. Such a chance, Bloomah, for our little dolly, and how much longer can she go on sharing with her brothers, hey? If it's only Friday and Saturday nights it's not so bad, Shabbas and all. But in the week, in the week she can sleep in a big bed as big as we got all to ourselves. I tell

216

you, Bloomah, it's the best thing that ever happened. The best.'

And Bloomah said yes, of course, Hannah must do it. It would be good for her, ideal for her, what more could any mother want for her child?

But she cried when she went to bed and went on crying a long time. Hannah woke up twice in the night and heard her.

22

The worst part of it all for Bloomah was Hannah's eagerness. She had known as soon as she had looked at the child's face that someone had lit a fire inside her. There was an intensity in her, a blazing blue-eyed hunger that could not be ignored. Hannah actually wanted to go away to spend half her life with strangers, and looking at the life around her, Bloomah could not blame her.

She had tried to make a home of the two rooms and landing they rented in Antcliff Street, had tried desperately, but as the children grew and space shrank and her own strength ebbed away, the rooms had become harder and harder to keep tidy. Every movement in the cramped space was likely to send something toppling over, the rickety table, or the papers Nathan kept piled in the corner which no one was allowed to touch. It was rare that Nathan's earnings brought in enough to feed them properly, and there were more days that she could not work than days when she could, and Isaac was not the sort of master tailor to pay workers who didn't work. Even his own sister.

She had hoped after Lazar and Rivka had died, that Nathan would accept Alex's offer of the house in Sidney Street, but he had roared with a monumental rage when she had broached the idea.

'Take from him, from my younger brother I should take such favours? He can go to hell in a teapot, him and his favours! I don't take no favours. What sort of a man is it takes such things from his own younger brother? What sort of wife is it asks of a man he should make such an object of himself?' And so on, and so on.

217

So, Alex had shrugged and put Benjamin and his wife Sarah and their three children in the Sidney Street house, and given Bloomah a few shillings to help out a bit. (She never dared to take more in case Nathan found out; better to be hungry than put up with Nathan shouting questions because they had a chicken in the pot when he knew perfectly well he hadn't earned enough to buy even the giblets) and shaken his head and gone away to go on making money.

Bloomah tried to understand what made Nathan the way he was. He had refused, over and over again, to accept help from his own family. He was as he had been for the past twenty years, the poorest member. Even the children of Benjamin, the rabbinical scholar who lived entirely on his father-in-law's beneficence and his brother Alex's gifts, went better shod and fed than her children did. Yet Nathan would go cap in hand to the schnorrers' shop, to cringe before those high nosed aristocrats and their probings! How could a man be that way? How could he let his own children suffer because of his stubbornness? Bloomah too could ask unanswerable questions, but she asked them of herself, not the entire universe, the way Nathan did.

Sometimes she thought she glimpsed an answer. Nathan, she suspected, took pride in being so very poor, so severely hard done by, when his family were there to see. He was meticulous about attending every family function, everything at which Alex and Benjamin and Reuben and their wives and children might be. There he would stand ostentatious in his shabbiness alongside Reuben's polished paunch and Benjamin's neat gaberdine, Bloomah, miserable beside him in her eternal purple rep dress, the one he had got for her from the schnorrers' shop long ago, making her usual heavy contrast with her satin clad sisters-in-law, and he would shine with a sort of unctuousness. He seemed on these occasions to wear his poverty and his injustices with the passion of martyrdom. How could he have accepted help from Alex, which would spoil all that?

So Bloomah would sometimes say to herself as she sat unhappily with the women at a baby's circumcision party or at a wedding, feeling shame at the way her children's eyes lit up at the sight of the food that was so lavishly spread. But she never dared to speak such thoughts to Nathan. His anger would not be worth it. It had been a long time since Bloomah

218

had regarded Nathan with anything but wariness. Once, long ago, there had been love and a great deal of passion. Now there was just fatigue, bone deep fatigue, and an anxiety so constant and so all-pervading that she could not remember a time when she had not felt the knot of it in her belly.

Only the children gave her solace, her two boys, and above all her quiet Hannah. She would sometimes watch Hannah, sitting as she did, quiet and controlled on the edge of her brothers' noisy play, and try to fathom what the child was thinking. She knew that the roof had become Hannah's special place, and would sometimes stand in the shadow of the door of her room staring out of the landing window at the child's oblivious back, wondering what went on in that carroty head, and aching to ask her. But she never did.

So, when Hannah showed how clearly she wanted to go away for half the week – more than half the week – to another woman's company, Bloomah swallowed the pain of the loss and told herself the child could not be blamed for feeling so. What had Bloomah to offer that could possibly compare with Mary Lammeck's promise? She took a deep breath, and dragged herself from bed to wash all of Hannah's clothes, to take with her, and when the carriage arrived for her on Sunday morning (much to the amazement of all the other residents of Antcliff Street) kissed her cheek and said gruffly, 'Mind your manners,' and let her go. The gulf to next Friday yawned in front of her, terrifyingly empty, but she could not, would not, say a word about it.

So Hannah went, convinced that after all her mother didn't mind her departure, and that she had no idea how frightened Hannah was, how much she wanted to stay at home and live her usual life and never see the big house or Mrs Lammeck again. Momma, she told herself, in spite of her crying in the night wanted her to go as much as Poppa did. It was a bleak thought, but she swallowed it and went, leaving Bloomah to spend her Sunday in an even deeper silence than usual, and Nathan to harangue the world with questions until even he was too exhausted to go on. She was going to a marvellous new life and everyone, except Mary Lammeck, was miserable about it.

Mary Lammeck was incandescent with joy, as anyone who

had ever bothered to take notice would have known from her blank face and her total composure. She had told Emmanuel so casually that he hardly noticed when she said that she had decided to take in one of the children from the Settlement.

'An experiment,' she said, pouring coffee for him as they sat at breakfast on the Saturday morning before Hannah was due to arrive. 'If these girls can be taught to improve themselves, they will rear their own children to be more capable of absorbing the ways of this country, don't you think? If it works well perhaps other children could be taken into other houses....'

'Hmph,' said Emmanuel and looked at the clock. 'Three quarters of an hour, I want to be in good time for the service this morning. Albert's bringing his Amsterdam brother-in-law, and I want to arrange for him to dine here. Monday, I think. A child? What sort of child?'

'Oh, a scrap of a creature,' Mary said vaguely. 'Small and quiet, you know. I shall teach her to sew and such things, and she can cook with Mrs Sarson.'

'As long as the servants aren't upset by it, I suppose it is a good enough idea.' He swallowed the last of his coffee and wiped his moustache. 'Yes. Give you something to think about, too, I dare say. Make sure you've got the right shoes on this morning. I don't want you complaining all the way, like last week.'

It was a constant thorn in Emmanuel's side that the synagogue of which he was a leading congregant was so far from the fashionable purlieus of Eaton Square. He had considered property on the Bayswater side of Hyde Park, but the northern side was the wrong side, and that was all there was to it. Better to live in Eaton Square even if it did mean a half hour's walk every Sabbath.

There had been times when Emmanuel had considered taking his carriage to the end of Edgeware Road and walking the much shorter journey from there. Then he would shake his head. God could not be mocked; inevitably someone would see him descending from the vehicle, and then tongues would wag. A devout Jew never rode on the Sabbath, and although Emmanuel was privately less than convinced of the value of the laws of his religion he was well aware of the importance to his friends and neighbours of his outward observances. So he, and therefore Mary, walked to Bayswater every Sunday morning, through the Park, rain or shine, even though Mary often ended the journey hobbling, for fashionable shoes gave scant consideration to religious demands.

This morning, however, she walked with a spring, and was quite unaware of the cruel pinch of kid boots. Hannah was coming. Her red headed ten-year old was coming, tomorrow morning. Life was going to start again, from Sunday to Friday every week. For the first time in twenty years Mary Lammeck had something to look forward to.

At first Hannah was so overcome by the newness of it all that she seemed struck dumb. She watched as Mrs Lammeck's dressmakers measured her, and there and then, sitting in the little sewing room at the rear of the housekeeper's domain, cut and stitched for her two plain print dresses embellished with cotton lace collars and cuffs, and two sets of underwear, the drawers trimmed with blue ribbon. And her eyes opened wide.

'More when you come next week,' Mary promised her on Friday morning as she packed the basket the child was to take back with her to Antcliff Street. 'Show your Mama these, and I'm sure she will be pleased for you. And take her these as well.' She gave her another larger basket, with eggs and cheese and a cooked chicken and several pots of jam in it. 'For your little brothers, you know,' she said in the vague way that Hannah was already beginning to realize masked feelings of great intensity. 'Tell your Mama it is for your brothers, a little present from you, not from me.'

Mary had meant to be tactful in so instructing the child, but it had not worked as well as she had meant. When Hannah arrived at Antcliff Street in the carriage, stepping out of it with great aplomb, for having ridden in it every day since Sunday she was becoming quite at home there, she looked to Bloomah's eyes a different person. Mary's maid had cut her hair and arranged it, and now she had a crop of close curls that framed her face much more appealingly than the old unkempt mop had done, and she was wearing one of her new dresses with a fine woollen shawl over her shoulders and neat lace-tied shoes over warm black woollen stockings.

'You look like a servant girl,' Bloomah said shortly, unable to cope with the way Hannah seemed to glow in her new finery. 'No hat! Where's your black straw?'

'Mrs Lammeck doesn't like it,' Hannah said. 'She said I don't have to wear it if I don't like. She's getting me a new one.'

The gift for her brothers created a chill too. They seized on the treats in the basket, but Bloomah, straight faced and sullen, refused to touch anything. 'You brought it for your brothers,' she said flatly when Hannah tried to persuade her. 'Not for me.'

On that first visit home, Hannah lost some of the bloom she had acquired and returned to Eaton Square on Sunday morning with a deep sense of relief which made her feel more miserable than ever. She ought to feel bad, she thought, as she looked back at Antcliff Street from the carriage, trying not to cry. It would never do to let the staring children in the street, among whom she had spotted Rachel Levin and the Stern boys, see her weep.

But fortunately Bloomah saw her unshed tears, and they comforted her greatly. By the time Hannah returned the following week she had softened, and even though she had yet more new clothes, a handsome woollen coat and hat to match and a pair of stout walking boots together with a very pretty muff, Bloomah welcomed her warmly and with no jibes at all. Hannah had gained some weight, even in so short a time, and her cheeks were filling out to a more dimpled prettiness that made her brother Jake stare at her solemnly and treat her more politely than he ever had. At sixteen he was a strutting self confident boy, street-sharp, with an intimate knowledge of the tangle of alleys that interlaced the quarter, and an even more detailed awareness of the stalls in the market which were easy to pilfer and those which must be avoided. Once, he had regarded Hannah as part of the furniture of his life, of no more significance than the knob that pulled the front door open, but now, arriving as she did with gifts of woollen clothes and new boots and coats for her brothers as well as baskets of food, he realized that she was worthy of respect. And Hannah enjoyed that.

As for Nathan, he blossomed in the warmth of his daughter's good fortune. He took from her hand each week the envelope Mary gave her for him, smiled at the sight of the clothes and the food baskets, and began to strut a little. None

222

of his brothers' children had done so well for themselves! Not even Benjamin's David, who had won a scholarship to the City of London Boys' School, could be said to be as successful as Hannah was. So he smiled, and stopped shouting questions at the ceiling and everyone relaxed and basked for a little while in the warmth of his satisfaction.

The year slid along its grooves, March drifting into a blazing blue April, which made even Whitechapel feel a better place to be, and on into a hot summer. By September 1903, which was warmer still, Hannah had grown two inches and had filled out amazingly. She stood almost as tall as stocky Jake now, and next to her Solly looked positively squat. Not that they were not benefiting from Hannah's new life; indeed they were, in direct material ways. Week by week Mary sent supplies for them, gifts purchased on long and joyous expeditions she took with Hannah about the shops of the West End. She had a new purpose in her life now and even her long years of practice at looking imperturbable did not protect her. Her relations began to notice how much better she was looking, how much more cheerful, and actually commented on it to each other.

Hannah and Mary began to establish a pattern of life at Eaton Square. Hannah soon learned, as much from what Mary did not say as what she did, that the master of the house was a man to be avoided. It was not that he was particularly short tempered or disagreeable; indeed, on the few occasions that Hannah encountered Emmanuel he was affability itself, treating her with bluff politeness. He nodded at her monosyllabic answers to his questions (Hannah had realized at once that he was one of the Mrs Arbeiters of the world, given to asking but not to listening) and gave her a shilling from his pocket and chucked her under the chin and sent her away. She went gratefully. He was not alarming, but he was not particularly enticing company either. If Mary chose to keep her out of his sight, that suited her well enough.

So, she and Mary spent Sundays peaceably together, while Emmanuel was out on some sort of vague 'business'. Hannah had been puzzled at first, for she knew that offices and shops closed on Sundays. Only in Whitechapel where just Jews lived did some shops stay open and even they closed early. What sort of business was it that this big important man could be about on a Sunday?

223

After the first few weeks, she asked Mary who looked vague and said, 'Oh, people – just people,' and Hannah had to settle for that. But before the year was out she had discovered, by listening to the gossip in the kitchen, that Mr Emmanuel liked the company of lady people more than gentlemen people. That, as far as Ellen and Cook were concerned, was the way he spent his Sundays. She also realized very quickly that that was the way Mary liked it, for it gave them their tranquil afternoons with needle and thread or music lessons or reading lessons 'to widen her vocabulary' or, to Hannah's special delight, drawing lessons.

She soon showed an aptitude for art, especially the drawing of interesting gowns, and this, associated with her growing skills as a needlewoman, gave them both much pleasure. They planned clothes for Hannah, and with the dressmaker's assistance, made them up and were very content indeed with the results.

On Mondays and Wednesdays, Mary went to the Settlement as she had always done. Now that she had Hannah she would have gladly given up her charitable duties, but she was much too wise to do so. To let Davida suspect for a moment that she so much enjoyed the company of the child who had so insulted her would never have done, so she went serenely about her usual ways, leaving Hannah with much regret to the care of the housekeeper, Mrs Sarson.

Hannah spent those days learning to cook, once she had overcome Mrs Sarson's initial resistance to 'that charity child'. By the end of the year she was a capable hand with cakes, and was beginning to master the intricacies of pastry making and to understand the different ways of dealing with fish.

Though Hannah did not enjoy this aspect of her new education, she was wise enough to be silent on that score. She listened and learned and worked industriously at all she was asked to do, and at last received the grudging acceptance of the upper servants. The housemaids and footmen and bootboys, of course, ignored her. What else could they do to one who was of no greater status than they but who spent so much time with Madam? She was an anomaly and as such to be disregarded and despised.

Tuesdays and Thursdays were delightful days, for both Hannah and Mary. Then they wandered from shop to fashionable shop, and ate ices at Gunter's. To Hannah, Gunter's was splendid with its little tables at which the most beautifully dressed people ate ices and cakes and drank China tea out of perfect porcelain and chattered so busily they almost drowned the sound of the music played by the string quartet in the corner.

Hannah learned much about the city of her birth on those happy expeditions, discovering the beauties and excitement of Oxford Circus and Regent Street, Pall Mall and Piccadilly, the charms of Hyde Park and above all the theatre, for sometimes Mary took her to matinees. She would sit on the edge of her seat bewitched, watching the most beautiful actresses and unbelievably exquisite actors gyrate and dance or fall on their knees at each other in scenes of undying passion in which Hannah believed implicitly. She adored every moment. But she didn't plan to be an actress herself any more. Somehow that dream had burned out; she no longer needed it.

With each week that passed, Mary became ever more delighted with life. She had taken to her protégé because of her appearance, only her appearance. Red hair and blue eyes had opened the way for Hannah. To find therefore, as Mary did, that the child was an amusing chatterbox and therefore good company was a bonus she had not expected. She had wanted a doll to play with, a live doll to take the place of her dead one, and what she got was a genuine companion, someone with real warmth and real emotions who made her feel, for the first time in twenty years, that she was real herself. It was as though she had been encased in a transparent shell and Hannah was chipping away a gap ever more widely until Mary could emerge as a whole person again.

It was Daniel who first told her what had happened. He was paying a duty visit, for as a well brought up young man he knew the respect that was due to his aunts, and made the rounds of them punctiliously once a month. He watched her help Hannah with a piece of complicated knitting the child was struggling with, and then, when she had gone to her room up in the attic to fetch another ball of wool, said easily, 'That child clearly has made you very happy, Aunt Mary. Is she the same one who spat at Mama? The one I scooped up as she was running away?'

Mary reddened a little. 'Ah – What was that, dear? I don't quite remember. . . . '

Daniel laughed. 'Oh, come on, Aunt Mary. You can't bamboozle me! There can't be that many coppertops around. Mother told me you'd got a maggot in your head and taken in a charity child, but she never said it was this one.'

He grinned then, stretching out his legs and contemplating his boots with satisfaction. 'Mind you, under the circumstances I doubt she would. Would she?' He looked sideways at Mary with a wicked little glance, and Mary allowed herself a small smile in return. She had always had a very soft spot for this good looking nephew, even though he was the disagreeable Davida's son.

'It might be as well to say nothing of it,' she murmured. 'Of course your dear mother knows, but we don't discuss it, you know. I see no reason why we should.'

'Nor do I,' said Daniel heartily as Hannah came back. He smiled at her, and held out one hand and bade her come and talk to him.

Hannah, who had felt herself go hot all over the first time he had come visiting and who still went hot all over every succeeding time, stood at the door and folded her lips and shook her head, allowing herself to show her own will for the first time since arriving at Eaton Square. Mary looked surprised and Daniel amused as she blinked and turned and bobbed awkwardly at Mary and went away to hide until Daniel had gone.

Even when she reappeared after his departure, and Mary tried to discover why it was she had behaved so, she still kept her own counsel, and continued with unusual stubbornness to do so.

How could she do otherwise? Ever since that morning when Daniel Lammeck had caught her under her arms and lifted her high in the air to kick helplessly and impotently at him she had adored him. She saw him, very definitely, as the author of all her good fortune. If he had not so caught her, had not stopped her from escaping into Hanbury Street that March morning, she would not be here now, would she? That was why she thought so much about him, she told herself. That was why she thought him the handsomest, most agreeable person she had ever seen in all her life. And that was why he was at the core of every one of the stories and dreams with which she sent herself to sleep every night in her snug attic room.

23

Walking down to the corner shop was one of Bloomah's favourite activities. In the old days she'd gone rarely, sending Jake or Hannah when she had to because it was easier for them to ask Black Sophie to put it on the slate please, just for a day or two, than it was for her. On the occasions she'd had to do it she had stood there sick with shame, afraid to meet the other women's eyes and see their contempt, or worse, their pity; those had been bad days indeed. But not now, because of Hannah. She could walk down to the corner shop with her plaited straw bag in her hand and her chin up as high as any of her neighbour's.

Because of Hannah. She stopped at the chicken stall at the kerb outside the shop and tried not to think of Hannah. She chose a neat little fowl, just big enough for the five of them, yellow with fat and with a plump look that promised unlaid eggs, golden globes of deliciousness, lurking inside. She bought extra giblets, too, asking especially for *gorrigles*, the neck pieces; Hannah loved those after they'd been cooked in the soup and would sit happily for half an hour or more stripping the shreds of meat from the tiny bones with her teeth.

Not Hannah, she told herself. She won't be home to eat with us. Not till Friday. Today's only Tuesday. No Hannah till Friday. Don't think about her. Onions and carrots and potatoes at the vegetable stall alongside, big Joe scooping up the earth encrusted roots in his gleaming brass scoop so that they tumbled and rattled against the scales. A cabbage, with thick dark leaves, ideal for stuffing with minced soup meat from the butcher, to whom she could afford to go these days. Don't think of Hannah. And then Black Sophie's shop, smelling so powerfully of garlic pickles and salt herring and cream cheese and freshly baked bread that your mouth burst into saliva as you walked through the door.

They made way for her at the counter. Mrs Arbeiter of course – she was always there at this time of the morning, and Mrs Abrahams, and a clutch of younger wives with their small children bawling at their skirts. Bloomah nodded gravely at them and settled down to wait while one after the other they listed their wants, and watched eagle eyed as Sophie measured out cheese and weighed out ounces of tea into twists of heavy blue paper and bestowed a few broken biscuits on the children, while the women chattered. The women of the quarter didn't need a newspaper. They *were* a newspaper.

'So she was in labour twelve hours and nothing happening, I tell you even Mother Charnik from Christian Street, she said she'd never seen such a case, so they have to get the doctor out no less, from the hospital, you shouldn't know of such things and you know what he had to do?' The voice dropped, became confidential, and was overwhelmed by Jenny, who had the highest and shrillest voice of any of them. ' – So the teacher says to me, she says, he's a very bright boy, Mrs Fishman, you should understand so bright I haven't had one like him in years, and I want he should have his opportunities, so I'm putting his name down for the scholar-ship to Raine's Foundation School, and meanwhile we got to worry about buying the uniform, such a performance. You won't have such worries by your Morry, please God.'

And Mrs Kellerman, bristling. 'My Morry? Already he knows all his colours and can count up to twenty and only just walking, already so soon! Believe me, we'll have the same problem as you in spades, and before the boy's ten years old, that's for sure.'

' . . . and when the bandages came off, the agony! Six babies I had, and never do I know of such agony as from that leg! I said to Sam, I said, if your mother God rest her dear soul in peace had had half the suffering what I get, she'd never have got up and cooked and cleaned for you the way I do – the lazy *shloch* that she was.'

'My Sadie, already she's got three boys looking at her serious, such a dolly she is! Won't be fourteen till next High Holy Days. Please God no harm should come to her, and already she's such a well developed girl, we'll have to make a nice early *shidduch* for her, and how's by your Hannah, Mrs Lazar? Just a bit younger than my Sadie, ain't she? Give or take a month or two ... so how is she? She meeting nice boys and all where she is?'

The shop slithered into an expectant silence and Bloomah smiled as easily as she could. 'Hannah? She's very well, thank you. Getting very tall of course, and such a beauty – but thank God I don't have such problems with her as boys. At her age it would be a great worry to me, and I can imagine how you must worry, Mrs Arbeiter, believe me. It's not easy, girls working in the factories, to keep such an eye on them as is necessary. Hannah, thank God, is well looked after – '

'Oh, I'm not so sure,' Mrs Arbeiter said with a fine judicious air. 'Girls is interested in boys no matter how careful they get to be watched over. You was interested I dare say, and so was I, and why should our girls be any different? At least in the factories the girls meet only Jewish boys. In a place like your Hannah's she might meet anyone, God forbid.'

'It's a good Jewish house!' Bloomah said, stung into dropping her guard. 'The richest place you ever saw, believe me.'

'Sure, I know,' Mrs Arbeiter smiled sweetly, revealing blackened front teeth. 'But it's not like your Hannah is exactly living with them, eh? I mean, they have men servants, don't they? And they ain't Jewish boys, that's for sure. *Shagetses* every one of 'em – it must be a great worry to you. . . . ' And she swept out of the shop like a galleon in full sail, giving Bloomah no chance to riposte.

She went home feeling the weight of her loneliness more heavily than her laden shopping bag. Of course Mrs Arbeiter was right. What sort of life was it for a nice girl from a decent Jewish family, being in such an occupation? Poor they may always have been, she and Nathan, but they never had had any problems such as the one Mrs Arbeiter had so cruelly underlined. Hannah *was* exposed to influences that could damage her; might indeed get so involved with the servants in that house that she would marry out of the faith.

Don't be stupid, she told herself as she climbed the stairs to her flat. Don't be stupid. You know how it is there. That woman dotes on your Hannah. Treats her like her own child. There's no risk she'll ever let her come to such a harm as that. No risk. And anyway, she's changed Hannah so much she'd frighten off anybody who ever looked at her. She's not like

229

a child of mine any more.

That was the worst part of all for Bloomah. Not the shame of having to depend on the earnings of so young a child to keep the family, not the pain of missing her so cruelly from Sunday morning to Friday afternoon, but the pain of change. The scrawny little ten-year-old who had gone to be companion to Mrs Lammeck three years ago had disappeared inside the handsome, self-possessed young woman who came in her carriage each Friday afternoon laden with baskets of food and clothes and sometimes even more exotic gifts like a bottle of brandy and a couple of cigars for Nathan. Bloomah's Hannah had been dreamy but biddable, an untidy child with frizzy hair and a bouncing vigour who looked out at the world with unquenchable excitement behind her bright blue eyes. Mrs Lammeck's Hannah was quite different. Always polite and cheerful, never obviously dreamy and certainly never excited. She wore her hair brushed sleekly over her forehead now, its natural curl well controlled by the attentions of Mary's hairdresser. Her eyes were watchful. Her figure, well rounded and mature for nearly fourteen, looked neat and controlled beneath the expensive clothes, and she moved carefully, with none of the hoydenish bounce of her young years.

All of which of course had to happen, Bloomah told herself, as she unpacked her purchases and stored them away in the metal mesh food safe on the window to catch whatever cool breezes there were this hot August day. If she'd stayed here with us she'd still have grown up, wouldn't she?

It was not Hannah's emerging womanhood that hurt her. It was the remoteness of Hannah that edged its way under Bloomah's skin and made her so irritable on each of those much longed for yet miserable weekends. Hannah would sit beside the table in the front room, a cup of lemon tea and a slice of Bloomah's best cheesecake in front of her, and in every neat movement of her hands, every small and tidy bite, Bloomah read criticism. Hannah never said anything about the way they lived; about Nathan's noisy eating or the way the boys gobbled their food, nor about the flat, with its overcrowded furniture and the flies that could not be kept out and the reek of pine disinfectant that struggled to overwhelm the stench of vagrant cats on the stairs, against whom Bloomah fought an unending battle. She never complained at having to sleep on the sofa with broken springs, that had to be dragged out onto the landing at night, so that she need not share the front room with her brothers. But in Hannah's silence, Bloomah found pain. It shouldn't be that way, and she knew it. But she could do nothing about it, so she turned her distress against Hannah, feeling that in her silence she was scorning her parents, and her home.

Somewhere deep inside herself she knew she was wrong; that it was inevitable that Hannah would notice the difference between the luxury she knew all week and the poverty of her East End weekends, and that to blame the child for noticing was cruel. It was wrong, too, to blame her for her new manners, her tidy style of eating, her way of sitting with her knees together and her back straight, her hands clasped quietly in her lap. Clearly she had been taught to behave so by Mary Lammeck and it had become second nature to her. Under the circumstances Hannah could not help becoming better behaved than the people from whom she sprang, any more than she could be blamed for the way she spoke. As a child she had sounded like every other child of the quarter. Her speech had been nasal, tinged with that curious mixture of cockney and the sing-song intonation bought to London from the shtetls of Russia and Poland. Now she spoke in a well modulated voice, with neat, clipped vowels and the nasal sound quite gone. Is that something to resent in your own child? Bloomah would ask herself. Of course it isn't – but still she resented it, for it was Mary's teaching, Mary's way of life, Mary's ideas her own and only beloved girl was imbibing, not her mother's.

Bloomah took refuge from the confusion of love and deprivation and resentment that filled her in the only way she could. She remained silent. The long weekend would pass with her sitting there beside the table most of the time, not talking at all while Hannah tried to make conversation – another of the things she had been taught was the right way to behave. The harder Hannah tried, the more monosyllabic Bloomah became. Bloomah was aching to pour out all her fury and distress and then to hug her daughter close; but that she could not, indeed would not, do. I may be poor, she would think grimly, but I got my pride.

Inevitably her feelings about her daughter spilled over into her behaviour towards the rest of the family. Nathan, descending ever deeper into his own resentments, spent less and less time at home. There seemed little point in it, for Bloomah sat as silent with him as she did with Hannah. Each morning he disappeared with his packet of pens and paper, making a pathetic attempt to pretend he was going to work, and Bloomah watched him go and ached to be closer to him as much as she ached for Hannah, and was as incapable of letting him know.

As for the boys, they inhabited a world of their own. She cooked and cleaned for them, and washed their clothes, and let them be. Solly, a boisterous ten-year-old, found most of his joy in the streets just as his big brother had once done. He would come home from school, on the occasions he actually went (for he was an inveterate truant, and very good at not being caught), to take a slice of bread smeared with chicken fat and then run out into the street 'to play'. To him it was play, though to most of the neighbours what he and his cronies got up to was rather more sinister. They were accomplished petty thieves, young Solly and his friends, Barney and Issy, getting apples from street stalls and lollipops from corner shops, lifting handkerchiefs and old clothes and bric-a-brac of various sorts from busy stalls in Petticoat Lane, anything that could be tucked easily beneath a shabby jacket, then sold to other stalls further down the Lane. At home, though, Solly was silent, knowing well that silence was what Bloomah liked best. Or seemed to.

Sometimes he would go to the gym in Leman Street, a dispirited building containing little more than a roped-off open space and a few battered chairs. There he would watch his brother Jake sweating heavily as he tried to work up the skill he was sure he had somewhere deep inside him, if only he could get it out – the skill of hitting an opponent harder and faster than the opponent could hit him. Sometimes Uncle Alex would be there, too, watching the sweating would-be boxers with a sardonic look on his face, and when Solly saw him, he would melt away and take to the street again. Uncle Alex didn't approve of ten-year-olds in the gym, and had been known to make his disapproval felt. Although not a boxer himself, he still knew enough about the fight game to be able to handle even someone as tough and quick on his feet as young Solly, when he chose to.

Solly loved the gym. He loved the smell of sweat and old

232

rubber shoes and dust all overlaid heavily with the pungence of liniment. He loved the way the boxers grunted and snorted as they dodged around the ring, though most of the boys with real talent, the ones with the intelligence to see blows coming and to parry them rather than mere sluggers who just hit out, went to the better gym, the one that Solly had heard his Uncle Alex owned, down near Limehouse police station.

Solly knew that Jake took boxing with deadly seriousness. He was supposed to be a lathe operator for his Uncle Reuben but turned up at the factory as rarely as he could, complaining of aches and pains and ills galore to cover his absences: Reuben shrugged and said nothing. He didn't pay Jake, of course, if he didn't work, so why upset his sister-in-law by telling her of her older son's defections? Let him explain to her why he came home from work with no money to give her. It wasn't Reuben's problem.

Not that Jake ever did explain. Somehow he lurched from financial disaster to financial crisis and got through. There was always a side bet to be made, always a bit of dealing to be done in the Lane, above all always Uncle Alex to touch for a loan. Uncle Alex always came through. He would just nod, then shake his head and hand over the cash, and say nothing. It was, after all, another way of helping his stupid brother Nathan without his knowing it, and Alex, for all his busy life and his boxers and his thriving coffee stalls and his own dealings in and about Petticoat Lane still cared for his brother Nathan and, curiously, felt a guilt about him, though the rest of the family had long since stopped bothering about his complaints, regarding him simply as the family failure who deserved all that happened to him. But Alex felt sorry for his brother, and wanted to pay back the debt his parents had incurred; so, shelling out for Jake pleased him. The fact that it didn't do much for Jake, whatever it did for Nathan, did not escape him. But Alex was an observant man. He looked at his nephew with clear eyes and recognized his central tragedy; the possession of a huge ambition and no talent with which to achieve it. 'Poor devil,' he would think, and slip him a sovereign. 'Poor *shlemiel*. What'll he ever be? Not even a boxer.'

When Hannah came home for those painful yet so yearned for weekends, she would sit and listen to her mother's silence

233

and weave complex dreams in her head, about how one day she would change everything for them all, not only for Bloomah and Nathan but for Jake and Solly too. One day, when she was old enough, she'd find a way to make it better for all of them, just as it was better for her now. One day. Meanwhile, there was Mary Lammeck and the peace and luxury of life at Eaton Square to see her through the years of waiting.

<h1 style="text-align:center">24</h1>

Hannah was combing Mary's hair, and Mary sat with her eyes half shut, enjoying the sensation, peaceful and comfortable.

Now, Hannah wondered? If I ask her now will it be a good time? Or would it be too soon? If she has too much time to think about it, she'll get upset. If I leave it till just before, maybe it'll be easier. Or maybe she'll already have made a plan and be upset about changing it.

'Mrs Mary,' she said softly, turning the tortoiseshell comb with an expert glide of her wrist as she reached the end of a stroke. 'My Uncle Alex has sent me a letter.'

'A letter, Hannah? That's nice,' Mary said dreamily and then, a little more sharply, 'There's nothing wrong, I hope? You said everyone was well when you came back this week.'

'Oh, no, Mrs Mary, nothing at all. Everything was fine.'

Everything was just the same as ever, Bloomah seeming a little whiter and thinner and a little more tired, and as silent as ever, Nathan still haranguing the corners of the room, and the boys bigger and noisier but just the same old boys. Everything was fine.

'He's the one I told you about, you remember? The one who used to work in the theatre?'

Mary smiled, tilting her chin back so that Hannah could more easily reach the crown of her head. 'I remember. The one who's done so well. The one your father doesn't like.'

'Not doesn't *like*,' Hannah said, quick to Nathan's defence. 'Everyone likes Uncle Alex. It's just that he's Poppa's younger brother, you see, and he doesn't think ... it doesn't seem right that – well, you know how it is! Poppa gets upset if Uncle Alex tries to help, and Momma gets upset when Poppa gets upset, and then the boys shout as well and ...'

'And you're glad to get home to me, hmm, Hannah?' Mary smiled gently at her in the mirror, but there was a watchfulness behind her eyes. Even after all this time, seven years of having Hannah with her from Sunday to Friday, there was a shred of anxiety in her. Would she just not come back one Sunday? Would the carriage return without her, and bring instead a peremptory message to say she was going to stay with her parents now? Each week Mary would stand at the drawing room window, watching through the curtains until the horses came spanking round the Square to deliver Hannah at the front steps and would breathe again as the small figure appeared in the carriage door, foreshortened but unmistakeable. She had her Hannah back for another week, and her fragile happiness was secure. Till the next Friday came, and with it that nibble of jealousy and doubt that always came to fill the void left by the girl's departure. Even after seven years of returns.

'You know I'm always glad to see you, Mrs Mary,' Hannah said carefully. Home was Antcliff Street, happy as she was here in Eaton Square. Eaton Square she thought of as work. Home was where Bloomah and Nathan were, miserable though it was. Poor Mrs Mary! she thought now. Poor Mrs Mary!

'Uncle Alex's letter,' she said. 'He sent it to me here. I got it this morning.'

'That's nice,' Mary said, and waited, carefully blankfaced.

'It's his business,' Hannah said. 'I told you about his business?'

'Which one, Hannah?' Mary said, and her lips curved. After a moment Hannah smiled too.

'He's a busy person,' she said, still a little defensive. 'It's good to be busy. You've said that yourself.'

'But how busy can a man be?' Mary was smiling more widely than ever now, feeling somehow that there was no threat to her peace of mind in Alex Lazar's letter, and Hannah, swift as she always was at identifying Mary's thoughts, struck quickly.

'It's his tea shops,' she said, and put the comb down and began to braid Mary's hair. 'He's opening up one in the West

End now. It's his third one, and it's to be in Tottenham Court Road, and he's having a special party to launch it, with a gypsy band and all the family there, and he says he wants me to come. It's on Sunday afternoon. I thought you wouldn't mind, seeing all the family will be there. Can I tell him? He's got a telephone now, and he said I could ring him on it.'

The telephone was commonplace in Eaton Square and unsurprising to Hannah in that setting, but in East London, even in Hackney, they were a rarity. Hannah was quite sure her uncle was the only Jew in the whole district who had one, and was deeply impressed by it; just for once, she needed to impress Mary too. It wasn't easy to have anything with which to impress a Lammeck, not when you were a Lazar.

'Sunday afternoon?' Mary said blankly and looked at Hannah through the mirror, letting the appeal show in her face, but Hannah went on industriously braiding her hair, avoiding looking at her. 'This Sunday afternoon?'

'I would be back here about seven o'clock, I expect. Uncle Alex'll see to it that I get back all right. He's very careful.'

'I'm sure he is,' Mary said. 'Very careful. Sunday until seven?'

'About seven,' Hannah said, and pinned the braid carefully. 'There, does that feel right? It looks nice.'

'Very nice,' Mary said. 'In Tottenham Court Road, you say? I could come in the carriage.'

'It's the family,' Hannah said and this time lifted her eyes to look directly at Mary. 'Momma will be there. She doesn't often go anywhere now, but Uncle Alex insists this time. He's sending a carriage for everyone all the way to Antcliff Street. It's very important, he says.'

Mary nodded, her face still. 'Yes, of course. I do see that. His third tea shop, you say? That's very good, isn't it?'

'He had just a stall once, outside the Yiddish Theatre, you know? Just a stall, and now he's got a proper shop in Whitechapel Road and one in Mare Street, in Hackney. It's got marble topped tables, that one, and waitresses. They wear frilled aprons and caps just like your maids. It's very nice. And now this one in Tottenham Court Road. It's really very important.'

'Of course it is,' Mary said, and now she smiled. 'I'm sure you'll enjoy it very much. I'll still send the carriage on Sunday morning though, with a few things. I've got a dress for your mother.'

'Yes,' Hannah said. 'Thank you. That will be nice.' After a momentary pause, she bent and kissed Mary's cheek. It was not something she did very often, and Mary went pink with delight. 'Momma will be pleased, I know.'

If only I could share her, the way they do, Mary told herself bleakly, as she sat later that evening watching Hannah's fingers flickering in and out of the sewing in her lap. They share her with me, why can't I share her with them? She's theirs, not mine. I've had her for seven years, but she's still theirs.

The seven years had dealt generously with Hannah. Her hair had lost some of its carroty look and had settled to a deeper copper gloss that shone rich and clean from good food and careful washing, and her once pinched narrow face had filled out. She had a small pointed chin that looked unexpected under those round cheeks, but endearingly so, and her eyes remained as rich a blue as ever. Some blue eyed children settled to slaty grey in adolescence, Mary knew; she had seen many who had lost their childhood richness for a less exciting maturity. But not her Hannah. *Their* Hannah. She looked exactly as Mary's dead child, grown up, had been meant to look. She knew that now. For seven years she had been free to live, no longer trammelled by the memory of her dead baby, for she had a real child now, one who could move from awkward bony immaturity to young womanhood without damaging herself or Mary. She had breasts now, this replacement child of Mary's, surprisingly full ones for a girl of seventeen, and a rounded bottom that gave her back a hollowness that made the men who came to the house look and then look again. Mary had seen their eyes move across that rich shape, and felt her own lips curve with pleasure at the sight of them. Men *should* be bewitched by her Hannah, just as she had been herself, just as she still was. That was the way it ought to be. Mary did not feel at all perturbed at the idea of sharing Hannah with outsiders like that. Only with her own people. The thought of next Sunday deadened her spirits.

But it lifted Hannah's. She sat and sewed, setting tucks in a grey silk bodice for Mary, and though her head was bent and she seemed totally absorbed in her work, she was as uncomfortably aware of Mary's thoughts as if the woman had spoken them aloud. Hannah cared for her, indeed she did; how could she do otherwise? Her whole life had been changed by her. It had of course been Daniel who had been the real instrument of her good fortune; she still felt that, but she knew it was Mary's love for her that kept it so buoyant and she was genuinely grateful. Still, she couldn't give back the unstinting love that Mary so much wanted and pleaded for so wordlessly. That sort of love belonged to Bloomah. It was Bloomah Hannah worried about, Bloomah whose needs she fretted over. And Bloomah from whom she felt most parted between Sundays and Fridays.

Hannah often thought of her mother as the days went smoothly past on their elegantly oiled wheels. When she sat beside Mary's bed each morning with her own breakfast on a small table, as Mary took hers from a tray, and read letters aloud to her, she saw Bloomah at home in the crowded room in Antcliff Street, moving awkwardly between the huddled furniture, making her own breakfast of a slice of bread with caraway seeds and a scrape of cream cheese, alone because the boys had gone, Jake to his uncle's stick factory and Solly to his school, or the streets, and Nathan to wherever it was Nathan went each morning. It had been a long time, Hannah knew, since he had earned anything from his pen. The number of people who needed letters written in Russian and Polish had steadily dwindled, and anyway, more and more children were educated now. Parents who spoke only Yiddish had children who had learned good plain English at their Board schools, and they dealt with their families' legal forms, if any, and such letters as they needed. No one had a use for Nathan any more.

Bloomah sat alone in her room in Antcliff Street, staring out of the window at the cobbles and the passers by, eating bread and cheese, while her daughter sat beside a bed furnished with satin sheets and ate curled toast and rich farm butter and strawberry jam from the finest china, and thought about her, guiltily and miserably, and with an aching need that she knew she could never express.

For each Friday when she climbed the stairs to the family's two rooms and landing, and Mary's carriage went clattering away, Hannah pulled the shutter down. She and Bloomah spent most of their time together in silence. There might be the odd conversation that never did more than skim the surface of either mind. They would avoid each other's eyes and show none of their hunger for each other, for even after seven years neither Bloomah nor Hannah could forgive themselves for their defection of each other. And neither could they speak of their pain. The longer the silence between them went on, the harder it became to break it. Thank God, Hannah would think every Friday, for the men. Thank God for the way they niggled at each other, as Jake teased Solly about his cluster of girlfriends, and Solly jeered at Jake about his lack of any, and Nathan roared at all of them indiscriminately.

Now, sewing Mary's new gown, she deliberately closed her mind to the waves of anxiety Mary was directing at her, and thought about Uncle Alex and next Sunday. She saw him far too rarely, she thought now, not nearly as much as she would have liked. I wonder what it would be like to see him as often as I see Mrs Mary, she thought. I wonder what would happen if Daniel happened to walk by the new tea shop next Sunday, and happened to see me there, and happened to come in? She let her mind slide away into a lovely fantasy, one of the nicest she'd invented for a long time. Mary's clamouring silence at last receded from her mind, and she was comfortable again, as comfortable as she could be only when she had shut out all the real things there were, and was left with the pretences that she could control for herself. That was the best sort of living there was, for Hannah.

When Sunday afternoon came it was almost as good as one of her private imaginings. Riding up to the West End in Uncle Alex's carriage was somehow much more exciting than the ritual Sunday journey to Eaton Square. Her two brothers sat opposite her, resplendent in new celluloid collars and well oiled violet-scented hair. Her father gave them a running commentary on the passing scenery as though none of them had ever seen it before, and Bloomah sat beside her, silent as usual but looking remarkably handsome in her dark blue dress, the only one of the many that Mary had sent for her that she had ever seemed to like wearing. Hannah looked at her sideways and smiled, and Bloomah, without thinking, smiled back. For a moment a fragile thread of understanding hung in the air between them. Then Bloomah turned her

239

head and looked out of the window and it was gone, blown away in the chill draught. But never mind, Hannah thought, never mind. It will get better, when Momma feels better. She's looking better.

Which was a lie, of course. She wasn't. She was looking thinner every time Hannah saw her, a thinness which suited her, for her cheeks seemed translucent and young, the lines of her middle age and fatigue stretched out to invisibility on the taut skin, and her hair, still as thick and curly as it had been in her girlhood, exuberant over that sharpened little face. She looked handsome, but she did not look healthy.

They arrived at the same time as the carriage Uncle Alex had sent for Uncle Reuben's family. Hannah stood beside Bloomah as the cousins surged around them, kissing cheeks and exclaiming, smiling and nodding as Rachel and Leon and Rivka and Bertha, Hyman and Jack and Ann, a noisy gaggle of adolescents, carried their parents, the large and self satisfied Reuben and the eternally weary Minnie, triumphantly into Uncle Alex's new establishment.

Hannah stood in the door staring around her, and her mouth curved with delight. It was a beautiful place, really beautiful. Two of the walls were lined with engraved glass, great sweeps of fern and flowers and incredibly feathered birds depicted on each panel, and there was at the far end a wall as lavishly furnished in carved mahogany. The floor was a clattering terrazzo of white and black squares, and there were marble topped tables, each equipped with four wrought iron chairs. A long table covered with heavy damask had been set down the middle of the shop, laden with plates of rolls with smoked salmon on them, and rolls with pickled herrings on them and rolls with cream cheese and fresh cucumber on them, and rolls with heaven knows what else on them. There were cakes of all sorts, and bowls piled high with fresh fruit. There were mountains of sweet biscuits, and sweets in brilliant colours and chocolates and more bowls of fruit. There were two great shining samovars, steaming seductively, and the table was draped with so much smilax and trailing maidenhair fern that the cloth beneath could only just be seen.

Uncle Reuben's collection stood poised for a moment and then surged forward in a mass, with Hannah's brothers very close behind them, and joined their Uncle Benjamin and

Aunt Sarah who were already swooping around the table with plates at the ready, to chatter and exclaim over the riches they were offered, while several large men in very expensive looking dark suits and matching wives, friends of Uncle Alex, helped themselves equally avidly from the other side of the table.

'So, Hannah, dolly? What do you say, hmm?' Uncle Alex had appeared at her side, and she turned to him eagerly and lifted her cheek to be kissed. He smelled as always of bay rum and chypre combined, and his eyes glinted at her from beneath his prematurely white hair. His face, round and jovial, so much younger and healthier looking than any of his brothers, beamed at her as he took her by both shoulders and held her away from him to stare at her.

'Such a girl!' he said and shook his head in mock disbelief. 'How come such a misery as Nathan should produce such a beauty, hey? You look good enough to eat on dry toast without any butter, dolly. So tell me, what do you think?'

'It's beautiful, Uncle Alex,' Hannah said truthfully, and turned to look again at the tea shop and the marble tables around which the families had scattered to settle to the serious business of demolishing Alex's heapings of provisions. 'Really beautiful.'

'Got class, hey?' Alex peered at her sharply, and his eyebrows quirked. She laughed and said, 'It's lovely . . . I said it was.'

'But dolly, has it got the right – you know what I mean! Who else do I have I can ask such a question, hey? Everyone else in this family, they think I'm the *gunsa macher*, the big one, the know all. Me, I'm the maven to them. No one knows better than Alex. But *you* don't think that, on account you hang around with the real thing, the ones who got so much class it's crawling out o' their *tochusses* you should forgive the expression.'

'Listen, Uncle Alex,' Hannah said earnestly. 'It's *beautiful*. It's the nicest tea shop I ever saw.'

'Peeh pah pooh, a tea shop! Of course it is! Better fixed up than Gunter's, better than Gatti's, better than all them! See those potted palms there? Cost me more'n your Mrs Lammeck pays her servants a week, believe me, and that's a lot. And that band – you hear that band?' No one could fail to hear it, playing as it was a very lively mazurka with

241

enormous gusto, the players in their exaggeratedly sleeved cream silk shirts and red cummerbunds and trousers tucked into shiny boots leaping and stamping about till the crystal chandelier overhead rang with the excitement. 'Cost me more'n she pays for *two* weeks' wages! It's not that I'm asking, dolly. I want to know, does it have *class*? Like at your Mrs Lammeck's house? I want my tea shop should look like her drawing room, you understand me? Not like Gunter's, but like *real* class.'

Hannah looked at the glittering scene in front of her and conjured up the quiet expanse of the Eaton Square drawing room with its velvet sofas and the hand blocked Chinese wallpapers and its all pervading silence and laughed aloud and said, 'Mrs Lameck's drawing room, Uncle Alex? It's *better* – much better.'

He put his arm about her shoulders and hugged her and pulled her away to collect a heaped plate of food she knew she'd never be able to finish and then sat her at a table with her cousins Charlotte and David, two of Uncle Benjamin's brood, while he went rushing about from one group to another, here insisting that someone take more cheesecake, there heaping a plate with cherries, all the time chivvying his sweating waitresses in their over-frilled uniforms to feed everyone faster and faster and more and more. And Hannah watched him and enjoyed him because he was patently enjoying himself so much. He was dressed in his best clothes, a suit of dark green checks and very gleaming white shirt and even more gleaming patent leather shoes and his face out-shone both with sweat and excitement. He had been white haired now for almost three years, and it suited him, that great crest of frosty waves; beneath it his face was the same young one she had always known, and his voice was the same booming cheerful sound that had lifted her childhood spirits whenever she heard it. She did love him dearly, she told herself, watching him. It's so easy and comfortable to love Uncle Alex. Not like Momma....

She pushed that thought away and turned to talk to her cousins, though it wasn't easy; David was a serious minded young person who was an even more assiduous Talmudic scholar than his father, dark eyed and thin faced and very intense, and rather scornful of females, and Charlotte was interested only in possible husbands. Since none were present at this solely family party she was patently bored, so when Alex returned to slide one hand under Hannah's elbow and take her away Hannah was grateful.

He led her to the end of the room to the curtained window that showed the darkening pavements of Tottenham Court Road outside, for it was now six o'clock and the autumn afternoon was dwindling.

'So, tell me, dolly,' he said. 'You really like my shop?'

'I love it, Uncle Alex,' she said and laughed at him, her eyes bright. 'You've made it beautiful. Those mirrors, you'd think it was a place twice as big as it is.'

'Four times,' he said, 'maybe five. And one day it will be. And I'll tell you something else. One day I'll have dozens.'

He swept his hand round in a comprehensive gesture, then reached into his pocket with the other hand to take out a slim gold case.

'Cigarette, dolly? No? Well, you will one day. All the classy ladies smoke now, they tell me. So, how goes it in your fancy Lammeck house, hmm? Enjoying life, are you?'

'Yes thank you, Uncle Alex. It's very nice.' She was cautious now, for she had always found it difficult to talk to Uncle Alex about her relationship with Mary Lammeck. He looked at her so much more knowingly than any other member of the family did, and seemed so much more aware than any of them. He knew, as none of the other uncles and aunts and cousins seemed to know, how anomalous her position was. Neither servant nor equal, she was an interloper in the Eaton Square household, and she knew it. Mary might regard her as her companion, almost as an adopted child; Mr Lammeck did not, seeing her only as his wife's personal maid. The other servants didn't quite know how to see her, regarding her as much less lofty than a real lady's maid would be and far from their equal. And Daniel – he was not to be thought of at all.

'Neither fish, nor fowl nor good red herring,' Alex said sapiently, and took out one of his cigarettes and lit it with a match taken from a gold Vesta box in his waistcoat pocket. The scent of the Turkish tobacco drifted over her head and she looked away, her face a little pink.

'I don't know what you mean,' she said a little stuffily.

'Oh, dolly, of course you do! You know exactly what I mean. Listen. I got ideas. You know that. I always have ideas, but this one, this is an idea and another again, it's so good.'

She smiled, glad he'd moved away from his previous tack. 'What idea?'

'I told you. I'm going to expand. Dozens of places like this I'm going to have, only bigger and better and classier. You know about class now, Hannah, hey? You've got style like no one else in this family ever had, nor'll ever hope to have, apart from me, o' course. So what d'you say, dolly? Isn't it time you left off being a servant to these fancy Yidden who reckon they're so much better than you and me, hey? Time you came and worked with your Uncle Alex and showed 'em what we can really do when we try? What d'you say, Hannah? Come and be my manageress. Here.'

25

In a way, it was Mary's own fault that Hannah was so well able to deceive her. Hannah had long ago learned to emulate Mary's tricks of hiding her true feelings behind a mask of calm uninterest. It had not been difficult for her, for had she not, from her own earliest childhood, taught herself to keep her own secrets behind a smooth quiet face? So it was that she was able to return to Eaton Square and assure Mary gravely that thank you, yes, she had enjoyed Uncle Alex's party, and no, there had been no problems, and should she fetch Mary's beaded bag now, so that she could explain exactly what repairs it was she wanted made to it? And show no sign of the turmoil into which Uncle Alex had thrown her.

They settled to another quiet Sunday evening, Mary in her usual comfortable high backed chair beside the fire, and Hannah on a broad stool at her feet, with no sound to disturb them but the muffled traffic from beyond the shrouded windows and the occasional crackle of coals in the grate. Mary watched Hannah dreamily, enjoying the way the firelight moved across her copper hair, and was content, and Hannah sewed the crystal beads on to the bag delicately and with sure movements and tried to decide what to do.

To work with Uncle Alex, in his business – it was an

awesome prospect. All through her childhood he had moved in and out of her life like a glittering river in a far prospect, sometimes showing only gleams of reflected light, sometimes rising to inundate the whole of the land like a sea tide, sometimes lying low and quiet; but always *there*. Even when he was away about his own business and no one in the family saw him for weeks, they talked about him, as long as Poppa wasn't there to hear, of course. Uncle Alex had done such and such, had you heard? Uncle Alex is starting up this and that, did you know? Uncle Alex, Uncle Alex, Uncle Alex. In the days before her life in Eaton Square had begun, he had been the only source of excitement in her existence, outside her own imaginings.

And now he was offering her the chance to be part of that life. To be almost his equal. He had made that very clear.

'I'm not looking for a dogsbody, Hannah, get that straight. I can get anyone for that – the streets are lousy with people I can get to work for me for flumpence. That's not what I want. I need a partner, a real helper, you understand? Someone I can trust. So, I got no children. I have to look to the rest of the family, don't I? My brothers' children. And what do I see? All respect, dolly, but Jake and Solly I don't find interesting. Good boys, I'm sure. Got a bit o' charm about them, I suppose, and your Momma and Poppa love 'em, but they ain't what I need, though mind you, Solly might be a useful little welter weight one of these days. But a partner in business – no, that he ain't. As for Reuben's lot – trouble with them is they all stick together like bulls' eyes in a paper bag. You got one, you got the lot. And I don't want Reuben knowing no more about my affairs than is strictly necessary. As for Benjamin's three ... '

He lifted his eyes to the ceiling. 'Bella's courting, so count her out, a rabbi I don't need, and a girl who thinks of nothing but catching a husband I also don't have a use for. And then I look at you, and what do I see?'

She had said nothing, and he had grinned then, his face creasing with delight.

'I see a right careful madam,' he said. 'Never say a word, do you, until you got something useful to say? I like that. A person that's good at keeping her own business to herself'll be just as good about keeping mine. I got a long way to go, Hannah. Come with me, what do you say? There aren't that many chances for a girl, after all. Are there?'

Not many chances for a girl. Hannah sat and sewed and tried to see how her life would be if she didn't go with Uncle Alex. Stay here with Mrs Mary? For how long? And to what end? There were servants in the house who had worked here for years, twice as long as she had herself or even longer. She saw them moving about the great house like the well-trained shadows they were, giving no signs of having any life of their own beyond the brooms and dusters they pushed for the Lammecks. What sort of future did they have that was any better than their anonymous past? Was that what would happen to her? That Mary needed her and relied on her she knew, but there could be no guarantees of future happiness in that. Mary herself was under the domination of Emmanuel, that remote and unpredictable figure who still sometimes stopped Hannah when he met her in the hall and pinched her cheek and gave her shillings, as though she were yet a child. But suppose one day he took it into his head to send her away? Then what? Back to Bloomah in Antcliff Street. Back to Momma. And a job in Uncle Reuben's or Uncle Isaac's factory, grey shawled and grey faced with fatigue, spending her day in the reek of tailor's soap and the steam from the great goose irons and human sweat and wool fat and machine oil.

She sewed a little faster. Or go with Uncle Alex, to the excitement of a totally novel sort of life. Running first his new tea shop. 'Just to get the feel of the way they run, these places,' he had said. 'And then help me get the next few off the ground. Me, I got other business to sort out. I got a couple of boys with so much talent they drip it out when they sweat, and I'm going to set up fights for them as'll bring the whole boxing fraternity to a standstill. But I need time for that. Someone I can trust here.'

But how can I leave her? Hannah looked up at Mary, who smiled back at her and then rested her head comfortably against her chair back and closed her eyes to nap a little. How can I? She'll be ... impossible.

And Daniel. That would be impossible too. Not to see him once a month, when he came visiting, and sat beside his aunt chatting about the family and about his visits to theatres and parties, and carefully not talking about his mother. Not to be able to feed her imaginings with that regular injection of his presence; that would be misery.

But be honest, Hannah, one part of her mind admonished herself, be honest. Isn't it time you stopped this nonsense? You're an adult now, seventeen years old. You can't go on telling yourself stories the way you used to on the lavatory roof. To imagine Daniel ... It's crazy.

Just as crazy as the way I used to imagine being rich and wearing beautiful gowns and living in a beautiful house. And that happened, didn't it? Or something a little like it.

A servant. That's all you are. A servant.

Mary stirred in her chair and opened her eyes and for a moment Hannah saw in Mary's sleep-startled face the reality of the older woman's feeling for her. There was a desperate longing in those pallid eyes, a passionate need that frightened her. She hooded her own eyes and looked back at her work and knew that the decision had been made. That look in Mary's eyes could not be ignored. To leave her now to do what she wanted to do would be more than selfish; it would be cruel, and that was something Hannah could not be.

And anyway, she told herself bleakly, what would Momma say? With Poppa so angry all the time with Uncle Alex? If she went to work for him, imagine the fuss. And where would she live? She thought of her warm neat room high in the attic of this house, and of Antcliff Street and marvelled at herself. How could she have ever thought it possible to listen to Uncle Alex's siren song? He'd find a way round all the problems, of course, or would think he could, just by finding her somewhere to live, telling her to shrug her shoulders at her father the way he did; but it could never be her way, which was the way of pleasing as many people as possible, excluding herself.

Oh, hell, Hannah thought uncharacteristically. Oh, damn. Oh dear.

But the making of decisions was taken from her, as events turned out.

She arrived as usual at Eaton Square on Sunday two weeks after Uncle Alex's party to find, to her amazement, that Emmanuel was closeted with Mary, and she was able to go to her room and take off her coat before presenting herself at the drawing room door, a reversal of her usual practice, for Mary could never bear to wait a moment longer than she had to to welcome her. When she did tap on the door and slip in quietly Emmanuel greeted her with a crisp nod and told her gruffly to come and make herself useful to her mistress.

He was sitting very upright on the sofa, with Mary looking anxious in her usual chair. Hannah went and stood behind her, her hands folded on her neat green skirt in front of her. She was looking particularly well today, she knew. The skirt was cut on the newest bell shaped lines, and made the most of her neat waist, and the lemon coloured frilled blouse lifted her hair to a richer gleam than usual. She was aware of Emmanuel's eyes lingering on her for a moment longer than he usually allowed. There would be no shillings and cheek pinchings any more, she realized suddenly, and looked down at her clasped hands, her face a little pink.

'Hannah, fetch a sheet of paper from the desk, and write down as I bid you,' he said and she obeyed, moving quickly across to the little escritoire in the far corner.

He began almost before she had returned, reeling off a list of names at breakneck speed. It was all she could do to keep up with him. Lords and earls and baronets jostled with the more familiar names of Goldsmith and Damont and Gubbay and her pencil flew over the page, making column after column in her small neat script. She had covered both sides of the large sheet before he stopped at last.

'You may add any that I may have overlooked, Mary,' he said at last and stood up. 'And remember, the theme is flight. I want the best decorations, and the best food and wine it's possible to get. Tell Levy at Lammeck Alley to arrange any extra money, and get him to fetch any extra stuff you may need. But for God's sake make it *right*. It's the first chance I've had to get him here and I want no nonsense, understand me? Only the best. I'll show Albert and his damned Davida what's what.'

He went leaving a silence behind him that lasted until Hannah said, 'What shall I do with this list, Mrs Mary?'

Mary sat still for a moment longer and then shook her head and looked miserably over her shoulder at Hannah.

'I wish you could throw it in the fire,' she said. Then, 'No, don't!' For Hannah had made a move in that direction. 'Heavens, that would be ... no, my dear, I must bite on the bullet, I suppose. I have to give a ball. Oh dear, oh dear, but

248

I have to give a ball.'

'Oh,' Hannah said, and her spirits tilted and then lifted at the sound of the word. A ball? here, in this quiet, dull house? Lavishly furnished as it was, large as it was, it had never had any pretensions to gaiety before. A ball – the very idea made her flood with excitement.

'You like that?' Mary said and smiled. 'Well, it's natural enough. Young people ... ' Her face clouded then. 'But I don't think it will be too agreeable for you, my love, for the work that has to be done is prodigious. It's the King, you see. He's agreed to come. Emmanuel came home in a towering excitement over it. He'd had lunch with the Rothschilds and the King was there and twitted him, I gather, on being a dull stick, and that made Emmanuel – well, you can imagine. So he said we are to have a ball, and the King will be here, only not officially of course. It's all to do with this aeroplane business. The man who crossed the Channel, you know? Emmanuel has some plans to organize regular journeys – some nonsense or other which I dare say'll prove to be anything but nonsense, for what he does he always does right. Heaven help me if I don't get this wretched ball of his right. I wish – oh well, wishes will get me nowhere. We must settle to planning.'

For the rest of the week she and Hannah concentrated on their plans for the ball, which was to be held a scant three weeks away. Invitations were to be printed and sent, decorations to be ordered, menus to be planned, flowers to be delivered, and it was Hannah who seemed to do the bulk of the work, for Mary became more and more distraught as the week wore on. That she loathed large and noisy entertainments Hannah knew, of course; everyone knew that. But that she could be quite so terrified of a party in her own home was, Hannah thought privately, a little ridiculous. But Mary was Mary, and had to be humoured. So, Hannah did all she could, encouraging her to rest whenever possible, and taking as many of the details from her back as she could.

And enjoyed herself immensely. She found within herself an energy for work and an ability to organize that slightly surprised her. She had always been tidy of course, keeping her room and her clothes pin neat, and liking order and method to her day, but she had never before had to perform the sort of task she was now performing, which involved doing a great many different things, some large and some very trivial, in a logical order, while remembering all that had to be remembered about them, and doing it all at high speed.

She did it and did it well, and did not even realize herself, at first, that in so doing she had taken on an air of authority. She gave instructions to servants in her normal soft voice and with courtesy, but with no hint of cajolery, taking it for granted that they would see her as Mary's spokesman in matters to do with the ball. Amazingly, they accepted her in that guise. The cook, who had hitherto ignored her most of the time, accepted the menu for the supper, over which Hannah and Mary had pored for a long evening, as perfectly reasonable, and the butler, who had shared the cook's disdain for the little Jew girl that Madame kept as a lap dog, now allowed her to tell him that she had ordered all the champagne that would be required for the ball, and would he please tell her when he would like it delivered, so that she could give the necessary instructions.

Some of her success was due not so much to her own abilities as to the fact that she had told them that the King was to be a guest at the ball. Mary had not told her not to say so, so she had, and it worked like yeast in dough, lifting the entire staff to a high excitement. The lower in the hierarchy they were, and the less likely actually to clap eyes on their corpulent monarch for themselves, the more tearing the excitement and the more air of importance they assumed.

Hannah listened to the undercurrents of excitement and marvelled. Just for a king, all this? It seemed to her to be absurd, for no one in the East End gave a fig for royalty. The important people in their lives were landlords and sweatshop owners and rabbis and shopkeepers who allowed credit; their interest in the doings of remote aristocrats and rulers (who weren't even worth considering anyway on account of they weren't Jewish) was minimal.

But here in Eaton Square everyone except Hannah seemed to be in a fever of excitement. Every evening Emmanuel catechized Mary at length about what preparations had been achieved that day and listened with his eyes narrowed as Hannah read out the information on her interminable lists. Mary herself showed her excitement in ever deepening gloom and anxiety, which she hid from Emmanuel, and the staff showed theirs by becoming ever more punctilious.

This was no time to risk being given your notice for sloppy work.

Daniel was perhaps the one who came the nearest of them all to sharing Hannah's unconcern about the King. He came as usual one afternoon for tea, and found Mary and Hannah with their heads bent over the ballroom design which had been sent in from the catering department at Harrods. It showed a number of facsimiles of Bleriot's aeroplane swooping over the Channel, which were to be made in quarter size and suspended from the ceiling, and also offered a number of pennants on which further depictions of the aeroplane were painted. There were to be streamers in the design of the French flag and plaster birds and paper clouds, and all round the walls of the great ballroom Channel waves made of grey-blue tulle. It all looked very exotic and, to Hannah's critical eye, somewhat excessive. Her own taste ran to simpler decorations.

'Why aeroplanes?' Daniel said, staring down at the hodgepodge on Mary's lap. 'Why not steamers? Much more fun. Why, you could put a model of one on rockers right down the centre of the supper room and serve the buffet in it and then if you're fortunate the duller guests will get seasick and go home and leave just a select few of us to enjoy the elbow room and the music.'

'It's Emmanuel's idea,' Mary said fretfully. 'He had some plan to start some sort of mail delivery service, I believe. Or is that cousin Louis Damont? I don't know. Anyway, it seems the King is very enamoured of flying machines, and that is why we are to have them. Should we have them in the supper room as well, then? I hadn't thought of it.'

'Not unless you can persuade all the bores to climb into them and keep out of my way,' he said, and smiled at Hannah. 'In fact, tell 'em all to stay away, and you and I shall dance all evening, Hannah, what say you?'

'I have much too much work to do,' Hannah said, a little primly, trying to ignore the way he had given words to her own current daydream. 'And we can't have aeroplanes in the supper room, Mrs Mary, because they'd impede the waiters and ... '

'I was only joshing,' Daniel said. 'Don't be so stuffy, Hannah! You're as bad as the rest of them, getting all into a lather just over a ball! What does it matter anyway?'

251

He went and leaned against the mantlepiece and kicked one of the coals in the grate with the toe of his boot, making sparks fly in the hot air. 'I'm bored out of my mind with balls.'

'The King is coming, Daniel! And he's never been here before,' Mary said.

'Lucky you. He's always coming to Mamma's parties, and a dead bore it all is, to be sure! Can't do this, mustn't do that – you shouldn't bother with it all, Aunt Mary. You've better things to do with your time, surely, than be like ... like everyone else and fuss over the Royals.'

'Do you talk so to your mother, Daniel?' Mary said with a flash of spirit. 'You'd surprise me if you did.'

'I'd surprise myself,' Daniel grimaced. 'Of course I don't. Can you imagine what happens at our house when the wretched man's coming? It's not his fault, I suppose. I mean, he might be quite an entertaining fellow. It's the fuss I loathe.'

'So do I,' Hannah said, almost without realizing she had spoken, and then went crimson as Daniel turned to stare at her.

'Dear me! So the mouse squeaks, does it?' he said and grinned. 'And here I was thinking you'd be in a great fuss and lather of excitement at the thought of seeing his boring majesty!'

'I'm too busy to be excited,' Hannah said and the mask came down over her face again as her colour subsided. 'Mrs Mary, shall I go and talk to Harrods on the telephone and tell them they can put it all in hand, then? There's not a lot of time, and if you're sure it's what you want ... '

'Are you sure, Hannah?' Mary said, her face creased with anxiety. 'Daniel seems not to think it right.'

'I'm quite sure, Mrs Mary,' Hannah said firmly. She didn't look at Daniel, but he picked up the message anyway and laughed and said easily, 'Oh, Aunt Mary, pay no attention to me. I'm bored and irritable and was just making mischief. They're splendid designs and I'm sure Uncle Emmanuel and the King will worship them and you for being so clever as to provide 'em. Put 'em in hand, at once, do, Hannah, and then come and tell me how many dances we shall have. What do you say? Do you like dancing?'

'I don't know,' Hannah said. 'I – I've never tried.' Liar, she thought. Liar, who knows every step to every dance there is, from reading about balls and listening to the servants and watching them practise in the servants' hall and then trying for yourself, alone up in the attic. Liar.

'Then it's high time you did!' Daniel said. 'Hey, Aunt Mary? Shall I teach your little amanuensis to step it lively? Come on.' He crossed the room and took Hannah's hand and, whistling the 'Blue Danube', dragged her across the carpet into a somewhat clumsy waltz.

She didn't believe it. This was the stuff of her dreams, having Daniel's arm round her waist, and one hand in his. Ridiculous, marvellous, mad – la, la, la, la*la*, la*la*, la*la*, la la la la*la*, la*la*, la*la* ... mad, ridiculous, marvellous!

Mary was glowing with delight, watching them, her chin lifted with an excitement that Hannah had never seen in her before, and after another moment of resistance she let go and followed Daniel's urging hand on her back, and followed his step. His whistling came breathily in her ear and warmed her face.

It was inevitable, of course. She had never been anything but totally circumspect in all her dealings in this house, had never in all the years she had been there behaved in any way but the demure and polite one she had learned so early in her life. And the first time she allowed herself to be otherwise, there was Emmanuel standing at the door watching her, his face rigid with disapproval.

26

Daniel saw him after a moment and then, very deliberately, took one more turn round the room before relinquishing his hold on Hannah.

'Hello, Uncle Emmanuel! You see how seriously I take your ball? Making sure I'm in good trim, getting my dancing knees oiled.'

'Yes,' Emmanuel said frostily. 'I see. Mary, how many replies have you had to your cards today? Lord Minton came into Lammeck Alley today and said he hadn't had a card for the ball, to the best of his knowledge.'

'Hannah?' Mary turned her head to look across appealingly to where Hannah was standing with her back to the window, so that her face was in shadow. 'You dealt with that for me, I think ...'

'Lord Minton's card went with the first batch, Mrs Mary,' Hannah said. 'And I have here the answer from Lady Minton, in this afternoon's post. Perhaps she hadn't mentioned it to him yet.'

'You see?' Mary said. 'I knew everything was in hand.'

'And we have had sixty-three replies so far,' Hannah went on. 'I imagine the rest will be here by the end of the week.'

'Quite the secretary, aren't we?' Emmanuel said. 'Well, Daniel, I dare say you've better things to do than wait about here. My regards to your mother. Mary, I want to talk to you.'

They left the room together, Hannah and Daniel, and she almost ran as the door closed behind them, hurrying for the stairs, but he caught up with her and grasped her wrist.

'You said you couldn't dance!' he said. 'Such a lie! You dance very well. We'll dance at the ball, shall we?'

'I shan't be there,' Hannah said. 'I mean, not for dancing. How can I be?'

'How can't you? You're always with Aunt Mary. I can't imagine her getting through the evening without you. Of course you'll be there. And we'll dance.'

Emmanuel's voice was raised suddenly. They heard the muffled sound of it from behind the closed drawing room door although the words could not be identified. Hannah's brows creased. That Mary and Emmanuel were not on close terms was common knowledge in the household, but they never raised their voices at each other. To hear Emmanuel shouting was not only strange to Hannah but alarming. She pulled her wrist away from Daniel's grasp and said quickly, 'I think you'd better go, don't you?'

He frowned. 'Are they fighting?'

'I don't know!' She allowed herself to sound pettish. 'I'm only a servant. How should I know?'

'A servant? Don't be silly. You're ...' He stopped. 'Different,' he said. 'Not a servant.'

'What else am I? A fetcher and carrier.'

'Not a servant. You call my aunt by her name, and anyway ... '

254

'That was what she asked me to do. She wanted me to call her just Mary, but I couldn't do that. Nor Aunt, so we made it Mrs. Mary and that seems best.'

'. . . and anyway, you're Jewish,' he went on as though she hadn't spoken. 'Jewish girls aren't servants. How can you be one?'

'Jewish girls aren't servants?' She felt anger bubble in her; anger at the way Emmanuel's voice was still raised behind the closed door, anger at her own confusion at the way Daniel was standing so close to her that she couldn't get away, because she had her back to the banisters, and a more general diffused anger at the confusion that had filled her ever since Uncle Alex had made his offer and she had had to refuse it. Now she indulged the feeling.

'Jewish girls are factory slaves, of course, working all the hours God gives in stinking workshops where they can't breathe properly, and never getting the chance to lift their eyes from what they're doing. Or they kill themselves trying to keep slum rooms half clean and their children alive in them, or they give up trying and die before they're forty, but they're not *servants*! That would never do, would it, for your sort? You sit in your big rich houses and go to the East End settlements and hand out your charity with your noses in the air and then talk about how awful it is down there, but you wouldn't ever demean a Jewish girl by turning her into one of your servants, would you? Unless you can do it in a special way, calling us a companion or something.'

He had been standing very still, his face expressionless. He held that stillness for a long moment after she came breathlessly to a stop. Then he said, quietly. 'I thought you cared for my aunt. She's been very good to you, I thought.'

'Of course I care for her!' To her fury she felt her eyes brighten with tears. 'Of course I do! She's been marvellous to me! She's done all she can to make me what I'm not, which is her own daughter. But I'm not, and I never can be. I'm a *servant*. But I do care.'

'You don't sound very caring.'

'What can you understand?' she said, and now she sounded tired. 'What can you understand about what it's like to be anyone but the person you are? You have a marvellous life.'

'How do you know?' It was his turn to sound angry. 'What do you know about anything to do with me? I go to

Lammeck Alley in the morning because they won't let me do anything I want to do and they're still trying to make up their minds about what I can be used for in their damned business, and I dance around my mother and aunts in the afternoons and do what I can to entertain myself in what's left of my life. What do you know about what it's like to be me?'

'I don't ,' she said, and at last her self-training and caution came back. 'I'm sorry to have spoken so. You're quite right. Please to excuse me.' She ducked under his arm and away towards the head of the stairs, but he went after her, and caught her again, this time around her waist.

There was a last shout from Emmanuel and then the drawing room door flew open and he came out, his broad face gleaming with sweat and his mouth turned down. At the sight of him Daniel turned and at last let her go, so that she could get away and to the stairs.

'What the hell are you doing, hanging around? If you want to go sniffing around skirts, go and do it in your mother's house,' Emmanuel said, and his voice was still loud. 'As for you ... ' He flicked his eyes at Hannah. 'You're getting a bit above yourself, aren't you? You'd better mind your manners. Go on in. You're wanted.' He jerked his head at the drawing room door, and then pushed past them and went stumping down the stairs, his back very straight.

After a moment Daniel said, 'I'm sorry. He ... that was appalling. I'm sorry.'

'You don't have to apologize,' she said, 'I told you, I'm only a servant,' and she went into the drawing room and closed the door behind her, quietly, and stood with her back to the panels looking across at Mary.

She was sitting as she had been when Hannah had last seen her, still in her armchair, her face quiet and expressionless. She lifted her eyes after a moment and looked at Hannah, and essayed a small smile.

'Dear me,' she said, and her voice sounded quite normal. 'Quite a fuss. Did you hear?'

'Just that Mr Lammeck was shouting,' Hannah said, and came across the room. 'Not what he said.'

'He wants me to invite Mrs Chantry to the ball. And Mrs Keppel, of course.'

'Mrs Keppel?' Hannah said.

'She's the King's whore,' Mary said in a conversational

256

tone. 'Didn't you know that?'

Hannah felt her face go pink but with amazement rather than shock. To hear Mary use such a word was as surprising as hearing the kitchen cat declaim Shakespeare.

'Just as Mrs Chantry is Emmanuel's. He didn't think I knew. Silly, really. He should have realized there were plenty of people to tell me. Davida . . . ' She smiled again at Hannah, her face as calm as if she were discussing the weather. 'The woman's got two children, it seems. Boys. He spends a lot on them.'

Hannah stood dumbly, unable to do anything even though it was clear that Mary was suffering a great deal. It had been a long time since Hannah had seen her quite so still, and quite so controlled.

'I don't want her here, of course. How could I want her? I said as much. But he says I've got to, and reminded me I've got no children, so –' She stood up. 'So you'd better send cards, Hannah. Will you do it as soon as you've dealt with the design business?'

'Yes,' Hannah said. 'If you want me to.'

'I want you to.'

'I'm sorry,' Hannah said after a moment.

'No need, my dear. No need. I'm used to it, really. Dealing with him, I mean. But I've got you and that helps.' She smiled then, a wide and brilliant look that made Hannah feel again that chill of alarm that came whenever Mary displayed her feeling for her too obviously. 'You make all the difference, you see. All the difference in the world. I can manage anything between Sundays and Fridays.'

The days between that afternoon and the ball were busy and Mary seemed to most onlookers to be her usual quiet self, but to Hannah's more experienced eye, it was as though a spring were being very slowly wound up inside her, taking her each day to a level of tautness that seemed the tightest she could reach, only to be increased yet more the next day. Her face was smooth and showed no concern at all as she went about her affairs, with Hannah watchful at her side, and her eyes seemed untroubled, but Hannah knew, and worried about her. It was like waiting for a thunderstorm to erupt.

On the day of the ball the house rang with activity.

Harrods' men rushed about setting up the decorations in the ballroom. Florists arrived in droves with great boxes of flowers. An army of servants polished everything in sight. The kitchens were a maelstrom of activity, with the regular staff as well as the extra people hired for the day falling over each other in their efforts. The supper room bulged with housemaids spreading tablecloths and arranging dishes, the pantry glittered with silver as the butler sorted out what dish should be used where, and the cellars were ablaze with light as the champagne was carefully stacked in ice baths.

Mary seemed unperturbed by the busyness and for a little while even Hannah began to believe that all would be well, until late in the afternoon when Emmanuel came back from Lammeck Alley, his face white with tension as he hurried up to his dressing room.

Hannah was in the ballroom checking on one of the pennants which had come adrift and needed repinning, and making sure that the last traces of French chalk had been polished from the expanse of gleaming wooden floor when one of the parlour maids came with a message that she was to go to Madam at once.

'Got a fit of the megrims,' the girl said over her shoulder as she bustled back to the kitchen to get her share of the special afternoon tea that had been provided for all the staff. 'Looks shockin', she does. Can't see 'er at no ball tonight and that's a fact.'

Hannah couldn't either, when she saw her. She was sitting on the chaise longue in her bedroom with her head thrown back against the cushions, her complexion yellowish grey. Her forehead was lightly beaded with sweat, and she seemed to be breathing much more quickly than she usually did.

Hannah took one look at her and then ran across the long corridor to tap on Emmanuel's dressing room door.

'Please tell Mr Lammeck Madam is ill,' she said to the valet. 'I think she needs a doctor.'

The next half hour was hubbub and hell. Emmanuel came rushing to Mary's room, and slammed the door behind him when he went in, leaving Hannah and the valet hovering outside uncertain of what to do. Again his voice was raised, and somewhere behind the blustering Hannah could hear Mary's voice, thin and weak. It was more than she could tolerate, standing out there in the heavily carpeted corridor with the scent of tuberoses and jasmine in her nostrils. She felt Mary's need of her as powerfully as if there had been a rope tied around her middle with Mary pulling on it, and she took a deep breath, pushed the door open and walked in quietly.

'This is sheer bloody nonsense,' Emmanuel was shouting. 'You're doing it just to spite me the way you have before and I won't let you get away with it. Do what you like tomorrow. Go into a bloody clinic for the next year for all I care, but tonight you stand in the reception line with me, and you smile and you look good and for once in your life you behave like a wife. I've kept you like a damned duchess for nearly thirty years. Now try and give me something back for my money, you hear me? Lying there like some puking infant!'

'Shall I send for the doctor, sir?' Hannah said loudly. 'I could send a footman, or telephone if you tell me which one you want called.'

'No bloody doctors!' Emmanuel was in his shirt sleeves, his collar lying in a ring on the back of his neck and making him look absurd. 'There's not a bloody thing wrong with the stupid bitch apart from bad temper.'

'I could send the carriage for the doctor if you'd prefer, sir,' Hannah said, her own terror mounting in her. Mary looked so appalling, and Emmanuel's fury was almost tangible, filling the room with a sort of mist.

'I've told you, she's not ill! This is just a ... Mary, sit up!'

Hannah looked at him for a moment and then took a deep breath and moved across to the chaise longue and knelt beside it so that she could slip one arm under Mary's back, and lift her gently, for she was trying to sit up unaided. The effort brought some colour back to her cheeks, and she seemed to be breathing more normally now.

'It's all right, Hannah,' she said. 'I shall be all right. Don't worry.'

'Do you want a doctor, Mrs Mary?' She said it quietly, urgently, touching Mary's face with one hand. It felt surprisingly cool under her fingers.

'No, I shall be all right. Emmanuel, I'll do my best, I really will. But I can't manage on my own, I told you. I need Hannah there. You've got to let her ...'

'I told you! No!' Emmanuel began to shout again. 'For

God's good sake, woman, what are you? Some sort of cripple you can't stand beside me without a crutch?'

'Call it that if you like.' Mary was taking deeper slower breaths now, and looking a little less pallid. 'Call it what you like. But I told you, I can't unless she's there.'

There was a short silence and then he threw his hands up in a gesture compounded of both fury and resignation. 'All right, all right! But for God's sake, get yourself ready, will you! It's getting late.' He went storming out, taking the valet with him, and slammed the door behind him.

There was a silence and then Mary smiled, a slow easy smile, and sat up, apparently without undue effort.

'He said you couldn't be at the ball,' she said after a moment. 'Said you were getting above yourself. Such a thing! As if you could! I've got a dress ready. In the far wardrobe.'

Hannah sat back on her heels and stared at the face so close to her own.

'Mrs Mary?' she said after a moment. 'Are you all right?'

'I shall be better once I see you dressed,' Mary said, and leaned back now on her cushions. 'I made up my mind to it, you see. I just couldn't see how I could manage to stand there unless you were there, so I had to show him, didn't I?'

Hannah stood up and folded her hands against her skirt, looking down at the quiet figure on the chaise longue.

'I wish you wouldn't,' she said after a moment.

'Wouldn't what?'

'Be so – I mean, it's only me. I can't do all that much.'

Mary smiled, and put out one hand. 'You have no idea what you can do, Hannah, my love. You make all the difference in the world to me. Just being you.'

Hannah shook her head. 'It's not right.'

'That I should love you so much? Why not right? You're like a daughter to me, Hannah, you must know that.'

'But I'm not your daughter.' She knew she sounded mulish and couldn't help it. 'Momma and Poppa ... '

There was a little silence and then Mary said, 'I know. Of course. Momma and Poppa. Never mind, Hannah. There's no need to fret over it. Just put on the dress. It's in the far wardrobe.'

For a long moment she stood there, trying to imagine it all. Tried to imagine shaking her head and turning and going away, back to Antcliff Street and telling them she'd come home, telling Uncle Alex she would go to his tea shop. But the imagining wouldn't take hold for alongside it there was another one happening deep in her mind, all by itself; herself in a ball gown, twisting and turning under a great crystal chandelier, beside a grey tulle sea and under decorated model aeroplanes hung from the ceiling, and the music and Daniel breathing on her cheek as he whistled the 'Blue Danube' in her ear. And while all that happened behind her eyes, in front of them lay Mary with her head thrown back on her cushions and her eyes wide and watchful in her pale face, willing her to do as she wanted.

And because Mary was weak, and had all the power of truly weak people, she won, just as she had won her battle with her husband. Hannah turned and went to the far wardrobe and took out the gown.

It was white raw silk looped with satin ribbons with a lace sweep across the bust and fringing the upper arms and she recognized at once one of her own designs, a drawing she had made one evening a few weeks before when they had sat side by side before the fire and Mary had coaxed her into showing her her 'dream dress'. She had been high spirited that night and happy, Hannah remembered now, and had been lavish with her pencil, making great curves of satin across the swirling skirt, and cutting the decolletage daringly low. It had looked wickedly expensive as just a drawing on a page. Now, lying across her arm in all its superb reality, it looked unbelievably sumptuous.

'There are satin shoes there too, and a beaded bag – see? It has that fringe you so much admired when we saw it in the *Ladies' Journal*.'

'You've thought of everything,' Hannah said, her voice rather flat, and Mary smiled and sat up, and swung her feet off the chaise longue to the floor.

'I know,' she said, and giggled like a child. 'It's been such fun hiding it all from you. I pray it fits. I gave it to Miss Winkworth with one of your other dresses for the measurements and she swore it's exactly the same. Do put it on, my love, and then I shall arrange your hair. A Gibson Girl knot will be best, I think. I have some gardenias for you, too. Oh, Hannah, isn't it fun?'

Despite all her misgivings, it was. The dress fitted perfectly, clinging to her long waist as though she had been poured into it, and making her rather heavy breasts look rich but exactly right above the swirl of the silken skirt.

'You have just the right shape for today's fashions, Hannah,' Mary said with satisfaction, and her delight in Hannah's appearance was infectious and made her feel, just for the moment, like the most lavishly rich lady who had ever existed. 'No one will look as you do tonight. No one.'

It was difficult to be as she usually was, when she followed Mary out of her bedroom half an hour later. She had sat quietly, wearing a plain cotton wrapper over her gown, while the maid set the room to rights, and then, after she had gone away, had dressed Mary's hair as carefully as she could, and helped her fasten her own gown, a confection of deep yellow satin and fringe that somehow managed to look rather dull, once it was on, despite the fact that it had cost the better part of a hundred pounds. But Mary was unconcerned with her own appearance; it was Hannah who mattered, Hannah around whom she fussed and fiddled, clearly happier than she had been for weeks. Soon she was to stand beside her husband at the top of her own staircase and greet her guests, among them her husband's mistress. She was to welcome a king who was pretending not to be one in such a manner that he would feel both respected and relaxed, a difficult feat that he always demanded of those of his subjects he treated as friends. She was to spend the whole evening pretending to be serene and happy, a formidable task for one of Mary's nature. Yet now all she cared about was the appearance of an East End charity girl who was neither family nor servant, a nothing of a girl who yet mattered more to her than husband or husband's mistress or any number of kings. It made Hannah feel exceedingly uneasy.

But when the time came, and she slipped out of the room to walk beside Mary as she made her way to the top of the staircase, she could not help feeling her heart lift in her throat, almost choking with excitement. Here was another of her fantasies taking solid reality. It was almost more than she could bear.

27

It grew hotter and hotter, and the scent of the dying flowers mingled with the smell of human sweat and champagne and cigars and made her feel a little sick; but it could have been the excitement that made her chest so tight and her belly so queasy. It was all so exactly as she had imagined it so often, the slow parade of people coming up the stairs to be greeted by their host and hostess at the top, the men in their penguin brilliance, the women in their deep cut gowns, so tight at the waist, so swirling at the skirt below the curve of their hips, and so gleaming of complexion and hair. She stood just behind Mary, where she could put out a hand to support her should Mary feel at all weak, and watched the glittering array as they murmured their way past.

At first, Emmanuel had looked at her with his face tight and cold, and yet with an expression in his eyes that alarmed her. There was a voracity about them as they swept down and over the gown that clung to her so closely, and then flicked back to stare into her eyes. It was as though he had taken the dress off with that look, and she felt exposed and ashamed.

But then he had ignored her, standing beside Mary as the guests started to arrive, all smiles and bonhomie, becoming ever more glistening of forehead and louder of laugh. Daniel arrived fairly early, behind his mother, who was looking quite ravishing in emerald satin, and with his father, Albert, beside him, together with a tall fair young man. He bent his head very slightly at Hannah, but she pretended she had not seen him, shifting her gaze to the girl who was walking beside Davida. She was tall and had very dark eyes under brows which swept up like parentheses, and which gave her a look of great hauteur. But she was beautiful, of that there was no question. Very slender, she was encased in rich creamy lace, and her shoulders sloped above her decolletage, gleaming like marble. Her hair, as dark as her eyes and very abundant, was piled on her small head making her long neck seem very fragile. The total effect was magnificent.

'Deawest Mawy, a splendid evening, such a cwush!' Davida murmured, kissing Mary's cheek and totally ignoring Hannah. But Hannah knew she had seen her, had noticed her gown and probably registered just how costly it was. 'Dear Leontine dined with us for the evening, and her dear brother Willem, you remember Willem I'm sure, from Amsterdam? Of course you do.' The tall young man behind Daniel bowed with a very Continental crispness. 'Come and kiss dear Mawy. Is she not looking quite divine? Daniel, dear one, come and kiss your aunt.'

She drew him forward, and somehow contrived to arrange him alongside Leontine so that they looked as though they were a couple. It was inevitable that as the crowd behind pushed onwards and upwards Leontine should set her hand on Daniel's, and be led by him into the ballroom. Almost at once they were dancing. Hannah could see them through the great double doors, and tried hard not to notice how very gracefully the tall girl moved, the way her back curved so deliciously under his guiding hand and how attentively he seemed to listen to her as they danced by, his head bent towards her.

'Margaret, how good to see you, so glad you could come,' Mary was saying to a stout woman in deep purple. 'And Peter, how well you look too, dear boy.'

Peter Lammeck, Alfred's son, a tall and rather thin young man looking very like his cousin Daniel, bent his head to kiss his aunt's cheek and smiled at Hannah, and she bobbed her head back in some confusion. She had seen him before, when he had come visiting Mary with Daniel but he had seemed a very quiet young man, with little to say for himself, and she was surprised that he had noticed her at all. She watched him go on into the ballroom and thought for a moment with a pang of her own brothers – stocky, rather short in stature and not at all as elegant as the young men of this family. What was it about these rich Jews that made them so different from the East End ones? The people at Uncle Alex's party seemed alien in comparison, an exotic chattering exuberant lot as unlike these langorous quiet creatures as she herself was unlike her brothers. It was all so strange that she felt more and more as if she were in one of her dreams, as though she were sitting high in a corner of the great ballroom staring down at all that was going on below.

The family were gathering in strength. Emmanuel's brothers, Albert and Alfred, instead of passing on into the ballroom as their wives and sons had done – Davida leading the way with great imperiousness – had stopped to stand behind Emmanuel, talking to each other and to him when he could be distracted from greeting newcomers. They looked like great birds, Hannah thought, with their glossy black tail coats and blindingly white shirt fronts decorated with diamond studs. They looked so alike too, all with dark hair receding over their high foreheads and greying at the temples, all olive of complexion and rotund of figure and with gold chains looped across their expanses of belly. They all had clean shaven cheeks, pendulous and a little shadowed by their dark beard growths, and they all looked exceedingly prosperous.

'Susan, and dear Ezra,' Mary was saying. 'How nice.' And she swayed a little as Susan kissed her, and Hannah, watchful and very quick, put her hand unobtrusively against her back and she steadied. 'Are the children well?'

'Very well, dear. Very well. Marcus is getting so tall, you'd be amazed. And Daphne is the sweetest little darling you ever saw – and little Rupert – oh, you should have heard what he said to his nurse this morning ...'

She chattered on and Hannah could feel the tension in Mary, who always suffered when her sisters-in-law talked of their children. Davida did it with malice, Hannah was sure, but on the occasions when she had heard Susan talk as she did now, she had felt nothing in her but genuine passion for her own children and total unawareness of the effect that such talk might have on a disappointed woman like Mary. Which was odd, Hannah thought now, listening to her, when you remembered that Susan had seen two of her own children die when they were babies. Women are very strange, she told herself as at last Susan and Ezra moved on, making way for the people behind. Very strange.

Her hand was still on Mary's back and she felt her stiffen and turned her head to look. She had been almost unaware of the butler's voice, intoning the names of each arrival, until now, but this time it seemed to be louder and much more enunciated than other names had been. 'Mrs Thomas Chantry,' he said. Mary tilted her chin and held out her hand.

'Mrs Chantry,' she murmured and though Hannah could

not see her face, standing as she was behind her, she knew as surely as if she had been staring at it that Mary looked serene and calm, and that her eyes had flicked away after the proper interval of time to the next guest.

Mrs Chantry, a large blonde woman with a cheerful face and small but very bright eyes moved on past Emmanuel. Hannah had to admire her, for she merely bent her head and went on into the ballroom, seeming quite unabashed by the fact that clearly everyone standing nearby, and most particularly the cluster of brothers standing behind her host, were well aware of the special relationship she enjoyed with him. Yet from her demeanour no one would have thought they were anything but the merest of acquaintances. It was a magnificent performance.

They kept on coming. Hannah stared with particular interest at Mrs Keppel, a dark eyed, dark haired beauty with a very friendly face who stood and chattered at Mary with such vivacity that no one seemed to notice that Mary hardly answered her, and also at the somewhat faded beauty of Lillie Langtry, arriving on the arm of a man who had cheeks that looked painted, so reddened were they by years of heavy drinking.

There were other famous faces too, faces she had seen in the illustrated journals, and on the picture post cards that the servants kept pinned up on the board in the servants' hall. It was a most fashionable party, and she could tell that Mary felt all the work and planning had been worthwhile as Emmanuel became more and more cheerful, and even seemed to look at her with some approval when next he caught her eye.

The music had been going for some time, waltz succeeding polka and then some of the newest ragtime tunes, freshly imported from America. Hannah listened to the irresistible beat, and made herself resist it, not moving a muscle as she stood there doggedly behind Mary. It wasn't easy but she did it. There was a little stir then, below in the hall. Emmanuel stiffened and so did his brothers, moving forwards to be nearer to him, and Hannah heard a booming voice from the crush of people below, and then a loud laugh.

Emmanuel almost visibly relaxed. Clearly he had, for a while, doubted whether the King would arrive at all, and the sound of that voice coming up to him from his own hallway reddened his face with pleasure and made him gleam ever more richly with satisfaction. The butler opened his mouth to announce the newest guest as he came up the stairs, a cigar in one hand, and his other resting on the shoulder of a tall young man, an equerry, but he shook his head at him, and obediently the butler closed his mouth.

'Sir,' said Emmanuel, and bobbed his head awkwardly. It was the first time he had greeted a reigning monarch in his own home. But Mary extended her hand.

'Good evening, sir,' she said quietly. 'So happy you could be with us.' The King smiled at her and wheezed a little and kissed her hand.

'My pleasure, ma'am,' he said, and his voice wheezed a little too. 'My pleasure. Evening, Lammeck. And bless my soul, here's the whole family turned out. Evening, gentlemen! And what's the world doing to you, hey? Got any offers for tomorrow's racing?'

'Not tomorrow's, sir,' Albert said. His voice was smooth as silk. 'Next year perhaps. The English successor to Louis Bleriot should be a good bet.'

The King laughed, throwing back his head and almost choking with delight. 'Damned good, Lammeck, damned good. You get your aeroplanes off the ground, damme, but you might get me up in one after all, damme if you mightn't.'

He moved into the ballroom, and with one accord, as though obeying a signal, they followed him. Anyone who arrived now would just have to find his own way to the host and hostess. The time for receiving lines was past.

Mary settled herself on a small gilt chair near the entrance to the conservatory, under a particularly large pennant which was swaying in the breeze caused by the whirling dancers, and which consequently created a cool place for her. The ballroom was exceedingly hot and Hannah could see that she was genuinely feeling unwell in it. However much she may have exaggerated her distress before in her bedroom, in order to get her own way with Emmanuel, it was clear that by no means all of it had been artifice. She looked yellowish, and her eyes seemed to be sunken in her face. Hannah took a small bottle of eau de cologne from her beaded bag and unobtrusively soaked a corner of her handkerchief in it and gave it to Mary to cool her forehead.

'You're a dear, Hannah, to know what it was I needed,' Mary said, and smiled at her. 'Now, when are you going to dance? There's no joy in being at a ball and not dancing. We must find a partner for you.' She stood up and looked about the room at the great press of people, and at once Hannah tugged at her elbow.

'Please not, Mrs Mary,' she said urgently. 'I'm perfectly happy here with you, truly I am. I don't want to dance.'

But it was no use. Mary had made up her mind, and with her usual weak stubbornness was not going to unmake it.

She beckoned, and Daniel moved out of the crush with Leontine on his arm and came towards them. Quite how Mary did it Hannah could not tell, but she managed to convey an unspoken message to Daniel which made him murmur something in Leontine's ear, so that she stopped and turned to a small group of girls who were chattering not far away, leaving Daniel to come alone to his aunt's side.

'Dear Daniel.' Mary smiled and tapped his wrist with her dance programme. 'Here is my little Hannah looking quite lovely, I'm sure you'll agree, and she's not torn herself away from my side once to dance. That won't do, will it? Will you take her out, and see to it she enjoys a little dancing?'

'Mrs Mary, I don't want to dance,' Hannah said almost angrily. 'Really, I'm perfectly happy with you. It's why I'm here.'

'You see the trouble she gives me?' Mary smiled, and took Hannah by the wrist and pulled her forwards. Daniel held out a hand and took Hannah's. Short of making an unseemly scuffle there was nothing she could do. She had to walk out onto the dance floor with him, as the orchestra, which had stopped to catch its breath, swung into another ragtime.

'There!' said Daniel. 'You're dancing! The lady who said she never did, and said she couldn't, who insisted she wouldn't be at this ball, and insisted she was just a servant. That gown, my dear Hannah, is no servant's frills, is it?'

'Mrs Mary is very kind to me,' she said as primly as she could, which was difficult for he was whirling her round. 'She insisted on this gown.'

'And very wisely too,' he said, and whirled her again. 'You look quite magnificent.'

'Not as magnificent as your other dancing partner.' She hated herself as soon as the words were out. What right had she to complain about his dancing partners? What right had she to say anything?

He looked down at her, holding her away from him so that he could see her face more clearly. 'Dear me,' he said. 'Do I detect a note of waspishness? How very unlike a servant girl!'

'You're getting boring,' she said, as coldly as she could. 'There is no need to keep on and on about that.'

'My previous dancing partner,' he said, as though she hadn't spoken at all, 'is my distant cousin. Her name is Leontine Damont, and she is very sweet and very beautiful and very very rich. My mother wishes me to marry her.'

'Really,' said Hannah, and concentrated on trying to follow his steps. There seemed very little else she could do, as the music became more insistent. Anyway, she wanted to concentrate on the here and now, on fantasies come true, or almost true.

It wasn't possible to concentrate. She could only react to feelings. It seemed to her that she was preternaturally aware of all that was happening in the big crowded ballroom around her. As they swung into yet another whirl she saw Davida standing beside the floor, Leontine by her side, her face a mask of anger, and as Daniel opened his mouth to say something Hannah said almost desperately, 'There's your mother. She wishes to speak to you, I think. You should go to her.' She tried to pull away from him so that he would have to stop, but he was much too determined to allow any such thing, and took her back into the press of dancers, laughing a little breathlessly.

'There!' he said as they reached the far side of the ballroom, and the music stopped at last. 'Now, have you had some supper? Let me take you down.'

'No,' she said, looking back over her shoulder to where Davida was standing. 'No, really. I must go back to Mrs Mary. Thank you for the dance. Excuse me – '

But she had no chance to retrace her steps, because Davida and Leontine were coming towards them, threading their way through the groups of people waiting for the next burst of music. Behind them came Mary, seeming casual and relaxed, but as Hannah could clearly see, well aware of Davida's state of mind.

'Daniel!' Davida sounded wrathful, even though her words were polite in the extreme. 'There you are, my dear. I could not imagine where you had lost yourself. Here's Leontine weady to go down to supper, and I shall join you, I think. Your papa is as usual talking to the King, I beg your pardon, I meant of course his good friend Mr Bertie, and will not be dislodged this next half hour. Come along, my dear.' She linked her arm in Daniel's, and moved expertly so that Leontine was available for his other arm and, totally ignoring Hannah, moved majestically towards the staircase.

But Mary was equally swift and equally courteous. 'Such a lovely idea, Davida. I too am ready for a little supper. Come along, Hannah, my dear. We shall all go down together if Daniel does not mind having such a gaggle of females to look after!'

'Not at all, Aunt Mary!' he said heartily. He smiled at her and stood back so that she and Hannah could lead the way.

It was as they reached the top of the stairs that Hannah realized that the King was standing there talking to Emmanuel and Albert. He turned as they came up to him and smiled at Mary.

'So, Mrs Lammeck? A splendid ball you are having, aren't you? Very enjoyable, very. And who might this pretty little charmer be, hey? One of the family? Or perhaps not, with such red hair as that. None of your lot got such a copper knob, have they, Lammeck?' He grinned at Emmanuel.

Emmanuel's face was blank, but Hannah felt sick again. The way he did not look at her, the way he tightened his nostrils, the set of his head, were enough to tell her how angry he was and that was terrifying. Yet at the same time, somewhere deep inside herself she wanted to laugh. I'm a servant, she thought. He said I was getting above myself, and now the King's asking him if I'm a relation because who invites servants to balls? She wanted to giggle aloud.

'Miss Hannah Lazar, sir,' said Mary's voice, and for the first time for many years Hannah felt their positions were reversed. She had become so used to looking after Mary, protecting Mary, covering up for Mary, that she had forgotten that in the very early days of their relationship it had been Mary who had looked after her; as now she looked after her again. 'My protégée, sir, and a very dear child. So caring of my welfare, I don't know how I would manage without her. She made most of the preparations for our ball tonight. Such a help to me ... '

The King smiled and reached out and pinched her cheek, and she could smell the cigar smoke on his fingers and schooled herself not to rear back, standing there looking as demure as she could, and she bobbed a little curtsey, at which he shook his head, but still jovial.

'No formality, my dear, not tonight,' he said. 'Plain Mr Bertie tonight.'

Behind Emmanuel Albert laughed suddenly. 'Now, sir, there's a sight for sore eyes!' he said. 'Did you ever see a thing like that!' The King turned and followed the direction of his nodding head and laughed too. The orchestra had started playing again, another sprightly ragtime tune, and in the middle of the floor, capering as though she were a lamb in a field, was an elderly woman with a very raddled and painted face in a crimson gown which was totally unsuitable for her age. Other dancers were giving her room, and laughing too, for she had no partner and was clearly rather the worse for wear, having been down to supper, and champagne, rather more often than a lady should.

'Oh heaven help us,' Emmanuel muttered. 'It's old Mrs Goldsmid. I told her son to keep her away.'

Albert laughed, as the other men crowded round the door to watch her, guffawing and grinning. 'No one tells *her* what to do, not even her son. He may have half the City by its financial ear, but she still calls the tune in their house. Poor devil.'

'Hannah, my dear, skip upstairs and fetch me something,' Mary whispered in Hannah's ear, and Hannah turned to look at her, red faced and relieved. She didn't know what was worse; the confrontation with the King, or the way the men were laughing at that stupid pathetic old woman in the ballroom.

'Of course, Mrs Mary,' she said. 'What do you want?'

'Anything you like. A handkerchief. Smelling salts. Anything, just to slip away, you see. Wait five minutes or so, and then bring whatever it is to me in the supper room. It will be better that way, I think.'

Hannah nodded eagerly, grateful and relieved, and marvelling again at how wise Mary could be when she had to. 'Of course I will, Mrs Mary. Are you sure you're all right?' She looked at her a little more closely. 'You do look awfully tired.'

'I am. But I'm all right. Don't fret. Just go and get me my whatever it is.' She turned back to the little knot of people at the ballroom door, leaving Hannah to slip away up the other staircase that led to the bedrooms on the storey above.

She stopped on the landing and looked down for a moment, saw Daniel looking around, and shrank back into the shadows of the banisters, glad he could not see her. Clever Mrs Mary. She had seen not only that it was best to get her out of Emmanuel's and the King's way, but also Daniel's, who seemed mischief bent tonight. She could have hit out at him physically, she felt so angry with him. It might amuse him to make a show of her in front of his mother and his precious Leontine Damont, she told herself as she went on her way to Mary's room, but it doesn't amuse me. I've got tomorrow and next week and next year to get through in this house. I think I hate Daniel Lammeck. When I was a child I knew no better than to think he was marvellous, but now I'm learning.

She sat down on the sofa in Mary's bedroom and took a deep breath. She could hear the music below and the smell of the ball drifted up to her; champagne and flowers and rich food and hot people, and again the excitement lifted in her. It was all very confused and worrying, but it *was* exciting. And she was really and truly living it. What more could any girl ask?

She leaned back on the sofa and in so doing brought herself in line with the mirror of Mary's dressing table. At the sight of herself she took a sharp breath and then stood up and moved closer to the expanse of bright glass.

I do look marvellous, she thought, almost in awe. I look really beautiful. My hair looks better than it ever has, so red and yet so dark, and my eyes are shining more than the lamps are and I look absolutely marvellous.

She turned and twisted in front of the mirror, throwing her head back to display the clean line of her throat and shoulders, and the curve of her waist and breasts and for one long delicious moment loved herself. She was all she had ever dreamed she would be. She was the heroine of her own reality, and it was the headiest moment of her entire life. Never mind Kings and Emmanuels or even Daniels. Hannah loved Hannah, just for a moment, and it was a good feeling.

And then she laughed. 'Silly,' she said aloud and made a

face in the mirror, crossing her eyes so that she could only see double, and sticking out her tongue, and then giggled again and took the smelling salts and a clean handkerchief from Mary's drawer, and turned to go. Enough of this nonsense. Mary was waiting for her.

The corridor was quiet as she ran along it, only the distant sounds of the music and chatter drifting up the stairs. She hummed the tune they were playing under her breath for a moment. Ta ta, tatatata – and danced a little shuffling step as she reached the stairhead.

'Quite the little sprite!' a voice said, and she was so startled that she almost tripped over her own feet. The King was standing at the top of the stairs grinning at her, his whiskers gleaming a little in the light that was thrown up the staircase from the floor beneath. He looked very large, suddenly, and she took a step back in some alarm.

'Now, why be so shy, my dear? A pretty little thing like you shouldn't be so shy! You're a beauty, you know that? You could make quite a little stir if you had the mind to, I'm thinking. You've an odd little face, but your colouring's superb, and you've a winning way with you! Come and give an old man a kiss, and smile a little, do. No need to look so solemn!'

She was terrified. He stood between her and the stairhead, her only means of escape, unless she ran back and went down the back stairs. She almost turned to go, and then remembered how ill lit the servants' stairs were and how far away from the rest of the house and people, and how easily he could follow her there. And then what?

There was only one thing to do. She took a deep breath and ran at him with her head down, so that she cannoned into his belly and left him gasping as she went down the stairs to the light and the noise and, above all, the people beneath.

28

'I don't understand,' Nathan said for the tenth time. 'I mean, how can a man understand such a thing? Seven years there's no problems, no word of any troubles and then pfft, in one night she's back here, looking like the sky fell on her head, and she says, "That's it"? She don't say why, she just says "That's it"! How can a man understand such a thing? I ask you, what sort of man is there could begin to ...'

'Nathan, be quiet.' Bloomah's voice was quiet and unemotional, but it had its effect, for Bloomah spoke so rarely and certainly never spoke so to Nathan that his words dried in his mouth with surprise.

Hannah was sitting very upright at the table with her hands folded in front of her on the red plush cloth. She was still wearing her coat, a well cut sensible cloth one that looked incongruous under the wilting gardenias in her hair. She felt drained, too tired now even to try to help them comprehend.

She had arrived at the door in a hansom cab, unheralded, at two in the morning, wearing a frivolous white raw silk and satin and lace ball gown under the sensible coat and with her face grey with tension. She had had to wake them up, inevitably waking an avidly curious Mrs Arbeiter as well, and then had to explain what had happened. That she had come home for good. That the seven fat years in Eaton Square were over. That all her golden fortune had shrivelled to nothing in a matter of half an hour of squabbling and accusations that had made her feel sick.

Of course they needed her help to understand. She tried not to think of it at all, but she could not prevent the pictures forming in front of her eyes, the whole scene re-enacted against the plush tablecloth at which she was staring: Daniel at the foot of the stairs as she reached the landing, his face creasing with surprise as he looked at her. Daniel putting out one hand towards her with so generous a gesture that she had just hurled herself at him and held on, desperately.

It had been stupid to be so alarmed, she knew that now. So a silly old man who stank of cigars and brandy had been familiar with her, had tried to kiss her. What was so terrible about that? She'd come across that sort of behaviour before, after all. There had been the footman who had stopped her on the back stairs one afternoon and thrust his spotty face at hers in an effort to fondle her. She had just laughed at him and pushed past, and that had been that. And the heavy winking, nudging chatter of the coachman. She had dealt easily enough with that simply by pretending she hadn't heard a word of it.

So why get so upset because another stupid man had tried another stupid trick? Because he was the King? Because she was as enraptured by his lofty position as any of the kitchen maids? Surely it couldn't be that.

It happened because Daniel held out his hand the way he did, a secret part of herself whispered. It was nothing to do with the King. It was to do with the opportunity to have Daniel hold on to you, the chance to set your face against his chest and hold on to him. That was why it happened. It was your own stupidity, no one else's, your own attempt to make a fantasy real. And all you did was destroy the best thing that ever happened to you in all your life, or would ever be likely to happen again.

Because inevitably Davida had appeared. Wherever Daniel was, Davida was likely to be nearby. And where Davida was, was Leontine.

Davida had lost her temper quite spectacularly, allowing her voice to rise shrilly, even forgetting her redundant R as she spat the words out, horrible words that had made Hannah feel as though someone had kicked her in the belly and robbed her of breath. She had made it clear that Hannah was a cheap servant girl, a jumped up self-seeking salacious slattern with designs on her betters, who had abused Mary's trust and care by setting her cap at the rich young nephew who came to visit, a man who was virtually engaged to be married, at that. She was little better than a tart, a street girl, a guttersnipe who polluted her benefactor's home. It made no difference that Daniel turned on his mother and tried to stop the flow of vituperation. It made no difference that Emmanuel appeared, and Leontine's brother Willem, and then even the King and a large number of the guests. She went on and on, as Hannah stood there, white and silent, letting it flow over her. She saw the faces around her, amused and avid and contemptuous, and it seemed that nowhere was there a friendly expression, any hint of concern for her. Daniel seemed overwhelmed more by embarrassment than anything else.

And then Mary was there, her eyes wide and frightened, quite stripped of her armour of expressionless calm, just as Emmanuel was saying in a tight, icy voice that she was to go; that Hannah was to go now. She was to take herself out of the house instanter, no time to be lost, now, now, *now*.

Hannah saw it all again, saw herself staring at Mary trying to argue with him, pulling on his arm, and he turning on her, painfully aware of the King standing there near him, and saying in that same tight small voice that there was to be no argument, the girl was going now.

Even the King, laughing genially and bidding Emmanuel not to make such a fuss, had no effect on him. Emmanuel was implacable and Mary's stricken face showed that she knew no performances on her part, no inveigling would overcome this decision. For one mad brief moment Hannah had looked at the King and caught his glance and she thought, 'I'll tell them, I'll say that I was frightened by the King and Daniel was only trying to help.' But the idea slipped away as fast as it had come. Who would believe her? And if they did, wouldn't it make it worse? Setting your cap at the nephew of your benefactor was bad enough; doing the same at a King – they'd chop her head off, she told herself wildly. I can't. I can't . . .

She felt herself fill with panic, yet she showed none of it. The footman who opened the front door to let her out after Emmanuel had shepherded his guests away from the fuss, leading the King to his smoking room for a 'little special brandy I have for you,' pushed her coat at her, and she looked up at him gratefully. It was the spotty one who had fumbled at her on the back stairs, and she wanted to laugh, but she didn't. She was just grateful for the look of pity on his face.

'Never mind, ducks,' he murmured as she pulled the coat across her shoulders. 'You'll get another place, certain sure. Madam'll see to it you gets a good character, even if 'e carries on ever so. Good luck to you, ducks.'

She looked over her shoulder for one brief moment, at the few people standing in the hallway and on the stairs, and then saw her. Mary was standing with both hands gripping the banister rail, staring down with her face quite still and expressionless again. Hannah lifted her hand in a small gesture and then, as the door swung wider to let in the cold air of the early September morning, shivered. The door closed behind her with a snap that pounded in her ears like a violent thud. It was over. Quite, quite over.

And now she had to make them understand, Nathan and Bloomah, sitting there staring at her across the table, their faces creased with confusion and bewilderment and, just a

276

little, fear. For Hannah's money had been the prop and stay of their lives; Jake's contribution was little enough, and no one talked any more about what Nathan could provide. There had been, for seven years, Hannah's envelope, and Hannah's baskets of food and clothes and Hannah's gifts. And now there was just Hannah, sitting in a white ball gown under a sensible coat looking as though she had been whipped.

'Your clothes,' Bloomah said. 'What are you going to do about clothes?'

Hannah looked down at herself, and then almost against her will smiled, a twisted little grin. 'I'll have to manage with this, I suppose!'

'Sell it,' Nathan said. 'Jake can take it down the Lane. Sell it. You'll get a good price.'

The door opened and Jake was standing there with Solly behind him, peering past him into the room, blinking in the light.

'Wassa matter?' Jake said. 'Heard all the talking. Wassa matter?'

'Nothing,' Hannah said, and stood up. 'Not a thing. I just came home, that's all. Go back to bed. We'll talk in the morning – later in the morning. Momma, Poppa, go to bed. Please. I'll sit here in the chair a while. I don't need the couch outside. We'll talk later.'

'I'll ask Mrs Arbeiter, can I have her small back room. It's the smallest there is, so maybe she won't want too much for it.'

'Tomorrow, Momma,' Hannah said. 'Please, not now. Please, go to bed.' Bloomah recognized the appeal in her voice and nodded and stood up. 'Nathan,' she said, and went across the room to the curtain which was pulled across their bed, to give what semblance they had of privacy. 'Boys, go already. You heard your sister. Tomorrow we talk. Go.'

They all went, Nathan still uncharacteristically silent, and at last she was alone. The gas light was blown out, and she was left to sit in the big armchair in the darkness to try to think of tomorrow, listening to Nathan's snores and watching the sky lighten behind the uncurtained window. Tomorrow. It was a Thursday tomorrow. It would be the first Thursday she had spent in her own home for seven years. It was a strange thought.

*

277

Behind the problems of getting together a new pattern of life was a much bigger one, too big to think about properly. She talked to Mrs Arbeiter, and persuaded her to rent the small back room downstairs so that she could have somewhere to sleep, promising her she'd pay the extra money as soon as she had a job. She sat at the table upstairs in her chemise and sewed furiously on one of Bloomah's old dresses, so that she'd have something to wear, while Jake took the ball gown to the second-hand clothes-sellers in the Lane. She sent Solly to Uncle Alex's to ask him if he could come over to see her, so that she could tell him she would take his job after all, though she did not tell Solly that, and she talked a lot to Bloomah, trying to persuade her that she had been thrown out of the Eaton Square house not because of some venality on her own part, but because of Emmanuel's capriciousness.

'I didn't do anything, Momma, believe me,' she said, lying staunchly. 'Not a thing, truly. It was just he was in a mood and he gets jealous. Mrs Mary is . . . I mean, she liked me, and he got jealous.'

It sounded believable and Bloomah believed it. And if I work at it, Hannah told herself, biting off the thread and tugging on the new seam she had made to test it, if I really try, I'll believe it too. Because anything is better than thinking they really imagined I was trying to catch Daniel. As if I would dream of such a thing.

As if you ever dreamed of anything else, her secret voice whispered at her jeeringly, maliciously. You sent yourself to sleep with that one every night.

No, she argued, no. She needed that argument to stop herself from thinking about what was really distressing her, the biggest problem of all; Mary's silence.

The weekend came and went, and they counted the money Jake had managed to get for the gown – a munificent five pounds, for it was a very remarkable garment – and paid the next month's rent out of it, and put the rest into Bloomah's purse to buy food for as long as it would last. But there was no word from Mary. Hannah had thought that she would send some sort of message, some comfort for what happened, but nothing came. No note, no parcel of her clothes, no money, nothing. It was as though the Eaton Square years had never been, as though Hannah had never lived there, and never been loved by Mary. She could not understand it.

Hadn't she been frightened of the passion that Mary had had for her? Hadn't she always had to do her best to hold back that need, that longing the older woman displayed? Could it all have died overnight, on one September night at a ball, just because her sister-in-law Davida had accused Hannah of flirting with her son?

The silence stretched into Monday. Hannah sat and stared out of the window at the street and tried to make a plan for her future, and for her family's future. Because to add to all her other sources of distress, Uncle Alex was away.

'Away?' she said to Solly, staring at him as he stood in the doorway, his round face agog with the weight of his message. 'How do you mean, away?'

'He's gone to America!' Solly said, his voice thick with awe. 'On a ship, to America. Ain't that something?'

'But I don't understand! He never said ...' Nathan sat upright, pretending he hadn't been half asleep in the big armchair. 'I ask you, what sort of family is it a brother goes to America, never says goodbye, nothing? What sort of man is it takes no time to tell no one what he's doing? Here's Reuben, I see him in the street only yesterday, he don't say nothing about Alex going to America, so maybe he knows and don't choose to tell me? What sort of family is it, for God's sake, to treat a man this way?'

'He's coming back,' Solly said portentously. It wasn't often he had as interesting a piece of news as this, and he intended to make the most of it. 'He's gone on business, see? Just for a little while.'

'Business? What sort of business takes a man to America he don't even tell his family? Dirty business, I'll tell you what, dirty business. No time to say goodbye to his brothers, to his nieces and nephews, no time to remember he's got relations that care about him?' Nathan was rapidly converting Alex into the adored young brother with whom he spent the greater part of his waking hours. 'How come he don't even send a note round?'

'If you listen, I'll tell you!' Solly said. 'It's boxing, see? There was this big fight planned in a place near New York.' He took a piece of paper from his pocket. 'Yeah, Atlantic City, see? Only they send Uncle Alex a cable, they got let down, and it's a big fight, and he got Kid Zimmerman signed up, ain't he? He's the big one. Kid Zimmerman got the best chance at the heavyweight title since Daniel Mendoza, they reckon at Leman Street. Anyway, they send this cable they got to have the Kid. Uncle Alex got just an hour to get to Tilbury, get the ship. So they goes and the fight's three days after they gets there, and then they're having other fights if the Kid wins, which Bernie down the gym, he says he reckons'll happen. He says maybe Uncle Alex gets back November, December, maybe not till after the New Year, even!'

'And no message!' Nathan said. 'No message, for his own family.'

'Bernie says he's sorry. He was supposed to tell everyone, but he's been too busy, you know how it is.' Solly turned to Hannah who was standing very straight and quiet by the window. 'So there you are, Hannah. No Uncle Alex for a while. What did you want him for?'

'It doesn't matter,' Hannah said. 'It really doesn't matter.'

29

Her Uncle Isaac gave her a job grudgingly, because he couldn't imagine what use he could get out of a girl of seventeen who had never worked in a factory. Still, she was his sister's child.

'At your age, you ought to have three four years good experience behind you,' he said fretfully. 'How can I treat you like an improver when you ain't even a beginner? Sit you with the new ones and they won't understand how come it is you're so old, sit you with the people you belong with, they get upset you ain't pulling your weight. But what can I do? For Bloomah, I got to do what's necessary.'

She swallowed her pride, and with it her nausea and started work. She walked from home for twenty minutes each morning to Isaac's new Spitalfields workshop, arriving at eight sharp, climbing the stairs with the other beshawled cold yawning girls.

That was when the nausea began; the smell was so thick she could taste it, a mixture of wool fat and machine oil and dirt and cats and mildew which combined to make a repellent stench. Not that the others seemed to notice; they had worked here for so long it was part of the ambience they carried round with them. They would seize the enamel mugs of tea that Isaac's wife Thin Sarah had ready for them (she was called Thin Sarah to distinguish her from her brother-in-law's wife Fat Sarah) and drink it with every evidence of enjoyment. Hannah couldn't. It wasn't just that she was used to using fine china which was clean as well as delicate; it was the cloying taste of it, so heavily sweet, laced with thick sugary condensed milk, poured from a battered tin. She would stand and hold the mug between her cold fingers and pretend to drink it, finding a chance to empty it into the slop bucket beneath the rickety table used for brewing tea, when no one was looking.

Then she would push back her rising gorge and settle at her bench and start to sew. Uncle Isaac had told her she had better be a felling hand since she had never used a machine – which cheered him a little since felling hands, paid on piece work rates, usually earned less than machinists. Set in front of her each morning was a great pile of heavy men's overcoats, all with their seams and hems to be oversewn with thick thread. Felling hands usually had to find their own thread, and wax for strengthening it, and needles, too, but Isaac, with a great show of magnanimity, told her he would see her right for the first month. 'After that, though, you buy your own like everyone else. It's worth it to you, believe me. The more you buy, the more you use, the more you earn.'

All day she sewed doggedly, seam after seam, until her fingers felt like raw meat from the pressure of the heavy needle and her shoulders ached with the effort of pushing her arms through the same set of motions, hour after hour. They stopped for 'a piece' at eleven, when she would unwrap and eat the breakfast Bloomah had prepared for her – a slice of bread, sometimes spread with margarine, sometimes with chicken fat, depending on the state of the family's finances, and she would drink strong tea without any milk in it, pretending that it was chicken fat on her bread, even when it wasn't, so that she wouldn't have to take the sickening condensed milk. Thin Sarah took it as a personal affront if anyone refused any of her offerings, and it wasn't worth antagonizing her; better to pretend to a religious objection to mixing milk and meat, an excuse her aunt would understand.

And then it was the seams again, with the heap of coats seeming not to diminish at all, as Isaac added more and more to her work pile. At one o'clock there was a fifteen minute dinner break; she ate the rest of Bloomah's offerings then if she had the appetite. Often she did not. Often she would sit over her packet of food staring at the wall with its blackened spots where flies had been swatted to flattened death, and think of the lunches she had shared with Mary – bowls of creamy mushroom soup and souffles and puddings and eggs poached on beds of buttered spinach ... She would shake her head and pull herself back to reality and gladly give her meal to any of the other girls who asked her for it.

The other girls were her only source of pleasure in each day. There were six of them at her bench, mostly of her own age, though one was older, a round faced cheerful creature of almost thirty who had been married once, but who had been widowed very early. She seemed unconcerned about her bereavement, or about the fact that she had to leave the only fruit of that short marriage, a little boy, with her mother while she earned their living.

'I much care,' she would say when one of the others sympathized with her because she had to come to work before her little boy had woken up. 'So I miss him this morning, he's that much happier to see me tonight. You win a few, you lose a few.' And she would start to sing in a rough little voice, always the same whining song, a lullaby, 'Schlaft, mein kindele, schlaft, mein kindele, schlaft, mein kindele, schlaft.'

'Shut up already, Cissie,' the others would cry. 'You'll send us all to sleep and then where do we go for next week's rent?' Cissie would laugh and go on with her hoarse little croon, until eight o'clock came. Time to go home, if they were lucky.

They talked a lot, of men, of course, but of other things too. There was Lena, a thin, very dark eyed girl of nineteen who was newly in love with one of the local lobbuses – or so Isaac labelled him, for he was a man of thirty with a taste for politics who was busily involved in trying to start a trade union in his cabinet-making workshop. She had caught his fire and talked about the need for a union here in Isaac's workshop.

'We need proper breaks, three times a day with half an hour for dinner and piece work rates what he doesn't change every time he feels like it, and a proper lavatory that's kept clean for us, and one of us to talk to him when things ain't done right.'

'I should cocoa!' said Cissie. 'I should bleedin' well cocoa! An' who's goin' to tell him that, eh? Who's going to stick that bell on the cat? Not bloody me, and not bloody you, either.' Jessie, the fat girl at the end of the table would shake her head in disapproval at Cissie's rough language and start to talk about clothes, and how you could get really lovely nets down at Barney the *Schmutterer's* place for less than a penny three farthings a remnant, if you went early on Sunday morning. The others would join in. They knew better than anyone that there was no chance ever of the workers in Isaac Levson's shop telling their guv'nor what to do. Tell him he had no right to change piece work rates when it suited him? Tell him he couldn't lay them off when he was short of work, couldn't make them work long overtime at the ordinary rates when the rush was on and he needed them, however late into the night it kept them there? The sky would rain sovereigns every day after dinner before that would happen. It made more sense to talk about penny three farthing bargains. That was a realizable hope.

Hannah sewed and listened and smiled when they spoke to her, and said little. She became a part of the furniture of the place, as much as the row of roaring sewing machines and the great goose irons steaming and stinking on the presser's bench. The others chattered on, leaving her in peace to think her own thoughts and dream her own dreams.

She was dreaming more than ever now, but these dreams were quite unlike her old ones. Never did she think of Eaton Square or the people there if she could help it, though sometimes a vagrant memory would creep past her guard and explode into her mind. But that was not often; mostly she had managed to lock that seven years of her life into a box, to be buried deep inside her.

Instead she dreamed of remote coral islands, surrounded by azure seas, where she lived alone. She would furnish her islands, exotic creations all her own, with meticulous detail, seeing every plant and every animal on them. She would watch herself through each tranquil day, seeing herself wake in a tent made of branches to run and swim in her perfect seas, and then to catch fish and cook them over fires she had built of drift wood, and then to catch butterflies so that she could set them free, or to pick flowers to arrange in her tent. On and on she went, weaving a remote and totally impossible world into which she could escape.

She grew thinner and thinner. Bloomah looked at her at the end of each day as she sat at the family table playing with her supper (for the less she ate the less she seemed to want to eat) and worried over her. But she said nothing. She knew better than to do that.

For life at Antcliff Street had been misery, that first few weeks. The first flush of delight at having Hannah back dissolved into petulance. If the girl was quiet, Bloomah suspected her of yearning for the other woman, for her lost Mary, and she would snap and complain, so that Hannah became even more withdrawn. And then, sometimes, she would start to nag at her, going on and on about how much Hannah must despise her home, after the way she used to live, and wasn't she ashamed of her parents, and how was she going to get on with her fancy ideas now?

Bloomah knew she was wrong to do it, knew it was unkind, knew above all that it estranged her daughter even more, but she could not stop herself. And Hannah on her part felt the sting of her mother's words because there was truth in them. She *did* loathe the narrow pinched poverty of Antcliff Street. She *did* hate the shabbiness and the dirt and the smells and the way her brothers and father seemed to take it all for granted and to have no ambition to better their lives. And she hated the way Bloomah had been defeated by her years of struggle in this cramped little place. At first Hannah had tried to help. She had suggested different ways of arranging the furniture, better ways of draping the windows, offered to clean and scrub, but Bloomah had flared up at that, and accused her of criticizing. So she had stopped trying. They settled for a sullen politeness that left both of them feeling cold and lonely. Life at Antcliff Street was undoubtedly misery.

October died in a splutter of yellow leaves in Victoria Park, and Hannah began to hope again. Soon, surely soon Uncle Alex would be back? Then she could go and tell him she wanted that job, wanted to find a better place to live, wanted to get away from Bloomah and Nathan and the boys, to be her own woman again. Soon surely, she would be free?

*

Her freedom came in a splutter of blood on the worn linoleum in front of the cooker on the landing.

It was a raw night in the middle of December, when the smell of sulphur was thick in the air. Hannah had walked back from Spitalfields with her head down and a scarf pulled over her nose, thinking of how much she would enjoy a hot bath, a real hot bath in a bathroom with hot towels and good soap and the smell of scent, the way it had been at Eaton Square. She had been too tired to stop herself remembering, letting her mind wander through the carpeted corridors and the warm firelit rooms; anything to take the chill of this winter darkness out of her bones.

She stopped at the corner shop to buy a loaf of fresh brown bread and some Dutch cheese, for today was pay day, and she had three gleaming half-crowns in her pocket. The week had been murderously busy, and she had worked at a rate which surprised even her, turning out fifteen felled coats a day, a considerable feat. Had she but known it, Isaac was complimenting himself on his newest felling hand; she was not only fast but neat, and she kept at it. Paying her seven shillings and sixpence for her week's work had been a pleasure, because she had earned more than three times that for him, and he knew it. Of course he had more sense than to let *her* know it.

The shop was warm and welcoming, the women standing about chattering as usual; whatever time of day it was, there was always someone at Black Sophie's. For once they didn't stop as she came in to stand staring at her, but nodded affably enough and went on with their gossip.

Hannah didn't linger with them. There was always the remote possibility that a message had come from Uncle Alex. And if not she would wrap herself up again in her heavy coat (the one memento of her Eaton Square days that she valued greatly, especially now that the weather had become so bitingly raw), and go to the public library in Watney Street. It was usually warm there, and they stayed open until nine o'clock on these winter nights. The library was free and sparsely occupied, and above all quiet, a comforting place, away from the miseries of Bloomah's silence and Nathan's armchair snores.

She pushed open the front door, stepping out of the wraiths of fog gratefully, and began to climb, wishing she could persuade her parents to invest in a small lamp for the dark turns. One of these days someone would fall and kill themselves in the dark, over the broken treads.

The landing was dark too, and she stopped, aware suddenly of something wrong. There was a bulkiness somewhere in front of her. She put out her hand, but felt nothing. After a moment she said, 'Momma?' in a small voice. There was no answer, and she said, 'Momma?' again and tilted her chin, but it was clear that she was alone in the house. She reached for the wall, and inched her way round the edge of the landing, somehow not daring to walk across the middle of it, though she knew it as well as she knew her own hand. The door to the living room was ajar and she pushed her way in and fumbled across to the fireplace to reach for the mantelshelf and the box of Vestas in the vase on the right hand side.

The match flared as she lit the gas. She looked round, puzzled. Usually when she got home the fire was burning and the table was laid for supper, and there was some smell of cooking, but tonight the place felt empty and still, as though no one had been here for a long time.

'Momma?' she said again, standing beside the table with the Vesta box in her hand as the gas overhead hissed down at her. She shook her head in irritation at her own timidity and went to the door. Bloomah must be in the other room, lying down, maybe on the boys' bed, having fallen asleep and slept longer than she meant.

She was lying huddled in front of the cooker, a saucepan in one outflung hand and potatoes and water splattered around her head. She looked very small and very crumpled and yet somehow curiously comfortable.

She was still breathing. When Hannah squatted beside her and reached out one terrified hand, she had thought at first she was not, but now she could see her chest just rising and could hear a faint sound of air moving through her parted lips. She was very white; even in the poor light thrown from the gas mantle in the living room Hannah could see that. She could also see that she was lying in a pool of blood. Her legs were spattered with it, and it had formed a cold clot beneath her apron, on the worn linoleum.

She had to run to the corner shop to get help. There was no

one downstairs, in Mrs Arbeiter's part of the house, no one anywhere about in the street, but at the corner shop there would be women and warmth and commonplace talk. Normality. So she ran, and burst in through the door breathlessly, her face white and her legs shaking beneath her.

Black Sophie was tidying up, yawning, waiting for the last of her customers to make their unwilling way out into the fog. Hannah looked at her worn old face and felt, suddenly, huge guilt. It wasn't right to upset her at the end of her day. She'd have to go somewhere else.

She pushed that silly notion away, and managed to catch her breath enough to tell them, to explain that Momma was lying on the linoleum in a clot of blood and please, *please* would someone do something ...

One of the women ran home to haul out her son and send him running as fast as he could to the hospital for an ambulance. Sophie herself, who reacted to every emergency with thoughts of food and drink, scrabbled under her untidy counter to find a small bottle of brandy, which she forced at Hannah so that she had to swallow some of the fiery stuff. It made her cough, which at least brought some colour back into her face, and made her legs feel less jellied. And then all of them came with her, back to the silent house at number nine.

Somewhere along the way, in all the excitement (for the women's exclaiming and shouting brought any number of neighbours to their windows), someone sent for Mother Charnik, the midwife from Christian Street. She arrived, panting, to drag her vast bulk in its rusty old black overcoat up the stairs to the landing.

The cluster of women made way for her respectfully, for she was not one to argue with, not Mother Charnik. She had delivered their babies, and sorted out their aches and pains for as long as they could remember. Hannah looked up at her, from her place at Bloomah's head where she was kneeling stroking the pallid forehead, and shuddered a little. Mother Charnik in that horrible overcoat had scarred her childhood with her ominous visits; when she had come to see Momma it meant Momma was ill and small Hannah had to creep about and Be Good. She remembered it all too painfully now, as though all the episodes of Bloomah's myriad illnesses had been woven into one huge one, the present one.

The old woman peered at her through narrow short sighted eyes, then flopped down on her knees beside Bloomah and without a word dragged her skirt up. Hannah wanted to reach out and hit her for handling her mother so; Bloomah who whatever else happened was always so modest, who would never let anyone see her when she took her dress off, not even her own daughter.

'Tsst,' the old woman said after a moment of fumbling. 'Tsst – give me a towel, one of you. Come on, you ain't made of schmaltz on a cold day, are you? Move already!'

'In the boys' room,' Hannah said, jerking her head, and one of the women ran and fetched a towel. Mother Charnik with swift and surprisingly delicate movements wadded it between Bloomah's legs, and held it there fast. They could all see the blood now, a slow purplish stain spreading sluggishly across the fabric. The women took a hissing breath and shook their heads and muttered. Hannah felt the coldness that was inside her start to rise, like a tide.

'Not good, dolly,' Mother Charnik said, and peered at her in the dim light. She was sweating and her forehead sent an oily gleam back at Hannah. 'Where's your poppa? Where's the boys?'

'I don't know,' Hannah said. 'They usually eat before I get home. Gone out maybe. I don't know.'

'Jake's at the gym in Leman Street and Nathan's playing solo down at Curly's,' one of the women said. 'My Sam's there with him. He told me he was going with Nathan.'

'Someone go fetch,' Mother Charnik ordered. 'There's a time a man plays solo, there's a time a man sits beside his wife God forbid it should be necessary.'

The ambulance arrived after what seemed to Hannah an eternity, its bell ringing importantly in the narrow street, and then everyone was out, the uncorseted women with their hair pinned up, wigless at this time of night, the children tousle headed from their beds, the men whispering and muttering at each other, shaking their heads with downturned mouths. They had hardly ever noticed Bloomah from one day's end to the next but tonight they appeared to watch her being carried out on a red blanketed stretcher to the high wheeled white ambulance with its two impatient high stepping horses misting the heavy air to an even thicker fog with their breath.

Bloomah died at the London Hospital fifteen minutes

before Nathan and Jake got there, and just after Solly arrived, wide eyed and guilty from the public house in the Mile End Road where he had no right to be at his age, and out of which one of the busy know-all neighbours had flushed him. They found Hannah sitting very still and straight on one of the wooden benches in the front hall, staring down at the tiled floor. The place reeked of lysol and hard carbolic soap and the high ceiling was misted with the fog that had come drifting in through the big doors. All Hannah could think of was the fact that in two days time it was her birthday. She would be eighteen.

30

The days went by in a mist even thicker than the all pervading fog. People came and went and murmured at her, 'I wish you long life,' the timeless ritual words of comfort. Hannah hated them for that. It implied that all she cared about when faced with the awesome fact of her mother's death was her own chance of life. As if that mattered. As if any of it mattered. Bloomah was dead, and she'd never been able to tell her how important she was, never been able to apologize or explain how much she really loved her, and needed her. And now she never would. The chance to pay her debt to that thin tired woman was gone for ever, and Hannah felt, with all the intensity of which she was capable, that she would bear the burden of that failure all her life. She had to bite her lips to prevent herself shouting as much at the repeated mumbles of 'I wish you long life,' 'I wish you long life.'

Nathan was at first stunned, not seeming to believe it had happened. He seemed to Hannah to shrink before her eyes that first night, sitting in the front room at Antcliff Street in his armchair and staring at the dead fireplace and saying absolutely nothing. Jake and Solly were silent too, but theirs was more the silence of uncertainty. Hannah realized that what was distressing and frightening them was not Bloomah's death, which they had not yet fully comprehended, but Nathan's silence and staring-eyed blankness.

The next day he began to change. The rabbi came and talked to him, and then his brother Reuben, and sister-in-law Minnie, and then Isaac and Thin Sarah, and the neighbours, all bending respectfully over him. He seemed to blossom under the warmth of their regard and became more himself again. He began to talk of the funeral arrangements and harry Hannah about the way everything should be done.

'There'll be food to prepare,' he said importantly. 'Bagels and salt herrings and hard boiled eggs for the mourners, when they come back from the burial grounds, and whisky. And then afterwards when the people come to the *shivah*, coffee and cakes. And we'll need a cloth over the mirror and a memorial candle and low chairs.'

'Hannah mustn't do it,' Thin Sarah said. 'She's a mourner too – ' And Nathan had peered at her, puzzled for a moment and then said vaguely, 'Oh yes. Hannah's a mourner too...'

The funeral was held at eleven in the morning. The carriage came with its black horses and Hannah wondered briefly who had paid for it. Reuben? Isaac? Certainly not Nathan. If Alex had been here, he would have covered it all, of course. And then she stopped caring as the men in their dark suits clustered round and the women started to wail and throw their hands up, and she took hold of her awareness and pushed it deep inside. Today was going to be hell and she could live through hell only by withdrawing from it.

They told her not to go to the burial grounds, that women never did. For a brief moment she almost rebelled, wanting to tell them that she too had the right to set her hand on the barrow that would hold the plain box in which Bloomah would be buried; she too had the right to push it to the grave, and then to throw in her handful of soul. But the flare of argument died as soon as it raised itself, and she stayed obediently with the women.

They bustled about importantly, setting plates with salt herring to symbolize tears, together with hard boiled eggs, symbols of the way the Jewish soul is toughened under stress, and round bagels to add their symbolism of life going on in its eternal circle, readying the house for the mourners' return from the cemetery, far away at Plashet in East Ham, the other side of Plaistow. They gossiped and bustled, well pleased with themselves, giving each other instructions and countermanding them with busy efficiency.

'Look at 'em,' Cissie said sourly, sitting beside Hannah. 'Just look at them. It's as good as a wedding or a Barmitzvah to them. Better. No presents to buy.' Hannah actually smiled and reached out and touched her hand. To have given up a morning's work to come to comfort her was friendship indeed and she was grateful for it. Even Uncle Isaac had made a face at the amount of time he was losing to go to his sister's funeral. Only a small complaint, but a complaint nonetheless. And Hannah knew it was justified. The loss of a day's money was a painful one. All the more reason to be grateful to Cissie.

The day wore on. The men returned and more and more people came pressing up the stairs to bring their offerings of freshly baked kugels and plavahs, food for the mourners, then to stay and gossip and drink tea and enjoy the unusual respite of a social occasion. A *shivah* it might be, but after all, everyone has to die and Bloomah *alovah shalom* hadn't had so bad a life. Three children almost full grown *c'nainah hora*, and thank God she didn't suffer too much, she went fast, please God by me it should be the same God forbid you should even think of dying, but you got to be practical, don't you?

The next day and the days after that were the same, punctuated by the sing song of prayers at morning, mid-day and evening. And all the time Nathan seemed to grow in stature. He developed an air of dignified mourning that made Hannah want to shout at him, to tell him Bloomah was dead, really *dead*, that he wasn't just playing a game pretending she was.

But she didn't, of course. He needed his moment of glory, standing there praying flanked by his sons at the forefront of the mourners, as the rabbi swayed and chanted over the flickering candles. Who was she to rob him of that?

It was on the fifth morning he came. She was sitting on the special low mourner's chair staring out of the window at the dirty grey sky. The fog had lifted at last. The boys had muttered something about needing to get some air, and after morning prayers were over had slipped out, promising to be back before midday. Nathan was dozing in his armchair, abandoning his own low chair with the excuse that his back was hurting him. She looked at his half open mouth and his unshaven cheeks (for mourners may not shave until the allotted time is past), and felt her anger at him bubble inside her again. It was as though she needed someone to blame for what had happened to Bloomah, someone apart from herself. Nathan with his air of self centred satisfaction made a good target. And then she hated herself for feeling so. He was suffering too, in his own way.

She turned her head as the door opened and stared at him, somehow unsurprised. It was as though she had known he'd be there, for there was no lurch inside her, no surge of breathtaking excitement of the sort she used to know when he came to Eaton Square.

'Hello, Daniel,' she said.

'Hannah.' He stood with his hat held before him, clutching the brim in both hands, and he looked as exotic as a parakeet, in spite of the fact that his coat and cravat were a respectful black. But the coat was so silken, and his linen was so blazingly white and his neat black bowler hat so impeccably brushed that he could not fail to look different from the other men who inhabited this sad sour corner of London.

'I'm so sad for you. I offer you my condolences.'

Thank you, she thought with passionate gratitude. Thank you for not wishing me a long life. But she said nothing, just sat and looked at him, her head slightly bent.

'You ... are you well? You look ... you don't look too well,' he said and then shook his head in impatience at his own ineptitude. 'Damn it, I'm a fool. Of course you don't. You've had a bad time. I heard when I came last night.'

'Last night?' Her voice was a little husky from fatigue.

'Yes. I came to fetch ... to tell you something. I saw the people and someone told me. They said the morning would be better if I had to talk privately. So I've come back.'

'What is it?' She was sitting very upright now, staring up at him. 'Mrs Mary?'

'I hate having to do this,' he said wretchedly. 'You've had enough to ... but what can I do? I can't help it.'

'Mrs Mary,' she said. It wasn't a question.

'Yes,' he said. 'She ... I told her I'd come to tell you. I couldn't refuse. I didn't want to come. Not till last night. But I have to do it.'

'You'd better explain.' She moved her head to indicate a chair beside the table. 'Sit down and tell me.'

'After they sent you away she got ill. Uncle Emmanuel said it was temper, but it went on and on, and it was Mrs

292

Sarson who called my Aunt Susan, and she came and said Aunt Mary needed a doctor, so Emmanuel had to agree. And of course he was wrong.'

'What is it?'

There was a small silence. Daniel looked at her, at the pinched white face over the black of her mourning clothes and thought, how can I tell her? How could she live with the knowledge of what Mary had done, and why she had done it? His father had made it clear to him yesterday: Mary had been systematically dosing herself with morphine laced chlorodyne and aspirin and whatever else she could find to dull her senses, including brandy, ever since Hannah had gone away. The doctor had been horrified, he'd said, at the cadaverous state she was in.

'If she'd jumped out of the window she couldn't have done herself more damage,' Albert Lammeck had said to Daniel, seeming unaware of the significance of what he had said. Daniel had felt himself go cold as he realized what had happened. And almost certainly why. But how could he explain it to Hannah? How could he put that burden of guilt on her? So he said the first thing that came into his head, which had a certain logic, for Mary had indeed seemed to his horrified eyes when he had seen her to have wasted away.

'Cancer,' he said and the word hung in the air between them.

'Cancer,' Hannah said after a long moment, almost dreamily. 'They told us that was what my mother had. Had it a long time. In her womb. It ate into an artery and she bled to death. Cancer.'

Daniel whitened. 'Please, Hannah, don't.'

'Is it too disagreeable for you?' she said harshly. 'Does it upset you? I'll try not to mention it again.'

He shook his head. 'I know how you must be feeling, and I'm truly ... well, it's Mary now. She's really very ill. It's as though ... to tell you the truth, I don't think she wanted to be well once you'd gone.' He could risk that much.

'She sent no messages.' Hannah knew her voice sounded stark and cold and didn't care at all. 'Not a word. Nothing.'

'Don't be a fool, Hannah,' he said sharply. 'You know perfectly well what Emmanuel's like when he gets a notion! He'd made up his mind to it that you were out, and that was that. Do you think he'd let her get any messages to you? Do you think she didn't try?'

Hannah was silent. He said even more wretchedly, 'And I, dammit, I should have realized she'd want some help, but I was so involved with my own affairs, I didn't see her for a while, so I didn't know. Or I'd have sent her messages to you. But I was busy ... '

'Busy with Leontine?' She grinned at him, a tight little grimace that showed how much she hated herself for the absurdity of even caring what his business had been.

There was another pause and then he said with all the dignity he could, 'Yes. With Leontine. There seemed no reason why I shouldn't please my family after that. No reason. The notice of our marriage next spring was put in *The Times* a month ago.'

'I didn't see it.' She grinned again, almost with real amusement. 'It isn't a newspaper we see much in this part of London. We're a long way from Eaton Square here.'

'Yes,' he said.

They sat silent then. Below, she heard the door slam as the boys came back, listened to them rattling up the stairs. She stood up.

'Jake, Solly,' she said. 'This is Mr Lammeck. Mr Lammeck, my brothers.'

'How d'you do,' he said punctiliously and held out his hand. 'I wish you a long life. My regrets at your bereavement.'

They glanced sideways at Hannah. She came round the table to stand beside them, almost protectively. She was as tall as them now, though much more fragile, yet she felt she had to look after them in the face of this exotic creature who so abashed them.

'Wassa marrer?' Nathan stirred in the armchair and sat up.

'I wish you long life, sir, and comfort in your loss,' Daniel said. He shook hands with Nathan who peered up at him owlishly from the depths of the chair. 'I am Daniel Lammeck, sir, a friend of your daughter.'

'He's come to tell me she's ill,' Hannah said harshly. 'Mrs Mary is ill.'

After a moment Daniel said, 'Dying.'

'Mrs Mary?' Nathan struggled to his feet, his hand at the small of his back. 'That one, that woman who threw my Hannah out, I should care she's dying? You come and tell a man who's mourning, who sits crying for the loss of his dear wife may her sweet soul rest in eternal peace, that another woman who treated my girl so bad is dying? You want I should care? A *choleria* on her, you hear me? The way she treated my Hannah, may she die at once and rot for ever!'

Hannah had gone white. She took a deep breath to speak, to cry Nathan down, but Daniel was too swift for her.

'I know how you must feel, sir. This is a dreadful time for you. I meant no disrespect, I do promise you. As for what my aunt did, believe me, she is not to blame. If any blame is to be apportioned it is to me, for not fighting hard at the time of our ... of what happened. It was all so quick, you see. One minute there we are at a ball, and the next there's Uncle Emmanuel shouting and the King there and ... '

It was as though there was no one else in the room, just herself and Daniel, as she felt the coldness in her begin to melt at the look on his face. When he ended awkwardly, 'I'm sorry. It was all my fault, and I'm sorry,' the last vestige of the ice dissolved. For five days now she had been wrapped in a veneer of bitter cold, and now it had gone. Now she had to think and decide for herself again, and not just stand by as things happened around her.

'It wasn't your fault,' she said. 'It wasn't anyone's. It just happened. Is she dying, Daniel, truly?'

'Yes.' He shook his head, his eyes suddenly bright. She wanted to go to him and hug him and soothe the tears away, but she stood very still, and without moving her eyes from Daniel's face said, 'Poppa? She's asking for me. And you heard ... it wasn't her fault. She's dying and she's asking for me.'

'Your mother's already dead!' Nathan shouted. 'You hear me? Your mother's already dead, and you got to sit here a week to mourn respectful for her, what do you mean, do I hear? What sort of question is that a girl asks her father, a bereaved man who sits with his face unshaven and his clothes torn? You want you should go already? It's mad, it's wicked, you should be ashamed of yourself.'

'Mrs Mary isn't dead. That's why I have to go.' She felt the stubbornness rise in her. She had to put it right with Mary. Bloomah had died with the words unspoken between them, leaving the guilt to lie heavy on Hannah's head. To let Mary do the same would be more than she could bear. She had to see her, had to tell her how much she cared. To let her disappear into the blackness with no word from Hannah would be to consign herself to the same darkness. So she told herself, deep inside, staring at Daniel beseechingly, knowing she was being over-dramatic, but needing to indulge herself.

'You go from here, and you never come back!' Nathan roared. 'You hear me? You understand what I'm saying? You got to stay here to look after me and your brothers, you can't go because some madam from the schnorrers' shop crooks a finger!'

'Mr Lazar, believe me, it isn't like that!' Daniel said. 'She isn't being ... I don't think I explained well. She's *dying*. The doctors say it's a matter of days. She looks so bad, and she's fretting for Hannah. All she wants is to say a few words. Believe me, I'll have her back in no time. A few hours, no more. My carriage is at the end of the street in Commercial Road. I can be there and back in hardly any time at all, before evening prayers tonight, I promise. Just a few hours.'

'She goes now, you don't bring her back, you hear me?' Nathan was standing very erect, his face suffused a deep red. It was as though all the feelings of the past days had coalesced into one single furious emotion, all of it directed at Hannah. She stared at him feeling the sick, all too familiar coldness rising in her belly. It seemed as if Nathan were someone else, not her father at all.

'Jake,' she said. 'Solly?'

Jake shook his head, his eyes troubled. 'You want to go, it's up to you. Poppa knows what's what, though, and if he says no, well ... ' His voice died away. Solly just shook his head and said nothing.

'You go and you don't come back. You got no more respect for your mother than you go running to someone else, not a week after she's in her grave, I got no use for you. Not now or ever. You understand me?' He thrust his hands behind his back with a theatrical gesture that was almost funny, but there was no humour at all in the expression on his face.

She couldn't help it. She lost her temper. 'You fool!' she shrieked at him. 'You half witted fool! Momma's *dead*. She's dead and buried! I can't do anything for her. But Mary isn't, and I'm going to her, and I'll be back tonight. And if you don't like it, I don't care, you hear me? I just don't care!'

296

31

They travelled to Eaton Square in silence, sitting as far apart in the carriage as it was possible to do. She was wearing an old black dress with the collar which had been ceremoniously cut at *Kesirah*, the ritual tearing of the mourner's garments, on the day of her mother's funeral, and with a grey shawl over her head. She was aware how shabby and poor she looked, and took a perverse pleasure in that. They would see, the people at Eaton Square, to what she had come. Not Mary, of course, but the others. Especially Emmanuel.

She tried to imagine how it would be with Mary. She would go up the broad thickly carpeted stairs and along the corridor with its niches and little marble statues and heavy oil paintings and bowls of flowers on gilt tables and tap on Mary's bedroom door and walk into its white and gold magnificence and stand beside her bed and ...

And what? She couldn't see Mary's face, however hard she tried. Just a blank on a pillow. She couldn't feel words in her, or any response that Mary might give her, and that distressed her. She stared out at the blur of passing traffic trying to compose herself, but it was difficult. The confusion of feelings in her could only be composed by tight control. All she could do was push the anxiety down and try to pretend it wasn't there.

To Daniel, sitting on the other side of the carriage and staring at her, she looked unapproachable, pale and thinner than he remembered her, with shadows at her temples. She had always been an amusing little thing in his eyes, someone who was part of his Aunt Mary's life and who made him feel comfortable and interested when he went to visit; it had only been in the past few months that he had noticed how attractive she was, with her heavy breasts and that curving waist. She looked beautiful still, even under that hideous shawl, and he wanted very much to reach out and touch her, to try to offer her some comfort in the tangled situation she was in, but he dared not. She sat wrapped in a silence that could not be broached.

The carriage came round the Square and the wheels muffled as they passed over the straw that had been set in the roadway. Hannah lifted her chin and for the first time a real awareness of the severity of Mary's state came to her. If they had strewn the street this way then indeed it was very bad. She began to feel sick.

Daniel seemed to be aware of the chink in her control. He helped her down from the carriage, and tucked his hand tightly into one elbow, and she was grateful for his support and leaned against him a little. So it was that they climbed the front steps and walked in through the open front door very close together, and the first Davida was aware of their presence was when she turned and saw them there, Daniel with his arm protectively around Hannah now, for he had realized as he crossed the threshold what had happened.

They were standing at the foot of the stairs, Davida and Emmanuel and Susan, with Ezra and Alfred and Albert behind them.

'Oh, God, she's dead,' Daniel said blankly.

Hannah tightened her shoulders, and took a deep breath. It had to be so; that was why she had not been able to see Mary's face when she thought of her. It had to be so, because someone somewhere wanted to punish her. Guilt and anger and shock meshed together to fill her with a sense of panic. She turned her face towards Daniel, and he put up his other hand to cradle her head against him.

'Daniel?' Davida said, and took a step forward. '*Daniel?* What is that ... what are you doing here with that creature? Get her out of here at once, you hear me? At once.'

'Mother, be quiet,' Daniel said, and his voice was harder than Hannah could ever remember hearing. 'Uncle Emmanuel, I'm sorry, so sorry. When ... '

'About an hour ago,' Susan said, and sniffed. Her eyes were red and her skin looked pouched with the tears she had shed. 'She was conscious, oh God, she was conscious. I thought people were always in a coma when they died, but I swear she knew what was happening and ... '

'Be quiet, Susan,' Albert said sharply. 'It's enough. I know you feel bad, but it's enough. Daniel, I don't know what you think you're playing at, but will you please – '

'Get that creature out of here!' Davida shrieked it, and though Albert put out his hand to stop her she couldn't be

298

controlled. She had gone a patchy red, and the words came out of her in a flood of fury. Everything she had said on the night of the ball she said again, only now she said it even more violently; Hannah was a whore, a street creature, a filthy object which polluted everything and everyone with which it came in contact, and if he didn't get her out of this house at once and throw her back in the muck from which he'd fetched her, then she, his mother, would personally see to it that …

'What, mother?' Daniel said, not moving, still holding Hannah's head against his chest. 'You'll do what, mother? Because I'm not going to do anything of the sort. She's going to be your daughter-in-law, and the sooner you stop that shrieking the sooner you'll get used to the idea.'

Hannah tried to move her head, tried to look up, but he was still holding her close. After a moment she stopped trying and remained very still. None of this was happening, of course. None of it. It was all one of the dreams, gone crazy.

'Not funny, Daniel.' It was Alfred's voice, heavy and tired. 'This is no time to make such stupid jokes. Your Uncle Emmanuel … '

'I'm sorry, Uncle, but you must see it isn't my fault. Aunt Mary asked for Hannah, so I went to fetch her. To have her treated so by Mama – you must see I couldn't help it.'

'You do as you choose,' Emmanuel said testily. 'Everyone can help everything. You chose to interfere in matters that don't concern you, so naturally your mother is angry. I'm angry. You had no right to bring that girl here.'

'I had every right!' Daniel said strongly. 'Aunt Mary asked me.'

'A dying woman, half out of her mind! What do you mean she asked? What did she know?' Emmanuel said. 'I put that girl out, and out she stays.'

'Then I stay out too,' Daniel said. 'I told you.'

Emmanuel shrugged. 'I'm not interested, Daniel. If you want to have family arguments, go home and have them there. Leave me in peace to bury my wife.'

'Until that creature goes he doesn't come home,' Davida said. Now her voice was very controlled. 'Understand me, Daniel? Whatever maggot it is you've taken into your head, you can get it out. You've gone mad, just for a moment you must have gone mad.' Her voice softened, began to wheedle a little. 'You were fond of your aunt, I know, and distress for her ... well, we can understand. And forgive. Now, Albert, get one of the footmen to send that wretched girl on her way and take us both home. Daniel needs some rest.'

'Mother, I told you!' Daniel said, his voice all sweet reason. 'You might as well get used to it. I told you! And I mean it.'

Now Hannah had to move. Dreams sometimes ran away with themselves, always had, even from her earliest days when she had first learned how to comfort herself with the splendour inside her own head, but this was going too far.

'Daniel,' she said, her voice husky again. 'Daniel, please stop this. And take me home.'

'You can't. You heard what your father said. You can't. Anyway, I've got other plans.'

She closed her eyes and took a deep breath. 'Take me home, please.'

'You heard her, Daniel,' Albert said. He moved across the hall towards them, and set one hand on Daniel's shoulder. He spoke more softly now, so that the others couldn't hear him. 'Do me a favour, son. Go, will you? We've got too much to do here to cope with, and your mother is in one of her ... I'll be home later, we'll talk then.' He looked at Hannah, and managed a small smile. 'You look done in, girl. This son of mine, you must forgive him. He doesn't always let his head take charge of what he's doing or saying. You must be upset about Mary too. You worked for her a long time.'

'Yes,' she said. 'Yes. A long time.'

'So, Daniel, on your way. I'll be at home tonight, after we've settled everything here. I'll talk to you then. Only do me a favour – keep out of your mother's way for a bit. Go on.'

To Hannah's intense relief Daniel obeyed. At the front door, he stopped for a moment, and said carefully, 'Uncle Emmanuel, I wish you long life.'

Emmanuel, who had started to go back upstairs, looked back at him. 'What? Oh, yes.' He went on walking with a very straight back and a certain spring in his step.

He's glad she's dead, Hannah thought. He's glad. Mrs Chantry, I suppose. Oh, Mrs Mary, I did love you so much. And I never said it properly. Momma, I want you, Mrs Mary –

300

She was weeping by the time they reached the foot of the steps outside, great sobs tightening her chest so that she could hardly breathe. Daniel increased his grip on her and waved down a passing hansom cab, for his carriage had gone, and almost lifted her into it and shouted something up at the driver before tucking himself in alongside her to put both arms round her and hold her close, letting her weep herself to a state of peace.

By the time the cab drew up with a jingle of harness at its destination she was in control again. Her eyes were red, but she was calm.

'Where are we?' she asked.

'The Cavendish. In Jermyn Street.' He jumped down and paid the driver and then helped her out. 'Come on.'

'But I want to go home.' she said. 'Please, Daniel. I must go home.'

'Later, perhaps.' He led her up the steps into the hallway of the hotel, a small and very elegant one, and she said no more. This was a new Daniel. There was nothing smooth about him, nothing obliging; he seemed to have a new power in him and she was grateful for it, for she was very tired, now. The past few weeks of her life had been enervating; the loss of her comfort with Mary, the grinding slog at her Uncle Isaac's factory, and now two deaths so close together that tragedy was almost overwhelmed by absurdity. There was a lassitude in her that welcomed this new and unexpected strength in Daniel, and she yielded to them both.

'Cor stone the bleedin' crows, and what the 'ell 'ave we got 'ere? Looks like somethin' the cat dragged in and was ashamed to drag out again. What ho, young Lammeck! How's your old Dad then? And that 'orse racin' uncle o' yours – what's 'is name. – Alfred?'

'Very well, thank you, Rosa. That is to say, we've had a death in the family and everything's a bit at sixes and sevens. Thought you might be able to help me.'

'Will if I can, I s'pose.' She was a tall woman wearing very fashionable clothes over a handsome figure, and she had a handsome face, too. She looked at Hannah with a considering expression, then grinned. 'Gawd, girl, if you don't sit down yer goin' to fall down, ain't yer? Come on. I don't know what 'e's bin up to but I'll find out soon enough.'

She turned and led the way to the wide staircase. Daniel

301

followed, his arm still round Hannah.

''Ad a death, 'ave yer? Bad luck, that. Anyone I know?'
'My Aunt Mary.'

She sniffed. 'Oh, that one. Emmanuel's missus, poor cow. Well, I don't suppose 'e'll cry long over 'er, not with Nellie Chantry to keep 'im comfortable.'

'Ye gods, Rosa, is there anything you don't know?'

'Not much. Not when it's got to do with the nobs, and your lot's nobs, ain't they? Friends o' the King, an' all that, and got more of the ready than's good for any man. Still, they're not a bad lot, as some of you Jews go. Civilized like. I've known a few, I can tell you. 'Ere you are. Tuck 'er up in 'ere, and I'll send up a bit o' something to eat later on.'

She led them into a large bedroom decorated in soft blues and greens. Hannah registered mirrors decorated with great curving carved lilies on the frames and cabinets with similar curves and swathes of curtains and patterned wallpaper. It looked and smelled like a haven of comfort.

'Who's that?' Hannah said when Rosa had gone, more out of shyness than because she really wanted to know. It felt odd to be here, in a bedroom, with Daniel.

She turned away to the window, pulling her shawl off her head as she went.

'Rosa Lewis? Don't you know her? No, I don't suppose you do.'   .

Daniel didn't seem at all shy, standing beside the fireplace. After a moment he bent and set a flame to the prepared paper from a box of Vestas in his pocket. Soon the cheerful crackle of burning wood filled the room.

'She's a great character. Best cook in the world – does all my mother's parties and nearly everyone else's besides. Runs this place, too, very select, very distinguished, and very easy going. If Rosa likes you, she doesn't ask questions.'

'And if she doesn't?'

'You don't get over the threshold. Hannah, come and sit down. Rosa was right. You do look done in. Come and rest, my dear child, and – '

'I am not your dear child.' She said it in a tight little voice.

'No, I'm sorry. It's just that you look at the moment like – '

'Nor am I . . . nor are you going to . . . ' She stopped and he laughed.

302

'Marry you? But I am. I've set my mind to it.'

She turned and looked at him then, still in the window embrasure so that her face was in shadow. He looked very sure of himself standing there with one arm resting on the mantelshelf, and the firelight lifting his cheeks to peaks and shadows.

'You're supposed to be engaged to Leontine. You told me. There was a notice in *The Times*.'

'What's that got to do with anything? I did it to please my mother. There seemed no reason not to. You'd gone, and it was all too boring and anyway, she nagged so. And Leontine's harmless enough, you know. Pretty girl, and all that. So I thought, why not?'

'And now you're thinking, why not me, is that it?'

He was silent for a moment and then he held out his hands to her.

'No. It's not as easy as that. I ... it seemed so right, you see. When mother was going on and on, I suddenly realized that that was what I wanted. I've never gone in for thinking much, Hannah, never had to, you see. I mean, there was always everthing *there*. Mama can be so, well, she's a very organized person, usually gets what she wants. So she told me what I wanted and I believed her. It's easier that way. But then you seemed to change, when I came to Aunt Mary's. You were different. That was why I came so often. Didn't you know?'

'Don't be stupid.' Her voice was a little unsteady. 'How could I know anything? Your aunt's servant.'

'Oh, don't start that nonsense again,' he said impatiently. 'It's boring. Hannah, I truly do love you, you know that? You ... oh, I don't know what it is. You make me feel good. That's why I told them I was going to marry you. Please, don't make a liar of me.' He smiled, but he looked anxious.

'It's crazy,' she said. 'Quite crazy. I'm just – who am I to marry you?'

'A nice Jewish girl,' he said, and grinned. 'Believe me, my mother'll come round. She was always worried that I might marry out of the religion. I think that was why she got so set on Leontine in the first place. Someone safe, you know. That and her money, of course.'

'I've no money,' she said, and wanted to giggle. 'I could

ask my father, I suppose. Good fathers are supposed to find a dowry for their daughters, aren't they? He might manage a couple of bagels ... '

Daniel grinned even more widely. 'That's better,' he said softly. 'That's much better. Come, Hannah, admit that you like me. You do, don't you? That's why I first noticed you, I think. You used to sit there with your sewing on your lap sending out messages.'

'Messages? I? I did no such thing!'

'But you did, my little love, you truly did! You sat there thinking I was marvellous, didn't you? You can't deny it – I used to feel it. That's why I first noticed, you see. It's why I love you now.'

You can make things happen just by wanting them, she thought, and stared at him in the firelight. You can make things real by making them false first. You just sit and dream, and make pictures in your head and if you do it with enough power and wanting the dreams get solid and move out of your head and into real life. Suddenly she was frightened. She loved him and she was frightened. She wanted Mary, she wanted Momma ...

Again she was crying and this time he came and picked her up and carried her across the room to put her on the bed, then sat beside her stroking her as she wept and wept, soaking the silken coverlet with her tears, and somewhere deep inside herself, almost bursting with excitement.

32

It was inevitable, of course. Her highly emotional state and fatigue, and his excitement and enormous self esteem at having successfully imposed his will on his mother, and the blue-green room in its firelight, with its sensuous curves and rich fabrics, were too much for them. They were too close together there on that bed for it to be otherwise.

He was kissing her wet face, and kissing her again and again, and she was responding with a warmth she didn't know she had in her. She had never explored the sexual possibilities of her own body, had never let herself dream about love making; in all her years of fantasizing about handsome shadow-faced lovers and sumptuous weddings she had always left herself and her dream partners at the bedroom door. She had shrunk from ever allowing herself to think what physical love might be like. Now she knew why she had been so circumspect.

It was because she had a vast reserve of sensuous response in her. His mouth slipping against her own wet mouth made her head sing. His tongue against hers started sensations in her belly she would never have imagined possible. His hands against her breasts as he pulled away the black mourning bodice were like a fire against her skin. Her nipples contracted so hard that they hurt and she whimpered a little with the pain of it when his lips touched them and that seemed to galvanize him. He tugged at her clothes and at his own with such speed that she had no time to think, even if she had wanted to, and then they were rolling on the silken counterpane in a welter of torn fabric and slippery skin as the firelight leaped in the grate and the sensations leaped in her groin to an even higher peak. The hurting went on as he thrust at her, and it was marvellous and she raised her hips to him, wanting to suffer, and relishing it. Somewhere at the back of her mind she felt she was assuaging her guilt for Bloomah and Mary; hurting like this meant she burned out some of the distress she had suffered at their loss. She needed the pain, and the fact that it was such pleasurable pain did not diminish its value.

Someone tapped the door, twice, but neither of them paid any attention. The fire burned down as the wood was consumed and the few coals that had been piled on it fell in with a soft crash to make red embers, and at last they lay there breathless and entwined. After a little while she shivered, and tried to pull one of the scattered garments over her bare breasts.

He laughed softly. 'Now you'll have to marry me,' he said. 'I've deflowered you! I've ruined you. No decent man will have you. You'll have to marry me.'

'Silly,' she murmured, and turned her head so that she could look into his face.

'You're quite a fiery lady, aren't you, Hannah?' he said lazily, and moved his head so that he could kiss her face, nuzzling against her cheek like a baby. 'I thought you so modest, so shy, and you turn out to be a man-eater.'

'Am I?' She stared at him, pulling her head back a little to get him into focus. 'What do you mean?'

'Don't you know?' He laughed again, and rolled over. 'Sweetheart, you're the most passionate woman I've ever come across.'

'Oh,' she said and was silent for a moment. 'Then there've been ... I mean, other times? Like this? Other people?'

'Darling girl, I'm twenty-seven, you know!' He looked amused. 'Not exactly a baby, after all.'

'No,' she said, and shivered again. 'I'm cold. I want to get dressed.'

'All right,' he said, and made no move.

'Please, Daniel, go away and leave me alone, will you? I want to get dressed.'

Again he laughed. 'After all we've done, you're shy? Oh, come on, Hannah!'

'I'm not twenty-seven,' she said with all the dignity she could. 'I'm eighteen. And I've never been – I've got no experience. Not like you.'

He put his arm across her, and began to nuzzle her cheek again. 'Sweetheart, please, don't fret yourself. We're getting married, remember? It's all right.'

'Is it?' She turned her head to look at him, and her eyes were opaque. 'Really?'

'Really, I told you. I've made up my mind.' He rolled off the crumpled bed and padded to the door to bring in the tray of tea and toast and small cakes that had been left there, along with a white silk wrapper.

'She's a discreet lady, our Rosa,' he said. 'Knows when to keep out of a man's way.' He looked at her in the dull light of the December afternoon, at the way her shape curved against the line of the window, and said suddenly, 'It's going to be marvellous, being us, Hannah. Isn't it?'

She stood very still for a moment and then smiled, slowly. She felt comfortable now, languorous and relaxed, though a ghost of pain still lingered. 'Yes,' she said, and he smiled too, a wide boyish grin, and for a moment their roles were reversed and she was reassuring him.

The next few hours were, for Hannah, the most precious she was ever to know with him. They pulled the curved chaise longue over to the fireplace, and Daniel replenished the grate until the flames leapt again, and they sat curled up

306

together, drinking their cold tea and eating their leathery toast. The afternoon drifted into an early evening and the window turned lilac, then violet and at last indigo before Daniel yawned and sat up.

'Darling Hannah,' he said. 'We have things to do. I must go and tell them at home, and find out what's happening about Aunt Mary's funeral and the *shivah*.'

'Poppa,' she said, and the afternoon's fragile joy shattered. 'The boys. I've got to go back, Daniel. I must.'

He was silent for a while, and then he said. 'Listen, Hannah. I think – I mean, I know he's your father and you know him best, but I think I'd better go and see him first, don't you? He's entitled to know from me what our plans are. Let me go and see him. I'll arrange with Rosa for you to stay here, and I'll come back as soon as possible. If you go and he chooses to go on being angry, it could be unpleasant for you. And I don't want that.'

There was enough fatigue still in her to make her agree. She knew, somewhere at a deep level, that she ought to go herself to face Nathan, to tell him that she was to be married, to explain, to ask him to forgive her for leaving when she had. But she was tired, and it had been, to say the least, an extraordinary afternoon. So she nodded and let him go.

It was, of course, the wrong decision. Nathan had been angry when Hannah had chosen to go to Mary, but it had not been a complete anger. He had been performing somewhat, showing the world how a bereaved man ought to feel and behave when faced with such a lack of daughterly complaisance. But now he was genuinely angry. When Daniel came back, chastened, from the East End he brought with him all Hannah's meagre possessions.

'There was nothing I could do,' he said, as she stood there looking at the plaited straw bag dangling from his hand. 'When I told him, he just said nothing, and then he went and took these things and put them in the bag, and walked out of the room. I'd have gone after him, but your brother Jake said I shouldn't. And I think he was right.'

'I see,' she said dully after a while. 'I see.'

It was over for Nathan and her; in truth it had been over almost eight years ago when he had given her to Mary. He had, in giving her to Mary, stolen something of Bloomah from her, while not giving her all of Mary. She had had a half life with both of them, and now they were both dead, and Nathan had turned his back on her. And it didn't seem to matter, all that much. She was so tired.

'The boys,' she said then, in the same dull voice. 'What did the boys say?'

'Jake says he wishes us happiness,' Daniel said, not looking at her, and she knew he lied.

'He didn't say anything, did he?'

There was a small silence and then Daniel said, 'I'm sorry. He was too startled, I think, really.' Daniel did his best, wanting to help her, but not knowing quite how. 'And your other brother is very young, of course. I don't think he quite understood.'

'Solly?' She managed a small grin at that, a tight little grimace. 'Solly not understand? You've got a lot to find out about Solly.'

'Yes,' he said, and after a moment, went over and put the straw bag on the blue-green silken counterpane.

Suddenly she was very frightened. In the muggy warmth of the luxurious room that had felt so sensual now seemed like a trap. She was aware of the cold air outside pressing against the windows. She felt she could see the serried rows of sooty roofs and chimneystacks stretching towards her from far away in the east where her only home lay, and she was afraid that the bubble in which she stood would burst, leaving her alone and cold and friendless in a bitter world. She shook inside, her courage crumbling within her.

She said nothing but he knew, and held out his hands to her and said, 'It will be all right, Hannah. We'll be married. It will be all right, I promise you.'

She shook her head, unable to believe him. Davida was outside the bubble too, her animosity pushing against it as much as the December night did, and she could not see Daniel pressuring her back. That she was passionately involved with him she knew; the shape of his head, the way the firelight reflected the planes of his face, the faint scent of him as he came and stood very close to her, all this was becoming part of her with every minute that passed. But for all her bedazzlement she was still able to see reality, and the reality behind Daniel's enormous sexual excitement was not strength, not safety, not the security she so ached for. It was only excitement. The core was not in him.

She clung to him all the same, putting up her face to be kissed, needing the reassurance of physical contact. And he, exultant, gave it to her, and found in her need enough encouragement to fuel his resolve. He would marry her, he would, no matter what Davida and his father and the whole damned tribe of Lammecks said or did.

In the moments when she was able to be detached, Hannah could understand that it was an absurd situation to be in, something out of a shilling shocker written for kitchen maids. Spurned by her father, alone in a rich hotel room with a handsome man who was about to challenge his rich parents in order to marry a penniless waif. It was enough to make you laugh, Hannah told herself a little wildly, if it didn't make you cry.

It was agreed that Hannah should stay in the room until Daniel could arrange their wedding, and both Rosa and Daniel waved away her protests about the cost.

'Don't you fuss, ducks,' Rosa said. 'Just be glad you got a real fella 'ere to care for you. There ain't that many walks in 'ere a miss and gets the chance to walk out to be made a missus. She'll need some clothes, young Lammeck, won't she? Can't 'ave 'er walking around the Cavendish lookin' worse dressed than the bleedin' maids. I'll fix somethin'.'

Hannah stopped arguing. There seemed little point, for Daniel was afire with his own resolve. It was as though something had entered into him to light his face and square his shoulders to a new swagger. She watched him and listened to him, a little overawed, for she had never in her best dreams ever imagined him as powerful as this. Or as loving. For there could be no doubt in her mind that he loved her. He missed no opportunity to sit close to her, to look at her, above all to touch her.

She stayed there for the next month, while Daniel bustled about their affairs, busy and important. He had to arrange for a wedding licence. She was under age and needed her father's consent but he told the registrar that like so many East End people his bride-to-be had no birth certificate, and was aged twenty-one. And it suited the registrar to believe him.

While all this was going on Hannah stayed in Jermyn Street unaware of what Daniel was doing on her behalf. She wanted, very much, to be part of the mourning days for Mary, but had to accept Daniel's insistence that she should go nowhere near Eaton Square.

'It's asking for trouble, darling,' he said. 'I know how you feel, but my Uncle Emmanuel ... you must see it's impossible. The place is seething with people, and he'd have no compunction at all about making a scene if he set eyes on you. You know that. And we're to be married, remember. I don't want to have any fights with him, or any of them, till it's a fait accompli.'

Because that was how it was to be. He had given her elaborate explanations about why it was best to keep quiet, and just go their own way, why forcing his family to agree that he should abandon Leontine in favour of Hannah would not be a wise move. Her spirits had sunk a little, for she had imagined him facing up to Davida. It would have been more dignified, more pleasing to her own sense of the fitness of things to do it that way, above all, more demonstrative of his strength. But it was, she had to agree, more discreet to go about it in this somewhat furtive fashion, and so had acquiesced.

The days slid by her in a soft blur. Indeed, she needed the time to recover her strength, for the months of hard work and penury and the great emotional unheaval of the last weeks had left her weak, almost ill. Rosa, shrewdly recognizing that, set her to tasks to pattern her day. She found sewing for her, and asked her to help arrange the flowers for the hotel and took her into the kitchens. 'Wives ought to know about cookin'.' Hannah was grateful to her. She had a rough tongue, a cruel malicious wit when she chose to display it, and a great deal of warmth, and she enveloped Hannah in it all and gave her time to recover.

And as the days went by, and her strength came back, she also had time to think.

She was learning that she was stronger than she had realized. That she could sit silently beside Daniel when he came to see her each evening and report on his day's doings and merely by being there, quiet and still, could rekindle his flagging energies and help extinguish his fears of his parents. No matter how set he was on having his own way, there was no doubt in her mind that he was afraid of them and dreaded the day when he would have to face them with what he had done. She had to give him the power to do so.

She was also learning that her own body was a source of vast delight, that there was a sweetness and excitement in reality that far outstripped the joys of her old dreams.

` At first she had demurred at making love again. Surely, she said to Daniel, surely if we are to be married, we should wait. But he had laughed, and after a while she had laughed too. It was nonsense, of course it was. Why deprive themselves of a satisfaction for which they both starved? Their nights – and often their early afternoons – when he could steal away from his desk at Lammeck Alley – became oases of pleasure for them, as they explored each other's bodies and their own responses with ever increasing subtlety and delight.

Hannah blossomed under such loving; she became sleek and handsome, her hair springing back into its old glory and her cheeks filling out and losing their translucent look.

But that was not all Hannah discovered about herself. She found she had a capacity for containing pain that she had not realized was part of her. She buried her feelings about Bloomah and Mary and about her father's rejection deep inside her, and looked only forwards, never backwards. She did it so well that when Daniel arrived triumphantly one afternoon with all her clothes from Eaton Square packed in a trunk by Mrs Sarson, whom he had coaxed to collect all these items for her, she calmly accepted them and sorted them out and made them over with never a thought of the days when they had been new and Mary had so delighted in providing them for her.

Yet there was another source of pain – the fact that Daniel was arranging for a wedding in a Register Office. She had never been deeply involved with religious life, for children learn from parents, and Nathan had been a lax attender of the synagogue services. He went of course on Rosh Hashanah and Yom Kippur, the High Holy Days, and very occasionally to ordinary services when a family member or a friend's son was Barmitzvah, but otherwise he had held himself aloof, and so inevitably did his wife and children. But that did not mean that Hannah did not care about the practices of her family's faith or that she could shrug away easily the accepted attitudes of the people of the East End. Marriages in Registry

Offices were not, in the eyes of the people of the quarter, marriages at all, and children born of them were regarded as *mumserim*, bastards, the offspring of fornicators.

'There is no other way,' Daniel said flatly. 'For my part, I don't care. All this fuss about synagogues, it bores me. And it's going to put one hell of a cat among the family pigeons. For both of us. But what else can I do? There isn't a rabbi anywhere in London who'd marry us without proof that you're Jewish – which means we have to show your parents' Hebrew marriage certificate. And not only would your father refuse to give it to you – it would come out, wouldn't it, that you're under age? Believe me. It can't be done. Later, maybe, when they all come round – and they will, of course – '

Hannah was not so sanguine about that, but she loved him and wanted him, and if he wanted to believe that his family would eventually be reconciled to their marriage, then she would help him by believing it too. But she had lain awake for many nights and thought what it would be like to marry someone and yet not really be married in the eyes of the people she knew. And it hurt. She told herself that as long as she and Daniel regarded themselves as properly married that would be all that mattered. Later they would put the seal of the rabbis on their union and surely that would help God to forgive them? You had to be practical in this life ...

So she would argue with herself as Daniel slept serenely beside her, his head thrust into her shoulder and one hand carelessly thrown over her breast, cupping it possessively even in his sleep, and try to stop the hurt from spreading from deep inside her. She knew that if she didn't control her distress, it would ruin everything, and she passionately wanted everything to be good and happy.

But although the pain was contained, it was still there. She knew that on her wedding day, a late December afternoon when the rain pelted down with a dreary insistence outside a green painted room in the despised Registry Office with Rosa and a couple of maids from the hotel standing witness for them, at a civil ceremony that would make her Daniel's wife. She should have been elevated with joy, standing there in her tailor made honey-coloured skirt and coat, with one hand in a handsome squirrel muff, a gift from Rosa, and the other holding her bell shaped skirt clear of her buttoned boots and with Daniel's gift of an elegant fur-trimmed bonnet on her head, but she wasn't. She was filled with an ominous mixture of guilt and dread of the future. How in God's name could she and Daniel ever be happy, when their marriage was based on such foundations?

33

But they were, in those early months. Daniel bought a house for them in a corner of Chelsea, not a very fashionable area but still very respectable. He took her there directly from the wedding, seen off in the hansom cab by a grinning Rosa who was spilling over with ribald jokes which Hannah tried not to hear.

From the moment she saw the house in Paultons Square at the western end of the King's Road, she knew it would be not just a place to live, but a haven in a very shaky world. It stood on the corner of the square, looking down Danvers Street to the occasional glimmer of the river at the far end, neat, white painted and trimmed with iron lace balconies on the upper floors. There was a small paved area at the foot of the kitchen steps and she peered down into it as they climbed to the front door and thought, 'I'll put plants there. Make a garden,' and felt suddenly very married.

Daniel had asked Mrs Sarson to find domestic staff for them, and in an obscure attempt to please dead Mary, she had gone to great trouble. Hannah found herself the mistress of a cheerful cook who was only a few years older than she was herself, and a general maid who was two years younger than Hannah, but very mature and hard working and determined to be the best general maid in the whole of Chelsea. Daniel had thought to have a valet, but Florrie, the maid, took him firmly in hand, and dealt with his clothes and his boots and his shaving water and bath water as firmly as she took care of Hannah and her needs, and that was that. They managed perfectly with just Florrie to attend to the house and their personal needs and Bet in the kitchen.

Which was just as well, because they were far from rich. Daniel had never had any money of his own; Albert had never seen any need for it, giving him as he did a handsome allowance, and knowing perfectly well that his mother provided for him lavishly in other ways. She had paid his club subscriptions, his servants' wages (for he had had his own valet of course as well as a groom to take care of his carriage and his horses), and on occasion, had sent him on costly holiday jaunts to Switzerland or Germany. But all that ceased when he married Hannah. Davida's fury was monumental, and she retreated into a vast sulk at Park Lane from which she sent furious letters to all her sisters-in-law and friends about the evil that had befallen her beloved son.

She had tried, very hard, to use financial pressure to bring Daniel to heel, but for once in her life was thwarted by her husband. Albert had always taken pride and pleasure in his Davida's sleek appearance and sparkling ways, but had learned to ignore her tiresome tantrums. Furthermore, he had a great affection for his only son. Daniel was very much like himself, dapper and charming and friendly, and not at all complicated to understand. And also Daniel had a faintly rakish way that his father secretly envied a little. Albert had a good life, wrapped in security, with his successful niche in his family's successful business, his splendid home and his elevated aristocratic friends and his gambling and his parties, but he had always hankered for a something a little more exciting, somehow, and when Daniel defied his mother and chose to marry a little guttersnipe from the East End in a Registry Office, Albert was, just a little, envious. Anyway, the girl was interesting. That red hair and those narrow blue eyes and that shapely little body stirred him too, and he would look at his daughter-in-law who had character as well as her oddly interesting looks, and was learning fast how to behave as Daniel's wife, with no hint of any East End vulgarity about her; and indeed, he would tell himself, riding home in his carriage along the King's Road after visiting them, indeed why should she not be perfectly *comme il faut*? Wasn't she raised as much by his own sister-in-law as by her own know-nothing nobody parents?

So, Albert ignored Davida's rages and complaints and nagging, and kept as close as ever to Daniel, arranging for him to have a slightly better title for the small amount of work he did at Lammeck Alley, so that he could be better paid for it. Albert's brothers, however, flatly refused to settle shares in the business on their nephew. As Emmanuel said, the control of the firm had, from the beginning, been tightly in the hands of the senior partners only, ever since old Bartholomew's day. They would not countenance so giddy a young man as Daniel having any real say in what happened in Lammeck Alley. He would simply have to wait until all the brothers were dead and the next generation had taken over.

'And,' said Ezra with satisfaction privately to Emmanuel, 'with my Marcus shaping up as he is, and Alfred's Peter being newly married and sensible with it, believe me, there's no risk Albert's Daniel will ever make trouble here. Anyway, we'll be around a long time yet, God willing.'

Daniel regarded himself as living in some penury, for he had been used to much less cramped quarters and his own vehicle and many luxuries which he had taken for granted. He had Given Up All For Love, he would sometimes think, and find pleasure in so doing. His Hannah was worth it, and made it less miserable than it might have been to hanker after more lavish days.

But from Hannah's point of view her life was one of great luxury indeed. It was not as new to her as it would have been to one of her brothers, of course; after seven years in Eaton Square she knew about luxury. But there, though she had eaten well, been dressed well, had slept on a soft bed, her role had been that of a pampered servant, no more. Here in Paultons Square she was the mistress, the queen of her domain, and how she relished it.

The first few months of her marriage, cold January and February and March, she spent blissfully shopping for curtains and furniture and kitchen fitments and cushions. Albert had taken her aside and given her a sizeable cheque, 'to make you comfortable, my dear. Get yourself a few new gowns.' She had smiled and taken it with appreciation. She was married now, and there was no reason why she should not accept a gift from her father-in-law. She would have accepted any gift at all from her own father, so why not Albert? And then she pushed away the thought of Nathan, as she was learning more and more easily to do, and settled to spending her riches on making home nicer for Daniel.

She did it well. In her drawing room were the curving lines of the Art Nouveau which was all the rage from Paris, the lily shapes, the green and yellow silk curtains and cushions, the Ambrose Heal furniture, but the walls were painted a cool white rather than hung with Mr Morris's wallpaper, and there was less furniture than there was in more fashionable establishments. Her dining room she modelled entirely on Eaton Square, as a sort of memorial to Mary. It was red walled and mahogany bedecked, heavy and a little stuffy in the old manner, but somehow it worked. The contrast between the two rooms delighted her, and met with Florrie's total approval, for she liked, she told her mistress with young severity, 'furniture as looks like furniture, none of that crinkle-crankle fall-down-as-soon-as-you-look-at-it-stuff you sees down at Schoolbred's in Tottenham Court Road – '

For Bet she provided the best that a modern kitchen could have, working her way through Harrod's kitchen list carefully, from One Mould Tin, copper, jelly, $1\frac{1}{4}$ pint, price five shillings and sixpence, via Six Wrought Iron Saucepans All Capacities prices from two shillings and fivepence to nine shillings net, to One Kneeling Mat (Waterproof), price one shilling and threepence. She enjoyed poring over the list with Bet and Florrie and prudently crossing out all that they felt they could do without, but then insisting that the best cooking stove, a Fletcher coal-gas range, should be provided to make Bet's job easier, and ordering a Bradford's Model Washing Wringing and Mangling Machine with Best Brass Capped India Rubber Rollers to make washday less arduous for Florrie. By the end of their third month with her, both her servants adored her. Hannah had managed that most difficult of tasks for ladies of a respectable class, that of Getting On Well With Staff, without even knowing it was difficult, or putting herself out in any way to do it. Daniel felt more and more certain that he had chosen wisely when he married her and began to talk to his father about the possibility of bringing Davida around to his way of thinking.

'She can't sulk for ever, can she?' he said. 'And I dare say once Leontine gets herself married off, as surely she will, for she's a good enough girl and she's got a handsome fortune for anyone who wants it, Mamma must see how absurd she's being.'

'Wait till you have children, my boy,' Albert advised. 'That's what will work the miracle. Don't rush it.' But Daniel persisted, sending his mother letters and flowers from time to time.

Not that he told Hannah that. He was not the most sensitive of young men, but he did realize that Hannah must be bitterly hurt by Davida's treatment of her. To have as your mother-in-law one who regarded you as a ragbag, a whore, a piece of filth, could not be easy. Yet Hannah never spoke a word against Davida, and showed only a nice respect for her father-in-law, for whom she was in fact developing a very real affection, for he was an easygoing pleasant man, and put himself out to please her.

Yet, try as she did, it was not possible to bury every atom of her distress over her father and brothers. Their silence gnawed at her and she went to a great deal of trouble to find out in every way she could how they fared.

At first she had to rely on cryptic notes sent to her by her Uncle Reuben, in reply to her long letters to him. 'Yr Pa and Bros is fit and well,' he wrote. Or, 'Yr Pa came in yest'day, looked alright.' Then to her intense relief her telephone rang one early April afternoon, and Uncle Alex's voice boomed at her from the ear piece.

'Uncle Alex!' she cried joyfully. 'You're back! Oh, I am so glad. Why were you so long away? And what happened? Are you well? And have you seen Poppa and the boys? And how did you find out where I lived and what the number here was?'

'Enough!' Uncle Alex's voice clacked tinnily at her, but sounded blessedly, wonderfully like Uncle Alex. 'This ain't no way we should talk after so long. Is it all right I should come and visit you? Your husband whoever he is won't mind?'

She laughed at that. 'My husband is Daniel Lammeck, surely someone told you? And of course he won't mind! Why on earth should he? When can you come?'

'Sure they told me. I heard nothing else since I come back. How's about now?'

'Now is perfect,' she said with delight, and hurried to the kitchen to ask Bet to make a special late lunch for her own uncle, who was just back in London from America and was coming to call. She felt a moment of pride in the fact that she had so splendid a relation all of her own; for once she did not have to feel inferior to all her husband's family.

He arrived in a large motor car that chugged around the Square with several small boys from the King's Road running alongside him and cheering. The car was a large open vehicle, with heavily padded green leather upholstery inside and gleaming brass fittings on its black paintwork. Alex sat in it very upright, holding onto the steering wheel with great nonchalance, a cigar stuck in his mouth to make an insolent angle under his heavily checked flat cap. His overcoat matched the cap, having the same checks only larger, and he was wearing large goggles. He looked every inch a modern man, and Hannah could have burst with delight at the sight of him, and almost hurled herself into his arms as he stepped down from the car, pulling off his heavy leather gauntlets as he did so.

'A welcome I expected, but this is more like an attack! Dolly, you look swell, real swell. Marriage suits you.'

'Uncle Alex, you look, oh, wonderful! And a car! And those goggles! Wonderful.'

He grinned at his car and patted it, as though it were a horse that could appreciate his love. 'Not bad, hey? De Dion Bouton.'

She looked puzzled and he laughed again. 'One day you'll know all about cars too, dolly. This husband of yours he'll get you one, and you'll drive everywhere like those American ladies. Some ladies, I'll tell you, but I never saw one who was a patch on you, dolly!' He pinched her cheek.

He sounded odd, she thought, speaking with more of a drawl that he used to, and peppering his speech with unfamiliar phrases, but she soon became used to it as he talked on and on, keeping her enthralled over lunch, and long into the afternoon. Indeed by the time he was ready to leave the new American sound had gone from his voice. He had stopped putting on his special little performance for her, and that made her feel very comfortable.

He had had a most exciting few months. The orginal boxing match for which he had rushed to Atlantic City had been a success and he had gone on to set up several more. Listening to him, Hannah could hear the excitement he had found in the New World, and the regret with which he had left it.

'You mean you mightn't have come back?' She looked blankly at him. 'Uncle Alex, you wouldn't leave us all here, would you?'

'Believe me, dolly, I thought of it, and then I realized people like me are ten a penny in New York! I deal a bit here

318

and there in Manhattan and I think I'm doing big and then all
of a sudden I meet another fella, doing even bigger, me all
over again! And I think, well, in London I know what I'm
doing, I know my way around, and I'm a bit special, you
know what I mean? Why should I start all over again some
place else, hey? I got my tea shops here, and a bit of action at
the theatre and all. And I tell you something else, I thought. I
can make my friends there in America, we can arrange things
anyway. It's no big deal.'
'Big what?'
He laughed. 'Big deal! The way they talk, these Americans,
it's great. I like it.'
'I noticed,' she said and smiled and he made a little grimace
and then laughed too.
'Oh, it is good to see you!' she said, and put her hand over
his impulsively. 'I needed you so much when ... ' She
·stopped and shook her head.
'I heard.' The laughter melted away. 'He's a fool, your
father, you know that? So it's sad, your friend Mrs Mary
goes and dies the same time as your Momma, it's sad. But it
ain't no crime you should go to see her, you're told she's
dying! I told Nathan, believe me I told him, he's a fool to you
and to himself. The last thing he needs is to cut himself away
from his only daughter now that Bloomah is dead, God rest
her poor soul in peace. But will the stupid *meshuggenah* listen?
Not him! He sits and sulks and he enjoys being hard done by.
He's made up his mind you're the bad one, so there he is with
no daughter, no son-in-law, no nothing.'
'Will he change his mind?'
There was a little silence and then Alex said gently, 'No,
dolly, I don't think he will. He made up his mind twenty odd
years ago that his family had treated him bad, and he wasn't
never going to forgive them. He never did. He made up his
mind I was a know-nothing upstart and he wasn't going to
take no help from such a brother, especially a younger
brother. So he never did. Not directly. And now he's made
up his mind again.'
'The boys then? What about them?'
He shrugged. 'They're all right. They got little jobs, you
know, pick up a few bob here and there. I give young Solly a
few quid when Nathan ain't looking, he pays the rent, gets
some food in, the same old business! I got to go backwards

to do my own brother a bit of good!'

'Will they talk to me again?'

'Of course they will! They got nothing against you, but they don't want to upset the old fool, so they don't answer your letters when you write, in case he finds out. You can understand.'

'Yes, I suppose so.' She sighed and leaned back in her chair. 'I just wish there was some way I could help a little. I sent some money, Daniel gave me some to send, but it was sent back. What can I do?'

'Same as me,' Alex said, and patted her hand. 'Same as me. Wait and see. It'll all come out in the wash. Most things do.'

'Uncle Alex, you remember you offered me a job?'

'Sure I remember. And you said no.'

'But I was going to say yes. When I left Mrs Mary – you were away, so I couldn't.' Alex hit the heel of his hand against his forehead. It was a gesture of mock fury, but Hannah could tell there was some real annoyance there. He truly had wanted her to work for him. 'What about the boys, Uncle Alex?' she asked. 'Couldn't one of them – '

He shook his head firmly. 'I love you, dolly. I love my relations. But I love business too, and I tell you, it wouldn't work. Managers they ain't, those two. Too lazy Jake, too unreliable young Solly.'

'Well, a job at least, for Solly!' she said again and put her hand on his. 'Please, Uncle Alex. He's got to leave school soon. I don't want him to have to work in a factory like Uncle Isaac's. I hated it. I wouldn't want to see him there. Bad enough Jake has to work with Uncle Reuben, can't you do something for Solly? Somewhere you could keep an eye on him?'

He shook his head at her, and stood up. 'It's time I was going. I got a meeting, a business meeting, you understand, in Whitechapel Road. Got an act I want to send over to America. I can make a few bob for myself this way, believe me. Agent, you know, for these burlesque houses. Okay, okay, I'll find a job for Solly. But nothing big, mind you, till the boy shows me he's got a bit of his sister's commonsense, and I ain't too hopeful, I tell you.'

He kissed her cheek with a smacking sound and she followed him out into the hall.

'It's a pity they can't see what a lovely life you've got for yourself here, dolly, the aunts, the uncles. My brother Reuben and his Minnie – they'd go *meshuggah* they saw this house!'

'They'd never come, the way they all feel about me now.' She followed him out of the front door to the doorstep, then stood and looked back into the hallway. The cool white paint, the drooping green fronds of palm in the corner, the flight of red carpeted stairs, did look pretty, and she would find pleasure in showing it all off to her aunts and uncles and cousins. But she couldn't imagine them ever coming.

'Who says they wouldn't?' Alex said, and kissed her cheek again. 'Sure they would! They ain't got no quarrel with you, dolly. Nathan they all understand and what he don't know won't hurt him. You ask 'em, they'll come and say nothing to Nathan, no harm done.'

Her chin lifted with delight at the idea. 'Really? Would they? Uncle Isaac and Aunt Minnie and all the rest?'

'Sure! They'd come. As long as Nathan wasn't told.'

'Then I shall!' she said. 'Uncle Alex, when shall it be? You tell me, because you'll be here too, won't you? We'll ask them all to come to tea.'

'Next Sunday.' He climbed into the seat of his car, with a swish of the skirts of his coat, scattering admiring small boys in all directions. 'Next Sunday, three o'clock. I'll bring 'em, every one. Make sure you got the samovar ready!'

And he was gone in a cloud of exhaust gas and noise, leaving her bursting with excitement at the thought of giving her first real tea party. Mrs Daniel Lammeck, At Home to her family!

34

Daniel was feeling very pleased with himself. He had set himself a target date by which he would bring his mother around and he was fully four months ahead of it. He had hoped by the end of the London season in late July to have persuaded Davida to accept his young wife to the point of being willing to introduce her into Society. Then, he had thought, by the autumn when the High Holy Days were over

321

and the winter season started they would be like any other young couple in London's rich Jewish circles, dining out in other people's houses, going to the theatre and opera and giving occasional crushes of their own. And, he thought shrewdly, they would be less strapped for money. Davida's purse strings would be loosened and he could have his own carriage again, even a car. It was time he had a car. His cousin Peter had one, and he was not working any harder at Lammeck Alley than Daniel was, or so Daniel told himself.

And now Davida was coming to visit! He hugged his success to himself like a child with a secret, and glowed whenever he thought about it, sitting at his desk in Lammeck Alley sorting through the piles of ledgers the junior clerks had brought for his approval.

In fact, his success had more to do with Davida's misery than his own powers of persuasion. She had thought at first that her feelings were lacerated beyond repair by Daniel's behaviour, and that she would never be able to forgive him or to accept his hateful guttersnipe, and all through the late winter weeks and early spring she had glowed with her self-righteous fury. But, as day succeeded day and it became ever more clear that Albert was not going to help her to make life difficult enough for Daniel to force him to leave his Hannah, loneliness for him filled her. In his bachelor days he had been busy with his clubs and his own friends and had come to sit with her and gossip no more than once or twice a week, but she missed him sorely, and once the family's interest had died down, and there was no one who would listen to her suffering and complaints, there was too much time to think about how much she missed him.

She missed Mary too, which was a disagreeable surprise. For years Davida had regarded Mary with contempt, considering her weak and stupid for putting up with Emmanuel's flagrant behaviour. The more Davida had ill used Mary, the more Davida had despised her for not standing pat and refusing to allow it. She had shed no tears at Mary's death, dismissing Ezra's Susan, who had, as 'merely sentimental'. But now she missed Mary, and often she remembered the days when she had visited Eaton Square and sat there chattering away for hours on end and found tears in her eyes.

So Daniel's patent willingness to forget the outrageous

things she had said to Hannah, and Davida knew perfectly well that she had used quite appalling language, was balm to her soul. Had anyone spoken so to her nephew Peter about his young wife Judith he would, she knew, never have had anything to do with that person again. Peter was quiet and spoke only rarely, but when he did it was to some purpose. Davida quailed when she thought how dreadful she would now feel if Daniel were like Peter.

But Daniel wasn't. He had coaxed and persuaded and cajoled at her till she felt her rage subside. Leontine Damont was still unmarried, and who knew what Davida might not be able to arrange? In time perhaps Daniel would see sense and tire of his Hannah, and though divorce was unheard of in respectable Jewish circles, there was a first time for everything. No one would think all that ill of a sensible young man shedding a guttersnipe of a wife who had trapped him into marriage in the first place. And, anyway, they weren't really married at all, in a sense. Davida knew perfectly well that a civil marriage was as legally binding as a religious one, but dissolving one would not be difficult, and any succeeding marriage Daniel made could be solemnized in a synagogue, properly, as though Hannah had never existed. So Davida thought more and more often, and so she began to make her plans. To be loving to Daniel, even at the cost of visiting his wretched Hannah, made good sense. So it was that she greeted Daniel with a gracious smile when he arrived to collect her from Park Lane at half past three on a bright Sunday afternoon when early daffodils and hyacinths scented the air from the window boxes and the trees in the park blushed a pale green with the promise of summer. He was very cheerful too, feeling particularly hopeful about the outlook for the afternoon, for Hannah had been playfully mysterious with him about her plans for the day.

'I'm having a tea party,' she said importantly. 'No, don't ask me who is coming. It's to be a surprise! It's my first real one, and I want you to be like one of the guests – I mean, I want it to be as new to you as it is to them so that you can tell me how it all is. Do you understand what I mean?'

He had laughed, and said he did, although he didn't quite, but was delighted all the same. Clearly she had chosen to invite some of the neighbours in Paultons Square, with whom they were now on nodding terms, and that would be splendid, for it would mean that when he arrived with Davida there would be others there to take some of the strain out of the situation.

'I've got a guest too,' he said and pinched her cheek. 'No, if you won't tell me who yours are, I shan't tell you who mine is. But you'll be pleased to see her, I know.'

And the less time you have to think about who will be here the better, he told himself shrewdly. If I say it's to be Mamma Hannah might stand on her pride and refuse to see her. A fait accompli will be much wiser.

Rosa Lewis, Hannah thought, who else? And smiled and said no more. Rosa would be fun to see again, and would impress the family – especially Uncle Alex – and Hannah had a childish desire to do that.

The ride from Park Lane to Paultons Square was agreeable in the sunshine. Daniel sat beside Davida, very dapper in his light flannel suit and round straw hat, feeling proud of his mother. She looked as handsome as any young man could wish a female companion to look, impeccably dressed in a hand tailored dark green merino coat and skirt under her duster coat and with her hat swathed in a motoring veil. Her face peeped out from folds of gauze which hid the softening of the jawline that the years had brought and her cheeks were whipped red by the crisp air. She looked delightful, and she knew it.

'Such a charmingly quaint corner, my dear,' Davida murmured, as the car chugged its stately way along the King's Road and turned left into Paultons Square, looking at the vista of flat fronted houses marching away round the four sides of the central garden. 'Later, of course you'll need to come back to London proper, but for the present, this is very nice. Which house is yours?'

'On the corner,' he said and frowned. 'There's a wretched char-a-banc left outside.'

'Yes dear, so there is. Perhaps someone is to have a ball and they have sent the extra servants in? Although they should have put the vehicle in the mews.'

'We don't have any mews,' he said shortly, as the chauffeur brought the car to a stop just in front of the char-a-banc, a gaudily painted open topped vehicle with two rows of polished wooden seats inside. The two horses tossed their heads and snorted, sending clouds of chaff and bran flying

324

from their nosebags. Sparrows came swooping down at once in a great twitter and Davida smiled forbearingly as she climbed out of the car, Daniel helping.

'Never mind, dear. You can send your servant out to tell them to take the thing away.' She looked back over her shoulder at the vehicle, so incongruous in the quiet square, as Daniel led the way up the steps to the front door.

He had to use his key to let them in, somewhat to his chagrin, for he had expected Florrie, neat and deft as usual in her frilled uniform, to appear at the door in immediate answer to his ring. As the door swung wide Florrie appeared at the foot of the stairs, looking a little flustered.

'Oh, sir,' she said. 'Oh, sir, sorry I couldn't get to the door in time, but they wants so much tea, you see, and I was just 'alfway up the stairs with ever such a big tray so I 'ad to go the rest of the way 'an I'm very sorry, sir.'

'It doesn't matter, Florrie,' Daniel said, puzzled and a bit impatient now. 'Just take Mrs Lammeck's coat now, will you? Mamma, will you need to tidy yourself before we go to the drawing room?'

'No dear,' Davida said sweetly. 'Don't discommode yourself.' She unpinned her hat and veil and gave it to Florrie who bobbed awkwardly. 'Such a sweet little house, to be sure! Perhaps you should tell your – tell Hannah to fix mirrors here in the hallway. It would make it seem so much less poky, don't you know.'

A remarkable noise was coming down the stairs. Daniel looked towards the drawing room door with a faint frown on his face as voices pealed very loudly above a great clatter of dishes.

'I can't imagine who is there with Hannah,' he said. The irritation that had crept into his voice was not lost on Davida. 'She said she had some people coming, but – '

'Her friends, no doubt,' Davida said, sweeter than ever. 'I shall be happy to meet them. Shall we go up?' She began to climb the stairs, holding her skirts away from the sides with some ostentation, for the staircase was barely half as wide as the one in Park Lane. Daniel followed although he would have preferred, had it been possible, to send Florrie up to fetch her mistress down to greet her guest.

Davida opened the drawing room door herself, not waiting for Daniel, and stood in the doorway looking in, with a faint smile on her face. And then her expression of well bred good manners froze into a chilly rictus.

The room was bursting with people. Hannah was sitting nearest the fire which was piled high with sea coal and pouring tea from a large pot. All around her were chairs and sofas tightly crammed with bodies. Daniel had never seen so many people in such a small space and he looked over Davida's shoulder and then pulled back at the heat that poured out at him. And at the smell.

The scent of naphtha from the moth balls used to store very best clothes was heavy in the hot air, and so was the smell of food – vast edifices of chopped herring sandwiches and egg sandwiches and cheese sandwiches and rolls covered with herring pieces and anchovies. There were slabs of cheesecake and strudel and honey cake and heaps of sugar biscuits. Everyone had laden plates on their laps.

Hannah looked up, then jumped to her feet, almost sending a plate of herring flying. 'Daniel! I thought you would have been home long ago. Oh! Mrs Lammeck!'

The room slid to a silence as heads craned to stare at the newcomers, and then after a moment, returned to their conversations. A thin woman with a very tired face talked in a high shrill whine to a very fat one who had a voice even higher and shriller and two men boomed at each other at the same time. A tall handsome girl wearing a red dress heavily trimmed with green frills and carrying food-laden plates in each hand shouted at a small boy who was trying to take food from the table by the fire, 'Leave orf, for Gawd's sake!' and then grinned at the newcomers.

'Allo! We 'aven't met, seein' I'm not family like the others, so I better interduce meself. I'm Cissie Weiss, used to work with Hannah in the factory. Nice to see you, you must be Daniel, eh? Lucky fella! She's a girl and three quarters, your Hannah! Insisted I should come today and bring my Lenny and all, a real *gutena shumah* she is! That's my Lenny over there – Lenny, will you lay off!' She swooped at the child and, putting down one plate of food, cuffed him, and he broke into a loud wail.

'Hannah!' Daniel said and at the sight of his face she felt her belly tighten.

She had realized as soon as she saw Davida standing there how silly she had been to keep her tea party a secret from

326

him. Had there been only themselves, he would have welcomed all the family warmly, she knew that. Daniel shared none of his mother's snobbery. But in the presence of his mother, that was different.

At the same time she felt her own pride struggling within her. These were her people, her family, her roots, and she had as much right to have them here, surely, as Daniel had a right to bring his mother. She lifted her chin and said, 'As you see, Daniel, everyone has arrived! Except Uncle Alex, I'm afraid, who had to remain in Hackney because of some problem to do with a concert he has organized for tonight. But everyone else is here, Aunt Minnie and Uncle Reuben and my mother's brother, Uncle Isaac, and there is my Uncle Benjamin. I don't think you ever met him, did you? And next to him his son David and – '

Doggedly she introduced them one by one. Charlotte, looking very pleased with herself as she sat beside a scrawny young man, some three inches shorter than she was, who was introduced as her fiancé, Monty Guz; her sister Bella, a quiet girl in unfortunate purple satin, who looked equally pleased with herself when Hannah presented her new young husband, Harry, a sad faced young man with a prematurely bald head; and serious young David, the Talmudic scholar, sitting with his yarmulka carefully placed at the very back of his head; and the seven noisiest and most lavishly dressed of them all, her Uncle Reuben's children Leon and Rachel and Ann and Rivka and Hyman and Jack and Bertha, and their assorted young companions to whom some of them were betrothed, and some of whom were only hoping (at which Minnie beamed for a moment and looked positively animated) and finally her brothers, Jake and Solly, who were standing behind her chair.

'I'm sure you'll be pleased as I am to see my brothers and the rest of my family here in our house at last, Daniel,' she said, and her chin was up even higher, but the anxiety showed in her face, which looked a little tight.

'Of course,' he said, and managed a smile. 'Mamma, I am sure you too will be happy to know my new ... relations.' He looked at her, prepared to weather another of her storms, and struggling to contain his fury with Hannah. Of all days to have invited such a ghastly crew; of all days!

To his amazement, Davida did nothing but smile, a thin

327

smile, accompanied by the smallest of nods at the whole room, but a smile none the less. He was so relieved that he became almost noisy, drawing her into the room, and urging her towards Hannah's chair which was the only one vacant. 'Well, isn't this splendid! Some tea, Mamma? Hannah, some tea, please, my love. And something to eat, perhaps.'

Cissie at once marched forwards with her plates at the ready, as the room burst into noise again. The children and grandchildren of Lazar and Rivka talked interminably when they were together because they were together so much. The seven cousins shouted and squabbled and contradicted each other and interrupted each other precisely as they did at home. A fugue of voices and shrill monologues filled the room again.

'I think, no, thank you, my dear,' Davida said weakly, and drew back from Cissie. 'No, I think – if you don't mind, Daniel, I will be on my way. I just wanted to call in for a few moments, you know, that is all. No, really, Mrs ... Weiss, I think you said, I really can't. Daniel dear, perhaps we can talk during the week, but I must go on now. Martha Damont is At Home this afternoon, with the Amsterdam cousins – the Willem Damonts you know – and she did so want me to call. I'll be on my way ... '

She smiled at the room in general, her eyes glazed so that she did not actually have to exchange glances with anyone, nodded, and then after a moment extended one limp hand to Hannah. 'Hannah,' she murmured, not looking at her, and then turned and went, Daniel following her after one last look over his shoulder at Hannah, who stood there as the chatter ricocheted around her head, and watched him go.

35

'You have absolutely no right to be angry!' she flared at him. 'None at all. Did you expect me to abandon my family just because I married you?'

'They abandoned you, didn't they? When it suited them,' Daniel said, and then as Hannah went a little white shook his head in irritation at himself. 'Dammit, I didn't mean that to sound the way it did. I know it was only your father who did, and I know that worries you. I'm sorry.' He came across the bedroom to put his hands on her shoulder, but she got up from the dressing table where she had been sitting brushing her hair and moved away to stand beside her washstand. She began to scrub at her hands, although she had already completed her preparations for bed.

'I'll say it again,' she said after a moment. 'And then no more. My relations are what they are. I'm sorry if they don't meet with your mother's approval, but I'm not going to apologize for that, do you understand me? I regret it because it makes things difficult for you. But it's no fault in me or in them that she feels that way. It's just that they're . . . different.'

He laughed then. 'Different? Oh, God, I'll say they're different! Did you *see* her face when she saw them all?' His grin invited her to share the joke, but she refused to look at him, and his face hardened again.

That night they slept far apart for the first time in the four months they had been married. It was as though there was a chasm in the middle of the big brass-framed double bed that neither would approach for fear of falling in.

Had Davida been able to see them she would have been well pleased with the effect of her visit to Paultons Square, a visit that had underlined her conviction that the Jews of the East End were of a different species from herself and should never have been allowed into England in the first place. It had also convinced her even more that it was her duty as a mother to separate her son from his so-called wife. If he didn't know what was good for him, she certainly did.

So, she started a new tack altogether with Daniel. She would be charming and friendly and quite uncritical, and show him by means of underlining the contrast between his past and his present how misguided he was. He must be coaxed back into the family fold, not harried. So she telephoned him each morning just before ten o'clock as soon as she had awakened and just before he left the house to go to Lammeck Alley, to chatter cheerfully and with every sign of warm affection. She talked of her friends, of other members of the family, of the busy doings of the Willem Damonts who were setting up an English office of their diamond business and therefore spending as much time in London as in Amsterdam, and of the assorted minutiae of her day. And he talked of office matters, and the people he met at lunch time and the gossip he picked up about mutual acquaintances, none of whom were known to Hannah, and never talked at all about his home life. Hannah would sit in her small morning room finishing her breakfast, able to hear every word he said. She ached to stop him, but never in any way would she interfere between Daniel and his mother. That was a problem that only he could sort out, and she bit her tongue and said not a word on the subject. And the silence grew between them.

Not that they argued. That first Sunday evening had been painful, their first real quarrel, but Hannah was too accustomed to behaving as other people wanted her to to persist in displaying anger at her much loved Daniel, and he for his part was much too sexually active to be able to maintain a fight with her for longer than a day or two. But a wound had been inflicted in the body of their love and it left a clumsy scar. The house in Paultons Square lost some of its comfort.

The weeks moved on into a blazing June when the tarred streets softened in the sunshine and horses stood with drooping heads at the kerb sides and people became irritable with each other. And Hannah found herself chafing at the pattern of her life. The house was finished now, and there was little for her to do in the running of it. The days yawned empty ahead of her though she sewed a good deal, making herself gowns and blouses and chemises, but her wardrobe was as full as she wanted it, and a puritan streak born of her penurious childhood forbade her to have more than she required. She did not even need all she had, for unlike most young brides she had no friends with whom to fill her indolent hours and so no one other than Daniel for whom to dress. Cissie, the only one of her erstwhile workmates with whom she still felt any rapport, was much too busy earning her own and Lenny's keep in Uncle Isaac's factory to spend any time with Hannah, and anyway the idea was ridiculous. The journey between Paultons Square and the East End was an arduous one, that took at least an hour even behind a fairly brisk cab horse. Hannah could not look to Cissie for companionship, nor, she felt, could she look to her neighbours. Questions would be asked about her antecedents, and about her life before her marriage, and she shrank from that. She was not ashamed of her past, nor of her family, but Davida's

330

expression that afternoon in Hannah's drawing room had told her all she needed to know about the way her neighbours would react. Better not to become involved with them at all than to tolerate their snubs.

Her discontentment was not lost on Daniel. He watched her and listened to her and knew she was distressed, but didn't know how to help. That wretched Sunday tea party still hung between them like a shadow, but there was nothing he felt he could do to dispel it. And because he was anxious, Davida blossomed. Even though he was punctilious about not discussing Hannah or his home life when they had their telephone conversations, or when they lunched together every Wednesday, a habit into which they had drifted, she could see Daniel's marriage crumbling before her eyes. And in her triumph became incautious.

She began to talk to Albert about her hopes. At first he let her prattle on, not bothering to try to sort out the meaning of her elliptical phrases, but after a while he did understand, and he disliked what he heard. The last thing Albert wanted was any further drama. He could imagine all too vividly the way his brothers would purse their lips and complain if Davida's hopes for a divorce blossomed. He could also imagine the repercussions. The Lammeck brothers had always treasured their royal friendship, not because they benefited in any obvious financial way – indeed they did not need to, for their business thrived – but because of its social value. There were people in England who sneered at the Jews, they all knew that. The older families, those who measured their lineage in hundreds of years rather than in mere generations, were cool in the extreme; there were many houses in London where Lammecks and Damonts, even Rothschilds and Sassoons, were regarded with contempt, and certainly never invited. Week after week the comical drawings in *Punch*, the journal of required reading for all with any pretensions to style, were littered with big-nosed caricatures. But the King's friends were privileged. To lose his cordiality would be a sad blow, and Albert had a shrewd idea that raffish though the King was, and fond of a night of gambling and womanizing, divorce in his circle would stick in his craw. There had been previous scandals, heaven knew, that had involved him, but that had been in the days when he was Prince of Wales. Now he was King and getting older too and far from well, and matters were different. Albert was quite sure that a divorce involving his son would cause the King to lose some of his affability, and that he was not to be thought of. He had to do something to block Davida.

It took longer than he thought. Indeed, by the time his ploys succeeded the King, his family's friend, was dead and London was in mourning, and wondering how life would be under raffish Edward's more prosaic son, George V. But that made no difference to Albert; he still had much to lose from a divorce scandal involving his son.

So it was that one late July afternoon at Lammeck Alley, Daniel was shaken out of his lethargy in a most surprising manner. His father and uncles sent for him at the end of the Senior Partners' monthly meeting. He was to come to the Board Room, Young Levy said, and no, he didn't know why.

Daniel looked questioningly at Young Levy (still called that, even after his thirty years with the firm) but he merely shook his head and went back to his tall desk. So Daniel went, trying to remember what he had done, or more likely not done, to merit so formal a summons. He was not, he knew, the most assiduous of the junior members of the firm. His cousin Peter, said to be a positive genius with figures, was much more industrious than he was, and Marcus, that square and rather silent youth who chose to spend his school holidays at Lammeck Alley, was said to know more about the diamond selling side of the business than anyone in the London branch of the family, almost as much as the Damonts who were the real diamond dealers of the City. The summons made his heart sink, but he entered the big panelled room with a jaunty step to show them how little he was concerned.

He listened to what they had to say with his face rigid with surprise.

'Shanghai?' he said at length. 'Shanghai?'

'Why not, m'boy?' Ezra said cheerfully. 'Why not?' He was cooling himself with a fan fashioned out of a dried palm leaf, and looked particularly oriental this warm afternoon, with the sallow complexion and liquid dark eyes with a faintly yellowish tinge to the whites that, more than fifty years ago, Bartholomew had brought with him when he came to open the London Office. Looking at him Daniel thought, 'I'm glad I look like Mamma's family,' and then wrenched his mind back to the present.

'We need a member of the family to keep an eye on what goes on there,' Ezra was saying. 'We're handling more and more tea, you know, and a good deal of silk, and I'm told the possibilities for textile manufacture are increasing daily. Ling Ho, who is the manager of the office at the moment, is a man of wide experience in these matters, and we want him to get out and about and buy textile plant and set up some factories of our own. That means we need someone to take over from him and we think it can be you. You'll have a reliable interpreter of course, but we will expect you to learn some Chinese, nothing too fancy, understand, just enough to follow the contracts. Ling Ho will be there if you need him. You will do very well, my boy! We've arranged to settle you in a house near the new Futan University, a very respectable area, and cool in the warm months, they say. Later, if you choose, you can find yourself a bigger place.'

Daniel shook his head, trying to collect his thoughts. He had visited abroad, of course – the spas of Germany, the more fashionable Swiss and French resorts, but the thought of going to China filled him with astonishment.

'You sail next month,' Alfred was saying. 'Stateroom will be booked by the firm, so all you need to worry about is getting your affairs here tidied up. Young Levy will see to selling your house, if that's what you want, though I'd suggest you rent it. They tell me that part of London is gettin' positively desirable. Odd, but there it is. Hang on to it and use the rents, that's what you ought to do.'

'Hannah,' Daniel began but his father leaned forwards and said carefully, 'Will of course go with you. Man needs his wife with him! Of course you must be together.'

Hannah's first reaction to Daniel's news was blank amazement. She who had never in her life been outside London, to travel so far? To spend so many weeks on a steamship crossing those myriad miles of water? She could not imagine it. She stared at him over the dinner table with her mouth half open in surprise.

'Shanghai,' she said 'Shanghai? Where is it?'

He laughed at that, the indulgent man of the world. 'Biggest city in China, and China's huge! It's a port of course, that's why we've got an office there. And we do a lot of trade, a lot of very good trade with the hinterland – the Yangtse valley, you understand. The city stands on the

333

Hwang Pu river on the Soochow Creek side but only fourteen miles or so from where it meets the Yangtse...' He had spent the remainder of his afternoon at Lammeck Alley eagerly gleaning all he could about the place from Young Levy. 'It's a very exciting place. There's a big International Settlement, with lots of Europeans. You'll like it, Hannah. You'll meet new people and make friends. You'll be very busy, I'm sure.'

They sat there staring at each other in the evening sunlight of their red walled dining room in Paultons Square in Chelsea, trying each in their own way to visualize life in remote Shanghai. Hannah thought of the crowded streets of the East End and tried to imagine them as Chinese streets decorated with shop signs like those she had seen occasionally in Limehouse, where the few Chinese people who lived in London clustered, but couldn't. Daniel tried to envisage the sort of life he would have as manager of the Lammeck office, in total command, making decisions, catered to and respected ... '

It was a heady vision. In Lammeck Alley he was just Albert's boy. He was well aware of the partners' opinion of him, and he could not blame them for it. He had never found what he had to do there exciting enough to make an effort over it. But as Office Manager in Shanghai, that would be different. There he would work hard, and enjoy it.

'You want to go?' Hannah said after a while, and picked up her spoon and began to eat her pudding. 'Please, Daniel, do finish. Bet will be mortified if she thinks you didn't like it. She's very proud of this recipe.'

Daniel began to eat, shovelling the food in without interest in what he was tasting.

'Yes, I think I do. It would be ... I think it would suit us both, don't you? Do us good.'

He looked at her carefully, wanting to say it but not knowing how. Good to get away for a while, just us. Good not to have to worry about relations, yours or mine. Then we can be comfortable again.

He didn't have to say it for she was thinking it too. It would be good to be far away from all the anxiety and the confusion. But not so good to be far away from Uncle Alex and Poppa and the boys. While she was in London there was always the chance, just a small chance, that Poppa would

334

relent and see her again. She shook her head, confused. Then, as she saw his anxious gaze fixed on her, she smiled.

'Yes, I think perhaps it will,' she said in a composed voice and bent her head to finish her pudding. Daniel grinned widely and held out his plate for a second helping.

But once again, events overtook her. Accompanying Young Levy around the house making an inventory, for it had been agreed that Paultons Square would be rented fully furnished and staffed against the day when the young couple should return, she suddenly felt odd. They had climbed the stairs slowly, for it was hot and the air hung moist and heavy everywhere. Suddenly her vision seemed to brighten and dazzle; the stairs in front of her bounced and tilted and she felt her gorge rise. Fortunately she fell backwards, against Young Levy who braced his elderly but wiry frame and caught her.

The excitement in the house was intense. Bet threw up her hands in horror and wept, while Florrie, more practical, ran down to the King's Road to fetch the doctor. Young Levy, alarmed by Mrs Lammeck's pallor, telephoned the office to tell Daniel to come home. He arrived, pale with anxiety and accompanied by Albert, only a short time after the doctor had finished his examination and was packing up his bag in the dressing room adjacent to the bedroom where Hannah lay.

'No need to look like that, young man!' the doctor said, as Daniel with Albert close behind him came rushing up the stairs. 'Nothing to get at all upset about. Put it down to the weather. No young woman in her state can expect to feel otherwise while it's so deucedly hot.'

'Her state?' Albert said sharply, pushing past Daniel.

The doctor grinned. 'You a member of the family? This young man's father, is it? Well, congratulations, sir. The young lady plans to make a grandfather of you. They will do it, you know, they will do it! I've left a prescription, Mr Lammeck, for a tonic for your wife, and for the rest, just make sure you get Miss Bishop booked. Best midwife in the district.' He turned to go.

'But they're sailing for Shanghai in a fortnight's time, doctor! They'll be there at least two years, you know, and –'

'Shanghai?' The doctor looked over his shoulder. 'Oh, dear me, no! No question of that! That girl takes a long voyage like that, and I won't answer for the consequences. No, she'll have to follow you, I'm afraid, if go you must, Mr Lammeck.' He looked at Daniel and grinned his sharp grin again. 'To tell you the truth, m'boy, I almost envy you. It ain't easy going through your wife's first pregnancy, you know, or any pregnancy come to that, all the fuss and the drama and dealing with her mother and her sisters and all. You go to your Shanghai and let her follow you once her babe is safely born and established in its health. Much the best plan, I do assure you. Good afternoon!'

36

Albert tried hard enough, heaven knew, to discover a way to persuade his brothers to change their plans, but he was hamstrung by his own previous deviousness. He had known perfectly well that if his brothers suspected that he had pressed for Daniel's appointment to the important Shanghai branch simply in order to protect his marriage from Davida's meddling, they would have had no part of it.

Instead he had used all his eloquence to convince them that his boy was eager for advancement, that he had settled well and was more than ready for this step forwards. To try and pull him out now simply because his wife was not fit to travel would make them exceedingly suspicious, and as the junior of the four senior partners, he was in no position to upset them. Anyway, he did not wish to. Albert had expensive tastes, and a disagreement with his brothers that might, just possibly, result in his losing his seat on the Senior Partners' Board was not to be contemplated. After all, they all knew that Lammeck and Damont wives understood the exigencies of the business. Why should Daniel's wife be treated any differently from, say, the wife of cousin Philip Damont, a nephew of their mother Augusta? He had been appointed to the Bombay Office the year before. When his wife Violet had been stricken with jaundice as soon as they arrived, they had simply arranged for her to be brought home again, leaving Philip alone in India for another two years, never contemplating the possibility that this was not the way to arrange matters. As far as the Lammeck brothers were concerned, business came first, second and last in every calculation; what the business needed the members of the firm needed and when they needed something, the wives accepted. So ran the creed at Lammeck Alley. Albert could do nothing.

The only comfort he had was that Davida at least recovered her spirits. Her fury when she had heard that Daniel and Hannah were to be swept out of her reach for two years had been monumental. Now that Hannah was to remain in London, her mood lifted.

'I take it you intend to look after the girl, then?' Albert said a little waspishly, unable to resist the barb, for she had given him some very uncomfortable hours this past fortnight. 'After all, she's going to give you a grandchild. Imagine that, Davida. You a grandmother!'

She swept over that magnificently. 'Oh, that should not be necessary. I am sure her own people will see she is fit enough. And I imagine you will be your usual foolish self and load her with money. Really, the way you let that girl bamboozle you is little short of – '

'I give what I give from my own choice,' he said shortly. 'She never asks, and never has. And for my part, I'm glad there's to be a grandchild. I've only the one son, after all.' Another barb, for Daniel's lack of brothers and sisters was due entirely to Davida's refusal after his birth 'ever to go through all that again', a matter which had caused Albert not a little distress. Again, she ignored him.

'I'm sure it will be the making of him.' She nodded in great satisfaction. 'He's had a bad time lately and – yes, the making of him.' Prudently she forbore to say what she had intended to about Hannah, because Albert was looking thunderous now, and Hannah was not worth having an argument over. 'I must see to it that I order some goods for him from the Army and Navy Stores. They'll know what I should pack.'

Hannah, at home in the heat of Paultons Square, was wretched. She had, absurdly, not considered the possibility that she might become pregnant. It was not that she was ignorant of the facts of parenthood; far from it. But she and Daniel had reached a tacit agreement that they would not wish for children too soon, and he had, in his lovemaking, taken care to protect her. And she had fully trusted him. So the realization that his care had failed and a child had been conceived had come as a most disagreeable surprise. And the fact that it had come at just this time did not help to make her any happier about it. All of which contributed not a little to the fact that she was now feeling far from well, and spent a large part of her day white faced and miserable sitting in her wrapper by her open window and trying not to vomit. Florrie and Bet hovered over her with tempting dishes, but she grew thinner before their eyes. The enormous relief they had felt when they realized that their much loved mistress was not, after all, going to disappear into some heathen wilderness gave way to grave concern for her.

It was not entirely her pregnancy and the hot weather which made her feel so low; it was Daniel too. Somewhere deep inside herself she had taken it for granted that once Daniel realized that there was no possibility of her accompanying him he would refuse to go. He had only to say to his uncles that he was sorry, but his place was by his wife's side, and that of his son or daughter.

But he didn't. He talked about it, of course, sitting beside her in the evening when he returned from the Alley, and holding her hand, but he did nothing. He said he would tell them he could not go, but not yet.

'Let's see how you are by the end of the week,' he said optimistically. 'Maybe you'll feel better. Maybe we can find a different doctor who'll see that what you need is a long sea voyage to set you up.'

Another doctor came and said the same, that travel to a country like China would undoubtedly kill the baby and would do a great deal of harm to Hannah's own health too. Still Daniel did not tell his uncles he would not go. At last she had to accept the situation for what it was.

'Please, Daniel,' she said, needing to give him permission to do as he chose, and knowing that the best way was to make him believe he was acting to please her. 'Please, it won't be for long. As soon as the baby's born, and big enough to travel, I'll book a place on the next steamer, truly I will. It won't be long. The doctor said it will be born in January, and by the spring, just a few months really, I'll be there. And you'll be busy, too busy to miss me.'

Daniel looked at her and frowned and then shook his head

and frowned again, but in the end said he agreed.

'It's not that I want to leave you, my love,' he said. 'You know that, don't you? It's just that, oh, at Lammeck Alley I'm nothing. But a couple of years in Shanghai and who knows? They'll give me a proper partnership as soon as I come back, I'm sure of that, and then we'll be sitting pretty. I mean, if I'm to be a family man, I've got to think of the future.'

'Yes.' She leaned back in her chair as another wave of nausea overcame her. The truth was, she knew, that Daniel had become enormously excited at the prospect of travelling so far. In the last few weeks he had thought of little else. She had seen him sitting with a blank expression on his face, and had known he was imagining himself there in exotic China, giving his lordly orders, making vast sums of money to send back to the coffers in Lammeck Alley to impress his uncles. She recognized what was happening to him. She, who had depended so heavily on fantasy all through her young years, knew the dream world into which her husband had retreated.

But unlike her, he could not relinquish his dream when circumstances made it unrealizable, and she could not, for all the sense of impending doom that filled her when she contemplated his departure, spoil it for him by making demands of her own. She knew that she could make him refuse to go. They were still very young and very much in love and he needed her in many ways, not least as a lover, and she could very easily make him realize that leaving her would make him unhappy. But she did not.

Because her pregnancy was making her feel so ill, they stopped lovemaking, and that added to his willingness to go. It was not that she did not want him; indeed she did. They would lie side by side on those hot summer nights, not touching. She knew he wanted her, but feared to harm her, and waited for her to make the first move. But she, feeling that ever present nausea, could not, and so they lay there and eventually slept, uneasily alone together and unfulfilled.

The days shrivelled away. Two nights before his departure they were sitting in the drawing room before the open window. There had been a few grumbles of thunder and Hannah was tense and nervous, waiting for the storm to blow itself into life and waiting, too, for him to go. She loved him, she didn't want to lose him, but the delay in his departure seemed intolerable. It would be easier if he went now, this second, she thought, resting her head on her chair back, and left me to get over this wretched business on my own.

He looked at her in the deepening twilight, at the way her hair, unpinned now, lay on her shoulders, and at the shadows under her eyes and wanted her very badly indeed. His body was tense with need. He had to lean back in his chair and stretch his shoulders very deliberately, concentrating his mind on the sensations his back muscles gave him, in order to keep his thoughts away from his genitals. When she stirred in her chair, opened her eyes and smiled at him, his body leaped again, and it took all the control he had to stop himself reaching out to seize her. She, less perceptive than she usually was, because she felt so low, said sleepily, 'Dear one, you must be very stuffy sitting here with me. Go for a walk, love, do. I'll be all right on my own.'

And because he was lonely and hungry for sexual reassurance he went to see Leontine. 'After all,' he told himself, walking through the hot still air of the busy streets towards her house in Knightsbridge, 'After all, she's an old friend. I've got to say goodbye.'

They said goodbye. Leontine behaved with sweet forbearance, as though he had never jilted her, for not only had she been reared to accept unacceptable male behaviour as always forgiveable, she still felt exceedingly attracted to him. He sat and talked to her for over an hour, never speaking of Hannah but about Shanghai, and how his life there would be. At last, he leaned forwards and touched her hand and said, 'Write to me, Leontine? I'd like to think we were still friends.' She promised she would, and they parted with a chaste kiss on her cheek that still managed to leave Leontine almost breathless. She watched him from her drawing room window as he went swinging away through the midnight streets towards his wife. 'Interesting,' she thought. 'Perhaps Aunt Davida was right. She said it would all work out, and maybe it will.'

Their parting, when it came, was almost perfunctory. Hannah was as felled by her sickness as ever when he got up very early in the morning of the day the Ocean Steamship company ship 'Priam' was to sail for Shanghai, calling at Colombo and Hong Kong, a journey that would take him almost seven weeks, but all he could think about was the risk of missing the boat train to Liverpool, from Euston Station. He rushed about the bedroom in a great frenzy of activity and she managed to drag herself up and put on her wrapper and get Florrie to come and help him with his last minute packing, in order to settle him.

They ate a brief breakfast, or rather he did, for she could manage only tea, and then, suddenly, the cab was at the door and they could hear the cabman complaining and panting as he carried the trunks and cases out to the four wheeler, supervised by Florrie. Daniel jumped to his feet, wiped his mouth on his napkin and looked around anxiously for his hat, a handsome new straw hat that he had bought expressly to travel in.

'Time to go, my love,' he said, almost distractedly. 'Can't miss the boat train, the ship goes on the late afternoon tide and they said it might be early. Dammit, where did I put that ... oh, there it is ... ' He seized the carpet bag containing his immediate necessaries and came and stood beside her where she sat at the table.

'Come and wave me off, then,' he said. 'No one will notice you aren't dressed yet if you stand well back in the doorway.'

'No,' she said. 'No, I don't think I will. I'll say goodbye here.' She put up her face to be kissed. After a moment he bent and brushed her cheek with his lips.

'I'll write as soon as we touch port,' he said huskily and turned and went. She sat listening for a long time after the rattle of the horse's hooves and jingle of its harness had died away.

It was both easier and harder than she had thought it would be. Easier to live without him, because she went on feeling ill for some weeks after he had left. Harder because hers was so disagreeable a pregnancy. It surprised her for she had seen enough of pregnant women in the East End to know that child-bearing was not an illness. The women of Antcliff Street had gone about on their daily business as their bellies burgeoned and had shown no hint of the misery she was suffering. The women at Uncle Isaac's factory, too, had gone on cheerfully working as their months passed, just pushing their stools further away from their work benches as the baby grew. They had not spent hour after hour battling with nausea.

'Hyperemesis gravidarum,' the doctor told her, when Florrie ignored Hannah's instruction not to fuss, and sent for him. 'You need some special treatment, young lady, if you aren't to lose this infant. Who d'you have here to take care of you, apart from servants? Mother, mother-in-law?'

Hannah managed a wisp of a smile at that and shook her head. 'I'll be all right. I don't need anyone.'

'Indeed you do,' the doctor said vigorously. 'Indeed you do. I'll send Miss Bishop.'

Miss Bishop proved to be a small termagant of a woman with legs bowed by childhood rickets and a round face adorned with glasses. Hannah looked at her severe navy dress and blindingly white apron and thought her formidable at first, but soon discovered her to be a most gentle and caring creature, whose tight little mouth could relax into a smile of particular sweetness. She set about Hannah with fearsome equipment, giving her rectal injections of sugar and salt water, an experience which Hannah felt too miserable to find as shaming as she might have done, and sat over her and fed her very slowly and with a great deal of gentle encouragement on dry toast and arrowroot. Florrie and Bet relaxed as Hannah slowly got better, and began to look less waiflike and pallid. By the time September had wheeled into a blustery October, and she had had several letters from Daniel in Shanghai, she felt much better.

Albert was punctilious in his care of her. She may not have had a mother or mother-in-law to share her distress, but she certainly had a father-in-law. He came to see her each week, to pay the account books presented to him by Bet and Florrie, who kept the household running on ball bearings, and to quiz Hannah about any other needs she might have.

'This isn't a gift, you understand,' he would say as he put crisp five pound notes into her small japanned cash box. 'This is the part of Daniel's salary that it was agreed should be paid directly to you. Now, if there is anything else you need you must let me know.'

She had another source of masculine help. Uncle Alex emerged from a flurry of his own business affairs – he had

342

been sending a number of English music hall acts across to New York to take part in vaudeville and burlesque shows there – to descend on Paultons Square with boxes full of smoked salmon and cheesecake and other assorted delicacies, none of which Hannah could face.

'Far be it from me to criticize your husband, dolly,' he said, 'so I won't. But I tell you, if I had that one here, I'd tie him into knots! Leaving a girl alone in such a state. So listen, who you got to take care of you, hey?'

'Florrie and Bet,' Hannah said. 'Now, do stop. They're all anyone could want, they're marvellous to me. And Mr Lammeck, Daniel's father, he comes every week to pay the bills.'

'You don't need no bills paid by him when you got me,' Uncle Alex said.

They wrangled amiably for a while about money, she steadfastly refusing to accept any. At last he gave in and instead talked about the news from the East End.

'Your father's gone to stay with your Uncle Benjamin, in Sidney Street,' he told her. 'The boys, too. They got the space there now Bella and Charlotte's married, and anyway they had to leave Antcliff Street – trouble with the landlord.'

Leave Antcliff Street? The home of her childhood? She tried to imagine her father living amicably with his brother Benjamin and couldn't, until Uncle Alex grinned and said, 'I got the place fixed up real nice. Benjamin and Sarah and young David live downstairs, your lot upstairs. They got separate doors, even. I boxed in the staircase, all fancy and modern, like the duplexes they got in America. I fixed it all up, with water in the upstairs kitchen, the lot.' And she knew Uncle Alex had once again found a way to provide his stubborn brother Nathan with care. She leaned forwards and kissed him gratefully. It was good to know they had a better place to live at last. Bloomah would have liked to live in the bigger flat too, but that was not a thought that could be faced, so Hannah pushed it away.

'And young Solly's working with me,' Alex went on. 'Sharp as a bloody needle that one, but he doesn't always prick my length of tweed, you know what I mean? I reckon he does as well for himself in my time as he does for me. Still and all, I'll teach him.' He nodded severely and then grinned, and she felt better about Solly.

The weeks wore on, as her waistline spread and she began

343

to think about preparing for the baby. Until now she had avoided thinking about it, as a person, and she tried now to decide whether she wanted a girl or a boy – and had to face the unpalatable truth that she did not want either. She was just not ready for a child, not ready to cope with the needs of yet another person. She wanted Daniel and wanted him badly. How could she look forward to the birth of a child feeling as lonely as she did? The hard fact was she resented the state of her health, and resented even more the cause of it. It would have been better to go with Daniel and let the baby die, she would think, and then feel sick with guilt at her own wickedness. So she tried not to think about the child at all, leaving it to Florrie to knit and sew clothes for it, which Florrie did with great satisfaction, and not a little skill. She had virtually adopted her mistress, it sometimes seemed, for all she was the younger of the two.

On a dark afternoon in November when the fog wove its yellow patterns round Paultons Square so thickly that she could not see across the square, a new dimension came into her life, to make the last weeks of her hated pregnancy less disagreeable.

Though she heard the doorbell ring and Florrie's footsteps pattering up from the kitchen to answer it, and the faint buzz of voices in the hallway, she did not move from her comfortable chair by the fireside. The sickness had left her completely now, much to her gratitude and Miss Bishop's approval when she visited each week, but she still suffered a good deal of lassitude and it was easier to sit still than to get to her feet to see who her unusual visitor might be; unusual because the doorbell hardly ever rang unexpectedly. She always knew when Uncle Alex or her father-in-law were coming, and Miss Bishop's visits were as regular as the sunrise. Even so, she could not summon up much curiosity until the door opened and Florrie said breathlessly, 'You got a caller, mum,' then stepped aside to let the visitor in.

She stood there in the doorway, a tall slender girl with dark hair and pale grey eyes which looked merry and a little impudent, framed in very thick dark lashes, and wearing an elegant gown of grey gaberdine under glossy furs. Her hat was very fashionable, wide brimmed and trimmed with drooping ostrich feathers. She looked expensive and petted and very charming, and she said in a slightly lisping husky

344

voice, 'Good evening, Mrs Lammeck! I'm Mrs Lammeck too. Isn't that delightful?'

37

'Judith?' Hannah said again. 'I think I have heard Daniel speak of you, but I can't be sure ... '

'Well, why should you?' the tall girl said affably, and began to peel off her gloves. 'Now, do ask me to sit down and be comfortable and ask your nice little maid to make us some tea and we shall have a lovely cosy chat.'

'Of course,' Hannah said, blushing a little at her own poor hospitality, and waved to a chair and then pulled the bellrope beside the fire. Florrie came in with suspicious promptitude and then went eagerly to make the tea for which she had been asked. Hannah sat and looked with curiosity at the girl now sitting opposite her.

'My dear, you look quite washed out, indeed you do! I cannot believe you always look so sad and sorry, indeed the gossip in the family is that you are a most delectable looking creature! And I am sure you usually are. Are you having a dreadful time of it with the infant?'

'Not very good,' Hannah said and sat up a little more straightly. Washed out? Sad and sorry? Oh dear. 'I've been very sick, I'm afraid. What do you mean, "gossip in the family"?'

Judith laughed, a loud and unselfconscious sound. 'Dear girl, you don't imagine, do you, that you can scoop up Aunt Davida's precious darling as you did and not be talked about? And in a Registry Office too! Why, to listen to some of the biddies, you'd think you were the scarlet woman in person. It's too delicious. You should hear my mother-in-law! And Aunt Susan! Oh, you'd enjoy it, I'm sure you would.'

Hannah stared, puzzled. She should have found this girl offensive, should have been mortified to hear the things she was saying, but she wasn't. Her directness and her cheerfulness took the sting out of the words, and anyway, it was very clear that she liked Hannah. Hannah decided that she was beginning to like her.

Judith leaned forwards. 'Now, you *have* worked out who I am, haven't you? My husband is Peter, such a darling, I do promise you, quiet and dour, you know, and altogether delicious. I do love him so! And his father is Alfred, who used to be Abdullah – no really! They came from India or some such place, you know, the Lammecks. Frightfully exotic. When I told my Mamma I was going to marry into that family she nearly swooned away! She's a Rothschild on her father's side you see, frightfully proper, and was quite sure I'd chosen to ally myself with a blackamoor! And of course my family were Ashkenazi and the Lammecks are Sephardi, quite different, the synagogue services, are they not? Or do you not bother to go? I'm sure I would not if it weren't for Peter. Anyway, as I say, Mamma was so put out to know I was marrying a Lammeck, until she met my lovely Peter and saw how adorable he is. And of course discovered how very rich the Lammecks are. So you see, we are cousins, are we not?'

'I suppose we are,' Hannah said.

'My dear, I do so feel for you,' Judith said, as the tea arrived and Florrie busied herself about serving it. 'The year before last,' she shuddered prettily, 'I was sitting about just like you and feeling quite, quite dreadful and looking worse. Why, if Peter so much as kissed me I almost swooned! As for anything more, well! Poor darling, he *did* have a bad time of it! Still, you don't have *that* worry, do you, with your Daniel away? Though it must be hateful for you, for I'm sure you love him as dearly as I do my Peter. I am so sad for you. And there's horrid Aunt Davida doing nothing to comfort you! Not that having her about would comfort anyone, of course! Anyway, that is why I am here. Dear Uncle Albert told me how alone you are, and said it would not do and he is quite right – ah, thank you!' She beamed up at Florrie who had given her her tea, and Florrie went pink and bobbed, and reluctantly went away to tell Bet that Missus had a new friend come to visit who talked ever so free considering she was a lady, but was really ever so nice.

'I would have come sooner had I known where to find you, but wretched Aunt D would not say, of course! I do dislike that silly lady, you know! She made such trouble for my poor Mama-in-law when I went out pavement chalking – '

'Pavement chalking?' Hannah said, quite at sea. This girl's

346

prattle was very engaging but very confusing too.

Judith laughed. 'Oh, my dear, such fun! As soon as your babe is born and you are free again you must come with me! The Suffragettes, don't you know! I'm a great supporter, indeed I am. It's quite a fashionable thing to do, for the more daring of us, you know! Last year, once I took my Charles off the breast and could get out again, I became madly interested. I mean, why *should* these wretched men have it all their own way? They are spoiled and horrid. Well, not my Peter, of course, and I dare say not your Daniel, but the rest of them. So when it all started, the votes for women thing, I thought it a great lark, and joined, and Aunt D! – well, she made the most frightful fuss and told Mama-in-law she should control me! Me! Margaret Lammeck control me! Can you imagine!'

Hannah laughed, almost against her will. She was feeling better by the minute.

'So, I did more, of course! I went out in the very early morning and chalked messages about the rally in Hyde Park all over the pavement outside Aunt D's house in Park Lane. She was so put about, it was delightful! And of course when I sent a letter full of pepper to Mr Churchill and he was telling her all about it at one of her stuffy dinner parties and he said how dreadful it was, I laughed so much I nearly choked and she knew at once I had done it, and was so mortified! But I really mustn't rattle on so! Tell me about you, everything now! For if we are to be friends, and I am determined we shall, then we must know all about each other.'

And tell her Hannah did. She had never thought herself able to be as relaxed with anyone as she became with Judith that foggy November afternoon. The fire burned cheerfully between them and the fog pressed against the window panes and they sat in the glow of a small rose-shaped lamp and chattered over their cooling tea. Judith heard all about Nathan and Solly and Jake and sympathized deeply, for she had never had brothers of her own but had always wanted them and her own parents were dead, and Judith told Hannah about her delightful baby Charles, an 'eighteen month old armful of heaven' and her friends – who often found her rather shocking, with her wilful attachment to the Suffragettes – and then Hannah spoke of her Uncle Alex, describing him in such terms that Judith declared herself quite in love with him, and both talked about clothes and housekeeping and servants and thoroughly enjoyed themselves.

It was precisely what Hannah had needed, and after Judith went away with promises to return another afternoon, she slept better than she had since her pregnancy had begun and without for one moment thinking about her unease about Daniel, whose letters had become less and less informative as the weeks went by.

Judith for her part went and told her Uncle Albert that she had done all she could to cheer up his sad little daughter-in-law, and would continue to do all she could, for she was a sweet girl indeed.

She did not add that it gave her a perverse pleasure to upset her Aunt Davida, but Albert was well aware that this was part of Judith's attachment to Hannah. He did not mind in the least as long as she became attached. He had been worried about the girl. To be able to relinquish some of Hannah's care to his niece was a relief to him, so he stopped visiting Paultons Square quite so frequently, sending the money by the hand of Young Levy instead.

The year turned on its axis, and 1911 rang in with the usual New Year's Eve mixture of excitement and depression. Hannah spent it alone in the house, insisting that both Florrie and Bet go out with their friends. 'I shall be all right,' she assured them. 'I have almost four weeks to go yet, so don't worry. And *go* or I shall be angry.'

She sat beside her fire and heard the bells ringing, muffled, from the dark streets outside and tried not to cry. Judith had visited that afternoon and done all she could to cheer her, but it was an impossible task. The first anniversary of her wedding had come and gone, and Daniel had not been there. And the first anniversary of the deaths of Bloomah and Mary had come and gone, too. New Year's Eve came as a culmination of her sadness. No one, not even Judith, could have lifted her from her despondency.

When her labour pains started, in the small hours of the first of January, she did not identify them for what they were. She put them down to her general unease. She had been having vague contractions for some weeks, her belly hardening when she made extra physical efforts like climbing the stairs, or walking down to the flower seller on the corner. She thought at first these were the same, but by the time dawn lifted itself sluggishly over the chimney pots of the houses across the square she realized that these were different. There was a rhythm now, and that meant that the time had come.

Miss Bishop arrived, fetched by Florrie at nine o'clock in a state of towering excitement, and the doctor came, but both pronounced it early yet – the baby would not be born for some time. She lay in bed all through that long Saturday, listening to the waves of contraction in her belly, and trying, still, not to think of the baby that would result from them. She didn't want it, yet she could not bring herself to admit that fact. All she could do was lie there tense and blank faced, staring at the cloud-scudding sky above the chimney tops outside her window.

Probably it was her own tension and control that contributed to the delay, for the pains went on, became more and more disagreeable, and yet, Miss Bishop said when she came to examine her again, there was no progress.

'You'll have to wait, that's all,' she said as she settled the covers round Hannah's body again. 'This one's in no hurry.'

Twenty-four hours longer it went on, and she became more and more tense, more and more resentful of the cause of her pain, and by early on Monday morning could no longer contain her feelings.

'I hate it, I hate it, I hate it,' she shouted at the doctor, as with Miss Bishop he set about the business of persuading the infant to emerge from her taut and resisting body. 'I hate it!'

'They all do, my dear,' the doctor said cheerily. 'There's no woman yet who ever enjoyed her labour pains, but it'll be worth it for the baby.'

'I hate it!' she said again, wanting him to know it was the baby she hated, not merely the pain, but he ignored her, busying himself about her pelvis as though she didn't inhabit it, as though she wasn't a person at all, only a container which would deliver to him some treasure which he greatly desired.

It was still not to be; after an hour of nagging her to push, they desisted, and told her the baby would not be born until tomorrow after all. She wept bitterly, as much from exhaustion as anything else.

In midafternoon, when blessedly her pains seemed to have slackened, she suddenly felt an aching need for the comfort of someone beside her. Not Florrie or Bet, good to her as they were. To Hannah it seemed that they were like the doctor and Miss Bishop, concerned only with the baby and not at all with her. She needed someone who would hate the baby as much as she did, and would love her, only Hannah, herself.

She told Florrie to send a telegram to her father. Had she not been exhausted with the past two days of labour she would never have considered it, but she was no longer herself, no longer sensible Hannah who knew what to do. She hadn't been that Hannah for a long time, not since Daniel went away. She was a childish Hannah, lonely and frightened, and she wanted her mother badly. And in her mother's absence she would have to settle for her father.

The telegram was sent, but no word came, none at all. She wept into her pillow, her face becoming pouched and soggy, and when the doctor came again she shrieked at him in her distress, but still he only patted her head and told her not to fret, and then turned his attention once again to her belly and its contents as though she were not there. She stopped trying, stopped caring, stopped thinking. There was just now, and the pain and the loneliness and the bitter anger at the anonymous lump inside her that, parasite that it was, drew what it needed from her helplessness and gave nothing back.

They took instruments to her, invading her body with the coldness of metal and pinning her to the bed when she tried to wriggle away from them, ignoring her cries of pain, and she sank into despair and wanted to die. There was nothing else that could bring any comfort, nothing at all.

And then, miraculously, it was complete. There had been a crescendo of sensation, and then they were washing her legs and belly and groin with warm water, and drying her with big soft towels and congratulating each other across her inert shape. And Miss Bishop was beside her, pulling on her arm, making her curve it to receive the blanketed parcel she was holding.

She looked down, almost amazed, to peer at the face that was framed in the folds. A reddish ugly face, streaked with yellow grease and blood spatters. A head covered in matted scraps of hair, and oddly misshapen. There were bruises too, on the temples, and the eyes were tightly closed and the mouth was twisting and turning, making ridiculous shapes under a dab of a nose. The mouth opened then and mewed like a sick kitten. She stared at it and then at Miss Bishop.

350

'A girl,' Miss Bishop said shortly, and snapped her rat-trap mouth closed, but her expression was kind. Hannah frowned a little and looked back at the infant.

It opened its eyes and stared, it seemed, straight at her, and she looked into the depths of blank darkness between the sparse lashes and felt a lurch of need and something she could not identify, a sort of hunger, perhaps. Automatically, she lifted the infant closer to her sweat-damp face and held its sticky cheek to hers and made an odd crooning noise in the back of her throat.

'I told you it would be worth it,' the doctor said triumphantly from the foot of the bed. 'Now, m'dear, we must put that one to the breast, for that will bring the afterbirth faster than anything. And then some stitches, I'm afraid, but I'll not hurt you any more than is necessary.'

Miss Bishop pulled her nightdress open, and for a moment she wanted to shout to her, '*No!* This is me! You can't do that to me!' but then the baby's cheek was against her bare skin, and the small misshapen head turned towards her, the mouth grimacing sideways. As the questing lips found the nipple, there was another surge of feeling, this time of enormous pleasure, almost as powerful as that she had felt when she and Daniel made love, and the doctor was saying triumphantly. 'There now! It never fails, here's the placenta! All right, Miss Bishop, put the babe in its cot and come and help me.'

To Hannah's amazement, when Miss Bishop took her bundle of blanket from her she felt bereft and reached her arms out after her and said, 'My baby, give her back. I want my baby.'

She had fallen in love, head over ears, desperately and unexpectedly in love. All the loneliness and fear and anger and despair of the months of her pregnancy coalesced in her, boiled up and emerged in a totally new form as adoration for the ugly object that Miss Bishop was putting down in the wicker cradle that Florrie had prepared.

'Give her back,' she said again, but Miss Bishop just shook her head.

'You can have her soon enough. First things first. We've got to get *you* right now. Can't leave you in that state. What shall you call her, then? Have you decided?'

The words came out without her realizing she had said

351

them. They hung in the air above her head and she contemplated them, surprised and pleased.

'Mary Bloomah,' she said. 'Mary Bloomah Lammeck. My daughter.'

38

It was some time before Daniel was able to admit to himself that he was a disappointed man, and when he did, the pit of misery into which he fell seemed that much darker and deeper.

From the moment he left London on the boat train for Liverpool, and settled into the comfort of his first class seat, he had lived on a peak of excitement that made him as breathless as if he had in fact been breathing thinner air. He looked out at the world through such a glitter of exhilaration that everything seemed tinged with a glamour he had never known before. Even when he had first launched himself upon London life, after leaving university, and had joined the best clubs and gone to the best restaurants and parties in the company of the richest and most attractive young people in town, it had not been like that journey to Shanghai. Now, he had a purpose in life; he was going to Run the Shanghai Office of the Lammeck Empire and that gave him a status in his own eyes that was hugely satisfying. He occupied the best stateroom on the *Priam*, a small but elegantly fitted passenger steamer, and became the object of awed attentions from the other passengers because of the fame of his name in commercial circles, and because of his obvious wealth; when Lammeck Alley sent its envoys travelling, it sent them in style. The result was that he became a minor celebrity on board. The pretty daughters of a tea planter on their way back to Ceylon after a holiday at home fluttered about him like adoring butterflies; the handsome widow on her way to housekeep for her brother in Hong Kong watched him with languorous inviting eyes; the captain took it for granted that Daniel would join him for pre-dinner drinks in his cabin every evening, and whatever he had to say the male passengers listened with flattering respect and the females

352

with wide eyed admiration. Long before they called at Colombo he was dizzy with self approval, and by the time he reached Hong Kong he felt himself to be one of the most successful of men. When Shanghai's teeming docks at last appeared over the rail of the ship he was impatient to get down to the business of setting the town on its ears.

His popularity helped a great deal in coping with his feelings about Hannah. There had been times when he had awakened in his cabin as it rolled its majestic way across the South China Sea or pushed uneasily through the Malacca Strait and found his body crying out for her. During the day it was easy to forget how long it had been since he had held her close to him, felt her skin hot under his touch, but at night, especially those sticky airless tropical nights, it was painful to remember the satisfaction he had found with her, the way her need for him could turn his already clamouring hunger into a roar of sensual satisfaction that left them both gasping. He learned to deal with his needs as best he could, turning over afterwards into an uneasy sleep during which he dreamed of himself as the King of the Shanghai office, burning out his physical demands in sheer hard work.

The excitement lasted for a few days after he landed. There was the big car with its liveried chauffeur waiting outside the customs shed to drive him to his hotel on the Bund, the great waterfront thoroughfare lined with offices and banks and stores, and the exotic strangeness of it all, Chinese in western dress, of course, but also many in the traditional robes of the mandarin, and coolies with rickshaws as well as modern cars and trams. There was excitement in living in the exceedingly luxurious hotel too, since his house was not quite ready, and also in the flattering attentions of the International Settlement hostesses who were very quick with invitations to parties and soirees and dinners.

But that was not enough, for there was the office, too. He presented himself on the first morning at his usual London time of ten o'clock, or he would have done so had he not been delayed by the press of traffic. It was almost a quarter past ten when he walked into the outer office of Lammeck and Sons and told the young man in the perfect black morning coat and sponge bag trousers of a City of London stockbroker that he wanted Ling Ho. He felt rather than saw the young man's eyes flicker over his alpaca jacket and trousers, both already a shade creased in the heat of the summer morning, but dismissed that; clearly junior members of the staff were expected to dress in a particular manner, no matter what the weather. The same could not, would not, be expected of the manager.

He found Ling Ho in his office, a rotund, imperious looking man with glossily brushed thick hair looking startlingly white over his sallow skin, and a smooth smile which did not at all change the alert eyes behind the thick glasses which shielded them. He too was wearing immaculate City black and perfect linen, and showed no signs of being at all uncomfortable in the heat. Daniel felt even more crumpled and casual than he actually was, and became a little haughty in consequence, giving Ling Ho only a perfunctory bow in response to his elaborate speech of welcome and cutting him short when he took breath to continue the orotund phrases so dear to the Chinese heart, by walking over to the window to look out into the teeming street beneath.

'Quite a busy part of town you're in here,' he said.

Ling Ho's mouth tightened very slightly but he showed no other sign of disapproval at the way his welcome had been truncated. 'It was busier at nine o'clock this morning when the office day starts here,' he said smoothly. 'People in Shanghai are very punctilious about their time keeping, and therefore the streets are particularly thronged at that time.'

He spoke fluent English with no trace of an accent, and Daniel felt his irritation increase, not only at the implied criticism of his own lateness but at the sense of inadequacy that swept over him. Would he ever be able to speak Chinese as fluently as this smooth faced man spoke his language?

Ling Ho took him around the office, introducing him to one round-faced smiling oriental after another, each of them rising from their desks to bow neatly, immediately to return to their industrious writing in ledgers, wasting not a second longer than was demanded by politeness. Had he thought about it, he would surely have realized that there would be no other Englishmen but himself in the office, but he had not thought about it, and loneliness suddenly swept over him in a wave of homesickness, a longing for Hannah in particular, but also for the sight of the old familiar office at Lammeck Alley with its pale faced, slightly shabby clerks. Here there was no hint of shabbiness. The lowliest clerk was as neatly

354

dressed in the prevailing uniform of black and grey as Ling Ho himself, and each showed a particular pride in his situation. As they moved from desk to desk, Ling Ho's courteously modulated voice murmuring unmemorable Chinese names in his ear, he became more and more uneasy. And more and more stiff as a result.

By the time they reached the last office, that of Ling Ho's nephew, Daniel was no longer able to be sensible at all. Kim Ching Wong, very like his uncle except that his hair was black and his glasses not quite so pebble thick, stood up at once and bowed, and began a speech of welcome similar to the one his uncle had started, but Daniel brushed that aside.

'Yes, very nice of you, absolutely,' he said. 'I'm delighted to be here too. Now, about my office – I rather think this one would suit me. Two windows, you see – I like plenty of light.'

Kim Ching Wong did not look at his uncle but immediately bowed again, and stepped out from behind the desk.

'Of course, Mr Lammeck. We will arrange the movement of the furniture at once. The room we had prepared for you is at the other end of the corridor, and you will find me there at any time you choose.' Again he bowed to Daniel, and then he and his uncle went quietly away. Almost immediately two of the black coated clerks arrived and with neat and economical movements began to take the ledgers and papers from the desk and carry them away. Two blue coated workers followed them. In a matter of minutes new furniture, rather more elegant than that which had been there, stood in place and Daniel had the office of his choice.

By now he had realized that he had caused great offence to both Ling Ho and Kim Ching Wong, making them lose face in front of their juniors, and he much regretted it. But even as the regrets came into his mind, he pushed them away. Begin as you mean to go on, he told himself. You're the manager here; they might as well learn it now as later.

Their courtesy remained unfailing, all through that day and the next and the next, as the two senior men took him through the work of the Shanghai branch of Lammeck and Sons. They brought him ledgers and murmured facts at him; they told him of the godowns in Hong Kew, north east of the city, which were crammed roof high with Lammeck goods, cotton and silk, sugar, tea and rice, and spices galore. They gave him sheets of figures to do with the establishment of cotton-spinning mills and weaving sheds; they talked of gold exchanges and the rates of pay for the coolies they employed. But though they seemed to be giving him the information he needed somehow the core of it eluded him. They spoke carefully in their impeccable English, answered his questions courteously, their eyes blank behind their glasses, as he struggled to organize it all in his head. And the harder he tried, the more he floundered.

It was particularly infuriating because he knew it was not his fault. He had never been a particularly eager businessman, often sitting half asleep at Lammeck Alley when the senior partners talked of deals and contracts, finding no excitement in making a buying and selling arrangement that netted the firm some three per cent, and then getting worked up because of a shrewd move that lifted the profit to three and a half. Still, he was no fool and he was experienced. He had been at Lammeck Alley long enough to speak the language of commerce, to understand how the system worked, yet he could not grasp the way the Shanghai branch operated. He would sit there in the office he had commandeered from Kim Ching Wong, with the two unfailingly polite Chinese on each side of him, and want to shout with frustration, because somehow they were not telling him all he needed to know. They were withholding vital information and he knew it, but because he did not know what the information was there was no way he could begin to extract it from them. At the end of each sweaty maddening day he would fling out of the office with his head in a whirl and his bad temper showing in every line of his body. What made it worse was the fact that he knew those over-controlled and perfectly mannered Chinese despised him for it, and he could do nothing about it.

The evenings were his only source of relief. The Imperial Hotel was awash with Western faces and he would hurl himself into the bar and order large gins and then sit on the wide terrace overlooking the Bund and watch the rickshaws bouncing between the big cars and the trams on their way to the haunts of the foreigners – the English Club, the Race Club, the Opera House – and would unwind to the silly chatter of the expatriates around him. He would dress for dinner in his best evening coat and wander down to eat a large meal, ostentatiously refusing even to try the local foods.

356

At first he went to the houses of the eager hostesses, but he soon discovered they were even more boring than London hostesses. They were provincial as well as drearily middle-aged and all seemed to have daughters to dangle before his eyes. He didn't want any daughter-dangling here any more than he did at home, and he was tired of explaining that he was married, that his wife had not accompanied him because of her health. So he turned away from the big low houses with their cool enclosed verandahs in the International Settlement, seeking more agreeable diversions.

Some nights he went to the Majestic Hotel, to sit in the gilt and marble bedecked Empire Banqueting Suite beside the sunken dance floor, with its coloured lanterns and jasmine bedecked tables, but that grew boring too. So, he began to go to Bubbling Wells Road, taking a rickshaw there, to visit the gambling houses.

It was absurd that he found any entertainment there, for he had never been a gambler. When his father and his uncles talked with relish of roulette and vingt-et-un, or had crowed over their racing coups, he had been remote and uninterested, but now the excitement of it began to waken in him. To sit and watch men betting vast sums in gold was enough fun to start with, but then he began to bet himself, at first wagering only modest string of Chinese cash. The excitement bit as he had some modest wins, and he began to do as the other rich expatriates did and gambled in English gold, piling sovereigns on the tables with a casual flick of the wrist that was somehow as exciting as collecting a win. There was little else to do with his money, after all; he could only eat and drink so much, and anyway, the firm was paying his hotel bills until his house was ready.

It was his recklessness that attracted them, the sleek girls in their skin tight cheongsams with the high necks and hip high slits at the sides, who stood about the gambling houses looking cool and elegant and unapproachable until a particularly lucky player caught a girl's eye, and she would come to stand beside him, her jasmine scent heavy and her rouged lips and black-outlined eyes an invitation that was hard to refuse.

At first he ignored them, until one of the other gamblers, a young man who worked for the Cathay Land Company which had offices next door to Lammeck's on the Bund and who also lived at the Imperial Hotel, asked him to dine one night, and brought along two of the girls as dinner companions. Daniel's eyebrows creased at the sight of them, one wearing vivid emerald and the other in deep crimson, but uncannily alike in every other respect. Jimmy Trent had laughed at him.

'Dear old chap, they're just for fun, don't you know! Don't speak a word of decent lingo, apart from yes and no, and no trouble to anyone. But a man needs a companion now and again, or he'll go out of his mind in this place. And anyway, everyone does.'

Looking around, Daniel had to agree that everyone did. At table after table in the big gambling house restaurant there were Western men, Germans and French, a lot of Dutch and Belgians, and not a few Englishmen eating and drinking and laughing, accompanied by these sallow skinned dark eyed creatures in their onion skin dresses which displayed every detail of their bodies. The lift of nipples on tiny breasts, the small indentations in the middle of the small domed bellies, the curve of the buttocks and groin were as clear as if they had been varnished. It was difficult for a man not to find comfort in looking at them, particularly a lonely and bewildered young man who was badly in need of his wife.

The girl in crimson clung to him more and more as after dinner he began to play again. He was on a winning streak. As sovereign after sovereign was pushed over the table to him, other girls clustered around, but the one with whom Jimmy had provided him as a dinner companion was too sharp for them. She remained by his side as though she had been sewn there, and somehow managed to reach out and take some of his winnings with such easy charm and such a wicked little glance from those hooded dark eyes that he had only laughed, a little drunkenly, for he'd taken in more than usual tonight, and let her slip the money into the top of her stockings.

She came back to the Imperial with him that night as though it was the most natural thing in the world, and followed him into his room. Even before he had time to take off his jacket she had slipped out of the cheongsam and precious silk stockings which were her only garments. Her face remained unreadable; no hint of a smile on those marble smooth cheeks, no expression in those narrow black eyes. Just a small perfect body, with breasts that looked like apples,

358

so neat and round were they, and a spring of hips over a round belly above a neat triangle of dark hair that he could not but stare at. He stood there and said loudly, 'Hannah,' at the girl who nodded, quite uncomprehending, and then came towards him and with the same neat, methodical movements with which she had removed her own clothes began to remove his.

'Hannah,' he said again. 'Damn it, she's having a baby. It's really not . . . ' But she went on, carefully unbuttoning his shirt and he stood there feeling his senses move in him and remembering all too dismally the lonely nights at sea and since his arrival. 'Dammit,' he thought, his gin-fuzzed mind slipping its cogs as he tried to concentrate. 'A man needs a woman. Can't go on just playing on his own, can he?'

He said it aloud then. 'Can't go on playing on my own, can I?'

By some quirk of coincidence she used one of her only two English words, and used the right one, responding to the question in his voice or perhaps to the hopelessness in him. 'No,' she said prettily and for the first time smiled, and lifted her face to his and kissed him, her tongue flickering expertly into his mouth.

There seemed no reason to stop once that first time was behind him. It was more than a fortnight before he learned her name was Yü Soo, that she was seventeen years old and that she came from Korea, information he gathered from Jimmy, whose own girl, Soo-Niang Pei, had learned to speak some English and translated for her friend. By that time it was all such a fait accompli that when he moved into his own bungalow, now ready at last in the northern part of the International Settlement, she moved in with him.

Somehow he managed not to think about Hannah, in all this. When he ran his hands over Yü Soo's satin smooth jasmine scented body, and she began to work her skills on him – and heaven knew she was an expert at her craft, with hands and lips and tongue that could arouse a man so fast that he could hardly catch his breath, and then bring him to another climax almost immediately after his first – he shut out of his memory entirely the way Hannah's body had felt, the way she had loved him with an uncalculating passion that was as unlike Yü Soo's attentions as Lammeck Alley was unlike the office on the Bund. He also stopped writing full letters to Hannah. How could he pour out all his misery about what was happening at the office when he had Yü Soo to fill his nights? How could he offer more than scrappy comments on the weather, and his own vague 'busyness' when he was living the way he was? The short, widely spaced letters and the refusal to think about Hannah and home became the only way he could go on coping with days that became more and more complex, and loneliness that had begun to make him feel as though life no longer had any savour.

The office situation became worse and worse; there was the day when a major order was lost to them, an order which would have emptied their biggest spice godown at a great profit, because the necessary paper work was missing. It was found tucked into his own private ledger, where he could have sworn it had not been when last he had used it, but there was nothing he could do. It was his ledger, and the missing order was there, and he could not remember where he had last seen it. It must have been his fault. And why go on and on about it, when the damage was done? And then there was the day when he – or someone unidentified – had entered a wrong date into his desk diary and therefore he failed to keep an appointment with a senior official from Shantung Province who could have brought them enormous trade in silk, and so caused that self important mandarin such huge offence that he took his business down the street, to Mocatta's. There were messages that somehow never reached their destination, plans that went horribly astray, sums of money that did not add up as they should. He knew that it was not his own oversights that had caused the errors, that Ling Ho and Kim Ching Wong were somehow involved, but they were so polite, so full of neat explanations, so commiserating in his anger, so careful not to make it seem they were blaming him, that he could do nothing but shout in impotent rage to which they listened with impassive courtesy and with no sign of the disapproval he knew was warranted. After such days, going home to his bleak bungalow was only made possible by the fact that Yü Soo was waiting there, smooth and silky and always ready to comfort him. That the comfort she gave him was merely the exhaustion that came after their extended bouts of sometimes savage lovemaking did not matter. It was comfort of a sort. He would settle for that.

When the cable came telling him of his daughter's birth it was brought to him when he was lying in bed, with Yü Soo asleep beside him.

39

Hannah was sitting up in bed with her knees spread wide to make a little hollow in the bedclothes in which the baby could lie, just looking at her, when the door opened and there he was, standing awkwardly and twisting a large brimmed hat between his hands. He was wearing a ill fitting suit of flecked tweeds and was sweating slightly and looking very uncomfortable.

'Solly!' she said joyously and held out both hands to him. 'I'm so glad you came!' She smiled widely at him. Already, only three days after Mary Bloomah's birth, she was looking herself again, with her pallor lifted faintly and her hair, washed and brushed, lying richly on her shoulders. 'I sent a message for Poppa but – well, never mind. You've come and I'm so glad.'

'It wasn't that we didn't want to come sooner, Hannah,' Solly said earnestly. 'Honestly. I mean, maybe Poppa would've come, what with it being a telegram. I mean, he's funny – sometimes you can get him if you makes things important, you know what I mean?'

She smiled at that. He may be only fifteen, she thought, but he's got a very shrewd awareness of Poppa's sense of the dramatic. 'I know.'

'But there was the siege an' all, and there was Mr Churchill standin' there with one of our cups and saucers in his hand and staring out at the soldiers from our window, and Poppa thinkin' any minute the shots'll come in and ...'

She stared at him in bewilderment. 'What on earth are you talking about?'

'The siege! The siege of Sidney Street! And Peter the Painter and all! Haven't you heard? About how they brought in the Scots Guards an' all, all togged up for battle, after that there Sergeant Leeson the copper, you know – after he got shot an' – you must've heard!'

She shook her head, bemused. 'I've heard nothing.'

'Papers was full of it. Monday it was, an' the whole street in an uproar, believe me it was a real *gunsah megilla*. And Poppa so busy, on account our house was right opposite, wasn't it? That's why Mr Churchill wanted to come up and watch from there – and Poppa told him all about how he was in the army and got a medal an' all in Siberia.'

She almost laughed then. 'I can imagine. But why was he there? And Scots Guards and guns – I don't understand.'

'Anarchists!' said Solly triumphantly, greatly enjoying being in a position to impart such momentous news. 'I thought you'd have heard about *them*! The papers've been on and on about it – ' His face lengthened for a moment. 'Some of the street kids, the *goyim*, you know? they been lying waiting for us, the Yiddisher boys, wanting to beat us up, saying we're anarchists like Peter the Painter, and the ones that got burned – whatsits, Svaas and Marks. I've had a couple o' good fights over it, I can tell you – so's Jake. But what can you do? The fellas that was in the siege was anarchists, no arguing that, and they was Yidden too. So, what can you expect? Uncle Benjamin, he worries about it. He says one of these days the *goyim'll* turn against us and make big trouble in the East End. He says they hate us because we're Jews, but I don't know – it's only when we make a bob or two they get bothered. They'll hate Uncle Alex more'n they'll hate us, seeing we ain't got fivepence to rattle between us.'

'And you say that all this was why Poppa didn't come to see me?' she said. Anarchists and Jew baiting outbreaks in the East End were important of course, but not as important as her own feelings at the moment. 'Will he come now it's all over? It *is* all over, isn't it?'

'Yes, it's over.' Solly sounded disappointed. 'They burned the house down, see, and Mrs Gershon – it's her house, they'd taken lodgings with her, and she got suspicious, told the coppers round at Arbour Square and there you were, they all turned out with guns – she's gone to stay with Mrs Cohen, Joey Cohen's mother, you remember her? No? Well, he's a mate of mine – anyway, they said they'll fix her house for her, the police and all since she was so helpful, and she's going back. Peter the Painter – he was the leader of the three of them – he got away. So unless he comes back, it's over – '

'Will Poppa come now to see me? And his granddaughter?' She looked down at Mary Bloomah sleeping comfortably between her knees in her hollow of sheets.

Solly peered at the baby with a fifteen-year-old's uninterest and after a moment shook his head.

'I asked him. I'm sorry, Hannah, but he really – he's got this notion, you see, that you ran out on him. Goes on and on about people abandoning people, and if we say anything, me and Jake, he gets nasty, so we don't say nothing. But Jake said I should come to see you and I asked Uncle Alex to give me the time, and he said fine.'

He stood up. 'And I'd better be going, I got things to do.'

'Back to Uncle Alex?' she said, and he looked a little shamefaced.

'Well, later on I will. But I thought, now I'm here, up West, I'd have a bit of a look around.'

She lectured him with all the authority of the big sister, insisting he go straight back to his job and he made a face, but said he would and then kissed her awkwardly and promised to come again. Jake would come as soon as he could, on Sunday, probably.

'And don't worry about Poppa,' he said at the door. 'We'll look after him, silly old ... well, we'll look after him.'

Judith came often during those first days, finally bringing her own baby with her 'to introduce them, for they are relatives, after all!' and then sat and gossiped cheerfully for the rest of the afternoon as Charles, a large and very active child, crawled about the floor and pulled over everything on which he could get his hands. Hannah, primed to be interested in babies by her own new motherhood, was fascinated by him and thought him singularly handsome with his dark curls and large serious dark eyes rather turned down at the corners, which gave him a mournful look which disappeared entirely when he laughed, which was often, at which point his eyes seemed to disappear altogether into delighted slits.

Judith explained to her about the drama in the East End about which Solly had spoken and which had so confused her, but which he had in essence got right. There had been a hunt on for some time for 'anarchists', politically active

363

people, many of them Jews, who were, it was said, trying to inflame the workers of the East End in order to bring about the end of the British Government. Three known anarchists had hidden themselves in Sidney Street and been flushed out violently.

'It's all nonsense, of course,' Judith said airily. 'Those people in the East End are altogether too feeble to do anything! I mean they had strikes years ago because the sweat shops were so bad, and yet nothing came of it! They didn't get involved with anarchists then and I doubt they will now. They're still as pathetic as ever they were.'

'Not precisely pathetic,' Hannah said quietly. 'Very hard put to it to be anything but what they are, I would say. It's not easy to be so poor that you can't buy food, or pay your rent. And when you get a job, you do it, however bad it is, because it's better than having nothing. If most of the people in the factory I worked in met anarchists, they'd pay no attention, but it wouldn't be because they were feeble. It would be because they were practical.'

'Oh, dear Hannah, I'm so sorry! I quite forgot that you – I mean that you came from the East End. It must be quite dreadful. And I have no right to speak of it at all, for what do I know! Only what I've heard the olds say, my parents-in-law you know, and Uncle Albert and Aunt Davida. They said the poor Jews who're coming in ought to be sent back to where they came from. It sounds very cruel to me.'

'It is,' Hannah said shortly, and picked up her baby and held her close. 'I'm glad my Mary B wasn't born there as I was – I'm one of the lucky ones, and so shall she be.'

'Is that what you're going to call her?' Judith cried in delight, glad to be able to escape from what was proving to be dangerous conversation. 'How delicious. Mary B. Shall you spell it as a word – I mean, Mary Bee – that makes her sound like a lovely bundle of fuzz who makes things which are sweet. It's lovely!'

'I've never written it down,' Hannah said, and laughed. 'Mary Bee, like a honey bee? Yes, that's what I'll call her, always. I like it.'

At that moment, Charles pulled over the fire irons with a great clatter and broke into a wail of alarm. His mother pounced on him to hug him close and make soothing noises and then bore him off to his nurse, who was sitting cosily downstairs gossiping over kitchen tea, and went off to go to the Opera with her darling Peter leaving Hannah feeling once more alone and lonely. Judith was full of affection and genuine concern and they *were* friends, but the gulf that yawned between their different experiences of life was almost uncrossable. She, Hannah, could understand Judith and her life and past, but never would Judith understand hers. Hannah inhabited a different world from everyone else, and she felt bleak in it.

Until Uncle Alex came to visit, with hampers full of food and armfuls of flowers and great piles of assorted toys and baby clothes. He had enjoyed himself hugely going from shop to shop all along Regent Street and had brought her the spoils of a most lavish afternoon. Her bed was piled high with it all, and Bet and Florrie giggled with delight as they bore it all away.

'You know you're the first to do it, don't you? The first child in this generation you've provided! Your father must be a lunatic, a real *meshugganer* not to want to come rushing here and take the credit that's due to the first grandfather among us. But him, all of a sudden he's the leading expert on radical politics, on account he had Winston Churchill drink his tea in front of his window and listen to him rabbiting on about anarchists, much he knows, the *shlemiel*! It makes you sick to listen to him, believe me, sounding like he's more of a politician than bloody Asquith you should excuse the expression and about politics he won't know nothin' as long as he's got a *tochus* to sit on – Hannah dolly, you look marvellous, your baby looks marvellous, I could bust a *kishka*, I'm that proud of you!'

And indeed he looked it, his round face creased with pleasure and his hair standing up in a great aureole. Hannah relaxed and smiled back at him.

'So, have you heard from your young husband, already? Does he know that he's a poppa?'

She looked down at the baby on her lap so that she didn't have to look at him.

'Of course he knows,' she said. 'A cable was sent as soon as she was born.'

'Have you heard from him already? He's sent a cable back?'

'Not yet.'

'Not yet? For God's sake, what's the matter with the boy? Here's you sitting here all on your own and he ain't sent no cable saying at least thank you for your trouble? What sort of man is this, for God's sake?'

'Uncle Alex, please don't!' She looked up at him and shook her head. 'A cable will come, of course it will.'

It was the first time she had admitted to anyone that Daniel had not responded to the news. No one knew either how scrappy and short his letters had become, how little contact she felt with him when she seized the heavy envelopes as soon as they arrived, and studied them with an eager hope that was always flattened as she scanned the lines scrawled so swiftly. It was bad enough knowing that the best part of two months lay between the time of their writing and her reading of them; to feel the emptiness in them was even worse.

Now she looked at Uncle Alex, and said again, 'Please don't fuss,' and then stopped as once more the door opened and Florrie let in another caller.

'Oh!' she said blankly. 'Mr Lammeck. How good of you to come! I didn't expect you again so soon.'

Albert had come the day after Mary Bee's birth, and stayed a few minutes and then, after putting many more five pound notes than usual into the japanned black box had gone off, silent and preoccupied. She had not felt he was particularly delighted with the sight of his new granddaughter and had felt a chill as she watched him go. And now he was back, barely a week later. 'Have you met my Uncle? Uncle Alex, Mr Albert Lammeck. Mr Lammeck, this is Mr Alexander Lazar.'

Uncle Alex stood up and sketched a sort of bow. As Hannah looked at the two men she felt a little surge of extra affection for her uncle. He was dressed, as usual, in an extreme of fashion, his suit a particularly strong shade of light chocolate, and was wearing a wide cravat with a diamond headed stick pin in it. He had elastic sided brown boots, and on both hands wore large gold rings, one with a positively massive diamond in it, the other with a tiger's eye, very large and very rich looking. Her father-in-law, on the other hand, looked sober and morose in his eternal black coat over sponge bag trousers, the City dress that he always wore, and the expression on his face was sour, not at all like

Uncle Alex's cheerful grin.

'How d'do,' he said gruffly and then turned towards Hannah. 'I thought to find you alone, m'dear,' he said. 'Thought we could talk a little.'

'Oh, Uncle Alex can hear anything we have to talk about!' she said in a louder voice than usual, stung by Albert Lammeck's casual rudeness. How dare he try to hustle her own relations away? It was like that awful Sunday last year all over again, when Davida had been so clearly offended by the sight of Hannah's cluster of cousins and aunts and uncles.

'That's it!' Uncle Alex said, and sat down with a little thump, flicking an understanding look at Hannah. 'Take a seat, Mr Lammeck! Take a seat! And *mazeltov* on your lovely granddaughter!'

'No, I won't stay,' Albert said, and moved back to the door. 'Just thought I'd call in you know, and ... I'll come back another time, since you're busy. Just a few family matters.'

He was feeling wretched. He had felt all through Hannah's pregnancy an increasing guilt at her distress; had seen clearly how much she needed her husband with her, and was angry with himself for being the one who had engineered matters so that they were parted. He had become quite fond of the girl, dammit, and it was no pleasure to know that he'd treated her damned nearly as badly as Davida had.

This afternoon had been the last straw. Ezra had told him flatly that his son had turned out to be worse than useless in the Shanghai Office, and was to be brought back.

'Look, Albert, family is family, but the firm can't be played about with! And you had no right to tell us he could manage it there when Ling Ho has told us it's plain as the nose on his face that the boy just doesn't have it in him. There's been nothing but muckups and lost money since he got there. He's got to come back. I've talked to Alfred and he agrees. We'll send Margaret's nephew, you know the chap I mean, Joseph Gubbay. He'll make a much better job of it. Your Daniel's got to come back.'

Davida's triumph when she had heard the news was galling. She let a smile spread across her face until she looked like a cat that had got the cream and he snapped, 'Well, there's no need to think you can make any more trouble for the boy! They've got a baby now, and if you meddle...'

'Oh, baby, pooh!' she said. 'If all the bastard babies this family has dropped around were added up it would no doubt provide enough clerks to fill Lammeck Alley twice over. I'm a practical woman, Albert, there's the difference between us. You're so sentimental it really is embarrassing. Once the boy is home then we'll see to it that things change. It's quite absurd to have him tied as he is, quite absurd.'

Now he had to come and tell Hannah that after all, the lonely misery of the past months had been to no point. She was not going to follow her husband to the glories of Shanghai and his respected job in the firm. She was to face a future with a husband who would never be more than a junior member of the family firm, however old he became in the service of Lammeck Alley. Her sacrifice had been totally wasted. He was to come back to her with his tail between his legs, branded as useless by his own family. 'Damned family,' he had thought uncharacteristically for a short moment, sitting in his car on the way to Paultons Square. 'Damned family! As if it mattered that the boy just doesn't care for business.'

But he could not convince himself. The firm had been the heart of his life for as long as he could remember, and at bottom he was disgusted with his only son for letting him down so badly in the eyes of his brothers.

By the time he reached Hannah with his news, he was in no good humour, and the sight of her vulgar self-satisfied uncle had done nothing to improve his temper. Nor did what the wretched man had to say help matters.

For Alex Lazer, in his usual blunt way, launched himself into a clear account of his views on the way his niece had been treated by her in-laws. Left alone to have her baby without any female companionship, what sort of family was that, he asked. She had no mother, surely her mother-in-law could have come to see the girl occasionally, help her, advise her?

'Uncle Alex, please!' Hannah said, aghast at both his sudden attack on her father-in-law and at the mere thought of Davida coming to advise and help her. 'Do stop, please!'

But it was too late. Albert Lammeck went white with fury, then turned and stomped out of the house, slamming the door behind him with very uncharacteristic ill manners.

40

It was early in February, a blustery day that sent rubbish swirling in the gutters around the square and made passersby hurry along with their heads down and their shoulders hunched against the wind, when Hannah suddenly decided that the time had come to do something more positive about her father.

She had been sitting in her drawing room staring out at the street while Mary Bee lay sleeping in the small moses basket that Judith had given as her birth present. Wherever she went about the house, she took the basket with her, wanting her baby always beside her; not for her the usual Lammeck practice of putting a baby in a special room all on its own. She hated the idea of a nursery as much as she hated the idea of a nurse, and had flatly refused to have either, to Florrie's and Bet's delight, for it meant that they were allowed to help with the care of the child. It also protected them from that bane of every servant's life, the presence of a self satisfied nurse. They complimented each other on Madam's wisdom and made sure that Hannah had all the help she could possibly need.

Which was why she often found that time hung heavy on her hands. Mary Bee was an easy baby, who slept a great deal ('because she had a long birth,' Miss Bishop said knowledgeably. 'These babies need time to get over it,') and took her feeds without fuss. However long Hannah stretched out the business of unbuttoning her blouse and providing her with her needs, and bathing her and changing her clothes, great tracts of the day remained unused. She yearned for the time when Mary Bee would be like Charles, large and active and in constant need of attention and play, and then felt guilty for wishing her baby's life away.

Guilt was very much a part of her feeling for Mary Bee. She would sit and stare down at the crumpled face on its lace trimmed pallet, at the way the soft fuzz of reddish hair misted the small skull – now a more natural shape – consumed by distress at the way she had felt about her during the long months of pregnancy. To have hated her so much – it had been wicked, wicked. Hannah would slip her little finger into Mary Bee's minute fist and swear she would make it up to her. She would have all any child could ever need, to repay her for the loss of love while she was growing inside her wicked mother.

She had been feeling particularly bad that February afternoon. It would still be four weeks before Daniel's ship would reach Liverpool; an eternity of time, and though she was impatient to see him, she was nervous too. Albert had said nothing about why Daniel was coming back; had only told her curtly two weeks ago that he was, but she realized it was for no happy reason, and was apprehensive. It was no wonder then that depression had come down like a cloud to settle over her. Tears were very near the surface as she moved away to the window to look at the world outside. She found herself thinking of the street she had once looked out on when she had been a child. Antcliff Street had been mean and narrow, with its twin rows of small flat fronted houses and tired inhabitants, and Paultons Square was pretty with its central tree fringed garden and obviously prosperous passersby; yet somehow there were similarities. The same grey stone and battered brick, the same sooty air, the same London 'feel' about it. She wanted, suddenly and desperately, to see Antcliff Street again.

Florrie showed no hint of surprise when she was told to call a four wheeler, and obediently whistled one up from the King's Road and helped Hannah to settle in it, with Mary Bee warmly bundled in a shawl on one arm. Hannah sat in the corner of the cab, leaning back against the dusty leather squabs and staring dreamily out of the window as the horse made the long trot to the East End. The streets became first richer and then meaner, and the short winter afternoon shrank into twilight as gaslights began to plop into life along the streets as the lamplighter went by, his long pole over his shoulder. She was going home and the thought made her feel good.

She went first to Antcliff Street, leaving the cab waiting at the corner of Bromehead Road and paying the driver a handsome tip to go and get himself a drink.

'I'll want you to take me back in an hour or so,' she told him. 'And I'll pay you the rest of the fare when we get there, so wait for me.' She knew she would never find another cab for hire in this part of London and needed to keep her escape route open. She might have told herself on the journey that she was going home, but she knew perfectly well that she was doing nothing of the sort.

She knocked on the door of number nine and stood on the pavement waiting, staring at the dark fanlight above the door with Mary Bee warm against her chest, and thought in an almost detached way, 'This is ridiculous. Quite ridiculous.' She didn't move though, and the fanlight sprang into life as someone inside brought a light.

The door opened a crack, and Mrs Arbeiter's face peered out, suspicious and ferocious at the same time, and stared at her for a moment. Then the door opened wide and a gust of the old familiar smell hit Hannah, food first, *greben*, and fried fish and garlic-scented cucumbers, and then the heavy reek of the carbolic used to scrub the stairs and a hint of cats and mildew too. At once Hannah was swept back into her childhood. She was ten years old, small and vulnerable to attack from this large and formidable woman.

'Hello, Mrs Arbeiter,' she said in a small voice.

'I don't believe it! I don't believe it, believe me, I don't! Hannah, is it, little Hannah come back all rich and beautiful? Such clothes, you look marvellous! And a baby, someone said you had a baby, heard it from Solly, they said, but I said, who can know what goes on in the West End, how can you be sure? So how are you? What's the baby's name? Is it a good baby? What is it? How come you're here when your Poppa don't live here no more?'

She still doesn't wait for answers, Hannah thought, and giggled softly and held Mary Bee out towards her.

'She's a little girl,' she said proudly. 'I've called her...'

Mrs Arbeiter was peering into the bundle. 'Well, never mind, dolly, next time, please God, a *bris*.' Hannah's face reddened, but she bit her tongue. Stupid woman! Mrs Arbeiter went on, 'You want I should make some supper for you? I got some lovely fried plaice, lovely, done it just this morning, believe me it's as white as snow, with a bissel cucumber, maybe, you'll eat, be comfortable....'

Hannah shook her head. 'Thank you, Mrs Arbeiter, but it was just...' She floundered and then tried again, and the words came out all wrong. It wasn't what she meant to say at all.

'I brought Mary Bee to show Momma.'

There was a little silence and Mrs Arbeiter drew back into the shadows of the lamplit hallway. She looked perturbed. 'You shouldn't say such things. Let her rest easy in her grave, already. You shouldn't say such things.'

'I'm sorry ... I didn't mean ... it's just that I wanted to come back to where I was born, you see, with my own baby. I ... it's hard to explain. I just wanted to show her...' She held Mary Bee closer again. The baby stirred and whimpered in her sleep and then settled.

'*Meshuggah*, you ask me,' the old woman said. '*Meshuggah*. You got a decent place to live now, Alex told me, real fancy place, and you want to bring a baby to show her a place like this? *Meshuggah*. Crazy.' She went padding away along the passage way to her kitchen door, her broken carpet slippers slapping on the worn lino. 'Go up already if you want. There ain't no one up there. Your Uncle Alex he pays the rent for me, uses the place to keep some of his stuff. Got no one living up there now since your Poppa and the boys went over to Sidney Street.'

Hannah climbed the stairs, feeling a little withdrawn and dreamy again, the way she had on the journey here. It was as though this was someone else, not her at all.

The stairs were narrower than she remembered, and she marvelled at that a little. She had been full grown when she left, after all; it wasn't that long ago. But it felt small all the same, as though she had not been here for a very long time, since she was small herself.

The landing above was dark and she hesitated for a moment, remembering suddenly the night she had come here and it had been dark, because Bloomah had been dying on the floor. She shook her head at herself and walked steadfastly across the space to the door.

It wasn't quite dark yet, and she could see fairly easily. It looked odd, with the furniture that she had known so well all gone, and smaller, just as the stairs had been. There were piles of cardboard boxes and wooden crates scattered about. She stared at them and tried to see Bloomah sitting up against her pillows in the big bed while she, Hannah, sat curled beside the fire, but there was nothing there, only wooden boxes which stubbornly refused to give way to her imaginings. Once she had been able to see all she wanted to, just by switching on the special ability inside her own head, but now she couldn't. She shivered a little in the dank mildewy air and hugged Mary Bee.

The baby stirred in her arms and began to wail and Hannah thought with a small shock, 'She's hungry. It's getting late, she's hungry.'

She sat down on one of the crates, and there, in the silent twilit desolation of the empty room unbuttoned her coat and then her blouse and put Mary Bee to the breast. The sound of it filled the room, small slurping noises and smackings. Hannah enjoyed the sensation, as she always did, and felt, again as she always did, a small surge of guilt because feeding her baby felt so agreeably like lovemaking. She became relaxed and languorous, sitting staring over Mary Bee's head at the greasy window panes and not thinking much of anything but the sensation of the busy mouth against her bare skin.

And then, at last, Bloomah was there. Not in the bed, not sitting against the white pillows and looking exhausted and pallid, not at all visible in the way the contents of Hannah's dreams so often were, but just *there*, a presence that was as natural to Hannah as the baby's was. The room grew gradually darker as Mary Bee sucked greedily and her mother and her grandmother watched her and listened to the small burp and then the hiccup and at last to the slight snoring of her satiated sleep.

Hannah buttoned up her clothes and tucked her baby back in the crook of her arm and went downstairs to thank Mrs Arbeiter gravely, and smile at her, no matter how the silly woman chattered with her eternity of unanswerable questions. She had found what she had come for.

She almost went back at once to the cab. She stood for a moment, uncertain, on the kerb's edge and then walked out to Bromehead Road. But instead of turning right to where the cab horse stood dispiritedly nosing in his straw bag of chaff and oats, she turned left and went along the alley that led into Jubilee Street, and then on and around the corner into Sidney Street. She had come this far, and found Bloomah, and said her farewells to her. Surely to go back to Paultons Square without trying to see Nathan too would be foolish?

And Hannah Lammeck was not foolish, she told herself. Never foolish. Leave that to others.

But he wasn't there. Her Aunt Sarah and Uncle Benjamin greeted her, drawing her into their flat, making her sit down in the best armchair, exclaiming delightedly over her baby, though her cousin David barely looked up from his place at the table.

'You forget what little *menschela* they are,' Aunt Sarah murmured, and slid her vast bulk into an armchair beside her fire and held out her arms. Hannah, uneasily, gave her the bundle. Mary Bee opened her eyes and looked at her great-aunt and then burped rather loudly, dribbling a little milky curd down her chin. Even Uncle Benjamin laughed, his black skull cap dancing on the back of his head.

Their room was comfortable and cluttered, with a big highly polished brass samovar on a corner table, and a myriad of ornaments on the red plush-covered mantelshelf and on the several tables with their fringe bobbled cloths. Sarah, the rabbi's daughter, had brought a decent dowry into her marriage, and it showed. The fire was bright and well fed with big pieces of coal, not the dust and slack that had been her own family's fuel all through her childhood, and the gas light purred richly overhead. Uncle Alex looked after his scholarly brother well, it was clear. Hannah smiled affectionately at Uncle Benjamin. He was younger than her father and only a little older than Uncle Alex but somehow looked much older than both of them, his white beard framing his face to give him a serious patriarchal look.

'So, my dear, you go regularly to synagogue, you and your nice young husband? Which one do you go to? I imagine he's so rich, he must be Sephardi? They tell me the services they have at their Sephardi place – Bevis Marks, ain't it? – I hear it's very interesting. Not for me, of course, I got my own Bes Midrash and I'd never go nowhere else, but it's interesting, very interesting, what these Spanish do.'

She went a little pink. 'I don't go at all, Uncle Benjamin. It just isn't ... I've never been able ... ' She shrugged and stopped. He looked at her a little sadly, then pushed his wire rimmed glasses more firmly back on his nose and shook his head. But he said nothing and Sarah, more perceptive than she looked, said, 'So tell me, how does this little boychick behave? He eats well? He looks like he does.'

'Her name is Mary Bloomah,' Hannah said, the irritation rising in her again. 'Didn't Solly tell you she's a girl?' If Sarah too commiserated over her child's sex she'd lose her temper.

'Solly never said nothing. What a lovely little girl she is,' Aunt Sarah said placidly and crooned at the baby's face. 'Such a lovely baby. My first was a girl, too. Such a lovely way to start your family, with girls such a help to you.'

'If you're lucky,' David said sourly. 'I ain't noticed Bella and Charlotte coming round all that much these days.'

His mother smiled and shook her head. 'When you was little, believe me, David, they was helpful. Now they got their own husbands to look after, Gott se dank, and it's not so terrible, a boy should help his mother a *bissel* shopping now and again. I don't ask you should wash dishes, God forbid, do I? So stop your complaining already.' She smiled fondly at him. 'Such a genius at the books as he is,' she said to Hannah. 'Every minute he has to spend away from them he grudges. Such a good boy.' Hannah looked at David's sulky face and remembered herself helping her mother with dishes, while her brothers did nothing at all, and sighed a little. Nothing ever changes, she thought. Nothing ever changes.

'Poppa,' she said after a while. 'Is he ... ' She left the sentence unfinished to hang in the air above the red plush table cloth and David's books spread on it. No one said anything.

'The boys,' Hannah said then, almost desperately. 'Are the boys well?'

Sarah's face lifted. 'Ah, the boys! Always a laugh, always a joke – it's a pleasure to see them. They eat with us every night, you know? Their breakfast they fix themselves with what I leave ready, then they eat at night with us, and I tidy a bit for them in the day, believe me, they're all looked after, Hannah.'

She peered at Hannah over Mary Bee's sleeping form and her small eyes were bright and appealing.

'Believe me, you don't have nothing to worry about. I watch them real careful. I know what it is for men on their own – helpless they are, like little babies. But you don't need to worry. I take good care of them, and your Uncle Alex.' She glanced at her husband, now sitting in his own chair opposite David, with his head bent over a book. 'One way and another, you don't have to worry.'

'Thank you, Aunt Sarah,' Hannah said. She felt passionately grateful to her and went across the room to kiss the sweaty plump cheek and then take her baby back. 'Thank you. If ever you need me, tell Solly – he knows where to find me. I can always come. Even if he doesn't want me, I can always come.' Neither of them needed to explain who was meant by 'he'.

On the far side of the door, shrouded by a large red curtain hanging from a polished wooden rail on large brass rings, there was a muffled thump. David lifted his head.

'That's Uncle Nathan,' he said conversationally, and then returned to his work as though he had offered nothing more momentous than a comment on the weather. Hannah stood very still, her baby crooked in her arm, and Uncle Benjamin and Aunt Sarah lifted their heads, like dogs in a hunt pointing at their quarry.

Footsteps came slapping closer. The curtain billowed and a puff of smoke came from the fire as the door opened. Then the curtain was pushed aside and he came in, his hat in one hand.

He stood peering around the quiet room. 'So, what's happened here? Cat's got your tongues?' He sounded jovial, the way he used to sound when she was small and he had come home full of satisfaction because he had had several clients with important letters to be written.

Then he saw her and the joviality disappeared and he stared at her, his face blank of expression. It was as though she had never seen him before. He looked older than she remembered, for his beard was longer and more straggled and his hair, in the rich gaslight, looked greyer than it had. His face was fuller though; clearly Aunt Sarah's cooking agreed with him.

'Hello, Poppa,' she said, her voice husky. 'I brought your granddaughter to see you.' She held her out, like an offering. 'Mary Bloomah, Poppa. Your granddaughter.'

He stood staring at her, and then he said it as though it were a bad word, spitting it out. 'Mary? *Mary*? A *choleria* on you and your Mary!' He turned and went blindly through the curtain and slammed the door on the other side behind him, leaving her standing in the warm and silent room.

'It's a pity, you know,' Uncle Benjamin said after a while.

'Pity you didn't just tell him her second name, you know? He feels bad about the way he gave you to that Mary Lammeck, and now ... ' He shook his head. 'He's a funny man, my brother. Difficult, you know? Sarah, make some tea. Tea and a bit of kugel ... '

'No, thank you,' Hannah said, and the words only just came out, for her throat felt constricted. 'I – it's time to go. Please, take care of him, Aunt Sarah, Uncle Benjamin. Let me know if ... Take care of him.' She went out into the cold dark street, holding Mary Bee close to her, and ran to find her cab. She thought she was crying, but she wasn't. Her face was quite tight and still.

41

She had no way of knowing exactly when Daniel would be home. Albert, who might have been able to give her news, had become more remote since Mary Bee's birth and Uncle Alex's attack on him. He never came to the house now but always sent Young Levy with her money. Nor could Levy tell her any more than she already knew, that Daniel had sailed from Shanghai in January and was therefore due in Liverpool sometime in February. No, he didn't know the name of the ship, all arrangements had been made from the Shanghai office – and no, he had not heard directly from Daniel. They would expect him in the office when they saw him, and clearly, as a Lammeck wife Young Levy expected her to be equally phlegmatic. She stared at his face, as wrinkled as a winter apple, and at his sparse white hair and sighed; no point in getting angry with him. He was as much at the beck and call of the lords of Lammeck Alley as she was, as Daniel was. She would just have to wait.

He arrived one evening just after her early dinner. She had settled Mary Bee for the night in her small basket and was sitting up in her bedroom beside the fire there. It seemed unnecessary to light the drawing room fire just for her, she had told Florrie, and they needed the bedroom warm for the baby. She was sewing a dress of white lawn for Mary Bee, wearing a comfortable but not particularly handsome wrapper, and with her hair unpinned, when she heard the rattle of horses' hooves outside and the bang of a cab door.

She lifted her head to listen and then, as no more happened, returned to her sewing. Whoever it was clearly was not coming to her house, for although there was still a certain amount of street noise, there had been no knock at the door.

She sat quietly sewing and when the bedroom door opened did not raise her head, but said only, 'Just a moment, Florrie. Let me finish this row.'

'Well, there's a welcome!' His voice sounded very loud in the quiet room and her chin jerked up.

'Daniel? Daniel!' She jumped to her feet and stood there clutching her sewing in one hand and staring at him.

He looks dreadful, she thought immediately. What's happened to him? He had lost weight and had an unattractive boniness about him. His skin seemed to have thickened and changed colour. He looked faintly yellowish and his eyes were bloodshot.

He came into the room and dropped his coat on the chair against the wall. 'My luggage can come up in the morning,' he said. 'I thought you'd have come to Euston at least to meet the boat train, if you didn't feel up to coming to Liverpool.'

'But I didn't know when you were coming!' She shook her head in puzzlement. 'Why didn't you let me know which ship you were on?'

'Don't be ridiculous,' he said curtly. 'You only had to check at Lammeck Alley. Or was that too much trouble?'

She felt as though she had been slapped and stared at him in even greater puzzlement. He sounded so angry, so cold and so very far away. 'Of course it wasn't! I mean, I tried and they said – '

'It really doesn't matter,' he said. 'You weren't there and that's all there is to it. At least Florrie was at the front door letting the cat out when I got here, so I didn't have to ring like a stranger. How are you, Hannah?'

'I'm . . . ' Again she shook her head and turned to put down her sewing, carefully smoothing it for something to do.

'I'm very well,' she said then and turned to look at him. 'Mary Bee, she's over there.'

'Who?' he said. He had approached the fire now, standing close to it, obviously cold, and she said quietly, 'Your daughter, Daniel. Mary Bloomah Lammeck. I've taken to

378

calling her Mary Bee. She's over there.'

'Yes.' He looked across the room to the moses basket in its warm dim corner, but he made no move. She felt fear rise in her. Surely something dreadful had happened?

'Daniel,' she said then. 'Daniel – I've missed you so much.' She put out a hand and set it on his sleeve, almost timidly. He pulled his arm away and turned to the fire to hold out his hands to the glow and rub them together, not looking at her. Something *had* gone dreadfully wrong, she told herself. Dreadfully, appallingly wrong.

'Daniel, what is it? What's the matter?'

'What do you mean, what's the matter? Dammit, I'm cold and I'm tired. I've had a hell of a journey. I've been on the move for the best part of seven weeks, and you ask me what's the matter? Have you no imagination at all?'

It was as though he were trying to work himself up into a righteous anger, for he went on and on, about how cold he was, and how tired, and how difficult the journey had been. She said nothing, just standing and staring at him and that seemed to make him even angrier.

'For God's sake, don't stand there gawping at me like that! What did you expect me to do? Fall on your neck, full of the joys of spring?'

'Yes,' she said quietly. 'Yes, I think I did. I've missed you. I thought you'd have missed me.'

He said nothing, just standing there staring at her. The glow from the fire and the lamp beside her chair shadowed his face and she could not see him clearly. For a moment it seemed to her that he was going to step forward and put his arms around her, that the last few minutes had been just a nightmare born of his fatigue, but then the hope shrivelled as he pushed past her and went to pick up his coat.

'I'd better go and see my mother,' he said harshly. 'She'll have been expecting me today, I know that!'

'And she didn't meet you at Liverpool, or even Euston?' she flashed, stung, but he said nothing, shrugging into his coat.

'I'll be back later,' he said. 'Don't wait up,' and was gone, leaving her standing there in her wrapper and staring at the door he had left swinging open behind him. She was almost in a state of shock, she was so bewildered.

*

God knew he had tried. In the first revulsion of feeling he had had when that cable had arrived, he had flung himself out of bed and had written a dozen pages to Hannah, pouring out his contrition, his misery, his self loathing. But just before he had finished it Yü Soo had awakened and come to stand naked behind him, weaving her hands sinuously through his hair. He lost his temper at himself, and directed it all at her, hitting out at her as though she were no more than a pet dog that had misbehaved, shouting his rage, and telling her to go, to get out of his house and his life. At first she just cowered away from him, amazed, and then, as she realized at last that she was being thrown out she hurled herself at him, her fingers clawing with great precision, and scratched his face and his back cruelly. She kicked at his belly and pulled his hair until they were both rolling on the floor spitting and swearing, each as naked as the other for she had pulled his dressing gown from his back. His houseboy pulled them apart, his face split with a huge grin of sheer enjoyment that had inflamed Daniel's rage even more. He flung the houseboy out too.

He had gone back to bed then, shaking and feeling sick and curled up there, trying to collect himself and regain his self control. It was time he went to the office. Friday was settling day, and he had to be there, for he was still struggling to understand the complex system of payments and discounts to customers and buyers. He had to be there. But the morning had gone on and he had been unable to move, feeling thoroughly ill.

Perhaps he had been incubating the fever, anyway; perhaps it was his own misery and the horrible scene with Yü Soo that lowered his resistance and allowed the germ to take hold. Whatever it was, by mid afternoon he was raving with fever, shouting for help which did not come. When he dragged himself to the kitchen to fetch water for his raging thirst, he found that every pot and pan was gone, and when he went to his desk to see what had happened there he found the sheets of his letter to Hannah ripped and strewn about the floor, and his cash box shattered and empty. But he had been past caring then, too ill to want anything but immediate death.

They sent no one from the office to see why he was absent. Ling Ho, he later realized, had been delighted with such further evidence of the foreigner's laxity. There he had lain, feverish, often delirious, his head and limbs aching ferociously all through Friday and Saturday, becoming ever more dehydrated and ill. By the time Jimmy had arrived to collect him for a pre-arranged game of golf on Sunday afternoon, he was lying in his own excrement, nearly comatose.

He had recovered reasonably fast, once the horrified Jimmy had sent for a doctor, and found a couple of new servants to take care of him. By the end of the week thinner, sallow of complexion and feeling weaker than a sick dog, he had gone creeping back to the Bund as miserable as he had ever been in his life. Those weeks of exhilaration when he had sailed in the *Priam* and contemplated the world of responsibility and success awaiting him in Shanghai seemed an eternity ago. Now he was defeated and miserable and almost past caring about anything or anyone.

Even Hannah. Had the letter he had written that January afternoon remained intact, he might have sent it to her and if he had his return home could have been tolerable. Painful, but tolerable. They would have had some sort of structure on which to recreate, however painfully, their lost past.

But the letter had been irretrievably lost, and he could not write another. He could not even send a cable, for he found waiting for him at the office when he returned a cable to himself, given to him by the ever courteous Ling Ho with one of his polite bows, recalling him to London. His reaction to that had made him hate himself even more, for his eyes had filled with tears compounded both of his fever-induced weakness and his bitter disappointment, and not a little shame that Ling Ho, the author of so much of his pain, should see them. Once again, he turned his self hate and anger away, in the wrong direction, aiming it at Hannah, far away and oh-so-innocent at home in London. Let her find out for herself that I'm coming back, he had thought, as he contemplated the wreck of his high hopes, and felt the weakness deep in his bones. Let her find out and come and meet me, and sort it all out. If she loves me, she will. It was unreasonable, ridiculous, childish, but he could not help that. It was how he felt, and he was in no condition to do anything but act on his feelings, as a child does.

He had left the office and taken the first available steamer home, not even telling them in Lammeck Alley which ship it was, leaving that sort of detail to Ling Ho. He was too tired and unhappy to care.

His unhappiness had grown all through his journey home. He looked back over his behaviour of the past few months and felt as though he had fallen into a great chasm of misery. He had written Hannah such meagre letters, because of that damned whore; how could he write lovingly to the wife of his heart who had just borne him his first child when he had been sharing with that olive skinned and oh-so-knowing body experiences that belonged to Hannah alone? How could he even face her when he got home? He paced the decks night after night as the ship heaved through rocking winter seas, hating himself and wallowing even more in his own self disgust.

From Liverpool onwards, as the train fled through the darkening Midlands towards the warmth and lights of London, a change came over him, once again taking his shame and guilt and turning it outwards. The dock there had been awash with people greeting passengers; on all sides couples were hugging, women weeping with delight, children leaping about with excitement, while he stood waiting to see his luggage through the customs shed, alone and lonely. She should have come to Liverpool, he told himself absurdly. She should have somehow known he was coming, and been there to hold him.

As the train went on its way he formed words in his head to match the rattle of the wheels over the lines: 'She should have been *there*, she should have been *there*, she should have been *there* ... '

At Euston there were more tearful greetings on the platform for other passengers, and eager parties shouting for porters and rushing away to comfort and happiness through the tendrils of steam that filled the echoing station. He had deliberately topped up his fury, converting the last of his guilt into her fault. How could he have cared what had happened when she cared so little that she couldn't be bothered to come from Chelsea to Euston?

By the time his cab reached his front door, his rage had been monumental.

The sight of her sitting there beneath the lamp, her bent head lit to a rich bronze beneath the lamplight and her figure voluptuous in its maternity under that thin wrapper had nearly ruined it all. He had wanted to go and throw himself at her feet and confess all and be shriven. But he had to hold on to his hard won rage and punish her for his own behaviour. There was no other way he could cope with his distress. So, he turned and ran from her, clattering down the stairs, slamming the door behind him, refusing to look at her stricken face another moment.

Now, as another cab sped through the busy lamplit London streets, he felt his rage diminishing. He was tired, quite desperately tired. He needed comfort more than any man ever had. He thought of his mother and her dark knowing eyes and the way she would chatter on and on without saying a word about Hannah, yet managing to imply that he was in some sort of thrall to her. That could not be borne. It would be so unfair to Hannah, he thought ridiculously, and shook his head at his own confusion and almost without thinking tapped on the roof of the hansom. When the driver looked down through the open flap Daniel gave him another address, instead of the Park Lane one. The man said equably, 'Righto, Guv,' and the flap snapped shut again and he leaned back in the cab and thought, 'Why did I do that?' and shut his eyes with fatigue. He didn't know why but never mind. He'd feel better later probably. Surely he'd feel better later?

It was not often that Leontine Damont was at home on a winter evening. She worked hard at holding her place in society and at enhancing it, and felt herself a failure if she did not have at least three competing invitations for the same evening. She needed her frequent trips to Baden Baden and Nice to recover, for she lived a punishing schedule of balls and dinners and crushes and opera visits for most of the year. But tonight she had stayed at home, because she had visited the dentist that afternoon and had suffered some pain at his hands. So, when her butler came quietly to announce Mr Daniel Lammeck she was sitting beside her drawing room fire in a crimson peignoir and thinking only of going to bed early with one of those splendid new cachets that Aunt Davida had brought home from Paris on her last visit, to help her sleep.

She stood up to greet him, with her hands held out in a pose that she knew was inviting and which showed her long white arms to advantage. Daniel, responding to her clear invitation, and because he felt no real emotion for her, unlike the confused and very important feeling he had for Hannah, walked straight up to her and put his own arms around her and kissed her with all the hunger that he had been holding back for so long. He did not precisely pretend she was anyone other than Leontine, a good enough girl he had known most of his life, but it was Hannah he thought of as he held her with her head thrown back against his arm, almost devouring her.

Nightmares again. It was like the time when Bloomah had died, and then Mary had too, only now it was worse, for now there was Mary Bee to think of and she became restless and fretful, needing to be held close and fed often, though Hannah's milk suffered badly. But she concentrated her whole mind on Mary Bee and her demands, willing her body to produce what the child needed, and refusing to think at all about Daniel.

They came in the early morning, when the sky was still heavy with darkness, though there was a promise in the east of light to come, knocking on the door so loudly that Florrie was terrified and came to her room to call her before answering it. She had not gone to bed but had stayed in the armchair into which she had folded herself after Daniel had gone, trying to think of why he had been so strange, and cried. There she had fallen asleep at last, exhausted and frightened.

And then there was Florrie, her flannel wrapper pulled around her and her face looking very childish under the hair in its curling rags, shaking her and saying, 'Oh, mum, please mum, there's such a bangin' at the door, and it's only six o'clock, mum, and I'm scared to go. I got such a bad feelin' in me. Please, mum, should I answer it? It's only six o'clock, mum, and no one comes till seven, not even the milkman.'

She stood on the doorstep with Florrie close behind her peering over her shoulder, and looked at the tall man in his shining mackintosh cape, with the rain dripping off the hem of it, and holding his helmet in his hand. She knew at once.

'Daniel,' she said in a flat voice. 'Daniel.'

The policeman had been regretful, very. He tried as

carefully as he could to make it easy for her, but how could it be easy? Daniel had come and gone so swiftly last night and in such a strange and unhappy way, and now there was this policeman telling her there had been an accident, that he had been found crumpled at the foot of the river steps by Chelsea Reach, his head bruised and his face in the water. He must have missed his footing in the dark and fallen. The blow on his head had done it, so far as they could tell, he told her earnestly as though that would comfort her, a blow that must have knocked him unconscious and that was why he'd not been able to pull his face out of the water as the tide lifted. She had swayed and he put out one huge hand to steady her, but she pushed him away. She lifted her chin as the baby began to cry, and said, 'I must go – my baby. Florrie, give him some tea. I'll come as soon as I can.'

It had gone on all morning, the telephone calls from Lammeck Alley and then the people coming and going, Florrie red eyed and soggy with tears, and Bet silent and frightened, both trying to help as best they could. Albert, white with control and looking at her with such fury in his eyes that she felt sick, and Uncle Alex, appearing somehow from nowhere and being noisy and bustling and blessedly wonderfully normal, and Mary Bee crying and crying and seeming insatiable however often she fed her, and she knew that she was pushing her nipple into the gaping little cavern of a mouth as much to comfort herself as to soothe her baby.

More policemen, more questions. Had he been ill? Odd in any way? Oh, just returned from abroad, was it? Oh, that affected some gentlemen badly, of course. No, they meant nothing, madam, of course not. Unexplained death, you see, madam, out of our hands, but I'm sure we'll do all we can to make it easy for you, madam, deal mostly with his father, I think. He says he'll take care of things. Deepest sympathy, madam, from all the force, I'm sure, at Chelsea Reach Station … tragedy to happen, hope you feel better soon and … and they talked themselves out of the house and out of her life, leaving her to cope with a fretful baby, and her own sick cold terror, and a blank future.

She was eighteen years old and had a two-month-old baby, and she was a widow. It took a lot of getting used to, that.

385

BOOK FOUR

Changing

42

The man sitting beside Hannah in the swaying crowded train was sucking his teeth mournfully as he read his newspaper. Hannah tried not to listen but even the rattle of the train could not drown the repulsive sound. She tried to read the headlines over his shoulder as a distraction, but that did not help because they were all about the gas attacks at Hill 60 and the Second Battle of Ypres. The War dominated everything as it was; to start reading casualty lists at eight in the morning was more than could be asked of even the most patriotic citizens.

She turned her head to stare out of the grimy window at the black walls of the tunnel, at the way the cables swooped and curved as the train rocketed by them, and made herself think of more pleasant things. Mary Bee this morning, for example, crawling into bed with her and making a great tangle of bedclothes and lace trimmed nightdress and demanding biscuits from the tea tray that Florrie had brought at six o'clock, and kicking her heels with fury when she was told they would spoil her breakfast. Little monkey! Hannah thought fondly. She had of course got her biscuits. I suppose I do spoil her a little but who can blame me? She's so very adorable, all red curls and wide blue eyes and a skin as firm and downy as a peach. And anyway, she only has me. No one but me.

That was an ever recurring theme in her thoughts about Mary Bee, her debt to her. She had tried, heavens, how she had tried, not to feel guilt about her daughter's fatherless state, tried to tell herself it was not a fault in her, Hannah, that had left Mary Bee to grow through her baby years to her sturdy almost five-year-old self without a father to care for her, but in a sense it *was* her fault.

Again she wrenched her thoughts away and remembered the previous evening instead. That had been fun, even though it had been quite unlike the old days, before the War – was that only eighteen months ago? – when going to the theatre had been an event of high fashion. Last night they had groped their way there through the blackout, taking a bus to the Gaiety rather than the car, and had worn just ordinary frocks, she and Judith, while Peter had been in his office suit, all stuffy grey and sober tie. But they had laughed a lot for the play was fun and the music delicious, with George Grossmith as handsome as ever and the comedian Leslie Henson with his odd croaking voice exceedingly funny. She hummed the tune she had liked so much under her breath; ' ... they'll never believe me – they'll never believe me ... that from this great big world you've chosen me ... '

The train slowed, came into Mansion House Station and the crowded seats heaved like a field of corn in a wind as passengers, looking tired even before the day's work had begun, got out and more came piling in. She relaxed. Not far now to Liverpool Street and the day's work.

Last night. Judith and Peter. Better not to think about last night with Peter sitting there between them. She and Judith had laughed and chatted during the intervals as they always did, yet she had been so aware of Peter's physical presence beside her, of the warmth of his body as his arm touched hers, of the way he looked at her sometimes in the dimness and how his eyes glinted with shared delight in what was happening on the stage. Don't think about that.

Peter and Judith. What would she have done without them these past four years? It had been Judith who had got Mary Bee Couturiere off the ground. She had listened to Hannah's tentative plans to make her living with the only real skill she had, her needle, and had sent so many of her fashionable friends trekking out to Paultons Square that for the first year of the business's existence Hannah had no time for anything but measuring and cutting and sewing and fitting, and of course looking after her daughter. As Judith had said, the two Mary Bees would be too much for anyone but Hannah Lammeck, who, she told everyone she met from Park Lane tea parties to East End suffragette meetings, was the hardest working woman she knew. In her loving generosity Judith filled her own wardrobe with Mary Bee frocks and cloaks and lingerie, and saw to it that everyone else she knew did the same.

And Peter. It had been he who had opened up the other half of her business, the factory in Artillery Lane to which the train was now carrying her. As soon as the War had started on that sweltering August afternoon, he had said, 'They'll need uniforms. Lots of uniforms. Find yourself premises, Hannah, get yourself some workers, I'll see to it you get the contracts.' In the past fifteen months since the factory had first switched on the banks of lights over the sewing machines and set the great goose-irons over the hissing gas jets, they had turned out more than fifty thousand VAD uniforms for the government, making money at a rate she would never have thought possible.

It worried her, the prosperity this hateful war had brought with it. The three years of struggle with Mary Bee Couturiere had been rewarded much less handsomely, in spite of demanding twice the effort, and still brought in a much smaller income though she still spent a good deal of time looking after it. But Peter had shaken his head at her in that dry way of his when she had said as much to him and told her shortly not to be so silly.

'There's no crime in being prosperous,' he said. 'If you did bad work, skimped on the contracts, I'd be as hard on you as anyone else. But you do good work. That's why you're paid so well. Enjoy it.'

Hard working Peter, growing more and more tired in his job in Whitehall, controlling so much of the government's war effort, handling so many contracts for war production; Lammeck Alley must miss him badly. They had only Marcus now to hold the fort, with the senior partners getting older and more inflexible with so many of the Lammeck and Damont nephews and cousins and in-laws in the army and navy. There were rumours that Marcus Lammeck too was getting restless and was talking of joining the Royal Flying Corps. Not that she cared about what happened at Lammeck Alley. Hannah Lammeck she may be, but not one of them cared for her or ever gave her a thought, apart from Peter and Judith, so why should she care? Yet she was, she had to admit, a little interested.

Liverpool Street at last, and, relieved, she joined the river of humanity that poured out of the stuffy train, walking with long easy strides for she was wearing one of her own 1914 creations but without the hobble underskirt that had been

391

such a stylish feature then. She had ripped it out and now wore only the over-tunic which reached just below mid calf, and gave her legs ample room to move. Fashion was totally irrelevant in wartime, of course, but she had been pleased with the idea when it came to her, liking the look of the neat attenuated skirt with the pretty flare and been even more pleased when more and more women followed suit. Now she was surrounded by busy females wearing sensible tailor-mades and tunic dresses. Some of them were even hatless, here in the City, though most, like herself, still felt naked without at least a small head hugger. No need for feathers now of course; that sort of frivolity belonged to the lost world of 1913 and before.

She breathed more deeply now, looking up at the milky blue April sky, and the sparrows that swooped so busily. There were fewer easy pickings for them these days, with so many horses gone to the Front; the hordes of chattering small birds that used to feed so richly under the noses of great dray animals who sent clouds of grain flying from their nosebags. Now, the sparrows had to seek elsewhere for sustenance.

She passed the tea shop on the corner of Bishopsgate, and glanced inside, smiling at the steamy walls and crowded marble-topped tables and the bustling waitresses. Uncle Alex had prospered too, for he had had the good sense to open his shops (now more than forty of them, exactly like this one, scattered about London) from six in the morning till midnight. That way the people who worked the nightshifts in munitions factories could get their dinners, and the people who worked during the day, starting too early for landladies to bother to put themselves out, got their breakfasts too. But he was doing his bit for the War effort as well. Each week he spent a large amount of time in Whitehall, sitting on committees that planned the victualling of the army at the Front and the feeding of vast numbers of soldiers in training at home. He had become an expert in mass catering, all because of a now vanished coffee stall outside the Yiddish theatre in Whitechapel. It was an amusing thought, and Hannah's lips quirked as she crossed the road, dodging open topped buses and the hooting vans and cabs.

Uncle Alex. He had saved her sanity in those dreadful days after Daniel's death, seeing her through the hell of the inquest, protecting her from Albert and Davida's wrath, when they had both turned on her on that awful day, accusing her of hounding their beloved only child to his early death. He sat beside her protectively as she sat *shivah* for Daniel for the full week, alone because Albert and Davida insisted on sitting their mourning days without her, at Park Lane. Albert's rejection of her had hurt, for she had thought he had become fond of her, but she understood it, dimly. He had to consider Davida, after all. Even at the cost of losing contact with his grandchild. So Uncle Alex had helped her through that dreadful week, and later it had been he who had finally pulled her out of her desperate misery when she had come so close to despair that she had contemplated, quite seriously, following her Daniel into whatever oblivion he now inhabited.

'Listen, dolly,' Uncle Alex had said to her that evening, five years before. 'You got to stop all this, you hear me? It's wicked, that's what it is. Wicked.'

'Wicked?' She had peered up at him through swollen eyelids. 'Wicked? I don't know what you mean.'

'Who do you think you are, dolly?' he had said earnestly, sitting facing her with his knees spread wide to accommodate his burgeoning belly. 'Eh? Who do you think you are? Some fancy lady that don't have to suffer on account she's some sort of special creation God made to amuse himself? That you ain't, dolly! I'll tell you who you are. You're Bloomah's daughter. You're my mother Rivka's granddaughter. They had troubles too, believe me, they had troubles. My Momma Rivka *Aleva ha-shalom* had to pick up everything she ever had to call her own to come and live in the stinkin' East End of a city that didn't want her or hers with people whose language she couldn't understand and who despised her and spat on her, and start again. Bloomah, God rest her soul, had to live in a lousy couple of rooms with a feckless husband who was as much use as a bloody sick headache to her, and work her *kishkas* out for her children. What satisfaction did she ever have in her life? And the women before them had it bad, just as bad. Worse, some of them. They really knew what *tsorus* was. There was one of the grandmothers, I don't know who, but I was told when I was a boy, one of the old *boobahs* in the family, had to give her baby boy away to relations to stop the Tsar getting him for his army. There was others who got themselves burned out by lousy Cossacks on account they'd committed the terrible crime of being Jews. There was some that was raped and killed – why else did they run the way they did and bring us all here, hey? So that you could live and your baby Mary Bee could live and keep us all going, till next time and the time after. Because the times keep coming, the bad times. They always have, and me, I reckon they always will. Right now the *goyim* are treating us fair enough, not too much hating, just a bit of nagging on account of some *meshugganeh* anarchists. But they'll start again, you see if they don't. They always have, and then there'll be work for you to do, and for Mary Bee and for all of us. Who are you now to fold up under your private trouble? Sure I know, you're suffering, oh God, but you're suffering. But that's what Jews is for, dolly. You got to suffer and try again, you hear me? And not only try again, but do better than anyone else. On account that's the only way we've got to show them what we're all about. Not just surviving but winning. Beating the lot of them.'

He leaned even further forwards to pinch her thin cheek. 'Like me, dolly, like me. You got to do the same. So cry a *bissel*, lie in your bed at night and cry a *bissel*, and then get up in the morning and get on with living.'

Somehow she had. She looked at his broad face and gleaming eyes, almost hidden now in the folds of expensively fed flesh and felt the strength and love in him and nodded and held onto him and cried bitterly for a long time. But it had been the last time that she had cried during the day. She wept at night, night after night, crying herself to her lonely sleep, but never again during the day did anyone see tears on her cheeks. They saw only concentration and seriousness, and then, as the months grew into years, sometimes laughter. Even now, after almost five years, she still wept at night occasionally, but it was less painful now, more a melancholy remembering of missed joys than the angry bitterness of the early years. She had filled her days with work, right from that evening when Uncle Alex had picked her up and dusted her off and set her on the road again.

Not at the tea shops. She had suggested that, but he had shaken his head.

'Dolly, would I ever like to have you! I tell you, I could make you the best bloody tea shop manageress the business

394

ever had, you should forgive the language. But that would be good for me, not for you. What you got to have is something of your own. And, love you as I do and care about you as I do, there ain't no way anyone owns Alex Lazar's business but Alex Lazar. Not even you, dolly. Anyway, you *need* something of your own. I'm here to tell you that there ain't no satisfaction in this world like your own business. You take your own hands and your own head and you use 'em to build something that wasn't never there before. Me, I got my tea shops, and my artiste's agency, and a couple o' this and few o' that besides, and I look at the offices and at the books and I say to myself, Alex Lazar, I says, that's *creation*. God you ain't, but you got that spark he gave you, and you've used it right. You got to do the same, dolly. You got to love Hannah Lammeck the way I love Alex Lazar, you understand me? Even if you don't understand it don't matter. You will one of these days.'

So Mary Bee Couturiere had been born, and thrived. The business made enough to pay the cost of running the house (at least she owned that, her only inheritance from her brief marriage) and to pay Florrie and Bet and later the girls who came to sit and sew beside her. To pay for the sewing machine and pressing table and materials which she put in the red walled dining room now her workshop, she sold her dining room furniture and that first year she had made enough to pay back to Uncle Alex his initial investment.

He stood and looked at her holding out the cheque to him, her chin up a little, and for one dreadful moment, she was afraid he was going to refuse it. If he had, the whole edifice would have crumbled, for she knew now the truth of what he had told her that April evening. That the full ownership of her own business had to be hers, that any feeling that he still had a share in it would somehow have diminished her achievement. She had fought back and won, and he had to take his money back to prove that she had. He understood. He took the cheque and solemnly gave her a receipt, and then took her out to dinner at Keppner's restaurant, and fed her on quantities of salt beef and apple strudel, and made her laugh a lot.

Now Mary Bee Couturiere operated smoothly and was still keeping busy in spite of the shortage of silks and satins and feathers and beads and sequins, and in spite of the guilty consciences of the fashionable women which kept them away from their dressmakers. And there was also Artillery Lane.

She stopped on the front step and looked up at the blank faced building and took a deep breath. The war was hateful. The fact they had to make uniforms for girls who would spend their time in them dealing with men who had been shot at and bayonetted or gassed by other men was sickening. But the hard fact could not be denied: Hannah Lammeck now owned her own factory, and employed fifty people in it and had a thickening bank balance to cushion the future for Mary Bee, safe at home now with Bet and Florrie to look after her. It was a warming thought.

'You're early, Hannah!' Cissie Weiss came thumping up the stairs behind her, panting a little. She'd put on weight since she'd agreed with joy to come and work for Hannah instead of Isaac Levson, but it suited her. She looked regal in her handsome green suit and with her mass of black hair pinned up. 'Bleedin' kid – you think I could get him out of bed this morning? Not Lennie Weiss! He reckons he's old enough to do what the hell he likes, and going to school ain't what he likes. I said to Joe Cohen at the paper shop this morning, I told him, that kid'll be enough to make me take him at his word one of these days and marry him. Maybe with a father to beat the *tochus* off him, we'd get somewhere. Seen the papers?'

'No thanks, Cissie,' Hannah said. They went together into the cluttered little office at the back of the factory, Hannah switching on the lights as she went. 'I've got enough to worry about. The more I read the papers, the worse I feel. Look, if that girl – what's her name, Jessie Cantor – if she's late again she'll have to go. I know it's hard to get people who're any good, but she's a bad influence.'

Cissie hung up her coat and pinned on her supervisor's overall. 'Glad to give that one the push,' she said with relish. 'She's a trouble maker. And I've got a couple of girls from down my street might do as fellin' hands, if I give 'em a bit of training. Listen, last night there was seventeen bolts of serge came in – I checked 'em and three of 'em's faulty. Bad dye errors. So, what do I do? Try and run 'em in on the cut and hope they don't show too much, or send 'em back? Thing is, if we do that, we'll run out of work for the third bench of machines, and they're on piece work and won't take it kindly.'

'Damn.' Hannah said. 'I knew I shouldn't have left early. If I'd have been here I could have sent them back right away. Look, I'll call the dyers. See what they can do to replace them. Three pieces, you say? It's a lot, and the next delivery not due till – ' She ruffled through the papers on her cluttered desk. 'Next Wednesday. Not good. I might have to send one of the men over – '

'Be better if you call Mr Lammeck, wouldn't it?' Cissie said. 'He gets them moving faster'n any of 'em. Or shall I?'

Hannah kept her head down, staring at the delivery note in her hand. Call Peter. She could say thank you again for last night as well as ask his help to sort out the bad delivery. Calling Peter would be a very agreeable thing to do, which was a very good reason why she should not do it.

All the same, as soon as the big clock on the far wall showed nine o'clock and she could count on him being there in his office, she closed her office door against the roar of the machines and the workers' chattering voices, and asked the operator to put her through to the Ministry of Supply.

43

'Dearest Hannah,' Judith said, 'I am utterly and totally exhausted. I can't tell you how it's been this past week – I've had every morning at Aunt Susan's, rolling bandages. You should just *see* them all, the old ones, solemnly dressed up in vast white aprons and nurses' white veils, every inch the ladies of the lamp, sitting there with the maids bringing in tea and cakes every five minutes to restore their strength, and moaning all the time about how frightful it is with all the butlers and footmen gone off to the army! I can't tell you how difficult it is to keep a straight face, but for all that it *is* hard work. They make me do all the really difficult bits like cutting the gauze and then humping the boxes of finished bandages away. Then in the afternoons if it isn't slipper-making at my revered Mama-in-law, it's sewing pillow cases at the Goldsmiths' or packing chocolates and cigarettes into

397

parcels for the Front at the Willem Damonts. And then I've been out three evenings this week at fund-raising balls. Truly darling, I am positively wrung out!'

She didn't look it. She sat opposite Hannah at the corner table at Uncle Alex's Bishopsgate tea shop eating her poached eggs on toast with every evidence of enjoyment, and looking very beautiful indeed. Even though she had done all she could to look 'ordinary', regarding it as immoral to look expensively dressed in wartime, removing every piece of trimming from her blue hand tailored suit, it still looked what it was, superbly cut and made of the most costly fabric Paris could provide. Her hair was as luxuriant as ever and her skin as unblemished and warmly coloured. It was small wonder that so many of the tired workers eating their frugal lunches watched her covertly over the rims of their tea cups.

'So, darling,' Judith finished her poached eggs and reached with gusto for her currant bun, 'I can't *tell* you how grateful I am that you have time to take care of my poor Peter. The poor angel works so hard all day he's entitled to a little relaxation in the evening and with me so busy on war work and organizing the fund-raising balls and all, I'm no pleasure to be with for he so *loathes* the social scene. And the darling does so enjoy his stuffy old music! It's so sweet of you to go with him and sit through it.'

'But I like Elgar,' Hannah bent her head over her own tea cup. This was awful. Her weekly visits with Peter to the Queen's Hall in Langham Place were a rainbow of colour in a world that was grey. To be thanked by Peter's wife for doing the thing she most wanted to do, which was to be alone with him, was beyond bearing.

'Really, Judith,' she said now, almost desperately. 'I love the music. It's been no hardship. But I won't be able to any more.'

'Oh, darling, why not?' Judith opened her eyes wide. 'He'll be quite *desolé*! He told me, you're much nicer to go to concerts with than I am. I chatter so much I spoil his enjoyment, and you, he said, are positively tranquil. You mustn't stop going, you mustn't. If you'd said you loathed the music of course it would be different, though even then I'd beg you to go on, as though it were war work, don't you know!' She laughed with great merriment. 'Indeed, I insist that you do. It *is* your war work. Well, I know the factory is

398

too, of course, but – well, you need the rest, and so does Peter, and you both enjoy it, so that is that!'

She gathered up her gloves and pushed back her chair. 'Dear heart, I must go! I promised Charles that I would take him to the Zoo this afternoon. I'll tell you what! I'll go along and collect Mary Bee, too, and take her. I'm sure she'll adore it, little wretch that she is, and then we can go to tea at Gunter's and I shall give them masses of cakes and ices and make them thoroughly sick and we shall all have a blissful time! Then you need not fret about rushing home to Mary Bee, you can go straight to meet Peter in Whitehall and have some dinner before you go to the concert! There, it's all arranged, and I must go. Thank you for lunch, sweet one. Too, too delicious.'

Hannah watched her go, and gave up fighting her conscience. Perhaps she was being foolish, after all. Peter seemed to see no threat in their evenings spent without Judith, so why should she? Clearly he did not recognize the electricity in her that she felt in him, so all she had to do was control her own reactions, and just go on being the Peter Lammecks' dear cousin Hannah, their good old friend, and not make any unnecessary problems.

It's probably all my own fault, she told herself as she paid her bill and walked back to the factory. I've been alone too long and I see things that aren't there and want things I shouldn't.

And the concerts *were* a delight. A haze of delight. He'd been so matter of fact about it that first evening, as indeed he was on every other succeeding one. 'I have tickets for the eight o'clock performance, and Judith as usual is gadding about on one of her things, so you shall come and hear it with me,' as though it were the most natural thing in the world. She had let the music wrap her in its comfort and sing its shapes into her tired brain and been totally content in a way she could never remember being, even when Daniel had been alive. There was a placidity in Peter, a still centre that sent waves of peace out to her, and quelled the anxiety that was so much a part of her now that she did not even realize it was there, until Peter dispelled it with his presence.

He had sent her home in a cab before going home himself that evening, and he said, almost as an afterthought as he closed the door on her, 'Next Monday. I'll meet you here, at half past seven. Then we'll have time for a glass of sherry before they start. It's rather light and pleasant next week. Pomp and Circumstance, inter alia. Very patriotic of course. Never mind. We'll still enjoy it. Goodnight.'

She enjoyed it as he'd said she would, and gone the next Monday and the Monday after that too, as they drifted into a pattern, a drink before the concert at the Langham Hotel, watching the khaki clad figures of young officers on leave being fêted by the usual clusters of eager girls, and then the music, and afterwards back to the hotel for a little late supper. They ate little, for usually both of them were too tired to bother much about food by the end of the day, and both had busy days to face on the morrow. The long social evenings and self indulgence that led to fuddled weary mornings were long since lost, though the roistering officers and their friends did their best to carry on the old traditions. Peter would watch them sombrely and then catch her eye and smile a little wryly, and say nothing.

Perhaps tonight he would be a little more cheerful than he had been last week? He had shown his usual calm face to her, but she had been aware of tension, of uncertainty of some kind inside him and had fretted all week about it. Tonight, perhaps, he would feel better, be himself again?

They listened to the music as usual and then went on to the Langham, not talking much at all until they ordered their meal. Then, one soldier in particular caught their eye, a tall young man who laughed a lot with a great deal of exuberance and was particularly noisy, and seemed, too, to be more than a little drunk. Certainly he was exceedingly clumsy and knocked things from the table and laughed uproariously when his companions fielded them for him. They seemed less elated than he was, and after a while Hannah said quietly, 'I think he's blind, you know.'

They watched for a little longer and then Peter bent his head sharply, not wanting to watch any more.

'Yes,' he said. 'He's blind. That's quite a performance he's putting on.'

'They're really incredible, these boys. That's all they are, most of them, children. I feel sick sometimes. I dare not think about what's happening, it's so ugly. I keep saying to myself, just finish today. That's all. Tomorrow can take care of itself. Just finish today.'

'But it can't take care of itself,' he said. 'It's got to be looked after. That boy's looked after some of the tomorrows. That's why he's here now, blind as a mole and fumbling in the dark and laughing his head off so that we can sit here and think that he's drunk.' His voice sounded harsher than it usually did. She looked at him and tried to see what lay behind his words, but his face was, as usual, unreadable.

'There's nothing more we can do than we're doing,' she said, almost defensively. 'I'm working as hard as I ever have, and so are you. Though it worries me that I make so much money out of it.'

He made a little gesture, almost literally brushing that aside. 'That's not important. It's only money. Not important. There's more to be done than we're doing.'

He looked at her, and she could see for the first time some tension in the muscles round his eyes. 'I sit at a desk with a telephone growing out of the end of my hand and I move thousands of yards of cloth and buttons and thread and tape and needles and tailor's chalk and out of the other end of the machine which I am comes uniforms and uniforms and uniforms. But it's not good enough.'

'Not good enough? What more can you do, for heaven's sake?' She let her voice rise a little. 'You're already doing an enormous job.'

'I should be wearing one,' he said, and bent his head again to contemplate the untouched food on his plate. 'I should be there at Hill 60 listening to that barrage and up to my knees in mud. I should be falling asleep not knowing if I'll ever wake up again. I should be taking the same chances they are.'

'Why?' She wanted to reach out and hold on to him physically. The war had alarmed her from the day it had started and she had spoken no more than the truth when she said that it made her sick to think about it. But so far it had not touched her personally. No one who was close to her had put on khaki and gone to be killed at Ypres. No one she cared about was facing German bombs and torpedoes at sea. She had to deal with nothing worse than shortages of familiar goods, and hard work, and making money. But now she was frightened, filled with plain cold terror that made her shoulders ache and the back of her neck feel as though a great weight had been put on it.

'Why, Peter? I can understand the boys getting excited and

needing to go. They've sat in schoolrooms waiting to grow up and for them it's a marvellous adventure. And the people who never do anything worth doing, who have no real use at home except for ordinary things, they're the ones the recruiting posters are after. Not you! You're doing an important job, Peter. If you left the Ministry who else could run the department the way you do? It's like oiled silk, the way things work. I know you're doing a vital job, and so do you if you think about it. Don't be infected by war fever, please. You're needed here.'

'There are any number of people who could do my job,' he said, still with his head down, staring at his hands on the table cloth in front of him. He was kneading small pieces of bread into grey bomb-shaped pellets. 'Old people. People who'd be no use at the Front, in the way I would be. Established people. Not Jews.'

She leaned back, chilled suddenly by the edge on his voice. 'Jews? What has that got to do with anything?'

Now he did look at her. 'You have to ask that? You? Don't you know what the people who came here before you put up with? Your parents, all their relations, all their friends, they came here like locusts, and they moved in, and they stayed. And my people, not my parents, I know, but a little further back, though not that much further back, it was the same with them. Old Bartholomew Lammeck came here from India, a funny little man wearing a proper suit of clothes for the first time in his life, more used to a turban than a top hat, he came here, and they let him come and stay, and now London's full of us. My people and your people. Hordes of us.'

'Well?' she said, 'What of it?'

'We have to do something about it. *Now*.' He shook his head and managed to smile a little. 'I suppose I do sound like a story out of the "Boys' Own Paper", but there it is. I'm grateful, you see. I feel I owe this country more than I can repay. That's one bit of it. And there's the selfish bit, too, of course. They don't like us, really, you know, the English – not yet. They're a funny lot, you see. They let us come and stay and looked at us sideways and didn't say much, but they didn't really take to us, and though we've been here long enough now to look like them – well, not all that different – and to talk like them and live like them, we're still that bit different and they don't really like or trust us. We make them uneasy. But if enough of us stand up and fight with them in this war, well, maybe they'll like us better. I've got roots here, Hannah. They don't go as deep yet as I'd like them to. Not deep enough to be really safe. I want to push them further in, and the only way I can do that is by putting on one of my own damned uniforms and going to that mess in France.'

She felt her eyes get hot as she watched his fingers, long flexible fingers, go on kneading the bread, making bomb after bomb, piling them neatly beside his plate. She didn't know what to say. She knew what he meant of course; she was as aware as he was of how unstable their hold was in the city of their birth. She had heard the gibes of 'Jewgirl!' shouted after her in the street. She had heard Judith making her light mocking jokes about the times she had been snubbed at fashionable parties because she was 'one of the Chosen, my dear, these Hebrews get in everywhere ... ' Had bitten her tongue when even Florrie who she knew was devoted to her personally made unthinking references to 'That there grocer, 'e's a right villain, always jewin' you down.' Only last month, there had been that fuss about Sir Edward Speyer. He'd been running the London underground train system for years, had made a superb job of it, but a whispering campaign had started, accusing him of being a spy, just because he was a Jew, and he'd had to resign. Peter was right. They did have to justify their presence in this country, had to prove themselves entitled to be here. Born here, but not belonging.

But that didn't help her dispel the sick fear she felt at the thought of Peter going to France. Let someone else go for you, she wanted to shout at him. Stay here and be safe and give me a reason for going on as I do. Let someone else go, not you.

That was precisely what she couldn't say, because that was precisely what he felt so strongly about; the fact that other people were going, taking risks that he was not. It was inevitable that he should feel so; people in general behaved so badly to apparently able-bodied men dressed in civilian clothes. There were girls who drew themselves aside with ostentatious disdain when such a man passed them in the street, others who spoke loudly and slightingly of 'shirkers';

and yet others, so she had heard, who gave white feathers to civilian men, as a label of cowardice. In such a fever of patriotism and recruiting posters and swaggering soldiers home on leave filling the streets, only the most insensitive could fail to be made uneasy. And Peter was far from insensitive.

She leaned forwards now and after a moment put her hand on his, wanting to stop the unceasing movement of his fingers.

'Peter. Please don't do anything hasty, will you? I think I know what you mean. I don't think you're right, but I know what you mean. Please take your time.'

'That's half my problem,' he said. 'I always do. I think everything through logically. It's an appalling habit. Makes you quite useless. Waiter! The bill, please.'

It didn't help that the waiter proved to be a middle aged woman, very neat and pleased with herself in frilly white cap and apron. More and more men's jobs were being filled by women. She felt the woman's slightly contemptuous stare at Peter as sharply as though the woman had actually spoken her thoughts aloud. *Oh, God, please stop him from going, please God.*

They came out into the street, pushing their way through the heavy blackout curtain and stood on the pavement trying to get used to the dark.

'Close your eyes,' he said. 'Keep them shut for a minute and then open them again. Then you'll be able to see.'

She obeyed. When she opened her eyes he was standing beside her, his face just a glimmer in the night for the moon had not yet risen. Without thinking, she put her hand on his arm and said, 'Peter, I do need you here so much. I know I'm selfish, but I do so not want you to go.' She felt her face go hot in the darkness. Mercifully, he couldn't see. He just said noncommittally, 'I know. Look, there aren't taxis anywhere, as far as I can see. Can you walk as far as Oxford Circus with me? I think we might do better there.'

She fell into step beside him, biting her lips with rage at herself. These Monday concert visits would have to stop if she couldn't trust her tongue better than this. It just wasn't safe. And maybe they'd stop anyway, if he acted as he was threatening to act. *Oh, God, please don't let him, don't let him.*

When it started it sounded as though it came from inside

her own head, it was so thin, so remote a ringing, and then it got louder and all at once there was a great rattle as a klaxon sounded nearby. She shrank back against the side of the building they were passing as footsteps went thundering by, seeming to come from all directions at once.

'What is it?' Peter was shouting, grabbing at someone as he ran by.

'Don't know, guv,' the man said breathlessly, and ran on as the wailing sound became louder and then louder still, and then, someone else passed them and shouted, 'Zeppelin raid! Come on, it's them bleedin' great airships, droppin' bleedin' great bombs! Come on and take cover!'

44

They discovered fairly soon that there was no need to be frightened after all, not there at Oxford Circus. They found a policeman who seemed slightly better informed than the passersby from whom Peter had tried to get some sort of coherent story, who told them that a Zeppelin had been seen at Stoke Newington and had dropped a fire bomb.

'Just by the railway station it was, sir,' the policeman said with relish, needing someone to whom to display his superior knowledge. 'Come up from Wanstead way, seemingly – no one saw 'er, seein' the moon ain't up, but they saw the fire right enough, and set off the alarms everywhere. 'My sarge, 'e says there's no need for no one 'round 'ere to get excited.' He sounded a little regretful, peering up at the black sky. ''E says it's all over to the East that there Zeppelin's going, and no one 'ere in the West End'll come to an atom of trouble on its account.'

'The East?' Hannah said, alarmed. 'Where in the East?'

'Last I heard, it was over to Hoxton way, Shoreditch like . . .'

'The factory,' Hannah said, and took a deep breath. 'Peter, the factory, there's no one there. No night watchman to put fires out. and we had a huge delivery on Friday, remember? I've got thousands of yards there.'

He stood in the darkness beside her, very still. She looked

at his profile and thought confusedly of what a stupid waste it would be if he took himself to France to be buried in mud, and what a waste it would be if the Zeppelin fired her factory with the cloth that Peter's office had sent to her, and what a waste it was to love someone else's husband as much as she loved Peter. It all boiled up together inside her to make her suddenly angry, and she took his arm and shook it and cried, 'Peter, don't just stand there like an idiot! Do something! Come to the factory. If they drop a fire bomb on it it'll be ... Peter!'

He looked down at her and said nothing, and then turned away to the kerb. Traffic had started to move again now that the panicky sirens and klaxons had stopped their din. After a moment he lifted his hand and waved, and out of the blackness a taxi cab with its flag up moved to his side.

'Come on,' he said shortly. She climbed in, shaky now and ashamed of herself. There had been no need to be so hateful to him, but she had been so frightened, and so much in need of reassurance. She turned her head to look at him in the dimness of the taxi and moved her hand to touch him but there was something very unapproachable about him now as he sat in his corner staring out of the window. She put her hand in her coat pocket and turned to stare out of her own window, as the taxi crawled through the darkness of London, up New Oxford Street to Holborn, and then on over the viaduct past St Pauls and through the City to London Wall and Liverpool Street.

She became more tense as the journey dragged on, listening to the chug of the taxi's noisy engine and peering upwards, trying to see signs of the dreaded Zeppelin, expecting at any moment to see the fat silvery maggot come creeping out from behind a cloud. But there was no sign of anything, only the newly risen moon, round and full just over the horizon.

When they reached Artillery Lane and she stepped out into the street she could smell it, and her chest constricted with sudden fear at the scent of charring timber and paint and something more sinister and chemical that she could not put a name to. She pulled her coat about her and without waiting for Peter, who was paying the cabman, ran down to the factory half way along the street.

He came after her, running along the pavement with loud

echoing footsteps as the taxi's engine throb revved and faded away in the distance, and stood beside her in the empty street.

'Looks all right,' he said. 'Though there's been – I can smell it.'

'Yes,' she said. 'And it's so quiet here, no one about at all. There are people living here, there ought to be some sound.'

Almost as though it were on cue, a ringing began, far away and then more loudly. Peter said almost casually, 'Fire engines.' They stood and listened as the noise drew a little closer and then sheered away north and east of them. 'Not all that close, after all.'

'Where is everybody?' she said, almost fretfully. 'Surely there ought to be someone about.'

'Sheltering, probably. Hiding under stairs. Shall we go in?'

She stood hesitantly on the pavement, feeling rather foolish. It was clear now that there had been no need to come at all, that she had panicked and been childishly rude to Peter all for nothing. She said awkwardly. 'No point now, I suppose. There's nothing happening.'

There was a sound of footsteps running from the Bishopsgate end of the street and someone came rushing up towards them. Peter whirled and shouted, but the man didn't stop, calling back over his shoulder as he went, 'Fire in Fashion Street, 'nother in Princelet Street and Pear Street, and the bugger's still at it.' And he was gone, still running full tilt.

'We'd better go inside,' Peter said then, and took her elbow. 'We can go up to the roof, see what's going on. Then we'll know if there's any need to worry about a fire here. You've got the keys?'

She fumbled in her bag. 'Yes, I came straight to the Langham from here tonight. Here they are.'

He led the way in, and she was glad to defer to his authority. Even though this was her factory, her business, it seemed right, somehow, to let him take charge. She followed him through the heavy door, and waited just inside as he swept his hand along the wall, looking for the light switch. The single naked bulb sprang into life above the stair well, and she looked about her at the familiar shabby green and cream paint, the flaking lino on the stairs and the cobwebbed corners and took a deep breath of the smell of machine oil and new cloth and dust. It was shabby and ugly and it had all the comfort of home, as much as Paultons Square with its fresh white paint and light curtains and familiar furniture.

He led the way up the stairs and unlocked the inner doors and switched on the single overhead light. The factory stretched there in front of her, the four banks of sewing machines shadowed and silent, the big pressing tables looming menacingly behind them.

'How can we get to the roof?' His voice sounded loud in the echoing space and she jumped a little.

'There's a fire escape out towards the back.' She led the way now, walking up an aisle between the machines. Ahead of her there was a rustle as mice scuttled away, but because he was there behind her she didn't mind. The fire escape door was bolted and had twisted a little, but it swung open after a moment's struggle and then they were out on the narrow iron stairway that led up to the roof and down to the yard below.

The roof had a small flat area bounded by a low brick parapet, and it looked eastwards towards the flats of the Lea river. She stood beside the parapet with her hands thrust deep in her pockets against the night air, which was chill even though it was now early summer, and stared out. He moved to stand behind her looking over her head.

The sky was very thick against the light of the moon, now lifting itself well over the horizon, and the rooftops beneath looked stark in the contrasts thrown by the shadows, gun metal grey and hard edged on the tiles. There were a few clouds, moving slowly away towards the west, and the air smelled both cold and sour, for the chemical odour of the fires was thicker here.

'Look,' Peter said quietly. 'Over there.' He pointed, his arm coming over her shoulder so that his hand brushed her cheek. 'Can you see?'

There was a glow where he was pointing, flickering a little against the dark sky. As her eyes became more accustomed to the light, she could see the drifts of smoke that were rising above it, curving elegantly against the light breeze.

'That must be on the other side of Commercial Street,' she said, trying to ignore the way her face held the memory of his touch. This was crazy, and getting crazier. 'Or further, maybe Brick Lane?'

'And there's another,' he said. Again she followed his pointing finger and saw, further away beyond the tangle of chimneys, another glow, leaping higher this time and licking the sky with yellow fingers of flame. 'That must be beyond Aldgate East Station. It looks as though they're moving away from here.'

'Yes,' she said. 'Maybe it's safe here after all. We can go.' But she didn't move and neither did he.

'They might curve back, of course,' he said after a moment. 'Isn't that what happened when they bombed Yarmouth? Went over the town and then came back and dropped more bombs after everyone thought they'd gone. I think we'd better wait and see. We're here now, after all.'

'What's the time?' she asked and he peered at his watch.

'Getting on for twelve.'

'So late? You'll be exhausted in the morning. You need your sleep,' she said, and turned to look at him. 'You work too hard to do without rest. We'll take the chance and go. It looks as though the excitement's over for tonight.'

Below them the sound started again, the frenetic shrieking of fire bells as an engine raced from Bishopsgate going east. He shook his head at her.

'No. Not quite. And what was it that man said, Fashion Street and Princelet Street? That's quite near here.'

'Just across the other side of Commercial Street.' She turned her head to try to peer northwards, on the other side of the chimney stack that lay to their left. Though she could see nothing there because of the bulk of the buildings in the way, the smell still came in gusts as the night breezes lifted and strengthened.

'The way the wind's blowing it could spread this way. Flying sparks. We'd better sit tight. Just a little longer, now we're here. Where's the fabric stock?'

'On the far side of the factory.' She shivered a little as she indicated the fire escape steps going down into the darkness below. 'It's filled the corner beyond my office, you know where I mean? It's the only space I have, but it's not a good place. Right near the door that leads to the stairs. If it ever went up, it'd block the way out.'

'Let me see,' he said. 'We might as well use the time we've got, and it's cold out here. Come on.' He led the way down the fire escape, moving slowly so that she could follow him safely.

Inside, the factory felt warm and stuffy in comparison with

the air on the roof, but after a moment she felt the cold again, and in spite of herself shivered again. The cloth bay loomed ahead of them beyond the little glass enclosed office and she went to switch on the light in there, but he shook his head.

'No need to unlock the office just to put the light on,' he said. 'And you'd need to put up blackout shutters. I can see well enough. It's not ideal to keep cloth here, I suppose, but I'm not sure you can put it anywhere else.'

He moved away from her, walking all round the factory, down one aisle and then another. She watched him in the thin light of the moon, at the way his narrow shoulders moved and his back held its erectness and thought, he's walking like a soldier already. *Please don't let him go.* I don't want him to be anywhere but where I can be near him – and then she turned away deliberately, forbidding herself to look at him, sitting down on a bolt of cloth and leaning back against the bulwark of piled bolts that lay behind it.

'Nowhere else you could put it,' he said as he came back. 'Hannah? Oh, there you are. You look like a frightened child in a haystack. Hiding.'

She shook her head. 'It's just somewhere to sit,' she said. 'I'm not hiding.'

'But you are frightened, aren't you?' He sat down beside her, and she pulled herself into as small a space as she could, tightening her muscles against him.

'Frightened? No, of course not. What have I got to be frightened of?' How could he not frighten her, she asked herself, screaming inside her own head. All I'm frightened of is that he might go away.

'I am,' he said. 'Air raids, even small ones, are very frightening indeed. Thinking of a man, just an ordinary man like me, sitting in an airship over my head where the moon and the clouds are and deliberately aiming explosives and firebombs at me, I find that very frightening indeed.'

She blinked and then shook her head at herself. She had actually, just for a moment, quite forgotten why they were here. An air raid. It seemed somehow unimportant now that she had seen how far from her factory the fires were. Now that she was sitting here in a cocoon of bolts of cloth with his body warm and close beside her.

'I suppose so. War is frightening. Every bit of it,' she said and then felt the words dragged out of her, much as she

410

wanted to keep them back. 'People one cares about going away to fight. Casualty lists in the papers.'

'I haven't gone yet,' he said. 'That's my problem. I haven't gone yet, though there's that man sitting up there over my head throwing bombs at me. Mad, isn't it? There he is and here I am, and there are men I know in France – quite mad.'

She couldn't help it, then. The threat seemed too big for her to contain her own need for him another moment, and his face was so close to hers in the thin light. 'Peter ... please, Peter. Don't go.' Her eyes were filling with tears and she couldn't stop them. 'Please, my dear, I do need you so.'

'Oh, God,' he said. 'Oh, God.' He bent his head and kissed her, his mouth feeling cold on hers, and she stopped thinking at all, stopped being angry with herself for her own lack of control over her thoughts, and let go completely. There was just now, and his closeness, and her own body screaming its need into her mind. She clung to him, feeling her curved fingers digging into the cloth of his coat.

For almost five years it had been corked down, that sensuousness that Daniel had first unstoppered, and far from dwindling in those lonely arid years it had flowered and come to a richness that, once released, could not be contained. She did not know what his feeling was, what his needs might be, and didn't even stop to consider them. She cared only for herself and just held onto him, and threw herself into their kisses and let time flow past her.

The cold didn't seem to matter as it struck her skin. Her coat and then her dress were there crumpled on the floor at her feet, and she could feel the roughness of the bolts of cloth against her bare shoulders, and then she was tugging at his clothes, feeling his skin warm under her fingers, his thighs and knees hard and bony against her softness, and they were together in one sudden urgent movement that came simultaneously from both of them, as far as she could tell. Yet even as she felt the excitement rising ever higher, felt her own hunger driving her further and further to satisfaction, she was watching herself, seeing herself on a blue green counterpane in a blue green hotel room, rolling and crying and hurting, but that was Daniel and this was Peter, and as at last the climax of her excitement came, hurling her breathlessly over the peak, she cried aloud, 'Peter!' And the image of Daniel

411

shattered and glittered inside her head and died in the glow that burned behind her eyes as she lay, panting, his weight on top of her.

45

'Oh, my dear one, what *can* I do? Not a thing. I mean I've talked till I'm blue, and he just listens the way he does, you know, and then carries on as though I had said nothing. My mother-in-law is in such a state of rage, I cannot tell you. And Alfred, he has tried all *he* can, even talking to the King's equerry. You know the man, Major thingummy. No, well, perhaps you don't, but he is quite a powerful sort of fellow, got the ear of the War Office Papa says. He spoke to Peter who made him agree not to interfere, and was really quite bucked that Peter is so patriotic.' Judith laughed a little, a tinkling sound that was painfully false. 'For my part, I have to say it is of course frightfully good that he is such a patriot.' She looked at Hannah sideways and smiled, but there was a bleakness in her face that made Hannah want to cry.

She didn't cry, only put her hand out and took Judith's and said, 'I'm sorry. I'm truly sorry.'

'It was such a shock, you see. France! I thought he'd just stay at the War Office. Such a surprise,' Judith said. 'No, Charles, my precious lamb, you'll spill your paint if you – there! I knew you would. Let me help. There, like that.'

She fussed a little over Charles and Mary Bee who were both enveloped in blue holland overalls and facing each other over the nursery table, painting books spread in front of them. Hannah watched her mopping the spilled water and scolding Charles lovingly, and then looked at Mary Bee, absorbed and silent for once as she spread crimson lake and burnt umber happily, and her mother tried to pretend that nothing had changed in her life and that everything was as it had always been, work and Mary Bee and –

And Judith and Peter. She wrenched her thoughts away, and looked now at Charles, standing there beside the table with his head bent a little, watching his mother's deft hands as she tried to repair the damage the water had done to his painting. He had sleek dark hair on a head that looked too large for his slender neck. The curve of the nape of that neck seemed to Hannah suddenly very touching, making her eyes fill with tears. And then she realized it was not just the defenceless small-boy look that had so pierced her, it was his likeness to Peter. He looked up then and caught her eye, and she stared at him, at his wide dark eyes and thin little face, and the way that same lock of hair that Peter had to control so carefully on his own adult head flopped over Charles' childish forehead, and she wanted to get up and turn and run away.

'Mamma,' Charles said. 'Is it true? Is Papa going to be a soldier in France?' But it was Hannah he stared at as he asked the question.

Judith's hands stopped moving and then started again. 'Yes, darling, I think so.' Her voice was rather loud. 'There! Now you can start your picture again.'

'Will he be killed, Mamma?'

'Charles, darling!' Judith stared at him wide eyed and then at Hannah and she laughed again, that same tinkling false laugh. 'Such questions these small people do ask! One hardly knows – dearest Charles, do get on with your painting. I'm sure it will be a perfectly beautiful one, and then Papa can put it up on the wall of his study, and be madly proud of you. Hannah, my angel, I must fly, I really must. Bless you for having Charles tonight. Say thank you to Aunt Hannah, my sweet. Nanny shall fetch him first thing in the morning. I couldn't refuse her the night off...' She faltered and swallowed and looked up at Hannah, her eyes very bright and smiling. 'Dear Nanny! Her fiancé, you see, off to France in the morning. Now, Charles, mind your manners.' She kissed his cheek and then Mary Bee's and Hannah's in a flurry of furs and scent and was gone, leaving the three of them to sit in silence listening to the sound of the engine as her car purred away.

'Will he be killed, Aunt Hannah?' Charles asked again after a while as though nothing had happened since he had first asked. He was still standing beside the table, his legs thin and bony under his blue holland overall, and his socks crumpled about his ankles. She put her arms out to him and said simply, 'Oh, dear Charles, I don't know. We none of us know what happens when there's a war on.'

413

But he did not come to her as he usually did. They had always been close, for she loved him as dearly as she did her own Mary Bee, and he was as comfortable curled up on Aunt Hannah's lap as he was on his mother's. But not this afternoon. He just looked at her and then climbed back on his chair and picked up his paintbrush again.

'My picture's better than yours!' Mary Bee said shrilly, leaning back to admire the confection of colour that she had created, but Charles, who could usually be trusted to rise to such taunts, said nothing but went on with his painting. Mary Bee, content to have established, however temporarily, her superiority over him, returned to her painting too. Silence slid into the room.

Hannah tried to relax into familiar comforts. The same old clock ticked loudly and with a faint whirr on the high mantelpiece, the battered wooden table in the middle of the room looked as solid and comfortable as it always had, the worn red carpet on the floor was littered as always with Mary Bee's toys and books and the place, as ever, spelled peace and comfort as no other room in the house could. Yet she could not be comfortable, not now that she knew it was inevitable. He was to go.

She leaned forwards and put some more coal on the fire. It was still early September but it was getting chilly already, and it was pleasant to have the fire glowing in the nursery these evenings, as the sun slanted its late golden glow across the square.

He was to go. He had at last said so, to everyone. The sword that had been hanging over her head these past ten weeks had fallen, and curiously, she felt less badly than she had feared she would – or at least was able to behave as though she did.

It had been a very painful time, as the heavy summer months dragged past, day succeeding effortful day so slowly that sometimes she felt as though the world had stopped turning on its axis. Every moment of that night at the beginning of June was carved into her memory. She had long since stopped trying not to think about it. She had to think of it; there was nothing else that mattered half so much. So she often sat and remembered, looking back on every detail, from the concert with the strains of Elgar wrapping her round and the laughing blind soldier and the ridiculous way they had reacted to the Zeppelin (ridiculous because that had been so minor a raid, compared with the ones that had come later) to that incredible hour they had spent among the bolts of cloth in the factory. She thought sometimes of that cloth, and the uniforms it had gone to make. Had any of the passion that had so filled them both when they had used the cloth as their couch imbued those stiff folds with emotion? Did any of those VADs scampering so busily about their wards ever find their spirits stirring at the sight of the men they were caring for, the way hers had that dark night in Artillery Lane? It was a stupid thought, but it somehow gave her peace of mind, for it made the episode seem governed by fate, something over which she had no control at all.

Though of course she had, and once they had emerged from their hour of madness she had exercised it with adamantine determination. She had refused to allow him to put her in a taxi, insisting on going alone to Bishopsgate station to find a late driver there. She had refused to speak to him on the telephone the next day, the day after that, or indeed on any day at all. She had contented herself with writing only one letter to his office, short and crisp, asking him – indeed demanding – that they remain always apart, and that nothing, absolutely nothing, be done to distress Judith.

She had prevailed. Telephone calls stopped. All her dealings with the Ministry of Supply were taken over by Peter's deputy, James Chesterton, and Peter was never available to join in on those evenings when she could not refuse Judith's invitations.

Judith had seemed unaware of the change in their social life. She exclaimed, of course, over how much busier darling Peter was these days, and how long he had to work at his dismal office, and so often, just as she exclaimed over the fact that Hannah too was over-working, often staying at her factory until almost midnight to get urgent orders out, and going in on Saturdays and Sundays too to cope with all the paper work. More and more now, though, she sat amid the machinists, pushing the heavy fabric under the bouncing iron foot as the wheels whirled, losing herself in the drudgery of boring repetitive labour.

The worst part had been the loneliness, not just the loneliness that came from not seeing Peter any more, but the loneliness that came from the barrier that she had erected between herself and Judith. She had vowed to herself, with all the fervour of which she was capable, that nothing she ever did would hurt Judith. She poured every scrap of energy she had into being the same as she had always been when they met. The burden of guilt that she bore with her made it difficult, but in a way more satisfying. The harder it was to keep Judith unaware of her own unhappiness the more virtue there was in succeeding.

And so the weeks went on, as Judith chattered about her fund-raising and bandage rolling and the children and poor dear overworked Peter, and Hannah listened and sympathized and said nothing significant at all, though she began to wonder, painfully, whether all her efforts to keep Judith happy had been wasted after all, for Judith changed, became edgy and nervous and brighter, more the chatterbox than ever. As June gave way to July and the war news became gloomier, she broke down at last and told Hannah of the real cause of her distress, the fact that Peter was determined to join the army in France.

Week after week it had gone on, Hannah having to listen to Judith talking about the arguments that were going on in every Lammeck and Damont household in London in anxious attempts to convince Peter that his sacrifice was unnecessary. It was not entirely selfishness on the part of the family either, as Judith was at pains to point out. Peter was doing a valuable job, as well as spending much of what little spare time he had in family affairs. With only Marcus to run the complexities of Lammeck Alley, Peter was a vital cog in the family wheel, but just as vital in Whitehall. Hannah listened and said nothing, for she knew all too well that she had no right to say anything. The last thing Peter had said to her was, 'I shall be joining the army, Hannah. I have to. But don't think, please, that this evening has anything to do with it.' Of course she was immediately convinced that it had. He had been talking of joining but would he have done so if she hadn't behaved as she had? Of course not, she told herself, listening to Judith. Of course not. Now, because of my treachery, our treachery, he feels he has to go. She hated herself with a dreary misery that made the days creep by even more slowly.

And today it was a fait accompli. Judith had discovered this morning that he had been going to training sessions on weekends when she had thought he was working in Whitehall. He was to go to France next Thursday.

Next Thursday. That evening as she helped Florrie put the children to bed she thought about it. The next day as she supervised their breakfast and settled the day's household tasks she thought about it. All that day and the next as she busied herself at the factory she thought about it, and on Thursday afternoon, she could contain herself no longer. She had to see him go, not speak to him, but just see him. She had to.

Victoria Station was a wash of khaki and steam and noise. She stood just inside the great concourse staring into the hubbub and her heart slipped in her chest and she thought, I can't. But then a girl near her asked one of the harassed station staff where the embarkation trains were going from and he waved her towards the thickest part of the crowd, and almost without volition Hannah followed her as she went plunging into the melée.

The feeling of the place was extraordinary. It seemed almost as though they were going on cheerful holidays, these khaki clad men with great packs on their backs, shouting and laughing and roaring their jokes at each other as if the whole expedition was some great lark. But that was only the surface of the layered scene. Just below the level of joking men there were women smiling and nodding and chattering, but they stood with their shoulders very closely hunched as though a cold wind were blowing through the station; it was fear, not cold, that lifted the muscles into that tension and tightened the smiles on their faces. And then there were children, some carried on their soldier fathers' backs. Hannah saw small face after small face as she pushed her way along the edge of the crowd towards platform seven, and none of them were smiling. They looked peaky and solemn, their eyes wide and somehow blank.

Here and there she could see the glimpses of the bottom layer of all, people in tears of fear and horror and foreknowledge. A middle aged woman, wearing a very smart hat over a sable coat, was clutching a brown paper bag full of fruit. As someone pushed past her the bag broke and apples went tumbling about the platform and she stood there making no

417

effort to pick them up, letting tears of acute distress run down her cheeks. Hannah stared at her and the young man standing helpless and embarrassed beside her in the clean and polished uniform of the very new officer, and she felt a stab of the same pain the woman was feeling. They were all so helpless in the face of the madness which had overtaken their world, the madness that was turning France into a pandemonium of bloody mud, that all they could do was weep at the tragedy of fallen apples.

The crowd behind her pushed her onwards, and she began to panic, afraid suddenly that they would see her, Judith and Peter. She didn't want to be seen by him, and she certainly did not want to observe their parting. She had been mad to come, and couldn't think why she had. She turned against the pushing tide behind her and began to battle her way back.

As she pushed her way at last out of the thickest part of the crowd, coming out by Smith's bookstall at the front of the concourse, she heard Judith's voice high and clear above the hubbub, and so determinedly bright it had the quality of polished glass. It might have shattered at a touch.

'Darling Hannah, I knew you would come! I just knew you could not let him go without being here. Peter, my angel, here she is, come to scold you for being so wilful as to go, and to wish you well. Aren't you, Hannah?'

They were standing side by side at the bookstall, where Judith had just brought a sheaf of magazines for him. He looked at her and nodded, his face quite still.

'Hallo, Hannah. Thank you for coming.'

Judith moved away to the chocolate stall to buy the most expensive boxes they had and Hannah looked at her briefly and said, 'I didn't mean to come. I don't know why I did. I shouldn't have. Let me go, now. I wish you well, and – oh, God, I must go.'

'No,' He put out one hand and held onto her. 'You can't. Judith would be bitterly hurt. She needs you. Stay.'

She looked at him, at the way the peak of his flat khaki cap sat so neatly on his forehead, at his shining buttons and the polished Sam Browne and the neat luggage at his side and could not see him at all, somehow. He was like every other soldier in this maelstrom of officers and men; just another chess piece in khaki, like the embarrassed youth with the mother who was weeping over her apples, like the nearby corporal in boots so bright they could mirror the face of the child he had perched on his shoulder, like every single one of them. She stared at him, her forehead creased. Who was he? Why was she here?

Judith came back and began to cram the magazines and chocolate into Peter's side pack. He said nothing, letting her do it, and then as she stood up he said gently, 'It will be all right, my love. It will be all right. Whatever happens. We'll be *all right.*'

She looked at him, her eyes wide and sparkling. She was as beautiful as ever, as elegantly dressed as ever, as perfectly head-turning as ever, and every line of her body spoke of the misery that was in her. Hannah stepped back, feeling sick with shame. This girl was her friend and she had used her so badly, and she wanted to blurt it all out, wanted to tell her what had happened that night in June in Artillery Lane, anything to shift the guilt from her own back, to let someone else suffer it. She bit her tongue so hard that she tasted salt blood.

'Remember what I told you,' Peter was saying, softly but so clearly that even above all the noise around them Hannah heard every word. 'Whatever happens, we two will be all right.'

He turned then and looked at Hannah and smiled. For a moment it was the Peter of the Monday concerts again, the Peter who had been her beloved friend these past five years, the Peter she loved and needed so much.

'Take care of her, Hannah. And of Charles. And they'll take care of you.' He bent and picked up his bags and his side pack and looked again at Judith, who was standing very still and straight. He bobbed his head and then turned and went, pushing his way into the crowd and disappearing into the sea of khaki. Judith and Hannah stood side by side and watched him go, and went on watching the crowd long after they knew his train had steamed out of the vast station, leaving wreaths of grey smoke tendrils to float about the iron tracery of the roof far over their heads.

46

If I can bear it for three weeks, it will be all right, Hannah would tell herself. Just for three weeks. And then would feel sick at the reason for feeling so.

It had been Cissie who had put the notion into her head, Cissie all unknowing and cheerfully chattering to the finishers as they worked late over a batch of uniforms due to be shipped out to Etaples on the midnight train to the coast.

'Three weeks,' Cissie had said. 'That's what they say, you know, three weeks is all anyone lasts out on the Front now. Wounded or worse they are, inside o' three weeks.'

Hannah, who had been sitting in her office with the door open, checking delivery notes, felt her throat tighten so that she almost retched. She got up and pushed the door closed and then tried to concentrate on the delivery notes again: seventy-five yard bolts of blue serge, width forty-eight inches, quantity fifteen; hundred yard bolts blue striped white calico width thirty-six inches, quantity thirty-five; fifty yard bolts scarlet flannel width forty-eight inches, quantity fifteen, dammit, that meant they'd be short of red flannel for the capes, and she'd have to spend another hour on the phone. Three weeks? She'd read that too, somewhere, but had managed to forget it till now. Three weeks was the life expectancy of men at the front now that the battle of Loos had begun. Three weeks if they were lucky. Three weeks before they were sprawled in the mud or hanging over the barbed wire staring blank-eyed at the squalor of no-man's-land, or weeping with pain in the casualty clearing stations behind the lines, waiting to be shipped home, if they survived long enough, to be patched up ready to be sent back to start all over again.

The words kept repeating themselves in her head as she went about the day's work, checking the cut of the capes and the dresses, watching over the stitching of the aprons and caps, thinking, *three weeks, three weeks, three weeks.* If I can stop myself saying anything for three weeks, it will be all right.

It was a crazy thought, a totally illogical idea, but it sustained her. Each evening she went home to find Judith waiting there for her, for she had surrendered her control entirely with Hannah. With everyone else she was her old self, chattering, bright, full of busyness and excitement. The bandage rolling ladies of the West End commented to each other admiringly on how brave darling Judith Lammeck was, and how she was an example to all young wives, or more waspishly told each other it was remarkable how unmoved she seemed about her dear husband's absence; these days, young women were all hard selfishness, were they not? But to Hannah, Judith displayed her distress in all its rawness.

She would manage, somehow, to get herself to Paultons Square every evening in time to collect Charles to take him home, or sometimes, more and more often now, to kiss him goodnight as he curled up in the spare bed in Mary Bee's nursery. The two children were becoming inseparable, for now that Judith's nanny had gone to make munitions, leaving the house staffed only by maids who were not bright enough to be of much use doing war work, it was better for Charles and easier for Judith to let him spend his days with Florrie and Bet. There had been some desultory talk of Florrie going off to a factory but Bet had coaxed her out of it, and Florrie knew herself to be indispensable to Hannah's war work, and so stayed put. More and more Charles regarded Paultons Square as his second home and, inevitably, so did Judith.

Perhaps that was one of the reasons she was so unguarded with Hannah, or perhaps it was an awareness that Hannah shared her sense of loss. It would never have occurred to her that Hannah felt anything but cousinly affection for Peter; Hannah knew that, and it made her own situation that much more poignant, her guilt a greater weight on her mind. It was not eased by looking at Judith's exhausted little face, the eyes shadowed and dull.

They spent many evenings together – for Judith could not bring herself to go to fund-raising balls while Peter was at the Front. They sat facing each other on each side of the fireplace in the pretty white drawing room with its Heal's furniture and its sinuous shapes, often knitting, sometimes sewing, frequently just staring at the dull embers in the grate. It was almost as though they were an elderly married couple,

Hannah thought, and almost said as much to Judith, and then, as ever, did not. More and more Hannah was learning that superficial chatter was the only safe talk there was. She became, despite Judith's frequent company, more and more lonely.

Chanukah, the festival of lights, came and Judith's spirits lifted for a while. She hurled herself into planning entertainment for the children, giving them their daily gifts for the eight days of the holiday (which made them both tell Florrie and Bet, happily decorating their small tree in the kitchen, that Christmas might be all right, but it wasn't a patch on Chanukah, which went on for days and days and *days*) and being everything a mother and aunt should be. Hannah did all she could to be as eager, but it was becoming harder to dissimulate.

The three weeks she had so feared had long gone, and still Peter survived. He wrote long letters to Judith, and equally long ones to Hannah, filled with friendship but with no hint that there was anything more than that between them, and seemed well enough; he was acting as a supply officer behind the lines, but went up to the trenches quite often, he said, to ensure that all the men needed was getting through. Hannah would take a deep breath, trying to control the fear that rose in her as she read his words, reminding herself that by the time the letter reached her he had moved on, and would agree brightly with Judith that 'he seemed to be his old darling self, did he not?'

By the end of January she was beginning to feel better. As the memory of that June night receded, so did some of the guilt; it had happened, and that was that. It had not been premeditated, and clearly it had done no harm to anyone but herself. She was suffering, but Judith was obviously not. Letters came with punctilious regularity; Judith relaxed and became less fearful, more cheerful in the evenings in Paultons Square. Hannah was feeling better too, for had Peter not survived the horrors of the trenches for four months now? He might even get some leave soon. And then she would feel that stab of fear again and would think wildly, 'If he does, I'll have to go away – not see him. Take Mary Bee to the seaside perhaps.' She shook her head at her own idiocy, for who went to the seaside in the depths of winter?

In early February, Uncle Alex came to see her, for the first time in some weeks. He had been, he told her with not a little self importance, hectically busy.

'I tell you, dolly, feedin' that lot – it's like pushing mountains down the Commercial Road. Running forty restaurants is a pushover compared with it on account people're prepared to pay for what they get in a tea shop. But dealing with the army, it's like selling apples to a man with no teeth. They don't eat the stuff themselves, the officers that do the buying. So they don't see that the cost of it has to be what it is and they keep cuttin' back. So there's me with the farmers on one side screaming for top rates and the complaints about the bully beef and plum and apple jam from the soldiers on the other, and the officers in between – I tell you, I feel like a nut between two sets of crackers.'

But he was obviously in his element, busy and content, and he beamed at her over his still burgeoning belly and lit another cigar. He might look like the sort of war profiteer so many of the nastier current jokes were about, but he was working hard, and he clearly took pride in his contribution.

'I'll tell you why I come, dolly,' he said after a moment. 'It's Solly.'

She frowned sharply. 'Solly? What's the matter? He's not ill?'

He shook his head and grinned. 'Ill, that one? Tough as a pair of old boots. No dolly. It's just that he says he wants to join the army.'

She closed her eyes for a moment. 'Solly? But he's so young.' She herself was almost twenty-four and Solly twenty, but somehow when she thought of him she still saw the cheeky small boy with the grubby clothes and the watchful sideways look in his round eyes, not the weedy youth that he had become.

'I thought they'd turn him down, he's so scrawny, but they're not so fussy as they was, the recruiters. They said they'd take him. Trouble is, your father. Since Jake went up to Scotland on that training camp job there's only been Solly to take care of your father – I mean, Aunt Sarah really does it all, but you know what I mean. Nathan's got to think it's his own life and his own boys – he don't take no help from relations if he can help it. If he knows it – you know what I mean?'

'I know what you mean.' She was silent for a while.

'What do I do?'

'I did what I could. Asked Nathan if he'd bury the hatchet, now you're a widow. I thought, if he's got you maybe he'll let Solly go. And Solly, he's getting very upset, stuck at home. Four times some stupid bitch gives him a white feather in the street, he feels it, the boy.'

'What did Poppa say?' She had felt a moment of lifting pleasure. Could they pick up the old threads again, she and Nathan? But Uncle Alex shook his head.

'That one! O' course he won't. So, all I can do is try to get some sort of army job for young Solly that don't take him to France. London's full of bleedin' officers in fancy uniforms that don't never get mud on their boots. So I thought these officers, they got to have batmen, drivers and that, eh? I got my contacts, but I used 'em a lot already to get favours, got three o' the boys from the gym into the regiments they wanted that way, Jews though they are, and I can't keep on pullin' the same bits o' string without breakin' 'em. So I thought, maybe you could ask your father-in-law. That *ferstinkeneh mumser*'s done little enough for you and his granddaughter. So maybe he can do something for her uncle, hey?'

She shook her head, reddening. 'Dear Uncle Alex, you can't mean it: They haven't spoken to me for five years. Not since Daniel died. His mother took it into her head that I'd – that it was something I did that made him ... that ... ' She shook her head. 'Please, I can't. It's not that I don't want to help. You know I do. But not that way.'

He made a small grimace, and finished his cup of tea. 'Well, if you can't you can't. I'll pull on my own bits of string again. But I ain't too hopeful, I tell you.'

'I could ask Judith,' she said after a moment. 'Her father-in-law, Alfred, he might. He's got some sort of pull at the War Office. He tried to keep Peter away from France that way, but Peter wouldn't have it of course.' She tilted her chin with a moment of pride, and Uncle Alex looked at her sharply.

'Is that a fact? All these people with consciences, what's the sense of it? You don't have to go to France to get yourself spitted to be useful. I reckon you do a better job bein' a bit less heroic and a lot more practical,' he said. 'You think that Alfred'd do something for young Solly? It's not just for your father, you know. I know the recruiters took him, but you only got to look at the boy to know he wouldn't last five minutes out there.'

'I'll ask Judith,' Hannah felt the weight of hopelessness settle on her again. It had been easing as the weeks went by, but now this. Solly at the Front to worry about as well as Peter? It had been a small comfort that Jake had been selected for a job as a training corporal in the north when he had joined the army; she had thought then that for once God had been on her side. But now Solly – '

'I'll ask,' she repeated.

Being asked seemed to help Judith in a most remarkable way. She listened to Hannah's explanation of the problem and caught fire, just as the old Judith would have done.

'Of course we'll have to arrange it!' she said, and went chattering on about whom she would call and how it could be done, and left in a flurry of furs and plans.

For the next two weeks she was almost her old self again, busy, sparkling, seeming happy in her hard work, bustling from Whitehall office to rich house to Paultons Square and back again.

Charles seemed more content too, not waking in tears in the middle of the night as he had been doing, and Hannah, putting the children to bed one night, thought, it's all going to be all right. We can manage. I think we can manage. She hugged Charles and settled him on one side of her lap and Mary Bee on the other and began to read them their bedtime story.

It was one of those soft muggy evenings in February when mist thickened over the London chimney pots and the streets smelled of people's suppers and horses and the promise, some time soon, of spring when snowdrops and crocuses would appear in the sooty little front gardens of Chelsea. The children were warm and scented from their baths, and sleepy as they listened to her reading with slightly glazed eyes, both with their thumbs in their mouths, and Hannah felt a lift of sheer pleasure as she sat there, murmuring her story of Peter Rabbit and Flopsy, Mopsy and Cottontail. She heard the telephone ring below, heard Florrie's footsteps come toiling up from the kitchen to answer it, still reading and with no sense of anxiety in her. For weeks now every knock on the door, every ring of the telephone had made her stomach

425

lurch but tonight the sound did not. Even when Florrie's footsteps came up the stairs, and the door opened she felt no sense of doom. She just hugged the children and said, 'That's all for tonight, my darlings. Tomorrow we'll finish it. Now let Florrie tuck you in while I go and talk to whoever it is. Florrie?'

'It's that there Mildred, mum,' Florrie said. 'From Mrs Lammeck's 'ouse.' She looked at Hannah uneasily, but Hannah just smiled back, still a little dreamy herself from the story telling and the soft warm children. 'Sounds a bit put out, she does. I'll tuck 'em in, mum, while you go to talk to her. Come on you two, up the wooden hill to Bedfordshire.'

Mary Bee giggled and said shrilly, 'Soppy Florrie! We're already upstairs!' and Florrie laughed and Hannah went away leaving the warmth of the nursery behind her with a small pang. Mary Bee was growing so sturdy and tall; it was such a little time since she had been just an armful of hungry baby.

'Oh, mum,' Mildred's thin voice crackled at the end of the telephone. 'Oh, mum, what do we do? 'Ere's a telegram come for Missus and Cook's 'avin' the vapours cos she says she knows it's the master dead and mangled in that there 'orrible trench and what shall we do, mum, on account of Madam ain't 'ere, and I thought she might be there, and would want to know right away, wouldn't she, mum?'

47

Bereavement this time came easier because there was so much around her. There was Charles's still white face, determinedly showing no feeling at all as he went about the day's play and lessons with Miss Porteous, the visiting governess Hannah had employed for the children. There were Florrie and Bet looking drawn and streaked with tears. Above all, there was Judith, who had come to stay with Hannah and now sat in the big chair beside the nursery fire all day and stared at the embers and said nothing. Looking after Judith, coaxing her to eat and drink, urging her to go to bed at night and persuading her to get up again in the morning, above all dealing with the commiserating telephone calls and letters that came for her, gave Hannah little time to explore her own distress.

But it sat low in her belly, an amalgam of memories of the way she had felt when Daniel had died, her own still smouldering guilt about her relationship with Peter, her sadness for the disappearance of Judith's sparkle – for that had vanished at the moment the telegram had been put into her hands – and finally her private sense of confusion over the loss of Peter himself. When Daniel had died he had seemed to her to be snuffed out. There had been no lingering consciousness of his existence. It was as though he had never been. But then there had been all the trappings of death, a funeral, a *shivah*, to make it all real. For Peter there was just a piece of paper; no funeral, no special rites to mourn his passing (for Judith, showing her only spark of will, had refused to go to her parents-in-law's home to sit and mourn there, and certainly Hannah could not visit them). So he seemed to linger on in her world, shadowy, but with so strong a sense of his presence that sometimes she actually found herself looking up to see him. I'm going mad, she thought one night, frightened.

But she did not go mad. She just went doggedly on, working at the factory and dealing at home with the restructuring of their lives.

It was not easy, for Judith was so pliable. Whatever Hannah said she acquiesced. Hannah thought Judith should move into Paultons Square for a while? Then Judith would. Hannah thought that Judith should start sewing for something to do as the days crept by? Then Judith obediently took up her needle. Hannah thought Judith should eat and drink and bathe? Then Judith would. But she did nothing of her own will, and the weight of her became ever greater, until at last Hannah decided that she needed help. It was not right that there should be just herself looking after Judith and Charles; they needed contact with Peter's family.

Was it because they were themselves so stunned that they remained aloof? Certainly none of the Lammecks made any attempt to contact Judith at Hannah's house, though plenty of caring messages came from her friends and her own cousins. But her in-laws were silent, and because of her own remoteness from the clan it was difficult for Hannah to know how to cope.

She asked Uncle Alex what she should do. He sat over coffee with Hannah after Judith had gone to bed, his lips pursed as he considered.

'I tell you, it's crazy,' he said at length. 'How come people can behave so strange? Here's a man, his only son gets killed in the trenches, he don't make no effort to get in touch with his grandson, and his grandson's mother? Me, I ain't got no sons and I ain't got no grandsons, but believe me, dolly, if I'd lost the one there'd be nothing in this world'd keep me away. I can't understand it. These English Jews, I just can't fathom 'em.'

She smiled a little at that. 'What do you mean, English Jews? What are we but English Jews?'

He shook his head. 'We're different, dolly. We came from the shtetls with *gornicht mit gornicht*, with nothing in our pockets to call our own. All we had was each other, you know? You won't remember how it was, but I tell you, it was beautiful. A person arrives, got nothing but a few kopecks in his pockets, and the clothes on his back, and what does he do? He looks for his landsleit, the people from his shtetl in the old country, and when he finds them in Spital-fields or down the Commercial Road, Stepney way, they look after him. He gets married? They look after his wife and children God forbid trouble should come to him. And they're still doing it, though it's twenty, thirty years or more since some of 'em came here. All over the East End now there's people lookin' after soldiers' widows and children like they've always looked after widows and children. But these English Jews, these rich men in their big fancy houses who call kings and lords *their* landsleit, they leave their young widows like ... ' His voice trailed off in hopeless fury. 'I tell you I don't understand them. They make me sick!'

'They're upset themselves, I suppose,' Hannah said, feeling oddly impelled to defend the Lammecks and Damonts, thought they had used her in her time of loss as badly as they were using Judith now, and even though Judith was one of them in a way she, Hannah, had never been. 'Peter was special. I mean, everyone is, especially someone's only son, but there was more than that. He was special ... '

Her voice dwindled away a little and Alex shot her a sharp knowing little glance.

'But what do I do about Judith?' Hannah said. 'It worries

428

me – I mean suppose she gets ill? Or … '

She stopped, unable to give voice to her deeper fears, but as usual, Uncle Alex knew.

'That's a lot of nonsense,' he said sharply. 'I don't know the girl like I know you, but you treat her like she's a real friend, more than a relation, you know? That extra bit, which means she's a sensible girl like you. You didn't do nothing stupid after Daniel died, and neither will she. Believe me.'

She did, grateful to have his strength on which to hold, but she still felt it was necessary to do something about the fracture that had seemed to appear between Judith and her in-laws. Eventually, Uncle Alex agreed with her.

'They don't deserve no-one should go to so much trouble for them, the *shprauncy mumserim* they are, but you're right, I suppose. Listen, dolly, you got enough on your plate. I'll go see this Alfred myself, all right? I'll tell him you're worried, see what he's going to do.'

'Bless you,' she said and took a deep breath of relief. Having Uncle Alex there always on the edge of her life ready to be turned to in such moments of anxiety as this made all the difference to her. It was not that she called on him all that often, perhaps because he was there and available; it was just knowing that she could.

Alex came back two weeks later with his face thunderous with anger, and a sort of shame, and stomped into the dining room where she was sitting sewing a dress for Mary Bee with Judith sitting on the other side of the table sorting buttons. It was one of those monotonous and therefore comforting jobs that Hannah had learned to give to Judith, and sitting there in the dull heaviness of a March Sunday afternoon there was satisfaction for her too in listening to the click of the buttons as Judith dropped them into their boxes.

'Uncle Alex!' Hannah said, and looked at Judith. 'How nice to see you! Shall we go upstairs?' She indicated Judith's bent head with a glance but he seemed too angry to be aware of her concern.

'I tell you, Hannah, those *ferstinkeneh* Lammeck relations of yours! May the good God bring down on their stinkin' lousy heads the sort of *tsorus* they been askin' for, the selfish, stupid – '

'Uncle Alex, please!' Hannah said. 'We'll talk upstairs.' But to her amazement Judith looked up and said dully, 'It doesn't

429

matter, Hannah. Let him tell you.'

'Tell me what?' She looked at Judith and then shook her head. 'No need, Judith, is there?'

Judith managed a smile. 'Dear Hannah. Always expecting the best of people aren't you? I never did. Still don't. I know my in-laws better than you do, and I expected nothing from them.' She looked at Alex. 'Why did you go to see them?'

He hesitated, for the first time aware of having blundered. 'I'm a *shlemiel*, Mrs Lammeck, you know that? I wasn't thinking. You should forgive me. I went to see your in-laws on account of Hannah here thought it would be a good idea.'

Judith turned her dull gaze on Hannah, and Hannah shook her head irritably. 'Darling, I had to! There's the future to think about, yours and Charles's. You can't just ignore your family. Charles is their grandson.'

Judith bent her head to her buttons again, her fingers moving slowly among the mother-of-pearl and bone and glass. 'They know that. They'll have made sure his money is all right. You don't need to worry about that.'

Hannah reddened. 'I wasn't even thinking about money!' she said sharply. 'I was thinking about *him*. I know how you feel, Judith, but since Peter died, it's been as though Charles was forgotten. His father's dead and you, well, you might as well be in some ways, you've been so lost. I know you can't help it ... But he needs his family, his grandparents.'

Judith didn't raise her head. 'He's got you, Hannah. That's why I can indulge myself the way I have been this past six weeks.'

Almost sick with contrition Hannah ran round the table to kneel beside her. 'Oh, dear, *dear* Judith, I didn't mean that the way it must have sounded. I truly didn't. I just – you're so stricken, darling, and Charles is so small and helpless and there's only me, and I can't ... Peter asked me to look after you and I will, all my life I will, but I thought that looking after you meant making sure you had others, not only me. Charles's grandparents.'

'Grandparents!' Alex, sat down on the other side of the table. 'They ain't like other people, those Lammecks. Some grandparents.'

'What happened, then?' Hannah said, and looked at him, her hand still on Judith's arm, and then, even as the words came out, she shook her head at Alex and turned back to

Judith. 'Please, Judith, can you understand why I asked Uncle Alex to talk to them? It was for you, really, to ... to give you someone safe to look after you. Mary Bee and I – we've got Uncle Alex and I don't think we could have survived without him. I *know* we couldn't have. I want you to have someone as strong for yourself and Charles. That was why. Not because of *money*. I can always make a living for us. I know that now. It was Uncle Alex who showed me how. And Peter. But there's more to surviving than money.'

'It goes a long way to keeping body and soul together,' Uncle Alex said dryly and, incredibly, Judith laughed.

'Of course it does. And it matters a lot, but darling Hannah, you needn't give it a thought. I've a little of my own that my father left me. It's in trust for Charles, of course, and all Peter's money is mine while I live, and then Charles's, and I dare say that my parents-in-law have made sure Charles gets his fair share of the family trust. They always look after things like that because money's so easy. Charles is probably very rich, you see. One day I'll find out and let you know so that you needn't worry ... ' She stopped fiddling with buttons then and turned her head to look at Hannah. 'Dear Hannah, you needn't have sent your uncle to find someone for me to lean on. There's no one I need more than you. You've got enough strength for yourself and me and a hundred others besides. Don't you know that? You don't even need him. Does she?' She looked across at Uncle Alex.

'D'you have to tell her that?' he said gruffly. 'You think I don't know? She don't, but while she thinks she needs me, it makes me feel good.' He grinned crookedly at Hannah and suddenly she found she was crying. Then Judith was crying too, her arms hot around Hannah's neck. It was as though someone had opened the flood gates to let the held-back emotion out. And the two of them clung to each other with their faces wet and for the first time since the telegram had come allowed themselves the luxury of shared tears.

When at last Hannah lifted her head and dried her eyes she saw that Alex too was crying, sitting there with his hands set on each knee. She managed a watery smile and said, 'She said you were the strong one.'

'So I am,' he said and sniffed lusciously. 'Believe me, it takes a strong man to cry, and you two are enough to break anyone's heart. Such people, these Lammecks, that they deny

431

themselves not to see such lovely girls as you two.' He wiped his eyes on a large white handkerchief.

'What did happen?' Judith asked then and Uncle Alex settled down to one of his long dissertations, his delight in talking never more apparent, even though the subject matter clearly angered him.

'I'll tell you,' he said. 'I got there, right to their fancy house in Belgrave Square. There's three men working there, you know that? A butler, two footmen. I saw 'em and I thought, why ain't they in the army like my nebbish Solly who's so scrawny you could tie a knot in each leg? And then I see the butler's limping, so I feel bad on account the man's a cripple and I been thinking rotten things, and you know how that makes a man irritable, so I suppose – ' He looked like a child who had been caught stealing. ' – I suppose I come on a bit strong, you know? There's him sitting there, that Alfred, at his desk looking busy, and I just land into him. I know I shouldn't, I know I made it bad, but I don't know, there was such an atmosphere there, you know what I mean? Cold and, *English*.' He said it as though it was a bad word and Hannah said, 'But what else should there be? The family isn't like ours – it's been here a very long time.'

'I know, I know, but at the time I was, well, I was angry. I have a go at him, he tells me to mind my own business, gets me shown out. Says he'll deal in his own way with his grandson and that's that.' He stopped and then said, 'I can't blame him.'

'It doesn't matter,' Judith said. 'Honestly, it doesn't matter. He'll come round when he's ready. Once I've gone home to my own house.'

Hannah looked at her sharply. 'Is it because you're here that he's kept away?' she said, her voice edged with anger.

'Yes,' Judith said. 'They're all like that about you. They went on and on at me because I was your friend. I told them it was none of their concern. But ... ' She shrugged. 'They'll come to see me once I go back to my own house. Don't worry, Hannah.' She looked at Hannah's face then and closed her eyes in distress for a moment. 'Oh, darling, I didn't mean that! I didn't want you ever to know. I did what I wanted, you see, and told them to go jump in the Serpentine, but I'd have bitten my tongue off before I told you. Oh, I'm sorry!'

Hannah shook her head. 'It doesn't matter,' she said. 'I've

432

always known they hated me. It's just – it's being told, I suppose.'

'It's Davida. She's been like this about you ever since Daniel, you see. They all are, now. I mean they don't know you, do they? So they believed Davida and blame you for what happened to Daniel because it makes them feel better. They wouldn't if they knew you the way I do, of course. But they don't, so ... ' She put her hand out to touch Hannah. 'They aren't worth fretting over, darling. And don't fret over Charles either. Once I go home to my own house, they'll soon be coming to see him, I know that. They'll start agitating about what school they'll want to send him to, how he should be reared to go into the business as soon as he's old enough.'

Hannah sat back, contemplating her hands in her lap. She saw not her hands but Daniel, bored and spoiled, his face reflecting his discontent, going each day to Lammeck Alley. She saw how he had looked the night he came back from Shanghai. She saw the desiccated face of Young Levy who had given his whole life to serving Lammecks, and her own father-in-law's lined and yet unexpressive face, a face born to dissimulate in the business world bounded by Lammeck Alley. And she thought of Charles, small and thin, his socks crumpled about his ankles and his eyes dark and watchful under that lock of hair that so stubbornly refused to behave itself, Charles with the curving nape to his neck that made her eyes melt with love when she looked at it. She thought of the way he would sit on her lap with his thumb in his mouth listening when she read stories to him and to her own Mary Bee, and how the two children played together and squabbled together and grew together.

She lifted her head and said very deliberately to Judith, 'Don't go back to your house, Judith. Sell it. Come and live here with me and Mary Bee and Charles and Florrie and Bet. Never go back to the Lammecks again. We'll be the new Lammecks, you and I and the babies. Will you?'

Judith looked at her and then at Uncle Alex and without a moment's hesitation said calmly, 'Of course. I was so afraid you wouldn't ask me.'

49

It was remarkable how happy they were. The small house was filled to bursting with them all. The dining room continued to be the home of Mary Bee Couturiere, small business though it was doing these days as the demands the factory made on Hannah increased steadily, and the drawing room on the floor above, which had once been so cool and pretty became cluttered, for Judith brought some of her own furniture with her when she sold her house. But none of the clutter mattered to Hannah, because somehow it all felt so *right*.

She tried to work out what it was about the new arrangement that comforted her so and came to the rather surprising conclusion that it was because it was like the East End. Antcliff Street had been mean and narrow, where Paultons Square was wide and pretty; the flat that Nathan and Bloomah and she and her brothers had lived in had been shabby and ill furnished and dreadfully cramped, whereas Number 22 Paultons Square was solid and spacious, but it had been home in a very special way. When she remembered her distant childhood now it was an amalgam of smells of food and drying laundry and carbolic soap but particularly human bustle and purpose that she recalled, and it was that same feeling that now filled Paultons Square. They did not feel their neighbours on each side and in the street outside pressing in on them in the same way they had in Antcliff Street; but still it felt the same. Warm and human and reassuring.

It was decided that the children should go to school together, now that Mary Bee was gone six and Charles was nine. Each day they went, accompanied by Florrie, along the King's Road to a small private school. Each afternoon Florrie went to fetch them home again and then each evening all of them, the two mothers and the children and Florrie and Bet, would sit down together at the big scrubbed wooden table in the basement kitchen to eat the main meal of the day. Hannah had been adamant about that; the days were long since gone, she told Florrie and Bet firmly, when they could lead separate lives.

'Having servants rushing around and waiting on people who can do things for themselves doesn't make sense in wartime,' she said. 'We'll eat the same meals at the same time. We're a partnership, now.' This startled Judith at first, for she had always inhabited a world where servants were ever present but never considered as people like herself. But she was now so completely dependent on Hannah that she did not demur.

Hannah continued to run the factory and the remnants of her couturiere business, while Judith, feeling quite freed from any involvement with her past interests, chose to start work at the munitions factory in Woolwich, travelling each day on crowded workmen's trains and returning white faced with exhaustion to Chelsea each evening.

The change in Judith worried Hannah dreadfully at first. That she should grieve for the loss of Peter was inevitable, but that she should so totally reject her past self as well as her in-laws seemed strange, even mad, and that was very alarming. Then, dimly, Hannah realized what Judith was trying to do. She was trying to retain her hold on the future by killing the past. The Judith that Peter had known was to die as surely as Peter himself had died. The chattering, sparkling creature who had fluttered so gaily around the rich drawing rooms of the West End had to go, leaving behind a different person, just as the death of a caterpillar gave birth to a butterfly. But in Judith's case it was a reversal of that metamorphosis; the butterfly had given way to the dullest and most dogged of caterpillars.

Once she understood, Hannah stopped worrying. She had genuinely feared that Judith might, in her despair, destroy her own life, but now that she saw Judith had destroyed only part of it, Hannah felt they were safe. With Jake still safely busy in his Scottish training camp, and with Solly strutting triumphantly in his neat khaki uniform as the driver to a colonel at the War Office (the last favour Judith had ever asked of any of her Lammeck relations having been granted), they could relax. The worst had happened with Peter's death. They had nothing more to dread.

Or so Hannah thought. But just as the war was coming to an end the next blow fell. Years later, when Hannah looked back, she would marvel at how casually it had started.

She had spent a busy afternoon at the factory joyously supervising a change-over of machinery to handle lighter peacetime goods, for she had decided that once the war was over she would expand Mary Bee Couturiere into a wholesale manufacturing house. Once the war was over, she told herself shrewdly, every woman in the country would be yearning for new feminine clothes; she had to be ready for a deluge of orders.

She had gone home by taxi, indulging herself a little, for she felt more tired than she usually did and had a mild headache. It surprised her to feel so low. That she, who had gone home with enough energy to spare for playing with Mary Bee and Charles after the hardest days at the height of the war and her grief, should feel tired now surprised her. What surprised her even more was how much worse she felt by the time she reached Paultons Square. Her headache was thumping in her ears, her back and legs ached abominably, and she felt shivery though it was a sunny early October afternoon and she dragged herself up the front steps and put her key in the door feeling wretched.

Florrie took one look at her and bustled her off to bed. 'Depend on it, mum, it's this 'ere Spanish 'flu,' she said. 'I'm a'callin' of the doctor, that I am. The things I've 'eard said about it, it won't do to neglect it. Turns into the consumption overnight it does, if you don't watch it.'

'Nonsense,' Hannah said, dazed, and then, as she moved her head and a sharp pain shot through it, added weakly, 'Well, maybe bed would be ... Spanish 'flu? What's that?'

'Ain't you been reading the papers?' Florrie had her upstairs now, and was busy turning back the bed, and setting a match to the paper and sticks laid ready in the fireplace. 'They says that there's ever such a lot of it about, started in Spain it did, been going all over the place, like anything. India's terrible, really terrible, it said in my paper. People fallin' over in the streets.' She shot a look at Hannah who was swaying a little as she tried to unbutton her dress and prudently said no more. To tell her that the papers had said that Indian peasants were dying in their hundreds and thousands would hardly make her employer feel any better.

The next few days were a blur for Hannah. Her temperature shot up, and she became delirious, calling for Daniel, and even, once or twice, for Peter. She was to remember, afterwards, seeing Florrie's worried face looming over her distorted and huge, and Judith's too, and the doctor's, and then slipping away into the hot red darkness of the aches that filled her. She would wake in the night and stare wildly about her at the lamp burning low on the table beside Judith, who was dozing in the arm chair, and shout suddenly and Judith would hurry to her and bathe her forehead with cold water and murmur soothingly and she would fall asleep again to dream terrifying visions of great animals chasing her and huge towers built of glass bricks which changed colours horrifyingly and then collapsed about her in thundering roars of noise. And everywhere she hurt, her eyes, her ears, her very bones.

Then, one morning, she woke to the drumming sound of rain on her window and looked about her and was puzzled. The fire was burning low and the room smelled odd, sulphurous and heavy, and there was an armchair beside the table with someone asleep in it. She blinked and looked and said, 'Judith?' in a puzzled way and was surprised because her voice came out in a small croak.

Judith woke at once and came to the bedside and peered down at her and set her hand on her forehead and then smiled, her face lifting from thin tiredness to relief.

'Oh, he was right, thank God, he was right. The doctor said you'd be all right this morning. The crisis was last night and we were so frantic about you, darling, you've been so *ill*. I'm so glad you're better.'

Hannah blinked and tried to sit up. Her muscles felt like cotton wool and she could hardly move, but blessedly they did not hurt; it was just an all pervading weakness.

'Ill?' Her voice was a little stronger, but still husky. 'I – I remember, I think. Florrie said it was influenza.'

Judith was busy now, fetching the washbowl from the marble topped washstand in the window, and bathing her face with cool water. It felt marvellous and Hannah was grateful, suddenly aware of how sourly she smelled, of illness and sweat and fever.

'It's been awful,' Judith said. 'Quite awful. You'd got pneumonia, you see, on top of the influenza and the doctor said it was very grave, but there was no help he could get us

437

for you because all the nurses are so busy. We sent the children away, of course.'

'Away?' Hannah peered up at her, suddenly feeling tearful. 'Away? Mary Bee? Where is Mary Bee?'

'Now, don't fret,' Judith said soothingly. 'It's all right. It was just that we were so worried about you, and you've been ill for almost two weeks, you know, darling, and the doctor said we should get the children somewhere safe because the epidemic is spreading quite dreadfully. Bet had it and – '

'Bet?' Hannah closed her eyes weakly, and now tears did run down her cheeks and she could not stop them.

'The children have gone to Bet's sister Jessie, the one who lives at Thorpe Bay. She's got a seaside lodging house there, you remember? And with all her summer people gone she's got room. They're better there, I promise you. Charles writes the most delicious letters every day, I'll show you.'

Judith was helping her into a fresh nightgown now, and Hannah said in a muffled voice, 'Bet?'

Judith laughed at that. 'She's as tough as they come, our Bet. She was over it and up and about in a couple of days. Doctor says she had it very mildly.'

'And Florrie? And you?' Hannah was lying back on her pillows now, feeling much more comfortable. She coughed a little, trying to clear her voice, but it remained stubbornly husky. 'Are you all right? You look so tired. Have you been here with me all the time?'

Judith laughed lightly. 'I was bored on my own,' she said, but Hannah stared at her, and felt the ready tears of the invalid come bubbling up again. Judith looked pale and very tired. Her hair was dragged up to a rough knot on the top of her head and looked thin and lifeless, and her cheeks were shadowed deeply, as were the hollows of her throat. 'Florrie's fine. She's helped marvellously.'

'Please don't get ill, Judith,' Hannah said weakly and made no attempt to dry her tears. 'I couldn't bear it. Please be well, Judith.'

'Of course I'm all right,' Judith said, and then shook her head suddenly and almost as though the words spoke themselves, said 'It's because I'd rather not be that I am.'

'Rather not be?'

'It doesn't matter, my darling. I'm going to fetch you some breakfast. Sleep a little, and when I come back I'll bring you in the children's letters.'

It was to be a long time before they came home again. Although Hannah improved steadily from that morning on, recovering more and more of her strength each day, the pestilence reached out and touched them again.

By the middle of October, the papers told them, the death rate from the infection was up to three thousand a week in England alone, the toll more than taking the place of the casualty lists that had been so much a part of the newspapers' daily offerings for so long. No one was exempt. When Florrie showed the too familiar early symptoms and Bet rushed to fetch the doctor to her, they were told the doctor had died himself of the 'flu the day before, worn out by weeks of incessant night calls. There was no other doctor they could find to help, and anyway there seemed little a doctor could do. Everyone knew the only answer was bed and hope, though they tried various nostrums. The chemists' shops everywhere did a brisk trade in sulphur candles, used in pathetic attempts to keep the infection at bay, and cough mixtures and steam kettles for the pneumonia cases, and tonics to restore the tissues of those left weak and miserable as the tide of the disease receded and left them behind.

Fortunately Florrie, who like Bet and Hannah herself had been reared in the crowded infection-ridden streets of London, seemed to have the same sort of resilience Bet had. She recovered within a few days, and by the end of the week was creeping about the house again, weak but determined to do her usual day's work. But Judith was of quite a different order. When the 'flu touched her at last, its hot, greedy fingers probed deeply.

Hannah thought sometimes, as she sat in the same arm-chair that Judith had used to watch over her own fever-filled delirious days, that Judith had by sheer effort of will refused to succumb while Hannah had needed her. Now she lay against the white pillows, her face looking like that of a painted Dutch doll, the skin white and pinched around the high spots of colour in each cheek and with her eyes half open so that the whites showed, sickeningly, and with her breathing rasping in her taut throat. She seemed to Hannah to have gone somewhere far, far away. Hannah would call to her sometimes, when in the dark early morning hours her own residue of weakness built fear in her, calling her name urgently and tugging on her damp, hot hands, and after a while Judith would open her eyes unwillingly and stare, unfocused, at her and then close them again, wordless, untouched by Hannah's urgency, or by her love and fear and tears. It was as though she had already died.

So that when she did die quietly, one dark afternoon when the first of the winter fogs had come drifting stealthily over the roof tops, her skin almost mauve with lack of oxygen, it came as no shock. It was to Hannah as though it was something Judith had wanted, something she had planned from the very day that the telegram had come telling her that her life was over, lost in the mud of Verdun. All through the succeeding weeks, as she tried to pick up the pieces of life yet again, once more having to contemplate the pattern of bereavement, she comforted herself that way. She told herself that Judith was happy now. That she had been loaned to Hannah for just a little while, to help her make her own life livable, and now, her self-appointed task done, had thankfully gone home.

Usually Hannah would not have thought so confusedly, so sentimentally, for later, much later, when she was free of the deadening depression her own 'flu had left behind in her and had recovered from the shock of all the other losses that she was to sustain, she realized that she had been sentimental and foolish. But it helped her when she most needed help, and she was grateful for that.

For not only Judith died. Less than a fortnight after Judith's death the message came from Solly, garbled and frantic but clear enough. Nathan was in the London Hospital, in the adjoining ward to the one in which Bloomah had died a decade before him, delirious and ranting hoarsely as the pneumonia that followed the influenza virus into his racked lungs consumed him.

She stood and stared at the telegram in her hand and knew that this was the end. If the disease had killed Judith, how could it fail to collect Nathan, too, a man so much older, so much less able to withstand the strain of illness after his long suffering years? Though she had known he could not survive, might already be dead by the time she got there, she set out for the hospital, greatly to Florrie and Bet's despair, for she was still weak and fragile. She travelled there in a cold rattling cab behind a wheezing old horse for she could not find a motor cab to take her, so desperately hit were the drivers by the same virus that was killing everyone else. It was a long and tedious and miserable journey through grey wintry streets and all the way she tried to think of Nathan as she had known and loved him when she was small, not as the bad tempered worn out sick old man he had become and whom she was afraid to see again. But she need not have distressed herself so through the long ride, for by the time she reached the ward he was dead and his body long since removed.

She stood at the ward door as the sister told her shortly, for she was too rushed to be anything but perfunctory, that Bed Seventeen's son had removed him, and no, sister did not have any idea where the body had been taken.

Hannah went back to Paultons Square, huddled in the corner of the cold cab, trying as hard as she could to remember her father with some sort of feeling, but she could not. He was dead, and somewhere inside herself she felt dead, too. No Judith, no Nathan, not much of herself; and what did any of it matter anyway? Her 'flu-born depression settled over her like a thick wet blanket.

Worse was to come. Uncle Isaac, Bloomah's only brother and his tired wife, thin Sarah, joined Nathan in the cemetery, though their children managed to emerge alive and shaken from their attacks of the infection. Davida and Ezra and Margaret Lammeck died too, and many more. Spanish influenza had shown no special signs of favour to the rich well-fed and well-cared-for. If thousands died in the East End slums, hundreds died in West End mansions. When the end of it all had come, when Armistice night with its frenetic celebrations and fireworks and tears was over, when the third and final wave of the influenza spluttered out in the spring of 1919 and the totals were counted, they found that more people had died as the result of that invisible virus than had succumbed to all the soldiers' bullets and shells in the muddy squalor of France.

Not that Hannah cared about comparisons. Her two Apocalyptic horsemen, war and pestilence, had taken from her a mere handful of people, not millions, but she was to mourn them bitterly for a very long time. She was not left without comfort, for she had her Mary Bee, and also Charles. The Lammeck relations argued and shouted and set lawyers to work, but there was nothing they could do. Judith had left a watertight will, appointing Hannah as Charles's legal guardian with full control of all his finances and his education and his life. Judith, in dying, had given Peter's son to be Hannah's own as surely as if she had borne him of her own body.

And so another child moved from one side to the other of the family descended from Susannah and Tamar of Jerusalem.

BOOK FIVE

Fighting

49

'My God, just *look* at them, will you? Honestly, Mother, they're – '

'Mary Bee, if you say another word, I'll – '

'And if you call me that, I'll just walk out, I swear I will. You promised me you wouldn't.'

'All right, all *right*. Marie, then. If you say another word about what anyone else does or is wearing or says, then not a penny of next month's allowance do you get, you hear me?'

'I don't care; I shall go to Gramps and tell him. He'll give it to me.'

'Oh, no, you won't, young lady! And you'll find out what happens if you try such a trick. Now be quiet and behave. For heaven's sake, child, it's only for a few hours! Is it so difficult to be polite to a few people just for a little while? To please me? I know you only came to do me a favour, but don't ruin it, darling, please!'

I'm doing it again, Hannah thought, staring at Mary Bee's sulky little face. I try to be firm and I end up cajoling. Oh, damn, damn, damn. And she looks so lovely and can be so sweet when she wants to be, I want them all to see her at her best, not sulking like this.

'Darling, listen,' she said then. 'Just be sweet and charming to everyone for an hour or two, and then as soon as I can I'll cry off with headache or something and we can go home. How will that be?'

'Can we go to a nightclub afterwards, then? On the way home?' Mary Bee's chin lifted and her lips curved so that the dimple that punctuated one corner of her mouth showed very clearly. Hannah closed her eyes in exasperation and said, 'No! Are you mad! You're fifteen years old, and people of fifteen do not go to nightclubs. So stop this nonsense and behave yourself.'

The music changed, swinging into the newest Charleston

445

rhythm, and Charles, on Hannah's other side, got to his feet.

'Come on, fishface,' he said. 'Come and show 'em how it ought to be done.' He took Mary Bee's hand and pulled her onto the dance floor, winking briefly at Hannah over her shoulder, and Hannah smiled her gratitude at him and leaned back in the little gilt chair, aching to kick off her shoes but knowing it would hurt more to put them back on again.

It had been an exhausting day. When the invitation to Sally Lazar's wedding had come, a massive creation of thick imitation deckle-edged vellum and semi-opaque paper and gilt print and white satin ribbons, her own heart had sunk at the prospect. She had looked at the invitation and then at Mary Bee and said as brightly as she could, 'Darling! Such fun. One of our cousins is getting married.'

Mary Bee looked up from her breakfast and said hopefully, 'A Lammeck cousin? Or one of the Damonts?'

'No,' Hannah had said, her smile brighter than ever. 'My cousin Leon Lazar's daughter Sally.'

'Oh, God, Mother, not one of those awful East End crew! You can't be serious. You're not *going*, are you?'

'Not going? Not going? How come, not going?' Jake looked up from his own breakfast, a sizeable plateful of bagels which he bought in the East End, since no King's Road Baker had ever heard of such things. 'Whoever don't go to weddings?'

Mary Bee ignored him, as she usually did ignore her uncles. They had lived in her mother's house for six years, but she had steadfastly refused to treat them with anything but the coolest of disdain.

'It's up to you, I suppose, Mother,' she said, returning to her oranges. 'They're your family, I suppose.'

'The invitation is to all of us. You and Charles as well as me and your uncles.'

'Me? Are you mad?' Mary Bee stared at her. 'Me, go to that sort of vulgar brawl? I remember the last one you dragged me to, and I swore I'd never go to such a thing again as long as I live.'

'Pitchi putchi!' Jake said cheerfully. 'So what's so terrible about it? You'd go soon enough if it was madam the Earl's missus inviting you, so why not for Sally, the presser's daughter, hey?' He laughed fatly at his own wit and started on another bagel.

Mary Bee threw him a withering look. 'Earls' wives are called countesses,' she said coldly, unable to resist answering this time. 'And if Daphne asked me to something it wouldn't be a vulgar brawl.'

Hannah was staring at her, her brows tight. 'What do you mean, Daphne? How long have you been on first name terms with her?'

Mary Bee reddened a little. Her very white skin showed the changes in her emotions more clearly than she liked, for it made it difficult to hide all she wanted to hide, especially from her mother.

'Oh, we met at a party,' she said with a fine nonchalance. 'At the Ritz – oh, don't stare at me like that, Ma! I wasn't doing anything I shouldn't. It was the one Charles took me to, his friend David Gubbay's party for his twenty- first. You said I could go, and she was there and she talked to me, and was very nice, and why shouldn't I call her by her first name? She's my cousin, isn't she? Even though if you had your way I'd never see any of my really nice relatives.'

'I've never stopped you from seeing anyone you want to, or who wants to see you,' Hannah said, wearily. This was an old argument. 'I've told you that over and over, so don't, please, launch on that again, Mary Bee.'

'Don't call me that!' She jumped to her feet and glared at Hannah across the table. 'I'm not your trade mark! I'm not going around like an advertisement for your wretched dresses! I want to be called Marie, and you said you would.' She began to wail, and then turned and ran out of the room, slamming the door behind her.

'The sooner young Charles comes home for the holidays the better.' Florrie, who had just come in with a fresh pot of tea slapped it down in front of Hannah. 'He's the only one can get her to behave proper these days. Honestly, fifteen!'

The row over Sally Lazar's wedding was indeed settled by Charles when he came home. Only when Charles was home from school for the holidays did the house seem to pull together. It was not that he pushed himself in any way, not that he actually tried to smooth the turbulent waters. He was just his own quiet self, smiling and friendly, with his dark hair brushed cruelly hard to his head in an attempt to control the curl, but, fortunately, quite failing, and his eyes that smiled easily. And that was enough. Just because he was

447

there, people around him relaxed. Hannah accepted the invitation for them all, praying that Mary Bee – no, Marie, damn it – would come round, and said no more about it.

Charles cheerfully dressed himself up in his best morning coat, and set out his white tie and tails ready for the midday change that was an inevitable part of the proceedings, and to Hannah's intense relief Marie followed suit. She had chosen one of the best of her mother's designs for the morning and came downstairs a vision in beige knitted silk jersey, her long legs resplendent in beige silk stockings, and with a beige cloche hat, neatly trimmed with a hint of chocolate, pulled down over her nose. Her shoes and gloves were beige too and she had carefully masked her face with beige poudre Tokay and smelled faintly of Chanel's latest perfume.

Hannah stared at her and for a moment wanted to send her upstairs to wash her face and put on something more suitable for her age, like the charming navy and white sailor dress she had made for her last year. Wisely, she bit her tongue and was glad she had when Charles said easily, 'Dear Marie! Feelin' a touch off, are you? Never mind. I'll walk you slowly to the car. That'll bring the colour back into your poor little face.' Marie pouted at him, but rubbed off some of the powder.

The long car journey to the East End with Charles driving rather proudly – this was a new skill for him – had been the best part, with the children chattering about his school affairs, for Marie was avid for Eton gossip.

Hannah had hesitated about sending her much loved Charles away to school, wanting to keep him near her, but her guilt about the way his family had rejected him because he was her ward had overcome her. If his surviving grand-parents and his dead parents' cousins wanted to pretend he was not a Lammeck, that was up to them; but she knew he was, and he was to be reared as his own parents would have wished. Which meant Eton, for all Lammeck and Damont sons went there. So, she had driven him to Windsor one September morning and settled him in his new school, a diminutive, forlorn figure in his high collared shirt and scrappy trousers under the classic jacket and top hat. She wept all the way home again, but it had been the making of him in many ways, training him up to be what he was now, easy going, relaxed and charming.

Listening to Charles and Mary Bee chatter as they drove

through the deserted City of London towards Aldgate and Commercial Street she smiled at the back of their heads, and felt a great wave of love for them both wash over her. The years had not been easy since the war had ended, what with the struggle to get the business back on its feet once the factory took over dress mass production, but the children had been there to help her feel there was a point in all her labours. She had no one else but them to love so uncomplicatedly, for her brothers' laziness filled her with exasperation and she felt guilt, still, about Nathan. Having the children had helped soothe the long lonely nights when she would lie awake trying not to remember Peter and behind him, in the shadows of her memory, Daniel. She had made up her mind to it that that sort of love was over for her. She had brought nothing to her men but cold death, and she was never going to take the risk of loving again. So thank God for the children.

Until Marie had stopped being just a wilful spoiled child and had become the wilful spoiled young woman she now was. A naughty ten-year-old can be scolded and put to bed early. A naughty fifteen-year-old, Hannah was finding, was quite another story. She refused flatly to go away to a stuffy old girls' school, and demanded the right to stay at home and have governesses, if she must have an education (for which she frankly saw no use at all) and insisted on going out and about unchaperoned, a demand to which Hannah had not yet acceded and which caused most of the fights between them.

The one thing they did not fight about was Marie's decision to seek out her Lammeck relations. She knew, for Hannah had told her so, that there had been a split in the family long ago, though not really why, and that her father's relations chose not to acknowledge her mother. In her young years she had been content to accept that. But when she was thirteen she had slipped out of the house one afternoon and with all the aplomb of a person twice her age had taken a taxi to the house of Albert Lammeck, having found his address in the telephone book, and there introduced herself as his granddaughter.

Old Albert, long alone now, forgot the hatred his poor dead Davida had felt for the child's mother and her refusal to have any contact with the child she had borne, and fell instantly in love with Marie. He refused to see her mother, which suited Marie well enough for she enjoyed having the old man to herself, and began to bestow outrageously lavish gifts on the child. And Hannah said nothing at all, bitterly hurtful though Marie's behaviour was. She felt she had no right to stand between her own child and her other relatives however much she mistrusted them. Only once did she intervene, and that was when the presents became too lavish altogether. She insisted that Marie return Albert's gift of a diamond ring and wrote a stiff letter to him demanding that the practice stop, pointing out that while the child was under twenty-one she, her mother and legal guardian, had every right to exert such control. The old man had muttered and complained and told Marie how cruel her mother was, and gave her presents of money secretly, a fact which Hannah well knew and could do nothing about. Marie, of course, was in her glory. When she had trouble with her mother she could always run to her Gramps. Indeed, being a good mother to Marie was a very difficult thing to be, Hannah told herself, even when Charles was home, for Marie, like everyone else, loved Charles and wanted to please him.

But not today. However well it had started, it soon decayed into another of Marie's squalls. They arrived at the house of cousin Leon, in a neat terrace at the Hackney end of Shoreditch High Street (for Leon had come up in the world and was doing well with a factory of his own) to find it in an uproar. The living room had been rearranged so that there were chairs all round the walls, under the many heavy pictures of which Leon's wife Rae was so proud, and a large sofa under the window had been covered with a white damask tablecloth. The bride, a large girl with a somewhat bewildered expression on her face, was sitting in the middle of it, her white lace dress with its uneven handkerchief hem mid-calf length (to show her thick legs in white silk stockings and white kid ankle strap shoes) carefully arranged to display the richness of the design which was fussy in the extreme. Hannah, whose own taste and therefore designs tended towards severe simplicity of line, could not help glancing at Marie and saw the faint sneer on her face and felt a little coldness form in her chest. Today was going to be bad, whatever Charles did to keep the peace. The rest of the bride's outfit was fussy too, with a headress plentifully sprinkled with large satin lilies of the valley and twinkling sequins and a veil spotted with more sequins, and a massive heavily beribboned bouquet of already wilting gardenias and camellias and arum lillies, and she could feel Marie's rising contempt as clearly as if she had given words to it.

The centre of the room was filled with the inevitable food-laden table, round which neighbours and friends and family milled and grabbed and grasped and chewed at the tops of their voices. The room smelled powerfully of gefillte fish and brandy and sweet cakes and moth balls and cigars and perfume, and already a hint of sweat, for it was a warm day although it was still early spring.

By the time they reached the synagogue and had been bombarded with the usual oohs and aahs over how much Marie had grown, and the service under the canopy had been chanted and wept through, Marie was in a towering sulk. Charles was as he always was, quiet and amused and interested in all that went on around him and unfailingly polite to everyone, but for once this seemed to make Marie worse.

After the ceremony they went on to the wedding breakfast at two o'clock, a vast meal. Marie picked ostentatiously at her plate and ate nothing, while Charles ploughed his way happily through a heaped plate, and even took second helpings, much to the approval of Aunt Sarah and Uncle Benjamin on each side of him, while Marie grew crosser and crosser.

At home, afterwards, where they had gone to change into evening clothes for the rest of the day's celebration, the Dinner and Ball, she had thrown a tantrum and sworn she would not go back, but somehow Charles had managed to mollify her. Back they trundled, now in evening dress, to the same hired hall with its trimmings of balloons and trailing smilax and flowers and the false sweep of staircase at the far side where the wedding group were photographed in half a hundred poses.

Now, the second colossal meal having been served and eaten, as though none of the guests had been fed for a week, the dancing had taken over. Another half hour, Hannah promised herself, and I'll tell Marie we can go. Thank God tomorrow is Monday, and I can lose myself at the factory, and the plans for Buckingham Palace Gate. She sank herself for a while in a little reverie about how she would arrange her splendid newly leased showrooms, and began to feel better.

The music pounded on and on, and she nodded and smiled at the aunts and uncles and cousins as they whirled past, glad no one had come to sit beside her and gossip. She was almost hoarse with a day of talking to them all, for they were clearly proud of her and her success and everyone in the family and the family's families by marriage had gone out of his way to come and say, 'Please God by your lovely daughter and your boy,' and 'God willing we should always meet on such simchas.'

The music stopped and the sound of voices rose to fill the gap. Somewhere across the big ballroom someone started shouting for a horah, and the band good naturedly followed the rhythm of their clapping hands and burst into one of the old tunes. For a moment Hannah felt as though she was five years old again, sitting beside her parents at a neighbour's house and listening to the singing voices and the thumping stomping feet of the dancers in a circle, heads bobbing and knees bending as they went through the ancient rhythm. *Ha va nagilah, ha va nagilah* ...

She was watching indulgently as one after another they all joined in until the place was bursting with the noise of singing and stamping, and enjoying it in a slightly dazed way, when Charles came pushing through the hubbub looking a little crumpled but happy enough.

'Hello!' Hannah grinned at him. 'I thought you'd be trying this one!'

'No such luck, I'm afraid,' he said, and not for the first time she was startled by the deep note of his voice. Would she ever get used to that baritone sound? Surely she should have by now; he was seventeen after all. 'I'm just not clever enough to learn it. Where's Marie?'

She jerked her chin up at him. 'Marie? She was with you!'

'Oh, blast her!' Charles said softly and then shook his head, irritated. 'I told her not to be so silly and to come and sit with you. She was in one of her tempers over someone accidentally kicking her. I'll go and find her. She really is getting tiresome, Aunt Hannah. You'll have to do something – send her away to school, I reckon. It does me all the good in the world, you know.' And he went ploughing into the still stamping shouting dancers to look for Marie.

But Hannah knew he wouldn't find her. The wretched

child had made up her mind to leave, and leave she had. Her peach silk coat with its chinchilla fur collar had vanished from the cloakroom, and the tired part-time commissionaire at the door of the hall thought, though he wouldn't like to swear to it mind, that he'd seen the young lady goin' off down the Commercial Road. Looked very nice she did, he thought, when she put her coat on, and he'd said as much and had his head bitten off for his pains, so he didn't exactly look to see where she'd gone when she'd went off, I mean, what man would? But he thought she'd gone off down the Commercial Road, all the same ...

50

'I'll find her,' Charles said soothingly. 'Don't worry, Aunt Hannah, I'll *find* her. She's probably gone to the Bag o' Nails or somewhere like that.'

'Bag o' Nails?' Hannah stared at him. She felt sick with fright; it was silly for her to be so alarmed, for Mary Bee – Marie – wasn't a baby after all; she'd be all right, surely? But she is a baby, a secret voice somewhere deep inside her whispered. Only fifteen. A baby. 'What's that?'

'A night club,' Charles said briefly, shrugging into his coat. 'She's developed a passion for the wretched place. A dead bore, if you ask me, but there, our Marie never really asks anyone, does she? I'll find her, I promise. Don't worry. Go home, darling, and leave it to me.'

It was Uncle Alex who took her home. He had a gift for appearing at just the right moment, and now he came out into the little lobby, his thumbs hooked into the pockets of his white waistcoat and his head wreathed in smoke from the cigar clamped between his teeth, and grinned at her.

'Having fun, dolly? Where's that little girl of yours? Not a dance have I had with her, and I've got to do that before the night's over.'

As Charles explained, Alex's face lengthened. He shook his head at Hannah. 'I've told you, dolly, that little puss wants her *tochus* smacked. You spoil her, you always have. Listen, Charles, you go look. Make sure she ain't out in the streets, on account it's not a good time. There's been some trouble,'

'Trouble?' Hannah said sharply.

'Ah, nothin' new! The local *shaygetzes* got nothin' better to do, they roam around, pick on nice Yiddisher boys, beat 'em up. I've got an arrangement with the gym, they're gettin' a few of our boys together to keep an eye out, you know? But they're not out tonight and I'm told there was a bit of trouble over towards Arbour Square. So watch out for yourself, Charles, you dressed like that, they'll get funny if they see you. Take one of the others with you.'

'Oh, really Uncle Alex, no need!' Charles was at the door, his hand on the knob. 'She's probably picked up a taxi and gone to a night club. That's her latest craze.'

'Look in the streets first,' Alex said. 'Taxis there ain't a lot of around these parts.' Charles went, smiling reassuringly at Hannah over his shoulder. 'Come on, dolly. I'll take you home,' Alex said. 'I got the car round the corner.'

'Ours is here too,' Hannah said distractedly. 'I can't leave it here.'

'I'll deal with it,' Alex said soothingly. 'Relax. One of the boys'll drive it home for you. Don't worry, Charles'll find her, you'll give her a spanking, it's finished! You're tired, dolly, that's why you're worrying.'

But when they had been at home in Paultons Square more than an hour and there was still no sign of either Marie or Charles, he stopped being so soothing. Hannah sat hunched in the armchair beside the long dead fire and Alex stood at the window staring out and smoking steadily so that the room greyed with wreaths of tobacco mist.

'I'm going to call the police,' Hannah said at last, unable to bear it any longer. 'Something awful must have happened. We can't wait any longer.'

'Not police,' Alex said. 'That makes dramas, and please God, there ain't no need for dramas. Listen, where's this place he said she might have gone? I'll phone, see if anyone's seen her.'

'It's one in the morning!' Hannah said. 'You can't phone now.'

'Night clubs I can phone,' Alex said grimly. 'I don't go to them much, but that for them one o'clock in the morning ain't no time to worry about, that I know.'

The operator took some time to answer. Hannah sat on the

edge of her chair, watching Alex jiggle the earpiece rest, and wanting to shake him to hurry him up and knowing she was unjust for feeling so. Fear was building in her so that she felt as though her skin was stretched tightly over the maelstrom of feeling within and would burst at any moment and leave her a screaming wreck. She had to clench her fists to control herself. She was so intent on Alex's struggles with the telephone that she did not hear the front door open and close. Not until the drawing room door opened did she realize the wait was over. Hannah whirled and stared and Alex stood open-mouthed and then very quickly cradled the earpiece on the telephone and started forwards.

'My God, what happened? Bloody hell, the lousy *mumserim*. Hannah, call a doctor!'

'No,' Charles said, his voice husky. 'No. It's not as bad as it looks. Not as bad as it looks.' He stared at Hannah and shook his head. 'Believe me, Aunt Hannah, not as bad as it looks.'

His coat was torn and thick with mud. His white tie had disappeared from his collar which had sprung open and his shirt was smeared with mud and blood, most of which seemed to have come from his nose. His right cheek had a graze that ran from the corner of his eye to his jawline, and one eye was swollen and bruised. His hair was ruffled and had sprung back into its childish curliness, and the combination of that and his attempt to smile reassuringly at her was too much for Hannah. She felt the tears spill over and she held her hands out to him and almost wailed his name.

They helped him out of his coat and settled him in a chair, and Hannah ran to fetch water and a towel and gently cleaned his face as he sat patiently, trying not to wince. As he had said, it looked worse than it was. When she had finished it was clear that apart from a black eye and the graze no damage was done. His nose had bled ferociously, but was now staunched and had not been broken, and the graze was superficial, like those on his knuckles.

'I gave them as good as I got,' he said contemplating his own fists, and then looked up at Alex. 'Uncle Alex, for God's sake, *why*? I did nothing to them! I was just walking, looking for Marie.'

'What happened?' Alex said and sat on the arm of Charles' chair.

'I don't know.' Charles leaned back, tiredness in his voice

now. 'Five of 'em – thin fellows, no brawn on them at all. Looked half starved, to tell the truth. But there were five of them. They just jumped me, you know? I wasn't doing a thing. They were shouting first, standing at a coffee stall, and when I went by they shouted "sheenie" and "yid" at me and I took no notice. I just walked past but then they started again and I stared at 'em. Dammit, who wouldn't? And that seemed to do it, because they came all at once, the five of them. And that damned coffee stall man and the other people around, there were enough of 'em, they watched and they cheered them on. It was the most sickening unfair thing you can imagine. They *watched*! And they shouted too – "Kill the bloody sheenie! Kill the bloody sheenie!".'

He closed his eyes and Hannah suddenly saw the small six year old Charles standing beside the nursery table with his paint brush in his hand and his thin legs sticking out beneath his blue holland overall. 'Is Papa going to be killed?' he had asked, and he had looked just like this; young and serious and remote.

'Did you find Marie?' Alex said after a moment. He turned his head and stared at Hannah and shook his head lightly at her. She took a deep breath and pushed down the new wave of fear that his question had created in her.

Charles shook his head. 'I think she must have got her taxi. I'd been walking around for ages before this happened. In fact, I was sure she'd got away from the district and I was looking for a taxi myself, walking along Whitechapel Road, you know? I don't know where she is, but I'm sure she's not in the East End. At a nightclub probably, safe and sound.' Charles opened his eyes and stared at Alex. 'Why, Uncle Alex? What did I do to make them do that to me? Or me to them? I beat them, you know. The five of them – they went off in the end, and one of them got a fair old pasting from me, I promise you. I've been boxing at school. And one of them, I think I broke his nose. I felt it go, and that was awful because it was only a fight – I mean, I didn't want to do anything like that, but what could I do? There was only me and those other people were cheering them on, and no one shouted for me or helped, so what could I do? I just hit him as hard as I could, and I felt his nose crunch. *Why*? That's what I can't understand. I was just walking past.... '

There was a little silence. Alex put his hand on Charles'

head for one brief moment, then took it away. 'You're a Jew, my boy. A yid, a sheenie, a Jew. That's what you did. That was the insult.'

'Insult? How can it be an insult just to *be*? I know I was better dressed than they were, and that's a bit insulting, I suppose, if you can't dress up yourself. But it was a wedding, wasn't it? A wedding, people always dress up for weddings.'

'Especially Jews,' Alex said heavily, and got to his feet. 'Especially Jews. Whatever we do, we do bigger than other people and they don't always like it. And we're foreigners, remember? Lousy foreigners.'

Charles stared at him, and then grinned, a lopsided grin that made his eye twitch with pain as his grazed skin stretched. 'Me, a foreigner? How can I be a foreigner? Dammit, I can't even learn a foreign language! You must have heard what old Barnsley said about my French, and my Latin isn't much better. Me a foreigner? I'm English.'

Alex shook his head. 'You're a Jew, my boy. And they'll never forget it, even if you do.'

The front door opened again, making a muffled sound beyond the drawing room. All three of them lifted their heads at the same moment like birds in a field, startled and alert.

Marie came in and stood just inside the drawing room door, her head down as she watched herself peel off her gloves.

'Really, this is too absurd!' she said in a high drawling voice, very artificial and controlled. 'Waiting around for me like this. I just decided to go on, that was all! Too absurd.'

She lifted her head and stared at them all, and they stared back silently and then she saw Charles and her face blanked. She moved to peer more closely at his bruised eye.

'Charles? What's the matter? What is it?'

He looked at her and then at Hannah, and lifted his eyebrows in a mocking little grimace. 'What happened? I went looking for you, fish face, and got my own face pushed in for my pains.'

'You, looking for me? But I don't – '

'You heard what he said, Mary Bee.' Hannah stood behind Charles's chair, her hands on his shoulders. 'He went to look for you when you ran off that way and frightened me, and some hooligans set on him and did this. Because he was looking for you.'

Marie was on her knees now in front of Charles, staring up at him. Her face crumpled and she began to cry, looking as she always did when she was distressed, more like a five-year-old than her almost grown-up self, but this time Hannah was not beguiled. For years Mary Bee had only had to cry to reduce Hannah to total compliance. It had always seemed to her that her child was uniquely disadvantaged in having no father, and she would do anything to protect her from unhappiness. But not this time.

'Take a good look, young lady,' she said now. 'Take a close look. You did this.' And Marie shook her head and wept even more bitterly, putting her face down on Charles's knees.

'Oh Lor!' Charles said lightly, and pushed her head away, grinning at her lopsidedly because of his sore face. 'What a carry on! Do stop, ducky. You'll have all the crease out of my trousers. No need to make such a fuss. I'm all right. Bit shattered is all. And I'm not sorry it happened.'

'Not sorry?' Hannah said, and bent her head and set her cheek against his undamaged one. 'That's taking good heartedness too far.'

'No, it's not – oh, Marie, shut up for the love of Mike!' Mary Bee sniffed and wiped her face with the back of her hand, looking very woebegone. 'I mean – it was interesting,' Charles said.

'Interesting!' Alex gave a little snort of laughter. 'Interesting, the *shlemeil* says! Maybe they mashed his brains, eh? Interesting, he says!'

Charles stared up at the ceiling, speaking in a rather flat voice, almost to himself. 'It's this sheenie business. I've never had it, you see. No one ever said anything like that to me. It makes you think, doesn't it? It's interesting. . . . '

'No one at that school of yours never made no cracks about you, Charles? You amaze me,' Alex said dryly. 'You really do. I get around, my boy, and the places I go to, I find the same sort of people as your coffee stall heroes. Only they don't always act so honest and direct. It's a bit more on the side when you get to some of the high places. Like, they make arrangements for entertainments that don't include you, by goin' to the sort of clubs that don't admit Jews. Or they organize things that you ought to be part of on Friday

458

evenings or the High Holy Days, so that you got to be left out. And they stop talking when you come by and look at you sideways and grin and nod and borrow your money and sneer at you. Oh, I tell you, Charles, sometimes I'd rather have the coffee stall *shaygetzes* and their fists. With them you know where you are. With the polite *mumserim*, you can't get hold of nothing. And you never noticed that at your school?'

'I never look for it,' Charles said. 'And I think that sort of thing you have to look for. But people with fists, thin people who look as though they'd break in a high wind because they're so scrawny, going for a chap like me with their fists, that's *important*. Isn't it?'

'What's important now is getting you to bed, darling,' Hannah said. 'You'll feel like death in the morning if you don't get some sleep. Come on.'

'Charles, Mama,' Marie said in a husky voice. 'Please. I'm sorry. I didn't mean it. I'm truly sorry.'

Hannah looked down at her and then managed a small smile. 'No, love, I don't suppose you did. You never do, do you? Go to bed, too. It's almost two in the morning. And tomorrow's a working day for me, if not for you.'

'Me too,' Alex said, and stood up. 'I'll be on my way. Listen, Charles, my boy, keep out of trouble, you hear me? No more going alone to the East End. Even if this *meshug-genah* madam here goes adrift again. Let *her* be beaten up next time. It'll be her turn.' He shook his head at Mary Bee, but there was no real anger in it. No one was ever angry with her for long, and she looked very crestfallen indeed as she watched Charles get to his feet a little stiffly.

'Of course I'm going back,' Charles said. 'I've got to.'

'You've got to do nothing of the kind,' Hannah said sharply. 'You're not the sort to go in for revenge, Charles, for heaven's sake.'

He stared at her, his forehead creased. 'Revenge, Aunt Hannah? Of course not! I've done that. I mean, I gave them worse than they gave me. I told you, I broke that poor devil's nose! It's not that. It's just that I've got to find out. Uncle Alex said this sort of thing happens all the time. But I'm seventeen and it's never happened to me, and I've got to find out why and – well, just *why*. So I've got to go back.'

'Charles, don't be a *shlemeil*!' Alex said. 'You're one of the lucky ones, one of the golden ones. You never got spat at in the street? Great. You never got a cold shoulder? Better still. You don't have to go looking. Just be grateful you're sitting where you sit, and stay there. Only an idiot goes looking for trouble.'

'I'm not looking for trouble,' Charles said. There was a stubborn note in his voice now. 'Just information. I have to know *why*.'

'Bed,' Hannah said authoritatively. 'Bed for everyone, and especially you. You're worn out and you can't think straight when you're worn out. Come on.'

As she was falling asleep at last, an hour later, after seeing both the young ones settled in bed, and having hugged a contrite Mary Bee back to peace of mind, she thought suddenly, 'How did she get home again? She didn't have enough money with her to pay for two taxis. How did she get home?'

51

Something would have to be done about Marie. Even as she thought it, sitting alone at her early breakfast the next morning, Hannah made a wry little grimace. The child had won over her name, just as she won over everything. It wasn't good for her. She was becoming more than wilful; she was a danger to herself, and knowing it was largely her own fault that Marie was the way she was didn't help Hannah feel any better.

She went first to the factory in Artillery Lane to spend an hour with Cissie, who was still managing that complex operation with ever increasing efficiency, and then went on to Buckingham Palace Gate to check the new workshops and showrooms there. The ready-to-wear side of her business was thriving and was the source of the family's security. As long as women wanted cheap and cheerful dresses Artillery Lane would make a comfortable living for Hannah and the children as well as Cissie and Florrie and Bet and all the workers who spent their days with their heads bent over the machines and pressing tables. But it was the couture side of her activities that most satisfied Hannah, and always would.

To design beautiful garments for rich and beautiful people was a source of real joy to her, and not because her clients were rich and beautiful. She found a complex pleasure in taking handsome tweeds and luscious silks and frothy chiffons and converting them into new objects of clean shape and elegant line and harmonious colour. When she made her Mary Bee garments she was creating as any artist would, and she knew it. When she made her Artillery Lane garments, which didn't even have a trade mark (the shops that bought them put on their own labels) she was simply making a living.

The difference was important to her even though the couturiere business had made her once again an unwilling part of the clan upon which she had turned her back. Her customers included many of the established English aristocracy, but the merely rich came to her too, and that included Lammecks and Damonts and Gubbays and Rothschilds and all the rest of the great Jewish houses; and her attitude to them could not help but be coloured by her past experiences at the hands of Davida and Albert Lammeck. When a new customer heard her surname and was surprised and started asking questions about her connections with the Lammecks, she was evasive; polite but unforthcoming, though she knew they soon found out from each other and gossiped. She needed to remain remote.

But she had to admit they were a particular joy to dress, these connections of hers, with their lazy good looks and elegant bodies and the carriage that came from years of wealth and security and contentment. English beauties with their pallid fairness and their delicate skins faintly flushed with rose were subtle and interesting, but these Jewish women with their splendid complexions and large dark eyes and lustrous skins, still carrying, many of them, the hint of rich colour that Bartholomew had brought to England from the East all those long years ago, looked magnificent in Mary Bee creations. She would stand back and watch them preening and know that they were special and be angry with herself for admiring them the way she did. She ought to be as cool with them as she was with the English roses, just a couturiere, a creator to whom they turned for self-adornment and no more than that. But because she tried so hard to be the same with her Jewish clients as she was with the others, she

461

only succeeded in being even more remote and abrupt. She did not know it, but she had a reputation among many of her clients for 'difficultness'. Not that it mattered; it added to her distinction in their eyes. Having Hannah Lammeck ignore you showed you were being dressed in the most fashionable way possible.

Buckingham Palace Gate looked particularly satisfying this morning. The workmen she had set to rearranging and decorating the rooms had nearly finished. She stood in the marble entrance hall staring at the great curving staircase and feeling good, in spite of her fatigue. Her eyes were sandy with lack of sleep, for she had only dozed for a bare four hours or so, but still she felt good as she looked. The crimson carpet against the white marble of the stairs, the delicate curving iron balustrade, the little marble copies of Greek statuary in the staircase niches, it all looked exactly as she had visualized it. The great showroom, too, with its creamy wild silk covered walls and the massive crystal chandelier and the low white suede sofas and armchairs almost blending into the deep pile of the white carpet, all looked as muted and subtle and yet as exciting as she had planned. Her clothes would stand out magnificently against such a background and she felt a lift of sheer excitement as she imagined, for one brief moment, the first mannequin parade she would have, next month. The clothes were nearly ready, the invitations were out. It would be superb.

Then, even as she saw how the great showroom would look, another vision lifted itself against her eyes. Herself as a scrawny carrot-headed child crouching by a half dead fire in Antcliff Street drawing pictures of dresses on blue sugar bags. It was an odd experience, and she shook her head at herself, and went swiftly up the stairs to the workrooms and her office above.

By eleven o'clock her fatigue was forgotten. The work-rooms were purring with activity, the women sitting at the big tables with their needles flashing busily as they made buttonholes and felled seams and set in hand-made shoulder pads. Hardly any machine work was done at all here, unlike Artillery Lane, and the noise and reek of machine oil that was so much a part of that establishment was quite absent. There was just the scent of new linen and the hiss of the modern gas fires and the breath of coffee from the corner where the most junior girl kept the pot bubbling to sustain busy fingers through the day. There were plenty of people working, for Hannah was now able to offer apprenticeships to selected girls, and there were several eager fourteen-year-olds being taught to sew fine seams as well as pick up pins and make coffee.

She was absorbed in her costing sheets when one of the little apprentices came breathlessly to tell her there was a gentleman please madam, and she'd told him as how madam was busy, but he said he wouldn't take long and please could he come in?

Hannah made a little face. There were always salesmen pestering her to buy cottons and needles and pins. She had opened her mouth to tell the child to send the man away when he appeared in the doorway behind the girl and nodded unsmilingly at her.

'Thank you, Rita,' Hannah said composedly, and Rita looked over her shoulder and bobbed at the visitor and then at Hannah and went scuttling away, leaving the two of them staring at each other.

She knew at once who he was. They had not met directly for many years, in fact the last time she had actually seen him had been half her life time ago, at an afternoon soiree Mary had given at Eaton Square, and then she had hardly noticed him. But he was so like his sister, with a wide mouth that looked as though it would move very easily with none of the stiffness about the upper lip that was so common among the men who came to her showrooms with their wives, and with those deep clefts in his cheeks, that he was unmistakeable. On Daphne, the Countess, that look gave a raffish air, a sly horsiness that had always made Hannah uncomfortable when she came to choose clothes, and which had coloured her reaction when she heard that Marie had met her. But in this man the look was quite different. It made him quite startlingly attractive and mature even though she knew he was five years younger than herself. He looked like a most interesting man, and one she would like to know better. No, she whispered deep inside herself. No, that's the last thing you want. Lammecks are trouble and never forget it.

'Mr Marcus Lammeck.' Her tone was frosty. 'What can I do for you?'

'Mrs Hannah Lammeck,' he said gravely and bent his head.

463

'Good of you to remember me. It's been a great many years since we actually saw each other. An At Home at my Uncle Emmanuel's house as I recall. I hadn't realized you'd noticed me at all. You, of course, were quite unmistakeable.'

I'm right, she thought. His mouth does move easily, curling around words in a most interesting way.

'I recognized you because you look like your family,' she said, still chilly. 'Your sister is a client of mine.'

'Ah,' he murmured. 'The Countess – tiresome wench, isn't she?'

'I really couldn't say.' Hannah lifted one eyebrow a little. 'What can I do for you, Mr Lammeck?'

'May I sit down?'

'By all means.' But she made no effort to indicate a chair. He fetched one from against the wall, and settled himself on the other side of her desk.

'I feel as though I'm asking for a job, sitting here like this. Would I be any use as a dressmaker, do you think? They tell me lots of men are involved with fashion these days, Captain Molyneux, and so forth.'

'I have a great deal to do this morning, Mr Lammeck,' she said, glancing at her watch pointedly and then at him. He stared back, and she became suddenly very aware of how she looked. She was wearing one of her favourite dresses, a soft green crêpe with pleats falling in panels from the low slung pockets and with long wide cuffed sleeves that showed her slender wrists and fingers. She had had her hair cut in the newest close shingle, and it shone with a particularly coppery glint in the sunshine pouring in through the high windows of her office, and despite her fatigue, she knew she was looking well. She needed little makeup and rarely used it, but this morning she had used some mascara to darken her lashes, as much to cheer herself as because she particularly wanted to impress anyone.

And now she was worrying about impressing this man! It was maddening. She tightened her lips and said again, 'I really do have a great deal to do this morning.'

'Then I'd better get to the point, and I don't want to,' he said, and unexpectedly smiled, a wide smile that deepened the clefts of his cheeks making him look, paradoxically, younger. 'I've come to meddle in your affairs, Mrs Lammeck. I loathe doing it, but I think I must.'

'Oh?'

'It's my sister's fault, I suppose,' he said, and leaned back in his chair. 'She has no more sense than a flea, frankly, and since she married her wretched earl she's lost what little she ever had. She's taken up with your daughter, I'm afraid.'

She raised her chin a little. 'I know. Marie told me.'

'She *told* you?' For the first time he lost some of his air of relaxation. His brows came down to form a straight line over his dark eyes. 'You know and you don't *care?*'

'I didn't say that,' she retorted. 'I said I knew. But I fail to see what affair it is of yours whether I know anything, or what interest my daughter's behaviour is to you.'

'She looks a nice child, at bottom,' he said reflectively, almost as though he were talking about the qualities of a new car. 'Basically nice manners, but a little spoiled, I suspect. It worries me to see her with a hard drinking set like my sister's. I've told her, of course, but Daphne is quite imposs-ible since she married. If she'd done the sensible thing and settled down with the Goldsmid chap who fancied her, it would have been much better all round, and I told the family so at the time, but they were so dazzled by that damned earl business. So, she's lost what little sense she had, as I said, and I'm concerned to see a girl as young as yours hanging around with her lot. Very raffish, they are, Mrs Lammeck, very raffish. You ought to keep a closer eye on her.'

Hannah felt the muscles in her cheeks knot against her jaws, she was clenching her teeth so hard. To have this interesting looking man lecturing her made all her own anxieties about Marie even worse.

'I fail to see what concern it is of yours,' she said, her voice high and hard. 'I am well aware of my daughter's ... activities, and I don't need you or anyone else to come and tell me.'

'There! I said I loathed meddling in others' affairs.' He smiled again, friendly and relaxed. 'It does put people's backs up. But there are times when you must do what you must. And times when you have to take the risk of upsetting people. Take last night. There I was at the Manhattan, it's a most reprehensible place – Mrs Meyrick opened it last month after they let her out of prison, you know – and I wasn't too pleased to find myself there anyway. But a customer from Amsterdam wanted to go there, and what can we business people do? And almost the first person I recognize is your daughter. She looks very much as you did when I first saw you, you know. And I just had to do something. I walked up to the child, told her it's time she went home and put her in my own car. Daphne was past caring, frankly, and I dare say the party was getting a shade boring anyway, but really, the child shouldn't have agreed to go in a strange man's car so easily. I told her I was Daphne's brother, but there was no proof! She let me drive her home to your house, and swept out for all the world like a countess herself. She could teach Daphne a thing or two about aristocratic behaviour, I suspect, but I'm genuinely concerned about what Daphne might teach *her*. Do remember, won't you?'

He got to his feet. 'I'm fond of my sister, but I'm not stupid about her, and she's bad news for a girl as young as yours. So, there you are! I came to do my family duty, and now I've done it. I'm sure you'll keep a close watch on her in future and – '

'And you can get out!' Hannah said, luxuriating in lost temper. She felt the colour rising in her cheeks. 'How dare you come here and lecture me! Who do you think you are? The mere fact that I married your cousin and you run your family's business and lives doesn't give you any jurisdiction over me. Marie is my affair, and stays that way! I'll thank you to keep out of what doesn't concern you.'

'Oh, damn it,' he said quietly, so quietly that it stopped her in full flood. 'And I'd hoped I'd done it tactfully. Well, I suppose there's no way to be tactful in such a matter. I'm sorry, Mrs. Lammeck. I'd hoped we could become friends over this, but there it is. Good morning.' He turned and went quietly, closing the door behind him.

She spent the rest of the day in a blur, working smoothly but automatically, without giving her full mind to what she was doing. When the time came to go home she took a taxi instead of making her usual frugal journey by underground. It was not that she could not afford taxis; indeed she could, but there was a long memory of past penury in her and she hated to waste money unnecessarily.

This evening she sat at the back of the cab watching the traffic rush by and stared out unseeingly. That damned man!

As if she didn't know that Marie was a problem! Did he have to come and lecture her so? But he didn't, her secret voice whispered. He was really very charming about it, and it was a caring thing to do. Suppose it had been you in his position. Would you have gone to so much trouble for someone else's errant child? And instead of thanking him she'd chewed his head off. Oh damn, damn. Marie ought to be *spanked*.

But when she got home she forgot her rage because Marie was in such a state of anxiety.

'It's Charles, Mama!' Marie came rushing down the stairs to greet her as soon as she put her key in the lock. 'He's been gone all day, and I'm so worried!' She stood there with her eyes filled with ready tears and Hannah put one arm out and hugged her, almost automatically.

'Florrie!' she called, and Florrie came toiling up the stairs from the basement, wiping her hands on her apron.

'I've told her not to take on so, mum, but you know our Miss Marie, always works herself up, like she did when she was a baby. I told her, there'll be tears before bed if she don't stop it. No, don't you make faces at me, madam! No harm done, mum, I told him what you said, that he was to take it easy today, but he said he was right as a trivet and he had some business to see to and he was going out. He put some flour over his eye – he's a caution that one, but he was right, it did hide it real good! And off he went about eleven o'clock.'

'Where?'

'Back to that hateful East End,' Marie burst out and clutched at Hannah's dress rather dramatically. 'I told you it was an awful place, Mamma, and if we'd never gone to that horrible wedding, none of this would have happened.'

'Be quiet,' Hannah ordered. 'Florrie?'

'He said he had to see someone, and I asked who and he laughed and said not to worry, it wasn't no one as'd do any harm. Your cousin he said, but there, you've got a lot of them cousins, ain't you mum? And I couldn't say which it was, and with Mr Jake and Mr Solly not here there was no way I could work it out. But I wouldn't worry, mum, really I wouldn't and so I've been telling madam here all day. The way she's been goin' on! He's a good sensible boy, not like some I could mention as isn't a million miles away, and he'll come home safe and sound. He promised to be here for supper at seven and it's all Lombard Street to a China orange

467

he will. So you go and take your bath mum, and settle into your comfortables and I'll deal with you, Miss Marie. You can come and make the custard for dinner. Keep you occupied that will, and let Bet take the weight off her feet.'

At ten to seven Hannah heard his key in the door and came out of the drawing room to meet him. He was standing in the hall, unwinding his scarf from his neck. At first she couldn't see him properly, for he was standing with his back to the light that was coming through the glass panels of the front door. But then he turned to greet her and her chest seemed to lurch, for he looked so strange, so very unlike the Charles she had known and loved for so long. His usually neat hair was rumpled and his eyes, those sleepy smiling friendly eyes, were wide and seemed to have had a torch lit behind them. He looked as though he had been quite, quite changed, and she wasn't sure it was a change she liked.

52

'*Charles*, of all people,' Hannah said. 'How can such a thing happen to Charles? He's an intelligent boy, educated.' She shook her head. 'You're not helping, Uncle Alex,' she said with an edge to her voice. 'I asked you because you always know what's best, I've leaned on you for years and now you're just telling me there's nothing I can do? There's got to be.'

'For an intelligent woman you're being stupid,' Alex said, and leaned forwards across the vast expanse of his office desk. 'I'm telling you, the boy's been converted. Never mind that it's politics as much as religion – whatever it is, there ain't no way you can change the situation. Be glad it's no worse, is all.'

'No worse! He says he's leaving school! He wants to spend all his time in the East End with my cousin David, and when I get my hands on *him*, I'll – '

'You'll what?' Alex leaned back and shook his head at her. 'What can you do? The boy went to see him because he recognized the man's got a spirit in him. And so he has, one of the best Talmudic scholars this side of Omsk, got the

468

respect of more rabbis than I've had hot dinners.'

'And a bolshevik.'

'Listen, dolly, I don't know what he is, bolshevik, men-shevik, all I know he's interested in the Russian ideas. And why shouldn't he be? What does a Talmudic scholar have to lose preaching revolution? *Gornisht!* So he can enjoy himself dreaming crazy dreams about how everyone can have what everyone else gets. When you're a businessman like me, you can't afford such notions. But I don't grudge David his dreams – they don't do him no harm.'

'They've done Charles harm!' Hannah flashed, and got up restlessly and moved over to the window to stare down into Pall Mall. Alex had bought one of the handsomest buildings London could produce for his offices, and worked as he lived, in luxury. But all she could see when she looked down was Charles's pale face and wide bright eyes and the air of suppressed excitement that had been so much a part of him since the evening he had come back from his day spent with David Lazar in Sidney Street.

'What harm?' Alex said reasonably. 'Just tell me what harm! So the boy wants to leave Eton? Is that so terrible? Place costs a fortune, and as far as I can see ain't doing him a ha'porth of good. If he'd ever said he wanted some special sort of career that he had to have Eton education for, it'd be different. But I've talked to him, and he always said he had no special ideas about what he wanted to do. Said he'd probably finish up in Lammeck Alley like all the others.'

Hannah turned and stared at him. 'He said that?'

'He said that. And looked content enough to say it. It fretted me, I'll tell you. It sounds so defeated, you know? No spirit in it. A nice boy, your Charles. Good hearted and – nice, you know? But he had no guts in him. Lazy, easy, nice boy. But now – ' He shook his head. 'I saw him, you know? Last night over at David's. And it was ... I don't know. It made me feel good.'

'It made you feel – Oh, Uncle Alex, you're as bad as he is! I can't talk sense to him, and now I can't talk sense to you – '

'Listen to yourself, Hannah! Just listen! *You're* not talking sense! You're just displaying your own prejudices! What does it all add up to? The boy says he reckons he's been a parasite all these years. That the Eton people are parasites and he's had enough of 'em. He wants to learn about his own roots, his own people, and he's going to go to David every day to learn Hebrew and a bit of Jewish history. Is that so terrible for a Jewish boy? Your David, he says he wants to be a *Jew*, a real Jew, not a parlour one. He says he got beaten up for the way he was, so he wants to have the game as well as the name. Be a *real* Jew. And you know something? That makes me feel good.'

'Why? Because it salves your conscience about your own behaviour?'

He grinned. 'Now you're using you kopf! Sure, I'm a lazy *mumser*. Never go to *shul* unless I must, and I forget the last time I prayed of a morning. So, it does me good to see someone else doing it for me.'

'It's not the religion I mind, Uncle Alex. I might not be a devout person myself – if anything, I suppose I'm not really sure I even believe in God. Why should I? But that's my business, just as Charles's beliefs are his. It's the rest of it that frightens me. He talks so wildly, how he's going to change the world, get rid of the poverty and the landlords and share all the money. It's such *nonsense*. He told me I'm at risk of being a capitalist, you know that? Because of the factory. I told him that without me a lot of people wouldn't have jobs at all, and people without jobs are people without food. And he said that would all change one day, that the time would come when the workers would own everything – that it was a future worth fighting for. On and on he went. It scared me.'

'No need to be scared, dolly,' Uncle Alex said comfortably. 'Believe me, no need to be scared. At his age he's entitled to change the world. Leave him alone, and thank God you don't need any of his earnings like parents did in the old days. You can indulge him while he gets it out of his system. And when the time comes and he's got to earn his living, I'll find a place for him. So don't be scared.'

She tried not to be, but the change in Charles was so dramatic that it affected all of them. The old laziness that had been so charming was gone. He was up before any of them each morning ('Praying,' Florrie told her in a low voice. 'With them leather straps and all that on his head and on his hands, real peculiar, he looks. I never meant to see him but he left his bedroom door open,') and refused to eat the sort of food they provided. Hannah had never bothered with kashrus; her mother had, of course, for all the East End people did, but Mary, in common with many of the richer

West End Jews, had been very lax about the biblical dietary laws, and Daniel had cared even less. Now, Charles demanded his own special china, and ate only vegetables and fruit and bread and cheese. He would eat no meat or fish for fear it was not kosher, and that ruffled Bet dreadfully. It ruffled Florrie too, and also, inevitably, Marie.

For days she crept about the house lackadaisically, doing all that her mother or Florrie and Bet asked of her. The only time Marie was so complaisant was when she was ill, and they watched her fearfully. But then, one evening, she burst into tears when Charles came home from the East End, where he now spent every day, and begged him to be as he had used to be, because she couldn't bear it.

'And it's all my fault,' she wept. 'If you hadn't had to go looking for me you wouldn't have had your head beaten by those horrible men and you wouldn't be acting so crazily now.'

Then it was Charles's turn to lose his temper. He told her she was an arrogant spoiled baby to take to herself the credit for what had happened to him. That she would do better to stop beating her breast and carrying on as though she were God himself, changing other people's lives, and set about changing her own by doing as he did, and learning something of her Jewish heritage.

'You're ignorant and stupid,' he said scathingly, and she went white at the scorn in his voice. 'When the revolution comes people like you will be – well, there'll be no place for you. You've got to change now before it's too late. And if you've got an atom of sense in that empty head of yours you will.'

Hannah lost her temper then, for Marie looked so stricken. She launched into him for his selfishness, and he went white too, and said in a clipped cold voice that he would leave the house and go and live where he belonged, among the real people of the East End.

They made it up, of course, for Hannah cooled as fast as she had boiled over, and managed to talk both the children down to calmness. In the end it was agreed that Charles would go on as he had chosen, attending David's East End Yeshivah each day, and going to his political meetings in the evenings, and that no one would criticize him for it; at home, however, he would stop criticizing Marie, or Hannah herself.

So an uneasy peace descended on Paultons Square. Marie spent her days with her governess, and her evenings drooping about the house or going to bed early with a book, while Hannah worked longer hours than ever getting everything ready for the first mannequin display of her new collection at Buckingham Palace Gate.

The night before the showing at Buckingham Palace Gate, she worked until almost midnight to make sure all was ready. She had known she would have that sort of day, and had asked Marie to come with her. 'I'd love you to see the dress rehearsal, darling,' she'd said. 'I'd value your opinion.' But Marie had pleaded a headache, and Hannah had gone without her.

She came home to find Florrie in a state of great confusion, standing in the hallway in her flannel wrapper and curling papers, and Marcus Lammeck in her drawing room, with Marie in her room refusing to talk to anyone.

'I've done it again,' Marcus Lammeck said, standing in the middle of the drawing room with his overcoat slung over one arm and his top hat gleaming in his hand. 'I had to.' He was wearing evening dress, and looked tired. She wanted to put her hand out to him, but she didn't. She stood by the door and said only, 'Marie?'

'Marie,' he said, then shook his head. 'I had no intention of ever meddling again, but damn it, the child was behaving appallingly. At my sister's house, I'm afraid. Half drunk, carrying on like a – well, you would have meddled yourself. So, I brought her home. Only this time she argued.'

He touched his cheek and for the first time Hannah saw that there was a scratch there. She closed her eyes for a moment.

'Oh, what *am* I to do?' She looked at him miserably. She was too tired to be angry, too distressed to be anything but honest. 'She's so unhappy and so am I, and since Charles . . . I just don't know what to do.'

'Will you let me advise you?'

She stood very quietly there looking at him. He had not moved, still standing with his overcoat thrown over one arm and his hat dangling from the other hand, and she thought confusedly, such a nice face. So comfortable. A nice face.

Wearily she said, 'I'm not coping well on my own, am I? I thought I could, but she's almost defeated me. Advice would

472

be welcome.'

'Let me talk to her grandfather. He's a difficult man, I know, and he's behaved badly to you, but he's got some influence over Marie. I've found out that much. I think if *he* suggests to her that she should go away to school, some-where that sounds exciting, like Paris, or Switzerland, she might go. She's at an age when she'll want to do things to upset you, you see, so if you suggest a school, she'll fuss. If my Uncle Albert does, however, she'll want it.'

She stared at him and then rubbed her face with one hand. It felt numb, she was so tired.

'You seem to understand her better than I do.'

He smiled then and the mobile mouth curled and the parallel clefts appeared in his cheeks. She thought again, nice face. Nice.

'That's because I don't love her too much,' he said. 'Which is why it's easy for me to see what she needs. You'll let me do it?'

'Yes please.' She managed a smile. 'And – ' She stopped and then shook her head.

'Yes?' He quirked his head at her, waiting.

'Nothing – I mean, would you care for some coffee, or a drink perhaps?'

He shook his head. 'You weren't going to say that, were you?'

'Yes, of course.'

'Try again.'

She made a little face. 'No, I wasn't. I was going to say I'm sorry. And thank you. And I hope you can forget how rude I was last time we met.'

He put his hat down very carefully on a small table, and threw his coat over the back of the chair beside the dead fire and sat down with a sigh of relief, stretching his legs out and throwing back his head against the chair back.

'Thank heaven for that,' he said. 'Now you come and sit down, and we'll start from the beginning again. It's the only place to start. And I'll have that drink you weren't going to offer. Whisky if you have it. You have something too. You need it.'

'Oh,' she said, a little blankly and then, with a spurt of irritation, 'Help yourself. The table in the corner.' She sat down in the other armchair, kicking off her shoes and throwing her own head back to rest as he had.

'Better and better,' he said, and went to fetch drinks. He brought her the same as his own, whisky with a splash of soda, and though she rarely drank anything so powerful, she took it gratefully.

'Now,' he said, coming back to his chair. 'Where shall we begin?'

'Where shall we – Don't talk riddles, please. I'm too tired.'

'We've a lot to learn about each other,' he said. 'Friends need to know a lot about each other, and if we're to be friends, then the sooner we fill in all the gaps the better. Shall I start telling you about me, or would you rather start telling me about you? I know a lot already, of course – '

'Like what?' She had taken very little of the whisky but already it was warming her, making her feel easier.

'Like you married my cousin and he left you a widow with a baby. Very stupid of him.'

'Stupid! That's a harsh word.'

'No, it isn't. I knew Daniel better than you might think. A charming chap, but not the most sensible of people. I hope you haven't gone on mourning him all these years?'

She looked at him over the rim of her glass, but said nothing. She should have been offended but somehow she wasn't. The whisky, she thought a little confusedly. Or tiredness?

'I've wondered why you haven't married again, you see,' he went on. 'I've kept an eye on you, as much as I could. When Judith left Charles to you, and everyone was in such an uproar, I told them then it would be all right, that I'd see no harm came to him, so I've had to watch out for you.'

She opened her eyes wider and stared at him then, her relaxation disappearing. 'You've been *spying* on me? Because of Charles?'

He laughed. 'Such a dramatic word! Not spying, just watching. Not that it was necessary. I told them all very early on that there was no need to worry over Charles. He's been better with you than he would have been with anyone else in the family. He's a lucky boy to have you for a mother.'

'I'd rather he'd had his own parents,' she said, and her voice was flat.

'I know,' he said gravely. 'They were special people. And Peter told me...'

474

There was a little silence.

'Peter told you what?' She sat very still, feeling a warmth growing deep inside her that she knew was not the whisky.

'That you were special,' Marcus said simply. 'That's all. That you were special. I knew anyway, of course.'

'That I'm special?' Her voice was a little unsteady, but she could do nothing about it.

'No. That I look forward to finding out for myself. I mean that he loved you, and you him.'

She felt the warmth rise higher and higher, filling her belly and then her chest, and then to her own fury felt it spill over into tears. She stared at him, holding her face as still as she could, and keeping her eyes wide open to prevent the tears from spilling out, and he looked back at her with that same grave look and said quietly, 'It's all right, you know. There's no need to feel bad about it. It helped him, I think. He loved Judith but he needed to love you too. It was inevitable. Just as his dying was. Those were bad times and you made them better for him. Hannah, will you believe me? It's all right. Don't look so . . . like that. Please. I need you to look happy. I really do.'

'Do you?' she said, and the tears that had hovered withdrew, leaving only the warmth behind. 'Why?'

He smiled then, that wide and easy smile that made him look so young. 'You'll find out,' he said. 'You'll find out. Now go to bed. You're exhausted. You look as though you need sleep more than anything else in the world. I'll see you tomorrow, after I've spoken to Uncle Albert. Tomorrow evening, over dinner. I'll call for you at Buckingham Palace Gate. Goodnight, Hannah.' And he was gone, leaving her sitting in her armchair and staring at the opposite one and trying to collect her thoughts into some sort of coherence.

53

In years to come Hannah was to look back on that summer of 1925 as though it had been preserved in golden amber. Though there were the children to worry about, especially Charles, it was a glorious time in every other way. The business was thriving; the first collection from the new showrooms caused a furore, and she found herself in demand in a way she had never been before. Women who regularly dressed in Paris, with Coco Chanel or Poiret, Lanvin or Worth, demanded Mary Bee clothes, and wore them everywhere. She was photographed wherever she went and bombarded with requests from the newspapers to write articles on What the Modern Girl Should Think, and What the Modern Woman Needs to Know, and a great many other things which had nothing whatsoever to do with her skill as dressmaker. Of course, she refused all such offers, having far too much to do to be interested in becoming any sort of journalist, but she was flattered and amused all the same, and found herself basking in her new found fame.

For the first time since she had moved into the house more than fifteen years before, Hannah agreed to make it over, and decorators and builders descended. The kitchens were equipped with the newest electrical equipment, including a refrigerator which made Bet's eyes open wide, and central heating was installed with radiators in every room, much to Florrie's gratification after fifteen years of hauling coal scuttles. The drawing room was stripped of its old fashioned art nouveau decor, somewhat to Hannah's regret, for she had always been particularly fond of it, and replaced with the newest rage in furnishings, which was cubist. There was square furniture upholstered in vividly coloured geometric patterns, piles of jazzy cushions, curtains which bedazzled the eye. Florrie was enchanted with it all, and no less enchanted with the dining room, which Hannah made as snowy as her showrooms, all in white and gleaming chrome and glass. Even her bedroom was done over in shimmering mauves and lilacs, and a new bathroom added in which she had a special shower built, all very daring and American. Jake's and Solly's rooms, too, were totally redecorated, since they had seized on an offer by Uncle Alex to spend some time in New York 'keeping an eye on his interests'. Hannah knew that Uncle Alex had created the job for them; and although she felt a certain amount of guilt about how relieved she was to have her house less crowded, she did not feel as badly about their departure as she might. She spent a great deal of money and enjoyed herself hugely, looking forward with glee to Jake's and Solly's exclamations when they returned from New

York and Marie's response to it all when she came home from Lausanne.

For Marcus had manipulated Albert exactly as he said he would. Marie, offered the chance of finishing school in Switzerland, was entranced with the idea. The word school on her mother's lips, she said, made her think of hockey sticks and long hikes in the country that gave you hideous muscles, but a Swiss finishing school, where she'd meet the most divine people and really learn about life and the world was something else. Hannah, suitably coached by Marcus, primmed her lips and looked doubtful, and allowed Marie to coax her into giving her consent.

Seeing her off had been misery, a hectic farewell at Victoria Station where Marie caught the boat train.

Hannah had been controlling her anxiety and distress at parting with her beloved only daughter so well that she had given no thought to where their final farewells must take place. When they actually arrived at the station in Uncle Alex's Hispano Suiza she felt her belly lurch in that all too familiar painful fashion. The station swarmed with fashionable people rushing to catch the boat trains or the Flèche d'Or through to Paris, but as she looked at it the scene seemed to float out of focus and a picture came over it of the way it had looked the first time she had seen a traveller off here, eight years before. Then it had been khaki, everywhere, under clouds of steam and children with crying faces and women with dry eyes and apples rolling on the ground . . .

She jerked her thoughts away and helped Marie, who was flushed with the excitement of it all, to count her luggage, and soothed her when she announced dramatically that she had lost her dressing case and found it for her, and would not let herself remember.

At last Marie was ensconced in her first class compartment and the guard had been heavily tipped to take full care of the transfer of her luggage and her own safe conduct to the boat. As Hannah stood watching the train curve away down the line, she could control the memories no longer. She stood there, bereft, feeling the same sense of despair filling her as had filled her that last time, standing in this same station, with Judith at her side.

When she had turned to go, almost blinded by her own pain, he was standing there in what was becoming a familiar pose of his, his hands clasped together in front of him, his overcoat hanging over his arm and his hat in one hand.

'I thought you might be feeling it a bit,' he said. 'So I played hookey from Lammeck Alley. They can manage without me for a while, don't you think? Yes. So do I. Come on. We'll go and have a great big piggy tea at Gunter's and talk nonsense.'

And so they had, eating crumpets and jam and milles feuilles and licking their sticky fingers and laughing, so that she had gone home to Paultons Square calm and relaxed, genuinely happy that Marie was safely on her way.

Once Marie had gone, life with Charles became easier. He continued to be passionate about his new found beliefs, especially the political ones; he sat opposite her at meals, his elbows on the table, talking lucidly and with great excitement about his dream of a new world, and she sat and listened and watched his eager face, and began, slowly, to understand.

All her life she had known about poverty and hunger and misery. She had been born into it, and grown through it and out of it. Now she was comfortably off by means of her own talent and the pain of her deprived childhood had long since left her. Indeed, if she thought about it at all, it was to be glad that she had been so toughened in her early years. If she had not been so, would she have had the strength, the energy, the sheer application to have reached the point she now stood upon? Listening to Charles, she realized how different it was for him. Protected from his birth by the comfort of money and love, his world had been a good and caring place, marred only by the blind inevitability of war that had stolen his parents from him. Meeting for the first time in his eighteenth year, as he now had, the sight and smell of poverty, it had felled him. It had not been only his beating at the hands of those street boys which had affected his conversion; it had been his own later observations in those narrow mean streets that swarmed around Whitechapel Road and Commercial Road. And, now, talking to Hannah, he managed to communicate to her his anger and his passion and his solid determination to change it all.

'If I persuade just one man that he owns his own soul and the work of his hands, Aunt Hannah, it will be worth it. If I can fight and destroy just one of the men who steal their

478

hearts from them as they steal their labour, then I shall have been born for something.' The high flown words were robbed of any banality by his sheer passion, his total conviction that he was right, and she listened and thought, and slowly stopped worrying about him. The way of life he had chosen might not be one she would have chosen for him, but it was his, and it filled him with satisfaction and striving. In his anger and distress and hunger for justice he was a very happy young man. What more could she want for a child she had always loved?

And all through that golden summer, while Charles learned and argued and listened to David and ranted at his meetings, and Marie danced and chattered with other girls in her Swiss school, and Florrie and Bet purred happily about the house in Paultons Square, Hannah fell more and more deeply in love.

She had never meant to. She was the woman who had made up her mind. She was the woman who was never going to love again. She was going to be celibate for the rest of her life, she had told herself; devoted to her work and her children. No man with a curling mouth and clefts in his cheeks was ever going to change that.

Was he?

But he made arrangements for her that were so irresistible that she could not demur, though she did try, often. But what was she to do when he announced he had such treasures as opening night tickets for the newest Noel Coward revue, 'On With The Dance!' Or when he arrived at Buckingham Palace Gate just as she was leaving at the end of the day, and drove her off to summer-warm Maidenhead to eat supper at Skindles, and then punt along the dark river while a gramophone played 'Poor Little Rich Girl' in the bow? Such treatment was irresistible and at last she gave up trying to resist. When she caught sight of his familiar figure standing in the hall waiting for her, his hands clasped in front of him, she let her stomach turn over and made no effort to control the excitement. When the telephone rang and she knew it was he, she hurried to answer it. He had slotted himself into her life as though a place had been carved out for him, long ago, and had just been waiting to be filled.

He never said anything about their relationship, even though they became closer and closer. They would talk about

479

everything and anything – world news, the art shows, the newest ballets and plays and music and food and wine and books. They shared silly jokes and puns. They chattered about their acquaintances. Yet close as they became in friendship, still there remained a barrier between them, and that puzzled Hannah. She knew he cared about her, and found her exciting. She would see his eyes on her across a room and feel her skin redden at the unmistakable message that was in his glance; she would feel his hand on her arm as he led her to a theatre seat, and she knew the electricity that leapt in her at his touch communicated itself back to him. Yet he said nothing.

Until one night in late October. She was feeling depressed, for the summer holidays had been a disappointment to her. Hannah had been looking forward to Marie's return home with enormous excitement, and then, out of the blue, there had been a laconic telegram from Lausanne announcing that Marie had been invited to spend the holidays at the Riviera villa of Comte Hugo de Marechal, the father of her dearest friend at school, so she could not come to London after all. Hannah had managed with considerable difficulty to telephone her, waiting hours to get a line, and Marie had been cheerful and friendly, but clearly amazed that her mother could possibly expect her to come home to London when she had the chance to go to Cap Ferrat with such madly fashionable people.

'*Ma chère Maman*,' she had carolled in the thin crackling little whine that the telephone made of her voice. 'You said I could come here to be properly finished, and if you fuss over letting me take up the opportunities that come my way, how can I possibly benefit? *Tu comprends, Maman? C'est necessaire!*'

Hannah had comprehended and said no more. The child was happy, and that was what mattered, but Hannah had been disconsolate, and Charles had been of little help, absorbed as he was in his own doings. Hannah had tried talking to cousin David about him to see if he could persuade the boy to spend more time at home and with his old friends. It worried her that he was so intent on his new learning that he had no fun at all. 'A boy of eighteen,' she told David, 'ought to enjoy himself *some* of the time, surely. Tell him to come to the theatre with me sometimes, David, or to a party. He's looking so pale and so – oh, so *anxious* it worries me.' But she got as little satisfaction from him as she had from Marie.

'Listen, Hannah,' David had said, sitting at his kitchen table with his elbows on it, and the inevitable book between them. 'You've got your life to live and your boy Charles has got his. He came to me to be taught, and it's a *mitzvah* to teach such a boy. You wanted that I should refuse? Tell him he'd be better off dancing the Charleston? How could I? Sure I knew it would worry you, that his ideas and attitudes wouldn't be comfortable for you, but Hannah, that's your problem, not his. If you try to change him, all you'll do is drive him away. And I'll tell you this much, that boy is someone so special that I regard him as my brother. If he told me he wanted to come and live here with me, then the door would be open to him.'

And Hannah looked round the small crowded kitchen with its lines of washing drying on the racks overhead, and the toys that littered the corners and the shabby furniture and knew there was no more she could do. David and his young wife Sonia had enough to cope with, what with their two small babies and the struggle to live on the few shillings David earned as a Talmudic teacher; she could not allow them to burden themselves with her Charles. And she knew that if she leaned too hard on Charles that he would come here, unaware as only a rich boy could be unaware of the responsibility and expense he would be.

By that evening in late October, she was restless and aware of a dragging discontent somewhere deep inside her. Her friendship with Marcus mattered enormously to her, but it was not enough. The old needs were stirring in her, the old hungers that she had so rigorously repressed all these years. She would stand sometimes in her bathroom after her shower and stare at her own naked body, still beautiful, even though she was so far past her thirtieth birthday; she saw enough of the bodies of her clients when they were being fitted to know that her own shape was good. Her breasts were as firm as they had ever been, rich and full and smooth, and her waist had not thickened nor had her hips and buttocks sagged. Yet it was a beauty that was wasted, and that, for the first time since Peter's death, depressed her. She began to be angry with Marcus for awakening her hunger while doing nothing to satisfy it.

She dressed that evening particularly carefully, in a daringly cut copper coloured silk dress. She put on makeup too, more carefully than usual, so that her eyes looked startlingly blue against the dark lashes, and her skin shone as though someone had put a light behind it. When Marcus looked at her as she came down the stairs to meet him, his eyes widened a little, but his face remained quite expressionless.

She chattered with great vivacity as the car purred through the King's Road and on past Sloane Square to Knightsbridge. He said little and now again she looked at his profile, clear against the passing lights of the shops and the traffic, and redoubled her efforts. Dammit, she thought deep inside herself, dammit, I'll show him. But she didn't know what she was going to show him.

The dance given by one of the younger Rothschilds was a particularly fashionable one, well attended by Lammecks and Damonts as well as by an assortment of county English. There had been a time, early in her friendship with Marcus, when she had resisted going to such parties; were not these the people who had once snubbed her, misused her, followed Davida's lead into treating her like a guttersnipe? But she had overcome that, because she had realized how irrelevant it all was now. The ancient snobberies and slights had died with the generation which had displayed them. These younger Lammecks and Damonts had long since forgotten the old scandals. For Hannah to remember them, she told herself, would be stupid. And she was not stupid. So she buried the old hurts, and went to the parties with Marcus, and usually enjoyed them, gossiping with him about the people there, though usually objecting strenuously to being treated as a celebrity, as hostesses were wont to try to do.

But tonight, Hannah yielded to her hostess's determination to treat her so and allowed herself to be drawn into a group of chattering and exceedingly expensively dressed people. She went on as she had begun with Marcus; she was vivacious and sparkling and almost surprised herself with the wit that came bubbling out of her, and the way she made the people around her laugh. And all the time she was aware of Marcus near her, watching and listening, and redoubled her efforts.

That people liked what they saw and heard was undoubted. They laughed a lot, and the group she was in grew larger, as more people drifted over to be where the centre of interest so clearly was, and after a while Marcus

482

spoke behind her. 'Hannah,' he said quietly. 'There is some-one who would like to meet you.'

She turned, feeling the group around her fall back a little, and looked at the man standing beside Marcus. He was rather short and had fair hair slicked fairly close to his head, and a face a little like Marcus's own, with deep clefts in the cheeks, but there was a petulance about his expression that was clearly all his own. He smiled, and that lifted the expression a little, and held out one hand.

'The Prince of Wales, Hannah,' Marcus murmured and she threw a glance at him and then to her own amazement, laughed. 'Do you know, I rather thought that was the case,' she said, and held out her own hand. 'You are not difficult to recognize, sir.'

The Prince looked a little blank, and there was a silence from the people behind her. Then he smiled again, and shook her hand warmly and laughed too. 'How do you do? I hope we shall be friends, Mrs Lammeck.'

'Hannah,' she said. 'My friends call me Hannah.'

'Ah, Hannah. How charming a name that is! Do you dance, Hannah?'

'Frequently,' she said, and he laughed again, as though she had been exquisitely witty, and as the music changed to a tango, stood back with one hand indicating the dance floor, so that she could lead the way.

All the time she was dancing she knew she was being watched and to her own amazement enjoyed the sensation, swooping and throwing back her head with all the elan she could muster. They moved through the staccato steps as though they had danced together many times, and he was indeed an elegant and adept dancer. She wanted to giggle and wished Marcus was near enough so that she could whisper some silly joke in his ear about the Prince pretending he was Rudolph Valentino and she behaving like Pola Negri. The idea was so absurd that she did laugh, and that seemed to please the Prince.

Afterwards, as the other dancers broke into a spatter of applause at the performance, he led the way back to the corner of the big room where there was a table at which he had been sitting, and insisted she join his party there, and she smiled brilliantly as the Prince introduced her to the various people sitting there.

'I have some champagne here, Hannah,' the Prince said. 'Or would you prefer a cocktail? Young Rothschild is quite disgusted with me, I have no doubt, for he's a noted wine bibber, but there, what can I do? I seem to have an affinity for gin, and I recommend the White Ladies. Rupert, do push that chap over there in this direction ... '

Hannah watched as the young man addressed as Rupert moved lazily away to fetch the waiter the Prince wanted and then, as he came back, felt her face redden. He was looking at her very directly with a sort of insolence in his expression, and she felt her lips tighten; he had no right to look at her so.

'And how is Marie, Mrs Lammeck?' he said in a high pitched and rather affected drawl as he came back to the table, followed by the waiter. 'Haven't seen her in an age, and she used to talk of you so much.'

'In Switzerland,' Hannah said sharply, and turned away, not wanting to talk to him, but he was not so easily put off.

'Such a charming daughter Mrs Lammeck has, sir,' he said, and his voice seemed higher than ever now. 'Prettiest little creature you ever set eyes on, very shapely. Not surprising of course, with so beautiful a mother.'

The Prince turned and looked at her. 'You have a grown daughter, Hannah? Bless me. I wouldn't have thought.'

'Indeed I have, sir. Perhaps you will let me present her one day. Now, if you will excuse me ... '

She got to her feet, suddenly tired of the silly game she had been playing. The people round this table were not her sort; they were either ten or more years her junior or pretending to be so, and the glossiness of them was no longer attractive and her head was beginning to ache a little. What had possessed her to put on so silly a performance on the dance floor as she had? She deserved to be reminded that she had an almost adult daughter, that she was too old for this sort of nonsense. Where was Marcus? She wanted to go home.

As though she had called his name aloud, he was there standing beside her shoulder. The Prince looked up and said, 'Ah, Lammeck, d'you know everyone?'

'How could he not?' Rupert said. 'My brother knows everyone in the world, sir, you know that! And disapproves of most of 'em! What ho, big brother! Going to tell me what a bad little boy I am? Or will that wait till later?'

'Depends on how bad a little boy you are,' Marcus said

equably. 'Hannah, my dear, you said that you had promised the Henriques we'd go on, and I rather think ... '

'What?' she said. 'Oh, yes, of course, the Henriques.'

'Oh, you can't take her away when I've only just met her!' the Prince said. 'Come, Hannah, do stay a little longer. I'm sure your friends will wait. Anyway they're probably here themselves – everyone *is* as far as I can see. Who was it did you say, Lammeck?'

'Some rather older people, sir,' Marcus said easily. 'Disapprove of the Charleston and cocktails, you know. We'd better go.'

'But we must meet again, Hannah.' The Prince stood up and took her hand and held it warmly. He was about her own height, and she was able to look him directly in the eye, which felt odd after being with Marcus who was several inches taller. 'I'm sure we could be very good friends, you and I,' he said, and his eyes crinkled with practised charm.

'I'm sure.' She nodded at the people at the table and moved away feeling safe and strong with Marcus at her side. 'Good night, sir.'

'I'm sorry about that,' Marcus said in a cold voice, as they approached the door. 'I'm truly sorry.'

'Actually I wanted to leave,' she said. 'I've got a headache. I'm glad to go.'

'I'm not apologizing for taking you away. I'm sorry because you had to meet those people.'

She laughed then. 'Meeting the Prince is supposed to be a special privilege, isn't it? I know when I met his grandfather people thought so. I don't imagine anything much has changed.'

Again she felt a wave of awareness of her age sweep over her. Thirty-three never used to feel so old, but now it did. She had met the Prince's grandfather and men she met at parties asked after her daughter.

'I hadn't met Rupert before,' she said then.

'And if I'd had my way you wouldn't have met him then,' Marcus said savagely. 'Oh, dammit, that's silly, I suppose. You'd have had to meet him sooner or later, if not at our wedding, but I didn't want you mixed up with that horrible lot there. It's all right for the Prince, he can hang around with any riff-raff he likes and get away with it, but for people like Rupert, they're a menace. There wasn't a woman at that table who hasn't had more lovers than she's had dinners, and most of 'em are – well, never mind ... '

They were standing now on the pavement outside the house while Marcus rummaged in his pockets for his car keys. She was staring at him, her face quite blank.

'What did you say?' she said after a moment. 'What did you say?'

'I said I'm sorry,' he said, 'and – '

'Our *wedding*?'

'Oh. That. Yes, I've been meaning to talk to you about that. Ah, here they are! Shall we go straight home, Hannah? Or would you like to go and eat supper somewhere else first?'

54

'I don't know why I won't,' she said again. 'I just won't. Can't.'

'But you're not a fool, Hannah! You're an intelligent woman with a good deal of commonsense, which is rare enough, God knows. You can't fob me off like that.'

She shook her head, and turned to stare out of the car window at the square outside, lying dark and ruffled in the October night. The wind was not high but it was enough to keep the yellowed leaves on the plane trees in constant uneasy movement, and the whispering seemed to echo her own uncertainty. She watched a few of the leaves go bowling along the gutter from pool of lamplight to pool of lamplight, straining her eyes a little to see them as they moved through the dark patches between.

'I'm not – ' she said, and turned her head to look at him. 'Listen, Marcus. Please listen. Don't interrupt or even think until I've finished, and I'll try the best I can to explain. I care a lot for you. You're the best friend I've got, I think, even better than Cissie at the factory, and you know how important she is to me. Since you arrived I've been happy. Excited, too. You're very exciting. I – damn, this bit's difficult. I got excited enough to be angry with you because you didn't do anything about it – no, don't *move*, I'm having enough problems. Just listen. I like you as a friend. I'm excited by you and I think you'd be a ... I think I want you as a lover. Dammit, I know I do. *No.* Keep still. But I don't want you as a husband. I've done that once. And ... well, I've done that once.'

Now he made no attempt to move, peering at her in the darkness. After a while he said carefully, 'Let me understand this. You're saying that the problem is not that you don't love me?'

'That's what I'm saying.'

'Then you do love me?'

She took a deep breath. 'I think – I'm not sure. That's part of the problem. I *want* you, I know that much. But I'm not sure I really love you. Enough.'

'Enough for what?' She felt him smile in the darkness and a spurt of anger lifted in her.

'Don't be indulgent at me! Enough not to make – not to make a mess of it. Look at my history, damn you, and then think again! I'm not just a silly girl you've picked up, someone who's young and inexperienced.'

'You're hardly old,' he said dryly.

'Almost thirty-four.'

'Hardly old.'

'I feel it, sometimes. Often. Marie is almost sixteen. She's a worry to me, the way almost grown daughters *are* worries to their mothers. I'm getting older.'

'Why should you be any different?'

'You're five years younger than I am.'

'So?'

'So, it worries me. I made a mess of two other men's lives, your own *cousins*, damn it. You should be glad I'm not about to rush headlong into doing the same for you.'

'Oh, come on, this is perfectly ridiculous!' He sounded genuinely angry. 'Just what do you see yourself as? Some sort of lethal black widow spider who destroys her mates?'

'You can laugh if you like, but it's true. Daniel ... ' She tried to go on, and she couldn't, feeling the tears tightening her throat and keeping the words dammed back.

'Hannah, listen to me. Please, my love, listen.' She could feel his breath warm on her cheek, but he did not touch her. 'I knew Daniel. Better than you did, for all you married him. He was a ... oh, he was a flawed person, I suppose. I know we all are, in some form or another, but in him it was

487

different. It ran so deep it had to destroy him. Really, my aunt had destroyed him long before he met you. I think you were the best thing that happened to him. If he'd done as my aunt wanted and married Leontine Damont do you think he'd have been any happier?'

'He'd be alive,' she said. Her voice sounded very loud in her own ears. 'He'd be alive.'

'Sometimes being alive is to get the worst of it,' he said. 'Easy to say when you're living, I know, but it wasn't your fault. You must believe that.'

'I've told myself that lots of times, Marcus. I used to lie awake at night and try to understand, to see whether it was my fault, Mary Bee's for being conceived when she was, that Daniel ... that it happened. And I'd tell myself I wasn't God, that Uncle Alex was right when he told me I wasn't to blame. But there's another part that doesn't listen. The guilty part.'

'Guilt! You and your guilts, Hannah! As long as I've known you I've felt that in you, that need to expiate all the time. What is it about you that makes you take everyone else's shame and fear the way you do?'

She managed to smile in the darkness. 'You sound like Uncle Alex. He says it's always been like that. That Jews used to be blamed for everything so much that now they blame themselves before anyone else gets the chance.' She imitated Alex's gruff tone. 'On account of we're quicker on the uptake. So he says.'

'He may be right. Don't change the subject, Hannah. I've asked you to marry me.'

She looked away from him then. 'I don't think I can. Marry you, that is ... ' And deliberately, she left the end of her sentence open, fixing her eyes on his face now, trying to see the expression on it in the dark interior of the car.

He was silent for a long moment and then he said carefully, 'I think you'd better say it all clearly. Are you offering something different? I don't want to jump to any conclusions that might be – embarrassing.'

'It's not all that unusual,' she said, almost defensively. 'You said all those women at the Rothschild dance had them, more than they'd had dinners. Why not me?'

'Because you're not one of that crowd,' he said, and the contempt in his voice was icy. 'Promiscuous pieces of – of

488

garbage! They're the richest most cossetted women there are in this whole damned country and they behave like pigs in straw. They'll do anything with anyone for no reason. They don't even have *need* to redeem them. They do it casually carelessly and – they're sickening. They've as much notion of love and loyalty and trust and – and decency as a dog. Less.'

'So!' She tried to sound light and relaxed, and managed to sound in her own ears only silly. 'It's clear you don't want to consider my offer.'

'I am offering you all I can which is everything. My love, my total concern for your happiness and welfare, my complete involvement in everything that matters to you. What are you offering in return? Just sex? That isn't enough, Hannah. Not for you, and certainly not for me. You demean yourself by suggesting it.'

'Demean myself?' She sounded very bitter then. 'There was a time when your family would have said that was impossible. That I was already so low I could go no lower.'

He was very still beside her, and then he said in a voice that was icy, 'I will not tolerate this. To refuse me as a husband because of what my older relations did would be an outrageous insult. I don't think you mean to offer *that*, whatever else you're offering.'

'I'm sorry,' she said after a moment. 'That was wrong of me, I suppose. But it still hurts. It still sits in my mind. I can't help it. They hated me. Perhaps some still do.'

He made an impatient gesture in the darkness, and she saw the glint of light on his hand. 'It's no reason to refuse me. No reason to suggest – whatever it is you're suggesting. Family connections mean nothing between us. There's just you and me. And what you seem to be suggesting is not an answer I can take. You must not speak to me in such terms.'

'You sound very biblical,' she said and took a deep breath. 'Very proper. I meant no wickedness, you know. I was trying only to be honest. There wasn't only Daniel, you see. There was Peter. But of course, in your eyes, that was – that was behaving like those women you so loathe, wasn't it? What was it you said? Pigs in straw? Like a dog? That was how it was with Peter and me, I suppose.'

'Oh, no, please stop, Hannah! This isn't what was supposed to happen! I love you! I want everything to be perfect for you, and I can't bear it that we've degenerated into this sort of horrible squabble. Please.'

'I'm sorry. I didn't mean to be unkind,' she said, a little dully. 'I only wanted to explain to you that I don't feel able to marry you. I'd be afraid. I've done enough harm to your cousins. To hurt you too would be . . . I can't bear it.'

She struggled with the car door for a moment and then managed to get it open and tumbled out, and ran up the steps to the house, fumbling blindly in her bag for her key as she went.

He didn't follow her. And long after she was inside, sitting curled up in her new white armchair and staring blindly at the curtained window she heard the engine purr into life and the car go whispering away through the sound of the wind blown trees.

It could not be the same of course. It was not that he stayed away from her. He phoned her and told her there was a private viewing at a gallery of Sonia Delaunay's newest work from Paris, and could she come, and sent her flowers and saw to it that she was invited to the same dinner parties as he was; most London hostesses were fond of him, and willing to oblige him, even if they had their eyes on him for their own nieces or daughters. He invited her to theatres, to films, to concerts, just as he always had.

But it wasn't the same. The intimacy was gone, and she missed it dreadfully. Her sense of loss was not helped by her own anger at herself. She would lie in bed night after night unable to sleep, asking herself, why was I so stupid? Why didn't I say I'd marry him? Who do I think I am, that I'm afraid I'll hurt him if I marry him? He's not stupid; he can look after himself, and I want him! And he's right about the old feuds. They don't matter any more. It's him I want, not families, not revenge . . .

And she would turn and bury her face in her pillow, trying to ignore the hunger that now bit so slyly at her whenever her guard was down. It had been a long time indeed since she had been so aware of her own sexuality, and it was not an awareness she enjoyed at all.

Marie came home for Christmas in a flurry of excitement, bringing with her a French girl and a German one, whom she introduced as her dearest chums in all the world. They spent the four weeks of the vacation rushing about London shops and hotel thé dansants, and gossiping and giggling. Hannah was delighted to see Marie looking so happy, and was pleased she had such close friends to share her holiday with, but she felt a little bereft as well, for somehow there was no time for any talk between them at all. Marie was always fast asleep when Hannah left for Buckingham Palace Gate each morning and when Hannah came home at night she had already gone bustling off with her friends.

At first Hannah was anxious about the people the girls met, remembering all too painfully Marie's involvement with Marcus's sister, but then she discovered that the German girl, Mercedes von Aachen, had relatives at the German Embassy, who were entertaining the three girls a great deal.

'They are the cousins of my father,' she told Hannah in her prettily accented voice. 'And when they heard that Papa and Mama had to be away from Berlin during my holiday, they agreed that they would ensure I should be content here in London, which of course I am with you, Gnädige Frau. I have also been told by my aunt, the Baroness von Aachen, that I must meet some of her relatives here, since she is English, you know.'

'Oh?' Hannah said politely.

'Indeed. She was Fraulein Leontine Damont, of an excellent family here, I am told. She says to me I must visit some of her relations and she has given me some addresses.' Mercedes began to leaf through her notebook to show Hannah the people on whom she was to call.

Hannah said nothing, making no comment about the fact that she knew the names of all the people listed and was grateful that the French girl, Henrietta de la Tour, also had London connections, and was more clamorous about visiting them, so that the trio did not in fact visit Leontine's friends as much as they might have done.

'Not that it makes any difference to me,' Hannah would tell herself. 'Why should it? It's all so long ago now. It doesn't matter. And I'm glad Leontine married and is happy. I'm glad.' But it was difficult to believe herself.

Charles had chosen to go away for the Christmas holiday. He told Hannah bluntly that he could not bear the fuss that was made about it, with Florrie and Bet decorating a tree for themselves in the kitchen and insisting on distributing presents which of course Hannah reciprocated.

'It's all so *wrong*,' he told her earnestly. 'We're Jews, and anyway, it's a pagan fertility rite. I don't believe in God, you know – no, I know it sounds complicated but it isn't. The longer I study the Talmud and Hebrew the more I realize that what matters is the Jewish *people*, not the God they invented for themselves, and it's the people I care about. And because I do, I can't stand this Christmas rubbish. I'm going to go and stay with David in the East End. Please, Aunt Hannah. They've asked me, and it's what I want.'

She did not argue, but insisted he take a kosher food hamper with him as a Chanukah present ('Which they'll value if you don't,' she told him sharply) and made the best of the holiday that she could. She was, to her own distress, actually relieved when the four weeks were over and Marie returned cheerfully to Lausanne, leaving her with a casual kiss and never a backward look as she ran for her train at Victoria.

The year turned slowly through a biting winter to a chilly spring, and she worked harder and harder, and went out less and less. Marcus still telephoned occasionally, but she had made up her mind that she must wean herself from even his friendship. When she saw him she still felt that sickening leap of physical excitement and need, still had to bottle up her feelings behind a bland glass-smooth exterior. He called less frequently now, as the labour crisis had deepened and strikes began to loom on the horizon. Lammecks owned large blocks of shares in several coal mines as well as steel mills and other factory interests, and as labour unrest bubbled and heaved all through that dull spring of 1926, Marcus became busy as a mediator and spokesman for several of the owners. She read about him in *The Times* and listened to Florrie exclaiming over the things she had heard about him on the kitchen wireless and said nothing. She had set herself the task of forgetting Marcus Lammeck, and the best way to begin was never to talk to anyone about him.

When, on May 4, a General Strike was declared she decided to go on working and that any of her workers who could not get in because of the lack of buses and trains would still be paid. Cissie told her roundly that she was a fool, that most of the workers would take advantage of her goodwill, but she was stubborn.

And her stubbornness was justified. Many of them did struggle in, some walking the long grey miles from Hackney and Whitechapel to Buckingham Palace Gate as well as to the Artillery Lane factory, and Hannah felt a glow of pride. Other workers might be complaining bitterly of exploitation and bosses' greed, but hers saw the business as she did, as a co-operative venture that mattered to all of them, and supported her in spite of exhortations from pickets and street shouters to come out and stay out.

When the call came early on a Saturday morning she was at Artillery Lane, supervising the loading of a lorry she'd managed to borrow from Uncle Alex to deliver garments waiting for urgent despatch to Birmingham which couldn't go by train, as they usually did. The boy who came lurching into the back yard of the factory looked drunk at first and then she saw that in fact he was exhausted. His face was dirty and bloodstained, and he'd obviously been in a fight. She took him by the shoulder when she heard him asking one of the men loading the lorry for 'Charlie's Auntie Hannah'.

'What is it?' she said urgently with a sudden spurt of fear. 'Is Charles hurt? Is he ill?'

'He's bin beat up,' the boy said, and pulled away from her, and turned to go lurching on his way again. 'Made me promise I'd tell yer, so I did. In the London 'Ospital, under police guard. Got took there from the docks. Said I was to tell yer.'

55

The ward they sent her into was long and cluttered, with fireplaces at each end in which big coal fires burned, for it was a cold May. Nurses in blue print dresses and frilled lace caps and stiff starched aprons bustled by, rustling with every movement, and ignored her as she stood hovering between the big double doors. The ranks of beds on each side ran away to the far end in diminishing red blanketed oblongs, and the faces that lay on the pillows all looked the same, drawn and blank and ageless, hollow simulacra of men. The place smelled of soap and cold air and carbolic and a thicker ominous sweetness that stirred fear in her belly, and because she was afraid she lost her temper, and marched up to one of the nurses and took her by the elbow.

The girl reared back, offended by her touch, and stared at her frostily.

'I want to see Charles Lammeck,' Hannah said sharply. 'Immediately.'

'Visiting time this afternoon, two o'clock,' the nurse said. 'You'll have to come back then.'

'I was sent for, to see my son, my ward,' Hannah said. 'I was told he was injured. I insist on seeing him at once.'

'Insist?' the nurse said, and looked at her with a blank face. 'You can't insist. It's up to the doctor.'

'To hell with the doctor,' Hannah said. She turned and marched into the ward, looking from side to side at the beds she passed. The men in them stared back at her incuriously, as though she wasn't actually there. The nurse followed her, expostulating, but Hannah ignored her and marched on. As she reached the middle of the ward someone who was sitting beside one of the beds stood up and she stared and realized he was a policeman, though he looked odd, for he had his helmet in one hand so that his head looked naked and vulnerable.

'The young man says it's him you're looking for,' he said in a hoarse whisper, then reddened as the nurse stared at him with an icy glare, and Hannah thought absurdly, 'He's very young, scared.'

She came to stand at the foot of the bed and stared down at it, and at first she could not see anything but the glow of the red blanket and the whiteness of the pillow and then, slowly, she was able to focus more closely.

He was almost unrecognizable. One eye was completely closed as the tissues around it had swollen to such proportions that the skin seemed to be stretched as tight as the skin of a rubber balloon. It was almost as brightly coloured as a balloon, too, a blur of purple and red and blue, and the discoloration stretched right down one side of his face. His lips were blackened and cracked, and there was a streak of blood running from one corner of his mouth. His nose was swollen, looking as broad as a baby's, and she could see that it was blocked with cotton wool. One arm was encased in plaster, and lay awkwardly on the bed beside him as though

494

it was not part of him at all.

'Oh, my God.' Her voice sounded loud in the quiet ward. She felt rather than saw some of the men in the other beds turn to stare at her. 'Oh, my God. What happened?'

'Can't say, madam.' The young policeman sounded embarrassed. 'They sent me to stay with him till he could give me a statement, like, and they could charge him and all, they said, but they never said what the charges were. I only just got sent here, after the worst of the fight was over.' He looked down at the bed.

'Charles?' Hannah moved round the bed and crouched beside it so that her head was on a level with his. 'Charles, darling, what happened to you?'

He swivelled his one good eye towards her and his cracked lips seemed to lift a little. She felt tears rise in her. He was clearly trying to smile, though obviously it hurt him for he winced. Still he went on trying.

'I'll see the doctor, darling, find out what happened,' she said, and he took a sharp little breath and said in a cracked voice, 'No, he's mad at me. Don't ask him ... mad at me.'

'Mad at – what do you mean? A doctor looks after people. I'll find him and he can tell me. Oh, darling, I'm so – ' She bent her head and kissed his cheek, delicately, terrified of hurting him, but needing to have some sort of physical contact.

The nurse came back with a white coated man in tow. Hannah stood and stared at him with all the anger she had in her lifting her chin and said sharply, 'You are the doctor looking after my ward?'

'I am indeed,' he said and his voice was loud and heavy at the same time. 'And you have no right to come pushing your way here in this manner.'

'What has happened to him? I insist you tell me at once. He is under the age of twenty-one, and as his legal guardian, I insist on my right to be told all that pertains to his welfare.'

'Under twenty-one, is he?' the doctor said contemptuously. 'Then you, madam, should take better care of what he gets up to. The state he is in he frankly deserves to be in and I'm not afraid to tell you so! To come down here to the slums and try to meddle in matters that don't concern him, and then to fight with public spirited citizens who have come to try to keep this country going while those damned strikers try to destroy it! You should be ashamed to have a ward who behaves in so appalling a manner.'

An odd little sound came from the bed behind her. After a moment she realized that Charles was laughing.

'I told you he was mad at me,' Charles said in that rough hoarse little voice. 'Told you. Capitalist pig that he is.'

'Pah!' the doctor said, and suddenly Hannah wanted to laugh too for he looked so pompous and absurd in his white coat and with his face set in a scowl of disapproval. But she did not laugh, and looked instead at the policeman.

'Can I take him away from here to get proper medical care elsewhere?' she said. 'You mentioned charges – what charges?'

'Can't say, madam. Just charges in connection with an affray down the docks is all I know. And probably speaking out of turn to say that much.' He looked at her wretchedly, his smooth young face suffused with patchy red.

She turned back to the doctor. 'You will tell me the extent of his injuries, please. I will not discuss with you the manner in which they were sustained. I want only the *medical* information, so that I can arrange to have him cared for by my own physician.'

The doctor glared at her with his face reddening too, so that he was an older stouter parody of the young policeman, and she stared back at him, her eyes wide, using all the will she had to outface him. After a moment he said loudly, 'Fractured radius, three cracked ribs, superficial soft tissue injuries to the face, fractured nose, possible fractured skull. You move him at your own risk.' He flashed a contemptuous glance at Charles as though to say that for his part he could not care less what risk he was exposed to.

'Thank you. And the name of your superior? The specialist who is in charge of the case?'

The doctor reddened even more, opened his mouth as though to speak, then turned away, and said to the nurse sharply, 'If arrangements are made to remove this patient without my consent, see to it that this policeman's sergeant is called. He is not to be removed until I say so.' He went marching away down the avenue of beds with the nurse scurrying importantly behind him.

'Nice piece of work he is,' the policeman said in a low voice. 'Would you care to sit down here, madam? I can move away a bit – I mean, as long as I keep him in sight it'll be all right. I don't see why that doctor had to be so hard, that I don't. There was lots o' these public school boys came down the docks to do some work. Why pick on him like that?'

'Because he didn't come to strike break,' Hannah said, and looked ruefully at Charles. 'Did you, my love? He came to stand with the pickets, I imagine.' Charles looked at her with his only available eye gleaming, and again tried to smile.

'Oh,' the policeman said blankly. 'Oh. Educated boy like that? Standing with the pickets? That's a funny way to go on.'

'Not funny,' Hannah said. 'Just angry.' She looked at Charles again and felt a surge of pride. A fighter. Not a whiner who only talked and complained but a fighter too. Her Charles. Wrong headed perhaps – and she wasn't sure of that, to be honest – but a fighter.

'I'll be back,' she said to Charles and smiled briefly at the policeman. 'I'll make arrangements, darling. Get it all sorted out. Try to rest.' Again she kissed his cheek, and turned and went, hurrying back down the ward and feeling the eyes of the men in the beds on her back, and curiously, a wave of approval, and she thought, 'They don't like that doctor either. They're glad I argued with him.' She smiled as one of the men she passed grinned at her and made a thumbs-up signal.

She managed to find a sweetshop with a little sign outside proclaiming, 'You may telephone from here,' and started to try to arrange Charles's care. She began with her own family doctor, in the King's Road, but he was away for the weekend, she was told, and his housekeeper suggested another. She called him only to be told that he was unable to involve himself in a hospital case. 'And if the injuries are as you say, he's better off where he is than at home,' the little voice clacked in her ear. 'Not a case I can accept responsibility for.' She called the factory in Artillery Lane, but Cissie had gone, and she realized with a shock how late it was, after eleven, and she had told Cissie she could close the factory once the orders had been loaded and the lorries despatched. She tried Alex next, but he was in Liverpool trying to sort out the unloading of some of his more urgent tea supplies. David? Perhaps David could help, she thought briefly though she knew she was being absurd. What she needed was someone who would scoop her Charles out of that horrible huge ward full of hollow faced men, away from that pompous doctor, away from the police, away from all the trouble he was in. And David couldn't do that.

She held the phone in her hand, her forefinger hooked over the rest and the earpiece held against her chest, trying to understand why she was so unwilling to do what she knew was the only answer to her dilemma. The shop owner peered at her curiously over the piles of dummy boxes of chocolates and dusty toffee tins that cluttered the counter and sniffed mournfully at her. Hannah stared back and then released the rest. When the operator's voice answered she gave Marcus's number wearily. What else could she do? And why shouldn't she? Why be so upset at the idea? He would want to help, she knew that; indeed he would be bitterly distressed if he thought she had not sought his aid.

He was not at Lammeck Alley, but they found his secretary for her, a sensible young man she had talked to before, and she found herself spilling it all out. Charles was hurt, being badly cared for in the London Hospital, there was some problem with the police; 'He was involved with a picket line,' she said mendaciously, knowing the young man would assume as everyone else did that a well-off young man like Charles would inevitably be a strike-breaker rather than a supporter. At once the secretary was all concern: Mr Lammeck was at the airport at Waddon overseeing the delivery of gold bullion which had to be flown in because of the strike. The secretary would see to it that he met her at the hospital as soon as he returned. Three hours, he said apologetically, no more than that. She was to wait.

She paid for her calls and walked out into the street and stood there, her coat pulled up against her ears, for she was cold now in spite of the sunshine. Three hours. Three hours in this grey dingy road with its grey ugly people shuffling along the wide pavements, and the curious emptiness of the roadway, for there were none of the buses and lorries that usually thronged it, and few private cars either. The strike was now five days old and even the most eager of lift givers and parcel and letter deliverers had lost some of their heart. But there was nothing more she could do. No one but Marcus could help her extricate Charles from his bondage in that pile of carbolic smelling buildings. She would have to wait, and fill in the time somehow.

An old woman went by her, almost cannoning into her, and Hannah stepped back muttering an apology. The old woman looked up briefly, her eyes gleaming under the heavy fringe of her old fashioned wig and said automatically '*Gut shabbos.*' Hannah said '*Gut shabbos,*' equally automatically and then thought, almost surprised, 'It's Saturday. *Shabbos.* People in synagogues.' She realized this was one of the reasons for the emptiness of the street. She remembered how it used to be in Antcliff Street, long ago, when people put on their best clothes and went trooping off to the synagogue on the corner, peacocking a little if they had something new to wear, gossiping busily, cuffing the children as they skipped and squabbled, and how empty the street became after they had gone by. Sometimes, when he had been in one of his unusual moods of goodwill, Nathan would announce that he was going to *shul*, and anyone who wanted to come too was welcome, and then she would put on her coat and that hateful pancake of a black straw hat (she could almost feel its scratchy edge against her forehead now as she remembered) and go with him to sit in the gallery staring down at all that went on below and from which she was excluded. *Shul* in those days had been a sort of treat, a break in the dullness of the ordinary week, and she felt a great wave of nostalgia for it.

The wind blew a little gust, sending dust swirling around her ankles and again she shivered and looked at her watch. After a moment she pushed her hands deeper into her coat pockets and began to walk, down East Mount Street, then along Raven Row and into Sidney Street.

It wasn't too long a walk; along Sidney Street, through Sidney Square and then left into Commercial Road, and then there it was, looking just as it had when she was a child. But much smaller.

She stood outside for a moment. Two old men, long bearded and with their white hair in tight curls over their ears under wide brimmed black hats, and a few small boys in ill fitting clothes, stared at her. She smiled at them but they stared unsmilingly back. After a moment she pushed past them, for they made no effort to make way for her, and went in through the double doors she remembered so well.

She could hear them beyond the inner doors, that odd and interesting familiar combination of wailing and jubilation, the rise and fall of chanting voices with an undertow of chatter. She took a deep breath and then began to climb the rickety wooden staircase that led to the women's gallery.

It was not full; there were only a few little knots of women scattered about. Old ones with shawled heads and a little cluster of young ones in very modern cheap cloche hats, clearly a party come to hear a boy say his Barmitzvah portion, and a few small girls with their heads together whispering busily and giggling in stifled little shrieks which made their mothers turn and hiss at them. Hannah stood there for a moment as they all turned and stared at her and then moved down to the front row, picking up a prayer book as she went.

She turned the pages, enjoying the feel of the thin rustling paper beneath her fingers and letting her eyes slide over the heavy black symbols, as incomprehensible to her now as they had been almost thirty years ago when she had sat here in that horrible hat and heavy coat and painfully large boots, watching Poppa down there below with the men. He had laughed at her when she had asked why she couldn't learn Hebrew like Jake and Solly, and had told her it was enough a girl should learn about running a decent Jewish home and not to fill her head with such a thing as Hebrew lessons.

'Be happy,' she heard his voice come into the back of her mind. 'Be happy, Hannelah, don't worry about reading. What good did it ever do me, I want to know? Tell me one good thing ever came from all the hours I spent sweating over my *chumash* or studying the Siddur, and I'll let you suffer like I did, God forbid I ever should ... ' She closed her eyes for a moment and then opened them and stared down into the synagogue below.

It was as though she had never grown up. There they were, packed together as close as they had always been, swaying and bobbing, their *tallus* clad shoulders making a pattern against the blackness of their suits. Row upon row of striped prayer shawls, row upon row of fringes, some long, some short, some hanging free, some flung back over the shoulders, row upon row of covered heads, yarmulkas and bowlers, homburgs and caps, and in the box in front of the Bimah on which the rabbi and cantor stood, three glossy top hats looking as full of pride as though they themselves were sentient beings.

The smell enveloped her, mothballs and oil from the heating stoves and cooking, for the old women near her reeked powerfully of the fish they had fried and the chicken soup they had prepared and the livers and onions they had chopped yesterday afternoon ready for the Sabbath. The sound wrapped around her too; women's voices whispering nearby, rich baritone and tenor voices singing below, old cracked voices praying. It was like crawling back into the past, and she took a deep breath and at last relaxed.

'Perhaps I should go to *shul* more often,' she thought after a while, almost dreamily, watching the men as the swaying went on. 'I've left too much of yesterday behind. I don't belong there where I am.' She thought of Paultons Square and Buckingham Palace Gate, trying to make them feel alien inside her head, but it didn't work. They *were* where she belonged and no amount of nostalgia, sitting here in the stuffy heat of a tiny East End synagogue, could alter that. She belonged in the West End as much as she had ever belonged here, more in fact. She had only spent ten years of her life here in the middle of the poverty and fervour that so filled this small rackety building, and almost a quarter of a century on the other side of London. How could she try to convince herself that this was what she needed, and what she missed? She was just being sentimental, she told herself, trying to rub off the dreaminess that still filled her.

The service went on and on, and she sat there, listening, watching, trying to clear her head, and then stopped trying. She just let it roll over her, the ancient rhythms and sounds. Somehow they did what it was she most needed done. They took the fear and doubt and loneliness they found there and wrapped it all in a silken shell of peace. All gone, she thought. All gone. I'm not frightened any more because it doesn't really matter any more. Charles will live as he must, and do what he must, and so will Marie, and I must do what I must and I know now that I want Marcus and it doesn't *matter* anyway – it's only me, today, and has no relevance. All this is about what happened yesterday, hundreds and thousands of yesterdays full of frightened anxious doubting people, and they lived and died while the music and rhythm and the chanting went on and here it still is. And tomorrow when we're all gone it will still be here, the swaying and that sound and that smell and these people. It just doesn't matter at all.

It was a very comfortable feeling to have.

56

Marcus arrived at the hospital almost half an hour before she had hoped he would, his car sliding to the curb just beyond where she stood waiting for him, huddled against the main doorway at the top of the flight of entrance steps.

'Where?' he said, offering no other greeting. She said nothing and led the way inside the building, and on towards the ward where Charles was.

Marcus stopped at the door of the small office beside the ward entrance and with silken courtesy asked a nurse to find Sister for him, smiled briefly at Hannah and said, 'Go and wait with him. I won't be long.' She went obediently. He was here, and she felt safe and free and almost elated, and somewhere deep underneath, intensely happy. To be happy in such a situation was both selfish and stupid, yet there it was, and she could do nothing about it. She did not try.

Charles was asleep and the young policeman beside him almost half asleep, but he alerted as she came in and tried to offer her his chair. She shook her head at him and perched on the edge of the locker beside Charles, and leaned there, glad to see he was resting.

He woke after a few minutes, turning his head to see her, almost as though he knew she would be there.

'Hello,' she said softly.

'Hello,' he said and his voice sounded less difficult now. She was relieved by that for he had sounded almost choked before. Now he sounded only rather thick, like a child with a cold in his nose. 'I ought to say I'm sorry. For worrying you.'

'No need to fret over that,' she said.

'I'm not sorry, though. For worrying you, of course. But not for the fight. It was a *marvellous* fight.' He moved his head on his pillow and grimaced a little at the discomfort and she said quickly, 'Please, don't upset yourself, darling. Just rest.'

'I want to talk!' He sounded petulant, like a tired child. 'They can bash me as much as they like but they can't do anything to the inside of my head, can they? And inside my head – ' he closed his one good eye for a moment, ' – it's *marvellous* in there.'

The young policeman looked at her, his face troubled. 'I don't think as I'd encourage him to talk too much, madam,' he said a little diffidently. 'I mean, I ought to take down anything he says, I suppose.' He brightened then. 'Mind you, he hasn't been charged with anything yet, so maybe it don't matter.'

'Thank you,' she said, and smiled at him. A nice boy, she thought. Not all that much older than Charles, to look at him.

'Aunt Hannah,' Charles said suddenly. 'I saw some people from school.'

'School?'

'Eton,' he said irritably, and moved his head awkwardly again. 'Eton, of course. There was that chap Julian Lammeck, and the Gubbay twins, carrying on as though it was a great lark. Driving lorries and going onto the docks trying to run the pickets down. I climbed on the cab, and there they were, and I was so amazed I fell off. Why them, Aunt Hannah? They're Jews too, how can they try to break a legitimate strike like that?'

'Darling, please don't fret yourself,' she began but he stared at her with such ferocity that she stopped and took a deep breath. 'I don't see what difference it makes, their being Jewish,' she said carefully after a moment. 'I'm not sure what it is you mean.'

'How can they? Don't they know what it's like for these people? Don't they understand what poverty does to people? How Jews have suffered, are still suffering? And they come and drive lorries like all the rest of these damned capitalists –'

'Darling, they're ... what do you expect? Anyone who knows you've been in a fight involving pickets assumes that you've been fighting against them! Eton boys, it's natural. Try not to worry over it, please.'

'They ought to know,' he said, his voice rising fretfully. 'They ought to know. They're traitors, to behave so. I'm glad I hit them.'

'Was that how you got hurt?'

He lay still for a moment and then managed another of his painful smiles. 'Yes. Yes it was. Marvellous. They didn't know what hit them, *marvellous*. But then the others got involved.'

503

'Others?'

'People,' he said vaguely, 'and police,' and then looked at the young policeman at the other side of his bed and said no more, and the boy in uniform blinked and looked confused and then turned his head to stare pointedly down the ward.

They were quiet for a while, as Hannah too looked towards the ward doors to see if Marcus were coming. Then Charles said suddenly, 'I'm being Barmitzvah, Aunt Hannah.'

She stared down at him, amazed. 'Bar – but when you were at school, you flatly refused to have anything to do with it! I asked you, and people were very angry with me because I didn't insist when you said you didn't want it.'

She frowned, suddenly, remembering. 'Uncle Alex said you'd be sorry, if I let you have your own way, and he was right – '

'Yes,' Charles said and his voice sounded more tired now. 'He often is, isn't he? I'm sorry. I didn't know any better then. I was ashamed of being a Jew, you see. At school people didn't talk about it, so I thought it was a shameful thing. I knew so little, anyway, I didn't understand. Now I know. Now I understand, I'm going to be Barmitzvah. Not because of God, you see. Because of Jews. That's why David's arranging it. Soon.'

He closed his eyes and seemed to fall asleep as suddenly as a baby. She watched his chest rise and fall and the peace that had filled her since the hour she had spent at the synagogue began to dissipate and make way for the old familiar anxiety. Would he always confuse her like this?

At last Marcus came, walking quietly down the ward with a tall man in a neat dark suit beside him. He smiled reassuringly at her as he came up to the bed.

'Hannah, my dear, it's all arranged. Charles is to be transferred to a nursing home in Harley Street. An ambulance has been ordered. Dr Jaeger here is in charge of his care, and is happy to take him into his private clinic. Dr Jaeger, Mrs Lammeck.'

She bent her head in acknowledgement. The tall man smiled a little remotely and then moved to stand beside Charles, and took his wrist between his fingers to count his pulse.

'Constable,' Marcus said, and the policeman stood up. 'I

have been speaking to your Sergeant Forbes on the telephone. He's waiting for you to call in. You can return to your station, but speak to him first.'

'But I was told to stay here until I was relieved, sir, and –'

'I know,' Marcus said, still very soothing. 'And you're quite right to be unsure. That's why I arranged for your sergeant to speak to you on the telephone. You place the call yourself, and then you'll know it's all straightforward, won't you?' Though he still looked dubious the policeman yielded to the note of authority in Marcus's voice and did as he was bid.

'Solicitor's there already,' Marcus said briefly in response to Hannah's puzzled gaze. 'Young Peterson had alerted him, sensible chap, and he'd already done some investigating before I got here. It's all fine, my dear. You can stop looking so desperate. He's going to be all right.'

'I'm not desperate,' she said, but she felt the tightness in her face and knew he was right.

The transfer to Harley Street was uneventful, the ambulance moving through the half empty streets without hindrance, and once she saw Charles safely tucked into bed in a handsome single room, already bedecked with flowers and warm and scented, as unlike the bleakness of the London Hospital as it was possible for a room to be, she took a deep breath and realized just how tense she had been. The doctor assured her gravely that the boy was all right, bruised and a little battered but no worse harm done.

'His nose may have a certain – ha – shall we say characterful look about it henceforth. I set it as neatly as I could, but of course it isn't easy always to ensure a perfect cosmetic result. His skull is not broken, we've now had time to look carefully at his X-rays, so you can be reassured on that score. The fracture of the radius is a simple one and should heal without any dramatic problems. Try to keep him out of trouble once I send him home to you, in a few days, I think. And relax yourself, my dear lady.' He smiled that somewhat remote smile again and bowed her out. Marcus took her elbow in a warm grip and led her down to his car, and took her home.

Not until she sat in her own armchair beside her own fire, with an anxious faced Florrie bringing her tea, could she take in all that had happened. Marcus explained to her that there had been an intention of charging Charles with wilful obstruction of the police in the execution of their duty but that the Lammeck Alley solicitor, a much experienced man, had managed to persuade them that this was unnecessary since the boy was merely hot headed and infected with the current craziness. There would be no further problems, the solicitor had assured the police blandly – well brought up boy you know, and all that – and faced with the lawyer's authoritative superiority and the fact that his client was obviously very rich they had allowed themselves to be persuaded. Charges were dropped.

When he had finished his reassurances Hannah looked at Marcus and smiled, or tried to, but only managed a grimace as the tears exploded at last. He put his arms out and she crept into them and wept until she was exhausted.

'It's silly, isn't it?' he said after a while.

'What is?' By now she was sitting back in her own chair, her head thrown back against the cushions, feeling the puffiness around her eyes, aware of the tear stains on her cheeks and not caring, almost revelling in her exhaustion.

'You treat me like a husband,' he said. 'When there's trouble, you call me. You want me, and you need me, but you won't marry me.'

'I tried to do everything myself first – ' she began.

'And had to call me. Hannah, stop being so silly. Marry me. You know you'll have to eventually.'

'Yes,' she said, and let her eyes, tired as they were, move so that she could see him. 'I decided that this morning in the synagogue.'

He sat very still, only looking at her, and after a long moment opened his mouth to speak, but all he said was, 'The synagogue? Were you so frightened?'

'Perhaps. But I needed reminding. Who I am. What I am. I thought that there – ' She shrugged.

'And what you got was a revelation telling you to marry me?'

She smiled then. 'No. Not a revelation. I just realized that it's all so – that it's not important. What I do, what anyone does, it's all so temporary, I might as well do what I want. Does that sound selfish?'

'No, only sensible. Not very flattering to me, of course,

506

but sensible.'

'Then I'm being sensible.' She laughed then, a little unsteadily. 'Hell of a way to start a marriage.'

'It doesn't matter how it starts,' he said, and moved towards her for the first time, putting out a hand to take hers. 'It'll be how it goes on that will be important.'

They decided not to tell anyone yet of their plans. 'Let Charles get well,' she said. 'Let me see how things are with him, and then we'll see where we are. Please?' He agreed, content enough to do as she wanted. He seemed to be as he always was to outsiders, but she knew the difference in him. He was, she realized, incandescent with happiness. His calmness, his relaxed speech, everything about him bespoke a deeply happy man, and she felt humble and almost afraid of her own power since she had made him so, and could destroy his happiness as easily as she had created it. She was still unsure of herself, still confused by her own feelings, still feared at a very deep level that somehow she would destroy him as she had destroyed two of his cousins, men she had loved dearly too. She tried to believe that this was mere superstition, that it had no basis in any reality, as he continually assured her. It wasn't easy, but she managed it by letting go, by not trying, just as she had stopped trying that morning in the synagogue.

Charles came home at the end of the week, not long after the strike had ended, looking much better with his swollen eye almost healed and his scratches almost gone, though his nose was still rather puffy. He was dejected because the strike had, he assured them, failed.

'The bastards have won again,' he said passionately that evening over dinner to which Marcus had come. 'Those damned bosses have robbed the working man.'

'Not quite,' Marcus said quietly, and launched himself into an account of the issues raised by the strike, as seen from the side of the owners. Charles lifted his head and listened and then, pushing his plate to one side, leaned both elbows on the table and began to harangue Marcus about the evil of his ways. Marcus listened and now and again, when he could, interpolated a comment of his own, or a rebuttal, while Hannah sat and listened and curiously, gloried in it. Her boy, her Charles, was able to listen and learn as well as to defend his views, confused though some of them were, though his speech was adorned with a good deal of the sort of political claptrap she had heard spouted at Speakers' Corner many times and had read in newspapers. He had clearly come to no intellectual harm from his conversion to religious and political fervour, and though it was equally clear there would always be anxieties about him, that he would never spend his life in quiet safe backwaters, still, she had reared him well. He was becoming a successful person in his own eyes and therefore in hers. He had, she suddenly realized, watching him as he talked on and on in the light of that spring evening, almost finished his journey from childhood to manhood. The downiness on his cheeks was a sturdier growth; his voice was heavy with a new maturity and his body was as muscled and active as his mind. 'I'm free,' she thought. 'I can do what I choose. Marry as soon as I choose.'

Free except for Marie. She felt a pang of acute guilt as her daughter's name came slipping into her mind. Since she went away, all she had felt was relief at her absence. She knew she should miss her, but she didn't. And yet, in an odd way, she did.

'Marcus,' she said, when Charles, still tiring easily as convalescents do, had gone to bed early. 'I don't want to tell Marie of our plans in a letter. I want to tell her myself.'

'She'll be home for the holidays soon, though, won't she? Tell her then?'

Hannah shook her head. 'She's going to Berlin. To the Von Aachens. I can't say no, really. They're her close friends now.'

He sat silently for a while and then he said, easily, 'Then we'll go to Lausanne and tell her there. As soon as you feel happy about leaving Charles. We'll fly to Paris, shall we? And then take the Rome Express to Lausanne. And maybe, afterwards, go to Rome, just for a holiday. Would you like that, Hannah?'

She looked at him, facing her across her chrome and glass table in her white dining room, at the solidity of him and the sureness of him and felt the leap inside her that she had once been afraid of, even a little ashamed of, but now welcomed for its promise of joy to come.

'Yes please,' she said. 'And I rather think I'd like to be

married before we go, Marcus. Because I'm not sure I can wait much longer, and you won't – you want me to make an honest man of you, don't you? So, how soon can it be? I'm not asking Marie's permission to marry you, you see. I'm just telling her.'

57

It really was a silly plan in some ways; they both agreed that, yet still they did it. They would have a civil marriage at a Registry Office first, of which no one but Bet and Florrie who were to be witnesses would have an inkling, and then after returning from their journey to Lausanne, a 'proper wedding'. A synagogue wedding under a canopy, with all their friends and relations crowding round, and a noisy party afterwards. 'I like it,' Marcus said with relish. 'Honeymoon first, God's permission afterwards. It's got style.' Hannah laughed and accused him of being a hypocrite, since surely what they were doing made her as wicked in the eyes of religion as those women at the Rothschild's party, an argument into which he refused to enter. 'I have my standards,' he said with a heavy imitation of a pompous professor. 'And I don't need to defend them.'

She laughed again. They laughed a lot during those weeks while they waited for the formalities to be sorted out, though they both worked hard too. She organized the Artillery Lane factory as tightly as she could, giving Cissie reams of instructions to keep her going during Hannah's first holiday from the place, and at Buckingham Palace Gate arranged that there should be a close-down for most of the time she was away. It was the easiest way to do it, and had the added virtue of making her clients even more eager to place orders for later in the year. Hannah had discovered that being captious and masterful with her customers, far from driving them into the arms of other couturieres, made them cling to her even more closely.

Marcus too was busy, sorting out his complex Lammeck Alley activities, for now that the old uncles had retired he ran the business almost singlehanded, though the place was staffed as it always had been with young Lammeck and Damont cousins and nephews. He had not had a holiday for a very long time, so there was much to be done. But he found time in the middle of it all to arrange for Charles to go away for a while.

'You've had a rougher time than you realize, my boy,' he said, when broaching his idea to Charles. 'I think you need some time to catch your breath and the chance to learn a little more. We have an office in Amsterdam – it's run by a sensible chap, Piet Damont. His son, I'm told, is a considerable Talmudic scholar, very involved with the community there, and a bit of an historian. You're so interested in Jewish matters now I thought you'd like to stay with him for a while, and learn as well as relax. The boy's a couple of years older than you – Henk, they call him. I think you'll like him.'

To Hannah's relief, Charles agreed. She saw him off from Liverpool Street Station, on his way to Harwich and the boat for the Hook of Holland, with a warm hug and a supply of money which he tried to refuse, but which she insisted he take.

So, when the day came, in early June, for her civil wedding to Marcus, she was ready in every way she could be, or so she told herself. The factory and the workshop organized, Charles in Amsterdam, Marie safely in Lausanne where they would soon see her. She was ready.

Yet she sat at her dressing table that morning staring at herself in her mirror, trying to fight down an acute desire to run out of the house and away, away to anywhere except Caxton Hall in Westminster where Marcus was waiting for her. She wanted to abandon everything, not only the thought of being married again, but work and children and house and relations. But why? It's not that they're all that much of a burden, she told her reflection. Are they? Marie's so far away, and Charles, too, and even Jake and Solly, still in New York and apparently happy there, and Uncle Alex – what sort of a burden is Uncle Alex? It's the reverse, surely – he regards *me* as someone he has to worry about. And the aunts and uncles and cousins in the East End, do I worry over them? Of course I don't. So what am I on about, thinking of them as a burden I want to abandon?

Her reflection stared back at her, blankly, and she examined her face slowly, feature by feature, until she manage to slip out of her own body and become someone else. It was as though she were not the red headed woman with the blue eyes sitting in front of the mirror, but a totally alien being who stood behind the red headed woman and looked at her, mocking her, disliking her.

Florrie came bustling in with a tray of tea, looking exceedingly smart in a grey silk dress with a matching hat with a cockade up the side.

'Oh, mum,' she scolded. 'There's you sitting there and not half dressed and me and Bet ready this half hour. The car's already here, and the chauffeur's having his tea, so you get a move on do! I'll pour your tea – oh, I'm that excited, I can hardly breathe! Bet's as white as your shirt, she's so overtook by it all. You getting married, mum, it's wonderful, and high time and you should a' done it long ago, but never mind. The best always comes to them as waits, and Mr Lammeck he's really the best, and isn't it lovely you ain't changing your name, mum? Now there's your tea, and I'll just help you step into your costume, and it's as nice a piece of silk as I've ever set eyes on and no mistake.'

She chattered on, and Hannah obeyed her urging, putting on her new lime green suit, and thinking, you too. You and Bet, I have to please you two as well. What about me? Where do I fit in? What about what I want? And then felt fury at her own stupidity for she did want Marcus, she wanted him very much indeed. He was offering her the first chance of simple uncomplicated happiness she had ever had. No one in the background to spoil it or be hurt (Marie? No, not even Marie). No echoes of Davida's cruelty or Judith's pain. Why be so uncertain?

It went on, all through the journey to Westminster in Marcus's new car, a rakish Bentley in cream and chocolate with long sweeping mudguards and deep leather-upholstered seats into which she sank with a sense of great luxury, and even after she was climbing the steps, Bet and Florrie solemn-faced and rigid with excitement behind her.

Marcus was waiting and she looked at him consideringly, still the sharp-eyed mocking creature who had stared at her reflection in the mirror, not her own red headed, blue eyed self. Who was she? Who was he?

He did not smile, but took her hand gravely and that made it worse, somehow, for she was wearing gloves and he

511

seemed remote through the thin fabric, a stranger. She took a deep breath and almost whispered it aloud. 'I'm going to run. I can't. Too many people to think about. I can't run.'

What happened then she could never remember. She had walked up the steps and Marcus had been there and taken her hand and then she had walked out, her hand tucked into his elbow and with a new ring on her finger and she was married, or so they told her, and she stood blinking in the sunshine as Florrie and Bet fluttered and giggled and wept, and she stared at them and thought, *why*? And did not know what she was questioning, let alone what the answer was.

They lunched at the Savoy, just the four of them, an idea of Marcus's, for he had told Hannah this was not their real wedding day and it would be a treat for Florrie and Bet, and she had agreed, grateful to him for being as aware of their importance in her life as she was. But then Florrie and Bet were in a taxi on their way back to Paultons Square, weeping happily and bidding her goodbye, and she and Marcus were driving out to Waddon to be flown to Paris. Once more strangeness swept in and she was lost in it. He seemed to understand, for he said little, holding her gloved hand lightly, and she was grateful. Time, she whispered in her head, give me time.

Paris, the drive from the airfield, the echoing steam filled railway station glowing in the dark of the evening like a miniature inferno. She shivered a little despite the warmth of the June night and he smiled briefly at her as the blue clad porters loaded their luggage into the train, and she tried to smile back. It was difficult.

They had their own first class wagon-lit, an elegant little compartment heavily panelled in walnut and full of chrome mirrors and little shelves and hooks and cupboards. They had their own adjoining bathroom too, for Marcus had used all Lammeck Alley's influence to obtain the compartment usually reserved for directors of the railroad. She undressed in there, slowly, very aware of him waiting for her in the compartment, and yet not excited. I wanted this, she told herself. Didn't I? I ached for him. I've wanted to go to bed with him for so long, yet now, I don't care. I'm tired. I just want to go to sleep. I'm numb. I don't want to. I don't want to ...

He was not in the sleeping compartment when she pushed

open the little swinging door, and she stood there as the train began to move to the accompaniment of a distant hiss of steam and the sound of the departure whistle and muffled shouts from the platform, feeling the train beneath her begin to pick up speed, standing in the swaying rattle listening, but all she could hear now was the wheels chattering over the rails as the train looped its stately way out through the Paris suburbs, going south-east towards Lausanne; diddly *dum*, diddly *dum*, diddly *dum*, diddly *dum*. It echoed madly in her head and she shook it irritably, and moved towards the bed the wagon-lit attendant had made ready for them, a handsome double sized bunk with crisp linen sheets and plump pillows, and slid in between the covers.

Marcus came in from the corridor, and she looked at him questioningly.

'I was smoking,' he said briefly and went into the bathroom, first turning off the light in the compartment, so that she lay there in the darkness trying to relax, trying to pretend to herself she was eager and hungry and ready for him, but the line of light around the bathroom door mocked her in the blackness, and she could not untie the knots in her belly.

The train rattled on, noisily sometimes, then more rhythmically for a while, and then chattered furiously again as a new tangle of points attacked the wheels and she tried not to listen because the interrupted rhythm irritated her, made her edgier than ever. Then the bathroom door opened and he came through and suddenly it was quite dark, as he switched off that light too.

She felt him move across the small compartment and then sit down beside her on the bunk, and after a moment he said, 'Shall I lie down, Hannah? Or would you be happier if I stretched out on the bench there on the other side? You're tired, I think.'

'Yes,' she said, and breathed in sharply through her nose so that she made a small hissing sound. 'Yes. Dreadfully tired.'

'Shall I, then?'

She was silent for a moment. 'No, Marcus, of course not. Come to bed. We'll sleep, and I'll be better. I'm just tired, that's all.'

'I know,' he said and she felt his hand on her cheek for a moment, as light as a breath. 'I know.'

He lay there beside her very still, his hands hooked

together behind his head, and she was filled with a great wash of gratitude to him, and then was more tense than ever because gratitude was not enough. What have I done, she shrieked silently into the blackness, what have I *done*? Why am I married? Marcus lay breathing quietly beside her and said nothing.

She must have dozed then, for the rhythm of the train changed and the swaying seemed to increase and she was rocking, lightly and easily, and it was a good safe feeling, a peaceful feeling and then, slowly and gradually, an exciting feeling. She was lying on a huge cloud of a cushion, a soft, silken cushion and she was being swayed from side to side so that there was a sweep of pleasure as she came down from one peak of the rocking, and then another as she rose again to the next and she was singing inside her head, and watching Marcus's face somewhere in the blackness above her, a smiling happy face.

The rhythm changed, became noisy and uneven and suddenly she was wide awake in the darkness of a moving train in the middle of France with Marcus there beside her, and she needed him then with all the urgency she had been suppressing for so long. She lifted herself on one elbow and tried to see him in the darkness and couldn't, and moved her head forward, searchingly, and felt his breath on her cheek.

'Marcus,' she said and felt his head turn towards her and find hers and she opened her mouth and reached for him with it and found his cheek, and then, still searching, his mouth, and clung to him, pushing her tongue against his greedily. For a moment he lay there and then she felt the surge of response in him as she moved even closer, but he pulled his head away and said questioningly, 'Hannah? Are you sure? Quite sure?'

She laughed then, a silly childish laugh, and put her hands on each side of his face and kissed him again and still he seemed uncertain, and she slid her hand down his neck and across his chest, and then on to his belly, pushing his silk pyjamas aside and then there was no doubt in either of them. They were rolling with the rhythm of the train, first against it and then with it, and the swaying of the bunk beneath them seemed to meld with the movements of their own bodies and then, somehow, they were part of the train as well as of each other. The whole world was movement and excitement and noise and great sweeping breathless drops and rises from peak to peak, and she laughed aloud again, a loud and breathless sound this time as at last the final doubts died, and with them the horrible mocking black creature who had dogged her all day. It was all *right*, at last. It could not be more right.

58

'Now this,' said Uncle Alex with huge satisfaction, 'is what I call a *wedding*!' He leaned back in his chair and hooked his thumbs into his waistcoat pockets and grinned at her. 'Real style, that's what it is, real style.'

She slid a glance at Marcus, mockingly, and he raised his eyebrows at her in a parody of husbandly reproof.

'To tell you the truth, Uncle Alex, I had remarkably little to do with it all,' Hannah said sweetly. 'Marie, and Marcus, were the ones who were most busy. He's a bit of a bully, you know.'

'She's lying in her teeth,' Marcus said. 'Ignore the woman – she's only my wife – and come and have another drink with me. You're looking a bit too sober for my liking.' The two men weaved their way across the crowded floor towards a bar which had been set up on the far side.

Hannah watched them go, smiling a little indulgently, happy to see them so comfortable together, and then smiled even more widely as Jake went swooping by with a Damont cousin in his arms, dancing with all the New York style he could muster. Since coming back from his eighteen months there with Solly, he'd been more American than the movies, something which had helped a lot with Marie. She had scorned her uncles while they were London East Enders, but New York East Siders were different – they had a special classiness of their own that made them socially acceptable to her, and she was very gracious with them these days.

Indeed, she was very gracious with everyone, Hannah thought happily, sweeping the crowded floor with her gaze, looking for her. It had been difficult, that meeting at Lausanne, over six months ago. Hannah had been afraid that

Marie would sulk and be difficult, or worse still refuse to accept Marcus as a stepfather, for their previous encounters had not been happy ones. But to her intense relief Marie had not only accepted him, she had been delighted with her mother's news.

'Does that make Daphne my aunt, then?' she demanded. 'I would like that, having a countess for an aunt, and you couldn't stop me from being friends with my own aunt, could you, Marcus!' She had laughed at that, giving him a wicked little sideways glance. 'I mean, you were madly annoyed with me for going to her parties, weren't you? And sent me home like a baby. But you couldn't do that if she were my aunt, could you?'

'You were younger then, my dear,' he had said gravely, 'and less aware of the ways of the world. Now you've been here to school and learned a little more, I think you'll understand more about how to behave, and also why I was so tiresome when last we met. I shan't be a nasty step-papa, I promise you.'

'I shouldn't let you be,' she had said airily, and for a moment Hannah had felt her belly lurch with apprehension, but then relaxed as she realized all would be well. Marcus would be tactful with her and Marie was genuinely pleased about their marriage, and threw herself with great delight into the business of planning the wedding. Hannah was glad to let her do so, for it gave the child something to keep her busy after her time at the school ended in September, and also to keep her mind off the change in her personal fortunes. For in August Albert died. He was not all that old, just reaching his sixtieth birthday, but he had chosen to retire from Lammeck Alley when his brothers did, though they were older than he and ready to do so, and somehow he had never really found his life worth living after that. He had left the bulk of his fortune to his granddaughter, Mary Bloomah Lammeck, to be hers absolutely when she reached her eighteenth birthday.

Hannah had been shocked by that. It was not that she did not want her child to be the heiress to such a sum (for Albert, although he had been a prodigal spender, had left a sizeable fortune). Any mother would want it for her daughter. But she knew her girl, and it frightened her to think of her having the use of so much at so young an age. Marcus shared her

516

concern, and it was he who told Marie of her inheritance in such a way that she did not fully realize how much it was, nor that she could have control of it in just over a year's time.

'The less she knows the better,' Marcus said. 'I'll see to the investments, and we'll try to keep any fuss about it to a minimum. Let her have her head with the wedding, my love, and that will help.'

Marie had indeed shown a remarkable skill for one so young in planning a big party, and Hannah had greatly enjoyed watching her busy with her lists and her plans and her estimates and her suggested menus and her decoration schemes. It was all so like the way she had been herself all those years ago planning Mary's ball for the old King.

There had been one altercation to mar everyone's pleasure in the coming wedding, and that had been Hannah's insistence that all her East End relatives be invited. Marie's brow had darkened in the old childish way, and she had expostulated bitterly, but Hannah had been adamant. It had been Marcus who had managed to persuade Marie that having an invitation list that covered every sort of society was extremely chic. He pointed out the way his sister the countess filled her parties with crooners and jazz players and boxers, anyone who was fashionable, and managed to convince Marie that a party that included Uncle Reuben and Aunt Minnie's great brood with all their husbands and wives and in-laws and children would be as chic as any number of jazz players and boxers. Amazingly she believed him.

'I'd rather leave Daphne and Rupert out,' Marcus had said to Hannah over dinner at his flat that evening. 'How I ever came to have so disreputable a pair as my closest kin I'll never know. Someone up there must hate me. Mind you, they say the same about me – they think me intensely boring. Still, what can I do? They're my sister and brother and Marie would never forgive me if I didn't ask her wretched countess of a new aunt! You don't want that ice, do you Hannah, my darling? Say you don't and come to bed.'

That was the silliest part of that summer and autumn and early winter of 1926; their pretence that they were not yet married. It would have made no difference to anyone at all if they had chosen to set up house together as soon as they came home from Lausanne, indeed Florrie and Bet expected him to move in to Paultons Square. But, perversely, they chose to wait until the 'proper' wedding was over. So, all through those long months each of them lived in their own home, and worked at their own work. They made love whenever they could, either at Marcus's flat or at Paultons Square on the rare occasions when no one was at home to interrupt or disturb them. It was mad, but it was fun, and it also had another function; it gave Hannah the time she had so badly needed. Time to make the move from her old life to her new one, time to realize that she was not some sort of threat to Marcus, that she could be, eventually, the happy successful wife she so wanted to be.

And now, sitting here at her own wedding party at the Savoy Hotel, watching the great banqueting suite pulsating with people dancing to celebrate her happiness, she felt deeply content. The metamorphosis was complete, she told herself. She was happy, and she could go on being happy.

The music changed and the floor thinned out a little and she could see the children across on the other side of the room. 'I shouldn't call them that,' she thought, and smiled at herself. Children, with Charles, newly home from his prolonged stay in Amsterdam, so tall and handsome, and Marie so exquisitely grown up as she was! Seventeen now. It didn't seem possible.

They were standing side by side near the bar where Marcus was still talking to Uncle Alex, and there was something in the way Charles was hovering over Marie that made Hannah more watchful for a moment. He had been different somehow, since coming home, still besotted with his politics, of course, though less involved with religion. It seemed as though his long period of study with Henk Damont in Amsterdam had burned that passion out of him. He had been Barmitzvah as he had said he would be, shortly after returning to London, at a quiet service one very wet morning at a synagogue where none of the family was particularly well known, so that there was the minimum of fuss, and then had spent less and less time with David at his yeshivah, much to David's regret, though he did not question it. Charles no longer wished to study the word of God? All right, that was his affair and God's. He, David, would turn his attention to his own boy Lionel, a precocious lad of nearly seven. One day *he* would be David's great scholar, since Charles had decided to abdicate that role.

518

Charles instead began to work at a settlement, in Jubilee Street, not far from David's home, running a youth club for the local children and teaching them politics with every chance he got. But it was mostly in the evenings that he was really busy. His days were largely his own and once Marie had come home he had taken to spending more and more time with her, helping her with her planning, running errands for her willingly. Hannah had been delighted to see it. She had tried to rear them as happy brother and sister, and she had been sad when a split appeared between them as it had after he had left Eton. To see them so close again now was warming. But she watched them now across the ball-room floor and wondered. Brother and sister? Was it really like that? Or had it changed? There was something about Charles's posture as he stood watchfully beside Marie that made her dubious.

Marie was talking to a tall young man, and Hannah wondered who it was. She could not see clearly from this distance and he had his back to her. She got up, pushing aside the table bedecked with flowers at which she had been sitting, and began to move across towards the little group there by the bar.

But Marcus was back. He slid his hand under her elbow and bent his head and whispered, 'Isn't this exciting? Imagine, married! At last!'

'Idiot!' she said, and lifted her face and kissed him, and he grinned at her, cheerfully. 'Where were you heading so purposefully?'

'What? Oh, Marie. I thought – I wanted to tell her how lovely she looks. And how beautifully everything went. And how happy I was in the synagogue this morning. All those things.'

'And I thought you were going to scold her,' he said lightly. 'You had that mother-hen look on your face.'

'I suppose so,' she said consideringly, and then made a face. 'I was a bit bothered. Charles – ' She turned her head to look for them again. 'Look at him. He looks so ... I'm not sure. What do you think?'

The dancers who had been clustered in the way moved a little and she could see where the trio had been, but only Charles was there now and she frowned, for he was leaning against the bar looking, she thought, rather pale.

519

'I thought Marie was there,' she said, and began to move again towards Charles. Marcus followed her.

'Hello, my boy,' Marcus said. 'Why so pale, why so wan, alone and palely loitering? Has the Belle Dame – whoever she was – been at you?'

Charles looked up and made a little grimace. 'Do me a favour, Uncle Marcus, I can do without the gags. I'm just a bit bored, if you must know. I know it's your wedding, but really, all this – ' he swept his hand out in a comprehensive gesture. 'It's really obscene, isn't it?'

'Obscene?' Marcus said, interested. 'Where? Who's being obscene?'

Charles shook his head irritably. 'You know quite well what I mean, I've said it often enough.'

'Yes, you've said it. And you're right, up to a point. A lot of rich people stuffing themselves and drinking too much when half the world is starving. But there are other values as well as concern for the poor, you know.'

'I don't know of any,' Charles said harshly.

'Oh, family feeling, and giving pleasure to others, and rites of passage to make people happy about the way their experience changes – things like that! You can't make the poor any happier just by making the better off miserable.'

'That's a specious argument, and well you know it,' Charles began hotly, but Hannah moved between them and took each of them by the elbow. 'I'm damned if I'll have politics at my wedding,' she said lightly. 'Charles, my love, where's Marie? I wanted to tell her how clever and lovely and altogether splendid she – '

'Gone,' Charles said shortly.

Hannah's eyebrows snapped down. 'Gone? Where?'

He looked at her with a sharp little glance from dark eyes that seemed suddenly to be thick with tears, though he was quite dry eyed. 'She's got a tendency to slope off from weddings, hasn't she, our Marie? But no need for any worries, so don't look like that! She's gone with your brother, Marcus. He's taking her on to a party. Apparently the Prince of Wales will be there, no less, and you know our Marie. Can't resist a name and never could. Told me to tell you, so I'm telling you.' He pulled away from her a little abruptly and moved across the big room to sit beside David and his family and talk earnestly to them.

Hannah watched him go and frowned and then Marcus said softly, 'Oh dear,' and she turned and looked up at him, her forehead creased.

'I think I know what's happening to our Charles,' Marcus said. 'Bad enough the poor chap's been bitten by this wretched political bug. Add love on and he's really floundering.'

She turned to him and put her arms up so that they could dance, for the music had started again and she could see her cousin Leon moving purposefully towards her and she wanted to talk.

They moved through a few turns, dancing easily and comfortably as they always did, enjoying the contact with each other, and then she said abruptly, 'Do you really think that's what's happened? They grew up together. People who were children together don't fall in love, do they?'

'It's been known,' he said. 'And they've been apart a lot lately. She's changed a lot, you know. Since Lausanne. Much less petulant, and very – oh, I suppose poised is the word. I don't like it, sounds like a damned magazine, but it fits her. She's a very handsome young lady, your Marie, and very beguiling. I can see he'd be bowled over by the change in her.'

'Has he changed, too, then? I thought he had. He seems bigger, somehow, since he got back from Holland. And just as involved with his ideas, but less, well, childish about them than he was. They seem more a part of him. Will it be all right for him, Marcus? Will she see the change in him and be bowled over too?'

'Darling, I don't know.' He held her close as the music changed yet again, sliding into a very romantic waltz. 'And stop trying to be Mrs God. I know you'd like to run their lives for them and make it all cozy and tidy, but you can't. Leave them to sort out their own feelings, and concentrate on ours. Have you told me today how much you love me?'

'Can't you remember?'

'I don't choose to. Tell me now.'

She told him, and they danced closer still and she felt her cheek against his and his back strong and relaxed under her fingers and knew she was blessed. But even while she revelled in her own happiness, dancing at her own wedding, she watched Charles sitting alone now on the far side of the room and staring down at his fingers and thought about her Marie, out somewhere with Rupert. It shouldn't worry her, for Rupert was a grown man, well able to take care of any girl he escorted. So why was she worried?

It's a habit, she told herself, and looked up at Marcus and kissed his cheek. A bad habit, worrying about Marie. High time I stopped it. She'll be fine.

59

'So, then what happens?' the Prince said, enthralled. Marcus looked across the room and caught Hannah's eye and she nearly exploded into laughter but somehow managed to keep her face straight.

'What happens?' Sadie said. 'I tell you, it's like nothing you never saw in your whole life! They go *meshuggah* – '

'*Meshuggah*?' murmured the Prince.

'Crazy! Mad!' Sadie made a face, twisting her cheeks and mouth into an extraordinary grimace and crossing her eyes ferociously and the Prince blinked. 'They carry on like there's never been no fish brought into the place before, they jump up and down, they holler, they swear, you should forgive me mentioning such vulgarity to such a person as yourself, they hit each other sometimes but mind you, no hard feelings. Business is business and when it looks like someone else is gettin' a barrel of herring you got a fancy for, and what you knows is the best, sure you get *broigus* and hit out a bit – '

'Broigus?'

'Oy, Your Majesty, imagine me giving you a lesson in Yiddish!' Sadie beamed hugely. '*Broigus* means annoyed, put out, not very pleased, you know?'

'I'm beginning to know,' the Prince said. 'Now, what was that other word you told me? *Maven*. One who knows. I trust I'm beginning to be a *maven* – and to help you be a *maven* – Mrs Lazar, may I explain to you that it isn't correct to address me as majesty. Sir will do.'

Marcus had moved across the room to stand beside Hannah. He murmured in her ear, 'I don't think I *believe* this. I know he fusses about democracy and getting to know the

522

people, but finding out from Cousin Sadie how to run a fish shop in the Mile End Road is taking it to the outside edge of enough – she'll be offering to take him with her to Billingsgate next.'

'I tell you, sir, Your Majesty,' Sadie said with an even wider beam, leaning forwards to tap the Prince's arm with a large red hand much bedecked with garnets. 'I'll tell you what. You feel like getting up a bit early one morning? I'll take you down the market, show you the ropes! We'll buy the fish, you'll come back to my place, have a cupper coffee, an onion platsel maybe, and a nice bit fried halibut – '

'Too kind, but I rather think that will be difficult. Other demands you know, other demands, although it's all so interesting, Mrs Lazar, I truly regret it is not possible. But I wish your business every success in the future, indeed I do. I trust you will – er – always get the barrels of herrings that you fancy.'

'From your mouth to God's ears!' Sadie said and clasped her hands together prayerfully.

Someone on the other side of the room changed the record on the gramophone and the rhythms of the 'Black Bottom' scattered people into dancing couples and the Prince turned away to talk to Lady Ingham. Sadie sat and fanned herself happily, revelling at being at so smart a party. 'Although,' she later told her enthralled customers, 'it wasn't what you might call a proper catered affair. I mean, no food as you'd notice, just a few bits o' this and that on a plate, and more cocktails than I've had chicken soup, I tell you. Still, what do you expect of these fancy people?'

Hannah relaxed. She'd been doubtful about this party but Marcus had insisted and he had been right. He had become one of the Prince of Wales's most trusted advisers during the year they had been married, even though Marcus disapproved of some of the Prince's other friends, and was not afraid to say so, but the Prince respected his views and allowed him to say what he thought. They saw a great deal of him though usually within the same close circle of familiar people. But Marcus had told her the Prince wanted to know more about other people in his country, and it had been Marcus's idea that they give a party that mixed both sides of their family, to give the Prince the chance he wanted. So here were several of the Lazar clan, including David and his Sonia,

523

together with the regular aristocratic crowd. It shouldn't have worked, but it did.

Later, as they undressed for bed they talked lazily and comfortably of how it had all gone, of what Lord Ingham had said to David Lazar and how well David had put him in his place when he had tried to condescend, of the splendour of Cissie's new dress – for she had been a particularly successful member of the party, quite captivating the Prince with her talk of life in Artillery Lane – and how well Florrie and Bet had managed.

'I wish the children had been here, though,' Hannah said. She was sitting at her dressing table cleaning her face with cream, and he laughed as he looked at her, for she had made a mask of the thick white stuff, and her eyes peered through like holes in snow.

'Children!' he said. 'You don't look more than a child yourself, like that! Do stop it, love. You try too hard with those two. They're all right.'

'Are they?' She wiped her face carefully with cotton swabs, watching him through the mirror all the time. 'Are you sure, Marcus? I wish I could be.'

He threw his hands in the air in mock despair and now it was her turn to laugh for he was wearing only his socks, neatly held in place with sock suspenders, and the effect was ludicrous. 'What more do you want, Hannah? They're engaged! Isn't that what you thought would be the best thing for both of them? Why do you go on worrying so much?'

'Put your dressing gown on, do. I can't talk sense while you're prancing around like that. I suppose you're right. It all seems well enough, but somehow I don't know. I still worry. And they weren't here tonight and ... oh, well.'

Long after he had fallen asleep and was snoring softly beside her, his head pushed into the curve of her neck as always, she lay awake still thinking about Charles and Marie. They had come bursting into the house on a hot June afternoon, their hair bedraggled and their clothes dripping wet, because, they had said, they had fallen in the Serpentine while having a boat battle with a crowd of friends. 'And,' announced Marie, all wide eyes and excitement, 'He positively saved my life, darling Charles, and I realized he wasn't just my big brother after all, and I'm going to marry him. So there!' Charles had stood there, his face white and rigid with

524

joy and his dark eyes looking as though someone had switched on a light behind them, and Hannah had laughed and cried together, she was so delighted for them.

But that had been six months ago. As the summer went on and they went away, all four of them, to a villa in Mentone which belonged to Julian Damont and which most of the family borrowed from time to time, and came back to plunge into the business of their hectic working autumn, she had become chilled and anxious. Marie seemed happy enough, singing a great deal, and being cheerful and friendly with everyone, and behaving very affectionately towards Charles in front of them all, but Charles seemed less serene. Sometimes Hannah would notice him watching Marie with a brooding sort of stare and then, as he realized she was looking at him, would smile reassuringly and try to look unconcerned. And there were times when Charles, headlong into one of his favourite political discussions with Marcus, who was always willing to defend his own capitalist viewpoint cheerfully against Charles's passionate attacks, would redden and falter and give up when Marie yawned at him or seemed sulky and bored.

But as Marcus said, they seemed content enough, though they both slid off the subject when Hannah tried to discover what their future plans were: did they want to marry this year? Next? Where would they live? Would Charles continue with his settlement work, or had he thought of something else to do? Marie would sparkle and laugh and kiss Charles's cheek and hug him and say, 'Oh, Mother, dear one, do stop rushing us! We've lots of time yet, haven't we, my angel? I'm not eighteen yet, and Charles isn't all that much more. We'll get round to it. It's just so lovely being engaged, I want to enjoy that.' Charles would just look at her with his face devoid of expression and say nothing.

And of course Marie was right. They *were* both very young to marry. There *was* plenty of time. But surely, Hannah would ask herself, surely that isn't the way young people in love talk? They don't say sensible things like that. They want what they want when they want it. It's just not ringing right, somehow. Not ringing right at all.

She had stifled her anxiety and learned to stifle her questions too, and was a little rewarded when Charles started to work full time as a welfare officer for his settlement, dealing with the needs of the old and ill people as well as the young ones in the Jubilee Street area, becoming busier. He left the house each morning at the same time she and Marcus left for their respective work, leaving Marie to sleep until later, and came home long after they did, on some evenings working until almost midnight. But Marie seemed not to mind his absence too much, and filled her days with shopping and chattering on the telephone with her girlfriends and going to matinees and afternoon concerts. And on the evenings that Charles was working late, she announced she would go with him to his silly old settlement and work too.

'I might as well,' she said, pouting a little, 'Mightn't I, Charles?' She looked at him challengingly, her eyes very bright, and he glanced back and smiled briefly. 'I mean, if he insists on doing such a job what can I do, poor little creature that I am? Put up with it, I suppose!' She laughed, a very merry little sound and began to talk of the dreadfully exciting gossip about her friend's marvellous new fiancé, who was a film actor from California and given to violent attacks of jealousy which made him behave very excitingly indeed. 'She had a black eye yesterday when I saw her at Fortnum's,' she said with great relish. '*Too* marvellous.'

She had been invited to spend the Christmas holiday in Paris with Daphne. Marcus had not been very pleased with the idea. Since his marriage he had seen little of his sister or his brother Rupert, and though he and Hannah did not talk about them, she knew that he found their ways ever more distasteful. She read of Daphne's doings herself sometimes, in the gossip columns, and felt keenly for Marcus, for there was no question but that Daphne had become a very talked about lady indeed. She saw little of her husband and seemed to devote her time to spending her considerable fortune as fast as she could. Her mother, Susan, had persuaded her own father to leave the bulk of his money, made in diamond trading on the Amsterdam bourse, to his only granddaughter, since Susan had been of the opinion that her sons would be well provided for by their Lammeck connections but that her daughter needed extra care. She had died content in the knowledge that her dear Daphne was safe for life, although, Hannah sometimes told herself, she would spin in her grave if she knew the efforts Daphne seemed to be making to spend all she had before she was forty.

Rupert seemed to be no better. Because Marcus had shown himself from his earliest youth to be capable and hard working, while Rupert had been a lazy, butterfly-minded boy from his earliest school days, Ezra, their father, had in his wisdom seen fit to leave the bulk of his money to his younger son before dying in the same 'flu epidemic that had killed his wife. It had been inevitable that the three of them should have split as they had; Marcus had to earn his living. He had done so handsomely, and was now a major shareholder at Lammeck Alley in his own right. He had gained his security by his own efforts. Daphne and Rupert, however, were of a different metal entirely, living lavishly on their income and sometimes even dipping into capital, behaviour that shocked the financial side of Marcus severely. Rupert at least worked sometimes, which redeemed him a little in Marcus's eyes. As a Lammeck he had almost automatically inherited a job at Lammeck Alley, and did in fact come drifting into the office occasionally, to try his hand at being an assistant sales director. His work was of small value but at least he tried, so sometimes Marcus was still hopeful for him. But he still could not approve of his social activities, any more than he could approve of his sister's.

But Marie adored them both, and it was difficult to give her any good reason why she should not spend time with them. They were her stepfather's family, how could they be bad company? There had never been any obvious breach, nothing on which Hannah or Marcus could base an embargo, so dislike the situation though they did they said nothing.

'Better to leave her to get bored,' Marcus counselled. 'Or for them to get bored with her. And anyway, once she marries Charles it will be all right.'

She returned from Paris after Christmas, looking tired and a little drawn in spite of swearing she'd had a super, fantastic, marvellous, glory-making time, while Charles looked paler and thinner than ever. He had worked every night rather than just three or four a week, to keep himself busy while she was away.

Tonight, as she lay in bed beside her peacefully sleeping husband, Hannah tried yet again to convince herself that all was well with her much loved children. Since Christmas it had seemed better, with Marie a little quieter and not so bubbly and Charles less busy at the Settlement and spending more time at home with them all. Hannah had felt better until tonight, when she had come downstairs to check all was ready for the party, to be told by Florrie that Miss Marie had gone out at seven o'clock and never said where she was going, and Charles had come in from his settlement just after, and when he had been told Marie was out, had gone right out again himself.

All through the evening that had nagged at the back of her mind; they had not said definitely that they would be at her special party, but both had known it was important for her and Marcus, a sort of social experiment. It had been taken for granted that the young Lammecks would be there beside the older ones to see it through.

Not a fair assumption, I suppose, she told herself now in the darkness. I shouldn't have taken it for granted. I'm sure they would have stayed in if I'd asked them to.

She slept at last, and woke to the uneasy light of heavy snow on the rooftops opposite her bedroom window. It made her restless, and even though it was still only seven thirty, and she usually did not get up until eight, she slid out of Marcus's sleeping grasp and showered and dressed.

As she came back into the bedroom to sit at the dressing table and put on a little makeup, he woke, and reached out to pinch her bottom approvingly as she passed the bed.

'You're early,' he said, yawning.

'I woke early – couldn't sleep.'

'You should have woken me. I'd have thought of something to keep us busy till breakfast.'

'That was why I didn't. I love you, my darling, but seven in the morning isn't exactly my best time of day ... Marcus ... '

'Mm?' He was out of bed now, padding into the bathroom.

'I've been thinking about Charles. I know there's no way he'll ever work with Lammecks in the office but maybe there's some sort of job you could suggest for him that would let him earn a little more and at the same time feel comfortable? He'll never go into any sort of business of course, but – I thought, this welfare job he does. Don't some of the Lammeck factories use people for jobs like that?'

'Yes, but I doubt he'd agree to take one, and anyway, I'm not sure that I would want him to work for us. We've done

528

quite well with our plants, less trouble with the workers than most of our competitors and I want to keep it that way. Let Charles loose in among 'em and we'll start having unions and strikes and heaven knows what. I love you dearly, Hannah, and I care a lot for Charles, but I'm a business man, remember. There's a limit to what I can do, ought to do, to please you. Anyway, he's happy enough where he is. What difference would it make if he did get another job, anyway?'

'Maybe they could get married,' she said after a moment. 'I know he's got money of his own to live on, and of course Marie has hers, but I don't think Charles will agree to use it. I tried to talk to him about his own money once and he got furious, told me to give it away. As for Marie –' she stopped. 'I suppose we'll have to tell her now. It's been six weeks since her birthday. She's got a lot of money. Have we any right not to let her know?'

He came back into the bedroom wrapped in his bathrobe, rubbing his newly washed head dry with a towel. 'There's no obligation to tell her,' he said. 'I've talked to Peterson and he agrees with us. The longer it is before she realizes how much she has, the better. And once she does know, Hannah, do you think that will help? If Charles won't live on his own inherited money when he gets married, you can be damned sure he won't live on his wife's.'

She got up and tweaked her skirt into place. 'I suppose you're right. Oh, damn, I wish I could stop fretting over them. It was just ... last night ... '

'I told you, darling. No point in worrying. If there is anything to worry about, you'll know soon enough. Go have breakfast, and read the papers, and stop being a mother hen. You make a better business woman, believe me.'

He was right about one thing. She'd find out soon enough if there was anything to worry about. She found out as soon as she got downstairs.

60

When Hannah came into the dining room Charles was sitting in the window embrasure, staring out at the snow. She blinked and she looked at him for the combination of white furnishings within and the icy glitter from outside dazzled her for a moment. He seemed to be surrounded by little points of light himself and she had to put her hand up to shade her eyes.

'Charles? Have you had your breakfast? No, that's silly of me, Florrie hasn't brought any yet. She shouldn't be long though. Do come and sit down, and tell me what sort of day you had. I haven't seen you since this time yesterday.' *I won't ask him where he was last night, I won't.* 'What happened to that old lady you were telling me about? Did you manage to get the eviction order changed?'

'She's gone,' he said, and his voice sounded flat and very ordinary. There was no special emotion in it, but there was an odd note all the same, and she looked at him sharply.

'Oh, I am sorry, Charles! After all you've done, too.'

Florrie came bustling in with her trolley and began to slap things on the table, toast and the coffee pot and boiled eggs in their neat little cups, complaining bitterly all the while about the coldness of the morning and the iciness of the back steps when she put her foot out to fetch in the milk. Hannah murmured a good morning. Charles said nothing until the door closed behind her. Then still sitting in the window embrasure and still using that same ordinary flat voice he said again, 'She's gone.'

'Yes, I heard you. And I'm sorry.' Hannah began to pour coffee. 'I know you were very worried about her, poor thing. Did you manage to find another room for her? Or did she have to go into the workhouse? I do hope not.'

'Not my old woman,' he said, a little impatient now. 'Marie.'

She put her coffee cup down with a little clatter. 'What did you say?'

'Marie. She's gone.'

'Gone? Where?' Absurdly, she looked around the room as though Marie were there somewhere hiding behind the furniture. 'I don't understand.'

He sighed, irritably, as though she were a wilful stupid child he was trying to teach the alphabet, and turned his head to look at her. 'Will Marcus be long? I don't want to have to go through this twice.'

Fear took hold of her, making her belly feel as cold as the street outside.

'Charles! Tell me at once what all this is.' But he ignored her and went to the door and opened it and called, 'Marcus!'

'Coming!' Marcus was already half way down the stairs. 'Good God, boy, no need to hustle me! What's the matter with everyone this morning? It's only quarter past eight, we're no later than we usually are. Earlier if anything. Morning, Charles. Florrie! Bring me some tea, can't cope with coffee this morning. Too much last night, indigestion. Hannah, love, where're the papers? I want to see *The Times*.'

'Marcus, Marie has gone,' Charles said loudly and Marcus stopped at once, standing still like a child playing a game of statues, half bent to sit down.

After a long moment, he sat down, and Hannah, moving automatically, poured a cup of coffee and pushed it at him. She did it every morning, and even though she knew he didn't want it this morning, had heard him ask for tea, she still did it.

'You'd better explain, I think,' Marcus said quietly. 'And Charles, you'll feel better if you come and sit down and have some coffee. Come on, boy.'

Surprisingly, he did, coming to sit in his usual chair between them, facing the empty one which was Marie's, on the rare occasions she took breakfast with them.

'I ... last night,' he began and then stopped and shook his head. Marcus pushed the coffee cup at him and Charles drank thirstily, spilling the coffee a little on the table cloth, for his hand was shaking.

'I can't start with last night,' he said at length. 'That was just the end of it, really. I – look, I'll tell you all of it, but for Christ's sake, don't interrupt. I couldn't stand that. Questions when I've finished.'

Florrie came in with a teapot and extra toast for Marcus, and they sat in silence till she'd gone and then he started. His voice remained as flat and commonplace as it had been all the time, but underneath it Hannah could feel the painful control in him, and it was that which distressed her almost as much as what he told them.

'It was all right, at first. Marvellous. Happy and all. Talked a lot, we did, about how it was when we were small, and about my mother. She remembered her as much as I did, you see, but different things, and it helped, having her telling me what she remembered. Made Mama more ... complete, you know? I remember her as shadowy bits. Like a jigsaw puzzle with some of the pieces lost. It spoils the picture. And Marie filled in a lot of the pieces for me. That was marvellous. And she let me talk about what mattered to me, about all the bad things there are in the world, and I thought she was learning and beginning to care properly and understand. About how destructive it was to be so rich and comfortable and, well, anyway, I thought she was as happy as I was. But then – '

He stopped and Hannah opened her mouth to say something but Marcus slid his hand under the table and grasped her knee hard, and she closed her mouth again, grateful to him.

'I suppose it was natural she'd get bored. I mean, the settlement work's great for me, but ... she's a girl. Different. And it's mucky sometimes. People smell, you know? They can't always help it and anyway, what does it matter? But it bothered Marie and she said she'd go out with her friends, that she wouldn't bore me having to see them because she knew I loathed 'em and she wouldn't inflict them on me, but that they were her friends and, well, it was a matter of ... of justice and equality, wasn't it? You can't believe things that matter about how people should be treated and not treat the people you love that way. I mean, equality and freedom isn't just for the masses, it's for individuals. Me and you, and Marie. So she wanted to see her friends and I didn't, so I said fine, and she started to go out in the evenings with them while I was working and she said it was great but not to be stuffy and tell you because you'd taken a hate to Rupert and would stop her seeing him just because of some stupid family feud. And I – ' He looked up at Marcus miserably. ' – I believed her.'

Marcus lifted his eyebrows at Charles, clearly asking permission to speak, and Charles nodded. 'No feud,' Marcus said, 'but I can't deny I'm not – I don't think he's a good friend for Marie.'

'Nor did I. I said so, and she said I was stuffy too and we argued ... and then we made it up.' He bent his head and his neck began to redden as a tide of colour rose and Hannah felt another wave of acute embarrassment. I shouldn't be told this. It's not right I should know. It was something between them.

'After that – I – what could I do? I'd behaved dreadfully, taking advantage of her. She said I hadn't, though.' He looked at Marcus and it clearly took some courage to do so. 'I – she said that, Marcus. Said that it was more her than me, and that it was only sex and to stop being so stuffy and stupid and old and anyway I – anyway I wasn't the only one who ... But I didn't know what to do. It was the first time for *me*, you see, and – ' He shook his head and then with a curiously childlike gesture rubbed his mouth.

'Well, after that, it was impossible. I couldn't say, don't do this, don't do that, could I? And I couldn't come and talk to you, though I wanted to. Not after what I'd done. I felt filthy. Wicked. Like an oppressor.'

'No,' Hannah said. She could not help it. He couldn't be allowed to go on like that, hating himself. If she had been there with them, seen what had happened, she couldn't have been more certain that he was in no way the instigator in whatever had been between them. 'No.'

He looked at her and for one brief moment managed to smile.

'That's how I felt, anyway. Which is why she's been going around with him these past three months, parties and all, and you thought she was with me. So there it is.'

There was a long silence and then Marcus said carefully, 'And now what? You say she's gone?'

'There's nothing you can do,' he said drearily. 'She married him, you see. In France at Christmas. I didn't know myself till last night. I knew something had happened, because she stopped – I mean, stopped caring whether I said anything to you or not. It helped a bit that. I mean, I'd felt before I was keeping quiet to please her. At least since Christmas it's been to please *you*. I didn't want to upset you, you see. And I couldn't see what difference it'd make if you did know she was going around with Rupert. Making you unhappy wouldn't make me any happier. I think I've known for weeks she wasn't going to marry me. But when she told me last night she'd married *him*, well, that was different.'

'Married,' Hannah said. 'Married. Rupert. Married.'

'In France?' Marcus said sharply. 'Are you sure about that? It was legal?'

'Oh, I think so. I'm sure it was. Daphne helped them, I gather. She's got an apartment there somewhere near the Rue St Denis, hasn't she? Oh, she let them say they lived there and that made it legal. Anyway, it's a proper marriage. They stayed together all through Christmas at the apartment and then ever since – she hasn't always slept at home, you see. It used to drive me wild!' He slammed his elbows on the table so that the dishes rattled and put his face in his hands. 'I knew she was up to something but it never occurred to me that – ' He took a deep breath and sat up again. 'Anyway last night, she got a message from Rupert, it seems, and ran off, and I got worried and went after her because Florrie told me she'd heard Marie tell the cab driver an address and I went there to have it out with her. I thought it was rotten of her to leave last night, you see, what with your party and all and I was going to tell her so. But that bastard Rupert was there, and that was how it all came out.'

'Hannah, I'll look more into this,' Marcus said and leaned over and took her hand in his. 'Please, darling, try not to panic. She's under age and – '

'But what's the point?' she said drearily. 'You heard what Charles said. They went through some sort of legal ceremony in France. And anyway, if it's what she wants, what can we do? What should we do? Charles, I'm truly truly sorry. She's treated you appallingly and I'm sick with shame.'

'No. Aunt Hannah, please don't cry. It isn't your fault! She's just – it's not even Marie's fault.' He was crouching beside her now. 'Please Aunt Hannah, don't cry or I shall too. It's all ... let it be. It's happened. Let it be.'

'What are they going to do?' Marcus asked, and Charles squeezed Hannah's hand and stood up.

'I don't know – well, not for sure. Last night she told me I could – she said she was going to stay with Rupert and I could do what I liked. Tell you or not. She's a married woman now and I can't do anything. So I came away. I walked around for hours. I couldn't come and interrupt your

534

party, could I?'

'*Bloody* party,' Hannah said violently. 'Of course you could. You're more important than any party.'

'Well, I couldn't. And when I did get in you'd gone to bed and your light was off and I thought, why wake you? News like this keeps, doesn't it?'

'Charles. I . . . thank you, Charles,' Marcus said. He put his arms around the boy's shoulders and held him close, hugging him, and after a rigid moment Charles bent his head and began to cry on Marcus's shoulder, silently and helplessly, his shoulders moving clumsily with the savageness of his tears.

Outside the snow began again. Hannah sat and stared out at it and thought of nothing at all but the falling flakes and the way they looped and danced and thudded silently against the glass of the window, and the weight of the grey sky looming over the eerie whiteness of the ground beneath.

'We'll have to go and see them, Hannah,' Marcus said, after Charles had agreed to go up to bed. He'd sat up all night apparently, just sitting and staring out into the square, and now he was exhausted. Hannah had told Florrie, of course; she had to and anyway Florrie had always been part of Marie's life. She had as much right to know as anyone else. She had primmed her mouth and said sharply, 'Well, there was no way she was ever going to do anything to please anyone but herself, mum, and there's an end of it, so don't you go blaming yourself, for no one never had a better upbringing.'

'I suppose so,' Hannah said and then closed her eyes. 'I feel so unnatural, Marcus! She's my daughter and I love her but all I feel is fury at the way she's treated Charles. How could she be so cruel? How could she? And why don't I care more about what she's done, and about her happiness? It's not right.'

'It's right and it's natural,' Marcus said firmly. 'And it's sensible. There's nothing you can do to change Marie. She is what she's always been, and I suspect it was to be. A totally self-centred person, beautiful and vivacious and charming and wholly selfish. It's just one of those things. But Charles is different. And never forget he's as much your child as she is. You may not have borne him, but he is your son.'

'Yes,' she said drearily. 'Yes. And I've got to go and see

Marie and remember she's my daughter. Whatever she's done, she's still my girl.'

'You won't forget,' he said. 'Come on, love. I'll have to go via Lammeck Alley I'm afraid. There are some early appointments I'll have to sort out.'

'And I'll have to call Artillery Lane too,' she said, and rubbed her face distractedly. 'Damn, there are three big deliveries I wanted to be there to see on their way.'

'Then we'll stop there too,' Marcus said calmly. 'Work has to go on, and I doubt she'll be out of bed anyway, much before eleven. She never is here so why should she be in her own home?'

'Her own home,' Hannah said and shook her head wonderingly. 'I can't imagine it.'

When the car drew up in front of the building Hannah sat very still for a moment and then, as Marcus took her gloved hand and squeezed it hard, took a deep breath and smiled at him, albeit a little tremulously, and got out. It was in Sloane Street, a block of modern flats, and a uniformed commissionaire led them through a heavily carpeted lobby towards the ornate gilded lift.

'Expensive,' murmured Marcus, as the lift purred upwards. 'Very expensive. I can't imagine these flats cost much under three hundred a year.'

'Three hundred – are you sure?' Her forehead creased. 'Charles seemed convinced that this was their own flat. Is Rupert that well off?'

'I don't know. He had a sizeable income, but he's been a free agent for a long time now. He's twenty-six, remember. It's been more than five years since I had any involvement in his financial affairs.'

The door was opened by a maid in a very chic French uniform, very lacy and tight and Hannah thought of Florrie in her commodious aprons and how she would sniff at so fancy a creature and was, momentarily, amused. The flat was luxurious. Wide windows overlooked the street, and there were heavy pile carpets, glass and chrome furniture, and very modern paintings on the walls. It was untidy, however, with cushions hurled on the floor and a litter of unwashed glasses and overflowing ashtrays scattered about, which the maid seemed to regard with distaste and an air of unconcern, as though whoever was going to clean up, it would certainly

536

not be she.

They waited in the stuffy room, which smelled of cocktails and stale cigarette smoke, for ten minutes before at last a door opened and Marie came out, her hair rumpled and her face streaked with stale makeup. She was wrapped in a man's dressing gown. She stood and stared at them both for a moment and then made a face.

'Rupert,' she shouted, and kicked the door behind her. 'You'd better come. Storm warning's gone up.'

'There's no need for that sort of attitude, young woman,' Marcus said strongly. 'Let's get that clear for a start. We've come to see if you are well, to sort out what has been happening, and to do so in a civilized manner. There are not going to be any storms of our making. I hope there will be none of yours. I've better things to do with my energy and so has your mother. Is that understood?'

She stood and stared at him for a moment, looking very young suddenly, like a child who has been playing with her mother's makeup. Then she said awkwardly, 'Well, all right, all right. It was just that I thought...'

The door opened again and Rupert came out. He was wearing only pyjama trousers in a heavily brocaded black satin and had a sweater tied by its sleeves round his shoulders. He had a cigarette between his lips and looked half asleep.

'Well,' he said awkwardly and then produced a cheeky grin, trying to look as though he couldn't care less. 'My in-laws, as I live and breathe! Little Boy Blue blew his horn then, did he? Sent you looking for your little Bo Peep?'

'Charles told us that you two are married, if that's what you mean,' Hannah said quietly.

'Damn him,' Marie said viciously. 'I didn't want to make any fuss yet. No need to go meddling.'

'Not a word about Charles, Marie,' Hannah said firmly. 'I won't listen. Now, what is all this? Is it true you're married?'

'Yup!' Rupert said. 'Thought we might as well. Madly romantic and madly wicked. Catholic Church in Paris! How's that going to get to the old biddies round the family, hmm? But it's right and tight and legal, I promise you. Went through all the right French channels, that we did. You can't overset it.'

'I don't intend to try,' Hannah said.

There was a little silence and then Marie said carefully,

'You don't? But I thought you'd be furious! Aren't you?'

'I'm hurt,' Hannah said after a moment. 'I didn't think I was so difficult that you had to be so hole-in-the-corner. I didn't think Marcus was so difficult a stepfather either – but angry? What would be the point?'

Marie ran then, like a child, trotting across the room with her face split from side to side with a huge grin. 'Oh, Mama, I do love you! I didn't want to upset you, honestly I didn't, but Rupert said ... Well, you know how you are about him and Daphne, and it was such a lark, and there was the money and all – '

'Money?' Marcus said sharply.

She looked over Hannah's shoulder at him, hugging Hannah hard all the time. 'Well, you didn't tell me, did you? There was I getting a lot from Gramps when I was eighteen, and if Rupert hadn't found out at Lammeck Alley I'd never have known. I thought ... Rupert thought ... '

She faltered and looked back over her shoulder almost fearfully. 'Rupert?' she said.

'Well?' He was leaning against the bedroom door, his arms folded over his bare chest.

'You said, didn't you, they'd try and stop us on account of the money?'

He tilted his head, and squinted at them over the smoke rising from the cigarette between his lips. 'It occurred to me that you might. Why keep it so close to your chest, I asked myself? Is it to make sure the family money stays in the family? To let little old almost-brother Charles get it? It occurred to me – '

Hannah hardly saw Marcus move, he was so fast. Suddenly, he was standing in front of Rupert, his shoulders rigid with fury. She heard the sound rather than saw his hand move, and then Rupert was standing there, one hand to his face and his cigarette smouldering on the carpet at his feet.

'You apologize at once for that,' Marcus said, his voice unrecognizable to Hannah. 'At once, you hear me?'

There was a long silence and then Rupert shrugged sulkily and moved his hand from his face. Hannah could see the red weals left by the contact of Marcus's fingers.

'Well, for Christ's sake, Marcus! We're bloody Lammecks, aren't we? People who go on and on about money all the time! Why should you be any different? If it wasn't so, then it

538

wasn't, and I'm sorry, but you don't have to make such a drama.'

'But I do,' Marcus said, and came back to stand beside Hannah. 'Now listen to me. You two are married. All right, you're married. We won't interfere and can only hope the pair of you can be happy. I'll see to it that Peterson sorts out Marie's finances in such a way that she's protected from you. No, don't you dare say a word! I know about the sort of extravagance you're capable of, and Marie has to be protected. There'll be settlements and arrangements made. I'll see to it that he advises you on finding somewhere better than this to live, where you won't spend such a fortune, and we'll do all we can to see you on the right road. But be warned, Rupert. If ever you do anything to make Marie anything but very happy, I personally will deal with you. Do you understand me?'

There was another silence and then Rupert shrugged and muttered, 'Okay, okay! Leave me alone, will you? I've got a headache. I'm going to take my bath. Stop playing the big brother. Do me a favour, and leave me alone.'

Marie drew back from Hannah then and went back to stand beside Rupert, tucking her hand into his arm.

'It's such fun!' she said and her voice was high and fluting. 'Too too ridiculous. I mean, Mama, you're my sister-in-law now, aren't you? Isn't it too too delicious?'

61

22 Paultons Square,
Chelsea

2 January 1931

Dear Edie,

Well, here I am at last finding a minute to say thank you for the lovely stockings which fitted perfectly, and just the right colour to go with my new gunmetal costume with the coney collar that Madam gave me specially made to measure just like she does every Christmas, as always being very thoughtful. I was glad to hear that Kenneth is well and has got over his whooping cough so nicely, I always said as he was the strongest boy of all your children and would be a credit to us all and so he seems to be turning out what with his scholarship and all. I am sorry to hear your George has been playing about but that's men isn't it, even the best of them though I must say as how our Mr Marcus seems to be a different sort, but for my part I am glad enough I never did marry for all you keep on having a go at me about being an old maid in your letters ha ha! Anyway no need to go on over all that old ground it doesn't make for happy families does it. We go on here much as we always have with You-Know-Who coming to dinner twice this past month and behaving as always very handsome to me and Florrie leaving a very nice gratuity on his way out and when he does get to be King then we'll all be very lucky though not a word of ill would I wish on his father of course but you know what I mean. I cooked him a lovely turbot in hollandaise sauce and an ice pudding and trimmed it all very fancy and Madam said I was the best cook in London and was very nice about how it all went. She looks better now, at last, though she was so peaky poor lady all last year and it wasn't only the way she was after she had come out of hospital having had her operation after that miscarriage, I think it was the sadness of her tragic loss that got to her for after all with her older one behaving so funny it's natural she should want a baby of her own again, but as Florrie says maybe it was for the best seeing as how she's getting on a bit and you do see these funny babies born to older women though Madam isn't only thirty-eight and looks very young with it. We've been very busy here seeing as how Mr Jake and Mr Solly who you will remember are Madam's brothers and keep coming and going have been here over Christmas and all but they are going back to America soon lucky them but they've got their interests there now and doing very nicely it seems, certainly they look very well dressed and fatter than ever they both got a tendency that way not to say I haven't too lately, but as time goes on what can you expect. They say it is all the food they eat in New York and they come into my kitchen sometimes and try to tell me about cheesecakes and such things but I don't pay no attention they are just like you and George great ones for having a go. Mr Solly tells me all the time about the people he meets and he talked to Al Jolson he said and well I was that surprised because Mr Solly says he is a very hard

540

man but in his films he is so lovely. I saw Mammy last week at the Empire Leicester Square and it was lovely I cried and cried do go and see it when it gets to you there in Whitby though of course you'll have to wait a long time Whitby isn't exactly like London is it, my turn for a joke. I will write again soon and will tell them all at Thorpe Bay when I hear from you and do give the children my love and tell your George not to be so silly I will tell him myself when I come to you in the summer.

    Your loving sister,
        Bet

                            Lammeck Alley
                            17 March 1931

Mr Rupert Lammeck
Sir,
    I am in receipt of yours of the 13th inst. and have noted the contents carefully.
    I must tell you, however, that your request is not one to which we can accede. As has been explained to you on sundry earlier occasions the Settlements involving your wife's monies cannot be altered in any way except at her request and then only in certain circumstances.

                            Lammeck Alley
                            27 March 1931

Mrs Rupert Lammeck
Madam,
    I am in receipt of yours of the 19th inst. and have noted the contents carefully.
    It is of course possible to do as you request, and arrange earlier remittance of such sums as are due to you in this calendar year, but would respectfully beg that you reconsider your request. You will recall that last year you had drawn all income due for the year before the end of April, and this caused great embarrassment to your Trustees who are loath to act in any way that will jeopardize your long-term interests.
    The fact that they had to draw on capital for you to maintain you for the remainder of the year caused great

anxiety among the Trustees and we would sincerely trust that such a situation will not arise again.

I also trust that your husband can be helped to understand that matters to do with the Settlements are entirely a matter between yourself and your Trustees and it is not helpful in any way when he addresses somewhat vituperative letters to individual Trustees as he has done in the past.

22 Paultons Square,
Chelsea
11 April 1931

Dear Henk,

Thank you indeed for the cigars – a most welcome birthday present though I must say being twenty-three makes me feel exceedingly old. So much to do and a constant feeling of too little time in which to do it!

You ask about progress here – and I have to admit it is slow. God knows times are hard enough – people ought to be recruitable, for ever since the Wall Street debacle money has become tighter and tighter in the East End. But however much we talk to them we don't seem to be getting through. Street meetings get only desultory attention, organized hall meetings get even less, which leaves only door to door. We aren't helped too much by the activities of a new breakaway group from the Labour Party either. They're trying door to door recruitment, too, and seem to have a certain appeal we don't, probably because they don't have any connection with the old Bolshevik scandals of the past which linger on in people's minds here and frighten them. It's little use telling them we're different, they just don't seem to believe us. So Mosely's lot, that is the new group, seem to be making headway. I'll be watching their development most carefully.

I've heard from my stepfather through some of his connections that a cousin of his, who married into a German family (von Aachen they're called, do you know them?) has become involved with the German National Socialists, and that there is a possibility of their man Hitler getting support from the industrialists. They mentioned someone called Hugenberg. I'd be most interested to know of anything you pick up.

No, I am *not* returning to Yeshivah. That was, I now

realize, just a stage in my political development. I needed it, but I no longer do. My commitment now is entirely to the Party, and that being so I cannot involve myself in Talmudic studies however intellectually seductive they may be. Indeed, the more seductive they are, the more important it is that I keep well away. There is work to be done, and it must be done soon. I can't indulge myself with religion. It's a false comfort and saps energy from what most matters. But we've been through all this before, Henk, my dear old friend. Please let us not be deflected by such arguments now. We're much too good friends for that, and are in step with so many other important issues. My love to Miep,

    Yours ever,
      Charles

                     Hotel Magnifique,
                     Ostend,
                     Belgium
                     24 August 1933

Dear Uncle Alex,
    Just a line to let you know what a marvellous time we are having. We've taken over almost a whole floor here, as you can imagine, and with people in and out of each other's rooms all the time we're getting known as the crazy Englesi among all these French and Germans and what have you! The children are having a lovely time on the beach every day and we are too and the weather though not marvellous is thank God not so bad we can't have a good time. Charlotte's Monty isn't too well still, but then he always was a bad traveller, you'll remember the first time you sent us all on holiday it was the same. I'm sending you a card with this letter showing you our rooms in the hotel. I've marked them all with crosses and names so you can see we're really getting value for money. Believe me, Uncle Alex, we're all very appreciative, and please God you'll be able to come with us next year.
    Much love from Charlotte and Monty and children, Bella and Harry and children, and of course from David and Lionel, as well as me,

    Your loving niece,
      Sonia

WESTERN UNION CABLEGRAM NEW YORK NY 165AT
LIONEL LAZAR SHOREDITCH TOWN HALL LONDON
ENGLAND NOVEMBER 17TH 1933 PREPAID

MAZELTOV ON YOUR BARMITZVAH STOP MAY YOUR
FUTURE BE ALL YOU WISH YOURSELF STOP SORRY
CANNOT BE WITH YOU STOP MUCH LOVE UNCLES
SOLLY STOP JAKE

GPO GREETINGS TELEGRAM DIDSBURY MANCHESTER
NOVEMBER 17TH 1933 LAZAR SHOREDITCH TOWN HALL

MAZELTOV AND LOVE TO YOU DAVID AND SONIA ON
THIS SPECIAL DAY STOP MAY YOUR LIONEL BE ALL A
SON SHOULD BE STOP REGRET CANNOT BE WITH YOU
ON YOUR SIMCHA STOP URGENT BUSINESS IMPOSSIBLE
STOP CHEQUE FOLLOWS STOP LOVE UNCLE ALEX

News Chronicle Gossip Column, 1 January 1935

The New Years Honours List published today includes the name of Marcus Lammeck, Managing Director and senior partner of the noted city firm of Lammeck and Sons. His knighthood is regarded as long overdue by many of his City colleagues who know him to be a man of great integrity and dedication. Sources close to the new Sir Marcus whisper that it is his friendship with the Prince of Wales that has made him unwilling to accept this long overdue mark of appreciation for his services to business for fear he would be marked down as a mere courtier. However, the Prince prevailed upon him we are told as did many of his friends, pointing out that no one who knows Sir Marcus can be in any doubt of his fitness for such an honour. Lady Lammeck, who is the noted couturiere Mary Bee, is said to be pleased for her husband but will not be using her title in her own business. The family is not new to titles, of course, for that vivacious and well-known lady-about-town, Countess of Markmanor, whose husband the Earl is currently wintering in Italy, is Sir Marcus' sister. Last night, interviewed at the Kitcat Club Lady Daphne, was in the company of Beverley La Vere, who is dazzling West End audiences with his neat footwork in the chorus of Cole Porter's 'Anything Goes' at the Palace Theatre . . .

544

22 Paultons Square
Chelsea
17 October 1936

Dear Edie,

Well, I am sorry not to have answered yours sooner, but you didn't have to write so sharp to me just because I had missed one letter. When you don't know what is happening then you can't really say can you and you made me very upset the way you wrote and I had to stop Florrie writing to you very sharp indeed she was that upset at the way you made me cry but never mind I am used to being misunderstood by you Edie and really it's time you stopped to think before sounding off like that. I will tell you what has been happening and then perhaps you will understand why I have had no time or heart for letter writing of my own though if you read the papers properly you would have seen something about it I am sure and would understand and not write nasty to me. Anyway it started when our Mr Charles got very upset about this here Spanish War and was all set to go and fight though as I said to Florrie what business it is of his I really don't know but Madam was upset and asked him please not to it was bad enough his Dad was killed in the Great War and to please her would he keep out of it and he said he would but it was clear as a window he was very upset and was going to go anyway sooner or later and as I said to Florrie better sooner I'm sure because I remember last time that those who went early and got small wounds didn't die the way the young ones as went later did as well I remember because of Sam Chambers as I was going out with in 1915 as you'd remember if you had any heart instead of twitting me about having old maid ideas. Anyway, that is neither here nor there because as I say Mr Charles stayed here at home but was fretting dreadful you couldn't help but see it though he was going out every night as usual to all his meetings in the East End though why he doesn't find a nice girl and settle down I can't say. Then there was this dreadful march in the East End all those blackshirts and we was all that upset well you can imagine. I know you say some nasty things about Jews but I say speak as you find and my Madam has always been as kind and thoughtful as anyone could be and as I say to Florrie many's the time she's the most Christian lady I ever had to do with, speaking of kindness and good manners and that, anyway I was very upset because even those cousins of Madam that come here and aren't all you might expect such a lady as her to have have always been good to me and live and let live I say, and why have marchers in the Mile End Road got to go making trouble like that? It was big trouble too because the young Jews took it bad as is natural and turned out and fought them and of course our Mr Charles was there and it was just like last time only worse, you'll remember all those years ago I told you what happened in the General Strike when he got so hit about and got his nose broken which quite spoiled his face he used to be such a beautiful baby. This time he got hit even harder and his wrist got broken and the trouble was it was policemen he got fighting with because he said they was making it easy for them blackshirts instead of understanding that peaceable Jews got a right to live in their homes like any other Englishmen and Englishmen they are I don't care what you say. So of course there was big trouble and he was arrested and come to court and you must have seen it in the papers they was full of it with the *Daily Mail* being very nasty on account he's got such rich relations and the *News Chronicle* taking his side, it was all very upsetting one way and another because we had all those reporters coming here like anything. And then when he got home from the hospital Miss Marie was here with her husband who I can't like, it's no good he really puts my back up but she loves him I suppose so what can you say, well, they was here because Miss Marie had had a fight with him, Rupert I mean, and come home to her mum as she always does when it happens and it happens a bit too often that I can tell you, but she always goes back to him more fool her. And he'd come here to get her because they'd made it up. Anyway home comes our Mr Charles and I made a lovely dinner to celebrate, a really beautiful rib roast with a Yorkshire pudding it really was one of my best as light as you can imagine and there they are as happy as can be I thought and all of a sudden there's such a noise from the dining room and me and Florrie goes rushing up and there they are fighting on the floor, Rupert and Charles and it was dreadful with Marie crying and Sir Marcus as white as I've ever seen him he was that angry and to cut a long story sideways young Mr Charles is going to Spain after all and Marie and Rupert is going to live in America because he says there's going to be big wars again in Europe and he wants to get away while he can and why don't we get out he says so you can see what a nasty object he is. I'm glad to see the back of him though Madam is very upset on account of losing her Marie as she sees it, but I said to her, it's not the end of the world exactly, and she'll come home and don't our Mr Jake and Mr Solly keep coming and going between here and America but she's still that upset ...

35 East Thirty-Fifth Street,
New York,
USA

1 November 1936

Dear Hannah,

Hope this finds you as it leaves me, in the pink. Don't worry about our Charles. He'll come out on top, he always has, hasn't he? I hope we can visit come the New Year. Jake thinks it's possible, business here is beginning to pick up with bigger takes though the real money's gone out of boxing, as I was telling Uncle Alex when he was last here. It was good to see him, he's looking very well, I thought. I enclose a cutting from a newspaper here, very interesting isn't it? Do tell me what Marcus says, seeing he's a friend of his and all. People here keep asking me because I'm English, but I say to them from where should I know? Still it would be nice to have a bit of news so do ask Marcus. I'll look forward to hearing from you.

Your loving brother,
Solly

New York Post Gossip Column, 20 October 1936

Royal circles in Britain are still in a great turmoil, a little bird tells me, over our Mrs Wallis Simpson and the Prince of Wales. Will she be Queen Wallis, everyone is asking themselves, though not of course the ordinary British people who are being kept totally in the dark ...

Hotel Bristol
Nice

12 December 1936

Darling,

I'll be leaving here tonight, train to Paris, to sort out some financial matters for David, and then should be home by the weekend. I miss you – he's coping well enough, and she seems to be calmer now. It's been a horrible business and I'd rather have had no part of it, but he asked me, and I'm sorry for the poor devil. If someone had tried to stop me from marrying you, I'd have done the same, of course, so who am I to judge him? But all the same I'm sick about it. Still, we managed to get him away well enough from Fort Belvedere and he was grateful. I got some news out of Spain, so this expedition was as good for me as it was for David, since I discovered that Charles is *fine*. He's been given a staff job because his wrist is still weak and that's something to be grateful for. He was in Madrid when the attack came – Moroccans and Foreign Legionaires mostly I gather – but they evacuated the rebel staff and he went with them so he's safe and looks to stay so. Try not to fret, my darling. I'll be home as soon as I can.

The Times, 27 February 1939
Today both Britain and France formally recognized General Franco's government in Madrid.

News Chronicle, 7 March 1939
British members of the International Brigade are seen in this picture returning from Madrid. Inset – wounded men accompanied by British VADs

28A Southbridge East,
Tiburon,
San Francisco, Calif.

3 January 1940

Darling Ma,
Yes I know I should have written sooner but really, life is too too hectic. We spend so much time driving up to Hollywood, and it takes all day and then some, but *such* fun, we see a fair bit of all sorts of interesting people. Met Cary Grant last week, too divine. I think you'd adore him, I know I do, and then there was a party with Claudette Colbert, lots of lovely gossip, which I'll write to you as soon as I have the

time. Rupert's behaving rather well at the moment, because he really feels this is where we belong, you know, so much our sort of world and people are saying he could actually get some sort of work in films! He'd like that and I'd be green with envy, but there it is. Who wants a swollen pregnant female on their screens? Never mind, as soon as the baby's born I'll see what I can do – and do stop fussing, Ma! Of course I'll be all right. People have had babies before, though I can't imagine why they bother, it's so boring, isn't it? Hope you keep well and there's no bad war news. Rupert was right, wasn't he? We got out just in time.

62

'It feels so *ridiculous*,' Hannah said, staring down at the cable in her hand. 'I mean, I'm actually a grandmother! Knowing it was going to happen didn't mean much, but now it has I feel so odd.'

'Why should you be any different?' Cissie said comfortably. 'I got three o' the little *mumserim*, God bless 'em. Such lobbuses! My Lenny told me, last week, Stanley got sent home from school for selling aeroplanes.'

'Aeroplanes?' Hannah was diverted momentarily.

'Sure. Paper ones his sister made him. Sold 'em for tuppence each to the other kids and told 'em they'd protect 'em from the raids when they came. Right little villain he is.'

'He'll go far,' Hannah said absently and stared again at the cable. 'She doesn't say anything, just that it's a girl. No birth weight, no name, nothing.'

'Oh, Hannah, when'll you learn?' Cissie said. 'That Marie of yours, she's a naughty girl! Not a letter have you had from her for months and months, she just don't care. No good fretting over it. That's the way she is.'

'Yes,' Hannah said and tucked the cable in her pocket, smoothing it carefully first. 'I suppose so. Still, she let me know about the baby. That's something.'

They went on with the packing in silence, though Cissie coughed occasionally as the dust rose from the folds of fabric, and Hannah looked at her anxiously. She was looking haggard these days, every minute of her fifty years, and was a little thinner than she used to be, but she had refused to see a doctor and there was little Hannah could do to make her.

'That's it then.' Cissie straightened her back and looked around the empty showroom. 'They can take this as soon as they like. I'll do a check, shall I?'

'I'll come too,' Hannah said. Cissie looked at her sharply and said nothing, but nodded and together they came out of the workroom and began to go from floor to floor down through the old house.

It looked mournful in the June sunshine thrown through the tall windows, the pale patches on the walls where pictures had hung and bare boards on the stairs where once the thick pile carpets had been. Mirrors, drapes, everything had gone, packed up and sent for storage out to High Wycombe.

'Although,' Hannah had said, 'Why High Wycombe should be any safer than London, I don't know. They could as easily bomb there as here.' But they had gone on, systematically stripping the Buckingham Palace Gate house of every sign that Mary Bee Couturiere had filled it with busyness and work and purpose for fifteen years.

'That's it, then,' Cissie said when at last they stood on the steps. 'I'll be here in the morning with the keys to let the men pick the stuff up, and then I'll leave the keys at Artillery Lane. When will you be there?'

'As soon as I get through at Whitehall. It looks as though its going to be ATS uniforms, rather than WAAF ones.'

Cissie grimaced. 'Pity. I like blue better than khaki. That was one thing about the last do. Striped print and red and blue capes – it was a pleasure to work on, sort of. This time, all khaki – oh, well, *was machst du*? That's the way it is. G'ey g'zint Hannah. See you tomorrow.'

Hannah watched her go and thought again how ill she looked, and made up her mind to phone Lenny tonight. A good boy, Cissie's Lenny, successful and busy in his accountancy office, for Cissie had done him proud when it came to education, and living in great comfort in a handsome solid house in Willesden with his handsome solid wife and handsome solid children; a good boy who cared still about his mother, although his wife sniped at her a good deal, finding her East End voice and her raucous East End manners offensive to her sense of propriety. Nice Jewish women didn't behave like that, Lenny's wife thought, and was busy rearing her two daughters to be nice Jewish girls with a liking for silk underwear and respectable addresses and refined accents and disdain for their tough old grandmother.

Grandmother, Hannah thought now, as she turned and began to walk up towards the park. I'm a *grandmother*. It doesn't seem to bother Cissie, it never did, but maybe it's different when you actually see your own grandchild, hold her, know her.

She remembered herself suddenly, with the baby Mary Bloomah in her arms, sitting on a box in the ice cold dimness of the Antcliff Street house, feeding her, a memory so sharp she almost felt the small mouth pulling on her nipple, and she shivered, in spite of the warm sunshine, pulling her jacket across·her chest and walking faster.

The park was lovely, alive with people on this hot afternoon, and she let the smell of hot crushed grass and roses and syringa drift into her, enjoying the way the heat came and went on her face as she moved under the trees with their great leaf carapaces. Even the busy squads of men toiling over the digging of trenches and the filling of earth bags couldn't detract from the loveliness of the afternoon; and she wouldn't let them. They had lived with doubt and fear and then let-down for almost a year now. They had steeled themselves for bombs that had not come, and for battles which had not erupted, and now all the preparations seemed rather pointless, and far from alarming.

Even when she was at Whitehall, sitting in those vast echoing offices with those polite murmuring men talking about the methods of supply and collection that would be used when she started her uniform making again, she could not believe in this war. It wasn't like last time, when the casualty lists and the constant flurry of wounded soldiers at the railway stations were a constant reminder of what was going on over the Channel. This time it was different, a nothing war, an empty war. They were getting ready for nothing, nothing at all.

But as she reached the far side of St James's Park and began to walk towards Admiralty Arch, she knew she was deluding herself, and she knew why. It was a real war. Germany had moved into Holland two months ago now, and since then there had been nothing. Silence, total silence and the only way she could cope with it was by pretending it wasn't so. Really, he wasn't there, her Charles. He had not gone there to see Henk and make plans for joining the left wing forces in Germany. He hadn't told her that he had heard of things happening to Jews in Germany that had to be taken seriously, had to be dealt with. It wasn't true, it couldn't be. She had told him that, passionately, when the first refugees had begun to arrive, filling people's heads with tales of persecution.

'I don't believe it,' she said. 'They look all right, well fed and dressed and, they aren't like the people I knew in the bad days, Charles! Then they hadn't clothes to call their own, hardly, when they arrived at Tilbury with just a bag of bits and pieces, and starving into the bargain! These are cultured people, well fed,' she repeated. 'It's not true, it's not *true*.'

But of course it was. The old fires were smouldering again just as they had when her father had been a boy, at home in the shtetl in the old Pale, so long ago. For months now, even before Hitler had marched into Poland, they had been busy, the Lammeck and Damont women, the Rothschilds and Sassoons and Abrahams, the rich and safe ones, collecting money, arranging for friends to be scooped up and brought out of Germany and Poland and Czechoslovakia and Lithuania and Estonia and wherever else they could. It was bad and might get worse yet.

'No,' she whispered into the trees above her head in St James' Park as she walked on, faster, ignoring the way the exercise beaded her upper lip with sweat. 'No. It's all right. He's going to be all right. He'll come home soon.'

She tried to see him, tried to imagine him coming up through Paultons Square towards number 22, his curly hair riffling in the breeze, his injured leg kicking out to the left as it had ever since the battle of Teruel in Spain, when his knee had been shattered by rifle fire and been left permanently stiff. At least that had brought him safe home then, and though she had wept for him she had been glad too, for it meant, she had told herself, an end to it all. He would stay here, be ready to admit he'd done enough, might even learn to forget Marie and be happy with someone nice, marry, have babies.

But of course it wasn't like that. He wasn't going to come home to Paultons Square for he was still there in Holland, had been there almost six months, and there had been a total silence from him since May 10th.

Germans in Amsterdam. Soldiers with rifles and heavy grey helmets and heavy grey uniforms and heavy grey faces in Amsterdam. She could not imagine it, and tried to distract herself from her fears by remembering the Amsterdam she had fallen in love with in the spring of 1935 when Marcus had taken her there for one of their rare holidays.

They had taken the car, the big Bentley, crossed the Channel at Dover and had driven briefly through the north of France and on through the Flemish countryside to the Netherlands and the bulb fields. She could still remember it, the sea of colour and the great waves of scent that had broken over their heads. She had been drunk with daffodils, giddied with hyacinths and tulips and jonquils and narcissus and by the time they had passed Rotterdam and the Hague and come rolling through the flatness into Amsterdam she had been giggling and silly and he too had been skittish, making dreadful puns and roaring with laughter at them.

They had gone on like that all the time they were there, behaving like silly children as they walked through the streets of Amsterdam, leaning over the canal bridges to watch the barges beneath. The bells of the Westerkerk, as they walked slowly along the Prinsengracht, had made her cry deliciously, not a sad crying, but a happy moist emotionalism that, he told her, laughing, was sheer chocolate-boxery and she had laughed as well as cried and told him he was absolutely right, and that she was full of tinsel too, and held his hand and walked on over the cobbles, deeply happy.

And now there were German soldiers in those tall thin houses with the bell gables and the hooks above to carry up goods to the high floors, and in the restaurants with the fat waiters who waddled everywhere, almost falling over their too-long white aprons, and at the herring stalls on the corners of the bridges and in the Dam Square and on Waterlooplein.

And in the tight narrow streets of the old city where the Jews lived. They had gone, she and Marcus, almost accidentally to a service at the Spanish and Portuguese synagogue at the Jonas Daniel Miejerplein, not because either of them was particularly anxious about synagogue attendance, but because they had happened to be walking there that Saturday morning and seen the people go in, dressed in their best hats

553

and shining with soap and virtue, and almost without consulting each other had followed them. They had parted, she to sit in the gallery above and he to sit below in a borrowed *tallis* and his very English bowler hat on his head, and listened dreamily to the singing and prayers and come out blinking into the noonday sunshine, responding happily to the nods and smiles of the other congregants, and gone to eat a vast Dutch lunch which was anything but kosher with no sense of guilt or embarrassment. It had all felt so right, so comfortable, so natural. As she walked now through St James's Park in London five years later, where men in khaki sweated over filling bags with earth ready to protect buildings when the German bombs came, she remembered those Dutch people in their half circle city of water and cobblestones and bells and tried to imagine it filled with German soldiers. And could not. It was as though her mind could not take hold of the vision of that water-shimmering city being anything but flower filled and carillon-echoing and happy in the sunshine, and she knew she felt so because of Charles. While Amsterdam remained in her mind a peaceful place it was possible to face the fact, the cold bitter fact, that Charles was there and had not sent word since May 10th.

She reached Whitehall in time to almost collide on the steps with Marcus, who had arranged to meet her there. They went together to the third floor of the War Office, where they were to settle the plans for turning Artillery Lane into a uniform factory again. He looked a little pale. She took his arm and held it close for a second, and he smiled at her reassuringly.

'Darling, I've had a cable,' she said.

'Marie?'

'A girl. That's all it says. Nothing else. It came from Los Angeles, not San Francisco, so you were right, they have moved. I wish they'd let me know!'

'She's still getting her money through all right,' Marcus said, and squeezed her hand. 'We'll hear soon enough if there's anything really wrong. At least they let us know about the baby, Grandma Hannah! Never mind, darling, I still love you.' He kissed her cheek briefly, somewhat to the shock of a passing clerk, and led the way into the office.

They went afterwards to one of Uncle Alex's tea shops in the Strand and sat opposite each other sipping the thick brown brew that had made so large a part of Uncle Alex's fortune. After a while she put her cup down and said, 'Marcus – I think we're going to have to move, don't you?'

He looked at her briefly and smiled. 'I knew if I waited you'd see it. It's not going to be easy if the bombing does start, and – well, it's a responsibility. I thought it might be better to try to fix a flat somewhere nearer the factory.'

She grinned at him. 'Psychic. As ever. I talked to Cissie about it. We can convert half the top floor into quite a neat flat, she says. Now's the time to do it while there are still some people around to do some work. Marcus, I'm not wrong, am I? It is going to get worse, isn't it?'

'Yes,' he said after a moment, and put down his cup. 'Yes. I've been talking to people, War Office and Defence. There's no question of it. Dunkirk was a bad business, bloody marvellous but bad. And Hitler's sure to follow it up. The ones in the know are getting ready for a big push. Quite what it'll be we don't know, but it'll be big. So, we've got to make plans accordingly. And being near the factory is a good plan.'

'Is it near enough for you? To Lammeck Alley, I mean?'

'I'll be spending more time in Whitehall than Lammeck Alley,' he said. 'I . . . ' He looked at her sideways. 'I tried to join the air force but they wouldn't have me. I'm young enough, just, but they had another job for me.'

'Thank God,' she said and closed her eyes. 'Oh, Marcus, I'd have ... how could you without telling me? After last time, I – ' she shook her head, her throat filling with tears so that she couldn't speak.

'I know. That's why I had to try. As it is, I'm getting a uniformed job, but they'll never let me out of London, so don't panic. Army. They're putting me in as a major. Supply and munitions.'

He reached over the table and took her hand.

'If . . . if they try to send you to France . . . ' she shook her head again, still choked and this time he laughed, gently.

'Darling, it isn't that kind of war any more. No one's digging trenches in Flanders or round the Marne. They've pushed us out of France, and it's going to be a long time before we get back there. I'm certain of that. We won't sort the Germans out in mud baths this time. This time it'll be different, God help us all. And I'll stay in London, where I'll be safe, with you. As safe as any of us can be, I promise.'

63

'All right, all *right*,' Cissie said distractedly, and reached for a rag from the pile in the corner to wipe the woman's face and then hugged her briefly. 'I know what it's like, believe me I know. Mine went last week. But they're better off gone, believe me, better off.'

The woman sniffed again, thickly, and began to weep once more, the tears rolling down her face unchecked. Cissie looked at Hannah and grimaced.

'Let her go home,' Hannah said softly. 'She'll be better off there. Let Milly go with her.'

They sent the woman home, and the machines began to whirr again, but the pall of emotion still hung over the wide factory floor. It had been a dreadful morning, and Hannah shared the woman's misery even though she herself had not had a child involved in the exodus.

They had gone from Stepney Green station, the children, all those over five, with their big handwritten labels tied to their coats and their gas masks in cardboard boxes strung over their shoulders and bouncing on their bottoms as they walked and their suitcases and bags of food and sweets and apples clutched in their hands. They had looked bewildered, some of them, and a few had been crying but most of them were just as children always were, noisy, excited by the fuss going on around them, unaware of what it all meant, even the big ten- and eleven-year-olds. All was orderly until the evacuation officials herded the children off down to the platform and onto the trains and refused to let the mothers seeing them off come any further, when one by one the women burst into wailing. The children, looking back, saw then what was happening, and began to cry too, and then it was an inferno of noise, of sobs and shouts and tears, and a few children turned and ran back, dodging under the officials' arms, and found their mothers and clung to them and refused to go. Hannah saw one look at her child, a black-ringleted plump little girl of about seven, and then, sideways, at the other mothers around her and begin to back away out of the crowd, taking her child with her.

'I don't care!' she had cried shrilly as one of the evacuation officials came bustling up to try and take the child away from her. 'I don't care, they ain't sent no bombs yet, have they? So they won't send none now! And even if they do, it's better we should be together. A bomb's got your name on it, what difference you're here or you're in Devon? It's got your name on it! My Shirley's staying here with me.'

But there had been only two or three like that. The train had pulled out with its load of labelled children and the women had been left standing on the bridge watching the empty rails glinting in the sunshine and then, slowly, gone back to their homes or to their jobs. Hannah had been there to help transport the children of her workers from Spital-fields, and now she filled the car with the mothers who belonged to her and drove them back, silent, trying not to think of Marie and her baby, of Charles, of Cissie's three grandchildren now on their way to America, of all the other shattered families who were almost the first casualties of this war.

Life had become unbearably hectic as she tried to run the factory while reorganizing so many other aspects of daily living. The Paultons Square house had been closed. Bet had gone to live with her sister Edie and her husband in Whitby ('And I know it's a sin and a crime to say it, but I don't like her, I reely don't, not the way I like you and Florrie,' she had wept. 'But I got to go, because they can't run their business now the boys 've gone to the army and George's heart isn't what it was so I got no choice, but oh, Mum, I'm that miserable.') and Florrie had set to work to make the flat at the top of the factory habitable.

It was tiny, with just a small living room and a bedroom for Marcus and Hannah and a boxroom for Florrie to sleep in with a slip of a kitchen alongside. Florrie grumbled mightily about it all, but coped, somehow, and Hannah and Marcus had moved in one lunch hour, so that they would lose as little working time as possible. The furniture had been put into storage, and so had the silver and china and all the ornaments and paintings they had collected over the fourteen years of their marriage, leaving the flat spartan and cheerless; but they were there so rarely, only sleeping and eating, that they hardly noticed.

Hannah had put the factory on a three shift system in order to increase output and from five a.m., when the machines went on as the first workers arrived, until midnight, when they were switched off at the end of the third shift, she was there supervising the cutting, the distribution, the sewing and the finishing, as well as dealing with the usual office work. Cissie had tried to argue to say she would work longer hours but Hannah had been adamant.

'You know what the doctor said. You can keep out of a sanatorium if you promise to work only three hours a day. So that's all you're working.'

But it wasn't easy without her, for there was no one else so reliable, and Hannah went doggedly on, working all the hours she could, growing more and more tired. And it was not only the factory. There were the firewatching rotas too. Someone had to sit on the roof each night, wrapped in heavy blankets in the corrugated iron lean-to, dozing uneasily over flasks of tea, waiting for warnings to sound so that they could leap up and go to lean over the parapets and watch for the tell-tale gleams of smoke which showed where incendiaries had landed. Hannah took her own turn with Marcus, one night a week. And then there was the canteen, her bit of special war work, she called it, looking after the air raid wardens who spent the nights waiting for the warnings to go on.

And behind all that, the anxiety about the rest of the family. Not just Charles and Marie, but her brothers too. They had sent anxious letters and telegrams many times during the first months of the war, trying to decide whether to come home. Their barrage of doubts and questionings, going on and on, had been irritating for Marcus.

'If they want to stay put, they should stay and stop nagging us about it,' he had snapped one morning, when they had been awakened from their exhausted sleep at an unconscionably early hour by the ringing of the telephone, so that yet another of Solly's cables could be dictated by a bored operator. 'I'm damned if I'm going to salve their consciences for them. Talk to Uncle Alex about it, for God's sake, Hannah.'

She had, pushing her way into his office one Monday morning through crowds of chattering singers and dancers and actors. She had been startled to find him so besieged, and had said so, and he had laughed at her hugely, taking his cigar

558

from his mouth with an expansive gesture, waving it about.

'ENSA, dolly! I got myself involved with ENSA, well, sort of ENSA. Last time round it was catering, right? And I tell you something, I reckon I taught them a thing or two at the War Office on account of this time they don't need that sort of help. They got it organized already. And anyway, I'm getting on a bit now! Why should I kill myself doing work that ain't no fun no more? Catering ain't no fun no more, but this business, show business, that's different! That I like. I tell you the truth, if it wasn't I got my seventieth birthday past me, I'd go back to the old song and dance bit myself. I wasn't so bad when I was a boychick! But fifty years ago and now – it's different. But I still got my theatre interests, ain't I? I got my health and strength, ain't I? I got my connections, ain't I? There ain't many people knows so many people as I do. I can put a show together overnight with such stars, such style, such artistry, I can't be touched! So I went along to Drury Lane, told Basil Dean what I reckoned I could do, so he got me going, said I could look after the civilian side. I sent three shows last week to factories in the North and Midlands, lovely little shows they was, a singer or two, coupla novelty acts. Now I'm working up another couple for the evacuees, come Christmas.'

She laughed, at his own pleasure in his accomplishments, happy for a moment. Whatever happened, wars and tragedies, wandering children, lost homes, whatever happened Uncle Alex remained unchanged, even though he was now past seventy. She went round his desk and hugged him and he grinned at her and patted her cheek and for a moment or two they clung together in a bubble of contentment, pleased with themselves and each other.

But when she told him of her anxiety about her brothers, he shook his head crossly.

'Such *schlemiels*! I tell you they got no more sense than a pair of babies! I sent 'em to New York originally to get 'em outa your hair, to set themselves up, and now look at 'em! Can't think for themselves. I'll send 'em some cables'll make their hair stand on end.'

'Saying what? Come home or stay put?'

'Stay put,' he said crisply. 'They got to be outa their bleedin' minds not to. What good will they be here, either of 'em?'

Yet still she was, deep down, distressed that was how it

had turned out. Of course it was better that Jake and Solly should stay in New York. She had no home to offer them, and as Alex said, what good would they be here? Both too old for the army, even Solly who was two years her junior. They would be an additional worry, yet she felt obscurely that it would be better if they were all together. The war was a bad one, was going to get worse; they all ought to be *together*.

It was not only Jake and Solly's absence that disturbed her; it was the distress of her aunts and uncles and cousins as the younger members of the family were scattered. Young Lionel, David's son, had joined the army; at nineteen he was a tall well set-up lad, full of energy and pride in himself, for had he not passed his matriculation with flying colours and started to study law at London University? First he would fight in the army, he had told David and Sonia and old grandfather Benjamin, and then come back to finish his studies and be the first judge in the Lazar family. Reuben and Minnie's children and grandchildren too, had scattered, some going to the army and some sent away as evacuees. The East End seemed to shrink as the young faces disappeared. There were just the very old, and all the women and the babies; it seemed to Hannah sometimes like a ghost of its former self, the streets too empty, too quiet.

But life went on, somehow, as they went about their day to day work, waiting for – what? Since Dunkirk people had been sure that invasion was inevitable. Hitler had taken so much already, Norway and Denmark following Holland and Poland and France and most of the rest of Europe into his bag; why should he stop now? Twenty-two miles of Channel was all there was between him and us, the wiseacres told each other in pubs and tea shops and factory canteens, why should that stop him?

But it seemed to as a blazing June became a heavy July. The news picked up a little, as British bombers began night attacks on Germany, and that cheered some people, though Marcus shook his head when Hannah repeated to him the talk of the factory floor. 'They'll hit back,' he said wearily. 'Soon. They know it at the War Office. Very soon.'

It seemed to start almost casually, one hot August night after another, with the sirens throwing their ululating cry into the dark sky just at the time, everyone grumbled, when people had gone to bed to try to get some sleep. They tumbled out into their shelters, wrapped in sheets, or, sometimes, fancy outfits especially made to be 'Chic in the Shelter' as exhorted by the women's magazines, made cups of tea over primus stoves and then went stumbling back to bed when the all clear sounded, complaining bitterly because there had been so little reason to get up in the first place. 'Nuisance raids,' the papers dubbed them and everyone agreed, coming to work bleary eyed for lack of sleep, 'all because of them bleedin' sirens, shan't pay no never mind to 'em again, I shan't,' the workers told Hannah, and she shook her head at them and told them firmly that they should.

And then, in September, it all burst over their heads. It was a hot Saturday afternoon when the factories had closed for the well earned weekend break and Hannah had twenty-four hours of relaxation to look forward to before she had to go off to the canteen for her Sunday night stint. She had undressed to bathe herself in the woefully tiny bathroom that had been rigged up for them in their stuffy rooftop flat, and had just tied the sash of her bathrobe when she heard the sound begin, that familiar whine, starting far away to the East and then, very swiftly, taken up nearer and nearer, until the siren based on the fire station around the corner began, almost deafening her.

For a moment she stood there, tempted to ignore it; just another damned nuisance raid, that was all it was, surely? But then she remembered Marcus's anger when someone in the factory had challenged his insistence that they always take shelter whenever the sirens went. She sighed, and dressed again, irritable and sweatier than ever. If only Marcus was here! But he had had to go to Whitehall for a specially convened meeting to do with aircraft production. Florrie was out too, on one of her rare jaunts to the West End, little enough though there seemed to be to buy these days. Hannah made her way out of the flat, on her way to the steps and the shelter, alone.

She stopped though, at the top of the stairs, her head tilted listening to the sounds; the distant rumble of guns, and behind it a deeper more even burring that was something new. She frowned sharply and after a moment turned and went running up the last flight of stairs to the roof, to stand and stare out over to the east at the warm afternoon sky shimmering with heat.

At first she could not believe what she saw, but then she took a deep breath and stood very still, for the sky was almost black with planes. Hundreds and hundreds of planes. German planes.

64

It seemed to go on for ever, although in fact it was only a week or two, that first really bad time, though there would be other bad weeks to follow, later. But all she knew then was the eternity of it. It seemed the most natural thing in the world that within a few days, almost, they accepted the pattern of the days and nights as normal. They became totally matter of fact about vanished buildings and the stench of high explosives and dust and burst sewers and gas mains and the squalor of streets littered with debris and houses with half a room left bare to the open sky and wardens with red tired eyes and reception centres full of dazed bombed out people. The shops she usually bought from disappeared or looked alien with boarded up windows and chalked signs reading 'business as usual'. And she hardly noticed. Landmarks she had never really been aware of until they were gone vanished from her memory as they vanished from real existence. The gas didn't pop when she tried to boil a kettle, because the mains had gone and she just shrugged; the electric light failed to come on and water to run in the flat and she didn't even frown. She went through the days as serenely as though nothing unusual was happening. The workmen got the electricity fixed somehow when it failed, so she opened the factory again, and they went on doggedly turning out their khaki shirts and skirts and greatcoats as though they had never stopped. The gas company men managed to reconnect the supply, so they had hot food again and she forgot she had been hungry; the water came back so they could bath and she said nothing. She just went on, unflurried by any of it.

Because of Marcus. As long as he was all right, she was. And he would be all right, for the meetings and eternity of planning sessions which filled his days were no longer held in the upper floor offices in Whitehall, but in safe, deep shelters underneath Horseguards' Parade. Once he left the flat in the morning to go to his job she could relax; he was safe, just as he had promised he would be. The danger from the raids was here in the East End of London, and in the City, both far from where he was, and that gave her all the peace of mind she needed.

He, on the other hand, was far from happy, for Artillery Lane sometimes seemed to be right in the centre of the German target. Bombs came down in great showers, night after night, to flatten the surrounding streets and factories into dust. Yet, somehow, the factory survived, and went on working, which made it impossible for Marcus to prevail when he tried, and he did, very hard indeed, to persuade her to leave London.

'I'll be fine here,' he told her, holding her close as they curled up in their small shelter one night, watching the oil lamp swaying on its post as the distant thudding of the guns sent vibrations through them. 'But I go through hell knowing you're here. Please Hannah, go to Daphne! I know you don't like her much, but she's safe there in the village. I'd sleep easier if you were with her.'

'And I'd never sleep at all,' she said, and tightened her grip on him, twining her legs around his into a Laocöon knot. 'Can you see me sitting in a tiny village in the middle of Herefordshire with nothing to do but drink gin with Daphne? Don't be crazy, Marcus! This is where I belong, right here. I'm not going anywhere. I'm going to be fine too – as long as you are. I can cope with anything, and knowing you're safe with the brass hats makes me feel marvellous!'

The heatwave went on which didn't help, and a minor epidemic of gastro-enteritis hit the factory workers, making it almost impossible to go on working. Somehow, she and Florrie overcame that, by humping bucket after bucket of water up from the street standpipe to the lavatories; that went on for three days. And then, late one Friday afternoon, just as she was coming back from the bank with cash to pay the workers, the mains that fed the standpipe fractured somewhere back down the Commercial Road and the last trickles of water disappeared.

She paid everyone with Florrie to help her, and sent them all away, and they went with relief to scurry fearfully through the littered streets back to the false security of home. It didn't matter what happened overhead; if you were in your own familiar shelter, that you had dressed up a bit with gingham tablecloths and cushions and even the odd plant or two, you could manage to keep your chin up. So they went, glad to be free, glad to have their money in their hands, glad it was Friday.

Hannah hesitated after they had gone, wondering whether to go to Whitehall and wait there for Marcus to be free. He had said she could do that any time she liked, giving her a special card that would get her in past the sentry, but she decided not to do that. It was now five o'clock, and Marcus had said he thought he could be away not much after half past.

'We'll pretend we're real people again,' he said. 'Get dressed in ordinary clothes and go up to the West End and find somewhere to get a meal. There're one or two places which are still not quite decrepit, I'm told, in Greek Street. Try to be ready, my love. Tonight we'll play at being human again.'

She dressed, wishing she could bathe, but settling for the clean up with her last precious bottle of skin cleansing milk which was all she could manage, and even put on a little make up. It was the least she could do, she told herself, peering in the mirror at her pale face.

'Florrie,' she said as she came into the tiny living room. 'Don't hang around here. You can't eat or anything – no water. So you'd be better off going to Uncle Alex's place in Golders Green. I know you don't like going, but tonight, what else can you do?'

Florrie grimaced, but went willingly enough and Hannah hugged her briefly as she saw her off, filled as always with gratitude. Florrie never changed, always did what had to be done, and went on as though the German attacks were no more than another tiresome domestic upheaval of the sort she had coped with so well in the old days at Paultons Square. Now she stumped off to Alex's big house to find a bed somewhere in its tangle of rooms, which wasn't always easy, for he had opened his doors to anyone of the family who wanted to flee there.

'We might even come out ourselves, later,' Hannah called after Florrie's retreating back. 'We'll see how it goes tonight. Tell Uncle Alex if he's there. He should be back from

Liverpool now.'

Quite why she chose to spend the remaining half hour before she could expect to hear Marcus's feet on the stairs going through the cloth supplies she didn't know. She was dressed in one of her favourite dresses from well before the war, an apple green crêpe de chine with a matching coatee, and it was hardly suitable for scrabbling among bolts of khaki serge, but still she had to do something and that was something that had to be done. She made her way to the back of the factory floor, where the cloth was stored and crouched down to begin her work, a ledger resting on one knee as she began to count the bolts. It was an awkward position, especially in her high heeled pre-war shoes. She thought briefly, I ought to take them off, but didn't for fear of ruining her stockings. Silk stockings were not easy to come by these days.

The sirens startled her when they began. This time it did not start from far away as a gentle little whine but sprang into first life at the neighbouring fire station, suddenly blasting her ears so that she jumped. Her ledger went flying and so did she, tumbling forwards awkwardly and hitting her head on a corner of a cloth bolt. She lay stunned for a second as the siren shrieked above her head, filling her with a sense of urgency and she shook her head to clear it and tried to get up, only to find her ankle was twisted under her. She couldn't move without agony. The siren went on and on, joined now by other sounds, klaxons and, most ominous of all, the deep throated burr of planes, pulsating so heavily that she knew at once they were almost overhead.

She began to drag herself across the floor, ignoring the way her precious crêpe de chine dress snagged against the rough floor boards or the way tears sprang into her stockings, desperately trying to make her way across the factory floor to the door that led to the stairs and to the shelter.

Marcus! He must be almost here, almost at the front door, maybe on the stairs already. She must get to the stairs and Marcus, she thought, and felt her face wet, almost with surprise. The pain in her ankle was excrutiating, and it was making her cry without knowing it. She sniffed and rubbed her wet face and eyes against her shoulder, lifting her arm awkwardly, trying to see through the blur of her own tears.

The burring noise got louder, and so did other noises, great bursts of explosions and the high pitched whistle of falling bombs and she stopped and tried to sit up and lifted her head and called, 'Marcus?' – absurdly because she couldn't even hear her own voice above the din. If he had been on the stairs, he could not have heard her.

It got worse, louder and louder and the building shook, the floor beneath her seeming to tilt, and she flung her hands out to catch at something alongside her to keep her straight, to help her on the way to the door and what seemed to be safety and reassurance and all she could feel above her head was the floor again, and she thought furiously – 'Stupid! It's supposed to be underneath me – ' And then the floor hit her on the head, a huge flat handed blow that made her eyes seem to burst into great circles of light. And then there was nothing at all.

A cold wet weight on her foot, as she tried to run, tried to rush along the platform to catch the train. But it wasn't a train she was running for but a taxi with its flag up, and as she ran it turned away and she couldn't run after it because of the cold wet weight on her foot. She opened her mouth to call after the taxi, furious at the driver for not seeing her here on the station platform.

It stopped being a station platform and became a flower market. Roses. The scent of roses. 'Roses, roses all the way and myrtle dropped in their path like mad,' she heard someone say and tried to turn her head to see who it was, but the pillows under her neck got in the way and she couldn't move at all.

'Hannah.'

The cold wet weight was worse now. She flexed the muscles of her thigh, trying to move her foot away to be free of it, but no matter how hard she tried she couldn't do it and she was angry then and wanted to shout, but all that came out were little whimpers and she wanted to say loudly, 'Be quiet! Such a stupid noise!'

'Hannah, dolly, it's all right. It's all right. Keep still, dolly. The nurses say you got to keep still.'

Another voice, not a warm friendly familiar one with bubbles in it somewhere, but a cold voice with trickles of ice water in it. 'Lady Lammeck, you must stop that! If you keep moving that way you'll pull the drip down and then where will we be? Do keep still!'

'Hannah, dolly, open your eyes. Please, Hannah.'

She thought about that for a moment. Open her eyes? A strange request, for they were open, weren't they? She was staring at the taxi on the train lines at the end of the platform in the flower market...

She experimented, trying to open her eyes that were not closed, and discovered that she was wrong. They had been closed, quite tightly, and now that she was opening them the light that came in was hurtful. She closed them again, looking for the reassuring familiarity of the train lines and the flowery platform, but all she could see now was light. Platforms and trains and taxis had disappeared.

'Try again, Hannah,' the familiar voice said, and obediently she did and stared at the source. Uncle Alex, his face so blessedly familiar that she felt warm everywhere except where her foot was; that was still cold and wet and so heavy.

'Uncle Alex,' she said. Her voice sounded very odd, thick and croaking, just like the voice that had been so silly about the roses and the myrtle. 'Uncle Alex.'

'*Gott se dank!*' She saw he was crying, the pouches under his eyes wet and gleaming in the lamp light. 'I thought you'd never talk again, and that's a fact, dolly. *Gott se dank.*'

She looked at him consideringly and then turned her head, carefully, almost surprised to find it obeyed her. A long white room warm with light, with patches of red in tidy patterns and flowers in a vase. She frowned, knowing that what she saw was familiar yet not able to identify it. She turned her head back to Uncle Alex, looking at him with hope. He would know. He always knew.

'Uncle Alex?' He took her hand in his and it felt so comfortable there that at once she knew where she was and said carefully, 'Hospital?'

'Yes, dolly. Hospital.'

She lay and thought about that for a while, staring up at the ceiling high above her, watching a cobweb in a corner swaying in a faint breeze. 'Hospital,' she said again, still carefully.

'In Letchworth,' Uncle Alex said and she frowned at the cobweb which shook itself more vigorously in the breeze and told her nothing. There was haziness around the edges of the

567

cobweb and she thought, 'I'm tired,' and closed her eyes, but felt a wave of fear come with the drowsiness.

When she opened them again she knew somehow that she had been asleep for all she had been afraid to, and turned her head to look for Uncle Alex, to apologize for being so rude. He was sitting there, his head slumped to his chest and she wanted to laugh. He had fallen asleep too, was as rude as she was. She felt a wave of tenderness for him lift in her and wanted to touch him, but she could not reach, and let her hand fall back. But he seemed aware of her movement and lifted his head with a jerk and stared at her, his face a little blank from his sleep.

'Hello,' she said, and managed to smile, though it hurt a little, for her face felt stiff. 'Tell me what happened, Uncle Alex. I'm all – muddled.'

You can't be that muddled, a small lucid part of her mind told her rather pompously. Not if you know you're muddled.

His face seemed to crease a little, and he looked at her hand on the counterpane and then reached for it, holding it tight in his fingers. She wanted to pull away because his grip was hurting her.

'Factory got a direct hit,' he said, and his voice seemed louder than it needed to be. 'They found you in the street. Thrown out by the blast, you were. Fractured ankle, three ribs cracked, bruises. Bit of concussion.'

'Oh,' she said. Her ankle, that was the cold wet weight, of course. She tried to squint down at her foot, but all she could see was a hump in the bedding.

'A cast,' he said following her gaze. 'Plaster, you know? Like a great big boot. Looks silly, really, but it'll cure your break.'

'That's good,' she said drowsily, and yawned, and felt her eyes closing gently as sleep stole over her. It was a good feeling, not alarming at all, as it had been before, and she was just letting it slide over her head when she realized what it was that she hadn't said to him.

'Marcus,' she murmured, and hardly opened her eyes as she spoke. 'When will he be here?'

There was no answer and the sleep began to roll back from her eyes. Slowly she opened them and looked at Uncle Alex, there in the chair beside her. She said again, 'Marcus. He'll be here soon, won't he?'

He lifted his chin and looked at her and now the tears were there again on his pouched and lined cheeks and he stared at her for a moment and then shook his head, very definitely, from side to side like a clockwork doll. He looked so absurd she laughed, had to laugh.

'Dear Uncle Alex, don't be silly! When is he coming?'

'I ... he won't be coming,' Alex said, loud again. 'You might as well know now. I told 'em I'd be the one to tell you, and I got to. He was on the stairs, dolly, when the factory got hit. On the bloody stairs. They reckon he never knew what happened.'

65

For a long time she did not think about Marcus. She thought instead of unimportant things like her ankle, which refused to heal and which eventually needed operations to repair the damage that had been done, and about the fact that the doctors told her, regretfully, that she would never regain normal use of it, that it would always be stiff. That gave her something to sit and brood about, there in the small day room at the end of the long hospital ward, something she could encompass in her mind.

She thought, too, about her workers, worrying herself about them so that she needed sleeping pills night after night. Where would they all go now? Millie, who had been a finisher for her for twenty-five years, ever since the VAD uniform days, and Moishe the presser who had come to her as a club-footed boy of seventeen and was now working to keep his senile parents as well as a wife and a couple of children, and old Mrs Schneider whose efforts as a felling hand were of small value to production but who had been part of the place, the best tea maker, the one all the young girls relied on when they were worried about their boyfriends; who would employ her now, a woman of almost seventy?

And Florrie, what about Florrie, treking out from London to see her day after day, making the tiresome journey into Hertfordshire on slow erratic trains, standing around for hours on windy station platforms uncomplaining and eternally patient, what about her?

She would tease and worry at her thoughts, obsessively, and knew it was all she could do, for how could she allow other thoughts of the greatest hurt of all to come into her mind? If she once allowed herself to think of Marcus, she would be lost forever. She knew that. Only by resolutely turning her back on the abyss of pain and despair that Marcus now was could she go on living at all.

And, extraordinarily, that mattered. In later years when she could allow herself to look back on the autumn and winter of 1940 and the early spring of 1941, she would marvel at how she had never once contemplated the possibility of just dying, as she should have done that Friday afternoon in Artillery Lane.

She had listened to what Uncle Alex had to tell her, his voice angry and loud with the misery of it, about how Marcus had told the people at the War Office that he was taking his wife for a night out, and they were to let him go early, how the driver of the official car he always used had tried to persuade him to take shelter as the sirens went just as they reached Artillery Lane, how he had gone tearing headlong down the street to the factory as soon as he had realized how close the raid was, and how the bomb – a comparatively small one, as it turned out – hit the roof dead centre just after he had gone rushing in. The driver had tried to hold him back, had himself been blasted into a hole on the far side of the street because he had not gone to take shelter himself, but he had not been able to save Marcus.

Once Hannah had been told all that, she closed her mind on the information, wrapping it in silence, hiding it away. Alex, her most constant visitor, seemed to understand, for he said no more about Marcus at all. Once, one afternoon during that first month, he leaned forwards and held her hands together, cradling them in both of his, and said quietly, 'Dolly, I'm proud of you. You're a credit to yourself, to your family, to all Yidden. You're well named, boobalah, you know that? Lammeck, *lamech*, strong, in the old Hebrew. That's you. Strong and quiet and good. I love you, dolly. Take care of yourself, and what you can't take care of I will.' He had kissed her on both cheeks had gone, walking down the ward with that slight swagger of his, his heavy checked

570

coat swinging and leaving a trail of cigar smoke behind him. She almost cried that afternoon, sitting in a hospital ward full of yellow and bronze chrysanthemums, watching him go and feeling dreadfully alone. But she did not. *Lamech*, strong, I must be strong.

They let her go home in early November, limping heavily and holding onto a thick ebony stick that Uncle Alex had brought her, because she had become too restless to stay. The orthopaedic surgeon, an elderly man with finicky ways and a passion for complex joint surgery, had wanted her to stay, so that he could operate again. 'Might be able to get more mobility back,' he had said, but she had refused. As long as she could get about at all, that was good enough. She had no need for more. She needed home and peace and comfort now.

Home. Florrie had lit up when Hannah had told her she was going to open up Paultons Square again.

'I don't care if they do bomb us there,' she had said. 'Anyway, they haven't so far, so maybe they won't. It seems to be mostly the East End and the City and the docks. Anyway, I don't care. But you should go away, Florrie. Go to Whitby with Bet. You know she'd love you to be with her.'

But Florrie of course had flatly refused and had a happy fortnight getting all the furniture out of storage and cleaning the house from top to bottom.

On the day Hannah came home, the weather was the sort that she and Marcus had both loved, cold and crisp but very sunny, with the last of the leaves on the trees whispering in the sharp breeze. The air smelled clean, with none of that thick explosive smokiness that had been so much a part of the atmosphere at Artillery Lane. Uncle Alex helped her out of the car wordlessly, supporting her with one hand under her elbow, but she disengaged herself gently and stood there, leaning on her stick and staring up at the house. It was important to her that she walk in unaided, and he seemed to understand and stood back as she made her way slowly and painfully to the steps.

As she reached the top step, her control as tight as she could keep it, refusing to think of Marcus here, the front door of the house next door opened and someone came out. She stopped as she saw Hannah and smiled widely.

'Hello, Lady Lammeck! I am glad you're back! Oh, have you been hurt? I am sorry! Fall, was it?'

Hannah stared at her, a tall buxom woman with iron grey hair, trying to remember. She had never been on particularly close terms with her neighbours, and this one had come to live at number twenty only a couple of months before the war started, all so long ago, so forgotten. She couldn't even recall her name.

'No, not exactly,' she said now. 'I – it's nice to be home.'

'Will you be starting up your dressmaking again, by any chance?' the woman said brightly. 'I was just going to start coming to you for some dresses and lo and behold you stopped for the war! But not for the duration, I hope! I've got some absolutely stunning silks my son brought home for me from Shanghai and I'm absolutely dying to have them made up! *Do* say you're going to start again!'

Hannah looked at her consideringly and after a moment nodded. 'I might,' she said. 'Let me see the silks, I'll see what I can do.'

'Marvellous! Couldn't be more marvellous! I'll pop in tomorrow, after seven, if that's all right? Must dash now, war work you know! Got a first aid detachment waiting to be taught bandaging. See you tomorrow!' And she went rushing importantly down the Square as Hannah stood on her step and watched her go.

That was how it was that she began to live again. The factory was gone and had to be forgotten, and Marcus had gone and was not to be thought of, but Mary Bee Couturiere was still there, waiting to be part of her life again. When Cissie came out of the sanatorium she had had to go to at the end of 1941, after an alarming haemorrhage, to find that her Hackney house had been bombed and was uninhabitable, she came to live in Paultons Square with Hannah, and together they picked up the threads of the old days. They made up the precious hoarded fabrics that women brought them and altered and refurbished old dresses from the halcyon days of the thirties, and, later, when illicit supplies of parachute silk came on the black market, found themselves sewing that extraordinary material too.

Florrie went on as she always had, looking after them, cleaning the house and cooking their meagre rations with as much skill as she could muster and, when they needed her, joined in the sewing. Much of it was hand work, for sewing machines were hard to come by, and the only battered one they had frequently broke down, so there was ample work for all of them.

And, oddly, they were happy. They would sit, the three women, with the wireless playing 'Music While You Work' and 'Workers' Playtime', Cissie sometimes singing along with the familiar tunes in her gruff alto, and talk a little of unimportant things like weather and films and the books they were reading. They never discussed the war, never listened to the war news on the wireless together, tacitly agreeing to shut it out of their shared lives as much as they could. Hannah would read the papers at night, after she had gone to bed, and for all she knew the others did too, but whether she worried about setbacks in North Africa or found hope in news of successful RAF raids on Germany, she never said a word about it to them any more than they did to her. It was as though they had all agreed that they had fought their war, and lost it. Now they would just struggle on, somehow, letting others carry their share of the rest of it.

Nor did Hannah ever speak to Cissie and Florrie of her other distress, the continuing silence from Holland and from America. Once she had asked Uncle Alex to do what he could, to see if he could find out anything about what was happening in Holland but he had come back after six weeks, miserable and angry because despite his many contacts in Government offices he had drawn a total blank. There were some refugees trickling out, occasional escaped prisoners of war who managed to get away by sea to England, but none of them, it seemed, knew anything much about what was happening there, and certainly nothing about one young English Jew who had disappeared into Amsterdam.

As for Marie, all Hannah knew was that she still drew her regular income from the bank as arranged by the lawyers at Lammeck Alley. Peterson had come to see her shortly after she had come home from hospital, to tell her of her own financial situation, and of what was happening with Marie's money.

'Sir Marcus was a major shareholder in Lammeck and Sons, as you know, Lady Lammeck,' he had told her. 'Business at present is, of course, virtually at a standstill, except for those factories which have been turned over to munitions or other war production. All our overseas interests have been frozen for the duration, and quite what will happen there we are not in a position to know. But you need not be concerned about money. You have a handsome competence, very handsome indeed, and once this tiresome war is over, you will, I am sure, be better off than you now are. However – '

'It doesn't matter,' Hannah said flatly.' It really doesn't matter. I've always earned my own living, and I still can if I must.'

'Your factory, of course, was insured, I've checked on the policies and enemy action was covered, so there will be money there, although it may be some time yet before we get it for you.'

'I've told you, it doesn't matter,' Hannah said more sharply. 'We've got enough, Florrie and Cissie and me. We've got the house and we get our rations. We're not likely to get involved in black market buying.'

'I should hope not!' Peterson said, his face a mask of horror, and Hannah wanted to laugh for a moment. His probity was such a comfort, so cosy a reminder of the long ago days when the world could afford luxuries like virtue and honour and polite behaviour.

'I'm more concerned about my daughter,' she said now. 'Mrs Rupert Lammeck. I've heard nothing from her since – since a cable to say her baby was born. Nothing. Is she – have you heard?'

He shook his head, not looking at her. 'I am sorry, Lady Lammeck, but no. Not directly. I can only tell you that the arrangements for drawing her money were changed from the USA side at her request. We were asked to allow for cash to be drawn on any branch of the British American Bank, and we did that. I can tell you that it has been drawn from, let me see ... ' He consulted one of the mass of papers on his lap. 'Ah yes. San Diego. Seattle. Las Vegas. Ah – Chicago. Then San Diego again. Then New York and the last time, hum, Detroit.'

She frowned, puzzled, and he said gently, 'She seems to be moving about a good deal.'

'Yes. A good deal. And Rupert? Have you heard from him?'

574

'Nothing at all. We will have to make contact of course. His brother, your husband, has left him a small legacy. Carefully tied up, of course, but all the same...'

'Yes. Marcus would have done that,' she said, and sheered away from thoughts of Marcus again. 'Please, Mr Peterson, can you try to find out for me what has happened? I can't help being afraid. Maybe she's ill. I just can't understand the silence. Though if she were in trouble she'd be in touch, surely.'

'Surely,' Mr Peterson said dryly. 'Quite surely. I will of course do what I can. I will see to it that messages are left at every branch of the British American Bank to be delivered to Mrs Lammeck should she go to them. Then perhaps she will make contact.'

'Yes.'. She seized on that gratefully. 'Yes, please. Just ask them to tell her to cable me, or write to me or ... something. Anything. Just to know she's all right. She and the baby.'

'Your granddaughter, yes,' Mr Peterson said, and then coughed a little stiffly and said, 'I – I have not spoken to you since – since Sir Marcus...'

'Please, Mr Peterson, let's just take it as said, whatever it is. Please? I ... I appreciate your kindness, the kindness you've always shown me. Let's just stop there, shall we?'

'Of course,' he said, and began to pack his briefcase again. 'So, that is that. I am always available as you know. Just a telephone call or a letter and I will come at once to arrange anything you wish arranged. And as soon as I hear anything about Mrs Rupert Lammeck, I will of course let you know.'

But he never did, because there was silence still. All he could report as the months and then the years went by was that the income was being drawn regularly, and that was all. Clearly Marie was alive and well enough to go to her banks, wherever she was, and she certainly seemed to travel a lot, for the bank reports came from a bewildering number of places, but she was not, for some reason, prepared to communicate with her family in England. And there was nothing Hannah could do to make her.

She swallowed that distress too, sitting day after day quietly sewing in her dining room, while Cissie sat beside her singing under her breath, and thinking only of the stitches she was setting, of the length of a seam, the shape of a shoulder. She ate her meals and went occasionally to walk around the Square, wearing though it was, for her ankle still gave her a lot of pain. She listened to music on her wireless. Sometimes the family came to visit, brought in Uncle Alex's car, old Uncle Benjamin and David and Sonia, and whichever of Reuben and Minnie's vast brood was available, and they would drink tea and gossip of family matters and sometimes play solo among much badinage and arguments about who had played what card in the wrong way. It was, on the surface, a tranquil life, an oasis of peace in the middle of the conflagration of a terrible war. And no one looking at Hannah would have known the maelstrom that was beneath that quiet surface. Indeed, they told each other, all of them, Hannah was a marvel, a real marvel, taking her loss so well, not moaning like some would, and with both her children gone as well as her husband. *Nebbish*, a real *guteneh shumah* thinking only of others and not of herself, so good to Cissie and Florrie and her neighbours. And underneath it all she was in a turmoil.

A turmoil of guilt. What was it about her, Hannah would ask herself in the long dark nights, what was it about her that destroyed those she most loved? Daniel and Peter and Marcus, Marie and Charles, all gone, vanished into a past that existed only inside her head, that filled her with despair. What had she done to have earned so sharp a punishment? She had never been taught to believe in her God as a caring loving personage. Nathan had not been one who could give such a message to his children, consumed as he was with his own rage against the world and the God who had made it. No, God had never figured in her scheme of things, till now.

And the God she now found was an angry one, a vengeful one, paying her in hard coin for sins she could not know she had committed. So she would tell herself, trying to understand. What did I do? Why me? What did I do that made me so poisonous to those I love? Why do they die? Why do they go away?

She became more and more enmeshed in her view of herself as uniquely wicked, uniquely punished. The quieter and the more serene she was by day with other people, the more bitter and angry and hurt she was at night alone. And somehow, that helped. Whatever it was she had done, surely she was paying for it now? This cruel God could not do worse to her, could he?

It was a sort of comfort, for a little while. Until late one October evening in 1944.

66

It was an evening with a difference because Florrie and Cissie had gone out to the cinema on one of their rare expeditions. There had been a time when Florrie and Bet had gone to the pictures every Saturday night, but that had stopped in 1940, when Bet went away. After that it had seemed, Florrie said, unpatriotic to spend money on such rubbish when there was fighting going on. And anyway, not so much fun. But now, as the news of the war improved each day, and the end seemed actually to be a possibility, her doubts about the morality of such simple pleasures were eased, and she was willing to go, even though the flying bombs had started to make nuisances of themselves.

'They didn't get me the first time round when they was aiming their bombs right at me,' she had said firmly, putting on her hat and her sensible knitted gloves, for it was a cold evening, 'so they won't get me this time, sending them things off from the other side of the Channel like they do, and not knowing who they're going for. Stands to reason –'

They had tried to persuade Hannah to come too, but she would not. It was difficult to cope if her ankle caused her pain, as it so often did, when she was sitting in the middle of a crowded row and couldn't get out, she told them. She would stay home and listen to 'Saturday Night Theatre' on the wireless. 'You tell me all about it tomorrow, Florrie. And I'll have some cocoa ready for you when you get in.'

So she was alone, sitting in the drawing room, listening to the wireless in the dark. There was a pleasure in not curtaining the windows, in being able to see the faint moon haze out there. It was as though she were somehow defying the blackout.

The play was dull, and she had almost dozed off in her comfortable armchair when she heard the rattle of the knocker on the front door, and jumped in the darkness. After a moment it was repeated, and she sat there uneasily listening. Who would visit her so late on a Saturday evening? None of the family ever did. She began to be frightened, sitting there alone in the darkness. She got to her feet awkwardly to limp to the window and look out.

There was a tall figure on the doorstep. She could just see the silhouette as she craned her neck and as though he could see her, he turned and stared up at the window and she drew back, nervously.

He knocked again, and once more lifted his face to the window. As a rack of cloud moved away from the moon she could see him a little more clearly, a cadaverous face, with a lot of dark hair flopping over the forehead and very dark eyes that looked like blank hollows in that pallid skull. And she felt another lift of fear.

After a while she saw him put his hand in his pocket, and take out something and as she watched she realized he was writing, his head bent close over his hands so that he could see what he was doing. She heard the letter box rattle as he pushed something through and then he went walking slowly but purposefully down the steps. She watched him go and then slowly drew the curtains and switched on the lamp on the small occasional table before, almost unwillingly, going to the front door to see what he had pushed through.

It was the back of a cigarette packet. She stared down at the picture of the sailor with his heavy moustache, locked forever inside his rope entwined lifesaver, and the legend 'Players Please', and then turned it over, and read the heavy pencil scribble on the other side.

'I will return later, in the hope you are here. I have news of Charles and Henk.'

That was all. She stared blankly at it and then, sick with terror, scrabbled at the front door, dragging it open, limping out onto the steps as fast as she could, looking for him.

He had reached the far side of the Square, almost to the corner where the King's Road was, or someone had, for she could just see a moving figure – and she shouted at the top of her voice, 'Come back. Come back!' and stood there very still staring so hard that lights began to leap inside her straining eyes.

Miraculously he heard her, for he stopped and then turned and came back with the same slow walk, not seeming at all surprised to be so summoned, until he was standing at the foot of her steps looking up at her in the dimness.

'*Mevrouw* Lammeck?' he said. 'I beg your pardon, it should be, I think, Lady Lammeck.'

'Yes, no, it doesn't matter. You know Charles? You have news of Charles? Where is he? Is he coming?'

He was silent for a moment and then said again, 'I have news of Charles.'

'Please come in, come in and tell me. Oh, I am sorry I didn't answer sooner. I'm alone, you see. I was worried. Please, please come in.' She was gabbling in her excitement, and she reached forwards to seize him, to hurry him in, and almost tripped. He took her wrist in a firm grasp and steadied her, then led her into the house again.

'A drink, some cocoa. I have some whisky somewhere, maybe – '

'Nothing,' he said. 'Just some time. I have a message to give you. Then I must go.'

'Who are you? A friend of Charles? Oh, I can't tell you what hell it's been, all the time, so frightened, he's been gone so long, it's been over five years, you see. I've been so frightened, so – '

'Your husband?' the man said, and she looked at him, surprised he didn't know and then angry with herself for her own stupidity. Why should he know?

'He was killed in an air raid,' she said, stiffly, waiting for the words of commiseration that she so hated. But he only nodded and said, 'Ah,' calmly as though that were news he had expected.

'Then I need not wait to speak. I can tell you alone.'

'I don't understand.'

'It would have been better to tell you in company with him, but what is not possible cannot be possible.' He spoke perfect English but there was a precision about his speech and a purity of tone about his vowel sounds that made it clear he was not English. As though he heard her thoughts he bowed and said, 'I am Gerhard De Jongh, *Mevrouw* – Lady Lammeck. Of Amsterdam. Your servant, madam.'

'I ... Hannah,' she said. 'Call me Hannah.'

'It would not be proper,' he said gravely. 'I am younger than perhaps I seem. I am twenty-nine. Two years younger than Charles.'

'He's a friend? You know him well?'

'Friends, yes,' he said. 'Perhaps I sit down to speak to you?'

'Of course, I'm sorry, it's just that I'm . . . this way, please.'

She led him to the drawing room and he sat down neatly in a chair beside the lamplit table. She could see him clearly now, a thin man with heavy lines on his cheeks and very deep set eyes. He was right, he did look much older than twenty-nine and she felt suddenly very sad for him, wanting to touch him, and comfort him. He looked cold and hungry and in need of care. But then he leaned back in the chair with an easy movement that made him seem so in command of the situation that she could not offer him the food she would have done.

'Mr De Jongh,' she said carefully, 'I am glad indeed to see you. Perhaps, now, you will tell me what it is you know of my Charles?'

He stared at her for a long moment and then said sharply, 'You seem very comfortable here.'

'I – what? Yes, I suppose so.' She looked round the room, at the neat richness of it, the handsome well kept furniture, the bowl of late dahlias from the garden Florrie had set on the mantelpiece, and saw it through his eyes for a moment. It looked wealthy and very comfortable and she said again, 'Yes, I suppose so.'

'You have enough food?'

She frowned sharply. 'We have our rations.'

'Ah, yes, rations. English rations. Enough to live on, I believe. The people I see in the streets do not look hungry.'

'Yes, I suppose – Look, what is this? You said you had news of Charles and – '

'Yes, I have. But I am interested to see how little you English suffer. You share the war, yet you have enough food while our people starve, our children starve. Your streets are not filled with soldiers with guns.'

'There are soldiers everywhere,' she cried, stung, and he laughed.

'Your own soldiers! Those, of course. But no Germans.'

'No,' she said. 'No Germans. You are right, we are fortunate. But please, tell me. What news have you for me?'

He leaned back in the chair and pulled his raincoat open and she saw he was wearing a heavy sweater underneath it. His hand was bony and rather dirty, and she felt suddenly

580

very old. He seemed so young for all he was so tired and drawn.

'I have so much to tell you I hardly know where to begin,' he said. 'So much. I think perhaps I will have that whisky after all.'

She fetched it for him, trying not to think. Everything about his manner was filling her with dread, and when she gave him his drink she thought wildly for a moment as he stared up at her with those deep dark eyes, 'He doesn't know Charles at all. He's a thief, a murderer, come to kill me while I'm alone, he doesn't know Charles at all.' But he said, 'Thank you, *Mevrouw*,' gravely and she knew she was being foolish.

'Well?' she said, and he took a deep draught of his drink and then put the glass down beside him.

'I have known Charles Lammeck for many years,' he said. 'Indeed, he recruited me.'

'Recruited?'

'To the Party.'

'I see. Politics.'

'Yes. Politics. It is what this war is about, *Mevrouw*.' She felt the anger in him and was ashamed at the note of asperity that had crept into her voice.

'So, he recruited you to the Party. And you are friends?'

'Yes. He and Henk and I. For a long time. We talk together, laugh together, chase girls together.'

Her head lifted suddenly. 'Girls? He had girl friends? Oh, I'm so glad.'

'Because of your daughter? Yes, do not look so surprised. I know of that matter. He took it hard, I know. He told me all, and I had sympathy. These spoiled over-rich Jewish girls are all of a type.'

She reddened. 'You know nothing of the matter!'

'Don't I? Well, it is not important. As I say, we are friends. And we work together against the Nazis, in Holland, then in Germany. When the trouble starts, we three get back to Amsterdam just in time. Underground, you understand.'

'I'm not sure I do.'

He sighed, irritably. 'We are Jews and Communists! Both! You think the Germans care for such as we to be walking about easy? Of course not. So, we hide. We get a room in a house on the Kaisersgracht and we stay there all day, come out at night, go to meetings, try to organize the people. They will not be organized, many of them. Some, yes. But most are already too frightened. Still, we go on trying. And then it begins ... '

She did not ask him what had begun; she just sat there staring at him in the lamplight, waiting.

'First there were the rules of behaviour for Jews, where they may work, what they may do, the rules, the rules. And then the Dutch, some of them, not many but enough, began to buy their own safety by informing. They help the police collect the Jews to deport them. They help flush them out of houses where they hide. The old women, the children, the sick men, all of them. For a couple of guilders, another ration of potatoes.'

He took up his scotch again and drank thirstily and she took his glass from him and refilled it without a word. He took it with only a nod of thanks.

'We do what we can, Henk and Charles and I. Some we smuggle out. We get them to the little boats and we smuggle them out. Others we try, but we fail and Charles – oh, Charles becomes so angry. It is the most beautiful thing I have ever seen!' The deep eyes seemed to be alight. Whisky, she thought dully. I should have given him some food.

'What happened?' she said after a while, for he had stopped talking, sitting staring into his glass with his eyes very wide open.

'Hum? Oh, yes. What happened.' He drew one hand across his lips, a worried little small-boy sort of gesture. 'He went back to Germany.'

'Back to – but how? How could he do such a – '

'He said things were happening there that we did not know enough about. That we had to get news. That somehow we had to discover what they were doing with all the Jews who were being shifted out of Holland and why the Germans were doing it. It all seemed so ... he said it was a puzzle that must be cleared. We had heard of work camps, you see. We knew of those. But Charles said he believed something else was happening, and he wanted to know what it was. So, he went back to find out.'

'And how – I mean, what happened? Is he still there?'
'No.'
'Then where is he? For God's sake man, stop being so –

582

you're playing games with me and I want no more of it! If you have news, give it to me. No more of this. I can't take more of this.' She luxuriated in her anger, letting it wash over her, almost encouraging it. 'I've had more than enough of your ... your stupid sideways talk! Tell me what has happened to my Charles or go away! I have waited this long for news, I can wait longer. If you won't tell me, someone will, some time.'

'You want news? You want to know what he discovered? You want to hear how he got back to Amsterdam, last summer? How he looked? What he told me? Then, by God, you will. Every word of it. Every last word that I can tell you I will tell you, you comfortable English lady here in London where the Jews can live in their houses like other people and never be hurt. Where there are no German soldiers with guns in the streets!'

Later, much later, she tried to remember the actual words he had used. How he had explained to her in ordinary English in those precise tones of his the facts that Charles had collected, but she could not. All she could remember were the pictures inside her head, the pictures he had painted for her, sitting there in his raincoat in the armchair in her drawing room in Paultons Square.

She saw her Charles, thinner now, for he had been ill, buying forged papers with money he had begged from one of the Damont family before they all managed to leave Amsterdam to go to America, for the Willem Damonts were rich, very rich. She saw him travelling by roundabout routes to Berlin, posing as a Dutch schoolteacher with Nazi sympathies, looking for a connection of the Willem Damont who had given him the money he had needed. His sister, in fact. Leontine von Aachen.

Leontine Damont. Hannah sat and stared at him as the name came slipping off his tongue. Baroness Von Aachen, Daniel's Leontine. Marie's glamorous friend. Leontine von Aachen.

The story had gone on and on. How Charles had waited in Berlin cafés and walked in Berlin Streets, trying to find a chance to speak to her alone, working as a waiter, as a street sweeper, any work he could get, freed from service by the German authorities because of his tuberculosis.

'Tuberculosis?' she had whispered and Gerhard had looked

583

at her in irritated surprise at the interruption. Of course, tuberculosis. After two years in hiding in Amsterdam, half starved most of the time, bitterly cold, in damp rooms, no medical care, how else should it be? Did he not have it himself? Did not half Holland? Of course tuberculosis.

He had gone on then, as though she had not interrupted, telling how at last Charles had managed his objective which was to take the huge risk of speaking to the important Baroness von Aachen whose husband was such a pillar of the Third Reich, so busy a member of Adolf Hitler's advisory staff, and telling her that he knew her history, knew that her brother, her Jew brother of Amsterdam had gone safely to America, and that he, Charles, would, if necessary, denounce her for a Jew to the powers that be, unless she helped him.

Helped him. Such strange help it was that he wanted. To go to work in one of those camps to which the Jews of Holland were being sent. That was what he wanted, and she, terrified that the secret she had managed somehow to hide from the Nazis might be exposed, had been more than willing to help. So he had gone there, Gerhard said. Gone to a little village in Lower Saxony, not far from Celle. 'Belsen,' he said. 'A place called Belsen.'

She stared at him uncomprehendingly, and he had leaned back and laughed, then again, loudly, the whisky rattling in the sound.

'Well, it will be heard of soon enough,' he had said and then had gone on. And on and on, until she could bear it no longer and had tried to cover her ears, but he leaned forwards and pulled her hands away and made her listen.

She saw it all. The rows of huts, the people skeletally thin with eyes bigger and darker and even more remote than Gerhard's staring at her so burningly across her familiar drawing room. People who would kill each other for a crust. People who despaired so much that they threw themselves against the high tension wires that enclosed the place and burned with a reek of cooking flesh while soldiers in grey uniforms laughed and watched and made ribald jokes about feeding the remains to the watching blank-faced hordes in the compounds. About the stench from the high chimneys that belched their greasy black smoke into the soft skies of Lower Saxony while the local farm workers went serenely about their business and paid no attention at all. About the women

584

screaming as they were dragged from their children and pushed towards the waiting buses which had pictures of happy people painted on the blacked out windows. About the young women who were taken to the camp hospitals and could not, would not, say what happened to them when they came out again grey faced and blank eyed.

It went on and on until she felt first numb, and then, suddenly, hugely angry.

'You're a liar,' she said, shouting it at him. 'Liar! It's not true. I don't know why you're here, why you're telling me this ... this filth, but it's not true, and I won't listen to it.'

'I said the same,' he said, and nodded at her, solemn as a child in school. 'I said the same to Charles when he came back. I did not believe it could be true, but he had been there and he had seen.'

'I don't *believe* you,' she shouted again. 'I don't believe you! How could he have come back to Holland to tell you? And how are you here? It's all a mad lie and I don't know who you are and why you've come to tell me all this wickedness but I won't listen.'

'Oh, you can warm yourself with disbelief if you choose,' he said, and now he sounded weary. 'I tried the same. I could not see how he could have made such discoveries and got away to come back to us, but Charles is Charles. Resourceful is I believe the English word. Resourceful. He worked there, you see. On the ovens. Would you believe, on the ovens? He wanted to cry out, he wanted to make the people there cry out, to fight back, but they weren't people any more. They could not fight back, and where would be the profit in dying with them? So he scratched inside his throat with a pin, he told me, and spat blood, and the village doctor said he must go away from there, so he did. Resourceful, my friend Charles. I want some more scotch.'

'No,' she said, but he just grinned at her and got up and went to the table in the corner and fetched it for himself. She could not stop him, for she was now too frightened to do anything at all. A madman, come to tell her mad lies. Cold terror filled her legs and weakened her knees and made movement impossible.

'Henk and I, still in Amsterdam, feeling good because the Dutch went on strike, you know that? They went on strike, our dull Dutch workers who only care for their bellies and their sacks of potatoes, they went on strike! The German soldiers shot some of them for their pains but they went on strike and Henk and I were in the middle of that, so proud, so hopeful, and then Charles came back. Back to Amsterdam, and told us it all and we said he lied. We too said he lied. And then the strikes ... the Germans came and took Henk. I got away, you see. I got away.'

She said nothing, staring at him, at the face now even more pale, but with tight spots of colour in each cheek so that he looked doll like. 'I have to think of that, you know. I have to think of that all the time. I went to the organization and I told them I must get out and there was a chance now after Arnhem. Oh! God, but I am tired!' He peered at her, his eyes gleaming a little in the lamplight. 'So tired. I left them there. Henk taken by the Germans, and Charles in the little room in Kaisersgracht, on his own. I could stay no longer, so I left my friends. You hear me? I left my friends. Such a friend for such men to have.'

To her amazement she felt a sudden stab of pity for him. She did not believe what he was saying, could not believe, yet she felt sorry for him.

'And then on the little herring boat, sick as a dog on the North Sea there was a man, a sailor, and he told me the same tale. He had heard it from a seaman who had heard it in Hamburg. It isn't only that place in Saxony. There are others, full of Jews and gipsies. Full of Jews and gipsies ... '

He was very drunk now, standing swaying a little there in the middle of her drawing room and she thought, he's going to be sick on my carpet. He's going to be sick all over my carpet, and suddenly that mattered more than anything else. She got to her feet, awkwardly as usual because of her stiff ankle and said firmly, 'You must go now.'

He peered at her a little owlishly and then, very solemnly, nodded. 'Yes. I have told you, and I must go. Charles said I must tell you. He said he will hope to see you again soon. Holland will soon be liberated everywhere, not just the south, and he will return to London, he said. I have given you the message and now I must go.'

To her surprise, he did. He put down his glass, now empty again, and moving with the studied care of the very drunk walked to the door and along the passageway outside to the front door and let himself out. By the time she reached the

586

door after him, leaning on her stick, he was gone, walking along the pavement with his back very straight and very controlled, lifting each foot a little higher than was necessary, as drunken men do.

She watched him go, leaning heavily on her stick and thinking only of the way he was walking, and wondering, vaguely, whether he would fall over. But he reached the corner safely and turned it, disappearing into the greater blackness of the King's Road as the moon, once more, slid behind a cloud.

67

She tried very hard, to pretend nothing had happened. When Cissie and Florrie came home full of talk of the film, she behaved just as they expected her to, listening, smiling, making them their hot cocoa, saying goodnight, going to bed. But she lay awake a long time forcing herself to think of the work she had in hand. Mrs Jean Goldman's coat that she was making out of a pre-war brocade curtain, and Barbara Cohen's parachute silk wedding dress, anything to blank out the images that Gerhard De Jongh had etched in her mind.

But it was not possible to pretend it hadn't happened, that he had been just a madman, come out of nowhere, gone back to nowhere, leaving no more than a wraith behind. Everyone she looked at in the succeeding days seemed to be over-shadowed by that cadaverous face with the deep dark eyes; every thin child she saw in the street made her think of the children he had described in Belsen, every bent old man shuffling along the pavement made her recall the old men who had thrown themselves on the high tension wires.

Florrie and Cissie worried about her, asking anxiously whether her ankle was playing up again, whether she was sleeping, nagging her because she seemed not to have her usual appetite until, uncharacteristically, she lost her temper and shouted at them and there had been days of stiffness and unhappiness about the house, until she managed to coax them back into being comfortable again. But the old peace was gone; the shutting out of the war that they had managed for so long had failed and she knew it.

Eventually she did what she had always done when she was distressed. She went to Uncle Alex.

His seventy-five years sat lightly on him. He was just a little more lined and perhaps a little fatter, but not much. His hair was as white and crinkled and as thick as ever, his clothes as natty, and his tongue as sharp. He still spent half of each day at his Pall Mall office, keeping a close control on every aspect of his business. Theatre trade had fallen off in London because of the flying bombs, but was brisker than ever in the provinces and he had three tours traipsing the country with Rudolph Friml revivals and Priestley plays and was making money hand over fist. Even the restaurants were doing well, in spite of the continued shortages of food and in spite of his determined refusal to seek extras on the flourishing black market.

'It ain't so much I got an excess of virtue, dolly,' he told her earnestly. 'It's just that it's bad business. Sooner or later these shysters get themselves caught and then what? If I do it, I get labelled as another lousy Jew profiteer. Not me. I'll give 'em what I can get for the restaurants and they'll have to settle for that. It can't last much longer, this war. Then the food comes back again. The people want fun again and my restaurants make money again. Meanwhile I got this idea I might start a few dance halls. I think dance halls is where it's going to be, you know?'

She had listened and laughed and told him yes, maybe he was right, dance halls were a good idea, and he had launched himself happily into plans for them. Now, when she went to see him, she found him surrounded by eager bandleaders all trying to convince him that theirs was the one and only outfit that could possibly open his brand new place near Tottenham Court Road.

She stood in the doorway of his office leaning on her stick and he looked up and waved jovially at her and opened his mouth to say something and then looked more sharply and said to the men clustered round him, 'Later, fellas, later. Right now I got some urgent family business.' They had looked at her curiously and gone away, leaving her there with him fussing over her, leading her to a seat, shouting for his secretary to bring her tea.

'So, dolly? Tell me what's happened.'

'How do you know something's happened?'

'How do I know? Fifty years you been my girl, dolly. Fifty years my niece, and she asks me, how do I know? So I look at your face, I see your eyes, I know. What more do you want? Diagrams?'

She smiled for the first time since Gerhard De Jongh had come into her life three weeks before. 'No diagrams. Yes, I'm – look, this will take time. Are you busy right now? Shall we meet later? If you've got business.'

'It can wait. Business never comes to no harm you keep it cooking a *bissel*. Those fellas, they want me more'n I want them, so they'll sit out there and they'll stew a little and that'll improve their flavour and make 'em cheaper. Talking to you'll be good business. So talk, already.'

She talked, haltingly at first and then more fluently, telling him what had happened, and, eventually, all that Gerhard had told her. That had been hard to start with, hard to get the words out of her mouth, but gradually, as she reproduced those painful images, she began to feel better, and she realized, suddenly, that letting it all out was having a cathartic effect.

'I – I'm beginning to think his telling me helped him,' she said. 'I thought he was mad, vicious, imagining it, trying to make me ill, unhappy, but now ... Please, Uncle Alex, tell me I was right. That this man *was* crazy? That for some reason I don't know he was making it all up?'

Alex was silent, sitting behind his big polished desk and staring down at the cigar between his fingers.

'You know, I remember the last time, 1914. The stories they put around then. About Germans bayonetting Belgian babies, killing pregnant women, raping nuns, burning hospitals. You remember. And everyone talked about it, everyone said it was dreadful and told everyone else. And then, afterwards, we found it wasn't true. Atrocity stories, all to get us stirred up. Not true. So, slowly, everyone tells everyone else it ain't true and nobody believes it no more. You remember any of that?'

She shook her head impatiently. 'I don't know – what does it matter what people said in 1914? It's now I'm talking about.'

'It matters, dolly. You see, people don't forget that easy. Last time it was atrocity stories all made up? Then,' he shrugged, 'it's the same this time. That's what I said. At first.'

She was silent for a long moment looking at him carefully, her forehead creased, but he did not look at her. 'Uncle Alex! Are you saying – what are you saying?'

Now he did look at her, his old eyes a little rheumy and then managed a tight little grin.

'I wish you got about a bit more, dolly. Got to meet some of the refugees, you know? The ones that came here the past five years or so, the ones still managing to slip in. I meet 'em, you know? I'm on one of these committees, give a few shows for 'em for raising money – you get the picture. And I talk to them, and they tell me things, about camps, about killings, about Jews being gassed, and I go home at first, and I say to myself, ach, Belgian babies on bayonets, that's what this stuff is. *Boobahmeisers*, old stories told by sad people! Lost their money, lost their homes, got no one to look at them and say there's a rich important man, so they got to make themselves look important. This is what I tell myself at first. But then ... '

He was silent and she leaned forwards, pulling on his hand on the desk.

'Then?'

'Then I get it from the others. Refugees in Liverpool start telling me the same stories I get from refugees in London and in Cardiff and everywhere else I go to give them shows, and I begin to think. Alex, I think, you're being a fool. Maybe last time it was stories and there weren't no atrocities like the papers was full of, but maybe this time it's different. Maybe it did happen already, these terrible things. I don't see these *nebbish* refugees getting together planning fancy stories to tell everywhere! These are ordinary people that have suffered so much they're angry. They sometimes hate each other as much as they hate the people they left behind and the people here they have to rely on. They don't plot together, I say to myself. So I reckon the stories I hear are true. Got to be true.'

'You knew,' she said. 'You knew? And it's true?'

'I knew. And I told you. I think it's true.'

'And you did nothing *about* it? My God, Uncle Alex, you heard all this, and from the people who'd been there and you did nothing about it?'

'Don't be a *shlemeil*, Hannah! What do you want I should do? Go get myself a train, a ship, hop over to Berlin, knock on Hitler's door say, "Adolf, *boobalah*, you shouldn't do such unkind things to my *landsleit*"? You want I should do that?'

'But to say nothing, to hear such things and say *nothing*?'

'Others heard the stories, others here who know the refugees, they heard them too, and what do they do?'

'I don't care what they did! What about you? Couldn't you have – '

'*Oy vey is mir*, what does she want of my life? Sure I tried! I went to the papers, right? I tell the newspapers and much good it does me. They listen to me sure, these fancy editors. I'm Alex Lazar, so they listen and they nod and they tut-tut and they say, "Well, Mr Lazar," they say, "I agree if it's true it's a terrible terrible thing, but is it true? That's the question," they say. "You bring me evidence and then we'll publish in our pages! But we got to have proof. You must understand this." And I ask 'em what proof they want, there's the refugees, go talk to them. And they say, "Oh, refugees," they say, "damaged people, they get a little mad in the head from their loneliness, they suffer a little, they tend, poor souls, to exaggerate. Remember the atrocity stories from last time," they say. So what more can I do? Go around telling you, telling my family, listen, in Germany the Jews are being exterminated like bed bugs? Much good that will do. And anyway, as the editors say, and I have to listen to them, where's the proof? I seen no pictures, no papers, no *proof*. Just angry lonely people talking of what... Ach, what can I do?'

They sat there silently for a long time and then she said, 'Then this man, this Gerhard – '

Alex made a little grimace. 'He sounds like the real thing. Another refugee. It's always the same, dolly, in every generation. Jews suffer, and some get over it and use it, and some are destroyed by it. Me and you, we were lucky. The ones that are here from Germany now, they're the sort that can't do it. Most of 'em.'

They sat there for a long time in the darkening office, neither speaking. Hannah could hear the rattle of a typewriter from outside, a mournful yet comfortable sound and beyond that the traffic in the street below. She thought of her house in Paultons Square and Gerhard De Jongh's dark eyes gleaming at her in the lamplight and thought of Charles in a small room in one of the tall houses that fringe the canal on the Kaisersgracht in Amsterdam.

'Uncle Alex, what about Charles? Is there anything we can

591

do? Anything at all? The south of Holland is liberated. Is there any way you know of we can find out what's happening in Amsterdam? Maybe get him out, somehow? De Jongh got out, maybe we can get Charles out too?'

He sighed and leaned forwards and switched on his desk light. The room sprang into brilliance.

'I'll see what I can find out,' he said heavily. 'The refugee committee, they can do a bit, maybe. But only a bit. Don't count on it.'

'No,' she said. 'I won't count on it.'

He got up and went to the window and began fussing with the blind although it wasn't quite blackout time yet. She watched him dully, feeling very tired now. It was as though she had spent the last hour running up hills rather than sitting in this luxurious office, just talking.

'People should know,' she said abruptly. 'If it's true. They should be told.'

'So who will believe it, hey? Like I said, where's the proof? The word of a few disgruntled refugees?'

'I don't believe it,' she said loudly. He came back to the desk and stared at her sombrely for a moment and then shook his head.

'I'd rather not believe it either,' he said. 'I'm trying hard not to.'

'It's not because I don't want to...'

'Never mind, dolly, never mind. Listen, I'll try to find out from Amsterdam, if I can, but don't count on it, and I'll find this Gerhard too. Talk to him myself, match his stories with the others I heard. There's a place in Poland they talk about, Ausch something. I wrote it down somewhere. I'd like to talk to this De Jongh fella. Where do I start?'

'Start?' She blinked at him. 'How do you mean?'

'Where did he say he was staying?'

'He didn't.'

'That of course makes it easy. He didn't confuse us with the facts, hey?' He grinned at her like a nursemaid coaxing a smile from a fractious child. 'Okay, okay, I'll see what I can do. Keep your chin in the air, dolly. It's the only place for it. And remember, bad as it feels at the moment it's no worse than it's been the past five years. You never knew where Charles was then, what he was doing, maybe you don't know now. Remember that.'

She tried to, but each day she woke to the thought of Charles, seeing him in that small room in Amsterdam as surely as if she had actually been there. Each day as she sat and sewed and the wireless blared and Cissie sang and Florrie brought the endless cups of tea, she thought of Gerhard De Jongh, walking away into the darkness of Paultons Square and hating herself for letting him go.

And each day, behind those thoughts, were others. Guilt and anger and helplessness as she let Uncle Alex's words march through her mind over and over again. The Jews suffer in every generation. Some get over it and some are destroyed by it. We're the lucky ones, the lucky ones, the lucky ones.

The words went on pleating themselves in and out of her thoughts as Uncle Alex, week after week, reported failure. No news of Charles, no news of Henk and no news at all of Gerhard De Jongh, even though he must be, had to be, somewhere in England, if not in London. He threw all his considerable energy into the search, sending people from his office to comb the refugee societies' files, badgering the Home Office for news of aliens, going to refugee clubs in every town he happened to be in as he stumped about the country looking after his tours and his actors and musicians. But it was as though De Jongh had never really existed and as the year turned into a hopeful spring and everyone was telling everyone else that it was almost over, it couldn't be long now, peace would come, she began to believe it had never happened. That night last October had been a nightmare, a figment of her war weary imagination. No young man with a thin face and dark eyes had come to get drunk in her drawing room and tell her mad stories. She had dreamed it all up because of her anxiety about Charles.

Then, the talk about the war ending became more than hopeful gossip and changed to certainty, and the newspapers were filled with accounts of allied soldiers fanning out over Europe so fast that even the most dedicated of readers could hardly keep up with it. And at last soldiers marched into Buchenwald and Belsen and the pictures arrived.

It was a sunny day in high summer and Hannah had come limping down to breakfast to find Florrie standing in the hallway with the *Daily Mirror* open in her hands and her face stiff with shock.

'What is it, Florrie?' Hannah had said, as she safely negotiated the last step. 'What's happened? You look as though the cat's got your – '

Florrie looked up and tried, clumsily, to fold the paper, to stuff it in her apron pocket. Hannah stared at her, puzzled.

'Florrie?'

Florrie shook her head again and then, slowly, obviously realizing the absurdity of trying to hide such a thing as a newspaper, gave it to her and Hannah leaned against the banisters, propping her stick beside her, and smoothed the crumpled pages as Cissie came down the stairs behind her, humming under her breath.

And there they were, the pictures, the words, the proof that they had asked for, she and Uncle Alex and all the others who had listened to the tales of the refugees and not really believed them. The pictures of starved bodies piled like garbage in a field, of faces staring out from behind barbed wire fences, of gas ovens and heaps of discarded spectacles and false teeth and shoes and bodies, bodies, bodies. They stood there, the three English women in the sunlit hallway of a pretty house in Chelsea, with the scent of their morning coffee in their nostrils and read over each other's shoulders of the deaths of millions. Florrie turned and ran, stumbling a little as she went up the stairs, and they could hear her vomiting in the bathroom.

68

In some ways it was harder to recover from the second world war than it had been from the first. Hannah had thought then, back in 1918, that she was at the very nadir of her life with Peter dead and Judith dead, and she alone to bear the burden of living on. But there had been the children then, two urgent reasons for getting up each morning and trying to get through the day. And she had been younger, and with more essential power still in her, though she had not realized that at the time.

But this time she realized full well how drained she was. Physically, she was deeply weary, eroded by the constant arthritic pain in her leg and hip, legacy of the injury to her ankle. She learned to stand as tall as she could, to use her stick at all times, and to control her pain by not thinking about it. When it got too bad to allow her to sleep, she took aspirin, but that was all. She would not see doctors, however much Cissie and Florrie nagged her to do so, determined to cope with her state as best she could, knowing it to be permanent.

The effect could be seen on her. Not only did she move with a rigidity that was a marked contrast to her old lithe easiness, but her face had changed. Her mouth had become tighter with the corners downturned and there were lines cut between them and her nostrils. The copper colour of her hair had faded, and was now tinged with white, though it was as thick as ever, and she flatly refused to do as Cissie did and have it dyed. Cissie was marching through her sixties triumphantly, a vision of New Look clothes and waved hair and lavish makeup while Hannah was heralding her fifties, it seemed, by displaying her age rather than fighting it.

But it was the emotional burden that was the heaviest. For the first two years after the war was over she went on hoping, forlornly, though she knew she was absurd. Of course Charles was dead, it could not be otherwise. Maybe, she would tell herself in the long dark nights, maybe one day someone will turn up who will know what happened to him. Maybe Henk will come to the door and tell her that Charles was well, alive and well and living in some remote country suffering from amnesia, his past driven from his memory by the hell of a particular present. She drifted back into the comforting fantasy habits of her childhood, weaving complex stories in her head to explain away the pain of reality, making elaborate story structures in which Charles triumphed over and over again, all culminating in Charles coming home to her.

Uncle Alex went on trying but a tide of displaced people was unleashed in Europe and in all the chaos and recriminations and confusion tracking down the fate of one Englishman who had lived in Amsterdam was a herculean task. At last he did find the facts and that was a bad day for Hannah. For Charles had died not a hero's death, fighting the injustices and hates that had fuelled him for so long, but a pointless wasted one, alone in a charity ward coughing his tubercular lungs into a chipped enamel bowl.

For weeks after that news reached Paultons Square Hannah walked taller and straighter and more grimly than ever, and Cissie stopped singing. Her own TB had been cured, leaving her with a safely calcified spot on her right lung. She, sixty-five years old, was alive; Charles, who had been little more than thirty, was gone, and that shamed her. So Hannah had to comfort her too. Bad days, bad days.

And not helped by the silence from Marie. Lammeck Alley moved back into gear slowly, picking up the threads of business as the world shook itself and returned to normal living, and it took some time for Hannah to identify the person most likely to help her. Peterson had long since retired, grateful for a little peace at last. He was succeeded by a Damont cousin who was quite uninterested in past family history, and took little trouble to advise her. But, by means of persistent letters and phone calls, she at last persuaded him to give her what news he had.

It was scant. Mrs Rupert Lammeck had gone on drawing her income until 1944 and then stopped. No more had been heard of her. There was now an accumulation of funds in her name, although of course the amount could not be divulged to anyone, even Mrs Rupert Lammeck's mother.

'Dammit!' Hannah shouted at the smooth faced boy reciting this at her. 'Dammit, do you think I care about her money? I only want to know where she is, is she well? What about her child? That's all.' But he just shrugged; he knew no more.

She considered hiring a private detective, but Uncle Alex talked her out of that.

'It's a big country, dolly, and she was always on the move. Forget it, look it in the face and forget it. She don't want to know you no more. Sure it hurts, but who promised you a life with no hurts in it? Anyone did, he was a liar.'

She wrote long letters to her brothers in New York, asking them to see if they could find news of her, not because she really thought they could but because it was better than doing nothing. They wrote back, short scrappy little letters full of their own doings on the fringes of the boxing world that made it clear they could not find their niece and wouldn't know where to begin looking. And Hannah tried to do as Uncle Alex advised and live with her pain.

The early post war years were hard for all of them, quite

apart from any personal distress. Food was in shorter supply than it had ever been, and rationing seemed to be a permanent feature of British existence. Women who could get their hands on black market cloth came to Hannah but most of her work was the dispiriting making over of old garments, lengthening skirts to approximate Christian Dior's New Look, remaking lingerie so that every possible use was made of every scrap of fabric. But at last the forties died miserably and became the fifties and people began to talk more of the future and to plan for it instead of looking back over their shoulders.

As the years of austerity eased and money became more available, it sometimes seemed to Hannah that the new young people had forgotten all the pain that their predecessors had suffered for them. Who cared any more about her Charles, about Marcus and his bitter loss, and her and her constant pain, who gave a damn? She would look at the young ones strutting about the streets in their full skirted dresses and drainpipe trousers, lugging their portable radios around and bawling their ugly noisy songs and was filled with a resentment and anger that tightened her mouth even more. For a long time Hannah disliked herself and her world sorely.

In 1955 Cissie at last took the plunge about which she had been talking for years. She had said, when Lenny and his Nina had gone to America to bring their children home and had decided instead to stay there, that she would follow them, would make her future there. Somehow she had never found the courage. But when she heard that her oldest grandchild had become engaged, she could bear it no longer. She would go – and what was more, she would go by air.

How they ever got her into the cab and out to Heathrow to get on her plane Hannah never really knew. The excitement in Cissie was so high it was almost hysteria, and Florrie started crying over breakfast and didn't stop all day, and Hannah was tight lipped with misery, for Cissie was her dearest friend.

They said little when they parted, just hugging each other, and Hannah sat beside a still weeping Florrie in the cab going back to Paultons Square and asked herself dully why she bothered to go on living at all. It seemed so pointless now. What was left of all the hopes and plans of the early years?

What was there in this new world for which her Marcus and Charles had died that was worth living for? Nothing at all, she told herself, nothing at all.

Cissie wrote regularly at first, twice a week. Her letters punctuated Hannah's dreary days with interest, but as the years moved on they became fewer and scrappier. It was not that Cissie had forgotten Hannah, but she had a new purpose in her life now, Hannah supposed, and was too busy to write.

Hannah was genuinely glad for her, but it underlined her own lonely uselessness. What good was she to anyone? Uncle Alex, old as he was, was still vigorous, still busy though not with business. Now an indefatigable committee man, he spent all his waking hours raising money for the infant state of Israel, an activity which seemed to have injected him with ever more energy, if that were possible. Certainly he had no need of Hannah. As far as she could tell, her only use was as someone for Florrie to fuss over, someone to give purpose to *her* life. That she had none in her own seemed irrelevant to everyone.

Until one evening in June 1957. It had been a hot day though not as hot as the previous weeks had been; the country had sweltered in one of the hottest summers on record, and Hannah, like many people, was drained by it. She had been to a wedding at Edgware. One of Reuben and Minnie's great brood had married, and Hannah had sighed when the invitation had come, wearied by the thought of yet another family party, for they were a burgeoning and busy clan, the Lazars. Weddings and brisses and Barmitzvahs seemed to happen with every rising of the moon, interspersed with house warming parties as the young ones prospered and moved on, shaking the dust of the East End from their well shod feet for the lusher pastures of north west London.

It amused her sometimes to contemplate them, business men and accountants, factory owners and shopkeepers, with their befurred and scented wives and sulky faced expensively educated spoiled youngsters, talking earnestly to each other of University for young Sandra and Lawrence and Andrea and Vernon and Debra and Ivor. They who had left their schools at fourteen were going to see to it that their children would have a better life in this better new world. Being Jewish in London in the nineteen fifties was a comfortable and safe thing to be, for was there not, at last, a safe haven available in case anything went wrong? When the State of Israel had been born in 1948 some of the more politically minded of them shook their heads, worried about the long term outcome, but most of them breathed deep and told each other how marvellous it was and set about fund raising as part of their social lives, and generally felt good.

So, when invitations to weddings and parties came Hannah sighed and accepted. It would be hurtful not to, but she never wanted to go. Their closeness with their children and grand-children underlined too painfully her own solitude. And today had been no exception.

Florrie was away, gone to visit Bet in Whitby for her annual summer holiday, having left Hannah with long lists of emergency instructions, so she was alone in the house. The street outside was still shimmering with heat, even though it was now seven in the evening, for the day had sweltered. The reception had been a tea dance – tea dances were more fashionable now, because they were less ostentatious than the old East End style parties with mountains of food and hours of dancing. Those were considered vulgar, too reminiscent of the olds days in the *shtetls*. English Jews today aimed to be as English as they could be. Which meant control, and an awareness of what was high class behaviour and what was not. Really rich people (and the father of the bride as a record shop owner was becoming exceedingly rich) could make these more stylish modest parties without being thought cheapskates by the older generation while adhering to their own notions of what was proper. Hannah for one was grateful. And also grateful to be home.

She showered slowly, letting the water run over her, feeling some of the pain ease from her hip, and then went limping into the bedroom, not bothering to dry herself. Letting the water evaporate on her skin was cooling and she needed that. She caught a glimpse of herself in the dressing table mirror as she went past it and stopped to stare. The silence in the house enveloped her and for a moment time seemed to slip. It wasn't now, but long ago, when this room had been newly decorated, and she frowned sharply at the image in the mirror. Who was that, so tired looking and lined? Whose body was that with drooping breasts and thinning hair? What had happened to her? Inside she felt as she always had, but on the surface was a total stranger.

She shook her head and closed her eyes. When she opened them again the moment had passed. Just for a second it had seemed as it used to, with a small watching Hannah sitting in the corner of the room jeering at her, commenting cruelly on her, making her feel like a totally different person. She could not cope with that feeling again now; she would not. She moved away from the mirror purposefully and put on the cotton housecoat in which she was most comfortable.

At first she thought she imagined it when the bell rang downstairs. With Florrie away, there was no one who would call on her at seven on a Sunday evening, and for a moment she felt a surge of fear, a memory of that night thirteen years before when Gerhard De Jongh had come.

'Silly,' she said aloud, and pushed her feet into her slippers and began the slow painful descent of the stairs.

The bell rang again, impatiently, a double ring, and she said aloud, 'All right, all right! I'm coming!' even though she knew she could not be heard. She could see a shape against the stained glass insets on the door and she squinted a little, trying to identify who it might be, but the shape was ill defined, refracted by the shattered light.

She stood in front of the door for a moment and then opened it cautiously a few inches.

The light was lowering now as the sun moved further down the sky and the figure in front of her was hard to see. She squinted again and said carefully, 'Yes?'

'I'm sorry to bother you, ma'am.' It was a soft drawling voice with an unfamiliar accent, a high voice. Hannah looked closer, puzzled. The figure was wearing trousers and a shirt and had a cloth cap on its head and she had thought, just for a moment, that it was a man. Now she could see the face, and relaxed a little. A round face, soft and young. A girl's.

'Yes?' she said again.

'I'm looking for a Lady Lammeck? I was told that this was the Lammeck home and ... but you are, aren't you? You're Lady Lammeck. I can see you are.'

Hannah frowned and stepped back a little, pushing the door almost closed.

'What d'you mean, you can see I am?' she said, sharply. 'You can't see me properly at all.'

The girl smiled widely, showing very white teeth. 'I can see your hair, ma'am. Red hair. Like mine.' She lifted her

600

hand and took her cap off and a tangle of hair fell over her shoulders, red coppery hair, just as Hannah's own had been.

She stood there for a long moment, listening to her pulse beating thickly in her ears, staring at the thin girl in her shabby shirt and trousers and with a mass of red hair framing her face, not daring to think, not daring to hope, only daring to breathe slowly, regularly, counting each breath. One, two, three.

'I'm Lee,' the girl said. 'Lee Lammeck. I said I'd come and find you, ever since I was a kid. And now I have. Do I call you grandma, or would you prefer something else?'

69

Lee was sitting on the floor, her knees hunched up and her arms hugging them, while Hannah sat very upright in her high backed chair on the other side of the fireplace. The small table with the remains of their supper stood to one side and Hannah looked at it and thought, I ought to clear that up. But she did not move.

Lee had been quite calm about it; she had come to London to find her grandmother, and she had every intention of staying with her, now that she had found her.

'You've got room, haven't you? Or would I be trouble to have around? I'm not usually. I'm used to living in other peoples houses.'

'No trouble at all,' Hannah said. 'And yes, I have room. Too much room.'

'I can see that.' She looked around consideringly. 'I was told you're rich, and you sure are. Looks like you're loaded, in fact.'

Hannah frowned a little at that. 'I don't talk about money,' she said stiffly.

Lee nodded. 'That sure as hell proves you got a lot of it. You can only ignore it when you're loaded. When you're not it sort of pushes itself at you, know what I mean?'

'I know,' Hannah said. 'I was born in the East End.'

'Oh? Where's that?'

'Where poor people are born.'

'I was born in San Francisco,' Lee said after a moment. 'Or so I'm told.'

Hannah took a deep breath. So far she had hardly dared to speak to the girl at all. Her own feelings were in far too great a turmoil to be able to say much and the girl herself seemed so contained and remote, somehow. So, she had offered her supper and Lee had accepted calmly and helped her make omelettes for them both, and chattered on about her journey, about how long it had taken her to save the money to buy an air ticket by working as a waitress and in a summer camp and as a baby sitter, and how dramatic the world looked from so far up and Hannah had listened and watched the girl's face and the way the light played on her hair and lit it to that familiar bronze sheen that used to look back at her from her own mirror.

And now she could wait no longer.

'Lee,' she said. 'Your mother. Tell me about Marie.'

The girl looked up at her. swinging her head so that the mass of hair covered half her face and she could hide behind it. All Hannah could see was one eye staring watchfully at her.

'What about her?'

'Where is she? Why hasn't she been in touch with me all these years? And Rupert, your father, what about him?'

'Oh, he's dead,' Lee said easily and looked away, staring at the window which the summer twilight was now deepening to a dusky blue.

'Oh,' Hannah said blankly, and felt a little chill inside her. Was this child as cold as she seemed? 'I'm sorry.'

Lee shrugged. 'Why should you be? I mean, from my point of view, gee, I never even saw him! He was gone before I was born, they told me, and I never knew anything about him till after he died.'

'They told you – who told you?'

'Aunt Pearl,' Lee said. 'I lived with Aunt Pearl, you see. In Sacramento. She took me after ... when I was four. I lived with her ever since, till she died last year. They tried to put me in a Home then, you know? In California they've got all these crazy laws about how old kids have to be to be left in peace to live on their own, and they tried to put me in a Home, like I'd done something, and I never did a thing I shouldn't! Aunt Pearl would'a killed me if I had. So when

602

she died, and they started talking about a Home I thought, hell, no, and I lit out.'

'Lit out?'

'Went to New York. Hitched, y'know? Wow, it was tough sometimes. Some of these truck drivers think that just because you want a ride you're . . . well never mind, Anyway, I got to New York and – '

'But Marie. Your mother,' Hannah said, holding onto the thread tightly. There was a lot to hear about Lee, but first things first, she told herself. First things first. 'Marie?'

Lee sat silently staring out at the dark square, then said abruptly, 'I'd rather not talk about her.'

The silence between them lengthened and then Lee said angrily, 'Oh, hell! What can I do? You were her mother so I guess . . . She took coke, okay? So Aunt Pearl said, anyway. Got into a whole coke bit and that did it.'

'I don't understand,' Hannah said carefully. 'I'm sorry, but I don't understand.'

'What don't you understand? That your daughter was a lousy addict? Spent most of her time so stoned she couldn't even talk, let alone take care of a kid? I remember it, you know that? I remember being in that apartment and she lying there breathing so loud I could . . . and so goddam hungry I didn't know . . . Aw, hell, she's dead, okay? And Aunt Pearl was her friend and she found her dead and took me in and that's all. Now, can we lay off my mother? I know you had to be told, but it . . . I just don't like to talk about it. I told you what I know, now leave it alone already.'

Hannah said nothing. There was nothing she could say. She sat in the darkening drawing room remembering and trying not to, seeing Marie in a high chair, Marie in a frilled white dress going to a children's party, Marie and Charles in blue holland overalls painting at the big nursery table.

'I'm sorry,' she said then. 'Sorry for you, sorry for me. Sorry for Marie. I don't know what I did wrong, but I . . . her father died when she was a baby, I . . . I did my best. But it wasn't enough.'

'Listen,' Lee said and there was a rough anger in her voice. 'I'll tell you what Aunt Pearl told me, okay? That some people are born to it, you know? Born to misery, I mean. That it is no one's fault it happens, that you can be the best friend that person ever had, the best kid, the best parent, I guess, but no matter what, they just don't make it. Aunt Pearl was the greatest friend anyone could have had. What she did for my mother, well, I'll tell you she was the greatest, fantastic. And she learned not to blame herself and she taught me not to blame myself, and now I'm telling you. None of this had anything to do with anyone except my mother, okay? You don't own people just because you care about 'em. You do what you can and the rest is up to them. That's what Aunt Pearl said.'

'Aunt Pearl sounds very special,' Hannah said quietly.

'She was. The best there was. She died bad, too, didn't deserve it. She had cancer in the breast. Awful.'

Lee stretched suddenly and yawned, opening her mouth wide and Hannah saw the gleam of her teeth in the darkness. 'And here I am. I got here! I always said I would. Aunt Pearl told me I had this high toned family back in London, and if I ever needed any help, go find 'em. So here I am. Jeeze, it wasn't easy, you know that? Getting a passport and all. I had to lie like crazy but I got it, and I raised the money and I kept out of their goddam Home and I made it! And from where I'm sitting that sure is something!'

'Indeed it is,' Hannah said, and felt a sudden warmth for this strange sharp girl. It wasn't just that she looked so like Hannah herself at her age. It was the determination in her, the strength in her that made Hannah feel good and whole again. Without thinking she put out one hand and said, 'I'm so glad you did. Glad you made it. I think I've been waiting for you.'

Lee sat still in the darkness for a moment and then she put out one hand too and took Hannah's in her rough young fingers.

'It's okay, then? You want me to stay?'

'I sure do,' Hannah said, and laughed softly in the dark room, enjoying her moment of affectionate mockery. 'I sure do.'

'Thanks most awfully,' Lee said with a neat imitation of an English voice. 'Thanks most awfully *awfully*.'

And so it was that at the age of sixty-four Hannah started to live again. It seemed to her sometimes, over the next ten years, that this was what she had been born for, what all the sad and painful years had been leading to, making a haven for

604

this tough little scrap of a girl who had, in her own way, suffered as much as her grandmother had. Nurturing her and teaching her and protecting her and loving her, watching her lose, slowly, her defensive edginess and become a laughing relaxed and happy person. That was what life was for. Even Florrie seemed to have a new lease on life with a young one in the house. She nagged less and sang more, and fussed over both of them with ill concealed delight.

Together they explored the East End where Hannah had been born, for Lee had a hunger for information about the past that was almost insatiable, and, slowly because of Hannah's arthritis, they walked through the Whitechapel Road and Commercial Road as Hannah told Lee stories of the old days, and how it had been to live in these tight, mean, hungry streets.

Many of them were gone now of course; where Antcliff Street had been there were now great tower blocks of flats set at angles in rough litter-covered grass. Sidney Street was still there and so was Jubilee Street, though largely rebuilt on the bombed sites of long dead houses and little shops, but Bromehead Road and Bromehead Street had gone, and the market stalls had gone. Now there were black and Asian faces where once had been Jewish side curls and old women in *sheitels* and men with their prayer shawls dangling beneath their waistcoats.

Lee stared and listened and asked questions and Hannah found herself, to her own surprise at first, talking about Charles and how he had come to these streets to fight for a better world for the people who had lived in them. How he had fought with the blackshirt marchers, how he had burned out his young life fighting, fighting, fighting. Lee had lifted her chin in exaltation at his story, and at last Hannah stopped mourning for the loss of Charles and was able to celebrate the fact that he had lived. So his life had been short? What matter when it had been so important and so well used? True, he had died alone and lonely in a foreign country. But what matter when he lived on now in this granddaughter of hers whom he would have loved as much as Lee had come to love his memory? Charles lived again, and lived well, because of Lee.

Lee and Uncle Alex took to each other with a delight that made Hannah want to weep with sheer pleasure. The old man, now almost ninety, would sit in his armchair when they went to visit him, and laugh and tease Lee as though he were still a sprightly sixty, and she teased him too, asking him why he had never married, just for the joy of hearing him giggle wickedly and tell her that he had been too clever.

'I tell you, dolly,' he would say in his thin old voice. 'I tell you, I had such girls! They were crazy for me, but I had my Hannah to worry over so what did I want with wives and more children? I had my Hannah and now she's got you. It all comes out in the wash, hey? That's what my Momma Rivka used to say, in the *heim*. It all comes out in the wash.'

One of Hannah's greatest delights was to discover that Lee had inherited her grandmother's gift for design and sewing. She told Hannah very quickly after arriving that she had no notion of being a layabout.

'I'm going to get a job,' she said. 'I'll find something to do. I gotta be independent, you know? I don't take no handouts from no one. I worked for Aunt Pearl, soon's I left school and I'll work now.'

'You don't have to, Lee,' Hannah said, tentatively. 'I don't mean I'll take care of you, though I would, gladly, but you've got your own money. Marie, your mother, only drew the income from hers. The capital's considerable by now, I imagine. All you have to do is go to Lammeck Alley. Once they know you're Marie's daughter, then, there it will be. You'll have all the money you need.'

'To hell with that,' Lee said, her voice flat. 'To hell with that. Much good it did my mother to have it. She didn't work for it, so she used it for junk. She killed herself with it. Didn't she? Not me. Not nohow, not ever. I'm going to work for my money. Anyway, I don't give a good goddam for money, not for itself. It's what you *do* that matters. What you create with your own head and your own hands. No handouts for me. I'm going to get work of my own.'

The work she got was in a dress shop and after listening to her and watching for a year, Hannah suggested, tentatively, that maybe it would be an idea to have a shop of her own.

'Not a handout,' she assured Lee hastily. 'I promise you not a handout. It's something that interests me, too, and maybe you could design your own, just as I did when I was Mary Bee Couturiere.'

And so it happened. By the time Uncle Alex died sweetly and contentedly in his sleep just after his ninety-first birthday, Lee had her shop just around the corner from Paultons Square in King's Road.

'Not the smartest place in the world, I grant you,' Hannah had said when they found the premises. 'But if you do good things people'll come to you, and districts change. You never know. King's Road could turn out to be a good place to have a shop.'

She was right, of course. By the time Lee's twenty-fifth birthday came, her boutique was regarded as one of the best in London. She had her own workshops behind it and was turning out clothes that every magazine wanted to write about and every smart woman wanted to wear. Never mind Courrèges and Quant, it was Lee Lammeck clothes they all wanted. And bought and talked about and feted Lee and she and Hannah laughed over the way it was all happening again.

Lee found a particular delight in tracing the similarities between herself and her grandmother's history, telling every interviewer that her grandmother had been to the 1920s what she, Lee, was now, forty years later.

And aged seventy-two, with her hair now completely white and her back as stiff as ever and her arthritis gripping her ever more tightly, Hannah found herself once again a person of fashion. It amused her immensely and when she planned a special birthday party for Lee, she made up an invitation list that was starred with famous names. Pop singers and photographers, actors and politicians, everyone who was anyone was invited. It was the biggest party of the year, one of the highlights of the Swinging Sixties world that London had become.

But Hannah did not invite only the rich and famous, any more than she had all those years ago when she and Marcus had entertained the Prince of Wales in their house in Paultons Square. She invited her cousins and their children too, though this time the difference between the children of Lazar and Rivka and the new aristocracy of England was difficult to see. For they came to the party in Paultons Square in their Bentleys and Mercedes, dressed and bejewelled as richly as anyone else, and spoke in the same voices with the same sort of words, expressing the same sort of sentiments. The differences had melted away in three generations. The poverty, the loneliness, the alienation of the immigrant East Enders were all gone.

One of the guests was Adam Lazar, the son of Lionel. A tall, quiet young man with a passion for learning that Hannah found very reminiscent of his long dead grandfather David and David's father, her Uncle Benjamin. He had been away working in America for the past five years and he and Lee had not met before.

Hannah watched them talk and laugh and dance together at Lee's twenty-fifth birthday party and knew that a new phase was about to begin, that a new generation was waiting to take the stage. And somewhere deep within herself she knew that the seeds of a new loneliness were being sown for her. And she was right, because in May 1967 Lee Lammeck married Dr Adam Lazar at the New West End synagogue at the smartest wedding of the year. Their shared relation, grandmother and great cousin Hannah was the most honoured guest. She sat at the top table as the other guests danced and ate and drank and danced again and watched them and thought her quiet thoughts. She was to be alone again, for Adam had an important research job to return to in California, and Lee was to accompany him. Hannah, almost seventy-five, could have gone with them; both begged her to, but she shook her head and patted their cheeks and told them, no.

'I belong here,' she said. 'Born and bred a Londoner, you know that. My parents and my grandparents had to wander, you have to wander. But me, I'm one of the few who stay put. So, I'm staying here. Come and visit me when you can. The house will always be here and I'll always be in it. *G'ey g'zint.*' And she smiled at herself for speaking Yiddish for she never had. But it was necessary, for that was what Uncle Alex would have said to them. '*G'ey g'zint.*' Go in good health.

And they went, with a good heart, Lee weeping a little, but glowing with the joy of having her Adam beside her. Hannah watched them walk through the departure gate at Heathrow Airport and turned away and went home to Florrie, now almost as arthritic as Hannah herself, alone, but not lonely. Lee might not be with her, but she was there in her world, and always a part of it. She had given Hannah reason to live and the reason was still there wherever Lee happened to be. So Hannah told herself as her taxi drew up outside the house in Paultons Square, and she went in tranquilly to make some supper for Florrie.

EPILOGUE

Returning

March 1980. A cold and blustery London morning with last year's leaves blowing along the gutters in little flurries and cars spraying up water as they swished past, their windscreen wipers working frantically. One of them, a big red one, spattered the small girl in the raincoat with muddy water and she squealed. Her mother looked at her and shushed her gently.

'You have to be quiet and polite this morning, honey,' she whispered, and pulled the rainhat more closely over her ears. The child wriggled and made a face.

Cars arriving, more cars, and people collecting in little groups, talking quietly. People in heavy black coats and ladies in neat hats and furs, all smiling small smiles, the sort that you smile when you want to but mustn't, or don't want to but must, the small girl decided. She tried not to yawn. If squealing was not polite, yawning must be worse.

People talked to her, were introduced and she smiled and nodded, not understanding who they all were but knowing she must be polite as Daddy pushed her gently forwards to shake hands. 'I'm ten years old,' she told them. 'Ten years old,' as they went on and on asking her, one after the other and smiling the way they did, small and tight.

And then there was praying and talking and she stopped listening, looking out at the sky that she could see through the high windows of the tall building they had all gone into and thinking how it would be tomorrow, going on a plane again. Three planes in three days. No one else in her grade at school at home had ever gone in three planes in three days, she was sure of that.

Walking again along muddy paths, all the people walking together, so close together that she could not see much more than the legs of the people in front. Anyway she didn't want to see. She knew what they were doing, for Daddy had told her, and it wasn't all that interesting. Or nice.

At last, they came back along the muddy paths, and the people were smiling more widely now, their shoulders less stiff, even laughing a little, as the men washed their hands at little fountains and nodded at each other.

And then it was over and they were ging back to their own car, the one Daddy had hired for today and there was someone calling after them.

'Lee? Adam? I knew it was you! I haven't seen you for, oh, years! How *are* you both? It's good to see you. I just wish it had been on a happier occasion.'

'Yes,' Mommy said, and the child looked up at her mother, a little surprised because she wasn't one who cried much and she was crying now. 'Yes.'

'You were close, I know,' the man said, and patted Mommy's hand. 'You'll miss her, but she had a good life, a good life. How old was she? Eighty-seven? And died peacefully in her sleep, just like old Uncle Alex, *alava ha-sholom*, you remember him? I tell you, we got good genes in this family, we live long, if we live in peace. And who is this? You haven't told me who this is.'

The child looked up at the man in his thick black overcoat and he smiled at her and she thought, I like his face, and she smiled too. He took off his hat and bent towards her, and wanting to be as polite as he was, she did the same, glad to pull the thing off anyway, for it made her ears itch. Her red hair came tumbling out and was blown about her face by the wind and she smiled at the man and said, 'Hi! I'm ten years old.'

He laughed. 'I was about to ask. And what do they call you?'

'Sukey,' she said. 'It's short though. Short, for all my name.'

'And what is all your name?'

Mommy and Daddy were smiling now. She could feel them standing there smiling at her, and she looked up at them and they nodded. It was all right to talk, to chatter on. The sad bits were over, now.

'Susannah Tamar,' she said. 'My name is Susannah Tamar Lazar, and I'm going to live in Jerusalem with my Mommy and Daddy, because he's going to work in a hospital there. Isn't that exciting?'

'Very exciting,' the man said, and Sukey pulled away from her Mommy's hand and went skipping along the path towards the car, leaving them to follow. Another airplane tomorrow, to go to Jerusalem. Very exciting. She began to sing.

GLOSSARY

Alav ha sholom: Literally, 'Peace to him or her'. Used whenever speaking of someone who is dead.

Ashkenazi: Jews of the Central and Eastern parts of Europe, most especially those of the Pale of Settlement, and Germany. (*See also* Sephardi.)

Bagel: A circular roll with a hole in the centre made of white flour and yeast, the dough being poached in hot water before baking, to make it particularly crisp.

Barmitzvah: Literally 'son of the commandment'; the rite of passage through which Jewish boys pass at the age of thirteen to permit them to join the community as full members.

Bimah: The central dais in the synagogue.

Blinis: Stuffed pancakes, sweet or savoury. Also known as blintzes.

Bissel: A little. (A *bissel* here, a *bissel* there – a little here, a little there.)

Bobbelah: A term of endearment, generally feminine of use, but, on occasion, directed at men. Derives from Russian Yiddish, as diminutive of buba – 'doll'.

Boobameiser: A grandmother's story (an old wives' tale).

Boychick: A small boy. Used sometimes to define a man with boyish ways.

Briss: Ritual circumcision of a baby boy.

Broigus: Offended, angry.

Chanukah: The Feast of Lights. An eight-day celebration observed in December and frequently coinciding with Christmas in the Christian calander. It commemorates the victory of the Maccabees, Jewish warriors who defeated the Syrians in 167 BC (See the Apocrypha, Book of the Maccabees I and II.)

Cheder: Schoolroom, where Hebrew is taught, only to boys in the old days but now to girls too.

Choleria: Literally cholera, but usually meaning a curse of

614

some kind or another. ('A choleria on him' means 'May a plague fall on him and destroy him'.)

Chuchum: Clever – a show-off sort of person.

Chumash: First five books of the bible (Pentateuch).

Chutspah: (many different spellings) Impudence, outrageous effrontery. Best defined by telling a story, e.g. 'A man killed both his parents and at his trial for murder begged for clemency on the grounds that he was an orphan'.

Dreying your kopf: Literally 'banging your head' – upsetting yourself.

Farbissen: Embittered, sullen, sour. Can be used as a noun – e.g. *farbissener*, an embittered man (for an embittered woman *farbissenah*).

Ferstinkener: Smelly. Used as an epithet to describe a disliked person, as well as literally to describe a smelly object/place.

Gefärlich: Busyness – doing.

Gefillte fish: Literally stuffed fish. A mixture of chopped white fish, onions, eggs, sometimes ground almonds or chopped apples, and seasoning, originally used to stuff carp before it was poached, now often poached or fried in small portions. Usually eaten with beetroot-flavoured horseradish sauce (chrane) and considered a great delicacy.

Gelt: Literally gold. Money.

Giveh: Showing off – swank.

Goldeneh medina: Literally the golden country. Usually used to define the USA to which the majority of the Jews of the Pale wished to emigrate.

Gonif (plural *gonovim*): Thief.

Gornicht mit gornicht: Literally 'nothing with nothing'.

Gott se dank: Thank God.

Goy: A gentile, a non-Jew.

Gunser macher: 'A big noise' – a busy person, either in reality or his own opinion!

Guteneh shumah: Literally a good person.

Gy gesund: Literally 'go in health' and by implication 'with a good heart and with a blessing'.

Haggadah: The collection of Jewish history, fables and folklore, assorted rabbinical writings, prayers – a whole library of Jewish culture.

Heim: Literally home. Often used to describe the place from which immigrants came to London (*see also* shtetl). Hence *heimish* or *heimisher* – homelike or in the style of the old home.

Halevai (sometimes pronounced 'aleavai', with a dropped aitch): Literally 'Please let it be so'.

Kaddish: A special prayer. The prayer at the end of the Sabbath service is a kaddish. Mourners say a kaddish for the dead. (Kiddush is another prayer used to sanctify the Sabbath and Holy Days and said before meals).

Kishke: Literally intestines. Guts.

Kopf: Head.

Kosher: Literally fit for use. Usually describes food prepared according to Jewish dietary laws.

Koyach: Strength.

Ladino: A vernacular used by Sephardi Jews (q.v.) deriving from Spanish, Portuguese, French, just as Yiddish (q.v.) derives from German and Russian.

Lavoyah: A funeral.

Lobbus: Lovable rogue.

Lockshen: Thin noodles, vermicelli. Traditionally served in chicken soup.

Lundsman (plural *landsleit*): Properly, land's man – one who comes from your land. A fellow Jew from the same *shtetl* in the *heim* (q.v.).

Magen David: The star of David. The symbol of Judaism.

Marrano: A converted Jew, from the Spanish word for pig.

Maven: Literally an expert. One who knows a great deal about a specific subject.

Mazel: Literally luck. Also part of the traditional greeting and congratulation, *mazel tov*.

Mechulah: Finished, without money. A person who goes bankrupt is *mechulah*.

Megillah: A long rigmarole, a spun-out tale, a false story. Originally for the Book of Esther which is a very long *megillah* indeed.

Mensch (plural *menschen*): Literally man, or men. But now used to describe a person of character, of stature or obvious worth. 'A real *mensch*' is a respect-worthy person.

Meshuggah: Literally mad. Used also as a noun *meshuggenah* – a mad person. Also *misheggass*, a madness, a crazy act.

Mezzuzah: A small container carrying a tiny scroll with the verses Deuteronomy vi, 4–9, xi, 13–21, and fastened to the doorposts of a house occupied by pious Jews.

Midrash: A collection of over a hundred books of Biblical

commentary.

Mishnah: One of the two parts of Talmud (the other is the Gemorrah). Contains the Law.

Mohel: A person who performs ritual circumcision (*see* Bris).

Mumser (plural *mumserim*). Literally bastard. So a bad person.

Nachus: Pride – especially in the doings of one's children.

Nebbish (also *nebbach* and other spellings): Pathetic. A pathetic person is a *nebbish*. When a person is ill, *nebbish*, he doesn't feel well. Widely used in many contexts to define a sad situation or person, but also a helpless person (a mentally handicapped individual is *nebbish*).

Oy vey is mir: Literally 'Oh woe is me!' A traditional Jewish cry of distress.

Putz: The male generative organ – expressed as a diminutive. (More insulting with the same meaning is *schmuck*.)

Rachmones: Pity. To show compassion.

Rosh Hashonah: The New Year festival, falling at the end of the growing and harvesting year, i.e. September, October.

Sairchel: Common sense, wisdom.

Sephardi: Jews deriving from Spanish and Portuguese communities. Often French nowadays. The old 'aristocracy' of Jews in some people's eyes. All, however, Ladino speaking (q.v.).

Shabbos: Sabbath. From sunset Friday to sunset Saturday.

Shachris: Evening prayers.

Shadchan: A matchmaker, active in the *heim* (q.v.).

Shaygets: A non-Jewish youth.

Shayne Mensch: Literallly 'pretty man' – a handsome person.

Sheitel: Wig worn by pious Jewish women who shaved their heads when they married, since a woman's hair is her 'crowning glory' and has erotic connotations which may no longer be allowed to be displayed once a girl marries.

Shidduch: A 'match', an engagement.

Shivah: The seven days of ritual mourning for the dead observed by the immediate members of the family.

Shlemeil: An idiot.

Shlep: Literally to drag, to carry on a long journey, a heavy load. Anything which gives a lot of trouble and takes a lot of effort.

Shmaltz: Literally fat. Used to describe cooking fat, especially chicken fat, but also for soft speech, and cooing talk.

Shnorrer: A beggar.

Shoin fertig: 'Make it,' finished, done.

Shprauncy: Fancy, showing off.

Shtetl: Literally a small town, a village. Used to describe the close-knit Jewish communities of the *heim* (q.v.) where the *landsleit* (q.v.) came from to enter their new homes in Britain and the USA, etc.

Shul: Synagogue.

Simcha: A happy occasion, for example a wedding.

Tallis: Prayer shawl, worn by men in synagogue.

Talmud: A collection of some sixty-three books encapsulating the Law, the customs, everything that matters to Judaism.

Tochus: Behind, bottom, arse, whichever you like.

Torah: The Five Books of Moses.

Tsitsis: Fringed garment worn at all times by orthodox Jews.

Tsorus: Literally trouble, suffering, unhappiness.

Was machst du: Literally 'What are you doing?' How goes things? How are you?, etc.

Yachner: A gossiping woman.

Yarmulkah: Skull cap worn by pious Jews, who keep their heads covered at all times.

Yenta: A vulgar woman. Often a *yenta* is also a *yachner* (q.v.).

Yeshivah: A Hebrew college, like a university when compared to a *chedar* (q.v.).

Yiddish: Diminutive term for Judisch-Deutsch, the vernacular developed by Jews living and working in Germany in past centuries, now used in other parts of the world, as the Jews dispersed even more widely.

Yom Kippur: The Day of Atonement. The most important Fast in the Jewish Year, occurring early in each New Year (*see* Rosh Hashonah).